D0773215

STEPHEN JONES is the winner of the World Fantasy Award, the Horror Writers of America Bram Stoker Award, and eight-time recipient of The British Fantasy Award. A full-time columnist, film-reviewer, television producer/director and horror movie publicist (*Hellraiser, Hellbound, Grave Misdemeanours, Nightbreed* etc.), he is the co-editor of *Horror: 100 Best Books, The Best Horror from Fantasy Tales, Gaslight & Ghosts, Now We Are Sick* and the *Fantasy Tales* and *Dark Voices* series, and compiler of *Clive Barker's The Nightbreed Chronicles, The Mammoth Book of Terror, Clive Barker's Shadows in Eden* and *James Herbert: By Horror Haunted*.

RAMSEY CAMPBELL is the most respected living British horror writer. After working in the civil service and public libraries, he became a full-time writer in 1973. He has written hundreds of short stories (his latest collection is titled *Waking Nightmares*) and the novels *The Doll Who Ate His Mother, The Face That Must Die, The Parasite, The Nameless, Incarnate, Obsession, The Hungry Moon, The Influence, Ancient Images, Midnight Sun* and *The Count of Eleven*. A multiple winner of both the World Fantasy Award and British Fantasy Award, he has also edited several anthologies, broadcasts weekly on Radio Merseyside as a film critic, and is President of the British Fantasy Society. He especially enjoys reading his stories to audiences.

BEST NEW

HORROR 2

BEST NEW
HORROR 2

Edited by
STEPHEN JONES
and
RAMSEY CAMPBELL

Carroll & Graf Publishers Inc
New York

First published in Great Britain 1991
First Carroll & Graf edition 1991

Carroll & Graf Publishers, Inc.
260 Fifth Avenue
New York
NY 10001

ISBN: 0–88184-736–4

CONTENTS

Necrology: 1990
STEPHEN JONES & KIM NEWMAN

ACKNOWLEDGEMENTS

THE EDITORS WOULD like to thank Avon Books, Pulphouse Publishing, and Chris Reed, for their help and support. Thanks are also due to the magazines *Locus* (Editor & Publisher Charles N. Brown, Locus Publications, P.O. Box 13305, Oakland, CA 94661, USA) and *Science Fiction Chronicle* (Editor & Publisher Andrew I. Porter, P.O. Box 2730, Brooklyn, NY 11202–0056, USA) which were used as reference sources in the Introduction and Necrology.

For
FORREST J ACKERMAN
father to all Famous Monsters

INTRODUCTION: HORROR IN 1990

IT WASN'T THE BEST of years; it wasn't the worst . . . And despite the multiplying prophecies of doom from the pundits, horror fiction continued to enjoy a healthy slice of the marketplace, although the total number of titles published was slightly down on the previous year.

In 1990 Stephen King remained productive, despite not having a new novel published. With more than 150,000 words added or restored to his 1978 apocalyptic SF/horror opus *The Stand* and a quartet of superb new novellas collected together in *Four Past Midnight*, there was plenty to keep his fans happy until the next blockbuster comes along.

Despite being dead for five years, V. C. (Virginia) Andrews continued to dominate the bestseller lists with *Web of Dreams* (in fact written by horror author Andrew Neiderman), and Dean R. Koontz was hot on her heels with *The Bad Place* (plus reissues of many of his earlier novels, the bulk of them originally published under various pseudonyms).

While Clive Barker had no new novel out he was represented by a trinity of movie tie-ins for his latest project as writer and director, *Nightbreed*: a reissue of the original short novel under the title of *Cabal: the Nightbreed*; a handsome coffee-table book of portraits and fiction vignettes, *Clive Barker's The Nightbreed Chronicles*; and *Clive Barker's Nightbreed: the Making of the Film*, which published the script along with interviews and photographs. Unfortunately, none of these (or even a *Nightbreed* computer game) saved the film from flopping at the box office on both sides of the Atlantic.

James Herbert was back at the top of the bestseller charts in Britain with his latest, *Creed*, about a sleazy paparazzo photographer who uncovers a cult of ancient demons, while the prolific Dan Simmons had two short stories published in limited editions of three hundred copies, *Entropy's Bed at Midnight* and *Banished Dreams*. Ramsey Campbell brought out two new books: *Midnight Sun*, a novel which drew comparisons with Machen and Blackwood, and *Needing Ghosts*, a novella which some readers found nightmarish, others hilarious. In the same Legend series Jonathan Carroll was as unpredictable as ever with his novella *Black Cocktail*.

On a slightly more mainstream note, Ray Bradbury's *A Graveyard for Lunatics* was a further instalment of his autobiographical fiction, set in 1950s Hollywood; Anne Rice's *The Witching Hour* chronicled the epic history of a family of witches over the centuries; and Robert McCammon's *Mine*, despite some great moments of psychological tension, saw the author moving away from supernatural horror towards the more popular thriller market.

Some publishers kept the dread word "horror" well away from their contributions to the field: Valerie Martin's *Mary Reilly* was a retelling of the Dr Jekyll and Mr Hyde story from the viewpoint of the doctor's maid; *Phantom*, by Susan Kay, was a fictional biography of the Phantom of the Opera; and James Lovegrove's first novel *The Hope* was composed of episodes (owing more to the splatterpunks than to William Hope Hodgson) set on a five-mile-long cruise ship adrift at sea for decades. Also standing somewhat aloof from their genre were Patrick McGrath's *Spider* and *Cold Eye* by Giles Blunt.

Most horror books, however, acknowledged their field. Brian Lumley treated his fans to *The House of Doors* and expanded his popular vampire trilogy with *Necroscope IV: Deadspeak*. More vampires figured in *The Stake* by Richard Laymon, and Tanith Lee dealt with a different kind at length in *The Blood of Roses*. S. P. Somtow's *Moon Dance* was a werewolf novel set in the American West during the nineteenth century, while the lyncanthropes in Charles L. Grant's *Stunts* were more contemporary. F. Paul Wilson's *Reborn* was his long-awaited sequel of sorts to *The Keep*; his novella *Pelts* was limited to just 552 copies. Graham Masterton's *Night Plague* was the third in his Night Warriors series. On the ghostly front, *The Promise* was another of Robert Westall's fine tales for young adults, while in *Rune* Christopher Fowler attempted to derive a novel from "Casting the Runes" without M. R. James' terseness and elegance of style.

It was good to see new work from veteran pulp writers: Robert Bloch brought out *Psycho House*, the third in his series about Mrs Bates' boy Norman, and *The Jekyll Legacy*, a Gothic mystery written in collaboration with Andre Norton; meanwhile Hugh B. Cave pursued his fascination with Caribbean voodoo in *The Lower Deep*. To celebrate the centenary of H. P. Lovecraft, publisher Donald M. Grant produced the first separate edition of *At the Mountains of Madness*, an expensive oversize hardcover illustrated in full colour by Fernando Duval.

Rex Miller's *Slice* once again featured detective Jack Eichord and everyone's favourite Vietnam psycho Chaingang Bunkowski. Many well-known horror writers had new books to their names: Peter James (*Sweet Heart*), Stephen Gallagher (*Rain*), Chet Williamson (*Reign*), John Farris (*Fiends*), John Coyne (*Child of Shadows*), T. M. Wright (*The School* and *Boundaries*), Ray Garton (*Trade Secrets*), Stephen Laws (*The Frighteners*), Brian Stableford (*The Werewolves of London*), the unstoppable Guy N. Smith (*Phobia*, *The Unseen* and *Carnivore*), and John Saul (*Second Child* and *Sleepwalk*). *Fairytales* by Steve Rasnic Tem appeared in a 300-copy edition, and David J. Schow could find only a British publisher for his superior second novel *The Shaft*.

Other noteworthy titles of 1990 included *Fire* by Alan Rodgers, *The Unseen* by Joe Citro, *The Vampire Files* by P. N. Elrod (three volumes confronting a hardboiled Chicago detective with vampirism during the Depression), *The Cartoonist* by Sean Costello, *October* by Al Sarrantonio, *Dead Voices* by Rick Hautala, and *Angel of Darkness* by Charles de Lint under his pseudonym Samuel M. Key. Kathryn Ptacek offered more Indian magic in *Ghost Dance*; Chelsea Quinn Yarbro, more historical horror from the Saint-Germain Chronicles in *Out of the House of Life*. A vampirish entity wiped out the members of a single family in Kim Newman's aptly titled *Bad Dreams*, and vampirism, voodoo, possession and reincarnation all combined in *Tempter* by Nancy Collins, the follow-up to her acclaimed debut novel *Sunglasses After Dark*. Steve Harris's *Adventureland* showed some promise among its derivations from King and Barker, while Michael Cadnum's debut *Nightlight* was impressively assured. Comic relief was provided by Terry Pratchett and Neil Gaiman in their hilarious *Good Omens*, which mercilessly lampooned the Satanic Apocalypse.

Demonstrating that horror is still a thriving market for the short form, David J. Schow had two substantial collections published, *Seeing Red* and *Lost Angels*, while *The Adventures of Lucius Leffing* continued the adventures of the late Joseph Payne Brennan's occult detective. *The Call and Other Stories* by Robert Westall and *Methods of Madness* by Ray Garton were both slightly disappointing, given each author's previous work, though less so than *A Fit of Shivers* by Joan Aiken. Michael Blumlein's *The Brains of Rats* lived up to the weirdness of its title story, and *Houses Without Doors* showed that Peter Straub's considerable talent extends to lengths shorter than the novel. *Blood and Grit* was a striking first small press collection by Simon Clark. Dan Simmons continued to proliferate with *Prayers to Broken Stones*, featuring thirteen stories with an introduction by Harlan Ellison, and Brian Lumley toured Lovecraft's dreamland in *Iced on Aran and Other Dreamquests*. Peter Haining disinterred and introduced *The Best Supernatural Stories of Wilkie Collins*.

1990 was a year for anthologies, with a huge variety of titles flooding the market. Marvin Kaye, ever reliable as an anthologist, put together fascinating contents for *Witches and Warlocks: Tales of Black Magic, Old & New* and *13 Plays of Ghosts and the Supernatural*, two volumes published only by the Science Fiction Book Club. *Dark Voices: the Best from the Pan Book of Horror Stories*, edited by Stephen Jones and Clarence Paget, collected thirteen stories from Britain's longest-running and most successful horror anthology series with introductions by contemporary writers in the field. The series subsequently entered its 31st year as *Dark Voices 2: the Pan Book of Horror* under the editorship of David Sutton and Stephen Jones. The same team were responsible for the move into America of the one-time small press magazine *Fantasy Tales*, which finally completed the transformation to a twice-yearly anthology format, and *The Best Horror from Fantasy Tales* saw American publication by Carroll & Graf.

The year's most prolific anthologist was, as usual, Martin H. Greenberg, who was involved with a whole host of titles: *Mummy Stories, Devil Worshippers, Ghosts of the Heartland, Western Ghosts, Cults of Horror, Phantom Regiments* (with Robert Adams), *Lovecraft's Legacy* (with Robert Weinberg), *The Rivals of Weird Tales* (a massive "instant remainder" collection with Weinberg and Stefan R. Dziemianowicz) and *Urban Horrors* (with William F. Nolan).

There were excellent stories to be found in *Alien Sex* edited by Ellen Datlow; *The Seaharp Hotel*, the third in the Greystone Bay series edited by Charles L. Grant; *Intensive Scare* edited by Karl Edward Wagner; *Walls of Fear* edited by Kathryn Cramer and *The Mammoth Book of Ghost Stories* edited by Richard Dalby. Predictably, commentators who had had nothing to say against all-male horror anthologies were quick to condemn two all-female books, *Skin of the Soul* edited by Lisa Tuttle and *Women of Darkness II* edited by Kathryn Ptacek. Paul M. Sammon's *Splatterpunks: Extreme Horror* was less representative of its chosen sub-genre than the title promised.

The Pulphouse publishing empire was among the most prolific of the year, and *Pulphouse: The Hardback Magazine Issue 7: Horror* and *9: Dark Fantasy* (both edited by Kristine Kathryn Rusch) featured an interesting mix of talents. An allegedly revised edition of *Weird Tales*, a facsimile volume edited by Peter Haining, differed little from the original 1976 edition. Worth noting were *Short Sharp Shocks* edited by Julian Lloyd Webber, *Hotter Blood: More Tales of Erotic Horror* edited by Jeff Gelb and Michael Garrett, and *The Man in Black: Macabre Stories from Fear on Four*, a tie-in with the (largely derivative and hack-ridden) BBC radio series.

On the banks of the mainstream could be found *When the Black Lotus*

Blooms edited by Elizabeth A. Saunders, featuring mostly new fiction and an introduction by Robert McCammon; *Black Water 2: More Tales of the Fantastic* edited by Alberto Manguel, which included sixty-four stories; and *The Omnibus of 20th-Century Ghost Stories* edited (and with a notably ill-informed introduction) by Robert Phillips, featuring a cover by Stanley Spencer and some out-of-the-way tales by such as Tennessee Williams, Denton Welch and Gertrude Atherton.

Two of the best anthologies of the year were *Digital Dreams* edited by David V. Barrett, ostensibly collecting science fiction tales about computers but featuring some memorable dark fantasy from the likes of Terry Pratchett and Garry Kilworth, and Thomas F. Monteleone's *Borderlands*, the first in a proposed series which showcased fine work by an impressive range of writers.

Although the series was dropped by its British publisher, Ellen Datlow's and Terri Windling's *The Year's Best Fantasy and Horror: Third Annual Collection* was a hefty selection of forty-seven stories and poems, along with knowledgeable end-of-the-year summaries, while Karl Edward Wagner's eclectic selection for *The Year's Best Horror Stories XVIII* produced the usual number of obscure gems. New "Best of the Year" collections were *Quick Chills: The Year's Best Horror Stories from the Small Press* Volume One edited by Peter Enfantino, featuring thirteen tales selected from semi-professional sources, and our own modest volume *Best New Horror*, which according to *Locus* suffered from being "slightly British-skewed".

In America, *Weird Tales* proved a worthy continuation of "The Unique Magazine", with some excellent stories presented in an attractive format. Although too much of the fiction in *Fear* was mediocre, the magazine continued to lead the market in the UK, despite the launch of such newsstand rivals as *Skeleton Crew* (which never really recovered from the sacking of its editor after the second issue) and *The Dark Half* (aimed principally at the horror video audience). Of the British magazines, *Interzone* published the most distinctive tales in the field.

Small press magazines proliferated, and there was worthwhile material to be discovered in a host of fanzines and semi-professional titles such as *After Hours, The Blood Review: The Journal of Horror Criticism, Cemetery Dance, Crypt of Cthulhu, Deathrealm, Eldritch Tales, Ghosts & Scholars, Grue, Haunts: Tales of Unexpected Horror and the Supernatural, Iniquities, Midnight Graffiti, Noctulpa, 2AM,* and the British Fantasy Society's *Dark Horizons* and *Winter Chills*.

The first issue of *Gauntlet: Exploring the Limits of Free Expression* lived up to its subtitle with fiction by Ray Garton, Steve Rasnic Tem, Harlan Ellison, William F. Nolan and Douglas Winter, and articles by Ray Bradbury, Ramsey Campbell, Rex Miller and Dan Simmons, amongst others.

Neil Barron's *Horror Literature: A Reader's Guide* was an expensive 600-page bibliographic reference book which included a lengthy section devoted to contemporary horror fiction. *The Weird Tale* by S. T. Joshi restricted itself to studying the work of Arthur Machen, Lord Dunsany, Algernon Blackwood, M. R. James, Ambrose Bierce and H. P. Lovecraft; a follow-up volume is planned. James Van Hise managed to exploit two authors in one book with *Stephen King and Clive Barker: The Illustrated Guide to the Masters of the Macabre*. King feels that too many books are being written about him, and Stephen Spignesi's *The Stephen King Quiz Book* is certainly one of them. Stanley J. Wiater continued in the footsteps of Doug Winter with *Dark Dreamers: Conversations with the Masters of Horror*, featuring twenty-four interviews with well-known horror writers.

On the film front, John McCarty's *The Modern Horror Film* covered much the same post-*Night of the Living Dead* ground as Kim Newman's *Nightmare Movies*. *Karloff and Lugosi: The Story of a Haunting Collaboration* was an in-depth comparison of the two actors by Gregory William Mank, and a worthy follow-up to the same author's *The Hollywood Hissables*. David J. Skal's *Hollywood Gothic: The Tangled Web of "Dracula" from Novel to Stage to Screen* provided fascinating insights into the making of both the US and Spanish versions of the 1931 *Dracula*. Stephen Rebello did an equally fine job on *Alfred Hitchcock and the Making of Psycho*, while Mike Budd's *The Cabinet of Dr Caligari: Text, Contexts, Histories* was exactly what its title described. *Invasion of the Body Snatchers* edited by Al LaValley featured the original script along with associational material, and *Plan 9 From Outer Space* was similarly enshrined, together with cast biographies and an Edward D. Wood filmography, by Tom Mason.

A real labour-of-love project was Philip J. Riley's series of facsimiles of the original shooting scripts for such Universal classics as *Frankenstein*, *Bride of Frankenstein*, *Son of Frankenstein*, *The Mummy* and *This Island Earth* (not to mention *Abbott and Costello Meet Frankenstein*), with introductions by Forrest J Ackerman, Vincent Price, John Landis, Valerie Hobson, Zita Johann, Jeff Morrow and others.

You either love him or hate him, but *Joe Bob Goes Back to the Drive-In* included the usual idiosyncratic movie reviews and satire which can be found every week in his *We Are The Weird* newsletter.

Two of the best art books of the year were *Blood and Iron*, showcasing the work of Les Edwards, and *H. R. Giger's Biomechanics*, introduced by Harlan Ellison.

The comics industry manifested the three persons of Clive Barker:

Tapping the Vein Book Three adapted his stories "The Midnight Meat Train" and "Scape-Goats", Book Four "Hell's Event" and "The Madonna". Even more popular were *Clive Barker's Hellraiser* and *Clive Barker's Night Breed*, both offering spin-off storylines from the author's two movie projects.

Neil Gaiman continued to develop *The Sandman* through such memorable mini-series as "The Dolls House" and "Dream Country", the former eight-part sequence ending up as a handsome graphic novel with an introduction by the ubiquitous Barker. Gaiman also did odd things with *Miracleman, Hellblazer* (in which he teamed up with artist Dave McKean) and a superb four-part series *The Books of Magic*. McKean was also responsible for the artwork in the hugely successful *Arkham Asylum*, and wrote and illustrated the first issue of the ten-part graphic magazine *Cages*.

Batman remained popular in graphic novel format. The inventive *Gotham by Gaslight* included an introduction by Robert Bloch, while *Batman 3-D* came complete with red and blue glasses and a headache. Gahan Wilson did a wonderful job illustrating the first of the new Classics Illustrated, *The Raven and Other Poems* by Edgar Allan Poe, and there were movie-inspired comics based on *Planet of the Apes, RoboCop, Total Recall, Darkman* and even *Aliens vs. Predator*! There was a welcome reissue of the best of the '50s EC Comics, including *Tales from the Crypt* and *Vault of Horror*.

The most commercially successful film of the year on both sides of the Atlantic was *Ghost*, which grossed more than $200 million. Other films that took more than $100 million at the box-office included *Teenage Mutant Ninja Turtles, Total Recall* and *Dick Tracy* – although, given their huge production costs, the latter two still have a long way to go before they make a profit.

The most popular horror film of the year was *Flatliners* ($60 million), closely followed by *Arachnophobia* and *Gremlins II: The New Batch*. Much further down the charts came *Darkman, Predator 2, Child's Play 2, Jacob's Ladder, The Exorcist III, Ghost Dad, Edward Scissorhands, Tales from the Darkside, The Guardian, Tremors, Graveyard Shift* and *The Witches*. *Vampire's Kiss* was an appealingly unrestrained comedy of psychosis, but the title was by far the best thing about *I Bought a Vampire Motorcycle*.

The big losers of the year included *Nightbreed, Leatherface: The Texas Chainsaw Massacre III*, the colour remake of *Night of the Living Dead*, Richard Stanley's first feature *Hardware, Brain Dead* (based on an unfilmed script by the late Charles Beaumont) and *Frankenhooker*. However, each of them took more than Roger Corman's comeback film as a director, *Frankenstein Unbound*. A surprise entry in the British chart was a reissue of *The Exorcist*, proving that it can still draw an audience nearly twenty years after it was made, perhaps because it is now banned in the UK on videocassette. The most powerful chills of the year were to be had from Joe Pesci's psychopath in *Goodfellas* and from George Sluizer's film *The Vanishing*, a sunlit tale of terror not unlike a bleaker Chabrol film than Chabrol has yet made.

David Lynch's *Twin Peaks* continued to delight and infuriate television viewers with its mysterious giants, singing dwarfs, possessed souls and the long-awaited revelation of just who did kill Laura Palmer. Malcolm Bradbury's three-part adaptation of Kingsley Amis' *The Green Man* for the BBC began well (if you discount the splattery preamble), but ultimately lacked the novel's severity and sense of the supernatural. Two other BBC films worth mentioning were *Frankenstein's Baby* because it was so terrible and the supernatural thriller *The Lorelei* because it was so good.

Just what we didn't need was yet another version of *The Phantom of the Opera*, but we got one anyway, filmed by Tony Richardson in France and Hungary. It starred Burt Lancaster and Charles Dance, who gave a ludicrously camp performance as the Phantom. To add insult to injury, we didn't even get to see his disfigured face during this tedious three-hour adaptation.

Among the worst of the new TV shows was the Canadian-made *Dracula: The Series*. Geordie Johnson played Alexander Lucard (get it?) as a contemporary Donald Trump of the vampire world (an idea which had already been used in Hammer's *The Satanic Rites of Dracula*). He is pursued by three typical teens and their know-it-all uncle through each shoddy half-hour episode.

Guest Speaker Robert Bloch received the Horror Writers of America's Life Achievement Award, presented in Providence in June. Dan Simmons' *Carrion Comfort* won the Superior Achievement in Novel; Nancy Collins picked up the First Novel award for *Sunglasses After Dark*; the Novelette award went to Joe R. Lansdale's "On the Far Side of the Cadillac Desert with Dead Folks" from *Book of the Dead*, and Robert R. McCammon's "Eat Me", from the same anthology, was the chosen short story. Richard Matheson's mammoth *Collected Stories* received the Collection award, while in the Non-Fiction category *Harlan Ellison's Watching* tied with *Horror: 100 Best Books* edited by Stephen Jones and Kim Newman.

Fantasycon XV, organised by the British Fantasy Society, returned to Birmingham in September, where *Carrion Comfort* also picked up the August Derleth Award for Best Novel. Co-Guest of Honour Joe Lansdale won the Best Short Fiction award for his *Book of the Dead* novelette, Carl Ford's *Dagon* was voted Best Small Press for the second year in succession, and *Indiana Jones and the Last Crusade* was Best Film, the last time an award in this category will be presented. Dave Carson again received one of his own statuettes as Best Artist, and Peter Coleborn was presented with the Special Award for his services to the Society.

The World Fantasy Awards were presented in Chicago in November, and R. A. Lafferty was justly honoured with the Life Achievement Award. Best Novel was found to be Jack Vance's *Lyonesse: Madouc*; "Great Work of Time" earned John Crowley the Best Novella award, while Best Short Story went to Steven Millhauser's "The Illusionist". *Richard Matheson's Collected Stories* was again honoured as Best Collection, and for the second year running the Best Anthology was considered to be *The Year's Best Fantasy Second Annual Collection* edited by Ellen Datlow and Terri Windling. Thomas Canty was voted Best Artist, the Special Award Professional went to publisher Mark Ziesing and the Non-Professional to *Grue* magazine.

The Collectors Award for 1990, presented by bookseller Barry R. Levin, went – not unsurprisingly – to Stephen King as "Most Collectable Author of the Year" and to Doubleday for the limited edition of the uncut *The Stand* as "Most Collectable Book of the Year".

1990 was another boom year for horror, but it could be the last for some time. The danger is that the much-vaunted recession in the publishing industry, coupled with continued pronouncements of a bottoming-out of the horror genre, could soon become a self-fulfilling prophecy.

1991 is the year when many publishers will begin cutting back on horror. Although the "name" authors will presumably survive, we could see a virtual disappearance of the mid-list (where most horror is published), resulting in fewer first novels appearing, contracts being cancelled, and the anthology experiencing yet another slump.

The genre is likely to fare no better in movies. All the major studios now realise they must cut back on the immense budgets of the past few years, and as few horror films are top earners, such effects-laden projects will be the first to go, once again becoming the province of the low-budget independent.

But it's not all doom and gloom. Horror fiction continues to thrive in the short form, with a wealth of new talent (particularly women writers) attracted to the field. There are still numerous outlets for new work, from newsstand magazines to the burgeoning small press. *Best New Horror* will be here with a representative sampling of many of the best practitioners working today.

THE EDITORS
APRIL, 1991

BEST NEW

HORROR 2

K. W. JETER

The First Time

K. W. JETER has been described by Ramsey Campbell as "one of the most versatile and uncompromising writers of imaginative fiction."

He considers himself "a Los Angeles kid" and lives and works in California. His controversial debut novel, *Dr Adder*, is generally considered to be the prototype for the "cyberpunk" movement in science fiction, and his mentor Philip K. Dick called it ". . . a stunning novel that destroys once and for all your conception of the limitations of science fiction."

His other genre-spanning books include *Farewell Horizontal*, *Infernal Devices*, *In the Land of the Dead*, *Dark Seeker*, *Mantis*, *Soul Eater*, *The Night Man* and *Madlands*. He has also scripted *Mister E*, a four-part graphic novel for DC Comics.

"The First Time" is only Jeter's second short story; it is a deeply disturbing view of coming of age, based on an article he read in *The Wall Street Journal* about US kids getting into trouble in Mexican border towns and some teenage memories of visits to Tijuana. It's not for the squeamish.

H IS FATHER AND HIS UNCLE DECIDED it was about time. Time for him to come along. They went down there on a regular basis, with their buddies, all of them laughing and drinking beer right in the car, having a good time even before they got there. When they left the house, laying a patch of rubber out by the curb, he'd lie on his bed upstairs and think about them—at least for a little while, till he fell asleep—think about the car heading out on the long straight road, where there was nothing on either side except the bare rock and dirt and the dried brown scrubby brush. With a cloud of dust rolling up behind them, his uncle Tommy could just floor it, one-handing the steering wheel, with nothing to do but keep it on the dotted line all the way down there. He lay with the side of his face pressed into the pillow, and thought of them driving, making good time, hour after hour, tossing the empties out the window, laughing and talking about mysterious things, things you only had to say the name of and everybody knew what you were talking about, without another word being said. Even with all the windows rolled down, the car would smell like beer and sweat, six guys together, one of them right off his shift at the place where they made the cinder blocks, the fine gray dust on his hands and matted in the dark black hair of his forearms. Driving and laughing all the way, until the bright lights came into view—he didn't know what happened after that. He closed his eyes and didn't see anything.

And when they got back—they always got back late at night, so even though they'd been gone nearly the whole weekend, and he'd gotten up and watched television and listened to his mom talking to her friends on the phone, and had something to eat and stuff like that, when his father and his uncle and their buddies got back, the noise of the car pulling up, with them still talking and laughing, but different now, slower and lower-pitched and satisfied—it was like it woke him up from the same sleep he'd fallen into when they'd left. All the other stuff was just what he'd been dreaming.

"You wanna come along?" his father had asked him, turning away from the TV. Just like that, no big deal, like asking him to fetch another beer from the fridge. "Me and Tommy and the guys—we're gonna go down there and see what's happening. Have a little fun."

He hadn't said anything back for a little while, but had just stared at the TV, the colors fluttering against the walls of the darkened room. His father hadn't had to say anything more than *down there*—he knew where that meant. A little knot, one he always had in his stomach, tightened and drew down something in his throat.

"Sure," he'd finally mumbled. The string with the knot in it looped down lower in his gut. His father just grunted and went on watching the TV.

He figured they'd decided it was time because he'd finally started high school. More than that, he'd just about finished his first year and had managed to stay out of whatever trouble his older brother had gotten into back then, finally causing him to drop out and go into the army and then god knew what—nobody had heard from his brother in a long time. So maybe it was as some kind of reward, for doing good, that they were going to take him along with them.

He didn't see what was so hard about it, about school. What made it worth a reward. All you had to do was keep your head down and not draw attention to yourself. And there was stuff to do that got you through the day: he was in the band, and that was okay. He played the baritone sax—it was pretty easy because they never got any real melodies to play, you just had to fart around in the background with everybody else. Where he sat was right in front of the trombone section, which was all older guys; he could hear them talking, making bets about which of the freshman girls would be the next to start shaving her legs. Plus they had a lot of jokes about the funny way flute players made their mouths go when they were playing. Would they still look that funny way when they had something else in their mouths? It embarrassed him because the flute players were right across from the sax section, and he could see the one he'd already been dating a couple of times.

One time, when they'd been alone, she'd given him a piece of paper that she'd had folded up in the back pocket of her jeans. The paper had gotten shaped round, the same shape as her butt, and he'd felt funny taking it and unfolding it. The paper was a mimeographed diagram that her minister at her Episcopalian youth group had given her and the rest of the girls in the group. It showed what parts of their bodies they could let a boy touch, at what stage. You had to be engaged, with a ring and everything, before you could unhook her bra. He'd kept the piece of paper, tucked in one of his books at home. In a way, it'd been kind of a relief, just to know what was expected of him.

It was what worried him about going down there, with his father and his uncle and the other guys—he didn't know what he was supposed to do when they got there. He lay awake the night before, wondering. He turned on the light and got out the piece of paper the girl who played the flute had given him, and looked at the dotted lines that made a sort of zone between the diagram's throat and navel, and another zone below that, that looked like a pair of underpants or the bottom half of a girl's two-piece swimsuit. Then he folded the paper back up and stuck it in the book where he kept it. He didn't think the diagram was going to do him any good where he was going.

"All right—let's get this show on the road." His uncle Tommy leaned out of the driver's-side window and slapped the door's metal. They always went down there in Tommy's car because it was the biggest, an old Dodge that wallowed like a boat even on the straightways. The other guys chipped in for the gas. "Come on—let's move on out." Tommy's big yellow grin was even looser; he'd already gotten into the six-pack stowed down on the floor.

For a moment, he thought they'd all forgotten about taking him along. There were already five guys in the car when it'd pulled up in front of the house, and his father would make the sixth. He stood on the porch, feeling a secret hope work at the knot in his gut.

"Aw, man—what the hell were you guys thinking of?" The voice of one of the guys in the car floated out, across the warm evening air. It was Bud, the one who worked at the cinder block factory. "There's no way you can stick seven of us in here, and then drive all the way down there."

The guy next to Bud, in the middle of the backseat, laughed. "Well, hell—maybe you can just sit on my lap, then."

"Yeah, well, you can just sit on this." Bud gave him the finger, then drained the last from a can of beer and dropped it onto the curb. Bud pushed the door open and got out. "You guys just have a fine old time without me. I got some other shit to take care of."

Tommy's grin grew wider. "Ol' Bud's feeling his age. Since that little sweetheart last time fucked up his back for him."

"Your ass."

From the porch, he watched Bud walking away, the blue glow of the streetlights making the cinder block dust on Bud's workshirt go all silver. He couldn't tell if Bud had been really mad—maybe about him coming along and taking up space in the car—or if it was just part of the joke. A lot of the time he couldn't tell whether his father and his buddies were joking or not.

"Come on—" His father had already gotten in the car, up front, elbow hanging over the sill of the door. "What're you waiting for?"

He slid in the back. The seat had dust from Bud's shirt on it, higher up than his own shoulders. "Here we go," said his father, as his head rocked back into the cinder block dust. The guy next to him, his father's buddy, peeled a beer off a six-pack and handed it to him. He held it without opening it, letting the cold seep into his hands as the streets pivoted around and swung behind the car, until they were past the last streetlight and onto the straight road heading for the southern hills.

All the way down there, they talked about baseball. Or football, shouting over the radio station that Tommy had turned up loud. He didn't listen to them, but leaned his shoulder against the door, gulping breath out of the wind, his face stung red. For a long while he thought there was something running alongside the car, a dog or something, but faster than a dog could run, because his uncle Tommy had the car easily wound up to over seventy. The dog, or whatever it was, loped in the shadows at the side of the road, a big grin like Tommy's across its muzzle, its bright spark eyes looking right at him. But when another car came along, going the other way, the headlights making a quick scoop over the road, the dog wasn't there. Just the rocks and brush zooming by, falling back into the dark behind them. He pushed his face farther out into the wind, eyes squinted, the roar swallowing up the voices inside the car. The dog's yellow eyes danced like coins out there, keeping alongside and smiling at him.

"All *right*—we have uh-*rived*." His uncle Tommy beat an empty beer can against the curve of the steering wheel, then pitched it outside.

He looked up ahead, craning his neck to see around his father in the front seat. He could see a bridge, with lights strung up along it. And more lights beyond it, the town on the other side. He dropped back in his seat, combing his hair down into place with his fingers.

The lights, when they got across the bridge, were like Christmas lights, strings of little colored bulbs laced over the doorways of the buildings and even across the street, dangling up above, pushing back the night sky. There were other lights, too, the kind you'd see anywhere, blinking arrows that pointed to one thing or another, big yellow squares with the plastic strips for the black letters to stick on, covered in chicken wire to keep people's hands off.

Tommy let the car crawl along, inching through the traffic that had swallowed them up soon as they'd hit the town. So many other cars, all of them moving so slow, that people crossing the street, going from the lit-up doorways on one side to those on the other, just threaded their way through. Or if they were young guys, and the cars were bumper to bumper, they'd slap their hands down on a hood and a trunk lid and just vault over, with a little running step on the ridge of the bumpers halfway across, and just laughing and shouting to each other the whole time.

Even though it was so loud in the street—with all the car radios blaring away, with everybody's windows rolled down, and the even louder music thumping out of the doorways—he felt a little drowsy somehow. He'd drunk the beer his father's buddy had given him, and a couple more after that, and had gone on staring out at the dark rolling by the whole way down here. Now the street's noise rolled over him like the slow waves at the ocean's surface, far above him.

"Bail out, kid—let's go!" The guy beside him, in the middle of the backseat, was pushing him in the arm. His head lolled for a moment, neck limp, before he snapped awake. He looked around and saw his father and his uncle and the other guys all getting out of the car. Rubbing his eyes, he pushed the door open and stumbled out.

He followed them up the alley where they'd parked, out toward the lights and noise rolling in the street. It wasn't as bright and loud at this end; they'd left most of the action a couple of blocks back.

His father and his uncle were already down the street, laughing and swapping punches as they went, little boxing moves with feints and shuffles, like a couple of teenagers or something. His uncle Tommy was always carrying on, doing stuff like that, but he'd never seen his father so wild and happy. They had their arms around each other's shoulders, and their faces and chests lit up red as they stepped into one of the doorways, his father sweeping back a curtain with his hand. The light that had spilled out into the street blinked away as the curtain fell back into place. He broke into a run to catch up with the others.

Some kind of a bar—that was what it looked like and smelled like, the smell of spilled beer and cigarette smoke that had soaked into everything and made the air a thick blue haze around the lights. The others were already sitting around a table, one of the booths at the side; they'd left room for him at the end, and he slid in beside his uncle Tommy.

The man came around from behind the bar with a tray of beers, squat brown bottles sweating through the crinkly foil labels. He didn't know whether his father had already ordered, or whether the bartender already knew what they wanted, from all the times they'd been here before. He wasn't sure he'd get served, but it didn't seem to matter here how young he was; the bartender put a beer down in front of him, too. He took a pull at it as he looked around at the empty stage at one end of the room, with heavy red curtains draped around it and big PA speakers at the side. The other booths, and some of the tables in the middle, were crowded with bottles, men elbowing them aside as they leaned forward and talked, dropping the butts of their cigarettes into the empties.

Somebody poked him—it felt like a broom handle—and he looked around and saw a face grinning at him. A man short enough to look him straight in the eye where he sat; the grin split open to show brown teeth, except for two in front that were shining gold. The little man poked him again, with two metal tubes that had wires hooked to them, running back to a box that hung from a strap around the man's neck.

"Yeah, yeah—just take 'em." His father waggled a finger at the tubes, while digging with the other hand into his inside coat pocket. "Just hold on to 'em now. This is how they make you a man in these parts." His father came up with a dollar bill from a roll in the coat pocket and handed it over to the little man.

The tubes were about the size of the inside of a toilet paper roll, but shiny, and hard and cold to the touch. He looked at them sitting in his hands, then glanced up when he saw the little man turning a crank at the side of the box hanging around his neck.

An electric shock jumped out of the tubes, stinging his palms. He dropped them and jerked away. He looked around and saw his father and his buddies all roaring with laughter. Right beside him, his uncle Tommy was slapping the table with one hand, turning red and choking on a swallow of beer.

"Here—give 'em here." His father traded another dollar bill for the tubes, the wires dangling between the bottles as he took them from the little man. "Let 'er rip."

The little man turned the crank on the box, digging into it to make it go round faster and faster. His father winced with the first surge, then squeezed the tubes harder, hands going whiteknuckled, teeth gritting together, lips drawn back. The crank on the box went around in a blur, until his father's hands flew open and the tubes clattered onto the table, knocking over one of the bottles. Beer foamed out and dribbled over the edge.

"Whoa! Jesus fucking Christ!" His father shook his hands, loose at the wrist. The guy sitting next over stuck out a palm and his father slapped it, grinning in triumph. The little man with the box did a kind of dance, laughing to show all the brown and gold teeth and pointing with a black-nailed finger. Then squatting down, the short legs bowing out, and cupping a hand to his crotch, acting like there was some cannonball-sized weight hanging there. The little man laughed and pointed to the man sitting in the booth again, then took another dollar bill and trotted away with the box and the tubes to another table.

He was looking at his father putting the roll of bills back into the coat pocket. His own hands still stung, and he wrapped them around the wet bottle in front of him to cool them.

"Yessir—that fucker'll sober you right up." His father signaled to the bartender. "I'm gonna need a couple more after that little bastard."

Somebody came walking over to the booth, but it wasn't the bartender. He looked up and saw one of the guys, one of his father's buddies—the guy hadn't been there the whole time they'd been messing around with the little man with the box.

"Lemme out." His uncle Tommy nudged him. "I think it's just about my turn."

He didn't know what his uncle meant, but he stood up and let Tommy slide out of the booth. The other guy took his place, sorting through the bottles on the table for the one that had been there before, that he hadn't finished.

Before he sat back down, he watched his uncle Tommy walking across the bar, squeezing past the backs of the chairs circled around the tables. There was a door in the corner with one of those wordless signs, a stick figure to indicate the men's room. But Tommy didn't head off toward that. His uncle pulled back the curtain hiding a doorway off to the side and disappeared behind it. He sat back down, but kept looking over at the curtain as he sipped at the beer that had grown warm in his hands.

Then—he didn't know how long it was—his uncle Tommy was back. Standing beside him, at the outside of the booth.

"Come on, fella—" Across the table, his father stabbed a thumb up in the air a couple of times. "Get up and let your old uncle siddown."

His uncle smelled different, sweat and something else. He got up, stepping back a little bit—the scent curled in his nostrils like something from an animal—and let his uncle slide into the booth.

He sat back down. His uncle Tommy had a big grin on his face. Around the table, he saw a couple of the other guys give a slow wink to each other, then tilt their beers up again.

Tommy glanced sidelong at him, then leaned over the table and spewed out a mouthful of blood. Enough of it to swamp across the tabletop, knocking the empty bottles over in the flood.

And he wasn't sitting in the booth then, next to his uncle. He'd jumped out of the booth, the way you would from the door of a rolling car; he stumbled and almost fell backward. Standing a couple of feet away, he listened to the men pounding the table and howling their laughter, louder than when the man with the box had shocked him.

"Tom, you shit-for-brains—" His father was red-faced, gasping for breath.

His uncle Tommy had a dribble of red going down his chin, like the finger of blood that had reached the edge of the table and dribbled over. Pretty drunk, his uncle smiled as he looked around the booth at the guys, pleased with the joke. His uncle turned and smiled at him, red seeping around the teeth in the sloppy grin.

The laughter dwindled away, the men shaking their heads and rubbing tears from the corners of their eyes. They all took long pulls at their beers. That was when he saw that there wasn't any room in the booth for him. They'd all shifted a little bit and taken up all the room; his uncle was sitting right at the end where he'd been.

They didn't say anything, but he knew what it meant. He turned around and looked across the bar, to the curtain that covered the doorway over there. It meant it was his turn now.

*

The woman ran her hand along the side of his neck. "You haven't been around here before, have you?" She smiled at him. Really smiled, not like she was laughing at him.

"No—" He shook his head. Her hand felt cool against the heat that had come rushing up under his skin. He pointed back over his shoulder. "I came with my dad, and his friends."

Her gaze moved past his eyes, up to where her fingers tangled around in his hair. "Uh-huh," she said. "I know your daddy."

She got up from the bed. He sat there watching her as she stood at a little shelf nailed to the wall. The shelf had a plasticframed mirror propped up on it, and a towel and a bar of soap. She watched herself taking off her dangly earrings, gold ones, drawing the curved hooks out. She laid them down in front of the little mirror.

"Well, you don't have to worry none." She spoke to the mirror. "There's always a first time. Then it's easy after that." She rubbed a smudge away from the corner of her eye. "You'll see."

When he'd pulled aside the curtain and stepped into the dark—away from the bar's light, its noise of laughing and talking falling behind him—he hadn't even been able to see where he was, until he'd felt the woman take his hand and lead him a little farther along, back to where the doors to a lot of little rooms were lit up by a bulb hanging from the hallway's ceiling. One of the doors had opened and a man had come out and shoved past him in the narrow space, and he'd caught a whiff of the smell off the man, the same as had been on his uncle Tommy when he'd come back out to the booth.

When the woman had closed the door and come over to the bed to sit close by him, he'd held his breath for a moment, because he thought the scent would be on her too, that raw smell, like sweat, only sharper. But she smelled sweet, like something splashed on from a bottle, the kind women always had on their dressers. That made him realize that she was the first woman, the first female thing, he'd been near, for what seemed like days. All the way down here—in the car with his father and his uncle and their buddies, packed up tight with them as they'd gone barreling along in the night, and then crowded around the table in the booth, the same night rolling through the street outside, until their sweat was all he could smell, right down into his throat.

"Here—you don't want to get that all mussed up." The woman had on a white slip—it shone in the dim light as she came back toward the bed. "Let's take it off." She bent down, her dark hair brushing against his face, and started unbuttoning his shirt.

He felt cold, the sweat across his arms and shoulders chilling in the room's air. The woman sat down and leaned back against the bed's pillow, dropping his shirt to the floor. "Come a little closer." She stretched out her arms toward him.

"You see . . . there's nothing to be afraid of." Her voice went down to a whisper, yet somehow it filled the little room; it ate up all the space, until there was just the bed and her on it.

"We'll go real slow, so you won't get scared." She smiled at him, her hand tracing down his rib cage. She was a lot older than him; this close to her, he could see the tiny wrinkles around her eyes, the skin that had gone soft and tissuey around the bone, dark underneath it. The sweet smell covered up something else; when he breathed her breath, it slid down his throat and stuck there.

"Look . . ." She took his hand and turned his arm around, the pale skin underneath showing. She drew a fingernail along the blue vein that ran down to the pulse ticking away in his wrist.

She dropped his hand and held out her own arm. For just a second—then she seemed to remember something. She lifted her hips to pull the slip up, then shimmied the rest of the way out of it like a quick snakeskin. She threw it on the floor with his shirt.

"Now look . . ." She traced the vein in her arm. Her fingernail left a long thin mark along it. She did it again, the mark going deeper. Then a dot of red welled up around her nail, in the middle of her forearm. She dug the nail in deeper, then peeled back the white skin, the line pulling open from the inside of her elbow to her wrist.

"Look," she whispered again. She held the arm up to his face. The room was so small now, the ceiling pressing against his neck, that he couldn't back away. "Look." She held the long slit open, her fingers pulling the skin and flesh back. The red made a net over her hand, collecting in thicker lines that coursed to the point of her elbow and trickled off. A red pool had formed between her knee and his, where their weight pressed the mattress down low.

The blue line inside her arm was brighter now, revealed. "Go on," she said. "Touch it." She leaned forward, bringing her mouth close to his ear. "You have to."

He reached out—slowly—and lay his fingertips on the blue line. For a moment he felt a shock, like the one the man in the bar had given him. But he didn't draw his hand away from the slit the woman held open to him. Under his fingertips he felt the tremble of the blood inside.

Her eyelids had drawn down, so that she looked at him through her lashes. Smiling. "Don't go . . ." He saw her tongue move across the edges of her teeth. "There's more . . ."

She had to let go of the edges, to guide him. The skin and flesh slid against his fingers, under the ridge of his knuckles. He could still see inside the opening, past her hand and his.

She teased a white strand away from the bone. "Here . . ." She looped his fingers under the tendon. As his fingers curled around it, stretching and lifting it past the glistening muscle, the hand at the end of the arm, her hand, curled also. The fingers bent, holding nothing, a soft gesture, a caress.

He could barely breathe. When the air came into his throat, it was heavy with the woman's sweet smell, and the other smell, the raw, sharper one that he'd caught off his uncle.

"See?" The woman bent her head low, looking up through her lashes into his eyes. Her breasts glowed with sweat. Her hair trailed across her open arm, the ends of the dark strands tangling in the blood. "See—it's not so bad, is it?"

She wanted him to say no, she wanted him to say it was okay. She didn't want him to be frightened. But he couldn't say anything. The smell had become a taste lying on his tongue. He finally managed to shake his head.

Her smile was a little bit sad. "Okay, then." She nodded slowly. "Come on."

The hand at the end of the arm had squeezed into a fist, a small one because her hands were so small. The blood that had trickled down into her palm seeped out from between the fingers and thumb. With her other hand, she closed his fingers around the white tendon tugged up from inside. She closed her grip around his wrist and pulled, until the tendon snapped, both ends coming free from their anchor on the bone.

She made him lift his hand up, the ends of the tendon dangling from where it lay across his fingers. She had tilted her head back, the cords in her throat drawn tight.

"Come on . . ." She leaned back against the pillow. She pulled him toward her. One of her hands lay on the mattress, palm upward, open again, red welling up from the slit in her arm. With her other hand she guided his hand. His fingers made red smears across the curve of her rib cage. "Here . . ." She forced his fingertips underneath. "You have to push hard." The skin parted and his fingers sank in, the thin bone of the rib sliding across the tips.

"That's right . . ." She nodded as she whispered, eyes closed. "Now you've got it. . . ."

Her hand slid down from his, down his wrist and trailing along his forearm. Not holding and guiding him any longer, but just touching him. He knew what she wanted him to do. His fingers curled around the rib, the blood streaming down to his elbow as the skin opened wider. He lifted and pulled, and the woman's rib cage came up toward him, the ones higher snapping free from her breastbone, all of them grinding softly against the hinge of her spine.

His hand moved inside, the wing of her ribs spreading back. Her skin parted in a curve running up between her breasts. He could see everything now, the shapes that hung suspended in the red space, close to each other, like soft nestled stones. The shapes trembled as his hand moved between them, the webs of sinew stretching, then peeling open, the spongy tissue easing around his hand and forearm.

He reached up higher, his body above hers now, balancing his weight on his other hand hard against the mattress, deep in the red pool along her side. Her knees pressed into the points of his hips.

He felt it then, trembling against his palm. His hand closed around it, and he saw it in her face as he squeezed it tight into his fist.

The skin parted further, the red line dividing her throat, to the hinge of her jaw. She lifted herself up from the pillow, curling around him, the opening soft against his chest. She wrapped her arm around his shoulders to hold him closer to her.

She tilted her head back, pressing her throat to his mouth. He opened his mouth, and his mouth was full, choking him until he had to swallow. The heat streaming across his face and down his own throat pulsed with the trembling inside his fist.

He swallowed again now, faster, the red heat opening inside him.

It was lying on the bed, not moving. He stood there looking at it. He couldn't even hear it breathing anymore. The only sound in the little room was a slow dripping from the edge of the mattress onto the floor.

He reached down, fingertip trembling, and touched its arm. Its hand lay open against the pillow, palm upward. Underneath the red, the flesh was white and cold. He touched the edge of the opening in its forearm. Already, the blue vein and the tendon had drawn back inside, almost hidden. The skin had started to close, the ends of the slit becoming a faint white line, that he couldn't even feel, though he left a smeared fingerprint there. He pulled back his hand, then he turned away from the bed and stumbled out into the hallway with the single light bulb hanging from the ceiling.

They looked up and saw him as he walked across the bar. He didn't push the empty chairs aside, but hit them with his legs, shoving his way past them.

His uncle Tommy scooted over, making room for him at the booth. He sat down hard, the back of his head striking the slick padding behind him.

They had all been laughing and talking just before, but they had gone quiet now. His father's buddies fumbled with the bottles in front of them, not wanting to look at him.

His father dug out a handkerchief, a blue checked one. "Here—" A quiet voice, the softest he'd ever heard his father say anything. His father held out the handkerchief across the table. "Clean yourself up a little."

He took the handkerchief. For a long time, he sat there and looked down at his hands and what was on them.

They were all laughing again, making noise to keep the dark pushed back. His father and his uncle and their buddies roared and shouted and pitched the empties out the windows. The car barreled along, cutting a straight line through the empty night.

He laid his face into the wind. Out there, the dog ran at the edge of the darkness, its teeth bared, its eyes like bright heated coins. It ran over the stones and dry brush, keeping pace with the car, never falling behind, heading for the same destination.

The wind tore the tears from his eyes. The headlights swept across the road ahead, and he thought of the piece of paper folded in the book in his bedroom. The piece of paper meant nothing now, he could tear it into a million pieces. She'd know, too, the girl who played the flute and who'd given the piece of paper to him. She'd know when she saw him again, she'd know that things were different now, and they could never be the same again. They'd be different for her now, too. She'd know.

The tears striped his face, pushed by the wind. He wept in rage and shame at what had been stolen from him. Rage and shame that the woman down there, in the little room at the end of the street with all the lights, would be dead, would get to know over and over again what it was to die. That was what she'd stolen from him, from all of them.

He wept with rage and shame that now he was like them, he was one of them. He opened his mouth and let the wind hammer into his throat, to get out the stink and taste of his own sweat, which was just like theirs now.

The dog ran beside the car, laughing as he wept with rage and shame. Rage and shame at what he knew now, rage and shame that now he knew he'd never die.

PETER STRAUB

A Short Guide to the City

PETER STRAUB is one of America's most popular authors. Born in Milwaukee, Wisconsin, he was a teacher before his first novel, *Marriages*, was published in 1973. Since then a string of popular best-sellers have appeared under his byline, including *Julia* (filmed as *Full Circle* aka *The Haunting of Julia*), *If You Could See Me Now*, *Ghost Story* (also filmed), *Shadowland*, *Floating Dragon*, *Under Venus*, *Koko* and *Mystery*. In 1977 he collaborated with his friend Stephen King on *The Talisman*.

A winner of both The British Fantasy Award and the World Fantasy Award, his most recent books are the short novel *Mrs God* and a collection of short stories, *Houses Without Doors*. The story that follows is taken from that collection and, as in much of Straub's superior fiction, the horror is hidden as subtext. However, it is no less powerful for its chilling subtlety and humour . . .

THE viaduct killer, named for the location where his victims' bodies have been discovered, is still at large. There have been six victims to date, found by children, people exercising their dogs, lovers, or—in one instance—by policemen. The bodies lay sprawled, their throats slashed, partially sheltered by one or another of the massive concrete supports at the top of the slope beneath the great bridge. We assume that the viaduct killer is a resident of the city, a voter, a renter or property owner, a product of the city's excellent public school system, perhaps even a parent of children who even now attend one of its seven elementary schools, three public high schools, two parochial schools, or single nondenominational private school. He may own a boat or belong to the Book-of-the-Month Club, he may frequent one or another of its many bars and taverns, he may have subscription tickets to the concert series put on by the city symphony orchestra. He may be a factory worker with a library ticket. He owns a car, perhaps two. He may swim in one of the city's public pools or the vast lake, punctuated with sailboats, during the hot moist August of the city.

For this is a Midwestern city, northern, with violent changes of season. The extremes of climate, from ten or twenty below zero to up around one hundred in the summer, cultivate an attitude of acceptance in its citizens, of insularity—it looks inward, not out, and few of its children leave for the more temperate, uncertain, and experimental cities of the eastern or western coasts. The city is proud of its modesty—it cherishes the ordinary, or what it sees as the ordinary, which is not. (It has had the same mayor for twenty-four years, a man of limited-to-average intelligence who has aged gracefully and has never had any other occupation of any sort.)

Ambition, the yearning for fame, position, and achievement, is discouraged here. One of its citizens became the head of a small foreign state, another a famous bandleader, yet another a Hollywood staple who for decades played the part of the star's best friend and confidant; this, it is felt, is enough, and besides, all of these people are now dead. The city has no literary tradition. Its only mirror is provided by its two newspapers, which have thick sports sections and are comfortable enough to be read in bed.

The city's characteristic mode is *denial*. For this reason, an odd fabulousness permeates every quarter of the city, a receptiveness to fable, to the unrecorded. A river runs through the center of the business district, as the Liffey runs through Dublin, the Seine through Paris, the Thames through London, and the Danube through Budapest, though our river is smaller and less consequential than any of these.

Our lives are ordinary and exemplary, the citizens would say. We take part in the life of the nation, history courses through us for all our immunity to the national illnesses: it is even possible that in our ordinary lives ... We too have had our pulse taken by the great national seers and opinion-makers, for in us you may find ...

Forty years ago, in winter, the body of a woman was found on the banks of the river. She had been raped and murdered, cast out of the human community—a prostitute, never identified—and the noises of struggle that must have accompanied her death went unnoticed by the patrons of the Green Woman Taproom, located directly above that point on the river where her body was discovered. It was an abnormally cold winter that year, a winter of shared misery, and within the Green Woman the music was loud, feverish, festive.

In that community, which is Irish and lives above its riverfront shops and bars, neighborhood children were supposed to have found a winged man huddling in a packing case, an aged man, half-starved, speaking a strange language none of the children knew. His wings were ragged and dirty, many of the feathers as cracked and threadbare as those of an old pigeon's, and his feet were dirty and swollen. *Ull! Li! Gack!* the children screamed at him, mocking the sounds that came from his mouth. They pelted him with rocks and snowballs, imagining that he had crawled up from that same river which sent chill damp—a damp as cold as cancer—into their bones and bedrooms, which gave them earaches and chilblains, which in summer bred rats and mosquitos.

One of the city's newspapers is Democratic, the other Republican. Both papers ritually endorse the mayor, who though consummately political has no recognizable politics. Both of the city's newspapers also support the Chief of Police, crediting him with keeping the city free of the kind of violence that has undermined so many other American cities. None of our citizens goes armed, and our church attendance is still far above the national average.

We are ambivalent about violence.

We have very few public statues, mostly of Civil War generals. On the lakefront, separated from the rest of the town by a six-lane expressway, stands the cubelike structure of the Arts Center, otherwise called the War Memorial. Its rooms are hung with mediocre paintings before which schoolchildren are led on tours by their teachers, most of whom were educated in our local school system.

Our teachers are satisfied, decent people, and the statistics about alcohol and drug abuse among both students and teachers are very encouraging.

There is no need to linger at the War Memorial.

Proceeding directly north, you soon find yourself among the orderly, impressive precincts of the wealthy. It was in this sector of the town, known generally as the East Side, that the brewers and tanners who made our city's first great fortunes set up their mansions. Their houses have a northern, Germanic, even Baltic look which is entirely appropriate to our climate. Of gray stone or red brick, the size of factories or prisons, these stately buildings seem to conceal that vein of fantasy that is actually our most crucial inheritance. But it may be that the style of life—the invisible, hidden life—of these inbred merchants is itself fantastic: the multitude of servants, the maids and coachmen, the cooks and laundresses, the private zoos, the elaborate dynastic marriages and fleets of cars, the rooms lined with silk wallpaper, the twenty-course meals, the underground wine cellars and bomb shelters. . . . Of course we do not know if all of these things are true, or even if some of them are true. Our society folk keep to themselves, and what we know of them we learn chiefly from the newspapers, where they are pictured at their balls, standing with their beautiful daughters before fountains of champagne. The private zoos have been broken up long ago. As citizens, we are free to walk down the avenues, past the magnificent houses, and to peer in through the gates at their coach houses and lawns. A uniformed man polishes a car, four tall young people in white play tennis on a private court.

The viaduct killer's victims have all been adult women.

While you continue moving north you will find that as the houses diminish in size the distance between them grows greater. Through the houses, now without gates and coach houses, you can glimpse a sheet of flat grayish-blue—the lake. The air is free, you breathe it in. That is freedom, breathing this air from the lake. Free people may invent themselves in any image, and you may imagine yourself a prince of the earth, walking with an easy stride. Your table is set with linen, china, crystal, and silver, and as you dine, as the servants pass among you with the serving trays, the talk is educated, enlightened, without prejudice of any sort. The table talk is mainly about ideas, it is true, ideas of a conservative cast. You deplore violence, you do not recognize it.

Further north lie suburbs, which are uninteresting.

If from the War Memorial you proceed south, you cross the viaduct. Beneath you is a valley—the valley is perhaps best seen in the dead of winter. All of our city welcomes winter, for our public buildings are gray stone fortresses which, on days when the temperature dips below zero and the old gray snow of previous storms swirls in the avenues, seem to blend with the leaden air and become dreamlike and cloudy. This is how they were meant to be seen. The valley is called . . . it is called the Valley. Red

17

flames tilt and waver at the tops of columns, and smoke pours from factory chimneys. The trees seem to be black. In the winter, the smoke from the factories becomes solid, like dark gray glaciers, and hangs in the dark air in defiance of gravity, like wings that are a light feathery gray at their tips and darken imperceptibly toward black, toward pitchy black at the point where these great frozen glaciers, these dirigibles, would join the body at the shoulder. The bodies of the great birds to which these wings are attached must be imagined.

In the old days of the city, the time of the private zoos, wolves were bred in the Valley. Wolves were in great demand in those days. Now the wolf-ranches have been entirely replaced by factories, by rough taverns owned by retired shop foremen, by spurs of the local railroad line, and by narrow streets lined with rickety frame houses and shoe-repair shops. Most of the old wolf-breeders were Polish, and though their kennels, grassy yards, and barbed-wire exercise runs have disappeared, at least one memory of their existence endures: the Valley's street signs are in the Polish language. Tourists are advised to skirt the Valley, and it is always recommended that photographs be confined to the interesting views obtained by looking down from the viaduct. The more courageous visitors, those in search of pungent experience, are cautiously directed to the taverns of the ex-foremen, in particular the oldest of these (the Rusty Nail and the Brace 'n' Bit), where the wooden floors have so softened and furred with lavings and scrubbings that the boards have come to resemble the pelts of long narrow short-haired animals. For the intrepid, these words of caution: do not dress conspicuously, and carry only small amounts of cash. Some working knowledge of Polish is also advised.

Continuing further south, we come to the Polish district proper, which also houses pockets of Estonians and Lithuanians. More than the city's sadly declining downtown area, this district has traditionally been regarded as the city's heart, and has remained unchanged for more than a hundred years. Here the visitor may wander freely among the markets and street fairs, delighting in the sight of well-bundled children rolling hoops, patriarchs in tall fur hats and long beards, and women gathering around the numerous communal water pumps. The sausages and stuffed cabbage sold at the food stalls may be eaten with impunity, and the local beer is said to be of an unrivaled purity. Violence in this district is invariably domestic, and the visitor may feel free to enter the frequent political discussions, which in any case partake of a nostalgic character. In late January or early February the "South Side" is at its best, with the younger people dressed in multilayered heavy woolen garments decorated with the "reindeer" or "snowflake" motif, and the older women of the community seemingly vying to see which of them can outdo the others in the thickness, blackness, and heaviness of her outergarments and in the severity of the traditional head scarf known as the babushka. In late winter the neatness and orderliness of these colorful folk may be seen at its best, for the wandering visitor will often see the bearded paterfamilias sweeping and shoveling not only his immaculate bit of sidewalk (for these houses are as close together as those of the wealthy along the lakefront, so near to one another that until very recently telephone service was regarded as an irrelevance), but his tiny front lawn as well, with its Marian shrines, crèches, ornamental objects such as elves, trolls, postboys, etc. It is not unknown for residents here to proffer the stranger an invitation to inspect their houses, in order to display the immaculate condition of the kitchen with its well-blackened wood stove and polished ornamental tiles, and perhaps even extend a thimble-glass of their own peach or plum brandy to the thirsty visitor.

Alcohol, with its associations of warmth and comfort, is ubiquitous here, and it is the rare family that does not devote some portion of the summer to the preparation of that winter's plenty.

For these people, violence is an internal matter, to be resolved within or exercised upon one's own body and soul or those of one's immediate family. The inhabitants of these neat, scrubbed little houses with their statues of Mary and cathedral tiles, the descendants of the hard-drinking wolf-breeders of another time, have long since abandoned the practice of crippling their children to ensure their continuing exposure to parental values, but self-mutilation has proved more difficult to eradicate. Few blind themselves now, but many a grandfather conceals a three-fingered hand within his embroidered mitten. Toes are another frequent target of self-punishment, and the prevalence of cheerful, even boisterous shops, always crowded with old men telling stories, which sell the hand-carved wooden legs known as "pegs" or "dollies," speaks of yet another. No one has ever suggested that the viaduct killer is a South Side resident.

The South Siders live in a profound relationship to violence, and its effects are invariably implosive rather than explosive. Once a decade, perhaps twice a decade, one member of a family will realize, out of what depths of cultural necessity the outsider can only hope to imagine, that the whole family must die—*be sacrificed*, to speak with greater accuracy. Axes, knives, bludgeons, bottles, babushkas, ancient derringers, virtually every imaginable implement has been used to carry out this aim. The houses in which this act of sacrifice has taken place are immediately if not instantly cleaned by the entire neighborhood, acting in concert. The bodies receive a Catholic burial in consecrated ground, and a mass is said in honor of both the victims and their murderer. A picture of the departed family is installed in the church which abuts Market Square, and for a year the house is kept clean and dust-free by the grandmothers of the neighborhood. Men young and old will quietly enter the house, sip the brandy of the "removed," as they are called, meditate, now and then switch on the wireless or the television set, and reflect on the darkness of earthly life. The departed are frequently said to appear to friends and neighbors, and often accurately predict the coming of storms and assist in the location of lost household objects, a treasured button or Mother's sewing needle. After the year has elapsed, the house is sold, most often to a young couple, a young blacksmith or market vendor and his bride, who find the furniture and even the clothing of the "removed" welcome additions to their small household.

Further south are suburbs and impoverished hamlets, which do not compel a visit.

Immediately west of the War Memorial is the city's downtown. Before its decline, this was the city's business district and administrative center, and the monuments of its affluence remain. Marching directly west on the wide avenue which begins at the expressway are the Federal Building, the Post Office, and the great edifice of City Hall. Each is an entire block long and constructed of granite blocks quarried far north in the state. Flights of marble stairs lead up to the massive doors of these structures, and crystal chandeliers can be seen through many of the windows. The facades are classical and severe, uniting in an architectural landscape of granite revetments and colonnades of pillars. (Within, these grand and inhuman buildings have long ago been carved and partitioned into warrens illuminated by bare light bulbs or flickering fluorescent tubing, each tiny office with its worn counter for petitioners and a stamped sign proclaiming its function: Tax & Excise, Dog Licenses, Passports, Graphs & Charts, Registry of Notary Publics, and the like. The larger rooms with chandeliers which face the avenue, reserved for civic receptions and banquets, are seldom used.)

In the next sequence of buildings are the Hall of Records, the Police Headquarters, and the Criminal Courts Building. Again, wide empty marble steps lead up to massive bronze doors, rows of columns, glittering windows which on wintry days reflect back the gray empty sky. Local craftsmen, many of them descendants of the city's original French settlers, forged and installed the decorative iron bars and grilles on the facade of the Criminal Courts Building.

After we pass the massive, nearly windowless brick facades of the Gas and Electric buildings, we reach the arching metal drawbridge over the river. Looking downriver, we can see its muddy banks and the lights of the terrace of the Green Woman Taproom, now a popular gathering place for the city's civil servants. (A few feet further east is the spot from which a disgruntled lunatic attempted and failed to assassinate President Dwight D. Eisenhower.) Further on stand the high cement walls of several breweries. The drawbridge has not been raised since 1956, when a corporate yacht passed through.

Beyond the drawbridge lies the old mercantile center of the city, with its adult bookstores, pornographic theaters, coffee shops, and its rank of old department stores. These now house discount outlets selling roofing tiles, mufflers and other auto parts, plumbing equipment, and cut-rate clothing, and most of their display windows have been boarded or bricked in since the civic disturbances of 1968. Various civic plans have failed to revive this area, though the cobblestones and gas street lamps installed in the optimistic mid-seventies can for the most part still be seen. Connoisseurs of the poignant will wish to take a moment to appreciate them, though they should seek to avoid the bands of ragged children that frequent this area at nightfall, for though these children are harmless they can become pressing in their pleas for small change.

Many of these children inhabit dwellings they have constructed themselves in the vacant lots between the adult bookstores and fast-food outlets of the old mercantile district, and the "tree houses" atop mounds of tires, most of them several stories high and utilizing fire escapes and flights of stairs scavenged from the old department stores, are of some architectural interest. The stranger should not attempt to penetrate these "children's cities," and on no account should offer them any more than the pocket change they request or display a camera, jewelry, or an expensive wristwatch. The truly intrepid tourist seeking excitement may hire one of these children to guide him to the diversions of his choice. Two dollars is the usual gratuity for this service.

It is not advisable to purchase any of the goods the children themselves may offer for sale, although they have been affected by the same self-consciousness evident in the impressive buildings on the other side of the river and do sell picture postcards of their largest and most eccentric constructions. It may be that the naive architecture of these tree houses represents the city's most authentic artistic expression, and the postcards, amateurish as most of them are, provide interesting, perhaps even valuable, documentation of this expression of what may be called folk art.

These industrious children of the mercantile area have ritualized their violence into highly formalized tattooing and "spontaneous" forays and raids into the tree houses of opposing tribes during which only superficial injuries are sustained, and it is not suspected that the viaduct killer comes from their number.

Further west are the remains of the city's museum and library, devastated during the civic disturbances, and beyond these pictur-esque, still-smoking hulls lies the ghetto. It is not advised to enter the ghetto on foot, though the tourist who has arranged to rent an automobile may safely drive through it after he has negotiated his toll at the gate house. The ghetto's residents are completely self-sustaining, and the attentive tourist who visits this district will observe the multitude of tents housing hospitals, wholesale food and drug warehouses, and the like. Within the ghetto are believed to be many fine poets, painters, and musicians, as well as the historians known as "memorists," who are the district's living encyclopedias and archivists. The "memorist's" tasks include the memorization of the works of the area's poets, painters, etc., for the district contains no printing presses or art-supply shops, and these inventive and self-reliant people have devised this method of preserving their works. It is not believed that a people capable of inventing the genre of "oral painting" could have spawned the viaduct killer, and in any case no ghetto resident is permitted access to any other area of the city.

The ghetto's relationship to violence is unknown.

Further west the annual snowfall increases greatly, for seven months of the year dropping an average of two point three feet of snow each month upon the shopping malls and paper mills which have concentrated here. Dust storms are common during the summers, and certain infectious viruses, to which the inhabitants have become immune, are carried in the water.

Still further west lies the Sports Complex.

The tourist who has ventured thus far is well advised to turn back at this point and return to our beginning, the War Memorial. Your car may be left in the ample and clearly posted parking lot on the Memorial's eastern side. From the Memorial's wide empty terraces, you are invited to look southeast, where a great unfinished bridge crosses half the span to the hamlets of Wyatt and Arnoldville. Construction was abandoned on this noble civic project, subsequently imitated by many cities in our western states and in Australia and Finland, immediately after the disturbances of 1968, when its lack of utility became apparent. When it was noticed that many families chose to eat their bag lunches on the Memorial's lakeside terraces in order to gaze silently at its great interrupted arc, the bridge was adopted as the symbol of the city, and its image decorates the city's many flags and medals.

The "Broken Span," as it is called, which hangs in the air like the great frozen wings above the Valley, serves no function but the symbolic. In itself and entirely by accident this great non-span memorializes violence, not only by serving as a reference to the workmen who lost their lives during its construction (its non-construction). It is not rounded or finished in any way, for labor on the bridge ended abruptly, even brutally, and from its truncated floating end dangle lengths of rusting iron webbing, thick wire cables weighted by chunks of cement, and bits of old planking material. In the days before access to the un-bridge was walled off by an electrified fence, two or three citizens each year elected to commit their suicides by leaping from the end of the span; and one must resort to a certain lexical violence when referring to it. Ghetto residents are said to have named it "Whitey," and the tree-house children call it "Ursula," after one of their own killed in the disturbances. South Siders refer to it as "The Ghost," civil servants, "The Beast," and East Siders simply as "that thing." The "Broken Span" has the violence of all unfinished things, of everything interrupted or left undone. In violence there is often the quality of *yearning*—the yearning for completion. For closure. For that which is absent and would if present bring to fulfillment. For the body without which the wing is a useless frozen ornament. It ought not to go unmentioned that most of the city's residents have never seen the "bridge" except in its representations, and for this majority the "bridge" is little more or less than a myth, being without any actual referent. It is pure idea.

Violence, it is felt though unspoken, is the physical form of sensitivity. The city believes this. Incompletion, the lack of referent which strands you in the realm of pure idea, demands release from itself. We are above all an American city, and what we believe most deeply we . . .

The victims of the viaduct killer, that citizen who excites our attention, who makes us breathless with outrage and causes our police force to ransack the humble dwellings along the riverbank, have all been adult women. These women in their middle years are taken from their lives and set like statues beside the pillar. Each morning there is more pedestrian traffic on the viaduct, in the frozen mornings men (mainly men) come with their lunches in paper bags, walking slowly along the cement walkway, not looking at one another, barely knowing what they are doing, looking down over the edge of the viaduct, looking away, dawdling, finally leaning like fishermen against the railing, waiting until they can no longer delay going to their jobs.

The visitor who has done so much and gone so far in this city may turn his back on the "Broken Span," the focus of civic pride, and look in a southwesterly direction past the six lanes of the expressway, perhaps on tiptoe (children may have to mount one of the convenient retaining walls). The dull flanks of the viaduct should just now be visible, with the heads and shoulders of the waiting men picked out in the gray air like brush strokes. The quality of their yearning, its expectancy, is visible even from here.

ELIZABETH MASSIE

Stephen

ELIZABETH MASSIE was born in Virginia and was a teacher for sixteen years. Her short fiction has appeared in many small press publications such as *The Horror Show, Grue, Deathrealm, 2AM, The Blood Review, New Blood* and *Iniquities*, along with the anthologies *Bringing Down the Moon, Women of Darkness, Borderlands, Obsessions, Dead End: City Limits, A Whisper of Blood* and *Still Dead*. Pan Books will publish her first novel, *Sineater*, in 1992.

She has also scripted a young people's drug abuse drama, *Rhymes and Reasons*, which was produced by the PBS Network and won a 1990 Parent's Choice Award. "Stephen" was nominated for the Horror Writers of America's Bram Stoker Award and is a memorable story of twisted love and obsession that breaks all the taboos.

MICHAEL AND STEPHEN SHARED A ROOM at the rehabilitation center. Michael was a young man with bright, frantically moving eyes and an outrageous sense of nonstop, bitter humor. He had been a student at the center for more than a year, and with his disability, would most likely be there much longer. This was true, also, for the others housed on the first floor of the west wing. Severe cases, all of them, living at the center, studying food services, auto mechanics, computer operating, art, and bookkeeping, none of them likely to secure a job when released because when hiring the disabled, businesses would usually go for the students who lived on east wing and on the second floors. The center had amazing gadgets which allowed people like Michael to work machines and press computer keys and dabble in acrylics, but the generic factory or office did not go in for space-aged, human-adaptive robotics. And Michael himself was a minor miracle of robotics.

Anne arrived at the center late, nearly ten thirty, although her meeting had been scheduled for ten o'clock. The cab dropped her off at the front walk and drove away, spraying fine gravel across her heels. Inside her shoes, her toes worked an awkward rhythm than neither kept them warm nor calmed her down. A cool November wind threw a piece of paper across the walk before her. On its tail followed the crumbled remains of a dead oak leaf. Anne's full skirt flipped and caught her legs in a tight embrace. It tugged, as if trying to pull her backward and away. In her mouth she tasted hair and sour fear. When she raked her fingers across her face the hair was gone, but not the fear.

The center was large and sterile, a modern bit of gray stone architecture. The largest building was marked with a sign to the left of the walkway. "Administrations and Admissions". Almost the entire front of this building was composed of plate glass with borders of stone. Anne could not see behind the glass for the harsh glare of morning sun, but in the wind the glass seemed to bulge and ripple.

Like a river.

Like water.

"Christ."

Anne scrunched her shoulders beneath the weight of her coat and glanced about for a place to sit and compose herself. Yes, she was late, but screw them if they wanted to complain about volunteer help. There were several benches just off the walkway, on the lawn, but she didn't want to sit in full view. And so she took the walk leading to the right, following along until it circled behind the main building beside what she assumed was a long, gray stone dormitory. The walk ended at a paved parking lot, marked off for visitors and deliveries. She crossed the lot, skirting cars and food trucks and large vans equipped for hauling wheelchairs, heading for a grove of trees on the other side. A lone man pushing an empty wheeled cot crossed in front of Anne and gave her a nod. She smiled slightly and then looked away.

The trees across the lot encircled a park. Picnic tables were clustered beneath the largest of the oaks, and concrete benches made a neat border about the pond in the center. The pond itself was small, no more than two acres, but it was dark and clearly deep. Dead cattails rattled on the water's edge. A short pier jutted into the water from the shore, with a weathered rowboat tethered to the end. Leaves were blown in spastic patterns on the black surface.

Anne sat on a bench and wrapped her fingers about her knees. There was no one else in the park. She looked at the brown grass at her feet, then at her hands on her knees, and then at the pond. The sight of the bobbing boat and the dull shimmering of the ripples made her stomach clamp. What a raw and ugly thing the pond was.

A cold thing, enticing and deadly, ready to suck someone under and drag them down into its lightless depths. Licking and smothering with its stinking embrace.

Phillip would have loved this pond.

Phillip would have thought it just right.

The fucking bastard.

If she was to go to the water's edge, she thought she might see his reflection there, grinning at her.

But she did not go. She sat on the concrete bench, her fingers turning purple with the chill, her breath steaming the air. She did not look at the pond again, but at the grass and her knees and the picnic tables. She studied the gentle slopes the paths made about the park, all accessible to wheeled means of movement. Accessible to the people who lived here. To the people Anne's mother had protected her from as a child; who her mother had hurried Anne away from on the street, whispering in her ear, "Don't stare, now, Anne. Polite people don't react. Do you hear me?

"There but for the grace of God go you, Anne. Don't look now. It's not nice."

Anne closed her eyes but the vision of the park and the tables and the sloped pathways stayed inside her eyes. She could hear the wind on the pond.

"Damn you, Mother," she said. "Damn you, Phillip."

She sat for another twenty minutes.

When she crossed the parking lot again, her eyes in the sun and her hands in her pockets, her muscles were steeled and her face carried a tight, professional smile.

Janet Warren welcomed Anne into the center at ten-fifty six, barely mentioning the tardiness. She took Anne into her office, and, as assistant administrator, explained the functions of the center. She gave Anne a brief summary of the students with whom Anne would work, then led her off to the west wing.

Anne entered Michael's room after Janet gave an obligatory tap on the door. Michael grunted and Anne walked in, still holding her coat, which Janet had offered to take, clutched tightly to her stomach.

"Michael," said Janet to the man on the bed. "This is Miss Zaccaria, the lady I said would be coming to help us out."

Michael propped up on his elbow, straightening himself, patting his blanket down about the urinary bag as if it were an egg in an Easter basket. He gave Anne a wide grin.

"Well, if it ain't my dream lady come to see me in the flesh!" he crowed. "Are you real or just a vision of delight?"

Anne licked her lips and looked back at Janet Warren. "Thank you, Mrs Warren. I'll be fine now. I'll let you know if we need anything."

"Hell, I know what I need," said Michael. "And she's standing right in front of me."

Janet nodded, her motion seeming to be both acknowledgment of what Anne had said and a sisterly confirmation of what she had come to do. Janet turned and left the room.

"Come on," said Michael, and Anne looked back at him.

"Come on? What do you mean?" There was only a small comfort in her professional ability at conversation. It wasn't enough to overcome her discomfort at seeing the physical form of Michael before her. He was legless, with hipbones flattened into a shovel-shaped protrusion. The thin blanket emphasized rather than hid his lower deformity. He was missing his right arm to the elbow, and there was no left arm at all. A steel hook clipped the air in cadence with the blinking of Michael's eyes.

"Come on and tell me. You ain't really no shrink, are you? I was expecting some shriveled up old bitch. You really is my dream lady, ain't you?"

Anne focused on Michael's face and took a slow breath. "No, sorry," she said. "I'm from Associated Psychological. I'm a clinical social worker."

Michael grappled with a button and pressed it with the point of his hook. The bed rolled toward Anne. She held her position.

"No, you ain't. I dreamed about you last night. Dreamed I still had my parts and you was eating them nice as you please."

Anne's face went instantly hot. She could have kicked herself for not being ready for anything. "I was told you've had a rough time these past months," she said. "Not getting along with the other students like you used to do. I'd like to help."

"Sure. Just sit on my face for a few hours."

Anne glanced at the withered body, then back at his face. Of all the students she would be working with through the volunteer-outreach program, Michael was the most disabled. "Is that all you think about, Michael? Sex?"

"When it comes to sex," he said. "All I can *do* is think." He laughed out loud and wheeled closer. "You like me?"

"I don't know you yet. I hope we'll like each other."

"Why you here? We got shrinks. Two of them. You on' field trip?"

"Field trip?"

"You know, like them school kids. Sometimes the local schools bring in the their junior high kids. Show them around. Let them take little look-sees. Tell them if they are bad enough and dive into shallow lakes or don't wear their seat belts, God'll make them just like us."

Anne cleared her throat, and loosened her coat from her waist. "First of all, I'm here on a volunteer program. Until the new center is finished down state, there will continue to be more students than can be properly provided for. The center called on our association to help out temporarily. You are a student with whom I've been asked to work."

"Student." Michael spit out the word. "I'm thirty one and I'm called a goddam student."

"Second," Anne said. "I'm not on a field trip. I'm not here to stare. I'm here to help."

Michael shook his head, then eased off his elbow to a prone position. "So who else is on your list besides me?"

Anne opened the folded paper Janet had given her. "Randy Carter, Julia Powell, Cora Grant . . ."

"Cora'll drive you ape-shit. She lost half her brain in some gun accident."

". . . and Ardie Whitesell. I might like Cora, Michael. Don't forget, I don't know her yet, either."

Michael sighed. "I don't need no shrink. What the fuck's your name?"

"Miss Zaccaria."

"Yeah, well, I'm okay. I don't need no shrink. Don't need one any more than old roomie over there." Michael tilted his head on his pillow, indicating a curtained corner of the room.

"Roomie?"

"Roommate. He don't need no shrink, neither. I don't 'cause I got things all figured out in this world. Nothing a little nookie can't cure." Michael looked at Anne and winked. "And roomie over there, he don't

29

need one 'cause he's in some kind of damn coma. Not much fun to have around, you know."

Anne frowned, only then aware of the mechanical sounds softly emanating from the corner. The drawn curtain was stiff and white, hanging from the ceiling-high rod like a starched shroud. "What's wrong with your roommate?"

"Hell, what ain't wrong? Come over here." With a hissing of his arm, Michael rose again and clutched the bed switch, tapping buttons in a short series, and the bed spun around. The legless man rolled to the curtain. Anne followed.

Michael shifted onto his right side and took the curtain in his hook. "Stephen's been here longer'n me. He ain't on no shrink's list." Michael pulled the curtain back.

It was not registering what was before her that allowed her to focus on it as long as she did. There were machines there, a good number of them, crowded around a tiny bed like rumbling and humming steel wolves about a lone prey. Aluminum racks stood on clawed feet, heavy bags of various colored liquids hanging from them, oozing their contents into thin, clear tubes. A portable heart monitor beeped. Behind it, a utility sink held to the wall, various antiseptics and lotions and balms cluttering the shelf above. The rails of the bed were pulled up to full height. At one end of the mattress was a thin blanket, folded back and tucked down. And at the other end, a thin pillow. And Stephen.

Anne's coat and paper dropped to the floor. "Oh my dear God."

"Weird, huh? I call him Head Honcho. I think he must be some doctor's experiment, you know, keeping him alive and all. Don't it beat all?"

On the pillow was a head, with black curled hair. Attached to the head, a neck, and below that a small piece of naked, ragged chest, barely large enough to house a heart and single lung. The chest heaved and shuddered, wires pulsing like obscene fishermen's lines. That was all there was of Stephen.

Anne's heart constricted painfully. She stepped backward.

"Nurses don't like him. Can't stand to touch him, 'though they shave him every three days. Doctor checks him nearly every day. Head Honcho don't do nothing but breathe. He ain't much but at least he don't complain about my music." Michael looked at Anne.

Anne turned away. Her stomach clenched, throwing fouled bile into her throat.

"Hey, you leaving?"

"I need to see the others," she managed. And she went out of the west wing to the faculty restroom, where she lost her control and her lunch.

It was three days before Anne could bring herself to visit the center again. The AP partners were asking her for her volunteer hours chart, and as the newest member of the firm, she couldn't shrug it off. And so she returned. Her pulse was heavy in her neck and the muscles of her back were tight, but she decided she would not allow herself more than passing acknowledgment of them.

She talked with Cora in the art room. Cora had little to say, but seemed pleased with the attention Anne gave her painting. Randy was in the recreation hall with Ardie, playing a heated game of billiards, wheeling about the table with teeth gritted and chins hovering over cue sticks. Anne told them she'd visit later, after the match. Julia was shopping with her daughter, and Michael was in the pool on a red inner tube.

"Hey, Miss Zaccaria!" he called when he saw Anne peering through the water-steamed glass of the door. "Want to come in for a swim? I'm faster in the water. Bet I could catch you in a split second. What do you say?"

Anne pushed the door open and felt the onslaught of chlorine-heated mist. She did not go any closer to the pool. "I never learned to swim, Michael. Besides, I'm not exactly dressed for swimming."

"I don't want you *dressed* for swimming. What fun would that be?"

Anne wiped moisture from her forehead. "How long do you plan to swim? I thought we could visit outside. The day's turned out pretty fair. It's not as cold as it has been."

"I'm finished now, ain't I, Cindy?"

The pool-side attendant, who had been watching Michael spin around on his tube, shrugged. "If you say so." She pulled Michael's wheeled bed from the wall and moved it to the pool steps. "Get over to the side so I can get you out."

"Hey, Miss Zaccaria, do me a favor. My blue jacket is in my room. It's one of those Member's Only things. Anyway, I'm not real crazy about wind, even when it's warm. Would you get the jacket for me? Door's unlocked."

Anne's head was nodding as she thought, 'Oh, Christ, yes, I mind.' "No problem," she said. She left the pool, telling herself the curtain was drawn.

They would always keep the curtain drawn.

Michael's door was indeed unlocked. The students of the center kept valuables in a communal vault, and the staff moved about the floor frequently, so chances of theft were slim. Anne went into the room, expecting the jacket to be in plain sight, prepared to lift it coolly and leave with her self esteem in tact.

But she did not see the jacket.

She checked Michael's small dresser, behind the straight-backed chair for visitors, in the plastic laundry basket beside the vacant spot where Michael's bed rested at night. It was not there.

Anne looked at the curtained corner. Certainly the jacket would not be behind the curtain. There was no reason to go there, no reason to look.

She walked to the curtain and edged over to the hemmed corner of the heavy material. 'It's not over there,' she thought. Her hands began to sweat. She could not swallow.

She pulled the curtain back slowly. And let her gaze move to the bed.

Again, it was a flash image that recorded itself on her startled retinas before she looked away. The head was in the same place, eyes closed, dark hair in flat curls. The neck. The breathing, scarred half-chest. Anne stared at the sink, counting, rubbing thumbs against index fingers, calming herself. She would look for Michael's jacket. There was a chair like that on Michael's side, and a laundry basket, although this one held no clothes, only white towels and washcloths. By the wall beside the sink was a pile of clothing, and Anne stepped closer to search through it. There were shirts, mostly, several pairs of shorts and underwear. And a blue jacket. Anne picked it up. She looked back at the small bed.

And the eyes in the head were open, and they were looking at her.

Anne's fingers clenched, driving nails into her palms. She blinked, and glanced back at the pile of clothes, pretending she hadn't seen the eyes. Chills raced tattoos up her shoulders, and adrenalin spoke loudly in her veins. 'Leave now.'

Her hands shook as they pawed through the clothes on the floor, acting as though she had more to find. 'Calm down. And leave.'

But the voice made her stop.

"I didn't mean to stare," it said.

Anne flinched, and slowly stood straight. She looked at the bed.

The eyes were still open, still watching her.

Her own mouth opened before she had a chance to stop it, and she said, "I was looking for Michael's jacket." 'Leave now!' cried the adrenalin. 'That thing did not say anything. It can't talk. It's comatose. It's brain dead. Leave *now*!'

The eyes blinked, and Anne saw the muscles on the neck contract in a swallowing reflex. "Yes," it said. And the eyes closed. The whole ragged body seemed to shudder and shrink. It had gone to sleep again.

The jacket worked in Anne's fingers. Michael was in the pool, waiting for her. 'It's brain dead, Anne. Get hold of yourself.' "Stephen?" she whispered.

But it did not open its eyes, nor move, and Anne took the jacket down to the pool where Michael was fuming about on his bed, spinning circles around the yawning attendant.

"So I store my stuff on Stephen's side of the room, 'cause he don't complain none. And when I get visitors they don't think I'm a slob. Nurses don't care. I get the stuff from over there into my laundry basket when it's really dirty."

Anne was in Michael's visitor's chair. He was on his side, his gaze alternating between her, his hook, and the curtain.

"He's never complained to you?"

Michael chuckled shallowly. "You serious? He's in a coma, I told you already. Listen to this, if you don't believe me." Michael reached for the sleek black cassette player on the night stand beside the bed. He pushed the switch, and an instant blast of heavy rock shattered the air. Above the shrieking guitars and pounding percussion, Anne could hear the sudden, angry calls from the neighboring students.

"Go, look, quick," Michael shouted over the music. "Go see before those damned nurses get here."

Anne shook her head, smiling tightly, brushing off the suggestion.

Michael would have none of it. "Shit, just go on and look at Dead-Head Honcho."

"I don't think it's my place to bother him."

"Get on now, the nurses are coming. I hear them damn squeaking shoes down the hall!"

Anne got up and looked behind the curtain. The head was silent and motionless. The eyes were closed.

"What'd I tell you? Deaf, dumb, blind, and in a coma. Sounds like hell to me, and God knows I seen hell up close myself."

"You have?" Anne went back to her chair. "What do you mean, you've seen it up close?"

"Look at me, Miss Zaccaria. You think the love of the Lord do this to me?"

There were then three nurses' heads at the door, clustered on the frame like Japanese beetles on a rose stem. "Turn that down, Michael, or the player's ours for the next week."

"Shit," said Michael. He grappled the button; pushed it off. "I ain't no goddam student!" he told the nurses who were already gone. "It's my business how loud I play my music!"

"Tell me about your accident," said Anne. But she was thinking, 'Hell, oh, yes, it must be like hell, living in a coma.

'But he's not in a coma. He is conscious. He is alive.

'And when you are already in hell, what is hell to that?'

Her next session with Michael was canceled because he was in the infirmary with the flu. And so Anne sought out Julia, and spent an hour with her, and then with Cora, who did not want to talk but wanted Anne to paint a picture of a horse for her. Randy and Ardie were again at the billiard table and would have nothing to do with her. Then she visited the faculty lounge, and listened with feigned interest to the disgruntled banter and rehab shop-talk. A few questions were directed her way, and she answered them as cordially as possible, but she wanted to talk about Stephen. She wanted to know what they knew.

But she could not make herself bring up the subject. And so she went to the west wing, and let herself into Michael's unlocked room.

She went to the curtain and took the edge in her fingers. Her face itched but she shook it off. 'No,' said the adrenalin. "Yes," she said. And she pulled the curtain back.

The tubes flowed, nutrients in, wastes out. The monitor beeped. Bags dripped and pumps growled softly. Anne moved to the end of the bed. She forced herself to see what was before her, what she needed to see, and not be distracted by the machinery about it.

The flesh of the chest twitched slightly and irregularly with the work of the wires. Every few seconds, the shuddering breath. It would be cold, Anne thought, yet the blanket was folded back at the foot of the bed, a regulation piece of linen which served no purpose to the form on the pillow. With the wires and tubes, a blanket would be a hindrance. The neck did not move; swallowing was for the wakeful. The head as well did not move, except for the faint pulsing of the nostrils, working mindlessly to perform their assigned job.

Anne moved her hands to the railing of the bed. She slid around, moving along the side to the head of the bed. Her feet felt the floor cautiously as if the tiles might creak. She reached the pillow; her hands fell from the railing. Her face itched and again she refused to give in to it.

Through fear-chapped lips, she said, "Stephen?"

The monitor beeped. The chest quivered.

"Stephen?"

The sleeping face drew up as if in pain, and then the eyes opened. As the lids widened, the muscles of the cheeks seemed to ease. He blinked. His eyes were slate blue.

"I hope I'm not bothering you," she said.

"No," he said. And the eyes fluttered closed, and Anne thought he was asleep again. Her hands went to her face and scratched anxiously. She pulled them down.

Stephen's eyes opened. "No, you aren't bothering me. Why would you think that?"

"You were sleeping."

"I always sleep."

"Oh," Anne said.

"You've been spending time with Michael. What do you think of him?"

"He's . . . fine. It's good to spend time with him."

The head nodded, barely, sliding up and down the pillow, obviously an effort. "You are Miss Zaccaria."

"Anne," she said.

"Anne," he repeated. His eyes closed.

"Do you want me to go now?"

His eyes remained closed. "If you wish."

"Do you want me to?"

"No."

And so she stood those very long minutes, watching Stephen slip into sleep, trying to absorb the reality of what was before her, counting the beepings of the heart monitor.

Again the eyes opened. "You are still here."

"Yes."

"How long has it been?"

"Only a few minutes."

"I'm sorry."

"No, that's all right. I don't mind."

Stephen sighed. "Why don't you sit? There is a chair over there somewhere."

"I'll stand."

"Michael is wrong. I do mind his music. I hate it."

"I could ask him to keep it down."

"It's not the volume. It is the music. Music was created for movement, for involvement. I feel a straight jacket around my soul when Michael plays his music."

Anne said nothing for a moment. Stephen looked away from her, and then back again.

"Why do you let them think you are comatose?" Anne asked.

"That way I can sleep. When I sleep, there are dreams."

"What kind of dreams?"

"Ever the clinical social worker," said Stephen. And for the first time, a small smile crossed his lips.

Anne smiled also. "That's me," she said.

"My dreams are my own," he said. "I would never share them."

"All right."

"And I would not ask you to share yours," he said.

"No," said Anne.

"I'm tired," he said.

And when she was certain he was asleep once again, Anne left.

"I liked college, my studies there. The psyche of the human is so infinite and fascinating. I thought I could do something with all I'd learned. But I wasn't smart enough to become a doctor."

"How do you know?"

Anne shrugged. "I know."

"And so you are a therapist," said Stephen.

"Yes. It's important. Helping people."

"How do you help?"

"I listen to them. I help them find new ways of seeing situations."

"Do you like your patients?"

"I don't call them patients. They are clients."

"Do you like them?"

"Michael asked me something like that when we first met. He wanted to know if I liked him."

"Do you?"

Anne crossed her feet and angled her face away from Stephen. There was a lint ball on the floor by the bed. The nurses and orderlies were obviously quick about their business here.

"Of course I do," she answered.

"That's good. If you like people you can help them."

"That's not a prerequisite, though. Liking them."

Stephen closed his eyes momentarily. Then he looked at Anne again. "You have a husband?"

"No."

"A boyfriend, certainly."

"No, not really. I've not wanted one." Anne hesitated. "It's not what you think."

"What do I think?"

"That I'm a lesbian or something."

"I haven't thought that."

"I'm not."

"You have family, though."

Anne's crossed arms drew in closer. Family, yes, she did. God knows what wonders she could have accomplished had it not been for her beloved family.

"A mother," she said. "An older brother."

"What are their names?"

"My mother is Audrey. My brother . . ." Suddenly Anne was acutely aware of the utility sink behind her. She could see it brimming with water, cold water, stopped up and ready . . . "My brother's name is Phillip."

"Are you close?"

Anne's shoulders flinched at the nearness of the sink. Dark water; thick, stinking, and hungry water. Eager. She swallowed, then looked down at her hands. 'Pathetic things,' she thought. She flexed them. 'Goddam it all.' She looked up at Stephen. His forehead was creased, with a barely discernible shadow over his eyes.

"Sure," she said. "We're close."

Then Stephen went to sleep. Anne stared at the dust ball, and at the tubes running from beneath Stephen's ribs. And her fingers, wanting to move forward, were stopped, and were locked onto her lap like a colony of trapped souls.

Janet Warren was chuckling as she ushered Anne into the office. "It's no big deal," she said, obviously seeing through Anne's tight smile. "Honestly, I just want to talk with you for a minute."

Anne took one of the chairs that sat before the desk; Janet sat on the edge of the desk.

"It's Julia," Janet said.

Anne recrossed her arms and frowned slightly. "Julia? What's wrong with her?"

"Now, don't get me wrong. Sorry, I don't need to talk with you like that. You know what you're doing, you know how people react sometimes. I'm sure you've had clients freak out during sessions, things like that."

Anne said, "Certainly."

"Julia went a little crazy after your last visit. She started throwing things; she even threatened bodily harm to herself if you came back again."

"Mrs Warren, certainly you don't think . . ."

"I don't think anything, Anne. We're in this together, remember? Julia has always been easily set off. It seems you remind her of someone she hated back when she was a child. In school, somewhere back then. You've done nothing wrong. As a matter of fact, you seem to be making real progress with Michael."

Anne tapped the rug lightly with the ball of her foot. "Michael likes to joke around. I seem to be a good receptacle for that."

"So be it," said Janet. "That could be just what he needs at this point."

"Yes, I believe so."

"So what I wanted to say was just forget about Julia for the time being. I'll get another volunteer assigned to her. With your own work at the Association, I'm sure a smaller volunteer load won't disappoint you."

Anne nodded, stood, and started for the door. She turned back. "Mrs Warren, what do you know about Stephen?"

"Stephen?"

"Michael's roommate."

"Ah, yes," Janet said. She slipped from the desk top and went around the desk to the swivel chair. She did not sit. "It may sound bad to say that we assigned Michael to that room because we didn't think any other student could tolerate Michael and his moods. Stephen's in a coma; you probably already know about that. We have brainwaves, and they seem quite active, but who can figure what kinds of unconscious states the human can fall into? But whatever it is, Stephen is not to be disturbed. I would appreciate it if you would remind Michael to stay on his side of the curtain."

"Of course I will," said Anne.

"Thanks."

Anne looked out the office door, toward the activity in the main hall. Several wheelchaired students were talking with visitors; family, possibly. She looked again at Janet. "Before Stephen came here, who was he? I mean, what did he do?"

Janet sat, and dug her fingers beneath a pile of manilla folders, in search for a particular one. "What? Oh, music, he was a musician. A pianist. On the way up, I was told. Into classical concerts, things like that. A pity."

It felt as though cold water had been poured over Anne's lungs. She held her breath and slid her balled fists into her pockets. "And what," she began, "happened to him?"

The phone burred on the desk, and Janet raised an apologetic hand to Anne before picking up the receiver. She dropped to her seat with her "hello", and Anne left the office.

Michael seemed glad to be out of the infirmary. He waggled his eyebrows at Anne as she came into the room and raised up on his elbow. "Miss Zaccaria! Did you miss me?"

Anne sat in the visitor's chair. "Sure, Michael. Are you feeling better?"

Michael snorted. "Not a whole *hell* of a lot better, but enough to get me out of there. God, you should see the nurses they have for us sick students. The old ones all look like Marines, and the young ones look like willing virgins. Like going from hot to cold and back to hot again all the time. It's enough to pop your nads, if you got some."

"Are you well enough to start back into the electronics program? You haven't done anything for nearly a month; and you know you can't stay unless you are working toward a future."

"I've been sick. I had my emotional problems, right? I mean, you can vouch for that. That's why you're here."

Anne scratched her calf. "You have to look at your goals, Michael. Without goals you just stay put in time, and don't make progress."

"I got a goal."

"What's that?"

"To get my butt scratched. You ever scratch your butt with a hook?"

Anne shook her head.

"You scratch my butt for me, Miss Zaccaria?"

"Michael, don't start . . ."

"I ain't trying to be gross, honest. I just got an itch."

"Michael, it's not my place to do that. There are nurses."

"Tell me about it. Okay, then my back. You scratch my back? Please?"

Anne felt her hands catch her elbows. She sat straight, shifting as far from Michael as she could without getting from the chair. "I'm not supposed to."

"Why?"

"I just can't. It's not professional. Therapists aren't supposed to touch clients."

"I'm not talking like you being my shrink now. Just my friend. Please. My back itches."

"No, Michael."

Michael was silent for a moment. He looked away from Anne, and studied a faint spot on his blanket. When he looked back, his face was pinched. "I ain't trying to be gross," he said softly. "How about my face? Can you scratch my nose for me?"

Anne, slowly, shook her head.

"Please," he said. "Nobody ever wants to touch me."

"I can't," said Anne.

Michael watched her, and then with a quick motion, he reached out and jabbed the play button on his tape player. Shrieking music cut the air. "Fine," he cried over it. "Sorry I asked. I didn't mean it, anyway. It was a joke. A butt scratch, shit, I just wanted a butt scratch for some jollies is all."

And then the nurses came and threatened Michael and he turned the music off.

"One of the last sets of visitors I had was quite a long time ago," said Stephen. "But it is one I'll never forget." He blinked, and his dark brows drew together, then apart. A strand of black, curled hair had been moved nearly into his eye, and Anne wondered what it would be like to reach out and push it back. "They were from a church. Pentecostal something. Holiness something. Young people, all of them. Neatly dressed, each in a pure white outfit that made me think of angry young angels. Even their Bibles were white. They didn't want to be here; I could hear them whispering behind the curtain. They were very frightened. But the leader, a young girl of about eighteen, quieted them, saying 'Even as you do it unto the least of the flock you do it unto Jesus.' And in they came, smiles flashing. The girl told me I needed to turn my life around, I needed to turn to the Lord. I told her I wasn't turning anywhere, couldn't she see that? She became flustered with my responses, then furious. I believe I was supposed to shake in the presence of their godly and bodily wholeness. Her face was as paled as her dress. When she finally ushered out her little group, she told me 'You better accept the love of the Lord. There isn't anyone else in this world who would love something like you.'"

"Christ, Stephen."

"No, it's all right," he said. His eyes closed, held, then opened slightly. "It was a long time ago."

"You said one of the last sets of visitors were the church people. Who were the last?"

"Two insurance salesmen. I saw who they were, and went to sleep. I think they were more than relieved. I've been asleep most of the time since."

"Stephen."

"It's all right," he said. "Really."

Stephen shut his eyes. Anne watched his face. The nurses had done only a fair job of shaving. There was a small red cut on his chin. Then Stephen looked at her.

"Why wouldn't you touch Michael?"

Anne started. "You were listening."

"Yes."

"I can't. It's not part of the job, you know. People might take it the wrong way."

"Why are you a counselor, Anne?"

"So I can help people."

"There are lots of ways to help. Doctors, physical therapists, teachers."

"Yes." 'But they have to touch people. I can't touch, not now, not ever. Phillip touched me. Sweet God, he touched me and touching is nothing but pain and . . .'

"Your family hoped you'd be a counselor?"

"No, I don't think it mattered to them." '. . . anger and disgust. Touching is filth, degradation. It is losing control.' Anne's feet planted squarely on the floor. She was ready to run. 'Touching is cold and hateful, like putrid, black water.'

"Tell me about your family."

"I already did."

"You have a mother. A brother."

"I already did!" Anne's hand flew to her mouth and pressed there. She had screamed. "Oh, God," she said then. "I'm sorry."

"It's all right."

Anne's throat felt swollen. She swallowed and it hurt. "I didn't mean to shout. It was rude."

"It's all right."

"Stephen," Anne began, and then hesitated. She inched herself forward on her chair. Stephen's eyes watched her calmly, and they were not eyes of a blue and frightening ocean, but of a blue and clear sky. She saw an understanding there, and she wanted to reach out for it.

She wanted it, but knew the only way to have it was to touch it.

She sat back. "Good-night, Stephen," she said.

"Good-night," he answered. And he slept.

Randy was being released from the center. The staff threw him a good-bye party, complete with balloons and ridiculous hats and noisemakers which Randy pretended to hate but obviously loved. He made a point of hooting his paper horn into the ear of everyone present. Randy had landed a job in the camera room of the local newspaper. His going away gift was a framed, fake newspaper front page, complete with the headline "RANDY MYERS, AKA CLARK KENT, SECURES POSITION AT DAILY PRESS." Beneath the caption was a large black and white photo of Randy, cigar in teeth, leaning over the billiard table. A cue stick was in his hand.

"I taught him everything he knows," said Michael, as he looped about among the partiers. "He ought to take me with him, or he'll just make a mess of things."

Anne left in the midst of the hubbub and went down to the pond behind the Administration Building. The sky was overcast, and mist covered the algaed water.

Water, the dark trough of fears.

She stood beside the edge. The wind buffeted her.

Her mind, wearied, could not hold back the rush of memories.

Phillip, as a boy, touching Anne in secret. First as a game, then as an obsession. Anne growing up, Phillip growing up ahead of her, and his touching becoming even more cruel. His body heavy and harsh; his immense organ tearing into her relentlessly. Anne crying each night, knowing he would come to her and would have no love for anything except the sensation of his own explosive release. Phillip swearing that if she told anyone, he would kill her.

Anne, promising herself over and over that if she was not killed, she would never let this happen again. She would not touch or be touched.

And then came the night when Phillip decided blood would make it more rewarding. He was tired of the same old thing; he said he was going to change Anne just a little, like a sculptor changing a piece of clay to make it better. With the door locked and his underwear in Anne's mouth, he carved. He took off her little toes, stopping the blood with matches and suturing with his mother's sewing kit. He decorated her abdomen with a toothed devil face into which he rubbed ink from Anne's cartridge pen. Across her breasts he etched, "Don't fuck with me." The ink finished it off.

The next morning, Mother wanted to know why there were stains on the sheets. She accused Anne of having a boyfriend in at night. She shook Anne until the confession was made. Anne took off her bedclothes and her slippers. Mother shrieked and wailed, clutching her hair and tearing hunks out. Then she said, "The grace of God has left you! You are one of those deformed creatures!"

Mother confronted Phillip.

Phillip killed Mother in the tub that evening with scalding water and an old shower curtain.

Then he had found Anne, hiding in the garage.

Anne doubled over and gagged on the bank of the pond. She could still taste the sludge and the slime from so many years ago. She drove her fists into the wall of her ribs, and with her head spinning, she retched violently. At her feet lay brown leaves, stirred into tiny, spiraling patterns by the wind and the spattering of her own vomit.

She wiped her mouth. She stood up. Her vision wavered, and it was difficult to stand straight.

She made her way to Michael's room.

Michael's tape player was on the bed table. Michael had left it on, though softly, and as Anne picked it up she could feel the faint hammering of the percussion. The player was slender and cool and Anne could wrap both hands about it easily. Much like Phillip's cock, when she was just a young girl. With a single jerk, she pulled the cord from the wall. The table teetered, then crashed to the floor. The music died in mid-beat.

Anne hauled the player, cord dragging, to Stephen's side of the room. There was sweat on her neck, and it dripped to her breasts and tickled like roach legs. She ignored it. Stephen was asleep.

Anne threw the player into the sink and it shattered on the dulled enamel.

"This is for you, Stephen," she said. "No more music. You won't have to suffer it anymore."

She ran the water until the heat of it steamed her face and stung her eyes. She grabbed up the pieces of broken player and squeezed them. Sharp edges cut into her hands and she let the blood run.

"And this is for you, Phillip. Goddam you to whatever hell there is in this world or the next."

She looked at Stephen's bed. He was awake, and watching her.

"Anne," he said.

Anne wiped her mouth with the back of her hand. Blood streaked her chin.

"Tell me, Anne."

"My brother killed my mother. Then he tried to kill me."

"Tell me."

Anne looked at the dead player in the sink. The hot water continued to run. Anne could barely catch her breath in the heat. She stepped back and licked the blood from her hands. "He tried to kill me. He was fucking me. Ever since I can remember, he was fucking me, hurting me, and enjoying it like any other boy would enjoy baseball." She turned to Stephen, and held out her wounded hands. "Touching is wrong. And he knew it. When Mother found out, he killed her. He took me down the back road to the water treatment plant, and threw me into the settling pool. It was not deep, but I could not swim, and the bottom was slick with sludge and it was rancid, Stephen, it was sewage and garbage, and I slipped under and under and every time I came up Phillip would lean over the rail and hit me with a broom handle. It was night, and I could no longer tell the difference between up and down, it was all black and putrid and I couldn't breathe. Phillip kept hitting me and hitting me. My blood ran into the sewage and when I screamed I swallowed the sludge."

Anne moved closer to Stephen's bed, her hands raised.

"Someone heard us. Phillip was stopped and arrested. I spent a good deal of time in the hospital, with concussions and infections. Phillip has since moved out of the country."

Stephen watched between her bloodied hands and her face.

"I wanted to help people," Anne said. "I don't think I ever can. Phillip has seen to that."

"Yes, you can."

"Tell me, Stephen. What can I do for you?"

Stephen sighed silently, his chest lifting then falling. His head rolled slightly to the left, and he stared at the light above the bed.

"Love me," he said finally.

"I do, Stephen."

His eyes blinked, the light reflecting tiny sparks. He looked back at Anne. His mouth opened, then closed. His jaw flexed and he licked his lips with his dry tongue. "Love me," he said.

Anne hesitated. Then slowly, she lowered the side rail of the bed. She knelt beside the bed and put her head onto the pillow beside Stephen. For a moment she held still, and then she brought her hand up to touch Stephen's lips with her fingers. They did not move, yet she could fee the soft blowing of his breath on her skin.

She moved back then. Stephen watched her. Then he said, "You knew about my music."

Anne nodded.

"My dreams are different now."

Anne nodded.

After a long moment, he said, "Anne, love me." His voice was certain, kind, and sad.

Anne touched her face and it was hot, and wet with the steam and her own sweat. She touched Stephen's face and it was fevered. She traced his cheekbone, his chin, his throat, and the damp, tendoned contour of his neck. She let her palm join her fingers, and felt slowly along his flesh among the myriad of tapes and tubes and wires. When she reached his heart, she pressed down. The beating quickened with the pressure, and Stephen moaned.

"That hurt," Anne said.

"No."

Anne stood straight. She unbuttoned her blouse and let it drop from her shoulders. She could not look at Stephen for fear of revulsion in his eyes. She removed her bra, and then slipped from her skirt and panties.

She looked at Stephen, and thought she saw him nod.

Anne climbed onto the foot of the bed. Beneath her knees the folded, unused blanket was cold. She moved forward, and bent over Stephen's body. Around her and beside her was the tangle of supports. Her body prickled; the veins in the backs of her hands flushed with icy fire. She tried to reach Stephen, but the web held her back.

"I can't," she said.

Stephen looked at her.

"These are in the way. I can't."

He said nothing.

And Anne, one by one, removed the web which kept her from him. She loosened the wires, she withdrew the needles, she pulled out the tubes. She touched the bruises and the marks on the pale skin. "I do love you," she said.

Anne lay with Stephen. Her hands were at first soft and tentative, then grew urgent, caressing his body, caressing her own. As she touched and probed and clutched, her fingers became his fingers. Gentle, intelligent fingers studying her and loving her.

Healing her.

She rode the current, rising and falling, her eyes closed. Stephen kissed her lips as she brought them to him, and her breasts as well, and as she lifted upward, he kissed the trembling, hot wetness between her thighs. She stretched her arms outward, reaching for the world, and then brought them down and about herself and Stephen, pulling inward to where there was nothing but them both. His breathing was heavy; her heart thundered. An electrical charge hummed in the pit of her stomach. It swelled and spread, moving downward. Anne opened her mouth to cry out silently to the ceiling. The charge stood her nerves on unbearable end, and it grew until it would hold no longer. The center of her being burst. She wailed with the pulses. And she fell, crumpled, when they were spent.

"Dear God," she whispered. She lay against Stephen, one hand entangled in the dark curls. Their warmth made her smile.

Her fear was gone.

Then she said, "Stephen, tell me. Only if you want. Why are you here? What put you in this place?"

Stephen said nothing. Anne hoped he had not slipped into sleep again.

"Stephen," she said, turning over, meaning to awaken him. "Tell me why you had to come to the center. What happened to you?"

Stephen said nothing. His closed eyes did not open.

Anne pressed her palm to his heart.

It was still.

The party was over. Back in the recreation hall, Anne could hear Michael tooting his paper horn and calling out, "Hey, Miss Zaccaria, where are you? I'm ready to give you that swimming lesson. What about you?"

The water in the pond did not move. The breeze had died down, and the mist was being replaced by an impenetrable fog that sucked the form and substance from the trees and the benches around the surface of the blackness.

There were leaves at her feet, and she kicked them off the edge of the bank and into the pond. Small circles radiated from the disturbances, little waves moving out and touching other waves.

Anne took off her shoes, and walked barefoot to the end of the pier. The boat was still moored there, full of leaves.

The deep water below was as dark as Stephen's hair.
Some have their dreams, others nightmares.
Stephen had his dreams now. Dreams without end.
Amen.
And Anne would now accept her nightmare.
The leaves on the water were kind, and parted at her entrance.

JONATHAN CARROLL

The Dead Love You

JONATHAN CARROLL prefers to remain mysterious to his readers. What we do know is that he has been described as "the most innovative and original fantasist today." He's an American who has lived overseas for almost twenty years, currently residing with his family in Vienna. He also has a bull terrier that doesn't talk.

He taught courses in world literature before becomming a full-time writer and has published six highly acclaimed novels to date: *The Land of Laughs*, *Voice of Our Shadow*, *Bones of the Moon*, *Sleeping in Flame*, *A Child Across the Sky* and *Outside the Dog Museum*, along with the novella *Black Cocktail* and a short story collection, only published in German translation, entitled *Die Panische Hand*. He won the World Fantasy Award in 1988 for his short story, "Friend's Best Man", a recent issue of *Weird Tales* was a Jonathan Carroll special, and he was Guest of Honour at the 1991 British Fantasy Convention.

None of which will prepare you for the story that follows, which was originally written for a stillborn anthology which Ramsey Campbell would have edited.

THE MOST FRIGHTENING sound in the world is your own heart beating. No one likes to talk about that, but it is true. In the midst of deep fear, it's a secret beast pounding a giant fist on some inner door, demanding to get out. A few minutes before the accident, I saw a line of graffiti written on a wall. In scragged white letters a foot high, it said, THE DEAD LOVE YOU. What did that mean? What kind of citizen would think it important enough to paint on a wall in the middle of the city? Easy enough to dismiss as a stunt, or a message to the world from a Grateful Dead fan, but I sensed it was something more.

My name is Anthea Powell. I am a semisuccessful career woman in her mid-thirties. My holdings include a few valuable stocks, a small condominium, and a bad heart condition. I've listened to my heartbeat for most of my adult life with both fear and fascination. It is my engine and constant reminder. I do not want the dead to love me, yet.

I was in a hurry to get across town. If you ask me why now, I can only answer, "Because." *Because* I thought I had to get there, because the clock in my car is always fast ... because I had to keep my appointment in Samarra. I knew the intersection, even knew the stoplight as a slow one. It was red when I got there, red when the white Fiat pulled up behind me. There was nothing else to do, so I looked in the mirror and saw the car, the man driving. He was wearing sunglasses, which made me smile because it was nine at night. Was he smiling, too? I don't remember. As the light changed, a bicycle came zooming by on my left side. At the same time, the Fiat sped up and tried to pass me on the right.

The bike was so close I was sure I'd hit it. The only thing to do was swerve right, into the car. Maybe I was wrong and wasn't *so* close to the bike. Maybe a lot of things. I smacked the Fiat and simultaneously heard a metallic crunch and loud boom: my right front tire blowing.

Feeling a car accident happening around you is a bitter, hopeless thing. As it's occurring you're shocked, but already beginning to regret all that comes afterward.

Punching the brakes, I swerved hard to get away, but that was only reflex.

Stopped, I watched the bicycle rider weave fast away up the street. I wanted to wring his neck. I wanted it to be thirty seconds ago so I could do it right this time. I wanted to run away and have a healthy car again.

A car door slammed. "God damn it!" an angry voice bellowed. The driver still had his sunglasses on, but the lower part of his face told all: a furiously moving mouth. He was very blond and flapping one arm up and down.

I opened the door and started to get out, but a sudden arrhythmia of my heart grabbed hold and for a moment I was frozen there, scared eyes closed.

"Lady, are you out of your fucking mind?"

"Could you just wait a minute?" Unconsciously I'd put both hands over my heart. I felt like a piece of paper being torn in half.

"*Wait*? Listen, lady, you just about took off the front end of my *car*. What am I going to wait for?"

"I have a bad heart."

"I have a bad *car*!"

The sound of a siren came up from behind and was on us in an instant.

For really the first time I looked up at the other driver. He'd taken the sunglasses off, and only then did I understand why he wore them: He was albino. Yellow hair on the edge of silver, transparent white eyebrows, pink skin. I don't know if he had the pink albino eyes. It was too dark to see them clearly.

What astounded me was how all of that human whiteness seemed to glow, pushing him forward from the evening dark around us. A phosphorescent toy or night-lite, glowing.

"Okay, what's the problem?" The policeman was big and burly, with a voice like a trailer truck shifting gears.

"The problem is she ran into my fucking car."

"Watch your mouth, Ace. There's a lady present."

I looked at the cop and tried to smile thanks. My heart had gone back into its silence. So I got slowly out of the car and stood between the two men.

"I was pulling out from the light when a man on a bicycle cut me off. I swerved to avoid him."

"Swerved right into me, you mean."

"That's true."

"Fuckin' A it's true!"

The policeman gave him a dour look and wrote things down on a big pad he took from his breast pocket. Everything on him was large: the pad, pen, the gun that sat brown and shiny on his wide hip. "And what were *you* doing, passing on the right?"

"She was going too slow. I had to get by."

"She wasn't *going* at all—she was trying to avoid the bicycle. You were wrong being there. That's why she hit you and that's what I'm putting in my report."

The albino's mouth opened once, then closed tightly. He couldn't believe what he was hearing. "That's absolute bullshit! How do you know what she's saying is true?"

"Because I got witnesses for one, and because I don't hear you denying any of it!"

"Where's these witnesses?"

The cop pointed to a group of people standing around his car, talking to his partner.

"They all say you pulled out too fast and tried to pass her on the right. Dangerous move, you know. Illegal, too. Means you're not going to have much of a case if this goes to court."

"I don't believe you're fucking telling me this!"

"I don't like your attitude, Whitey. Let's see your driver's license."

The other reached into his back pocket and brought out a beautiful red leather wallet. I saw a large decal on it for *Midnight*, that abominable horror film that is so popular these days.

"Now, *this* is interesting! You realize it's three months past due? You got an invalid driver's license and a probable reckless driving charge looking at you, Bruce, Bruce . . . Beetz? That's a hell of a name. You want to complain some more, Bruce Beetz?" The policeman winked at me. The albino saw it and his face looked like he'd swallowed a piece of pain.

As soon as I got home I drew a bath, my second of the evening. Baths are a secret love and constant indulgence. Like my hero Blanche Dubois, whenever something goes wrong, I turn on the tap. Hot, hot . . . as hot as possible. The doctors all say the shock isn't good for my heart, but it's one of the few times I say that's too damned bad. I keep thinking my heart has a mind of its own, anyway. Since it knows it's living inside me, it should be used to being dropped into cooking water whenever something makes its owner nervous.

I poured in a lovely big dollop of coconut oil bubble bath. Watching it swirl pearl and creamy through the water, I forgot a while about my crunched car and the angry man with the white hair. The angry white man with the white car.

After hanging my clothes up, I gratefully stepped into the smoking bubbles and got comfortable. A few heavy blinks later, I was sound asleep.

I dreamt I was in an unknown city, gray and sad enough on first sight and smell to be something Eastern, most probably Communist. Sofia or Prague, a foreign city in the truest sense of the word. A city of quiet, and anonymous pain. I had never been there, that was sure. More surprising was my companion. Tightly holding my hand was a little boy I didn't know: an albino dressed in blue jeans and a blue blazer, red sneakers, and a red St Louis Cardinals baseball cap.

"What's your name?"

"Bruce Beetz."

"How old are you?"

"Seven."

"Do you know where we're going?"

He frowned. "You're supposed to be taking me home."

"Where is that?"

He started to cry. I squeezed his hand and tried to smile reassuringly. But I really had no idea where we were or who he was, besides the little boy version of the man whose car I'd just hit.

The whole dream was so strange and ludicrous that I woke up laughing. I often fall asleep in the tub and haven't drowned yet, but waking with a giggle is *not* me.

I looked around the room with tired hot eyes, refocusing on what I'd lost to sleep. Nothing had changed around me. Then I looked in the tub. Floating there among the white bubbles was a little white plastic car—a Fiat Uno, just like Bruce Beetz's. Without touching it, I could see the front bumper had been carefully bent into the same twist as that of its big, real brother.

Terror.

A heart that shakes you like a tree in a storm warns that whatever word you hold on your tongue may be your last. So savor it and know it is the right one before you use it.

Terror.

The toy car terrified me. It was impossible, funny, the worst kind of threat. Had the white man actually come into my bathroom while I was sleeping and put it in my bath? Put it there when I was dreaming of holding his young hand in that strange and distant city?

Worse, was he still in my apartment?

Single women must take care of themselves these days. I keep two guns in my apartment, paranoid as that sounds. One under the bathtub, one behind my bed. They're licensed and I have practiced with them enough so that I know how to shoot someone if it is necessary.

Making sure the door was closed (it *had* been before I got into the tub), I dried myself quickly and slid my jeans and T-shirt on. The gun under the bath-tub is a thirty-eight and heavy in the hand. It is always loaded.

Cocking it, I crossed the room and opened the door. My heart was again banging on my chest's door.

I walked on tiptoe through the apartment. No one was there. I think I expected that, but it was wonderful knowing for sure. I looked in every hiding place, closet, under my bed . . . before saying "Okay."

When I was in the bathroom again a shiver went up my back like a cold fingernail. The albino had been in that room when I was *asleep*. Close enough to reach over and drop a toy car into my bathwater.

Even his seeing me naked wasn't as disturbing somehow as the idea of a white, white hand touching and getting wet from the water I was lying in.

The phone rang.

I picked up the extension next to the sink. "Anthea Powell?"

"Yes. Who is this?"

"A dead white Fiat. Remember? The guy you hit? The car in your tub? *Me*."

I still had the gun in my hand. I put it against the receiver, as if it might help.

"What do you want? What were you doing in my house?"

"You fucked up my car, Anthea. I'm collecting for that."

"What do you *want* from me?"

"What's mine. You owe me a lot of money."

"Then find out how much it'll cost to fix. Tell me and we'll figure something out."

"I don't want it fixed. I want a new one, *Anthea*. Buy me a new car and I'll leave you alone."

"Don't be ridiculous: I dented your front end."

"I want a new car, Anthea."

"Don't threaten me, *Bruce*. I remember your name. Don't forget I can call the police and tell them about this. Threatening phone calls, breaking into people's houses. . . . It wouldn't be hard finding you. I don't think there are too many albinos in town named Bruce Beetz!"

He laughed. "Brucey! You think that's my name? He's *dead*, honey. That driver's license I showed? It lapsed three months ago because old Bruce 'lapsed' then, too. I took it off his body and had it changed a little. He died in a car accident. Strange coincidence, huh?

"Do what I say, Anthea, or I'll eat your fucking face." He hung up.

I didn't sleep much that night. What dreams I had were all in black and white and took place in the new unknown city.

Young Bruce Beetz and I walked the De Chirico-lit streets— snow-white or cut in half by punishing, unforgiving shadows that scythed things into either light or darkness and nothing in between.

Nothing special happened and there was very little conversation. But I remember we were more comfortable with each other because I seemed to know where I was going. The boy sensed that and didn't whine or cry when I lost my way or got confused.

"What's your real name? You lied before; it's not Bruce."

He put his small hands over his face and laughed a lovely naughty kid's laugh.

"Are you mad at me?"

"Not at all. What *is* your name?"

"John Cray." He kept his hand in front of his face.

"Are you telling the truth this time?"

The hands dropped. He looked indignant. "Yes, John Cray. That's my name!"

Waking, I looked across the bed and saw a book lying on the pillow a few inches away. Too nervous, I hadn't read anything before falling asleep the night before. Grabbing the book, I tried to read the title through foggy, morning eyes: I'M COMING TO GET YOU.

It was a large-format children's book with little text but lots of pictures. I read it. A monster from another planet comes to Earth to eat a little boy. The story had a funny, sweet ending I would have loved if I'd read it in a different context. But I didn't own any children's books. And I hadn't read this one in bed last night. I'M COMING TO GET YOU.

When I finished, I put the book down and looked out the window. What could I do? Call the police and report a nonexistent "Bruce Beetz" who was terrorizing me? Pay him off for an accident he was partially responsible for? Wait for his next crazy move? What was his way of "eating [my] fucking face"?

The phone book. John Cray! Everything that had happened in the last twelve hours was so cuckoo, why *not* look in the phone book for the name of a little boy in a black and white dream?

There were two *John Crays* and one *J. Cray* listed. It was early Sunday morning. Time enough to track them all down and see.

I picked up the phone and dialed the first. The voice that answered was obviously black and not whom I was looking for, but I wanted to hear him say more than just "no", so . . .

"Is this John Crayon?"

"*Crayon?* No, John Cray, lady, John Tyrone *Cray*. What kinda name is that, Crayon? You think this is *Sesame Street*? You got yourself a wrong number, Big Bird." He laughed and hung up.

The next Cray number in the book was answered by a brittle-voiced old woman who said her husband, John had died six months ago.

I dialed *J. Cray* not expecting much. Another woman's voice answered.

"May I speak with John Cray, please?"

"He's not here now. Would you like to leave a message?"

"No, I'll call later." I smiled and hung up.

After puttering around the apartment for some hours, I went out to eat at my favorite restaurant.

Sunday brunch at Chez Uovo is a nice way to spend seven dollars. Go there a few times and soon they're greeting you like one of the gang and giving you free dessert if one of their fine pies is fresh out of the oven or you're looking sad.

I liked to sit by the window and watch the silent sidewalk traffic outside. Since it was midafternoon the place was half empty. Almost as soon as I sat down at my customary table, Walter, the headwaiter, came over and put a drink down in front of me.

"What's this?"

"I'm not supposed to tell you, Anthea. You're just supposed to drink it and be surprised."

I looked at the drink and smiled. It was a *kir*, but hooked on the side of the glass was a wedge of lime: my favorite drink in the world, although very few knew that. The last person I'd told was my old boyfriend, Victor Dixon. Was *he* here?

"Who sent it, Walter?"

"I'm not supposed to tell you that either, but I will. The guy at the bar in the great Gaultier jacket."

I looked up and saw a man at the bar, his back turned to me. He had dark hair and wore a cranberry-red jacket with black Cyrillic letters across the bottom. It was show-offy but wonderful, too. Victor Dixon never wore snazzy clothes.

"Who is he, Walter?"

"I don't know. He just ordered the drink and said you'd like it. Gave me five bucks to make it. Toodle-oo." Walter sauntered away, whistling the song "Love Is in the Air."

Who was he? How did he know about my secret, loved drink? All the time I waited for him to turn around, I felt a hot, sexy stone of expectation in my stomach. But he didn't turn and didn't turn. Finally I got annoyed waiting. He was mysterious and this scene was sexy, but I don't like long games, so I went back to looking out the window.

"May I join you?"

I turned and, taken aback by his sudden closeness, saw only the straight dark hair and aviator sunglasses. No, he had a good chin, too. A strong square chin.

"How did you know I like *kir* with lime?" He took off the sunglasses. It was Bruce Beetz.

"I know a lot about you, Anthea. You keep your diaphragm in a purple plastic case on the night table next to the bed. Eat only 'Bumblebee' brand tuna, and snore just a little when you sleep. Want to know anything else? Your father's name is Corkie. Corcoran Powell. Mother's dead, one brother and two sisters. I know a lot about you, Anthea."

"Why?"

He smiled, shrugged. "I have to know things about my people."

"Why am I one of your people, John?"

He stopped smiling. It was my turn.

"That's your name, isn't it? John Cray."

"How'd you know that?"

My hand was shaking in my lap. I tightened it hard, then relaxed. "Because I dreamed you. I don't know if you came out of my dream or went into it."

He stood up. "What the fuck are you talking about?"

"Where's your white hair, John Cray? Did it go away with Bruce Beetz?"

He stuck his finger out at me. "I studied you! I know a lot about you, Anthea!"

I shrugged, smiled. "So our accident wasn't an accident?"

He cut the air with his finger. "We don't make mistakes. We're always right with the people we choose!"

"Maybe I'm not people."

Walter watched Cray leave, then came over.

"That was a fast romance. What'd you tell him, Anthea, you got AIDS?"

I drank the last of the *kir* and held up the glass for another one. "Something like that. Did you ever see him before, Walter?"

"Nope. But he's certainly a good-looking guy."

"You mean good-looking woman."

Walter looked truly surprised. "No! I am a *champion* at guessing who's who these days. You cannot tell me that was a woman, Anthea."

I nodded and pushed my glass at him. "It was a woman. She works hard at *not* being one, but if you look and listen hard enough, you can tell."

"Your 'John Cray' is really Joanne Cray. She lives with another lez named Petra Hackett. Probably the one on the bicycle that night. They got setup situations like that that they've used before. Both of them are old actresses who didn't make it. So now the two of them got a good business terrifying people into doing whatever they want. It's a profitable approach these days."

"Terrify like how?"

He crossed his legs and took another of my cigarettes. "Like you name it. Big Push mostly."

"What's 'Big Push'?"

"Blackmail. I heard they kidnapped a kid once, but that's only hearsay. They specialize in scaring people into doing things. Like what they tried with you." He laughed and sat back in his chair. "Jesus, if they only knew who they were fucking with, huh?"

I straightened my skirt and pushed hair back over my ear. "What else?"

He looked at the pad on his knee. "Neither of them has a record because they got so many disguises. Most people think they're men! They also change cities all the time, move around a lot. But they got a good reputation."

"Are they for us? Are you sure?"

"They are absolutely for us. No question about it."

I nodded he could go. He got right up. "Can I do anything else for you, Ms Powell?" He was always eager to do more, one of his few nice qualities. Otherwise just another snoopy little rat who worked for me when I'd let him.

"No thank you. I'll be in touch."

He bowed, hat in hand, and left.

I sat back in my chair and looked out the window. I wanted to see for myself before I took them in. Other people's opinions aren't always my own. I liked the car in the tub and the book on the bed, but those might have been only inspired moments—the tenor who once reaches high C but then spends the rest of his career trying unsuccessfully to do it again. True inspiration isn't luck—it's genius. Only geniuses got in.

So I watched them. Bruce Beetz/John/Joanne Cray liked sexy stuff. Pick up people in a bar as a man, take them home either alone or to Peter (Petra), then pull some stunt there that was both hot and embarrassing to the unsuspecting victim. Simple stuff—take some photographs, then a few days later threaten to wave them around like the Libyan flag if the person didn't do what they asked.

More interesting, however, was the girls didn't always want money or the more obvious things. Sometimes it was simple humiliation. They made a snooty woman walk naked through a shopping mall and get arrested for indecent exposure. One poor man had to make an obvious pass at his son, thus ruining a lifelong wonderful relationship in a few hellish moments.

One afternoon sitting in my car outside their apartment building, I fell asleep and dreamed again of the child and the mysterious city. Only this time there were two children— Joanne Cray and Petra Hackett. Both held my hands and we walked happily through the anonymous, uninteresting streets.

"How much longer is it, Anthea?"

"Soon, Joanne. A few more blocks, I think."

"And I get to come, too?"

"Sure. Joanne asked and I said yes."

Joanne looked at Petra and walked around me to put her arm around her friend.

"Anthea always keeps her word." The two of them looked at me and smiled. I smiled back.

I know I am not a good storyteller. I could be, but it doesn't interest me. I purposely leave things out or ignore others if they don't interest me. I tell jokes terribly.

Anyway, this voice bores me. I am not Anthea Powell, although a real woman's similar fear and weakness interest me (and always incite others). I have pretended to be her often when I come here on my . . . trips. A middle-aged woman with a heart condition is a marvelous disguise. I have used her for hundreds of years. A good thing lasts forever! Like my slimy little detective. He is disgusting but efficient. And I did not even need to create him because he has been around as long as I. Loves his job, too. Loves finding all the boring dirt and gossip about people, loves the snooping, the setting up, the trap.

Are you confused? Good! Stick with me a while longer and you'll know everything. I could have held all this till the end. But I want you frowning now, knowing something is very wrong with your parachute even before actually pulling the cord and praying it opens. P.S. It won't.

I watched them for weeks. Both women were very good at telling the world things don't make sense and cruelty often comes in new colors. It is a talent, but there are more and more people who have it these days. Only the wrong survive. . . . Maybe it's like Hollywood in the Thirties—a lot of beautiful women dyed their hair like Lana Turner and sat around Schwab's waiting to be discovered, but very few of them ever got in the movies.

When I'd seen enough, I killed Petra Hackett. She wasn't as good at it as her lover and there really was only space for one. I killed her in their apartment while Joanne was away for the weekend.

When she returned on Sunday night, she found the table set with all their silver and linen and best crystal. I'd made a five-course dinner centered around a twenty-five-pound turkey. Petra sat in her chair in a mauve silk dress with the perfectly cooked, still-smoking turkey stuck over her head.

But Joanne passed the test with flying colors! She walked in and very coolly looked at the ruin of her life. I came out of the kitchen wearing a chef's cap and carrying the mince pie.

"Are you hungry? There's so much food."

She looked at me. "She's dead?"

"Choked on a Fiat." I pointed to my neck. "A little white one got stuck in her throat."

"Who are you?"

"Anthea Powell! One of your victims, Joanne!"

She smiled sadly. "I didn't do such good research this time, did I?"

I clapped my hands to my face. Mock dismay. "Just the *opposite*! You hit the jackpot this time. That's why you did what you did, all along. You two were looking for me! Want to come see?"

Coyly, she asked, "Something I want to see? I've been looking for *you*? That's funny."

"Absolutely. Come, I'll show you." I reached over and took her hand. It was warm and dry. I led us out of the apartment and down the stairs to the front door. "You really have no idea where we're going?"

She shrugged. "Maybe, but I'm not sure."

"We're almost there anyway. It's just around the corner."

Once outside again, I felt the hand shrink in my own until it was the size of a child's. I looked down at the girl with the white hair and squeezed her nice hand.

"What about Petra, Anthea? You said she could come, too."

"Well, sometimes you have to lie about things. I thought she could, but she can't. Are you angry?"

She shook her head. "Naah, she's a jerk. How much longer?"

"Two minutes."

In almost exactly two minutes we were there. We went into the building and down some stairs to the basement door. I opened it with a key and we walked into an almost totally black room.

"I can't see, Anthea!"

"Don't worry, honey. I know where I'm going."

I led us across the room with one hand out in front of me so as not to bump into anything. Almost at the far wall, I touched the ladder. "We're here."

I pulled her around and put her small hands on the first rung. "Just start to climb. It's twenty-five steps up. Real easy."

She started up. I went right behind her, just in case. Halfway there, you could smell something very sweet and sugary, almost sickening in its heaviness.

"Smells like cake."

"Just keep going, honey. We're almost there."

"I'm there! I can feel the top."

"Take a piece and taste it. It's your favorite."

"Chocolate! It's chocolate cake, Anthea!"

"That's right, Joanne. Now push through it. Everyone's waiting for you."

I heard a soft *smooshing* sound and then there was a blast of white light from above. Lots of voices cheering.

The girl had climbed to the top of the ladder. I went up behind her, into the light. People cheered. "Hooray, Joanne!"

I looked at everyone. Everyone who deserved to be here after so much good work. Wonderful souls. The shit of the earth.

"The dead love you, Joanne. Welcome home!"

HARLAN ELLISON

Jane Doe #112

NOVELIST, SHORT STORY author, screenwriter, editor, film and television critic, and lecturer, Harlan Ellison is arguably the most outspoken and controversial writer associated with the *fantastique* genre.

In a dynamic career that has spanned five decades, he is the multiple winner of almost every major award the field has to offer, including the Hugo, Nebula, Edgar, Bram Stoker, Writer's Guild of America, British Fantasy, and World Fantasy Awards.

His numerous books as either author or editor include *I Have No Mouth & I Must Scream, Dangerous Visions, Love Ain't Nothing But Sex Misspelled, The Glass Teat, Again, Dangerous Visions, Deathbird Stories, Shatterday, Angry Candy* and *Harlan Ellison's Watching*.

Ellison's fiction doesn't often stray into the horror arena, but when it does, as in the story that follows, you can expect something *very* special . . .

SHADOWS OF LIVES UNLIVED, as milky as opal glass, moved through the French Quarter that night. And one begged leave, and separated from the group to see an old friend.

Bourbon Street was only minimally less chaotic than usual. It was two days till the Spring Break deluge of horny fraternity boys and young women seemingly unable to keep their t-shirts on.

The queue outside Chris Owens's club moved swiftly for the last show. Inside, the entertainer was just starting the third chorus of "Rescue Me" when she looked out into the audience and saw the pale shadow of a face she hadn't seen in twenty years.

For a moment she faltered, but no one noticed. She had been a star on Bourbon Street for twenty years; they wouldn't know that the face staring up palely at her was that of a woman who had been dead for two decades.

Doris Burton sat in the smoky center of a cheering mob half-smashed on Hurricanes; and she stared up at Chris Owens with eyes as quietly gray and distant as the surface of the moon. The last time Chris had seen those eyes, they had been looking out of a newspaper article about the car crash over in Haskell County, when Doris had been killed.

Her parents wouldn't let her go over to the funeral. It was a piece of Texas distance, from Jones County over to Haskell. She had never forgotten Doris, and she had always felt guilty that she'd never gotten to say goodbye.

Now she felt the past worming its way into her present. It couldn't possibly be. She danced to the edge of the stage and looked directly at her. It *was* Doris. As she had been twenty years ago.

The woman in the audience was almost transparent in the bleed of light from the baby spots and pinlights washing Chris as she worked. Trying to keep up with the beat, Chris could swear she could see the table full of Kiwanis behind Doris. It threw her off . . . but no one would notice.

Doris moved her lips. *Hello, Chris.*

Then she smiled. That same gentle smile of an awkward young woman that had first bound them together as friends.

Chris felt her heart squeeze, and tears threatened to run her makeup. She fought back the sorrow, and smiled at her dead friend. Then Doris rose, made a tiny goodbye movement with her left hand, and left the club.

Chris Owens did not disappoint her audience that night. She never disappointed them. But she was only working at half the energy. Even so, they would never know.

That night, the Orleans Parish Morgue logged in its one hundred and twelfth unknown female subject. The toe was tagged JANE DOE

#112 and was laid on the cold tile floor in the hallway. As usual, the refrigerators were full.

Ben Laborde took his foot off the accelerator as he barreled north on the I-10 past St Charles Parish, and kicked the goddammed air conditioner one last time. It was dead. The mechanism on the '78 Corollas had been lemons when they were fresh off the showroom floor, and twelve years of inept service had not bettered the condition. Now it had given out totally; and Ben could feel the sweat beginning to form a *tsunami* at his hairline. He cranked down the window and was rewarded with a blast of mugginess off the elevated expressway that made him blink and painfully exhale hot breath. Off to his left the Bonnet Carré Spillway—actually seventeen miles of fetid swamp with a name far too high above its station—stretched behind him as an appropriate farewell to New Orleans, to Louisiana, to twenty-two years of an existence he was now in the process of chucking. The blue Toyota gathered speed again as he punched the accelerator, and he thought, *So long, N'wallins; I give you back to the 'gators.*

Somewhere north lay Chicago, and a fresh start.

When he thought back across the years, when he paused to contemplate how fast and how complexly he had lived, he sometimes thought he had been through half a dozen different existences. Half a dozen different lives, as memorable and filled with events as might have been endured by a basketball team with one extra guy waiting on the bench.

Now he was chucking it all. Again. For the half-dozenth time in his forty-one years.

Ben Laborde had run off when he was ten, had worked the crops across the bread basket of America, had schooled himself, had run with gangs of itinerant farm laborers, had gone into the Army at nineteen, had become an MP, had mustered out and been accepted to the FBI, had packed that in after four years and become a harness bull in the St Bernard Parish Sheriff's Department, had been promoted to Detective, and had had his tin pulled two years ago for throwing a pimp through the show window of an antique shop on Rue Toulouse. The pimp had been on the muscle with someone in the Department, and that was that for Detective Benjamin Paul Laborde.

He had become a repairman for ATMs, but two years fixing the bankteller machines had driven him most of the way into total craziness. And then, there was that group of pale gray people that kept following him . . .

He looked in the rearview. The expressway was nearly empty behind him. If he was being tracked, they had to be very good; and very far behind him. But the thought had impinged, and he cranked up the speed.

There had been six of them for the last year. Six men and women, as pale as the juice at the bottom of a bucket of steamed clams. But when he had seen them out of the corner of his eye the night before last, moving through the crowd on Bourbon Street, there had only been five.

He couldn't understand why he was so frightened of them.

He had thought more than once, more than a hundred times in the past year, that he should simply step into a doorway, wait for them to catch up, then brace them. But every time he started to do just that . . . the fear grabbed him.

So he had decided to chuck it all. Again. And go.

He wasn't at all certain if not having the Police Positive on his hip made any difference.

The nagging thought kept chewing on him: would a bullet stop them?

He ran, but the Corolla didn't have anything more to give. Still, it wasn't fast enough.

Chicago was dark. Perhaps a brownout. The city lay around him as ugly and desperate as he felt. The trip north had been uneventful, but nonetheless dismaying. Stopping only briefly for food and gas, he had driven straight through. Now he had to find a place to live, a new job of some menial sort till he could get his hooks set, and then—perhaps—he could decide what he wanted to be when he grew up.

As best he could discern, he hadn't been followed. (Yet when he had pulled in at a bar in Bloomington, Indiana, and had been sitting there nursing the Cutty and water, he had seen, in the backbar mirror, the street outside. And for a moment, five sickly white faces peering in at him.

(But when he had swiveled for a direct look, only the empty street lay beyond the window. He had paid up and left quickly.)

Laborde had never spent much time in Chicago. He barely knew the city. A few nights around Rush Street, some drinking with buddies in an apartment in a debutante's condo facing out on the Shore Drive, dinner one night in Old Town. But he had the sense that staying in the center of the city was not smart. He didn't know why, but he felt the push to keep going; and he did. Out the other side and into Evanston.

It was quieter here. Northwestern University, old homes lining Dempster Street, the headquarters of The Women's Christian Temperance Union. Maybe he'd take night courses. Get a job in a printing plant. Sell cars. Plenty of action and danger in those choices.

He drove through to Skokie and found a rooming house. It had been years since he'd stayed in a rooming house. Motels, that was the story now. Had been for forty years. He tried to remember where he'd last lived, in which town, in which life, that had provided rooming houses. He couldn't recall. Any more than he could recall when he'd owned a Studebaker Commander, the car that Raymond Loewy had designed. Or the last time he had heard *The Green Hornet* on the radio.

He was putting his underwear in the bureau drawer as these thoughts wafted through his mind. Studebaker? *The Green Hornet?* That was over when he'd been a kid. He was forty-one, not sixty. How the hell did he remember that stuff?

He heard footsteps in the hall. They weren't the halting steps of the woman who owned the hostel. She had been happy to get a boarder. But not even a need to accommodate her new tenant could have eliminated the arthritic pace she had set as she climbed the stairs ahead of him.

He stood with his hands on the drawer, listening.

The footsteps neared, then stopped outside his door. There was no lock on the door. It was a rooming house, not a motel. No chain, no double-latch, no security bolt. It was an old wooden door, and all the person on the other side had to do was turn the knob and enter.

He barely heard the tapping.

It was the rapping at a portal of something composed of mist and soft winds.

Laborde felt a sharp pain as he realized he had been clenching his teeth. His jaw muscles were rigid. His face hurt. Whatever he wanted to do, it was not to go over and open that door to the visitor.

He watched, without breathing, as the knob slowly turned and the door opened, a sliver of light at a time.

The door opened of its own weight after a moment, and Laborde saw a woman standing in the dimly lit hallway. She looked as if she were made of isinglass. He could see through her, see the hallway through her dim, pale shape. She stared at him with eyes the color of an infirmary nurse's uniform.

Isinglass? How could he remember something like that? They had used isinglass before they'd started putting real glass in car windows.

The woman said, "Jessie passed through in New Orleans. She was the oldest of us. She was the one wanted to find you the most."

His mouth was dry. His hands, still on the dresser drawer, were trembling.

"I don't know any Jessie," he said. The voice seemed to belong to someone else, someone far away on a mountainside, speaking into the wind.

"You knew her."

"No, I never, I've *never* known anyone named Jessie."

"You knew her better than anyone. Better than her mother or her father or any of us who traveled with her. You knew the best part of her. But she never got to tell you that."

He managed to close the drawer on his underwear. He found it *very* important, somehow, just to be able to close the drawer.

"I think you'd better let the landlady know you're here," he said, feeling ridiculous. How she had gotten in, he didn't know. Perhaps the old woman had let her in. Perhaps she had asked for him by name. How could she know his name?

She didn't answer. He had the awful desire to go to the door and *touch* her. It was continuing strange, the way the light shone through her. Not as if there were kliegs set off in the distance, with radiance projected toward her, but rather as if she were generating light from within. But what he saw as he looked at her, in that plain, shapeless dress, her hair hanging limp and milky around her shoulders, was a human being made of tracing paper, the image of the drawing behind shadowing through. He took a step toward her, hoping she would move.

She stood her ground, unblinking.

"Why have you been following me, all of you . . . there are six of you, aren't there?"

"No," she said, softly, "now there are only five. Jessie passed through." She paused, seemed to gather strength to speak, and added, "Very soon now, we'll *all* pass through. And then you'll be alone."

He felt an instant spike of anger. "I've *always* been alone!"

She shook her head. "You stole from us, but you've never been without us."

He touched her. He reached out and laid his fingertips on her cheek. She was cool to the touch, like a china bowl. But she was real, substantial. He had been thinking ghost, but that was ridiculous; he'd *known* it was ridiculous all along. From the first time he had seen them following him in New Orleans. Passersby had bumped into them, had acknowledged their existence, had moved aside for them. They weren't ghosts, whatever they were. And whatever it was, he was terrified of them . . . even though he knew they would not harm him. And, yes, a bullet would have done them.

"I'm leaving. Get out of my way."

"Aren't you curious?"

"Not enough to let you keep making me crazy. I'm going out of here, and you'd better not try to stop me."

She looked at him sadly; as a child looks at the last day of summer; as the sun goes down; as the street lights come on before bedtime; one beat before it all ends and the fun days retreat into memory. He thought that, in just that way, as she looked at him. It was the ending of a cycle, but he had no idea how that could be, or what cycle was done.

He moved a step closer to her. She stood in the doorway and did not move. "Get out of my way."

"I haven't the strength to stop you. You know that."

He pushed her, and she went back. He kept his hand on her sternum, pressing her back into the hall. She offered no resistance. It was like touching cool eggshell.

"This time you leave even your clothes behind?" she asked.

"This time I shake you clowns," he said, going down the hall, descending the stairs, opening the curtained front door, stepping out into the Illinois night, and seeing his car parked across the street. Surrounded by the other four.

As fragile as whispers, leaning against the car. Waiting for him.

Oh, Christ, he thought, *this isn't happening*.

"What the hell do you *want* off me?" he screamed. They said nothing, just watched. Three men and another woman. He could see the dark outline of his car through them.

He turned right and began running. He wasn't afraid, he was just frightened. It wasn't terror, it was only fear.

Abandon the underwear in the drawer. Lose the past life. Jettison the car. Get out of this existence. Forget the deposit on the room. Run away. Just . . . run away.

When he reached the end of the block, he saw the lights of a minimall. He rushed toward the light. Dark things have no shadows in sodium-vapor lights.

Behind him, the milky figure of the fifth one emerged from the rooming house and joined her traveling companions.

They caught up with him only three times in the next year. The first time in Cleveland. There were four of them. Three months later, he stepped off a Greyhound Scenicruiser at the Port Authority Terminal in Manhattan, and they were coming up the escalator to meet the bus. Two of them, a man and the woman who had confronted him in the rooming house in Skokie.

And finally, he came full circle. He went home.

Not to Chicago, not to New Orleans, not as far back as he could remember, but as far back as he had come. Seven miles south of Cedar Falls, Iowa—on the thin road out of Waterloo—back to Hudson. And it hadn't changed. Flat cornfield land, late in September after the oppressive heat had passed, into the time of jackets and zipping up.

Where his house had stood, now there was a weed-overgrown basement into which the upper floors had fallen as the fire had burned itself out. One wall remained, the saltbox slats gray and weathered.

He sat down on what had been the stone steps leading up to the front porch, and he laid down the cheap plastic shoulder bag that now contained all he owned in the world. And it was there that the last two of those who had dogged him came to have their talk.

He saw them coming down the dirt road between the fields of freshly harvested corn, the stalks creaking in the breeze, and he gave it up. Packed it in. No more getting in the flow, chasing the wind. No more. He sat and watched them coming up the road, tiny puffs of dust at each step. The day was on the wane, and he could see clouds through them, the horizon line, birds reaching for more sky.

They came up and stood staring at him, and he said, "Sit down, take a load off."

The man seemed to be a hundred years old. He smiled at Ben and said, "Thanks. It's been a hard trip." He slumped onto the stone step below. He wiped his forehead, but he wasn't perspiring.

The woman stood in front of him, and her expression was neither kind nor hard. It was simply the face of someone who had been traveling a long time, and was relieved to have reached her destination.

"Who are you?"

The woman looked at the old man and said, "We were never a high school girl named Doris Burton, who was supposed to've died in a car accident in West Texas, but didn't. We were never an asthmatic named Milford Sterbank, who worked for fifty years as a reweaver. And we never got to be Henry Cheatham, who drove a cab in Pittsburgh."

He watched them, looking from the man to the woman and back. "And which ones are you?"

The woman looked away for a moment. Laborde saw the setting sun through her chest. She said, "I would have been Barbara Lamartini. You passed through St Louis in 1943."

"I was born in '49."

The old man shook his head. "Much earlier. If you hadn't fought with the 2nd Division at Belleau Wood, I would have been Howard Strausser. We shared a trench for five minutes, June 1st, 1918."

"This is crazy."

"No," the woman said wearily, "this is just the end of it."

"The end of what?"

"The end of the last of us whose lives you've been using. The last soft gray man or woman left on a doorstep by your passing."

Laborde shook his head. It was gibberish. He knew he was at final moments with them, but what it all meant he could not fathom.

"For godsakes," he pleaded, "hasn't this gone on long enough? Haven't you sent me running long enough? What the hell have I ever done to you—any of you? I don't even know you!"

The old man, Howard Strausser, smiled sadly and said, "You never meant to be a thief. It isn't your fault, any more than it's our fault for finally coming after you, to get our lives back. But you did, you stole, and you left us behind. We've been husks. I'm the oldest left. Barbara is somewhere in the middle. You've been doing it for several hundred years, best we've been able to tell. When we found one another, there was a man who said he'd been panning gold at Sutter's Mill when you came by. I don't know as I believe him; his name was Chickie Moldanado, and he was something of a liar. It was the only memorable thing about him."

The woman added, "There's nothing much memorable about any of us."

"That's the key, do you see?" Howard Strausser said.

"No, I *don't* see," Laborde said.

"We were never *anything*. None of us."

He let his hands move helplessly in the air in front of them. "I don't know what any of this means. I just know I'm tired of . . . not of running . . . tired of, just, I don't know, tired of being *me*."

"You've never been you." Howard Strausser smiled kindly.

"Perhaps you can be you now," Barbara Lamartini said.

Laborde put his hands over his face. "Can't you just tell it simply? Please, for godsakes, just *simply*."

The woman nodded to the old man, who looked to be a hundred years old, and he said, "There are just some people who live life more fully than others. Take, oh, I don't know, take Scott Fitzgerald or Hemingway or Winston Churchill or Amelia Earhart. Everybody's heard their names, but how many people have read much Hemingway or Fitzgerald, or even Churchill's—" He stopped. The woman was giving him that look. He grinned sheepishly.

"There are just some people who *live* their lives at a fuller pace. And it's as if they've lived two or three lifetimes in the same time it takes others to get through just one mild, meager, colorless life, one sad and sorry—"

He stopped again.

"Barbara, you'd better do it. I've waited too long. I'm just running off at the mouth like an old fart."

She put a hand on his thin shoulder to comfort him, and said, "You were one of the passionate ones. You lived at a hotter level. And every now and then, every once in a while, you just leached off someone's life who wasn't up to the living of it. You're a magpie. You came by, whenever it was, 1492, 1756, 1889, 1943 . . . we don't know how far back you go . . . but you passed by, and someone wearing a life so loosely, so unused, that it just came off; and you wore it away, and added it on, and you just kept going, which way it didn't matter, without looking back, not even knowing.

"And, finally, the last of us followed the thread that was never broken, the umbilicus of each of us, and we came and found you, to try and get back what was left."

"Because it's clear," said Howard Strausser, "that you're tired of it. And don't know how to get out of it. But—"

They sighed almost as one, and Barbara Lamartini said, "There isn't enough of either of us left to take back. We'll be gone, passed through very soon."

"Then you're on your own," Howard Strausser said.

"You'll be living what portion has been allotted to you," the woman said, and Ben could see through the holes where her milky eyes had been.

And they sat there into the deepening twilight, in Hudson, Iowa; and they talked; and there was nothing he could do for them; and finally the woman said, "We don't blame you. It was our own damned fault. We just weren't up to the doing of it, the living of our own lives." What was left of her shrugged, and Laborde asked her to tell him all she could of the others they had known, so he could try to remember them and fit to their memories the parts of his own life that he had taken.

And by midnight, he was sitting there alone.

And he fell asleep, arms wrapped around himself, in the chilly September night, knowing that when he arose the next day, the first day of a fresh life, he would retrace his steps in many ways; and that one of the things he would do would be to return to New Orleans.

To go to the Parish Coroner, and to have exhumed the body of Jane Doe #112; to have it dug out of the black loam of Potter's Field near City Park and to carry it back to West Texas; to bury the child who had never been allowed to be Doris Burton where she would have lived her life. Pale as opal glass, she had passed through and whispered away, on the last night of the poor thing that had been her existence; seeking out the only friend she had been allowed to have, on a noisy street in the French Quarter.

The least he could do was to be her last friend, to carry her home by way of cheap restitution.

RAY GARTON

Shock Radio

SINCE THE MID-1980S, Ray Garton has been carving a niche for himself as one of the hot young writers of erotic horror fiction, although he actively resists the "Splatterpunk" label. After the early novels *Seductions* and *Darklings*, and a couple of movie novelizations, he hit his stride with *Live Girls* and *Crucifax Autumn*.

Since then he has published *Trade Secrets*, his first non-horror thriller, and *Lot Lizards*, a truck-stop vampire novel. His first collection of short fiction, *Methods of Madness*, has been nominated for a Bram Stoker Award and a novella from that collection, "Dr Krusadian's Method" (also a Stoker nominee), turns up in the anthology *Cafe Pergatorium*.

A New Age horror novel, *Dark Channel*, is due at the end of 1991 and he is currently working on *In a Dark Place*, a non-fiction book about a Connecticut family who moved into a house that used to be a funeral home, where they were plagued by the devil and his minions ("a la *Amityville Horror*").

Garton lives in Northern California with his wife Dawn and, as a hobby, has a collection of nearly 900 movies on video. "Other than that," he explains, "there is absolutely *nothing* interesting about me. I spend most of my time writing which, to anyone who doesn't write, is very boring. Hell, half the time it's boring to *me*."

We don't think you'll be bored by the story that follows . . .

T HE STUDIO WAS DARK but for a soft lamp over the console and, after being cued by the engineer who sat with the producer beyond a long rectangular window, the man leaned toward the microphone suspended before his face, touched his fingertips to the headphones through which he could hear his show's theme music and said, "You're listening to the Arthur Colton, Jr., Show and we're *back*! We have a few more minutes with my guest Melissa Cartwright, who is joining us by phone from Liberal Central, San Francisco, California. Miss Cart—excuse me . . . *Mizzz* Cartwright—is a writer, a feminist and, in my opinion, another of the whining castrators who has found a way to take out her aggressions *and* make a fast buck by writing a book about the evil that men do. Not people, but *men*, who, according to *Mizzz* Cartwright, are inherently *evil* simply because they have been born *men*." He smirked and winked at Harry, the engineer, who laughed silently beyond the glass.

"No, no, Arthur," Melissa Cartwright said, "that's *not* what I'm saying at all and you *know* it. I simply want to—"

"Let's go back to the phones." Arthur Colton, Jr., whose real name was Andy Craig, looked at the computer screen before him where the words TAMPA, FLA-FRIEND glowed in amber. "Tampa, Florida, you're on the air."

"Yeah, uh, Arthur?"

"Yessir, you're on the air."

"Yeah, Arthur, my name's Tom and I'm just calling, uuhhh, to tell you that you're, y'know, uh, right. You're *right*."

"I know I'm right, sir, that's why I'm the host and you're the caller. Do you have a question for our guest?"

"Yeah. I do. I'd like to ask Miss Carter—"

"Cartwright," Andy snapped. "Read my lips: Cart-*wright*."

"Yeah, okay, Miss Cartwright. I'd like to ask her exactly where she thinks women would be *without* men, huh? I mean, like, through *history*, y'know? Where do you think? And, uuhhh, I'll take my answer off the air."

Melissa Cartwright said, "I'm very sorry, Tom, this is not your fault, but I'm afraid there's been a misunderstanding here. It is *not* my opinion that men are inherently evil or dishonest or even ignorantly *wrong*. All I'm saying is that we have to find a way to—"

"It's very clear what you're saying, *Mizzz* Cartwright," Andy interrupted. "Your book, *Women in Crisis, Men in Power*—which, for those of you interested in this kind of whiney propaganda, is published by Putnam—is *clearly* the manifesto of someone who feels that *all* of our problems are the result of men and the *works* of men. Now, I would appreciate it if you'd answer my caller's question, which is quite straightforward. Okay? Oookay. Now, let's hear it."

She was silent for a long time—*too* long—and Andy was about to speak again to fill the dead air, but she spoke first. Slowly and coldly.

"I think that . . . to speculate on the position of women . . . without the presence of men . . . throughout history . . . would be asinine."

"Well, isn't that convenient." The screen read WINSTON-SALEM, NC-FOE. "Winston-Salem, you're on the air."

"Yeah, Arthur, I listen to your show a lot and I just wanna say that I think you're being a little hard on your guest, okay?"

"And why is *that*, sir?"

"Because I've read her book and, as a man, I can say that I think she's—"

"Wait-wait-*wait* a second here. You read her *book*? What, you *enjoy* being castrated? What, you *like* having a woman chew your balls off? And you call yourself a *man*?"

"That's exactly my point, Mr Colton, you're interviewing her and you probably haven't even read the book."

"Well, of *course* I haven't read the book! I *like* my balls!"

"But you rely on name-calling rather than discussion to make your point, when really you *have* no point to—"

Andy punched a button on the panel, cutting the caller off, and sneered, "You have a good time, sir."

Melissa Cartwright released an explosive breath over the phone and Andy could imagine her rolling her eyes as he flashed a grin at Harry; it was his this-is-good-radio grin.

"Redlands, California, you're on the air."

"Yes, Arthur?" an elderly woman said.

"You're on the air, ma'am, please get to your question."

"Well, I'd just like to say that I'm seventy-nine years old and I don't understand how your guest—what's her name? Cartwright?—can possibly suggest that all men are evil. Speaking from experience, I can say that I've—"

Miss Cartwright interrupted firmly: "I'm sorry, ma'am, but you and the rest of the listeners are being misled by Mr Colton. I am not saying that men are *evil*. I'm simply saying that our culture—along with many other cultures—has given women a back seat in *everything* and it's time to—"

"I'm sorry," Andy said as the theme music came up, "but we've run out of time. I'd like to thank my guest, Melissa Cartwright, whose book *Women in Crisis, Men in Power*, is, for some reason, number two on the New York *Times* nonfiction bestseller list. Thank you for joining us, *Mizzz* Cartwright, it's been an education, if nothing else. We're coming up on the news, then we'll be back with open lines. Stick around."

As Andy leaned back in his chair and removed his headphones, he heard Melissa Cartwright's pinched voice calling from them, "Mr Colton? Mr *Colton*?" He glanced at Tanya, the producer, waved toward the phone and picked up the receiver, saying, "Yes?"

She struggled to control her voice. "I'm very disappointed, Mr Colton. I was told you were going to interview me about my book. I didn't know this was going to be the broadcast equivalent of stocks and public humiliation. I didn't know it was going to be an inquisition."

"Oh, please, Ms Cartwright, don't take it personally. It's just the way I do the show."

She paused. "I'm sorry? Pardon me?"

He shook his head and chuckled. This always puzzled him. Didn't they understand it was just a *show*? That it was just *show business*? "Have you ever heard my show, Ms Cartwright?"

"No, I haven't. And after tonight, I have no intention of listening."

"Well, if you had," he said gently, "you'd realize that this is just the way the show goes, okay? I mean, *think* about it. My audience is made up of very conservative, aggressive people who want more than just an interview, okay? Otherwise they'd be listening to Larry King. They want *fireworks*, you know? So please, Ms Cartwright. Don't take this personally. I have nothing against you or your book or your opinion. In fact, you're probably right, *I* don't know. Anyway, I really appreciate your good sportsmanship. It's just show business, you know?"

Another pause, longer this time. "You appreciate *what*?"

"Your good sportsmanship."

She laughed, but it was an angry laugh. "Are you serious?"

"*Sure* I'm serious. Look, it's just a show, okay? I mean, you want compassion, call *Talk Net*. You want indepth questions, you go on *Nightline*. And on *my* show, you get confrontation and a lot of yelling."

"And name-calling and humiliation and some pretty obscene sexist insults."

"Well, that too. But you can't take it personally. It's the nature of the show. You got to make your point and plug your book, right? Myself? I think you're an interesting, intelligent woman. What I say on the show really means nothing."

A cold chuckle. "In other words . . . you're a whore." She hung up.

Andy rolled his eyes as he replaced the receiver. Why was it so hard for them to understand? Why did so many people get so upset? Not that he minded; they were his best publicity and stirred the controversy that made his show the number one late night radio talk show in the country. He just didn't understand what made them so furious. "About li'l ol' me," he muttered, leaving the studio and heading to the lounge for coffee.

Laurence Olivier had once played a hideous Nazi, but did anyone accuse him of actually *being* one? Of course not. They praised his performance; he was simply a great actor. Nobody accused Stephen King of being a sick bloodthirsty monster, did they? Well, maybe a few . . . but surely they didn't *really* believe it; he was just a very good writer. But when it came to The Arthur Colton, Jr., Show, otherwise rational people began to foam at the mouth, pound fists into palms and scream for a public hanging. It made no sense.

He'd used that argument with Katherine, a former girlfriend back in Cincinnati who had been irate about the content of his show. It hadn't worked.

"That's different!" she'd exclaimed. "What they do is fiction. Everyone *knows* that what Olivier and King do is *fiction*! You, however, are hosting a *talk show*! You're shaping opinions, *manipulating* them! You aren't writing a novel or acting in a movie. People *listen* to what you say. They respect it, they take it *seriously*. And for you to go on that show and say the barbaric things you say to boost your ratings—things you don't even *mean*—is obscene, Andy!"

It had just been a local show which, for the first four months, was just straight talk with a few guests and a couple hours of open phones; Andy had never expressed an opinion, just kept the conversation going. The ratings were bleak, so he'd listened carefully to his audience, looking for something he could use to breathe life into the show, trying to figure out what they wanted. One night it occurred to him: they were angry and they wanted to scream and shout and kick furniture and if they couldn't do it, they wanted someone to do it for them. His listeners were fed up with everything from crime and poverty to crooked politicians and unfair laws and they wanted someone with a voice—a loud, powerful voice—to represent them.

The following night, Andy opened his show differently than usual: "I've cancelled tonight's scheduled guests," he said, "because I want to talk about something, ladies and gentlemen. I . . . am mad . . . as *hell*!"

There wasn't an open line for more than thirty seconds that night. Liberals called to complain about his sudden change of attitude and his unfair generalizations and conservatives called to complain about the tit-sucking liberals. Blacks complained about whites and whites complained about blacks . . . and Asians and Iranians and American Indians. Men complained about women and women complained about men. AM radios throughout Cincinnati crackled with the wholesale condemnation of Jews and homosexuals and Democrats and Communists and drug dealers and feminists and homeless people and . . . and anyone who disagreed in any way with the caller. Cincinnati was angry and Andy Craig had given it an opportunity to throw a tantrum. Along with the city's anger, however, came a barrage of racial slurs and profanity which Andy, at first, edited during the seven second delay; but as the show continued that night, getting better by the minute, he left his finger off the button and let the bile flow. He knew he'd get yelled at for it but, in his gut, it felt right.

Two thirds of the way through the show, Dexter Grady, the station manager, burst into the engineer's booth and glared at Andy through the small square window; his face squirmed with anger as he waved his arms and yelled silently at the engineer. Moments later, the show broke, quite abruptly, for a commercial. Grady disappeared from the window and stormed into the studio shouting, demanding to know exactly who the fuck Andy thought he was, allowing all that Goddamned profanity to go out over the fucking radio. He yelled for quite some time, threatening not only to fire Andy, but to see to it that he never worked in Ohio again, not in a radio station, not even in a MacDonald's, and then—

—the phonecalls started to come in.

Grady had told the engineer to play a few songs, to go to some network programming, *anything*, just as long as he didn't go back to Andy's show.

And people complained. Oh, how they complained.

Andy stayed at the station and continued doing his late-night talk show for almost two years. It didn't last any longer because the sponsors got fed up with the show's controversy; the controversy was the only reason it lasted as long as it did . . .

In the lounge, Andy poked through a box of stale donuts left in front of the coffeepot and picked out a cruller, which he dipped into the black coffee he'd poured. He was a small, wiry man with short reddish-brown hair and a mustache between his slightly sunken cheeks. His skin was smooth and somewhat pale; he didn't get much sun. He chewed his cruller as he stared out the window at the black, light-smeared city nineteen stories below and listened to the news, which came over the P.A. He'd become addicted to the news; the more current his topics, the more riled his listeners became, and the more riled they became, the better were his ratings.

"You seen this?" Tanya asked, bursting into the lounge.

Andy turned as she tossed a section of the *Times* onto one of the round tables. It was opened to an article accompanied by a photograph of Andy; the headline read, DANGEROUS RADIO, DANGEROUS LISTENERS, OR BOTH?

"No, I haven't," Andy said, glancing over the article.

Tanya smirked. "It's great stuff. The kinda stuff that brings in new listeners, y'know? It was in this morning's edition and my buddy over at the *Times* says they've been getting phonecalls all day. I mean, *complaints*. Starting tomorrow, the letters to the Editor section'll probably be full of epistles from your loving fans for a couple weeks." She beamed at him through the smoke from her cigarette.

"Why? What's it say?"

She shrugged. "Oh, the usual bullshit. You're stirring up the masses, using sick jokes and faulty logic that *sounds* intelligent and reasonable to get them so upset that they're willing to *hand* over their freedoms to the first dictator that comes along. The usual bullshit. He says that you're—" She swept the paper up and raised a stiff forefinger. "—listen to this, '. . . sucking up ratings like a vampire sucks up blood, flashing his fangs all the way to the bank'. Isn't that *great*?" she laughed.

Andy grinned as he finished the cruller and plucked Tanya's cigarette from her fingers, taking a deep drag.

"I thought you quit," she said, slapping the paper down again.

"Just quit smoking my own. It's cheaper that way." He glanced at the clock.

"Don't worry, you got another six minutes." She started for the door as she said, "Got a great call for ya. A pro-choicer raving about the abortion laws."

"Man or woman?"

"Woman. A real bitch. Give her your Jerry Lewis speech." She winked at him as she went out the door.

Finishing Tanya's cigarette, Andy scanned the article. It accused him of stirring up hatred and racism, of helping to destroy the freedoms that made America great—especially the one freedom that provided for radio shows like his own—and suggested that his "careless and irresponsible form of broadcasting" could ultimately bring about "the downfall of American freedoms as we know them."

He chuckled bitterly as he sipped his coffee. He'd gotten the same response from the Cincinnati press since the day he'd changed the format of his show; they'd hated him.

But the *women* had loved him. Not just the women callers, but the women who attended his personal appearances . . . the women who wrote to him . . . the women he met in bars and restaurants and grocery stores who recognized his name or, better yet, his voice. Building his entire radio show around the political stance that riled his listeners the most—the one that would have sent most feminists into a convulsing, mouth-foaming seizure—Andy had more women hungry for his attention than ever before in his life. The change was so sudden and drastic that Andy had actually been relieved the day he'd come home and found Katherine stripping his apartment of her belongings.

"I can't live with you anymore," she said, throwing her toiletries into a satchel.

"But you don't live with me. We agreed you'd keep your apartment, I thought that was—"

"*Listen* to yourself!" she snapped, stabbing a forefinger at his chest. "You're such a *stickler* for details, like my fucking apartment. What difference does my *apartment* make? It's just a little section of a building in which I get my phonecalls and keep my *cat*! When I say I can't live with you anymore, I mean that I can't live with the fact that you're such a stickler for details and yet, when someone tries to point out the details of what you're doing, you blow up, or just *laugh*. I can't live with the fact that I'm wrapping my life around a person who can, so very *casually*, do such vicious damage to things that so many people have died to protect, things that have taken so many decades to finally realize and are already being dismantled fast enough as it is without any help from you! I can't live with you, Andy. And how you possibly can will be one of the greatest mysteries of my life." She was gone in ten minutes.

Half an hour later, he had a dinner date, and only a few hours after that, he had her in bed. Suddenly, life was good, *really* good. Suddenly, everything was going his way, and that included his break up with Katherine.

Then, a few months later, someone threw a brick through the windshield of his car at a red light. Not long after, the first death threat was phoned into the station, followed by a few more over the following months. At first it had, like everything else, worked in his favor and stirred up some publicity-grabbing controversy. But during the week of the second bomb threat received by the station, the sponsors began to drop like computer generated aliens in a video game and the manager and owners became so afraid for their lives that they saw no alternative but to let Andy go.

At first, he'd been very depressed. In fact, for a couple days, he hadn't left his apartment or answered the phone. But only two days after his firing had been announced, he was offered a job by TBN—Talk Broadcasting Network—the biggest talk radio network in the country. He'd responded with appropriate nonchalance, asking for a few days to give it some thought and talk it over with his agent; he needed the extra time to *get* an agent.

The network's offer was impressive: a nation-wide weeknight call-in talk show with timely guests covering controversial topics. Andy would have to move away from Cincinnati, of course, but that was okay. The only problem was Andy's certainty that the show would be watered down by the network to satisfy their sponsors, eliminating, at the very least, the profanity allowed on his show and, at the most, restricting his broadcasting style. But TBN surprised him. Countless polls had shown that, due to the overwhelming popularity of television, very few people listened to the radio unless they felt they were missing something unique or unusually popular, so the sponsors *wanted* Andy to be profane and aggressive and controversial and they didn't give a damn about his politics. Controversy usually attracted publicity, which *always* drew listeners. And listeners listened to advertisements.

After his recent experiences with bricks through windows and telephoned bomb threats, Andy was reluctant to use his real name on national radio, so, after acquiring the job and moving to the big city, he decided to come up with a pseudonym.

The Arthur Colton, Jr., Show began without fanfare, a strategic move by the network; they were confident that it would generate its own publicity and saw no reason to pay for any. They were right. The show created a wave of controversy and, within the first two weeks, inspired newspaper columnists across the country to write a column in response; some were positive, but most were vicious protests, some calling him a broadcasting whore who was willing to say anything, no matter how damaging or dangerous, that might garner a few more ratings points.

Once again, Andy was puzzled by his critics. He could understand if they just didn't *like* the show, but they made it sound *dangerous*. Didn't they understand that he wasn't really that person on the radio? He didn't even use his real voice anymore, let alone his real name; his radio voice was deeper, more authoritative than his regular speaking voice. And of *course* he didn't share the opinions of his radio alter ego; nobody *really* thought that way about everything, it was *ridiculous*, a caricature. In fact, Andy had very few opinions of his own. He watched the news and read papers only for the benefit of his show. He wasn't that concerned with world events; they were out of his hands. Didn't they realize that it was—

—"Just show business," he muttered, leaving the lounge with the paper and his coffee. He ducked into the control room where Tanya was occupied with a caller and didn't notice when he snatched up her cigarettes. In the studio, he tried to read the rest of the article, but the dim shadowy lighting only made his eyes water, so he leaned back in his chair with a sigh and pinched the bridge of his nose.

The night before, he'd gotten less than an hour of light dozing scattered between bouts of rolling and rutting in bed with a voluptuous, squealing coed named Debi, and that morning he'd had a brunch date with Jaretta, his hairdresser, who had agreed to grab a hotel room halfway through brunch so they wouldn't have to waste time deciding on his place or hers. Andy had seen them both before and would see them again, along with the several other women he saw regularly—Sherrie and Dina and Kaylee and Lynda and Melonie and Shawn—and the many others whom he had not yet met. His social life was better than it had been in Cincinnati despite the fact that he protected his identity and no longer used his celebrity status to impress women; it made no difference because, back in Cincinnati, he'd gained a lot of confidence with women, learned a lot about being funny and charming and tap dancing around commitment and exclusivity like Fred Astaire. And he was making a lot of money now, which didn't hurt a bit.

But tonight, he was taking a rest. After work he was going to call Sol's All-Nite Deli and order a pastrami and Swiss on an onion roll and one of Sol's fat dill pickles, take them home and eat them with a cup of hot tea in front of *Shane*, which was on the Late Late Movie, then he was going to sleep until noon. Maybe later. He lit a cigarette and sighed the smoke from his lungs, looking forward to his evening with relish.

"This is the Arthur Colton, Jr., Show and we are now entering the final hour of the show with open phones for those of you who have something to say. Anything you want. You got a gripe? You want to bitch about something? Give me a ring. Any questions? I'm almost *always* right, you know. Give me a call. And if you have a personal problem and would like to benefit from my experience, strength and wisdom, as the sniveling drunks say at AA meetings, don't hesitate to pick up the phone. Janice is calling from Witchita, Kansas. Janice, my dear, you're on the air."

"Yes, Arthur, I'm calling about your previous guest, Melissa Cartwright. I'm not a regular listener, but I heard Ms Cartwright was going to be on tonight and I'm a big fan of hers, so—"

"Why am I not surprised?"

"—I listened and I was very disappointed that you never allowed her to make her point. I mean, she is a very wise and warm person who has an open mind and she is *not* a man-hater. I think it's sad that you deprived your listeners of what she has to say, but I think it's indicative of a frightening trend in this country today toward *woman*-hating, a trend to which you seem to be a powerful contributor."

Andy smiled. This was the pro-choice woman Tanya had warned him about earlier. Andy didn't give a damn about abortion one way or the other—it meant *nothing* to him—but the great majority of his listeners were against it, and that was what mattered. It had been a hot topic ever since abortion laws had been reintroduced back in the eighties and he got a lot of calls for it, so he'd prepared a stock response—a funny, sarcastic, *angry* response—specifically for callers like Janice from Witchita.

"Janice, my dear, I may be a lot of things, but I am *not* a woman-hater. Women are my favorite living beings. Anyone who knows me will tell you that Arthur *loves* women. But I do not love *castrating* women. This is a free country, so you're entitled to your opinion just as I am, and *my* opinion is that *Mizzz* Cartwright *is* one of those castrating women. Believe me, I think there are plenty of men who *deserve* to have their balls chopped off, but not *all* of them, for crying out loud, and the women who think so are, in my opinion, no better than the psychotic *men who beat women*. Now. Why did you call? What's your question?"

"I don't really have a question, I just wanted to point out that this kind of attitude—the attitude you've exhibited on your show tonight—is greatly responsible for one of the most frightening changes to take place in this country in my lifetime."

"And what is that, praytell?"

"Within the last several years, laws have been passed in every state in the country stripping women of the right to do as they please with their bodies. Abortion has become a *crime*. It's like our bodies are now the property of the *state*! I don't see any laws prohibiting *men* from doing what they want with *their* bodies! How would you feel if a law was passed that *required* you to have a vasectomy? How would you like to be arrested if you weren't *circumcised*? And if you feel abortion is a moral crime, why can't you at least *give* women that choice? Why can't you allow them the *right* to commit that sin if they feel it's necessary?"

"Are you finished?" he asked calmly. "Is that your question? Because if it is, I have an answer."

"Yes. That's my question."

"First of all, that business about vasectomies and circumcision is just bullshit and I won't dignify it with a response. Okay, now. You and the women who agree with you claim that it is your right—your inalienable *right*—to do with your bodies as you wish. But I disagree, and I'll tell you why. Have you ever heard of Jerry Lewis?"

"Of course."

"Have you seen his Muscular Dystrophy Telethon?"

"Well . . . I'm familiar with it."

"Okay. Here's a man who has performed financial miracles for the battle against muscular dystrophy, and yet children continue to have their bodies withered by this disease. Do they have that *right*? Do they have the right to be crippled by this disease?"

"That's the most—"

"Do I have the *right* to get cancer?"

"That's the most—"

"Does my father have the *right* to have a stroke? Does my mother have the *right* to have a heart attack? Which they both *had*, and they are now *dead*."

"That is without a doubt the most—"

"What I'm saying is that our bodies are really not our *own*. When it comes right down to it, we don't *own* them. If we don't have the right to choose whether or not we get these horrible diseases or are stricken with these deadly ailments, what gives *you* the *right* to *kill* the life that is *growing* inside *your* body?"

"That is the most *ludicrous* thing I've *ever* heard in my *entire*—"

"Thank you for calling, Janice. We go to Tucson, Arizona, where David is waiting to speak with the *host*. David?"

"Hey, Arthur, it's great to talk with you, man, really."

"Thank you."

"I love your show and I think this country needs more people like you who's willing to tell it like, well, like, y'know, it *is*. I mean, I get so fed *up* with, like, all these liberal talk show hosts who ... well, who think this whole fucking country should be run by a bunch of communist faggots who ... who, um ... well, and women! They think the country can be run by, y'know, *women!* I mean, women like the one you had on tonight ... *what's* her name? The one who hates men?"

"Melissa Cartwright."

"Yeah, like women like her can *run* the damned country, I mean ... give me a *break*, okay?"

Andy smirked. Ignorant as he sounded, David was a typical listener—friend, not foe—and required a green light. "You're right on the money, David. You've got your fingers on the pulse of America and I appreciate your call. Paul in Anderson, California, what's on your mind?"

"I hear you get death threats."

"Pardon me?"

"I understand that you get threats against your life."

It was true; he still got some pretty scary threats. But his pseudonym and the anonymous nature of the network protected him. "Yes, that's true. There are people out there who don't like what I do and would like to kill me for it. Why, are you one of them?"

"Does it worry you?"

"Of *course* it worries me. Anti-American lunatics who want to kill me because of what I do? *Sure* that worries me."

"Well, I don't think you should be worried about that."

"And why's that, sir?"

"Because I don't think you'll be killed for what you do. I think you'll be killed for what you are."

The back of Andy's neck shriveled like a raisin and his hand trembled as he hit the button. "Rest well, sir, and be sure to take your medication regularly." He sighed heavily into the microphone. "Is the moon full, Tanya?"

She laughed beyond the glass.

"Tanya, of course, is my immensely talented producer, a lovely woman and a fine human being. You *see*? You see how *nice* I am to women? In fact, our next call is from a woman and her name is Mary. How are you tonight, Mary?"

"Oh . . . not so good, Arthur." Her voice was soft, breathy and tremulous.

One of his devoted female listeners with a personal problem. Arthur shifted in his chair, got comfortable. "First of all, I need you to speak up, dear. Okay?"

"O . . .kay."

"Now, tell me . . . what's wrong?"

"Well, it's about my boyfriend. He's . . . he's really hurt me, Arthur, and I just don't know—"

"Physically? Has he *hit* you?"

"Oh, no, no."

"Well, thank God for that. What's his problem, honey?"

"I don't know. I thought you could help. I listen to your show all the time and you seem so smart, so . . . worldly and wise."

"That I am. So how can I help you."

"All I want, see, is for him to let me into his life. And to let me let him into *my* life, see?"

Andy glanced over at Tanya and rolled his eyes. "Oookay, if you say so."

"I mean, we don't really share anything, you know?"

"Do you sleep together?"

"Yeah."

"That's sharing in my book."

"Yeah, but . . . but . . . well, it's little things. *Important* things. I don't know anything about him, about his life, his past. *Y'know*, those little things that make people close. And he doesn't *wanna* know anything about me. Like, what I want to do with my life and, well, what I've been *through*, I mean, just a year and half ago I was in a . . . in the hospital."

"Oh? Anything serious?"

"Well, I had some, um, a few nervous problems. It wasn't a . . . *regular* hospital. Um, it was a . . . a . . . ."

"You were in the cracker factory, Mary? Is that it? C'mon, spit it out."

She giggled. "Yeah. Guess so."

"Okay, so you blew a fuse for a while. How are you now?"

"I'm . . . well, I'm—" She sniffed a couple times. "—better. I'm doing better. Anyway, he just doesn't seem to . . . *feel* anything. You know. It's like he doesn't have any real *emotions*. And I also think he's sleeping around."

"Oh-ho, now, whoah, hold the phone. You mean, this guy is *your* boyfriend and he's sleeping with *other* women?"

"Uh-huh."

"Okay, now, honey, were you listening a few minutes ago when I said there are some guys who deserve to have their balls cut off?"

"Uh-huh."

"Well, this clown sounds like a prime candidate to me. So why don't you just chop the lousy bastard's gonads off and stuff 'em down his lying throat. And tell him Arthur Colton, Jr., said he deserved it."

Tanya grinned through the glass and made a scissor-like cutting motion with two fingers.

"Martha's been on hold for a while. Go ahead, Martha, you're on."

"Hello, Arthur, dear." An old woman. "Oh, my, I've listened to you for so long I feel like I know you." She said that every time. "I just called to tell you my son got that position I told you about a few weeks ago."

Oh, God, Andy thought. "Oh, really?" he asked.

"Yes. He and his wife are moving to New Jersey now, which is where the company's main plant is. Only problem is, they can't take their dogs with them and the children are *so* disappointed."

"Oh, too bad." He drummed his fingers on the console.

"And speaking of dogs, my Pookie is getting bigger every day. You remember the dachshund I got last month?"

"Mm-hm."

"Well, he's just as cute as a button and—"

"Take care, Martha, talk to you in a week or so. Keith in Provo, Utah."

"What gives you the right, man, what gives you the *right* to just dismiss people the way you do. You talk about freedom of speech, but you just cut people off like they're *nothing*. Who do you think you *are*? What gives you the *right*?"

"Well, I may not have the right, but I've got the button, which I'm gonna use . . . right . . . *now*. Lancaster, Pennsylvania, you're on."

"Yeah, Arthur, I hope you'll let me make my point and not cut me off."

"We'll see."

"I think maybe that last caller was onto something when he mentioned freedom of speech. You talk about it a lot, and yet your show is anything *but* an example of free speech because you hang up on anybody who disagrees with you before they've even made their point or asked their question. *That's* not freedom of speech. If you're so convinced you're right, why don't you let them speak? What are you afraid of? Why can't you *discuss* it with them?"

"Okay, okay, I get this question a lot. Listen, sir, when I talk about freedom of speech, I'm talking about freedom of speech *within the country*. This country was built on freedom of speech and continues to uphold that freedom, and it's one of the reasons I love my country so much."

"Continues to uphold—whatta you mea—what about *flag* burning?"

"Just hold onto your dick a second, sir, I'm getting to that. If you think I'm so anti-free speech, why do you *listen*? It's a *free country*, sir, you don't *have* to listen. If it weren't a free country, there might be a law requiring you to listen to me, but there's not, so why *do* you? I think it's because, deep down inside, even the people who hate me know, in their heart of hearts, that I'm right. As for flag burning, don't start with that bullshit argument the faggot liberals used back in the eighties when this whole thing came up. Freedom of speech doesn't mean freedom of *vandalism*. Men *died* for that flag and to burn it—"

"They died for what it *stands* for, there's a big—"

"And that flag *stands* for the thing for which they *died*, so to burn it has been made a crime, as it should be, and people are now in prison for it, where I hope they rot. It's barbaric, it's treasonous, and nothing less than criminal.

"Now *this* is what I'm sick of, sir, people like you who—look, I'll *tell* you why I run my show the way I do. Because I . . . love . . . my . . . *country*! And I'll explain that. Like I said, one of the things I love most about America is its freedom of speech. It's in the constitution, it was granted us by our forefathers. It is available to all who live here. I support it. But sometimes, ladies and gentlemen and Lancaster, Pennsylvania, *sometimes* it frustrates the hell out of me. Because this freedom is often abused by those who represent everything that is *un*-American. And I'm talking, now, about these people who think it's just fine and dandy to burn our flag, who think that it's just a piece of cloth and that burning it is a *statement*, when you and I, dear listener, *we* know that it's no different than *pissing* on our country, no different than *shitting* on the graves of those men who have given their lives so that ours might be free. Those who think *that* shouldn't be a crime—which it *is*—abuse the freedom of speech. And I'm talking about these women, these, these . . . okay, I'll say it, I'm not afraid . . .

these *sluts* who think they have the right to fuck everything that moves when they know full well they might get pregnant, then, and *then* . . . when they do . . . they feel they have the right to kill—to *scrape out* and *dispose of*—the very life they've created. These women who think abortion—which is *also* a crime—is a fine and dandy method of birth control because the life they've created just isn't con-*veeeenient* for them are abusing America's freedoms. And the list goes on. The faggots who continue spreading AIDS among innocent people. What, you think AIDS just *appears* in bags of plasma in some blood bank? You think it comes out of *nowhere*? Those queers who can't keep their dicks in their pants are abusing America's freedoms. The people who vote into office the liberal scum who pass laws requiring a white boss to hire a black employee when a white man is more qualified just because the black employee is *black*! Do *you* like that? *I* don't. I have nothing against blacks, some of my best friends are black, but some of my best friends are *white*, too! Those people—not the liberal scum, but the people who vote them into office—*those* people are abusing America's freedoms. And the Jews who have gained control of America's film and television industries so they can degrade the Christian values and beliefs that we all hold dear—*they* abuse America's freedoms. Those people make me sick. But I realize that they have just as much access to those freedoms as I do.

"However, folks, my show is not a country. It's *my* show. I'm in control here. Those people, those scumbags, those shitheels, they have all the rights they need, and they abuse them to hell and back. On *this* show, they do *not* have that right. And neither do the people who support them. My critics say I'm a danger to American freedoms but I say they're full of shit. My show is for the throbbing heart of America: the people who love and value their freedoms and use them as our forefathers *meant* them to be used. My show, sir, is *not* for people like you, and I would appreciate it if you didn't call again. Ever. In fact, I would appreciate it even more if you didn't *listen* anymore. And I would *especially* appreciate it if you would kindly take your fly-eaten, shit-soaked, un-American opinion and blow it out your ass. Have a *wonderful* evening." He hit the button. "And if this wasn't America—God *bless* her—I couldn't say that." He sighed heavily. "We've got a couple minutes of commercials, then we'll be back for more open phones. Stick around."

Andy looked up to see Harold and Tanya standing and applauding in the control room. It was one of the best—maybe *the* best—speech he'd ever given and he was exhilarated. He laughed, knowing that many of his listeners throughout the country were probably standing in front of their radios doing the same thing as Harold and Tanya. It tickled him pink.

*

. . . I don't think you'll be killed for what you do. I think you'll be killed for what you are . . .

. . . for what you are . . .

. . . what you are . . .

Andy shuddered. He'd never had any trouble leaving his work behind him when he went home, but as his cab drove through the warm, dark city, he couldn't shake that one call . . . one of the shortest calls of the night . . .

It haunted him.

He even remembered the caller: Paul from Anderson, California.

. . . I don't think you'll be killed for what you do. I think you'll be killed for what you are.

Andy leaned forward and said to the cab driver, "Right here, on this corner." The cab stopped and he walked into Sol's All Nite Deli where he heard Sex Talk with Dr Tracy Connor, the show that followed him on TBN. It was playing on the radio beside Sol's cash register.

"Andy!" Sol shouted with a grin and a wave. He was in his late sixties, short, fat, balding and loud.

"Hey, Solly, how you doing?"

"Shitty. I'm *shitty!* I been listening to this Arthur Colton shmuck. You hear him tonight?"

"Never listen, Sol."

"Aaaa." He swiped his meaty hand through the air, grimacing. "Dreck. That's what it is. Talkin' about how the Jews control movies and TV so we can destroy Christianity. What, like we haven't been through *enough*? Like we don't have enough troubles as it *is*? He's gotta stir the goyim sommore? Aaaa, *meshuganuh*."

"Why do you listen, Solly?"

He shrugged, stuck out his lower lip and cocked his head.

Andy grinned. "Well, if it's any help, Solly, I'm not Jewish and I think you're the bee's knees."

Sol laughed. "You want the usual?"

Andy nodded.

As he left the deli with his sandwich and pickle, Andy shook his head, puzzled. Why didn't they understand? And if they didn't understand, why did they listen?

As he walked into his dark apartment, his mouth watering for the sandwich, Andy was startled by the smell of a familiar perfume. He stood in the entryway a moment, staring into the dark, before he switched on the light.

"Andy?" The voice—a woman's—came from down the hall.

"Who's there?"

"It's me."

It was Sherrie. First, Andy rolled his eyes, knowing his plans for the night were shattered, then, heading down the hall, he shouted, "How the hell did you get in here?"

Andy froze in his bedroom doorway. The room was bathed in candlelight, and so was Sherrie, who lay on his brass bed wearing a sheer negligee that left little to the imagination. One knee was cocked up, one hand rested between her legs and her blond hair fell around her shoulders.

"Holy shit," Andy muttered with a smirk.

"I convinced the super to let me in," she whispered. "After all, he knows me, right? He's seen me before. It's all right, isn't it?"

"Wuh-well, I did sort of have other plans . . ."

She slid her hand up between her breasts and spread her legs. "Were your plans *this* good?"

"Ummm . . . no." As he entered the room, she stood and lifted a satchel from the floor, holding it between them, her eyes twinkling.

"I thought we'd try something different tonight."

"Different?" He tingled.

She nodded, dropped the satchel and embraced him, giving him a long, deep kiss as she began to remove his clothes. When he was naked, they moved to the bed, kissing again, and, removing something from the satchel, she told him to lie on his back.

Sherrie held up four lengths of velvet. "Have you ever been tied up?"

He laughed. "No. But I'll try anything once!" Smiling, Andy decided that *Shane* could go fuck himself.

Sherrie tied his wrists and ankles to the brass, put the satchel on the edge of the bed, then straddled him and began covering him with kisses. His cock was erect long before she took it in her mouth and began moving her head up and down on it as she ran her fingertips over his body like feathers.

Andy felt as if his brain were melting and he moaned deeply, moving his head back and forth, eyes closed.

She stopped.

He lifted his head as she fished through the satchel.

"You up for something *really* kinky?" she asked.

He gasped, "You kidding? *Sure!*"

She removed something long from the satchel.

A *vibrator*? he thought. *Oh, my God!*

There was a click and the object she held began to hum.

"Oh, my God," Andy moaned, dropping his head back on the pillow and closing his eyes.

She cupped his balls in her hand.

The electric hum continued.

Sherrie giggled.

Andy lifted his head, smiling, and saw it.

Its quivering blade caught the light as she lifted it.

An electric carving knife.

"What the—"

Sherrie grinned. "Arthur Colton, Jr., said you deserve this."

As her arm moved downward—so slowly, unbelievably slowly—Andy understood with terrifying clarity, remembered the call, remembered his response, and screamed, "No no wait you don't know you don't underst—"

He heard the sound.

He felt the pain.

Before he could react, something was stuffed into his mouth . . .

MICHAEL

MARSHALL SMITH

The Man Who Drew Cats

MICHAEL MARSHALL SMITH currently works as a Press Information Officer in Britain, although his early years were spent living in Australia, South Africa and the USA.

He has also worked as a writer and performer of revue comedy with The Throbbs on the BBC Radio 4 series *And Now in Colour* . . . and is currently working on a number of screen treatments and a novel. He cites Stephen King, Ramsey Campbell, Kingsley and Martin Amis as influences on his fiction.

"The Man Who Drew Cats" was the first story he has had published (other tales are forthcoming in *Darklands* and *Fantasy Tales*). He got the idea from watching a pavement chalk artist at work and seeing a child crying nearby. The original setting was Edinburgh, but he transferred the action to the Midwest and wrote the story in a day. It's a stunning debut of a promising new talent . . .

O LD TOM WAS A VERY TALL MAN. He was so tall he didn't even have a nickname for it. Ned Black, who was at least a head shorter, had been "Tower Block" since the sixth grade, and Jack, the owner of the Hog's Head Bar, had a sign up over the door saying "Mind Your Head, Ned". But Tom was just Tom. It was like he was so tall it didn't bear mentioning even for a joke: be a bit like ragging someone for breathing.

Course there were other reasons too for not ragging Tom about his height or anything else. The guys you'll find perched on stools round Jack's bar watching the ball game and buying beers, they've known each other for ever. Gone to Miss Stadler's school together, got under each other's Mom's feet, and double-dated together right up to giving each other's best man's speech. Kingstown is a small place, you understand, and the old boys who come regular to Jack's mostly spent their childhoods in the same tree-house. Course they'd gone their separate ways, up to a point: Pete was an accountant now, had a small office down Union Street just off the square and did pretty good, whereas Ned, well he was still pumping gas and changing oil and after forty years he did that pretty good too. Comes a time when men have known each other so long they forget what they do for a living most of the time because it just don't matter: when you talk there's a little bit of skimming stones down the quarry in second grade, a bit of dolling up to go to that first dance, and going to the housewarming when they moved ten years back. There's all that and more than you can say so none of it's important 'cept for having happened.

So we'll stop by and have a couple of beers and talk about the town and the playoffs and rag each other and the pleasure's just in shooting the breeze and it don't really matter what's said, just the fact that we're all still there to say it.

But Tom, he was different. We all remember the first time we saw him. It was a long hot summer like we haven't seen in the ten years since and we were lolling under the fans at Jack's and complaining about the tourists. And believe me, Kingstown gets its share in the summer even though it's not near the sea and we don't have a McDonald's and I'll be damned if I can figure out why folk'll go out of their way to see what's just a peaceful little town near some mountains. It was as hot as hell that afternoon and as much as a man could do to sit in his shirt-sleeves and drink the coolest beer he could find, and Jack's is the coolest for us, and always will be, I guess.

And then Tom walked in. His hair was already pretty white back then, and long, and his face was brown and tough with grey eyes like diamonds set in leather. He was dressed mainly in black with a long coat that made you hot just to look at it, but he looked comfortable like he carried his very own weather around with him and he was just fine. He got a beer and sat down at a table and read the town *Bugle* and that was that.

It was special because there wasn't anything special about it. Jack's Bar isn't exactly exclusive and we don't all turn round and stare at anyone new if they come in, but that place is like a monument to shared times and if a tourist couple comes in out of the heat and sits down nobody says anything and maybe nobody even notices at the front of their mind, but it's like there's a little island of the alien in the water and the currents don't just ebb and flow the way they usually do, if you get what I mean. But Tom he just walked in and sat down and it was all right because it was like he was there just like we were, and could've been for thirty years. He just sat and read his paper like part of the same river and everyone just carried on downstream the way they were.

Pretty soon he goes up for another beer and a few of us got talking to him. We got his name and what he did. Painting, he said, and after that it was just shooting the breeze. That quick. He came in that summer afternoon and just fell into the conversation like he'd been there all his life, and sometimes it was hard to imagine he hadn't been. Nobody knew where he came from, or where he'd been, and there was something very quiet about him, a real stillness. Open enough to have the best part of friendship but still somehow a man in a slightly different world. But he showed enough to get along real well with us, and a bunch of old friends don't often let someone in like that.

Anyway, he stayed that whole summer. Hired himself a place just round the corner from the square. Or so he said: I never saw it, I guess no one did. He was a private man, private like a steel door with four bars and a couple of six-inch padlocks, and when he left the square at the end of the day he could have vanished into thin air as soon as he turned the corner for all we knew. But he always came from that direction in the morning, with his easel on his back and paintbox under his arm. And he always wore that black coat like it was a part of him, but he always looked cool, and the funny thing was when you stood near him you could swear you felt cooler yourself. I remember Pete saying over a beer that it wouldn't surprise him none if, if it ever rained again, Tom walked round in his own column of dryness. Just foolish talk, but Tom made you think things like that.

Jack's bar looks right out onto the square, the kind of square towns don't have much anymore: big and dusty with old roads out at each corner, tall shops and houses on all the sides and some stone paving in the middle round a fountain that ain't worked in living memory. Well in the summer that old square is just full of out-of-towners in pink towelling jumpsuits and nasty jackets standing round saying "Wow" and taking pictures of our quaint old hall and our quaint old stores and even our quaint old selves if we stand still too long. And that year Tom would sit out near the fountain and paint and those people would stand and watch for hours.

But he didn't paint the houses or the square or the old Picture House. He painted animals, and painted them like you've never seen. Birds with huge blue speckled wings and cats with cutting green eyes and whatever he painted it looked like it was just coiled up on the canvas ready to fly away. He didn't do them in their normal colours, they were all reds and purples and deep blues and greens and yet they fair sparkled with life. It was a wonder to watch: he'd put up a fresh paper, sit looking at nothing in particular, then dip his brush into his paint and just draw a line, maybe red, maybe blue. Stroke by stroke you could see the animal build up in front of your eyes and yet when it was finished you couldn't believe it hadn't always been there. And when he'd finished he'd spray it with some stuff to fix the paints and put a price on it and you can believe me those paintings were sold before they hit the ground. Spreading businessmen from New Jersey or somesuch and their bored wives would come alive for maybe the first time in years and walk away with one of those paintings and their arms round each other, looking like they'd found a bit of something they'd forgotten they'd lost.

Come about six o'clock Tom would finish up and walk across to Jack's, looking like a sailing ship amongst rowing boats and saying yes, he'd be back again tomorrow and yes, he'd be happy to do a painting for them. And he'd get a beer and sit with us and watch the game and there'd be no paint on his fingers or his clothes, not a spot. I guess he'd got so much control over that paint it went where it was told and nowhere else.

I asked him once how he could bear to let those paintings go. I know if I'd been able to make anything that right in my whole life I couldn't let it go, I'd want to keep it to look at sometimes. He thought for a moment and then he said he believed it depends how much of yourself you've put into it. If you've gone deep down into yourself and pulled up what's inside and put it down, then you don't want to let it go: you want to check sometimes that it's still safely tied down. Comes a time when a painting's so right and so good that it's private, and no one'll understand it except the man who put it down. Only he is going to know what he's talking about. But the everyday paintings, well they were mainly just because he liked to paint animals, and liked for people to have them. He could only put a piece of himself into something he was going to sell, but they paid for the beers and I guess it's like the old boys in Jack's Bar: if you just like talking you don't always have to say something important.

Why animals? Well if you'd seen him with them I guess you wouldn't have to ask. He loved them, is all, and they loved him right back. The cats were always his favourites. My old Pa used to say that cats weren't nothing but sleeping machines put on the earth to do some of the human's sleeping for them, and whenever Tom worked in the square there'd always be a couple curled up near his feet. And whenever he did a chalk drawing he'd always do a cat.

Once in a while, you see, Tom seemed to get tired of painting on paper, and he'd get out some chalks and sit down on the baking flagstones and just do a drawing right there on the dusty rock. Now I've told you about his paintings, but these drawings were something else again. It was like because they couldn't be bought, but would just be washed away, he was putting more of himself into it, doing more than just shooting the breeze. They were just chalk on dusty stone and they were still in these weird colours but I tell you children wouldn't walk near them because they looked so real, and they weren't the only ones, either. People would just stand a few feet back and stare and you could see the wonder in their eyes and their open mouths. If they could've been bought there were people who would have sold their houses. And it's a funny thing but a couple of times when I walked over to open the store up in the mornings I saw a dead bird or two on top of those drawings, almost like they had landed on it and been so terrified to find themselves right on top of a cat they'd dropped dead of fright. But they must have been dumped there by some real cat, of course, because some of those birds looked like they'd been mauled a bit. I used to throw them in the bushes to tidy up and some of them were pretty broken up.

Old Tom was a godsend to a lot of mothers that summer who found they could leave their little ones by him, do their shopping in peace and maybe have a soda with their friends and come back to find the kids still sitting quietly watching Tom paint. He didn't mind them at all and would talk to them and make them laugh, and kids of that age laughing is one of the nicest sounds there is. They're young and curious and the world just spins round them and when they laugh the world seems a brighter place because it takes you back to the time when you knew no evil and everything was good, or if it wasn't, it would be over by tomorrow.

And here I guess I've finally come down to it, because there was one little boy who didn't laugh much, but just sat quiet and watchful, and I guess he probably understands more of what happened that summer than any of us, though maybe not in words he could tell.

His name was Billy McNeill, and he was Jim Valentine's kid. Jim used to be a mechanic, worked with Ned up at the gas station and did a bit of beat-up car racing after hours. Which is why his kid is called McNeill now: one Sunday Jim took a corner a mite too fast and the car rolled and the gas tank caught and they never did find all the wheels. A year later his Mary married again. God alone knows why, her folks warned her, her friends warned her, but I guess love must just have been blind. Sam McNeill's work schedule was at best pretty empty, and mostly he just drank and hung out with friends who maybe weren't always this side of the law. And I guess Mary had her own sad little miracle and got her sight back pretty soon because it wasn't long before Sam got a bit too free with his fists when the evenings got too long and he'd had a lot too many. You didn't see Mary around much anymore. In these parts people tend to stare at black eyes on a woman, and a deaf man could hear the whisperings of "We Told Her So" on the wind.

One morning Tom was sitting painting as usual and little Billy was sitting watching him. Usually he just wandered off after a while but this morning Mary was at the doctor's and she came over to collect him, walking quickly with her face lowered. But not low enough. I was watching from the store, it was kind of a slow morning. Tom's face never showed much, he was a man for a quiet smile and a raised eyebrow, but he looked shocked that morning, just for a moment. Mary's eyes were puffed and purple and there was a cut on her cheek an inch long. I guess we'd sort of gotten used to seeing her like that and if the truth be known some of the wives thought she'd got remarried a bit on the soon side and I suppose we may all have been a bit cold towards her, Jim Valentine having been so well-liked and all.

Tom looked from the little boy who never laughed as much as the others to his mom with her tired unhappy eyes and her beat-up face and his face went from shocked to stony and I can't describe any other way than that I seemed to feel a cold chill across my heart from right across the square. But then he smiled and ruffled Billy's hair and Mary took Billy's hand and they went off. They looked back once and Tom was still looking after them and he gave Billy a little wave and he waved back and mother and child smiled together.

That night in Jack's Tom put a quiet question about Mary and we told him the story and as he listened his face seemed to harden from within, his bright eyes becoming flat and dead. We told him that old Lou Lachance who lived next door to the McNeill's said that sometimes you could hear him shouting and her pleading till three in the morning and on still nights the sound of Billy crying for much longer still. Told him it was a shame, but what could you do? Folks keep themselves out of other people's faces round here, and I guess Sam and his roughneck drinking buddies didn't have much to fear from nearly-retireders like us anyhow. Told him it was a terrible thing, and none of us liked it, but these things happened.

Tom listened and didn't say a word. Just sat there in his black coat and listened to us pass the buck. After a while the talk sort of petered out and we sat and watched the bubbles in our beers. I guess the bottom line was that none of us had really thought about it much except as another chapter of small-town gossip and Jesus Christ did I feel ashamed about that by the time we'd finished telling it. Sitting there with Tom was no laughs at all at that moment. He had a real edge to him, and seemed more unknown than known that night. He just stared at his laced fingers for a long time, and then he began, real slow, to talk.

He'd been married once, he said, a long time ago, and he lived in a place called Stevensburg with his wife Rachel. And when he talked about her the air seemed to go softer and we all sat quiet and supped our beers and remembered how it had been way back when we first loved our own wives. He talked of her smile and the look in her eyes and when we all went home that night I guess there were a few wives who were surprised at how tight they got hugged and who went to sleep in their husband's arms feeling more loved and contented than they had in a long while.

He'd loved her and she him and for a few years they were the happiest people on earth. Then a third party had got involved. Tom didn't say his name, and he spoke real neutrally about him but it was a gentleness like silk wrapped round a knife. Anyway his wife, it seems, fell in love with him, or thought she had, or leastways she slept with him. In their bed, the bed they'd come to on their wedding night. And as Tom spoke these words some of us looked up at him, startled, like we'd been slapped across the face with pain. Rachel did what so many do and live to regret till their dying day. She was so mixed up and getting so much pressure from the other guy that she decided to plough on with the one mistake and make it the biggest in the world. She left Tom. He talked with her, pleaded even. It was almost impossible to imagine Tom ever doing that, but I guess the man we knew was a different man from the one he was remembering.

And so Tom had to carry on living in Stevensburg, walking the same tracks, seeing them around, wondering if she was as free and easy with him, if the light in her eyes was shining on him now. And each time the man saw Tom he'd look straight at him and crease a little twisted smile, a grin that said he knew about the pleading and he and his cronies had had a good laugh over the wedding bed and yes I'm going home with your wife tonight and I know just how she likes it, you want to compare notes? And then he'd turn and kiss Rachel on the mouth, his eyes on Tom, smiling. And she let him do it.

It had kept stupid old women in stories for weeks, the way Tom kept losing weight and his temper and the will to live. He took three months of it and then left without bothering to sell the house. Stevensburg was where he'd grown up and courted and loved and now wherever he turned the good times had rotted and hung like fly-blown corpses in all the cherished places. He'd never been back.

It took an hour to tell and then he stopped talking a while and lit a hundredth cigarette and Pete got us all some more beers. We were sitting sad and thoughtful, tired like we'd lived it ourselves. And I guess most of us had, some little bit of it. But had we ever loved anyone the way he'd loved her? I doubt it, not all of us put together. Pete set the beers down and Ned asked Tom why he hadn't just beaten the living shit out of the guy. Now no one else would have actually asked that, but Ned's a good guy, and I guess we were all with him in feeling a piece of that oldest and most crushing hatred in the world, the hate of a man who's lost the woman he loves to another, and we knew what Ned was saying. I'm not saying it's a good thing and I know you're not supposed to feel like that these days but show me a man who says he doesn't and I'll show you a liar. Love is the only feeling worth a tin shit but you've got to know that it comes from both sides of a man's character and the deeper it runs the darker the pools it draws from.

My guess is he just hated the man too much to hit him. Comes a time when that isn't enough, when nothing is ever going to be enough, and so you can't do anything at all. And as he talked the pain just flowed out like a river that wasn't ever going to be stopped, a river that had cut a channel through every corner of his soul. I learnt something that night that you can go your whole life without realizing: that there are things that can be done that can mess someone up so badly for so long that they just cannot be allowed, that there are some kinds of pain that you cannot suffer to be brought into the world. And then Tom was done telling and he raised a smile and said that in the end he hadn't done anything to the man except paint him a picture, which I didn't understand, but Tom looked like he'd talked all he was going to.

And so we got some more beers and shot some quiet pool before going home. But I guess we all knew what he'd been talking about. Billy McNeill was just a child. He should have been dancing through a world like a big funfair full of sunlight and sounds and instead he went home at night and saw his mom being beaten up by a man with shit for brains who struck out at a good woman because he was too twisted with ignorant stupidity to deal with the world. Most kids go to sleep thinking about bikes and climbing apple trees and skimming stones and he was lying there hearing splitting skin and knowing a brutal face was smiling as his mom got smashed in the stomach and then hit again as she threw up in the sink. Tom didn't say any of that, but he did. And we knew he was right.

The summer kept up bright and hot, and we all had our businesses to attend to. Jack sold a lot of beer and I sold a lot of ice cream (Sorry ma'am, just the three flavours, and no, Bubblegum Pistachio ain't one of them) and Ned fixed a whole bunch of cracked radiators. And Tom sat right out there in the square with a couple of cats by his feet and a crowd around him, magicking up animals in the sun.

And I think that after that night Mary maybe got a few more smiles as she did her shopping, and maybe a few more wives stopped to talk to her. She looked a lot better too: Sam had a job by the sound of it and her face healed up pretty soon. You could often see her standing holding Billy's hand as they watched Tom paint for a while before they went home. I think she realized they had a friend in him. Sometimes Billy was there all afternoon, and he was happy there in the sun by Tom's feet and oftentimes he'd pick up a piece of chalk and sit scrawling on the pavement. Sometimes I'd see Tom lean over and say something to him and he'd look up and smile a simple child's smile that beamed in the sunlight and I don't mind admitting I felt water pricking in these old eyes. The tourists kept coming and the sun kept shining and it was one of those summers that go on for ever and stick in a child's mind, and tell you what summer should be like for the rest of your life. And I'm damn sure it sticks in Billy's mind, just like it does in all of ours.

Because one morning Mary didn't come into the store, which had gotten to being a regular sort of thing, and Billy wasn't out there in the square. After the way things had been the last few weeks that could only be bad news and so I left the boy John in charge of the store and hurried over to have a word with Tom. I was kind of worried.

I was no more than halfway across to him when I saw Billy come running from the opposite corner of the square, going straight to Tom. He was crying fit to burst and just leapt up at Tom and clung to him, his arms wrapped tight round his neck. Then his mother came across from the same direction, running as best she could. She got to Tom and they just looked at each other. Mary's a real pretty girl but you wouldn't have believed it then. It looked like he'd actually broken her nose this time and blood was streaming out of her lip. She started sobbing, saying Sam had lost his job because he was back on the drink and what could she do and then suddenly there was a roar and I was shoved aside and Sam was standing there, still wearing his slippers, weaving back and forth and radiating the frightening aura of violence waiting to happen that keep men like him safe. He started shouting at Mary to take the kid the fuck back home and she just flinched and cowered closer to Tom like she was huddling round a fire to keep out the cold. This just got Sam even wilder and he staggered forward and told Tom to get the fuck out of it if he knew what was good for him, and grabbed Mary's arm and tried to yank her towards him, his face terrible with twisted rage.

Then Tom stood up. Now Tom was a tall man, but he wasn't a young man, and he was thin. Sam was thirty and built like a brick shithouse. When he did work it usually involved moving heavy things from one place to another, and his strength was supercharged by a whole pile of drunken nastiness. But at that moment the crowd stepped back as one and I suddenly felt very afraid for Sam McNeill. Tom looked like you could take anything you cared to him and it would just break, like a huge spike of granite wrapped in skin with two holes in the face where the rock showed through. And he was mad, not hot and blowing like Sam, but cold as ice.

There was a long pause. Then Sam weaved back a step and shouted, "You just come on home, you hear? Gonna be real trouble if you don't, Mary. Real trouble," and then stormed off across the square the way he came, knocking his way through the tourist vultures soaking up some spicy local colour.

Mary turned to Tom, looking so afraid it hurt to look, and said she guessed she'd better be going. Tom just stared at her for a moment and then spoke for the first time. "Do you love him?" Even if you wanted to, you ain't going to lie to eyes like that for fear something inside you will break. Real quiet she said, "No," and began crying softly as she took Billy's hand and walked slowly back across the square.

Tom packed up his stuff and walked over to Jack's. I went with him and had a beer but I had to get back to the shop and Tom just sat there like a trigger, silent and strung up tight as a drum. And somewhere down near the bottom of those still waters something was stirring. Something I thought I didn't want to see.

About an hour later it was lunchtime and I'd just left the shop to have a break and suddenly something whacked into the back of my legs and nearly knocked me down. It was Billy. It was Billy and he had a bruise round his eye that was already closing it up.

I knew what the only thing to do was and I did it. I took his hand and led him across to the bar, feeling a hard anger pushing against my throat. When he saw Tom, Billy ran to him again and Tom took him in his arms and looked over Billy's shoulder at me and I felt my own anger collapse utterly in the face of a fury I could never have generated. I tried to find a word like "angry" to describe it but they all just seemed like they were in the wrong language. All of a sudden I wanted to be somewhere else and it felt real cold standing there facing that stranger in a black coat.

Then the moment passed and Tom was holding the kid close, ruffling his hair and talking to him in a low voice, murmuring the words I thought only mothers knew. He dried Billy's tears and checked his eye and then he got off his stool, smiled down at him and said:

"And now I think it's time we did a bit of drawing, isn't it?" and, taking the kid's hand, he picked up his chalkbox and walked out into the square.

I don't know how many times I looked up and watched them that afternoon. They were sitting side by side on the stone, Billy's little hand wrapped round one of Tom's fingers, and Tom doing one of his chalk drawings. Every now and then Billy would reach across and add a little bit and Tom would smile and say something and Billy's gurgling laugh would float across the square. The store was real busy that afternoon and I was chained to that counter but I could tell by the size of the crowd that a lot of Tom was going into that picture, and maybe a bit of Billy too.

It was about four o'clock before I could take a break. I walked across the crowded square in the mid-afternoon heat and shouldered my way through to where they sat with a couple of cold Cokes. And when I saw it my mouth just dropped open and took a five minute vacation while I tried to take it in.

It was a cat all right, but not a normal cat. It was a life-size tiger. I'd never seen Tom do anything anywhere near that big before and as I stood there in the beating sun trying to get my mind round it it almost seemed to stand in three dimensions, a nearly living thing. Its stomach was very lean and thin, its tail seemed to twitch with colour, and as Tom worked on the eyes and jaws, his face set with a rigid concentration quite unlike his usual calm painting face, the snarling mask of the tiger came to life before my eyes. And I could see that he wasn't just putting a bit of himself in at all. This was a man at full stretch, giving all of himself and reaching down for more, pulling up bloody fistfuls and throwing them down. The tiger was all the rage I'd seen in his eyes and more and like his love for Rachel that rage just seemed bigger than any other man could know or comprehend. He was pouring it out and sculpting it into the lean and ravenous creature coming to pulsating life in front of us on the pavement, and the weird purples and blues and reds just made it seem more vibrant and alive.

I watched him working furiously on it, the boy sometimes helping, adding a tiny bit here and there that strangely seemed to add to it, and thought I understood what he'd meant that evening a few weeks back. He said he'd done a painting for the man who'd given him so much pain. Then, as now, he must have found what I guess you'd call something fancy like catharsis through his skill with chalks, had wrenched the pain up from within him and nailed it down onto something solid that he could walk away from. And now he was helping that little boy do the same, and the boy did look better, his bruised eye hardly showing with the wide smile on his face as he watched the big cat conjured up from nowhere in front of him.

We all just stood and watched, like something out of an old story, the simple folk and the wandering magical stranger. It always feels like you're giving a bit of yourself away when you praise someone else's creation, and it's often done grudgingly, but you could feel the awe that day like a warm wind. Comes a time when you realize something special is happening, something you're never going to see again, and there isn't anything you can do but watch.

Well I had to go back to the store after a while. I hated to go but, well, John is a good boy, married now of course, but in those days his head was full of girls and it didn't do to leave him alone in a busy shop for too long.

And so the long hot day drew slowly to a close. I kept the store open till eight, when the light began to turn and the square emptied out with all the tourists going away to write postcards and see if we didn't have even just a *little* McDonalds hidden away someplace. I guess Mary had troubles enough at home, realized where the boy would be and figured he was safer there than anywhere else, and I guess she was right.

Tom and Billy finished up drawing and then Tom sat and talked to him for some time. Then they got up and the kid walked slowly off to the corner of the square, looking back to wave at Tom a couple times. Tom stood and watched him go and when Billy had gone he stayed there a while, head down, looking like a huge black statue in the gathering dark. He looked kind of creepy out there and I don't mind telling you I was glad when he finally moved and started walking over towards Jack's. I ran out to catch up with him and drew level just as we passed the drawing. And then I had to stop. I just couldn't look at that and move at the same time.

Finished, the drawing was like nothing on earth, and I suppose that's exactly what it was. I can't hope to describe it to you, although I've seen it in my dreams many times in the last ten years. You had to be there, on that heavy summer night, had to know what was going on. Otherwise it's going to sound like it was just a drawing. That tiger was out and out terrifying. It looked so mean and hungry Christ I don't know what: it just looked like the darkest parts of your own mind, the pain and the fury and the vengeful hate nailed down in front of you for you to see, and I just stood there and shivered in the humid evening air.

"We did him a picture," Tom said quietly.

"Yeah," I said, and nodded. Like I said, I know what catharsis means and I thought I understood what he was saying. But I really didn't want to look at it much longer. "Let's go have a beer, yeah?"

The storm in Tom wasn't past, I could tell, and he still seemed to thrum with crackling emotions looking for an earth, but I thought the clouds might be breaking and I was glad.

And so we walked slowly over to Jack's and had a few beers and watched some pool being played. Tom seemed pretty tired, but still alert, and I relaxed a little. Come eleven most of the guys started going on their way and I was surprised to see Tom get another beer. Pete, Ned and I stayed on, and Jack of course, though we knew our loving wives would have something to say about that. It just didn't seem time to go. Outside it had gotten pretty dark, though the moon was keeping the square in a kind of twilight and the lights in the bar threw a pool of warmth out of the front window.

Then, about twelve o'clock, it happened, and I don't suppose any of us will ever see the same world we grew up in again. I've told this whole thing like it was just me who was there, but we all were, and we remember it together.

Because suddenly there was a wailing sound outside, a thin cutting cry, getting closer. Tom immediately snapped to his feet and stared out the window like he'd been waiting for it. As we looked out across the square we saw little Billy come running and we could see the blood on his face from there. Some of us got to get up but Tom snarled at us to stay there and so I guess we just stayed there, sitting back down like we'd been pushed. He strode out the door and into the square and the boy saw him and ran to him and Tom folded him in his cloak and held him close and warm. But he didn't come back in. He just stood there, and he was waiting for something.

Now there's a lot of crap talked about silences. I read novels when I've the time and you read things like "Time stood still" and so on and you just think bullshit it did. So I'll just say I don't think anyone in the world breathed in that next minute. There was no wind, no movement. The stillness and silence were there like you could touch them, but more than that: they were like that's all there was and all there ever had been.

We felt the slow red throb of violence from right across the square before we could even see the man. Then Sam came staggering into the square waving a bottle like a flag and cursing his head off. At first he couldn't see Tom and the boy because they were the opposite side of the fountain, and he ground to a wavering halt, but then he started shouting, rough jags of sound that seemed to strike against the silence and die instead of breaking it, and he started charging across the square and if ever there was a man with murder in his thoughts then it was Sam McNeill. He was like a man possessed, a man who'd given his soul the evening off. I wanted to shout to Tom to get the hell out of the way, to come inside, but the words wouldn't come out of my throat and we all just stood there, knuckles whitening as we clutched the bar and stared, our mouths open like we'd made a pact never to use them again. And Tom just stood there, watching Sam come towards him, getting closer, almost as far as the spot where Tom usually painted. And it felt like we were looking out of the window at a picture of something that happened long ago in another place and time and the closer Sam got the more I began to feel very very afraid for him.

It was at that moment that Sam stopped dead in his tracks, skidding forward like in some kid's cartoon, his shout dying off in his ragged throat. He was staring at the ground in front of him, his eyes wide and his mouth a stupid circle. And then he began to scream.

It was a high shrill noise like a woman and coming out of that bull of a man it sent fear racking down my spine. He started making thrashing movements like he was trying to move backwards but he just stayed where he was. His movements became unmistakable at about the same time his screams turned from terror to agony. He was trying to get his leg away from something.

Suddenly he seemed to fall forward on one knee, his other leg stuck out behind him and he raised his head and shrieked at the dark skies and we saw his face then and I'm not going to forget that face so long as I live. It was a face from before there were any words, the face behind our oldest fears and earliest nightmares, the face we're terrified of seeing on ourselves one night when we're alone in the dark and It finally comes out from under the bed to get us.

Then Sam fell on his face, his leg buckled up and still he thrashed and screamed and clawed at the ground with his hands, blood running from his broken fingernails as he twitched and struggled. Maybe the light was playing tricks, and my eyes were sparkling anyway on account of being too paralysed with fear to even blink, but as he thrashed less and less it became harder and harder to see him at all, and as the breeze whipped up stronger his screams began to sound a lot like the wind. But still he writhed and moaned and then suddenly there was the most godawful crunching sound and then there was no movement or sound anymore.

Like they were on a string our heads all turned together and we saw Tom still standing there, his coat flapping in the wind. He had a hand on Billy's shoulder and as we looked we could see that Mary was there too now and he had one arm round her as she sobbed into his coat.

I don't know how long we just sat there staring but then with one mind we were ejected off our seats and out of the bar. Pete and Ned ran to Tom but Jack and I went to where Sam had fallen and we stood and stared down and I tell you the rest of my life now seems like a build-up to and a climb-down from that moment.

We were standing in front of a chalk drawing of a tiger. Even now my scalp seems to tighten when I think of it, and my chest feels like someone punched a hole in it and tipped a gallon of iced water inside.

I'll just tell you the facts: Jack was there and he knows what we saw and what we didn't see.

What we didn't see was Sam McNeill. He just wasn't there, you know? We saw a drawing of a tiger in purples and greens, a little bit scuffed, and there was a lot more red round the mouth of that tiger than there had been that afternoon and I'm sure that if either of us could have dreamed of reaching out and touching it it would have been warm too.

And the hardest part to tell is this. I'd seen that drawing in the afternoon, and Jack had too, and we knew that when it was done it was lean and thin. And I swear to God that tiger wasn't thin anymore. What Jack and I were looking down at was one fat tiger.

After a while I looked up and across at Tom. He was still standing with Mary and Billy, but they weren't crying any more. Mary was hugging Billy so tight he squawked and Tom's face looked calm and alive and creased with a smile. And as we stood there the skies opened for the first time in months and a cool rain hammered down. At my feet colours began to run and lines became less distinct. Jack and I stood and watched till there was just pools of meaningless colours and then we walked slowly over to the others not even looking at the bottle lying on the ground and we all stood there a long time in the rain, facing each other, not saying a word.

Well that was ten years ago, near enough. After a while Mary took Billy home and they turned to give us a little wave before they turned the corner. The cuts on Billy's face healed real quick, and he's a good looking boy now: he looks a lot like his dad and he's already fooling about in cars. Helps me in the store sometimes. His mom ain't aged a day and looks wonderful. She never married again, but she looks real happy the way she is.

The rest of us just said a simple goodnight. Goodnight was all we could muster and maybe that's all there was to say. Then we walked off home in the directions of our wives. Tom gave me a small smile before he turned and walked off alone. I almost followed him, I wanted to say something, but in the end I just stood and watched him go. And that's how I'll always remember him best, because for a moment there was a spark in his eyes and I knew that some pain had been lifted deep down inside there somewhere. Then he walked and no one has seen him since, and like I said it's been about ten years now. He wasn't there in the square the next morning and he didn't come in for a beer. Like he'd never been, he just wasn't there. Except for the hole in our hearts: it's funny how much you can miss a quiet man.

We're all still here, of course, Jack, Ned, Pete and the boys, and all the same, if even older and greyer. Pete lost his wife and Ned retired but things go on the same. The tourists come in the summer and we sit on the stools and drink our cold beers and shoot the breeze about ballgames and families and how the world's going to shit and sometimes we'll draw close and talk about a night a long time ago and about paintings and cats and about the quietest man we ever knew, wondering where he is, and what he's doing. And we've had a six-pack in the back of the fridge for ten years now, and the minute he walks through that door and pulls up a stool, that's his.

MELANIE TEM

The Co-Op

MELANIE TEM lives in a nineteenth-century Victorian House in Denver, Colorado, with her writer husband, Steve Rasnic Tem. Her short stories were first published in various small press and literary magazines, and more recently she has appeared in such anthologies as *Women of the West, Women of Darkness I* and *II, Skin of the Soul, Dark Voices 3, Cold Shocks* and *Final Shadows*.

Her first novel, *Prodigal*, was published by Dell's new Abyss line in 1991, followed by *Blood Moon* from The Women's Press.

Melanie Tem is a social worker who works with abused and neglected children and disabled adults; "The Co-Op" could be considered to reflect some of the real-life horrors she encounters every day.

THE DIN OF THE CHILDREN in the basement rec room had been a white noise in the middle ground all afternoon, with occasional thunderous white-water surges like this one. Somebody was wailing, and two or three other piercing little voices were threatening to tell.

Outside was real water, rain in the streets, and more voices like water. A crowd was filling Cascadilla Street and, Julie supposed, the other streets of Ithaca, and flood waters were rising.

Steadying the baby against her body, where even in sleep she nuzzled for the breast, Julie started to get up to investigate the commotion in the basement. It was her house, and she'd noticed that up to a point everyone in the co-op parented everyone else's children. She liked that sense of community; it was one of the things, along with a need to be with other mothers who knew what she was going through, that had made her join the babysitting co-op the minute there'd been an opening.

But Diane, swearing, beat her to the basement door. Diane was tall, broad-shouldered, and obese, yet somehow she seemed emaciated; the many cracks and crevices in her flesh looked deep and gray, and there was always a sour odor about her. Three of the kids downstairs were Diane's, Julie thought, or four; unsuccessfully, she tried to remember their names or even which ones they were. Diane's voice carried even when she was engaged in ordinary conversation, and just now she was shrieking at the kids, competing with their noise but not noticeably diminishing it.

Julie frowned. She didn't like the way Diane talked to children, her own or anyone else's. That wasn't the way mothers should be. Mothers should be like Julie's mother: loving their children, loving motherhood, tired and cranky only once in a while. That was the kind of mother Julie wanted desperately to be, but it wasn't easy, in the middle of the night, when Megan wouldn't stop crying no matter what Julie did, or when she bit her breast, Julie was sure on purpose.

Her mother had never felt about her the way she often felt about Megan. Her mother had never said awful things to her, or wanted to hurt her, or wished she had never been born. Julie would never be as good a mother as her own mother had been.

But when she looked around her, no one else was, either, and this town fairly teemed with mothers and children. Everywhere she went, especially since Megan had been born, she saw them, was pulled into the milling crowds they formed. On the streets, in the stores, in the wet green parks of this town, mothers screamed mindlessly at their children or mindlessly ignored them, and the children howled and played and scratched at windows. Julie and her sisters had never acted like that.

Linda was talking to her. "Well, all I can say is, you better enjoy her while you can."

She'd said that before. Julie smiled somewhat vaguely and put a spoonful of Diane's orange Jell-o into her mouth. She was startled to discover something gooey in the middle and for a moment was afraid to know what it was. But then she knew, and it was only cream cheese.

Cautiously, she let the Jell-o dissolve inside her mouth. It left a thick film of cream cheese on her palette, like skin. Suddenly she was imagining that the cream cheese was fleshlike, and then it was hard to swallow.

Outside it was still raining; she was constantly aware of the rain. It rained a lot in central New York State, which might be why all the mothers she knew here had such pale and wet-looking skin. Julie glanced sadly at the fading watch-band stripe around her own wrist; since the baby had been born she hadn't been able to catch even what few hours of sunshine there were.

This house they'd moved into on Cascadilla Street was long and narrow, like a coffin. From where she sat, Julie could sight along the pinkish-brown living room wall, which had tiny dots in it like pores; along the kitchen wall with its bulbous cream-colored flowers; and out the high windows that overlooked the street. The streets and the sidewalks were slimy with rainwater; the crowds were without umbrellas, because they were used to this weather. The green of the trees was nearly black, and they dripped with coagulated precipitation; leaves curled like lips, exposing their pale undersides. There were rivers and lakes and streams and gulches everywhere around here, like exposed veins or hungry stretched mouths. It hadn't surprised Julie, though it had made her shudder, to learn that Cornell had one of the highest suicide rates of any campus in the country, particularly in the spring when the beckoning gulches were layered with heart-red and tongue-pink rhododendron.

Linda was still talking. "Like my mother always said, and of course I wouldn't listen to her, it only gets worse as they get older."

"I can hardly wait." The intended sarcasm was undercut by a real excitement, a real eagerness to see her daughter grow up, which made Julie feel terribly vulnerable. She managed to swallow the last of the orange-flavored cream cheese, though it left a gummy patina on her tongue and on the backs of her teeth. Gelatin, she suddenly remembered, was made from cows' and horses' hooves; she wondered whether that was still true or whether nowadays it was chemically constructed, and didn't know which she would prefer.

"This is great potato salad," Linda said. The whitish chunks of boiled potato and egg in her mouth looked like broken teeth. "Who made it this time?"

"I did," Julie admitted, almost shyly. She didn't know any of the co-op mothers very well yet, but they'd all been nice to her, and Linda especially had taken her under her wing.

"*Great* potato salad."

"Thanks."

"Nobody ever listens to their mamas about kids," Yolanda declared. Three-bean-salad juice dribbled from the corner of her mouth, looking like brown blood across her white lipstick and oddly colorless dark brown skin. When she wiped it off with a crumpled white napkin, it left a stain among other stains, and Julie looked away. "My mama had eight kids before she was thirty," Yolanda was saying. "She *knew* what she was talking about. But did I listen? Did any of us listen? I got six kids myself, and my oldest sister's got *twelve*!"

"Twelve children!" Julie whispered to her baby. "Twelve little monsters like you!"

In her lap, Megan was asleep, tiny fists balled at her ears and tiny jagged mouth wide open. Julie slid her index finger gently into the infant's mouth. She could just feel the minuscule ridges along the gum line where before long teeth would erupt. She'd heard that some babies were born with teeth.

Softly she rubbed at her daughter's nascent teeth, as though to push them back down. The baby opened her eyes, focused them directly on her, and clamped her mouth shut around her mother's finger. Though there were no teeth yet for biting or tearing her flesh, the baby's sucking was so strong that it hurt, and when she took her finger back it didn't come easily. Julie felt a little thrill of maternal horror.

In a sudden panic, she yanked her hand away. Too hard: her daughter's head twisted to one side, and she howled. Julie bent guiltily to kiss her, tasted the salt tears and the sweet-sour baby flesh. Fear that she had hurt her child, remorse that she had wanted to, clouded her thoughts like the fatigue that had been with her since the baby's birth. She was, she thought suddenly and clearly, being eaten alive.

"My mama died when I was seventeen of acute anemia. Like us kids sucked the blood right out of her. Like we just ate her right up."

Linda nodded. "That's how it is when you have kids. It's a matter of survival. Them or you."

"My mama did not know how to protect herself," Yolanda said sadly. "The doctors told her to eat raw liver, but she couldn't do it."

A small fair-haired woman named Kathy or Katie wrinkled her nose and made a delicate gagging sound. Kathy's skin was so fair that it seemed barely to cover her flesh, and the makeup around her nose and mouth was grainy. She had an odd, halting way of speaking, as if she could hardly remember one word after the next. Her blonde hair was firmly sprayed, but it still straggled around her face and neck so that it looked as if it were falling out, and her chipping nails had been painted with thick variegated polish, as if to hold them together. Her entire face and body looked rebuilt, reconstituted for viewing. "Probably," she said in her breathy voice to Yolanda, "it was"—she paused for a long time before she could collect her thoughts—"stress that killed her. Stress and fatigue and"—she stopped, ground her teeth across her lower lip—"and not knowing where she stopped and her children began."

"Occupational hazards of motherhood," Annette observed, and a glob of coleslaw slid out of her mouth onto the front of her gray business suit. Apparently she didn't notice, since she made no move to clean it off. She had announced at the beginning of the co-op meeting that she'd have to leave early for a lunch appointment; Julie tried to imagine her making corporate decisions with coleslaw and baby spittle patterning her vest. "It's certainly done us all in," Annette said.

"Not all yet," Linda said. "Julie still looks alive." She patted Julie's knee.

"I love my child," Julie said automatically. Megan was crying again, but half-heartedly now, and there were no tears, only noise.

"We all do," Linda said.

"You know all—those things you swore you'd never—say to your kids?" Kathy passed a hand over her face, jagged fingertips massaging at her own flesh as though she had a headache. She was sitting in the pale blue bar of light cast by the fluorescent fixture over the sink, and her teeth looked fluorescent themselves, and sharp. "I can't—help it. All that—stuff just flows out of my—mouth like milk flows out of your—breast when your—when your baby's born. I—can't help it."

"She's forgetting the words," Linda explained to Julie, quietly but with no real attempt not to be overheard. "We all do that sometimes, but Kathy's been at it longer than the rest of us. She's one of the organizers of the co-op. Her children are all grown. Her mind is going."

"Sometimes I have fantasies about these awful things I'd like to do to my kids," Annette said conversationally. "So far I haven't done anything really awful, but only because they'd take my broker's license if I did."

"I swore I'd never"—Kathy closed her eyes and allowed a long painful pause before she finally managed—"Spank. Or—eat. I swore I'd never do—what my mother did to me. But I do."

Yolanda nodded. "I swore none of that would ever happen to me."

"Well," someone said, "at least *you* didn't die of acute anemia, did you?"

"Close. Even though I did eat raw meat. Still do, right?" There were some knowing chuckles around the room. Julie's stomach churned, and indignantly she demanded, "Why'd you all have kids if you don't like raising them?"

Megan was regarding her with a murky blue gaze. Julie often wondered what she saw. Part of the baby's self, probably. An extension of her own mouth and her own bowel and her own lungs. A gigantic umbilical cord attaching the world to Megan.

Julie wondered if Megan would always see her like that. She thought of her own mother, emptied now by Alzheimer's, but still able sometimes to make fried chicken and chocolate chip cookies better than anybody.

Suddenly she realized that the lanky and very pregnant young woman on the sofa next to Yolanda, with even darker skin and an underlying pallor thick as chalk, must be Yolanda's daughter. Embarrassed by what she'd said about Yolanda and the others not wanting children, Julie added feebly, "I mean, six kids are a *lot*, no matter how much you love them."

"Actually," Yolanda said, "I had seven. One died."

Julie caught her breath. "I'm so sorry."

"Yeah, well, that's the only reason I'm here to tell about it. One more would've done me in for sure. There'd have been nothing left of me for the others. So the baby died for a good cause. 'She gave her life that others might live.' Right, Regina?"

She reached to pat the tall girl's hand, then her huge belly. Regina's coppery gaze, flat as the pennies on the eyes of a corpse, followed her mother's hand, and her lips pulled back from her teeth a little as if she couldn't control the muscles of her face. She said nothing.

Distant thunder shook the house in a regular beat like a pulse, and rain bled against the windows. Carefully cradling Megan against her own impulse to drop her, Julie got awkwardly to her feet and walked through the line of rooms to the windows. Cascadilla Street was filling up with water and with people; she could see that the crowd was entirely made up of mothers and children, some few of them garbed against the weather but most of them bare-headed, bare-faced, hair streaming, clothes adhering to the contours of their bodies which seemed to dissolve into the rain.

In the odd play of light between gray sky and shiny rising floodwaters, some of the mothers and children seemed to be gnawing at each other, tearing at each other's flesh or at each other's reflections. Through the thin cold glass, which was wet even on the inside when she put her free hand against it, Julie could hear them and she was sure Megan could, too, wordlessly shrieking at each other in the wind, moving closer. She shuddered and fumbled for the curtain cord, drew the heavy curtains, turned away from the windows.

She looked at the other mothers one by one, trying to decide whether they'd all known about Yolanda's sacrificed child. Probably they had, since she understood that the co-op had been going for some time, and since no one seemed surprised.

No one said anything, in fact. Yolanda's little confession lay in the room with them like the unburied corpse of her child. The mothers were eating. In the brief, companionable silence, Julie was surrounded by the wet sounds of the mothers chewing and swallowing, by the busy gurgling of Linda's digestive system so close beside her that it could have been her own, and by the blending white noises of the rain and the gathering crowd and the kids downstairs.

"It would be terrible to lose a child," Julie said aloud. Her cupped palm hovered just above her daughter's tiny head, where she could feel the hole that opened like a halo onto her brain.

"Sometimes," Kathy said, "it's either lose a child or lose— yourself. I mean, I—love my kids, but they were killing me."

"I don't think I could stand it," Julie said.

Linda looked at her, and Julie felt a chill pass through her even before Linda said, "We've all had a child die. Every one of us in this room has lost a child."

"And all our mothers did as well," Annette added.

"And all our daughters will, too," Yolanda finished. She put her arm around Regina, who tried feebly to pull away, then gave up and snuggled her enormous bulging body as best she could against her mother's scrawny one. "Guess you could say it runs in the family."

"It's one of the reasons this group formed," Linda said. "It's one of the things we have in common. It helps to be with other mothers who understand."

"How—how do you live through it?"

A look passed among the co-op members, a sisterly smile. It was Linda who said, "We don't, Julie. We didn't."

Julie laughed a little, experimentally, waiting for Linda and the others to join in, to explain the grisly joke to her. No one did. Finally she managed to say, "I feel that way sometimes myself. Raising kids is hard."

Kathy nodded. "When the baby cries all—night and you don't know what's wrong and you—know you're a terrible mother."

"When you just gave her a bath," Yolanda suggested, "and she shits all over herself again, and you're trying to get ready to go someplace."

"When she's two and you have to keep an eye on her every minute so she doesn't hurt herself or destroy your house," Linda said. "When she's six and the bully in the third grade keeps beating her up, or she's in the third grade and she bullies the six-year-olds."

"When she's twelve and failing seventh grade algebra and you have to go talk to the teacher again about her attitude." Annette shook her head appreciatively.

"When she's eighteen," Yolanda said pointedly, "and pregnant."

"I didn't like being pregnant in the first place," Julie said, her own resentment suddenly rising to meet theirs. She looked at the baby in her lap and tried to think of it as a stranger, an alien, an intruder. But the baby was part of her. As strong as the resentment was a huge hot love. "And labor was a bitch. They say you forget the pain, but you don't." She saw Regina's frightened look and was immediately sorry, but could think of no way to soften what she'd said. "I don't know why any of us have kids," she said.

"Oh," Kathy said airily. "I do. I—love my kids. You just have to—learn to cope, that's all."

"I don't know how." Julie's eyes were so full of tears she was afraid she'd drop the baby. She laid her down on the couch. Megan did not protest.

Yolanda had started talking again. Yolanda's voice was rough, as though her throat hurt. It was painful to listen to her, and she did talk a lot. "I was already way pregnant when my mama died, and after that she didn't have much to say to me, even though she did talk all the time. I wasn't a bit older than Regina is now when I had her. Barely eighteen. Now here she is, look at her, following right in her mama's footsteps but not listening to her mama at all. Look at her. Tired all the time. Sick all the time. The baby's eating her alive."

Julie did look at Regina, and was struck by how much Yolanda and Regina looked alike, mother and daughter, how closely they both must resemble the mother and grandmother who had died at the mouths of her children and who had not died.

Diane trudged loudly up the basement steps and slammed the door behind her. The latch didn't hold, and the door swung open again; Diane leaned back against it with all her considerable weight. Almost at once, the cacophony from the basement rose again. Julie thought uneasily of penned animals, of water in a cooking pot coming to a hard boil.

Kathy got up and, stumbling a little, made her way across the rooms to open the curtains again. Julie didn't say anything or try to stop her, though it was her house. The crowd outside was at the foot of the steps now, where the hill that the house sat on met the sidewalk. Julie held Megan up to the window so she could see, but the baby, of course, didn't look. She was screwing up her red little face and grunting vehemently. Julie felt a warm stickiness on the inside of her forearm and knew that the diaper was leaking, but didn't do anything about it. It wasn't important. It made no difference. She could clean the baby and herself, change the diaper, wash the clothes, clean the carpet, wash the windows, turn the co-op mothers out of her house, chase the crowd away from the steps, and the baby would just mess again.

Still leaning against the basement door, which gapped along the top, Diane sighed heavily. "How many times do you suppose I've done that over the years? For all the good it does."

"It would be worse if we didn't," Annette said serenely, glancing down at her folded hands as though she were consulting notes. "They'll thank us when they grow up."

"I don't know about that," Yolanda said. "My girl doesn't understand yet all the sacrifices I make for her, and here she is about to be a mama her own self."

Diane crossed to the littered table and filled a second plate. The paper of the plate got soggy almost immediately and bent around the edges; Julie watched a clot of cottage cheese fall to the floor, watched Diane step in it and smear it across the yellow and pink linoleum.

While the other mothers chatted around them, Linda said quietly to Julie, "I'm glad you decided to join the co-op. I think you have a lot to add, and I think you're ready for us."

Regina gasped and arched her back, gripped the arms of her chair, spread her legs and braced her feet against the floor. All eyes turned to her, even Megan's, and her mother said her name. "Regina? Honey? Is it time?"

"We need to get her to a hospital," Julie said, but she could see out the windows that Cascadilla Street was completely flooded and impassable now. Water was up over the curbs and the sidewalks, rain still falling so hard that it looked like viscous sheets, all of a piece. Mothers and children were so crowded and faceless that she couldn't tell one from another. Except that she saw Kathy join them, the stiff blonde hair getting stiffer in the rain, the thin skin parting to expose pale flesh, and Kathy's pale blond grown son beside her, nearly indistinguishable from her.

Regina cried out. Yolanda was standing over her, saying her name. The other mothers gathered around, murmuring, and the children began to come up from the basement.

Regina's baby was born on the kitchen floor, among the stains of food and the accumulating footprints of the mothers and their children. Julie watched, clutching her own baby, not knowing what to do. Labor was long and hard. There was a good deal of blood. Rain kept falling, and voices gathered. Children and mothers milled at the windows, inside and out, scratching at the glass and at each other, making wordless mewling sounds. Julie's daughter cried and cried in her arms.

When Regina's baby was born, it tore out part of her body with it, and left part of its new body inside hers. Julie saw the tissue and the blood. Regina screamed. Yolanda said her name. Julie slid her own daughter's tiny clawing hand into her mouth and bit down hard.

NICHOLAS ROYLE

Negatives

NICHOLAS ROYLE has sold around forty-five stories to a wide
variety of anthologies and magazines, including *Interzone*, *Fear*,
Fantasy Tales, *BBR*, *Reader's Digest*, *Gorezone*, *New Socialist*, *Dark
Fantasies*, *Year's Best Horror Stories*, *Cutting Edge*, *Book of the Dead*,
Obsessions and *Final Shadows*.

He was born in Sale, Cheshire, and is currently living in North
London. Two novels, *Counterparts* and *Saxophone Dreams* are
currently looking for a publisher, as is an anthology of new British
horror fiction, and he is working on a third novel entitled *The
Appetite*.

With stories of the calibre of "Negatives" and regular appearances in
the "Year's Best" anthologies, we don't think it will be too long before
his book-length work finds a market.

I F NIGHT-TIME MOTORWAY DRIVING didn't have such a numbing effect on the mind and the senses, he wouldn't have needed to wake himself up by accelerating down the inside lane and into trouble in the way that he did.

The queues out of London had begun thinning out near Luton and disappeared after Milton Keynes. There were still plenty of cars on the road but now they were moving at a proper speed.

He kept to a steady 70 in the inside lane, aware that it was a little too fast for the car over a long distance, and he would probably have to top up water and oil at Rothersthorpe or Watford Gap.

The road was straight; the distance to the next car in front remained constant. He'd tried listening to music but couldn't hear it over the noise of the engine. Now and again he looked over at the passenger seat and smiled at Melanie. Despite the noise and her conviction that she wouldn't, she'd managed to fall asleep.

For a brief moment he had a detached view of himself: sitting in a small chair hurtling through the darkness encased in this strange little shell called a car. It was like sitting in a chair at home and being taken somewhere. He felt as if he should be able to get up and go and make a coffee. The steering wheel and pedals seemed incidental. Then with a jolt he was back there driving the car again.

The road disappeared under the car, perfectly uniform from one bridge to the next. He opened his eyelids and wondered how long they'd been closed: a split second, or two or three seconds? He only needed to nod off for two seconds and unconsciously depress the accelerator and they'd be up the back end of the car in front. He knew he should stop but also knew he wasn't supposed to. Where would he stop if he decided to? On the hard shoulder, obviously, but where? After a mile, half a mile, a hundred yards? Its invariable aspect offered no invitation to pull in.

Instead, he shifted in the seat and straightened his back. Gently he accelerated. The car ahead was drawn into sharper focus. It was a Fiesta, a new model. He eased the pedal down further. He glanced in the mirror and saw just red lights; it must be reflecting the other carriageway; the vibration had caused it to slant; he straightened it.

He was suddenly right on top of the Fiesta.

With a tug on the steering wheel he missed the car in front and sheered into the middle lane. A horn blared, tyres screeched. There *were* cars behind him. He stood on the accelerator and leapt into the empty space ahead. A large BMW passed him on the outside, faces peering his way. Ignoring them, he concentrated on eating up the middle lane. Drowsiness snatched away, like a veil from a bold, thrusting sculpture, he bent over the steering wheel. Out of the corner of his eye he saw the speedometer needle leaning round the clockface to point at numbers it had not seen before.

The needle was just tipping at 98 when the back end suddenly collapsed at one side and the car began to veer.

His immediate reaction was enormous relief that Melanie was not with him. She'd been working out west and was going up in her own car to meet him there.

Although he detested actually going to work, he was glad when they'd had to move from the old office to new premises. It had taken two months to find suitable new office space and they'd ended up having to move right out of Soho (much to Egerton's regret) as far north as the Angel.

Linden had been pleased because it meant he could now drive to work and find somewhere to park. In Soho it had been impossible.

Of course, it meant sitting in traffic jams at the bottom of Holloway Road and where Essex Road joined Upper Street, but wasn't it nicer to be stuck in your own car rather than suffocating in a tube tunnel surrounded by the barely alive, still smelling of their beds?

He crunched into first and edged forward, but the Citroen in front had only been moving into space between it and the next car: the queue itself was not moving.

He realised he'd still got the choke out a fraction. He pressed it home and the revs dropped to normal. It was still running a little low; it could easily cut out waiting in a queue like this. Still, the man at the garage who'd tuned it only last week said it was better that it should be running too low rather than too high. It would keep his fuel consumption down and that had been quite a problem before. For a twelve-year-old Mini, the man had said, it wasn't in bad nick.

In front of him in the rear-view mirror he saw someone cross behind the car. He knew he was rolling back so he brought the clutch up and stepped on the gas. Then the queue started to move.

He parked in the private carpark in the courtyard of the new complex. The start of another week. He cursed at the thought of five more days in the company of Egerton. Five more days staring at that damned computer screen. He didn't know which he disliked the most—Egerton or the computer. That was a lie. The computer was not sentient; it had no excuse. (Come to think of it, Egerton was barely sentient either.)

Egerton was slowly climbing the stairs when Linden pushed open the ground-floor door. Not that the other man had, like Linden, just arrived—Egerton always got in at nine, an hour early—no, he'd come down to get the post so he could look at it before anyone else. That was why he was climbing the stairs so slowly, because he was devouring every bit of information the morning's delivery had to offer. Linden didn't care about the post—he wasn't in the slightest bit interested in the industry which employed him—it was Egerton's rapacious enthusiasm for everything connected with the job that irritated him.

"Good morning, Brian. How are you today? Did you have a nice weekend?"

Please somebody tell me why he has to be so bloody cheerful every Monday morning, Linden thought. The weekend, ah yes, the weekend—that precious island of time when he could escape. He knew Egerton often came in on Saturdays. He didn't ask why any more.

Egerton was grinning at him, waiting for an answer. He couldn't bring himself to speak to the man.

The computer was waiting for him. He sat down, switched it on and nothing happened.

"Good morning, Brian." Whitehead had come into the room. "It's down. You'll have to use the other one. You *were* working on floppies, weren't you? Just stick them in the other machine."

Linden nodded. Whitehead was the boss. He pretended to be everybody's equal. Until it came to writing out the salary cheques.

He worked without a break all morning. The computer had a green screen, which he wasn't used to. His eyes were tired by the time he'd saved all he'd done and was ready to go to lunch. One good thing about Egerton's keenness was that Linden never had to worry about the man inviting himself along to lunch: Egerton generally worked right through, occasionally getting in a McDonald's or a beanburger or something else equally Egerton-like.

When Linden tried to read his paper, waiting for his food to arrive, he found he couldn't concentrate properly. There were red dots all over the page. Wherever white was enclosed by black, like a b, an o, a p or an A, the little white space was now red. Consequently, the effect on a page of small newsprint was to turn the whole page red.

He worked all afternoon on the computer. Egerton annoyed him with his exaggerated mannerisms—grasping his chin, swinging his arms, clicking his fingers. When he wasn't striding around the office he was making telephone calls, mainly to the company's debtors. It was a matter of *personal* betrayal if someone had lapsed with an invoice payment. When Egerton uttered the company name he did so with chest-swelling pride.

Linden looked from the screen and grimaced at the tight little curls of blond hair on Egerton's head.

Driving home, Linden was tense. Occasionally he wavered over the red line in the middle of the road. A Triumph Vitesse barked its horn at him.

The red effect didn't wear off and allow Linden to read a book without straining his eyes until he was too tired to read anyway.

"It's the green, you see," Whitehead explained. "After looking at the green screen for long enough, you look away at something white and you see it as red. Green and red are the reverse of each other, or negatives or something. It's to do with that. Take a photo of a man in a red jumper and on the negative the jumper will be green."

Because the maintenance contract on the old computer had expired and Whitehead was too tight to get an engineer in, Linden had to work with the green screen all week. It only affects some people, Whitehead had said, but it's not dangerous and is only short term.

He knew he shouldn't sit in front of the machine for too long at any one time but try telling that to Whitehead. They had a big job on—correction: Linden had a big job on. He was editing a 400-page handbook and it had to be done by the end of the week. Each page resembled the next; three entries on a page, all with their identical lists of superfluous information. Every decimal point had to be checked. The spelling, as usual, was abysmal.

He ran off a hard copy of all he'd done, but the pages were bright red: it dazzled him. The material should be checked by someone else before it went off, but Egerton and Whitehead could barely spell their own names.

Negotiating Highbury Corner, Linden almost killed a pedestrian. He'd thought the old man was in his rear-view mirror, but the wrinkle-smoothing shock on the aged face when the Mini snarled forward brought Linden's foot crashing down on the brake pedal. The car juddered and stalled. Linden sank his head onto the wheel and waited for the old man and several bystanders to stop screaming at him.

As soon as he got in he went to the fridge for a long drink of cold milk. He opened the fridge door and recoiled. There were two bottles of blood on the shelf.

He washed and shaved to see if that would remove some of the tension. He looked awful in the mirror. His eyes were bloodshot.

He switched on the television, but the newsreaders' eyes were all bloodshot as well, and their red teeth made them look like they'd just been eating raw hamburgers with Egerton.

He got hungry but couldn't bring himself to touch the eggs which were all that he had in the way of food. He went out to a restaurant and ordered a salad. He shouted at the waitress: how dare she put tomato ketchup on his salad? Drawing angry red stares he stalked out of the restaurant and crossed the road to a fish and chip shop, but the woman started sprinkling little dried flecks of bloody dandruff onto his chips, so he left in disgust.

By morning there was milk in his fridge again and he could enjoy a normal breakfast before driving to work.

"Are you all right, Brian?" Whitehead wanted to know.

"Yes. Why?" he snapped.

"You look a bit harassed, that's all." Defensive. "You will get that editing done, won't you?"

There seemed to be more red cars on the roads than ever. The days were already getting shorter: as he drove up Holloway Road the premature sunset was turning low clouds vermilion.

He finished at the computer on Friday morning and spent the rest of the day checking the hard copy in spite of the eyestrain. There would be no use anyone else in the office proofing it. Although he considered himself underpaid for the work he was doing, he wanted to make sure it was right, in the unlikely event of someone, somewhere appreciating the hard work that had gone into the handbook.

He drove away from the Angel, down towards the roundabout. An enormous sense of release jostled with him for space in the Mini; the end of another week in the office, no more Egerton for two days, liberation from that infernal green computer screen. Since he'd finished on-screen editing before lunch, the effect had already begun to wear off.

He just had to call in at the flat to collect his bag and any messages, then head off up the A1 to the M1 and freedom. Melanie had been working out in W14 and so was going up in her own car. She would probably have been able to get away early, so would be first at the cottage. By the time he got there she'd have it all cosy for him.

The northbound lanes on Holloway Road were chock-a-block, as Linden knew the motorway would also be when he finally reached it. Through the windscreen he admired the beginnings of the sunset; the skies above Highgate were aglow with strange lilacs. Hadn't he seen yesterday's sunset in his rear-view mirror rather than through the windscreen? A small detail.

He reached the turn-off for Sussex Way and his flat. The traffic being as bad as it was, he was glad he'd put his bag in the car that morning and didn't have to make the detour to go and get it now.

He watched a Beetle worm its way out of a side street between two Escorts into the traffic-flow. If this was a stream of traffic then it was a stream of mud. He looked for the Beetle again: was it an old one with a tiny back window and semaphore indicators or a more recent model with big rear-light clusters and fat bumpers? But he couldn't see it and when he thought about it he couldn't remember if he'd caught sight of it in his rear-view mirror or through the windscreen.

On the other side of the road a red Escort nosed out from beside the snooker centre and was allowed to pass between two VW Beetles. The driver of the Escort waved her thanks. Behind Linden impatient drivers pipped their horns, making him jump: the queue in front of him had moved forward.

The traffic didn't get any better; when the M1 intersected the M25 and then merged with the M10, it got worse.

He asked Melanie to put on a tape. She chose the Organ Symphony; at least while they proceeded at 10 miles per hour he was able to hear it.

"Why don't you go to sleep?" he asked her.

"Your car's too noisy," she said. "I wouldn't be able to."

Every few hundred yards the congestion would just dissolve and Linden would get up to 30 or 40. However, it was always a brief respite and inexplicably the queue tightened up again. Eventually, though, thanks to the domestic attraction for the majority offered by places like Luton, Leighton Buzzard, Milton Keynes, Newport Pagnell and Bedford, there were fewer cars sharing the same lanes and all of them travelling at at least 65 miles per hour. The novelty soon wore off and the tedium of motorway driving set in, exacerbated by the fact that it was by now quite dark.

The tape clicked off, but since he hadn't been able to hear it for the last half hour he didn't bother putting another one on. He wished Melanie were with him to keep him awake. Would she be at the cottage yet, he wondered. He tried to guess who might be driving the Fiesta in front. What kind of person? He accelerated to get closer. A woman, he decided, but not like Melanie, more of a career woman, someone who saw great intrinsic worth in *belonging* to a company, a Company Girl. A female Egerton. He toed the accelerator again. Her hair would be fixed in a 'go-ahead' style like some kind of fossilized bird's nest, the brain-eggs long since hatched and flown the nest, leaving only the corporate gloss of cranial vacancy in her eyes.

He was suddenly right on top of the Fiesta.

When the back end collapsed at his side and the car began to swerve, he had no idea what had happened.

He glanced at the passenger seat and seized the steering wheel like the reins of a bolting horse. Steer into the skid, they always said. But what did that mean? Go with it or against it? He swung to the left, trying to aim the front of the car at the hard shoulder and braking as gently as he could without sliding into a new skid.

He never knew how close he came to being hit by the cars which flew past him as he shuddered to a halt on the hard shoulder. He didn't need to hold his hands out to see how much he was shaking: he was still holding the steering wheel and it was trembling, and not on account of the engine, which had stalled. Climbing over the empty seat, he got out on the passenger side, and walked unsteadily round the back of the car to see what had happened. A blowout. The back tyre on the driver's side was shredded. He could just make out the word REMOULD.

He got back in the car and told Melanie what had happened. She was calmer now; the shock had been greater for her since she'd been asleep when it had happened.

He took his spanner and a jack from the boot and set about taking the wheel off. The first nut was a bit difficult so he worked at the other three, which all came off after some effort. The first one wouldn't budge; the spanner's grip began to slide on the nut.

"Shit!" He leant against the Mini, watching the cars streaking past.

He tried the nut again but the spanner was now far too big for it; he was just wearing the edges away; if he continued, it would become impossible to remove.

Linden stopped for breath and looked back up the hard shoulder to see if he could still see the Mini. The car itself was invisible but the hazard lights flashed on and off and on again. They were much brighter than he would have imagined and he was grateful for them. He continued walking.

Cars sped past him, occupants' faces blank white spaces turned towards him, yet he'd never felt more alone. The sky was black, clouded over; the darkness of the land beyond the motorway uninterrupted by lights. Not even farmers lived here. People only drove through. He fastened all three buttons of his jacket and pulled up the collar. Where the hell was the emergency telephone? One just a few yards from his car was out of order. As was its opposite number which he had reached illegally by crossing the six lanes of the motorway.

Eventually he came upon a telephone which worked and he was able to call for assistance. It seemed so unlikely, that there should be a man waiting by a telephone to take his call and send another man out in a van to rescue him. And yet that was the system he paid for. He was of course glad now that he *had* subscribed.

He began to walk back. The cold penetrated his thin jacket. Cars swept by only a few feet away, making him feel vulnerable. He lost count of the bridges he passed under. The horizon failed to yield the flashing orange of his hazards. He began to worry that somehow he'd gone wrong. He'd not crossed back after running over to try the telephone on the other side. "Don't be stupid," he said out loud, but the sound of his voice, so feeble and vain, frightened him. He decided that he would turn back at the next bridge, and as the next bridge came into sight, so too did the hazard lights.

They belonged to a P-reg Ford Cortina. A woman with bad teeth sitting in the passenger seat threw him a nervous glance then looked away.

The Mini was another 200 yards further up. As he narrowed the gap from behind, a trick of the shadows cast by passing headlamps made it look like there were two people already sitting in the front seats.

He clambered in and waited for the van to arrive.

Each passing car shook the little Mini. He put some music on but imagined that it prevented him from hearing the footsteps of an interloper approaching the car. He pressed EJECT. Melanie said: "They won't be long."

It started to rain. Big fat drops exploded on the windscreen. He pictured Melanie at the cottage: making a drink, running a bath, watching the television. He wished he were with her. How long would it be before she started to worry? The rain rattled on the roof as if it were a tent. Suddenly a brilliant flash created a second's daylight in the night. Then the thunder began to roll, like a solo by a drunken timpanist.

When the serviceman arrived, Linden joined him in the teeming rain, but the man couldn't shift the nut either.

"It's only a mile to the next services," the man shouted over the noise of the storm. "I'll tow you there. It'll be easier. I'll be able to get this nut off. More space, more light."

Linden nodded and climbed into the cab as directed.

"It's not far," the man said, when he'd hitched up the back of the Mini to his truck. They moved off and stayed on the hard shoulder. After ten or fifteen minutes the lights of the services sparkled through the rain. Linden left the man to change the wheel and walked across the rain-slick tarmac to the complex.

In the self-service restaurant he sat down in a red plastic seat with a cup of stewed tea. He was alone in the place apart from a smartly dressed couple who stared miserably at each other's shoulders across a crumb-strewn table.

He stood looking at the telephones, wishing they'd gone to the trouble and expense of installing one in the cottage.

Crossing over the covered footbridge, he stopped in the middle and watched the traffic sweeping underneath in both directions. He felt like a pivot between the two carriageways, as if with his mind he could just switch them. A flash of lightning printed a colour negative on his retina, sending a shiver down his back and dropping a chilled weight in his stomach. With a vague sense of foreboding he reached the end of the bridge and walked down the steps. In the hall area a number of people were grouped around a video game. He joined the back of the group, which was murmuring its praise of the game-player. Someone moved to give Linden a better view. He stood behind a man with tight curly blond hair, whose hands, he now saw, were manipulating the game's joystick and firing button.

Ships and creatures fell from the top of the screen towards the bottom. The game-player had his own unit which he had to defend and from which he could attack the ships and creatures which if they came into contact with his unit would destroy it. The game was probably an old one, but the curly-haired man was obviously playing it extremely well to have attracted spectators.

The screen was bright green.

Linden was transfixed. He barely registered the man clicking his fingers as he relaxed between one attack and the next.

The screen seemed to get brighter, like a television in a darkening room.

Linden leaned closer. Slowly he began to turn his head to see the face of the man who was playing. But before he finished the turn he shot round the other way and barged his way out of the crowd, running for the doors.

His head pounding, he searched for his car. On the far side of the parking area he saw the serviceman's truck, its orange light still revolving. The man was bending down at the Mini's rear nearside, just tightening the last nut on the changed wheel.

"Quickly," Linden croaked. "I've got to go."

"All right, all right," the man said, kicking the wheel trim into place. "You've got to sign my forms."

The man walked too slowly to the cab of his truck and shuffled around some papers on a clipboard. Linden hovered at his shoulder.

"There," the man said, pointing with a stubby finger.

Linden leaned over. The paper was red. He looked at the man, who pointed again and rubbed a sore red eye with his free hand. Linden scrawled his signature.

"And there."

He signed again and dropped the pen onto the floor of the cab in his haste to get away.

He jumped into the Mini, rammed it into first, thrust the key into the ignition and started the engine as he released the handbrake and turned the wheel. He accelerated and stamped on the brake when he thought he was going to run the serviceman over: but he was behind him in the rear-view mirror, waving his arms and shouting something Linden couldn't hear. He screeched away and built up speed, aiming for the slip road to get back on the motorway. He ignored a road sign which he didn't recognise—a solid red circle—and sped between two bollards. The man's alarmed face receded to a fleck in his mirror.

The motorway was fairly clear so he accelerated straight into the centre lane, pressing the pedal to the floor. He soon caught up with the red lights ahead. Too quickly, in fact. Suddenly there were swarms of red lights apparently speeding towards him in all three lanes, as if reversing down the motorway at 70 miles per hour.

He turned to Melanie in bewilderment and fear.

But she wasn't there.

And within seconds neither was he.

THOMAS LIGOTTI

The Last Feast of Harlequin

AFTER YEARS TOILING in the small press field, Thomas Ligotti is finally making a name for himself with his unique and bizarre stories in such anthologies as *The Best Horror from Fantasy Tales*, *Prime Evil*, *Fine Frights*, *The Year's Best Fantasy and Horror* and, of course, *Best New Horror*.

He was born in Detroit and currently lives in nearby Michigan. His jobs have included grocery store clerk, working in the circulation office of a local newspaper, telephone interviewer for a marketing research firm, assistant teacher, and various editorial capacities for a reference book publisher.

His collection of short fiction, *Songs of a Dead Dreamer*, was published to great acclaim by Robinson and Carroll & Graf on both sides of the Atlantic, and it was recently followed by the equally remarkable *Grimscribe: His Lives and Works*.

The Washington Post has described Ligotti as "the most startling and unexpected literary discovery since Clive Barker"; when you read the story that follows, you'll understand why . . .

To the Memory of H.P. Lovecraft

I

MY INTEREST IN THE TOWN OF MIROCAW was first aroused when I heard that an annual festival was held there which promised to include, to some extent, the participation of clowns among its other elements of pageantry. A former colleague of mine, who is now attached to the anthropology department of a distant university, had read one of my recent articles ("The Clown Figure in American Media," *Journal of Popular Culture*), and wrote to me that he vaguely remembered reading or being told of a town somewhere in the state that held a kind of "Fool's Feast" every year, thinking that this might be pertinent to my peculiar line of study. It was, of course, more pertinent than he had reason to think, both to my academic aims in this area and to my personal pursuits.

Aside from my teaching, I had for some years been engaged in various anthropological projects with the primary ambition of articulating the significance of the clown figure in diverse cultural contexts. Every year for the past twenty years I have attended the pre-Lenten festivals that are held in various places throughout the southern United States. Every year I learned something more concerning the esoterics of celebration. In these studies I was an eager participant—along with playing my part as an anthropologist, I also took a place behind the clownish mask myself. And I cherished this role as I did nothing else in my life. To me the title of Clown has always carried connotations of a noble sort. I was an adroit jester, strangely enough, and had always taken pride in the skills I worked so diligently to develop.

I wrote to the State Department of Recreation, indicating what information I desired and exposing an enthusiastic urgency which came naturally to me on this topic. Many weeks later I received a tan envelope imprinted with a government logo. Inside was a pamphlet that catalogued all of the various seasonal festivities of which the state was officially aware, and I noted in passing that there were as many in late autumn and winter as in the warmer seasons. A letter inserted within the pamphlet explained to me that, according to their voluminous records, no festivals held in the town of Mirocaw had been officially registered. Their files, nonetheless, could be placed at my disposal if I should wish to research this or similar matters in connection with some definite project. At the time this offer was made I was already laboring under so many professional and personal burdens that, with a weary hand, I simply deposited the envelope and its contents in a drawer, never to be consulted again.

Some months later, however, I made an impulsive digression from my responsibilities and, rather haphazardly, took up the Mirocaw project. This happened as I was driving north one afternoon in late summer with the intention of examining some journals in the holdings of a library at another university. Once out of the city limits the scenery changed to sunny fields and farms, diverting my thoughts from the signs that I passed along the highway. Nevertheless, the subconscious scholar in me must have been regarding these with studious care. The name of a town loomed into my vision. Instantly the scholar retrieved certain records from some deep mental drawer, and I was faced with making a few hasty calculations as to whether there was enough time and motivation for an investigative side trip. But the exit sign was even hastier in making its appearance, and I soon found myself leaving the highway, recalling the roadsign's promise that the town was no more than seven miles east.

These seven miles included several confusing turns, the forced taking of a temporarily alternate route, and a destination not even visible until a steep rise had been fully ascended. On the descent another helpful sign informed me that I was within the city limits of Mirocaw. Some scattered houses on the outskirts of the town were the first structures I encountered. Beyond them the numerical highway became Townshend Street, the main avenue of Mirocaw.

The town impressed me as being much larger once I was within its limits than it had appeared from the prominence just outside. I saw that the general hilliness of the surrounding countryside was also an internal feature of Mirocaw. Here, though, the effect was different. The parts of the town did not look as if they adhered very well to one another. This condition might be blamed on the irregular topography of the town. Behind some of the old stores in the business district, steeply roofed houses had been erected on a sudden incline, their peaks appearing at an extraordinary elevation above the lower buildings. And because the foundations of these houses could not be glimpsed, they conveyed the illusion of being either precariously suspended in air, threatening to topple down, or else constructed with an unnatural loftiness in relation to their width and mass. This situation also created a weird distortion of perspective. The two levels of structures overlapped each other without giving a sense of depth, so that the houses, because of their higher elevation and nearness to the foreground buildings, did not appear diminished in size as background objects should. Consequently, a look of flatness, as in a photograph, predominated in this area. Indeed, Mirocaw could be compared to an album of old snapshots, particularly ones in which the camera had been upset in the process of photography, causing the pictures to develop on angle: a cone-roofed turret, like a pointed hat jauntily askew, peeked over the houses on a neighboring street; a billboard displaying a group of grinning vegetables tipped its contents slightly westward; cars abutting steep curbs seemed to be flying skyward in the glare-distorted windows of a five-and-ten; people leaned lethargically as they trod up and down sidewalks; and on that sunny day the clock tower, which at first I mistook for a church steeple, cast a long shadow that seemed to extend an impossible distance and wander into unlikely places in its progress across the town. I should say that perhaps the disharmonies of Mirocaw are more acutely affecting my imagination in retrospect than they were on that first day, when I was primarily concerned with locating the city hall or some other center of information.

I pulled around a corner and parked. Sliding over to the other side of the seat, I rolled down the window and called to a passerby: "Excuse me, sir," I said. The man, who was shabbily dressed and very old, paused for a moment without approaching the car. Though he had apparently responded to my call, his vacant expression did not betray the least awareness of my presence, and for a moment I thought it just a coincidence that he halted on the sidewalk at the same time I addressed him. His eyes were focused somewhere beyond me with a weary and imbecilic gaze. After a few moments he continued on his way and I said nothing to call him back, even though at the last second his face began to appear dimly familiar. Someone else finally came along who was able to direct me to the Mirocaw City Hall and Community Center.

The city hall turned out to be the building with the clock tower. Inside I stood at a counter behind which some people were working at desks and walking up and down a back hallway. On one wall was a poster for the state lottery: a jack-in-the-box with both hands grasping green bills. After a few moments, a tall, middle-aged woman came over to the counter.

"Can I help you?" she asked in a neutral, bureaucratic voice.

I explained that I had heard about the festival—saying nothing about being a nosy academic—and asked if she could provide me with further information or direct me to someone who could.

"Do you mean the one held in the winter?" she asked.

"How many of them are there?"

"Just that one."

"I suppose, then, that that's the one I mean." I smiled as if sharing a joke with her.

Without another word, she walked off into the back hallway. While she was absent I exchanged glances with several of the people behind the counter who periodically looked up from their work.

"There you are," she said when she returned, handing me a piece of paper that looked like the product of a cheap copy machine. *Please Come to the Fun*, it said in large letters. *Parades*, it went on, *Street Masquerade, Bands, The Winter Raffle*, and *The Coronation of the Winter Queen*. The page continued with the mention of a number of miscellaneous festivities. I read the words again. There was something about that imploring little "please" at the top of the announcement that made the whole affair seem like a charity function.

"When is it held? It doesn't say when the festival takes place."

"Most people already know that." She abruptly snatched the page from my hands and wrote something at the bottom. When she gave it back to me, I saw "Dec. 19–21" written in blue-green ink. I was immediately struck by an odd sense of scheduling on the part of the festival committee. There was, of course, solid anthropological and historical precedent for holding festivities around the winter solstice, but the timing of this particular event did not seem entirely practical.

"If you don't mind my asking, don't these days somewhat conflict with the regular holiday season? I mean, most people have enough going on at that time."

"It's just tradition," she said, as if invoking some venerable ancestry behind her words.

"That's very interesting," I said as much to myself as to her.

"Is there anything else?" she asked.

"Yes. Could you tell me if this festival has anything to do with clowns? I see there's something about a masquerade."

"Yes, of course there are some people in . . . costumes. I've never been in that position myself . . . that is, yes, there are clowns of a sort."

At that point my interest was definitely aroused, but I was not sure how much further I wanted to pursue it. I thanked the woman for her help and asked the best way to get back to the highway, not anxious to retrace the labyrinthine route by which I had entered the town. I walked back to my car with a whole flurry of half-formed questions, and as many vague and conflicting answers, cluttering my mind.

The directions the woman gave me necessitated passing through the south end of Mirocaw. There were not many people moving about in this section of town. Those that I did see, shuffling lethargically down a block of battered storefronts, exhibited the same sort of forlorn expression and manner as the old man from whom I had asked directions earlier. I must have been passing through a central artery of this area, for on either side stretched street after street of poorly tended yards and houses bowed with age and indifference. When I came to a stop at a streetcorner, one of the citizens of this slum passed in front of my car. This lean, morose, and epicene person turned my way and sneered outrageously with a taut little mouth, yet seemed to be looking at no one in particular. After progressing a few streets farther, I came to a road that led back to the highway. I felt detectably more comfortable as soon as I found myself traveling once again through the expanses of sun-drenched farmlands.

I reached the library with more than enough time for my research, and so I decided to make a scholarly detour to see what material I could find that might illuminate the winter festival held in Mirocaw. The library, one of the oldest in the state, included in its holding the entire run of the Mirocaw *Courier*. I thought this would be an excellent place to start. I soon found, however, that there was no handy way to research information from this newspaper, and I did not want to engage in a blind search for articles concerning a specific subject.

I next turned to the more organized resources of the newspapers for the larger cities located in the same county, which incidentally shares its name with Mirocaw. I uncovered very little about the town, and almost nothing concerning its festival, except in one general article on annual events in the area that erroneously attributed to Mirocaw a "large Middle-Eastern community" which every spring hosted a kind of ethnic jamboree. From what I had already observed, and from what I subsequently learned, the citizens of Mirocaw were solidly midwestern-American, the probable descendants in a direct line from some enterprising pack of New Englanders of the last century. There was one brief item devoted to a Mirocavian event, but this merely turned out to be an obituary notice for an old woman who had quietly taken her life around Christmas time. Thus, I returned home that day all but empty-handed on the subject of Mirocaw.

However, it was not long afterward that I received another letter from the former colleague of mine who had first led me to seek out Mirocaw and its festival. As it happened, he rediscovered the article that caused him to stir my interest in a local "Fool's Feast." This article had its sole appearance in an obscure festschrift of anthropology studies published in Amsterdam twenty years ago. Most of these papers were in Dutch, a few in German, and only one was in English: "The Last Feast of Harlequin: Preliminary Notes on a Local Festival." It was exciting, of course, finally to be able to read this study, but even more exciting was the name of its author: Dr Raymond Thoss.

II

Before proceeding any further, I should mention something about Thoss, and inevitably about myself. Over two decades ago, at my alma mater in Cambridge, Mass., Thoss was a professor of mine. Long before playing a role in the events I am about to describe, he was already one of the most important figures in my life. A striking personality, he inevitably influenced everyone who came in contact with him. I remember his lectures on social anthropology, how he turned that dim room into a brilliant and profound circus of learning. He moved in an uncannily brisk manner. When he swept his arm around to indicate some common term on the blackboard behind him, one felt he was presenting nothing less than an item of fantastic qualities and secret value. When he replaced his hand in the pocket of his old jacket this fleeting magic was once again stored away in its wellworn pouch, to be retrieved at the sorcerer's discretion. We sensed he was teaching us more than we could possibly learn, and that he himself was in possession of greater and deeper knowledge than he could possibly impart. On one occasion I summoned up the audacity to offer an interpretation—which was somewhat opposed to his own—regarding the tribal clowns of the Hopi Indians. I implied that personal experience as an amateur clown and special devotion to this study provided me with an insight possibly more valuable than his own. It was then he disclosed, casually and very obiter dicta, that he had actually acted in the role of one of these masked tribal fools and had celebrated with them the dance of the *kachinas*. In revealing these facts, however, he somehow managed not to add to the humiliation I had already inflicted upon myself. And for this I was grateful to him.

Thoss's activities were such that he sometimes became the object of gossip or romanticized speculation. He was a fieldworker par excellence, and his ability to insinuate himself into exotic cultures and situations, thereby gaining insights where other anthropologists merely collected data, was renowned. At various times in his career there had been rumors of his having "gone native" à la the Frank Hamilton Cushing legend. There were hints, which were not always irresponsible or cheaply glamorized, that he was involved in projects of a freakish sort, many of which focused on New England. It is a fact that he spent six months posing as a mental patient at an institution in western Massachusetts, gathering information on the "culture" of the psychically disturbed. When his book *Winter Solstice: The Longest Night of a Society* was published, the general opinion was that it was disappointingly subjective and impressionistic, and that, aside from a few moving but "poetically obscure" observations, there was nothing at all to give it value. Those who defended Thoss claimed he was a kind of super-anthropologist: while much of his work emphasized his own mind and feelings, his experience had in fact penetrated to a rich core of hard data which he had yet to disclose in objective discourse.

As a student of Thoss, I tended to support this latter estimation of him. For a variety of tenable and untenable reasons, I believed Thoss capable of unearthing hitherto inaccessible strata of human existence. So it was gratifying at first that this article entitled "The Last Feast of Harlequin" seemed to uphold the Thoss mystique, and in an area I personally found captivating.

Much of the content of the article I did not immediately comprehend, given its author's characteristic and often strategic obscurities. On first reading, the most interesting aspect of this brief study—the "notes" encompassed only twenty pages—was the general mood of the piece. Thoss's eccentricities were definitely present in these pages, but only as a struggling inner force which was definitely contained—incarcerated, I might say—by the somber rhythmic movements of his prose and by some gloomy references he occasionally called upon. Two references in particular shared a common theme. One was a quotation from Poe's "The Conqueror Worm," which Thoss employed as a rather sensational epigraph. The point of the epigraph, however, was nowhere echoed in the text of the article save in another passing reference. Thoss brought up the well-known genesis of the modern Christmas celebration, which of course descends from the Roman Saturnalia. Then, making it clear he had not yet observed the Mirocaw festival and had only gathered its nature from various informants, he established that it too contained many, even more overt, elements of the Saturnalia. Next he made what seemed to me a trivial and purely linguistic observation, one that had less to do with his main course of argument than it did with the equally peripheral Poe epigraph. He briefly mentioned that an early sect of the Syrian Gnostics called themselves "Saturnians" and believed, among other religious heresies, that mankind was created by angels who were in turn created by the Supreme Unknown. The angels, however, did not possess the power to make their creation an erect being and for a time he crawled upon the earth like a worm. Later, the Creator remedied this grotesque state of affairs. At the time I supposed that the symbolic correspondences of mankind's origins and ultimate condition being associated with worms, combined with a year-end festival recognizing the winter death of the earth, was the gist of this Thossian "insight," a poetic but scientifically valueless observation.

Other observations he made on the Mirocaw festival were also strictly etic; in other words, they were based on second-hand sources, hearsay testimony. Even at that juncture, however, I felt Thoss knew more than he disclosed; and, as I later discovered, he had indeed included information on certain aspects of Mirocaw which suggested he was already in possession of several keys which for the moment he was keeping securely in his own pocket. By then I myself possessed a most revealing morsel of knowledge. A note to the "Harlequin" article apprised the reader that the piece was only a fragment in rude form of a more wide-ranging work in preparation. This work was never seen by the world. My former professor had not published anything since his withdrawal from academic circulation some twenty years ago. Now I suspected where he had gone.

For the man I had asked for directions on the streets of Mirocaw, the man with the disconcertingly lethargic gaze, had very much resembled a superannuated version of Dr Raymond Thoss.

III

And now I have a confession to make. Despite my reasons for being enthusiastic about Mirocaw and its mysteries, especially its relationship to both Thoss and my own deepest concerns as a scholar—I contemplated the days ahead of me with no more than a feeling of frigid numbness and often with a sense of profound depression. Yet I had no reason to be surprised at this emotional state, which had little relevance to the outward events in my life but was determined by inward conditions that worked according to their own, quite enigmatic, seasons and cycles. For many years, at least since my university days, I have suffered from this dark malady, this recurrent despondency in which I would become buried when it came time for the earth to grow cold and bare and the skies heavy with shadows. Nevertheless, I pursued my plans, though somewhat mechanically, to visit Mirocaw during its festival days, for I superstitiously hoped that this activity might diminish the weight of my seasonal despair. In Mirocaw would be parades and parties and the opportunity to play the clown once again.

For weeks in advance I practiced my art, even perfecting a new feat of juggling magic, which was my special forte in foolery. I had my costumes cleaned, purchased fresh makeup, and was ready. I received permission from the university to cancel some of my classes prior to the holiday, explaining the nature of my project and the necessity of arriving in the town a few days before the festival began, in order to do some preliminary research, establish informants, and so on. Actually my plan was to postpone any formal inquiry until after the festival and to involve myself beforehand as much as possible in its activities. I would, of course, keep a journal during this time.

There was one resource I did want to consult, however. Specifically, I returned to that outstate library to examine those issues of the Mirocaw *Courier* dating from December two decades ago. One story in particular confirmed a point Thoss made in the "Harlequin" article, though the event it chronicled must have taken place after Thoss had written his study.

The *Courier* story appeared two weeks after the festival had ended for that year and was concerned with the disappearance of a woman named Elizabeth Beadle, the wife of Samuel Beadle, a hotel owner in Mirocaw. The county authorities speculated that this was another instance of the "holiday suicides" which seemed to occur with inordinate seasonal regularity in the Mirocaw region. Thoss documented this situation in his "Harlequin" article, though I suspected that today these deaths would be neatly categorized under the heading "seasonal affective disorder." In any case, the authorities searched a half-frozen lake near the outskirts of Mirocaw where they had found many successful suicides in years past. This year, however, no body was discovered. Alongside the article was a picture of Elizabeth Beadle. Even in the grainy microfilm reproduction one could detect a certain vibrancy and vitality in Mrs Beadle's face. That an hypothesis of "holiday suicide" should be so readily posited to explain her disappearance seemed strange and in some way unjust.

Thoss, in his brief article, wrote that every year there occured changes of a moral or spiritual cast which seemed to affect Mirocaw along with the usual winter metamorphosis. He was not precise about its origin or nature but stated, in typically mystifying fashion, that the effect of this "subseason" on the town was conspicuously negative. In addition to the number of suicides actually accomplished during this time, there was also a rise in treatment of "hypochondriacal" conditions, which was how the medical men of twenty years past characterized these cases in discussions with Thoss. This state of affairs would gradually worsen and finally reach a climax during the days scheduled for the Mirocaw festival. Thoss speculated that given the secretive nature of small towns, the situation was probably even more intensely pronounced than casual investigation could reveal.

The connection between the festival and this insidious subseasonal climate in Mirocaw was a point on which Thoss did not come to any rigid conclusions. He did write, nevertheless, that these two "climatic aspects" had had a parallel existence in the town's history as far back as available records could document. A late nineteenth-century history of Mirocaw County speaks of the town by its original name of New Colstead, and castigates the townspeople for holding a "ribald and soulless feast" to the exclusion of normal Christmas observances. (Thoss comments that the historian had mistakenly fused two distinct aspects of the season, their actual relationship being essentially antagonistic.) The "Harlequin" article did not trace the festival to its earliest appearance (this may not have been possible), though Thoss emphasized the New England origins of Mirocaw's founders. The festival, therefore, was one imported from this region and could reasonably be extended at least a century; that is, if it had not been brought over from the Old World, in which case its roots would become indefinite until further research could be done. Surely Thoss's allusion to the Syrian Gnostics suggested the latter possibility could not entirely be ruled out.

But it seemed to be the festival's source in New England that nourished Thoss's speculations. He wrote of this patch of geography as if it were an acceptable place to end the search. For him, the very words "New England" seemed to be stripped of all traditional connotations and had come to imply nothing less than a gateway to all lands, both known and suspected, and even to ages beyond the civilized history of the region. Having been educated partly in New England, I could somewhat understand this sentimental exaggeration, for indeed there are places that seem archaic beyond chronological measure, appearing to transcend relative standards of time and achieving a kind of absolute antiquity which cannot be logically fathomed. But how this vague suggestion related to a small town in the Midwest I could not imagine. Thoss himself observed that the residents of Mirocaw did not betray any mysteriously primitive consciousness. On the contrary, they appeared superficially unaware of the genesis of their winter merrymaking. That such a tradition had endured through the years, however, even eclipsing the conventional Christmas holiday, revealed a profound awareness of the festival's meaning and function.

I cannot deny that what I had learned about the Mirocaw festival did inspire a trite sense of fate, especially given the involvement of such an important figure from my past as Thoss. It was the first time in my academic career that I knew myself to be better suited than anyone else to discern the true meaning of scattered data, even if I could only attribute this special authority to chance circumstances.

Nevertheless, as I sat in that library on a morning in mid December I doubted for a moment the wisdom of setting out for Mirocaw rather than returning home, where the more familiar *rite de passage* of winter depression awaited me. My original scheme was to avoid the cyclical blues the season held for me, but it seemed this was also a part of the history of Mirocaw, only on a much larger scale. My emotional instability, however, was exactly what qualified me most for the particular field work ahead, though I did not take pride or consolation in the fact. And to retreat would have been to deny myself an opportunity that might never offer itself again. In retrospect, there seems to have been no fortuitous resolution to the decision I had to make. As it happened, I went ahead to the town.

IV

Just past noon, on December 18, I started driving toward Mirocaw. A blur of dull, earthen-coloured scenery extended in every direction. The snowfalls of late autumn had been sparse, and only a few white patches appeared in the harvested fields along the highway. The clouds were gray and abundant. Passing by a stretch of forest, I noticed the black, ragged clumps of abandoned nests clinging to the twisted mesh of bare branches. I thought I saw black birds skittering over the road ahead, but they were only dead leaves and they flew into the air as I drove by.

I approached Mirocaw from the south, entering the town from the direction I had left it on my visit the previous summer. This took me once again through that part of town which seemed to exist on the wrong side of some great invisible wall dividing the desirable sections of Mirocaw from the undesirable. As lurid as this district had appeared to me under the summer sun, in the thin light of that winter afternoon it degenerated into a pale phantom of itself. The frail stores and starved-looking houses suggested a borderline region between the material and nonmaterial worlds, with one sardonically wearing the mask of the other. I saw a few gaunt pedestrians who turned as I passed by, though seemingly not *because* I passed by, making my way up to the main street of Mirocaw.

Driving up the steep rise of Townshend Street, I found the sights there comparatively welcoming. The rolling avenues of the town were in readiness for the festival. Streetlights had their poles raveled with evergreen, the fresh boughs proudly conspicuous in a barren season. On the doors of many of the businesses on Townshend were holly wreaths, equally green but observably plastic. However, although there was nothing unusual in this traditional greenery of the season, it soon became apparent to me that Mirocaw had quite abandoned itself to this particular symbol of Yuletide. It was garishly in evidence everywhere. The windows of stores and houses were framed in green lights, green streamers hung down from storefront awnings, and the beacons of the Red Rooster Bar were peacock green floodlights. I supposed the residents of Mirocaw desired these decorations, but the effect was one of excess. An eerie emerald haze permeated the town, and faces looked slightly reptilian.

At the time I assumed that the prodigious evergreen, holly wreaths, and colored lights (if only of a single color) demonstrated an emphasis on the vegetable symbols of the Nordic Yuletide, which would inevitably be muddled into the winter festival of any northern country just as they had been adopted for the Christmas season. In his "Harlequin" article Thoss wrote of the pagan aspect of

137

Mirocaw's festival, likening it to the ritual of a fertility cult, with probable connections to chthonic divinities at some time in the past. But Thoss had mistaken, as I had, what was only part of the festival's significance for the whole.

The hotel at which I had made reservations was located on Townshend. It was an old building of brown brick, with an arched doorway and a pathetic coping intended to convey an impression of neoclassicism. I found a parking space in front and left my suitcases in the car.

When I first entered the hotel lobby it was empty. I thought perhaps the Mirocaw festival would have attracted enough visitors to at least bolster the business of its only hotel, but it seemed I was mistaken. Tapping a little bell, I leaned on the desk and turned to look at a small, traditionally decorated Christmas tree on a table near the entranceway. It was complete with shiny, egg-fragile bulbs; miniature candy canes; flat, laughing Santas with arms wide; a star on top nodding awkwardly against the delicate shoulder of an upper branch; and colored lights that bloomed out of flower-shaped sockets. For some reason this seemed to me a sorry little piece.

"May I help you?" said a young woman arriving from a room adjacent to the lobby.

I must have been staring rather intently at her, for she looked away and seemed quite uneasy. I could hardly imagine what to say to her or how to explain what I was thinking. In person she immediately radiated a chilling brilliance of manner and expression. But if this woman had not committed suicide twenty years before, as the newspaper article had suggested, neither had she aged in that time.

"Sarah," called a masculine voice from the invisible heights of a stairway. A tall, middle-aged man came down the steps. "I thought you were in your room," said the man, whom I took to be Samuel Beadle. Sarah, not Elizabeth, Beadle glanced sideways in my direction to indicate to her father that she was conducting the business of the hotel. Beadle apologized to me, and then excused the two of them for a moment while they went off to one side to continue their exchange.

I smiled and pretended everything was normal, while trying to remain within earshot of their conversation. They spoke in tones that suggested their conflict was a familiar one: Beadle's overprotective concern with his daughter's whereabouts and Sarah's frustrated understanding of certain restrictions placed upon her. The conversation ended, and Sarah ascended the stairs, turning for a moment to give me a facial pantomime of apology for the unprofessional scene that had just taken place.

"Now, sir, what can I do for you?" Beadle asked, almost demanded.

"Yes, I have a reservation. Actually, I'm a day early, if that doesn't present a problem." I gave the hotel the benefit of the doubt that its business might have been secretly flourishing.

"No problem at all, sir," he said, presenting me with the registration form, and then a brass-colored key dangling from a plastic disc bearing the number 44.

"Luggage?"

"Yes, it's in my car."

"I'll give you a hand with that."

While Beadle was settling me in my fourth-floor room it seemed an opportune moment to broach the subject of the festival, the holiday suicides, and perhaps, depending upon his reaction, the fate of his wife. I needed a respondent who had lived in the town for a good many years and who could enlighten me about the attitude of Mirocavians toward their season of sea-green lights.

"This is just fine," I said about the clean but somber room. "Nice view. I can see the bright green lights of Mirocaw just fine from up here. Is the town usually all decked out like this? For the festival, I mean."

"Yes, sir, for the festival," he replied mechanically.

"I imagine you'll probably be getting quite a few of us out-of-towners in the next couple days."

"Could be. Is there anything else?"

"Yes, there is. I wonder if you could tell me something about the festivities."

"Such as . . ."

"Well, you know, the clowns and so forth."

"Only clowns here are the ones that're . . . well, picked out, I suppose you would say."

"I don't understand."

"Excuse me, sir. I'm very busy right now. Is there anything else?"

I could think of nothing at the moment to perpetuate our conversation. Beadle wished me a good stay and left.

I unpacked my suitcases. In addition to regular clothing I had also brought along some of the items from my clown's wardrobe. Beadle's comment that clowns were "picked out" here left me wondering exactly what purpose these street masqueraders served in the festival. The clown figure has had so many meanings in different times and cultures. The jolly, well-loved joker familiar to most people is actually but one aspect of this protean creature. Madmen, hunchbacks, amputees, and other abnormals were once considered natural clowns; they were elected to fulfil a comic role which could allow others to see them as ludicrous rather than as terrible reminders of the forces of disorder in the world. But sometimes a cheerless jester was required to draw attention to this same disorder, as in the case of King Lear's morbid and honest fool, who of course was eventually hanged, and so much for his clownish wisdom. Clowns have often had ambiguous and sometimes contradictory roles to play. Thus, I knew enough not to brashly jump into costume and cry out, "Here I am again!"

That first day in Mirocaw I did not stray far from the hotel. I read and rested for a few hours and then ate at a nearby diner. Through the window beside my table I watched the winter night turn the soft green glow of the town into a harsh and almost totally new color as it contrasted with the darkness. The streets of Mirocaw seemed to me unusually busy for a small town at evening. Yet it was not the kind of activity one normally sees before an approaching Christmas holiday. This was not a crowd of bustling shoppers loaded with bright bags of presents. Their arms were empty, their hands shoved deep in their pockets against the cold, which nevertheless had not driven them to the solitude of their presumably warm houses. I watched them enter and exit store after store without buying; many merchants remained open late, and even the places that were closed had left their neons illuminated. The faces that passed the window of the diner were possibly just stiffened by the cold. I thought; frozen into deep frowns and nothing else. In the same window I saw the reflection of my own face. It was not the face of an adept clown; it was slack and flabby and at that moment seemed the face of someone less than alive. Outside was the town of Mirocaw, its streets dipping and rising with a lunatic severity, its citizens packing the sidewalks, its heart bathed in green: as promising a field of professional and personal challenge as I had ever encountered—and I was bored to the point of dread. I hurried back to my hotel room.

"Mirocaw has another coldness within its cold," I wrote in my journal that night. "Another set of buildings and streets that exists behind the visible town's facade like a world of disgraceful back alleys." I went on like this for about a page, across which I finally engraved a big "X." Then I went to bed.

In the morning I left my car at the hotel and walked toward the main business district a few blocks away. Mingling with the good people of Mirocaw seemed like the proper thing to do at that point in my scientific sojourn. But as I began laboriously walking up Townshend (the sidewalks were cramped with wandering pedestrians), a glimpse of someone suddenly replaced my haphazard plan with a more specific and immediate one. Through the crowd and about fifteen paces ahead was my goal.

"Dr Thoss," I called.

His head almost seemed to turn and look back in response to my shout, but I could not be certain. I pushed past several warmly wrapped bodies and green-scarved necks. Only to find that the object of my pursuit appeared to be maintaining the same distance from me, though I did not know if this was being done deliberately or not. At the next corner, the dark-coated Thoss abruptly turned right onto a steep street which led downward directly toward the dilapidated south end of Mirocaw. When I reached the corner I looked down the sidewalk and could see him very clearly from above. I also saw how he managed to stay so far ahead of me in a mob that had impeded my own progress. For some reason the people on the sidewalk made room so that he could move past them easily, without the usual jostling of bodies. It was not a dramatic physical avoidance, thought it seemed nonetheless intentional. Fighting the tight fabric of the throng, I continued to follow Thoss, losing and regaining sight of him.

By the time I reached the bottom of the sloping street the crowd had thinned out considerably, and after walking a block or so farther I found myself practically a lone pedestrian pacing behind a distant figure that I hoped was still Thoss. He was now walking quite swiftly and in a way that seemed to acknowledge my pursuit of him, though really it felt as if he were leading me as much as I was chasing him, I called his name a few more times at a volume he could not have failed to hear, assuming that deafness was not one of the changes to have come over him; he was, after all, not a young man, nor even a middle-aged one any longer.

Thoss suddenly crossed in the middle of the street. He walked a few more steps and entered a signless brick building between a liquor store and a repair shop of some kind. In the "Harlequin" article Thoss had mentioned that the people living in this section of Mirocaw maintained their own businesses, and that these were patronized almost exclusively by residents of the area. I could well believe this statement when I looked at these little sheds of commerce, for they had the same badly weathered appearance as their clientele. The formidable shoddiness of these buildings notwithstanding, I followed Thoss into the plain brick shell of what had been, or possibly still was, a diner.

Inside it was unusually dark. Even before my eyes made the adjustment I sensed that this was not a thriving restaurant cozily cluttered with chairs and tables—as was the establishment where I had eaten the night before—but a place with only a few disarranged furnishings, and very cold. It seemed colder, in fact, than the winter streets outside.

"Dr Thoss?" I called toward a lone table near the center of the long room. Perhaps four or five were sitting around the table, with some others blending into the dimness behind them. Scattered across the top of the table were some books and loose papers. Seated there was an old man indicating something in the pages before him, but it was not Thoss. Beside him were two youths whose wholesome features distinguished them from the grim weariness of the others. I approached the table and they all looked up at me. None of them showed a glimmer of emotion except the two boys, who exchanged worried and guilt-ridden glances with each other, as if they had just been discovered in some shameful act. They both suddenly burst from the table and ran into the dark background, where a light appeared briefly as they exited by a back door.

"I'm sorry," I said diffidently. "I thought I saw someone I knew come in here."

They said nothing. Out of a back room others began to emerge, no doubt interested in the source of the commotion. In a few moments the room was crowded with these tramp-like figures, all of them gazing emptily in the dimness. I was not at this point frightened of them; at least I was not afraid they would do me any physical harm. Actually, I felt as if it was quite within my power to pummel them easily into submission, their mousy faces almost inviting a succession of firm blows. But there were so many of them.

They slid slowly toward me in a worm-like mass. Their eyes seemed empty and unfocused, and I wondered a moment if they were even aware of my presence. Nevertheless, I was the center upon which their lethargic shuffling converged, their shoes scuffing softly along the bare floor. I began to deliver a number of hasty inanities as they continued to press toward me, their weak and unexpectedly odorless bodies nudging against mine. (I understood now why the people along the sidewalks seemed to instinctively avoid Thoss.) Unseen legs seemed to become entangled with my own; I staggered and then regained my balance. This sudden movement aroused me from a kind of mesmeric daze which I must have fallen into without being aware of it. I had intended to leave that dreary place long before events had reached such a juncture, but for some reason I could not focus my intentions strongly enough to cause myself to act. My mind had been drifting farther away as these slavish things approached. In a sudden surge of panic I pushed through their soft ranks and was outside.

The open air revived me to my former alertness, and I immediately started pacing swiftly up the hill. I was no longer sure that I had not simply imagined what had seemed, and at the same time did not seem, like a perilous moment. Had their movements been directed toward a harmful assault, or were they trying merely to intimidate me? As I reached the green-glazed main street of Mirocaw I really could not be sure what had just happened.

The sidewalks were still jammed with a multitude of pedestrians, but now they seemed to be moving and chattering in a more lively way. There was a kind of vitality that could only be attributed to the imminent festivities. A group of young men had begun celebrating prematurely and strode noisily across the street at midpoint, obviously intoxicated. From the laughter and joking among the still sober citizens I gathered that, mardi-gras style, public drunkenness was within the traditions of this winter festival. I looked for anything to indicate the beginnings of the Street Masquerade, but saw nothing: no brightly garbed harlequins or snow-white pierrots. Were the ceremonies even now in preparation for the coronation of the Winter Queen? "The Winter Queen," I wrote in my journal. "Figure of fertility invested with symbolic powers of revival and prosperity. Elected in the manner of a high school prom queen. Check for possible consort figure in the form of a representative from the underworld."

In the pre-darkness hours of December 19 I sat in my hotel room and wrote and thought and organized. I did not feel too badly, all things considered. The holiday excitement which was steadily rising in the streets below my window was definitely infecting me. I forced myself to take a short nap in anticipation of a long night. When I awoke, Mirocaw's annual feast had begun.

V

Shouting, commotion, carousing. Sleepily I went to the window and looked out over the town. It seemed all the lights of Mirocaw were shining, save in that section down the hill which became part of the black void of winter. And now the town's greenish tinge was even more pronounced, spreading everywhere like a great green rainbow that had melted from the sky and endured, phosphorescent, into the night. In the streets was the brightness of an artificial spring. The byways of Mirocaw vibrated with activity: on a nearby corner a brass band blared; marauding cars blew their horns and were sometimes mounted by laughing pedestrians; a man emerged from the Red Rooster Bar, threw up his arms, and crowed. I looked closely at the individual celebrants, searching for the vestments of clowns. Soon, delightedly, I saw them. The costume was red and white, with matching cap, and the face painted a noble alabaster. It almost seemed to be a clownish incarnation of that white-bearded and black-booted Christmas fool.

This particular fool, however, was not receiving the affection and respect usually accorded to a Santa Claus. My poor fellow-clown was in the middle of a circle of revelers who were pushing him back and forth from one to the other. The object of this abuse seemed to accept it somewhat willingly, but this little game nevertheless appeared to have humiliation as its purpose. "Only clowns here are the one's that're picked out," echoed Beadle's voice in my memory. "Picked *on*" seemed closer to the truth.

Packing myself in some heavy clothes, I went out into the green gleaming streets. Not far from the hotel I was stumbled into by a character with a wide blue and red grin and bright baggy clothes. Actually he had been shoved into me by some youths outside a drugstore.

"See the freak," said an obese and drunken fellow. "See the freak fall."

My first response was anger, and then fear as I saw two others flanking the fat drunk. They walked toward me and I tensed myself for a confrontation.

"This is a disgrace," one said, the neck of a wine bottle held loosely in his left hand.

But it was not to me they were speaking; it was to the clown, who had been pushed to the sidewalk. His persecutors helped him up with a sudden jerk and then splashed wine in his face. They ignored me altogether.

"Let him loose," the fat one said. "Crawl away, freak. Oh, he flies!"

The clown trotted off, becoming lost in the throng.

"Wait a minute," I said to the rowdy trio, who had started lumbering away. I quickly decided that it would probably be futile to ask them to explain what I had just witnessed, especially amid the noise and confusion of the festivities. In my best jovial fashion I proposed we all go someplace where I could buy them each a drink. They had no objection and in a short while we were all squeezed around a table in the Red Rooster.

Over several drinks I explained to them that I was from out of town, which pleased them no end for some reason. I told them there were some things I did not understand about their festival.

"I don't think there's anything *to* understand." the fat one said. "It's just what you see."

I asked him about the people dressed as clowns.

"Them? They're the freaks. It's their turn this year. Everyone takes their turn. Next year it might be mine. Or *yours*," he said, pointing at one of his friends across the table. "And when we find out which one you are—"

"You're not smart enough," said the defiant potential freak.

This was an important point: the fact that individuals who play the clowns remain, or at least attempted to remain, anonymous. This arrangement would help remove inhibitions a resident of Mirocaw might have about abusing his own neighbor or even a family relation.

From what I later observed, the extent of this abuse did not go beyond a kind of playful roughhousing. And even so, it was only the occasional group of rowdies who actually took advantage of this aspect of the festival, the majority of the citizens very much content to stay on the sidelines.

As far as being able to illuminate the meaning of this custom, my three young friends were quite useless. To them it was just amusement, as I imagine it was to the majority of Mirocavians. This was understandable. I suppose the average person would not be able to explain exactly how the profoundly familiar Christmas holiday came to be celebrated in its present form.

I left the bar alone and not unaffected by the drinks I had consumed there. Outside, the general merrymaking continued. Loud music emanated from several quarters. Mirocaw had fully transformed itself from a sedate small town to an enclave of Saturnalia within the dark immensity of a winter night. But Saturn is also the planetary symbol of melancholy and sterility, a clash of opposites contained within that single word. And as I wandered half-drunkenly down the street, I discovered that there was a conflict within the winter festival itself. This discovery indeed appeared to be that secret key which Thoss withheld in his study of the town. Oddly enough, it was through my unfamiliarity with the outward nature of the festival that I came to know its true nature.

I was mingling with the crowd on the street, warmly enjoying the confusion around me, when I saw a strangely designed creature lingering on the corner up ahead. It was one of the Mirocaw clowns. Its clothes were shabby and nondescript, almost in the style of a tramp-type clown, but not humorously exaggerated enough. The face, though, made up for the lackluster costume. I had never seen such a strange conception for a clown's countenance. The figure stood beneath a dim streetlight, and when it turned its head my way I realized why it seemed familiar. The thin, smooth, and pale head; the wide eyes; the oval-shaped features resembling nothing so much as the skull-faced, screaming creature in that famous painting (memory fails me). This clownish imitation rivalled the original in suggesting stricken realms of abject horror and despair: an inhuman likeness more proper to something under the earth than upon it.

From the first moment I saw this creature, I thought of those inhabitants of the ghetto down the hill. There was the same nauseating passivity and languor in its bearing. Perhaps if I had not been drinking earlier I would not have been bold enough to take the action I did. I decided to join in one of the upstanding traditions of the winter festival, for it annoyed me to see this morbid impostor of a clown standing up. When I reached the corner I laughingly pushed myself into the creature—"Whoops!"—who stumbled backward and ended up on the sidewalk. I laughed again and looked around for approval from the festivalers in the vicinity. No one, however, seemed to appreciate or even acknowledge what I had done. They did not laugh with me or point with amusement, but only passed by, perhaps walking a little faster until they were some distance from this streetcorner incident. I realized instantly I had violated some tacit rule of behaviour, though I had thought my action well within the common practice. The thought occured to me that I might even be apprehended and prosecuted for what in any other circumstances was certainly a criminal act. I turned around to help the clown back to his feet, hoping to somehow redeem my offense, but the creature was gone. Solemnly I walked away from the scene of my inadvertent crime and sought other streets away from its witnesses.

Along the various back avenues of Mirocaw I wandered, pausing exhaustedly at one point to sit at the counter of a small sandwich shop that was packed with customers. I ordered a cup of coffee to revive my overly alcoholed system. Warming my hands around the cup and sipping slowly from it, I watched the people outside as they passed the front window. It was well after midnight but the thick flow of passersby gave no indication that anyone was going home early. A carnival of profiles filed past the window and I was content simply to sit back and observe, until finally one of these faces made me start. It was that frightful little clown I had roughed up earlier. But although its face was familiar in its ghastly aspect, there was something different about it. And I wondered that there should be two such hideous freaks.

Quickly paying the man at the counter, I dashed out to get a second glimpse of the clown, who was now nowhere in sight. The dense crowd kept me from pursuing this figure with any speed, and I wondered how the clown could have made its way so easily ahead of me. Unless the crowd had instinctively allowed this creature to pass unhindered through its massive ranks, as it did for Thoss. In the process of searching for this particular freak, I discovered that interspersed among the celebrating populace of Mirocaw, which included the sanctioned festival clowns, there was not one or two, but a considerable number of these pale, wraith-like creatures. And they all drifted along the streets unmolested by even the rowdiest of revelers. I now understood one of the taboos of the festival. These other clowns were not to be disturbed and should even be avoided, much as were the residents of the slum at the edge of town. Nevertheless, I felt instinctively that the two groups of clowns were somehow identified with each other, even if the ghetto clowns were not welcome at Mirocaw's winter festival. Indeed, they were not simply part of the community and celebrating the season in their own way. To all appearances, this group of melancholy mummers constituted nothing less than an entirely independent festival—a festival within a festival.

Returning to my room, I entered my suppositions into the journal I was keeping for this venture. The following are excerpts:

There is a superstitiousness displayed by the residents of Mirocaw with regard to these people from the slum section, particularly as they lately appear in those dreadful faces signifying their own festival. What is the relationship between these simultaneous celebrations? Did one precede the other? If so, which? My opinion at this point—and I claim no conclusiveness for it—is that Mirocaw's winter festival is the later manifestation, that it appeared after the festival of those depressingly pallid clowns, in order to cover it up or mitigate its effect. The holiday suicides come to mind, and the subclimate Thoss wrote about, the disappearance of Elizabeth Beadle twenty years ago, and my own experience with this pariah clan existing outside yet within the community. Of my own experience with this emotionally deleterious subseason I would rather not speak at this time. Still not able to say whether or not my usual winter melancholy is the cause. On the general subject of mental health, I must consider Thoss's book about his stay in a psychiatric hospital (in western Mass., almost sure of that. Check on this book & Mirocaw's New England roots). The winter solstice is tomorrow, albeit sometime past midnight (how blurry these days and nights are becoming!). It is, of course, the day of the year in which night hours surpass daylight hours by the greatest margin. Note what this has to do with the suicides and a rise in psychic disorder. Recalling Thoss's list of documented suicides in his article, there seemed to be a recurrence of specific family names, as there very likely might be for any kind of data collected in a small town. Among these names was a Beadle or two. Perhaps, then, there is a geneological basis for the suicides which has nothing to do with Thoss's mystical subclimate, which is a colorful idea to be sure and one that seems fitting for this town of various outward and inward aspects, but is not a conception that can be substantiated.

One thing that seems certain, however, is the division of Mirocaw into two very distinct types of citizenry, resulting in two festivals and the appearance of similar clowns—a term now used in an extremely loose sense. But there is a connection, and I believe I have some idea of what it is. I said before that the normal residents of the town regard those from the ghetto, and especially their clown figures, with superstition. Yet it's more than that: there is fear, perhaps a kind of hatred—the particular kind of hatred resulting from some powerful and irrational memory. What threatens Mirocaw I think I can very well understand. I recall the incident earlier today in that vacant diner. "Vacant" is the appropriate word here, despite its contradiction of fact. The congregation of that half-lit room formed less a presence than an absence, even considering the oppressive number of them. Those eyes that did not or could not focus on anything, the pining lassitude of their faces, the lazy march of their feet. I was spiritually drained when I ran out of there. I then understood why these people and their activities are avoided.

I cannot question the wisdom of those ancestral Mirocavians who began the tradition of the winter festival and gave the town a pretext for celebration and social intercourse at a time when the consequences of brooding isolation are most severe, those longest and darkest days of the solstice. A mood of Christmas joviality obviously would not be sufficient to counter the menace of this season. But even so, there are still the suicides of individuals who are somehow cut off, I imagine, from the vitalizing activities of the festival.

It is the nature of this insidious subseason that seems to determine the outward forms of Mirocaw's winter festival: the optimistic greenery in a period of gray dormancy; the fertile promise of the Winter Queen; and, most interesting to my mind, the clowns. The bright clowns of Mirocaw who are treated so badly; they appear to serve as substitute figures for those dark-eyed mummers of the slums. Since the latter are feared for some power or influence they possess, they may still be symbolically confronted and conquered through their counterparts, who are elected for precisely this function. If I am right about this, I wonder to what extent there is a conscious awareness among the town's populace of this indirect show of aggression. Those three young men I spoke with tonight did not seem to possess much insight beyond seeing that there was a certain amount of robust fun in the festival's tradition. For that matter, how much awareness is there on the *other side* of these two antagonistic festivals? Too horrible to think of such a thing, but I must wonder if, for all their apparent aimlessness, those inhabitants of the ghetto are not the only ones who know what they are about. No denying that behind those inhumanly limp expressions there seems to lie a kind of obnoxious intelligence.

Now I realize the confusion of my present state, but as I wobbled from street to street tonight, watching those oval-mouthed clowns, I could not help feeling that all the merrymaking in Mirocaw was somehow allowed only by their sufferance. This I hope is no more than a fanciful Thossian intuition, the sort of idea that is curious and thought-provoking without ever seeming to gain the benefit of proof. I know my mind is not entirely lucid, but I feel that it may be possible to penetrate Mirocaw's many complexities and illuminate the hidden side of the festival season. In particular I must look for the significance of the other festival. Is it also some kind of fertility celebration? From what I have seen, the tenor of this "celebrating" sub-group is one of *anti*-fertility, if anything. How have they managed to keep from dying out completely over the years? How do they maintain their numbers?

But I was too tired to formulate any more of my sodden speculations. Falling onto my bed, I soon became lost in dreams of streets and faces.

VI

I was, of course, slightly hung over when I woke up late the next morning. The festival was still going strong, and loud blaring music outside roused me from a nightmare. It was a parade. A number of floats proceeded down Townshend, a familiar color predominating. There were theme floats of pilgrims and Indians, cowboys and Indians, and clowns of an orthodox type. In the middle of it all was the Winter Queen herself, freezing atop an icy throne. She waved in all directions. I even imagined she waved up at my dark window.

In the first few groggy moments of wakefulness I had no sympathy with my excitation of the previous night. But I discovered that my former enthusiasm had merely lain dormant, and soon returned with an even greater intensity. Never before had my mind and senses been so active during this usually inert time of year. At home I would have been playing lugubrious old records and looking out the window quite a bit. I was terribly grateful in a completely abstract way for my commitment to a meaningful mania. And I was eager to get to work after I had had some breakfast at the coffee shop.

When I got back to my room I discovered the door was unlocked. And there was something written on the dresser mirror. The writing was red and greasy, as if done with a clown's make-up pencil—my own, I realized. I read the legend, or rather I should say *riddle*, several times: "What buries itself before it is dead?" I looked at it for quite a while, very shaken at how vulnerable my holiday fortifications were. Was this supposed to be a warning of some kind? A threat to the effect that if I persisted in a certain course I would end up prematurely interred? I would have to be careful, I told myself. My

THOMAS LIGOTTI

resolution was to let nothing deter me from the inspired strategy I had conceived for myself. I wiped the mirror clean, for it was now needed for other purposes.

I spent the rest of the day devising a very special costume and the appropriate face to go with it. I easily shabbied up my overcoat with a torn pocket or two and a complete set of stains. Combined with blue jeans and a pair of rather scuffed-up shoes, I had a passable costume for a derelict. The face, however, was more difficult, for I had to experiment from memory. Remembering the screaming pierrot in that painting (*The Scream*, I now recall), helped me quite a bit. At nightfall I exited the hotel by the back stairway.

It was strange to walk down the crowded street in this gruesome disguise. Though I thought I would feel conspicuous, the actual experience was very close, I imagined, to one of complete invisibility. No one looked at me as I strolled by, or as they strolled by, or as we strolled by each other. I was a phantom—perhaps the ghost of festivals past, or those yet to come.

I had no clear idea where my disguise would take me that night, only vague expectations of gaining the confidence of my fellow specters and possibly in some way coming to know their secrets. For a while I would simply wander around in that lackadaisical manner I had learned from them, following their lead in any way they might indicate. And for the most part, this meant doing almost nothing and doing it silently. If I passed one of my kind on the sidewalk there was no speaking, no exchange of knowing looks, no recognition at all that I was aware of. We were there on the streets of Mirocaw to create a presence and nothing more. At least, this is how I came to feel about it. As I drifted along with my bodiless invisibility, I felt myself more and more becoming an empty, floating shape, seeing without being seen and walking without the interference of those grosser creatures who shared my world. It was not an experience completely without interest or even pleasure. The clown's shibboleth of "here we are again" took on a new meaning for me as I felt myself a novitiate of a more rarified order of harlequinry. And very soon the opportunity to make further progress along this path presented itself.

On the other side of the street, going the opposite direction, a pickup truck slowly passed, gently parting a sea of zigging and zagging celebrants. The cargo in the back of this truck was curious, for it was made up entirely of my fellow sectarians. Further down the street the truck stopped and another of them boarded it over the back gate. One block down I saw still another get on. Two blocks down, the truck made a U-turn at an intersection and headed in my direction.

I stood at the curb as I had seen the others do. I was not sure the truck would pick me up, thinking that somehow they knew I was an imposter. The truck did, however, slow down, almost coming to a stop when it reached me. The others were crowded on the floor of the truck bed. Most of them were just staring into nothingness with the usual indifference I had come to expect from their kind. But a few actually glanced at me with some anticipation. For a second I hesitated, not sure I wanted to pursue this ruse any further. At the last moment, some impulse sent me climbing up the back of the truck and squeezing myself in among the others.

There were only a few more to pick up before the truck headed for the outskirts of Mirocaw and beyond. At first I tried to maintain a clear orientation with respect to the town. But as we took turn after turn through the darkness of narrow country roads, I found myself unable to preserve any sense of direction. The majority of the others in the back of the truck exhibited no apparent awareness of their fellow passengers. Guardedly, I looked from face to ghostly face. A few of them spoke in short whispered phrases to others close by. I could not make out what they were saying but the tone of their voices was one of innocent normalcy, as if they were not of the hardened slum-herd of Mirocaw. Perhaps, I thought, these were thrill-seekers who had disguised themselves as I had done, or, more likely, initiates of some kind. Possibly they had received prior instructions at such meetings as I had stumbled onto the day before. It was also likely that among this crew were those very boys I had frightened into a precipitate exit from that old diner.

The truck was now speeding along a fairly open stretch of country, heading toward those higher hills that surrounded the now distant town of Mirocaw. The icy wind whipped around us, and I could not keep myself from trembling with cold. This definitely betrayed me as one of the newcomers among the group, for the two bodies that pressed against mine were rigidly still and even seemed to be radiating a frigidity of their own. I glanced ahead at the darkness into which we were rapidly progressing.

We had left all open country behind us now, and the road was enclosed by thick woods. The mass of bodies in the truck leaned into each other as we began traveling up a steep incline. Above us, at the top of the hill, were lights shining somewhere within the woods. When the road levelled off the truck made an abrupt turn, steering into what I thought was the roadside blackness or a great ditch. There was an unpaved path, however, upon which the truck proceeded toward the glowing in the near distance.

This glowing became brighter and sharper as we approached, flickering upon the trees and revealing stark detail where there had formerly been only smooth darkness. As the truck pulled into a clearing and came to a stop, I saw a loose assembly of figures, many of which held lanterns that beamed with a dazzling and frosty light. I stood up in the back of the truck to unboard as the others were doing. Glancing around from that height I saw approximately thirty more of those cadaverous clowns milling about. One of my fellow passengers spied me lingering in the truck and in a strangely high-pitched whisper told me to hurry, explaining something about the "apex of darkness." I thought again about this solstice night; it was technically the longest period of darkness of the year, even if not by a very significant margin from many other winter nights. Its true significance, though, was related to considerations having little to do with either statistics or the calendar.

I went over to the place where the others were forming into a tighter crowd, and in which there was a sense of expectancy in the subtle gestures and expressions of its individual members. Glances were now exchanged, the hand of one lightly touched the shoulder of another, and a pair of circled eyes gazed over to where two figures were setting their lanterns on the ground about six feet apart. The illumination of these lanterns revealed an opening in the earth. Eventually the awareness of everyone was focused on this roundish pit, and as if by prearranged signal we all began huddling around it. The only sounds were those of the wind and our own movements as we crushed frozen leaves and sticks underfoot.

Finally, when we had all surrounded this gaping hole, the first one jumped in, leaving our sight for a moment but then reappearing to take hold of a lantern which another one handed him from above. The miniature abyss filled with light, and I could see it was no more than six feet deep. Near the base of its inner wall the mouth of a tunnel was carved out. The figure holding the lantern stooped a little and disappeared into the passage.

One by one, then, the members of the crowd leaped into the darkness of this pit, and every fifth one took a lantern. I kept to the back of the group, for whatever subterranean activities were going to take place, I was sure I wanted to be on their periphery. When only about ten of us remained on the ground above, I maneuvered to let four of them precede me so that as the fifth I might receive a lantern. This was exactly how it worked out, for after I had leaped to the bottom of the hole a light was ritually handed down to me. Turning about face, I quickly entered the passageway. At that point I shook so with cold that I was neither curious nor afraid, but only grateful for the shelter.

I entered a long, gently sloping tunnel, just high enough for me to stand upright. It was considerably warmer down there than outside in the cold darkness of the woods. After a few moments I had sufficiently thawed out so that my concerns shifted from those of physical comfort to a sudden and justified preoccupation with my survival. As I walked

I held my lantern close to the sides of the tunnel. They were relatively smooth and even, as if the passage had not been made by manual digging but had been burrowed by something which left behind a clue to its dimensions in the tunnel's size and shape. This delirious idea came to me when I recalled the message that had been left on my bedroom mirror: "What buries itself before it is dead?"

I had to hurry along to keep up with those uncanny spelunkers who preceded me. The lanterns ahead bobbed with every step of their bearers, the lumbering procession seeming less and less real the farther we marched into that snug little tunnel. At some point I noticed the line ahead of me growing shorter. The processioners were emptying out into a cavernous chamber where I, too, soon arrived. This area was about thirty feet in height, its other dimensions approximating those of a large ballroom. Gazing into the distance above made me uncomfortably aware of how far we had descended into the earth. Unlike the smooth sides of the tunnel, the walls of this cavern looked jagged and irregular, as though they had been gnawed at. The earth had been removed, I assumed, either through the tunnel from which we had emerged, or else by way of one of the many other black openings that I saw around the edges of the chamber, for possibly they too led back to the surface.

But the structure of this chamber occupied my mind a great deal less than did its occupants. There to meet us on the floor of the great cavern was what must have been the entire slum population of Mirocaw, and more, all with the same eerily wide-eyed and oval-mouthed faces. They formed a circle around an altar-like object which had some kind of dark, leathery covering draped over it. Upon the altar, another covering of the same material concealed a lumpy form beneath.

And behind this form, looking down upon the altar, was the only figure whose face was not greased with makeup.

He wore a long snowy robe that was the same color as the wispy hair berimming his head. His arms were calmly at his sides. He made no movement. The man I once believed would penetrate great secrets stood before us with the same professorial bearing that had impressed me so many years ago, yet now I felt nothing but dread at the thought of what revelations lay pocketed within the abysmal folds of his magisterial attire. Had I really come here to challenge such a formidable figure? The name by which I knew him seemed itself insufficient to designate one of his stature. Rather I should name him by his other incarnations: god of all wisdom, scribe of all sacred books, father of all magicians, thrice great and more—rather I should call him *Thoth*.

He raised his cupped hands to his congregation and the ceremony was underway.

It was all very simple. The entire assembly, which had remained speechless until this moment, broke out in the most horrendous high-pitched singing that can be imagined. It was a choir of sorrow, of shrieking delirium, and of shame. The cavern rang shrilly with the dissonant, whining chorus. My voice, too, was added to the congregation's, trying to blend with their maimed music. But my singing could not imitate theirs, having a huskiness unlike their cacaphonous keening wail. To keep from exposing myself as an intruder I continued to mouth their words without sound. These words were a revelation of the moody malignancy which until then I had no more than sensed whenever in the presence of these figures. They were singing to the "unborn in paradise," to the "pure unlived lives." They sang a dirge for existence, for all its vital forms and seasons. Their ideals were those of darkness, chaos, and a melancholy half-existence consecrated to all the many shapes of death. A sea of thin, bloodless faces trembled and screamed with perverted hopes. And the robed, guiding figure at the heart of all this—elevated over the course of twenty years to the status of high priest—was the man from whom I had taken so many of my own life's principles. It would be useless to describe what I felt at that moment and a waste of the time I need to describe the events which followed.

The singing abruptly stopped and the towering white-haired figure began to speak. He was welcoming those of the new generation—twenty winters had passed since the "Pure Ones" had expanded their ranks. The word "pure" in this setting was a violence to what sense and composure I still retained, for nothing could have been more foul than what was to come. Thoss—and I employ this defunct identity only as a convenience—closed his sermon and moved back toward the dark-skinned altar. There, with all the flourish of his former life, he drew back the topmost covering. Beneath it was a limp-limbed effigy, a collapsed puppet sprawled upon the slab. I was standing toward the rear of the congregation and attempted to keep as close to the exit passage as I could. Thus, I did not see everything as clearly as I might have.

Thoss looked down over the crooked, doll-like form and then out at the gathering. I even imagined that he made knowing eye-contact with myself. He spread his arms and a stream of continuous and unintelligible words flowed from his moaning mouth. The congregation began to stir, not greatly but perceptibly. Until that moment there was a limit to what I believed was the evil of these people. They were, after all, only that. They were merely morbid, self-tortured souls with strange beliefs. If there was anything I had learned in all my years as an anthropologist it was that the world is infinitely rich in strange ideas, even to the point where the concept of strangeness itself had little meaning for me. But with the scene I then witnessed, my conscience bounded into a realm from which it will never return.

For now was the transformation scene, the culmination of every harlequinade.

It began slowly. There was increasing movement among those on the far side of the chamber from where I stood. Someone had fallen to the floor and the others in the area backed away. The voice at the altar continued its chanting. I tried to gain a better view but there were too many of them around me. Through the mass of obstructing bodies I caught only glimpses of what was taking place.

The one who had swooned to the floor of the chamber seemed to be losing all former shape and proportion. I thought it was a clown's trick. They were clowns, were they not? I myself could make four white balls transform into four black balls as I juggled them. And this was not my most astonishing feat of clownish magic. And is there not always a sleight-of-hand inherent in all ceremonies, often dependent on the transported delusions of the celebrants? This was a good show, I thought, and giggled to myself. The transformation scene of Harlequin throwing off his fool's facade. O God, Harlequin, do not move like that! Harlequin, where are your arms? And your legs have melted together and have begun squirming upon the floor. What horrible, mouthing umbilicus is that where your face should be? *What is it that buries itself before it is dead*? The almighty serpent of wisdom—the Conqueror Worm.

It now started happening all around the chamber. Individual members of the congregation would gaze emptily—caught for a moment in a frozen trance—and then collapse to the floor to begin the sickening metamorphosis. This happened with ever-increasing frequency the louder and more frantic Thoss chanted his insane prayer or curse. Then there began a writhing movement toward the altar, and Thoss welcomed the things as they curled their way to the altar-top. I knew now what lax figure lay upon it.

This was Kora and Persephone, the daughter of Ceres and the Winter Queen: the child abducted into the underworld of death. Except this child had no supernatural mother to save her, no living mother at all. For the sacrifice I witnessed was an echo of one that had occurred twenty years before, the carnival feast of the preceding generation—*O carne vale!* Now both mother and daughter had become victims of this subterranean sabbath. I finally realized this truth when the figure stirred upon the altar, lifted its head of icy beauty, and screamed at the sight of mute mouths closing around her.

I ran from the chamber into the tunnel. (There was nothing else that could be done, I have obsessively told myself.) Some of the others who had not yet changed began to pursue me. They would have caught up to me, I have no doubt, for I fell only a few yards into the passage. And for a moment I imagined that I too was about to undergo a transformation, but I had not been prepared as the others had been. When I heard the approaching footsteps of my pursuers I was sure there was an even worse fate facing me upon the altar. But the footsteps ceased and retreated. They had received an order in the voice of their high priest. I too heard the order, though I wish I had not, for until then I had imagined that Thoss did not remember who I was. It was that voice which taught me otherwise.

For the moment I was free to leave. I struggled to my feet and, having broken my lantern in the fall, retraced my way back through cloacal blackness.

Everything seemed to happen very quickly once I emerged from the tunnel and climbed up from the pit. I wiped the reeking greasepaint from my face as I ran through the woods and back to the road. A passing car stopped, though I gave it no other choice except to run me down.

"Thank you for stopping."

"What the hell are you doing out here?" the driver asked.

I caught my breath. "It was a joke. The festival. Friends thought it would be funny . . . Please drive on."

My ride let me off about a mile out of town, and from there I could find my way. It was the same way I had come into Mirocaw on my first visit the summer before. I stood for a while at the summit of that high hill just outside the city limits, looking down upon the busy little hamlet. The intensity of the festival had not abated, and would not until morning. I walked down toward the welcoming glow of green, slipped through the festivities unnoticed, and returned to the hotel. No one saw me go up to my room. Indeed, there was an atmosphere of absence and abandonment through that building, and the desk in the lobby was unattended.

I locked the door to my room and collapsed upon the bed.

VII

When I awoke the next morning I saw from my window that the town and surrounding countryside had been visited during the night by a snowstorm, one which was entirely unpredicted. The snow was still falling and blowing and gathering on the now deserted streets of Mirocaw. The festival was over. Everyone had gone home.

And this was exactly my own intention. Any action on my part concerning what I had seen the night before would have to wait until I was away from the town. I am still not sure it will do the slightest good to speak up like this. Any accusations I could make against the slum populous of Mirocaw would be resisted, as well they should be, as unbelievable. Perhaps in a very short while none of this will be my concern.

With packed suitcases in both hands I walked up to the front desk to check out. The man behind the desk was not Beadle and he had to fumble around to find my bill.

"Here we are. Everything all right?"

"Fine," I answered. "Is Mr Beadle around?"

"No, I'm afraid he's not back yet. Been out all night looking for his daughter. She's a very popular girl, being the Winter Queen and all that nonsense. Probably find she was at a party somewhere."

A little noise came out of my throat.

I threw my suitcases in the back seat of my car and got behind the wheel. On that morning nothing I could recall seemed real to me. The snow was falling and I watched it through my windshield, slow and silent and entrancing. I started up my car, routinely glancing in my rear view mirror. What I saw there is now vividly framed in my mind, as it was framed in the back window of my car when I turned to verify its reality.

In the middle of the street behind me, standing ankle-deep in snow, was Thoss and another figure. When I looked closely at the other I recognized him as one of the boys whom I surprised in that diner. But he had now taken on a corrupt and listless resemblance to his new family. Both he and Thoss stared at me, making no attempt to forestall my departure. Thoss knew that this was unnecessary.

I had to carry the image of those two dark figures in my mind as I drove back home. But only now has the full weight of my experience descended upon me. So far I have claimed illness in order to avoid my teaching schedule. To face the normal flow of life as I had formerly known it would be impossible. I am now very much under the influence of a season and a climate far colder and more barren than all the winters in human memory. And mentally retracing past events does not seem to have helped; I can feel myself sinking deeper into a velvety white abyss.

At certain times I could almost dissolve entirely into this inner realm of awful purity and emptiness. I remember those invisible moments when in disguise I drifted through the streets of Mirocaw, untouched by the drunken, noisy forms around me: untouchable. But instantly I recoil at this grotesque nostalgia, for I realize what is happening and what I do not want to be true, though Thoss proclaimed it was. I recall his command to those others as I lay helplessly prone in the tunnel. They could have apprehended me, but Thoss, my old master, called them back. His voice echoed throughout that cavern, and it now reverberates within my own psychic chambers of memory.

"He is one of us," it said. "He has *always* been one of us."

It is this voice which now fills my dreams and my days and my long winter nights. I have seen you, Dr Thoss, through the snow outside my window. Soon I will celebrate, alone, that last feast which will kill your words, only to prove how well I have learned their truth.

IAN R. MACLEOD

1/72nd Scale

IAN R. MACLEOD was born in Solihull, West Midlands and after taking a degree in Law at Birmingham Polytechnic, where he met his wife Gillian, he spent ten years working in the Civil Service.

He was nearly thirty by the time he started trying to get a novel published and despite receiving a number of rejection slips, he was truly hooked on writing. Through the wreckage of another couple of novels he began to experiment seriously with shorter fiction. There were more rejection slips, but they started to get more friendly.

"1/72nd Scale" was his first sale, although not, in the way that things inevitably work out, his first story to appear in print. In 1990 he summoned up the courage to quit work and devote more time to writing, with published work appearing in *Interzone, Weird Tales, Isaac Asimov's Science Fiction Magazine, Amazing Stories, Interzone The 5th Anthology* and *Best New SF 5*.

"I remember that I had Ramsey Campbell's story "The Chimney" in the back of my mind as a kind of role model of how you make an every day object gain a life of its own," recalls the author of "1/72nd Scale". Despite its strong horror premise, the story was nominated for a 1990 Nebula Award by the Science Fiction Writers of America.

D AVID MOVED INTO SIMON'S ROOM. Mum and Dad said they were determined not to let it become a shrine: Dad even promised to redecorate it anyhow David wanted. New paint, new curtains, Superman wallpaper, the lot. You have to try to forget the past, Dad said, enveloping him in his arms and the smell of his sweat, things that have been and gone. You're what counts now, Junior, our living son.

On a wet Sunday afternoon (the windows steamed, the air still thick with the fleshy smell of pork, an afternoon for headaches, boredom and family arguments if ever there was one) David took the small stepladder from the garage and lugged it up the stairs to Simon's room. One by one, he peeled Simon's posters from the walls, careful not to tear the corners as he separated them from yellowed Sellotape and blobs of Blutac. He rolled them into neat tubes, each held in place by an elastic band, humming along to Dire Straits on Simon's Sony portable as he did so. He was halfway through taking the dog-fighting aircraft down from the ceiling when Mum came in. The dusty prickly feel of the fragile models set his teeth on edge. They were like big insects.

"And what do you think you're doing?" Mum asked.

David left a Spitfire swinging on its thread and looked down. It was odd seeing her from above, the dark half moons beneath her eyes.

"I'm . . . just . . ."

Dire Straits were playing "Industrial Disease." Mum fussed angrily with the Sony, trying to turn it off. The volume soared. She jerked the plug out and turned to face him through the silence. "What makes you think this thing is yours, David? We can hear it blaring all through the bloody house. Just what do you think you're doing?"

"I'm sorry," he said. A worm of absurd laughter squirmed in his stomach. Here he was perched up on a stepladder, looking down at Mum as though he was seven feet tall. But he didn't climb down: he thought she probably wouldn't get angry with someone perched up on a ladder.

But Mum raged at him. Shouted and shouted and shouted. Her face went white as bone. Dad came up to see what the noise was, his shirt unbuttoned and creased from sleep, the sports pages crumpled in his right hand. He lifted David down from the ladder and said it was alright. This was what they'd agreed, okay?

Mum began to cry. She gave David a salty hug, saying she was sorry. Sorry. My darling. He felt stiff and awkward. His eyes, which had been flooding with tears a moment before, were suddenly as dry as the Sahara. So dry it hurt to blink.

Mum and Dad helped him finish clearing up Simon's models and posters. They smiled a lot and talked in loud, shaky voices. Little sis Victoria came and stood at the door to watch. It was like packing away the decorations after Christmas. Mum wrapped the planes up in tissues and put them carefully in a box. She gave a loud sob that sounded like a burp when she broke one of the propellers.

When they'd finished (just the bare furniture, the bare walls. Growing dark, but no one wanting to put the light on) Dad promised that he'd redecorate the room next weekend, or the weekend after at the latest. He'd have the place better than new. He ruffled David's hair in a big, bearlike gesture and slipped his other arm around Mum's waist. Better than new.

That was a year ago.

The outlines of Simon's posters still shadowed the ivy wallpaper. The ceiling was pinholed where his models had hung. Hard little patches of Humbrol enamel and polystyrene cement cratered the carpet around the desk in the bay window. There was even a faint greasy patch above the bed where Simon used to sit up reading his big boy's books. They, like the model aircraft, now slumbered in the attic. *The Association Football Yearbook, Aircraft of the Desert Campaign, Classic Cars 1945–1960, Tanks and Armoured Vehicles of the World, the Modeller's Handbook* . . . all gathering dust, darkness and spiders.

David still thought of it as Simon's room. He'd even called it that once or twice by accident. No one noticed. David's proper room, the room he'd had before Simon died, the room he still looked into on his way past it to the toilet, had been taken over by Victoria. What had once been his territory, landmarked by the laughing-face crack on the ceiling, the dip in the floorboards where the fireplace had once been, the corner where the sun pasted a bright orange triangle on summer evenings, was engulfed in frilly curtains, Snoopy lampshades and My Little Ponys. Not that Victoria seemed particularly happy with her new, smart bedroom. She would have been more than content to sleep in Simon's old room with his posters curling and yellowing like dry skin and his models gathering dust around her. Little Victoria had idolised Simon; laughed like a mad thing when he dandled her on his knee and tickled her, gazed in wonderment when he told her those clever stories he made up right out of his head.

David started Senior School in the autumn. Archbishop Lacy; the one Simon used to go to. It wasn't as bad as he'd feared, and for a while he even told himself that things were getting better at home as well. Then on a Thursday afternoon as he changed after Games (shower steam and sweat. Cowering in a corner of the changing rooms. Almost ripping his Y-fronts in his hurry to pull them up and hide his winkle) Mr Lewis the gamesmaster came over and handed him a brown window envelope addressed to his parents. David popped it into his blazer pocket and worried all the way home. No one else had got one and he couldn't think of anything he'd done sufficiently well to deserve special mention, although he could think of lots of things he'd done badly. He handed it straight to Mum when he came in, anxious to find out the worst. He waited by her as she stood reading it in the kitchen. The Blue Peter signature tune drifted in from the lounge. She finished and folded it in half, sharpening the crease with her nails. Then in half again. And again, until it was a fat, neat square. David gazed at it in admiration as Mum told him in a matter-of-fact voice that School wanted back the 100-metres swimming trophy that Simon had won the year before. For a moment, David felt a warm wave of relief break over him. Then he looked up and saw Mum's face.

There was a bitter argument between Mum and Dad and the School. In the end—after the local paper had run an article in its middle pages headlined "Heartless Request"—Archbishop Lacy agreed to buy a new trophy and let them keep the old one. It stayed on the fireplace in the lounge, regularly tarnishing and growing bright again as Mum attacked it with Duraglit. The headmaster gave several assembly talks about becoming too attached to possessions and Mr Lewis the gamesmaster made Thursday afternoons Hell for David in the special ways that only a gamesmaster can.

Senior School also meant Homework. As the nights lengthened and the first bangers echoed down the suburban streets David sat working at Simon's desk in the bay window. He always did his best and although he never came much above the middle of the class in any subject, his handwriting was often remarked on for its neatness and readability. He usually left the curtains open and had just the desk light (blue and white wicker shade. Stand of turned mahogany on a wrought-iron base. Good enough to have come from British Home Stores and all Simon's work. All of it) on so that he could see out. The streetlamp flashed through the hairy boughs of the monkey puzzle tree in the front garden. Dot, dot, dash. Dash, dash, dot. He often wondered if it was a message.

Sometimes, way past the time when she should have been asleep, Victoria's door would squeak open and her slippered feet would patter along the landing and half way down the stairs. There she would sit, hugging her knees and watching the TV light flicker through the frosted glass door of the lounge. Cracking open his door quietly and peering down through the top bannisters, David had seen her there. If the lounge door opened she would scamper back up and out of sight into her bedroom faster than a rabbit. Mum and Dad never knew. It was Victoria's secret, and in the little he said to her, David had no desire to prick that bubble. He guessed that she was probably waiting for Simon to return.

Dad came up one evening when David had just finished algebra and was turning to the agricultural revolution. He stood in the doorway, the light from the landing haloing what was left of his hair. A dark figure with one arm hidden, holding something big behind its back. For a wild moment, David felt his scalp prickle with incredible, irrational fear.

"How's Junior?" Dad said.

He ambled through the shadows of the room into the pool of yellow light where David sat.

"All right, thank you," David said. He didn't like being called Junior. No one had ever called him Junior when Simon was alive and he was now the eldest in any case.

"I've got a present for you. Guess what?"

"I don't know." David had discovered long ago that it was dangerous to guess presents. You said the thing you wanted it to be and upset people when you were wrong.

"Close your eyes."

There was a rustle of paper and a thin, scratchy rattle that he couldn't place. But it was eerily familiar.

"Now open them."

David composed his face into a suitable expression of happy surprise and opened his eyes.

It was a big, long box wrapped in squeaky folds of shrinkwrap plastic. An Airfix 1/72nd scale Flying Fortress.

David didn't have to pretend. He was genuinely astonished. Overawed. It was a big model, the biggest in the Airfix 1/72nd series. Simon (who always talked about these things; the steady pattern of triumphs that peppered his life. Each new obstacle mastered and overcome) had been planning to buy one when he'd finished the Lancaster he was working on and had saved up enough money from his paper round. Instead, the Lancaster remained an untidy jumble of plastic, and in one of those vicious conjunctions that are never supposed to happen to people like Simon, he and his bike chanced to share the same patch of tarmac on the High Street at the same moment as a Pickfords lorry turning right out of a service road. The bike had twisted into a half circle around the big wheels. Useless scrap.

"I'd never expected . . . I'd . . ." David opened and closed his mouth in the hope that more words would come out.

Dad put a large hand on his shoulder. "I knew you'd be pleased. I've got you all the paints it lists on the side of the box, the glue." Little tins pattered out onto the desk, each with a coloured lid. There were three silver. David could see from the picture on the side of the box that he was going to need a lot of silver. "And look at this." Dad flashed a craft knife close to his face. "Isn't that dinky? You'll have to promise to be careful, though."

"I promise."

"Take your time with it, Junior. I can't wait to see it finished." The big hand squeezed his shoulder, then let go. "Don't allow it to get in the way of your homework."

"Thanks, Dad. I won't."

"Don't I get a kiss?"

David gave him a kiss.

"Well, I'll leave you to it. I'll give you any help you want. Don't you think you should have the big light on? You'll strain your eyes."

"I'm fine."

Dad hovered by him for a moment, his lips moving and a vague look in his eyes as though he was searching for the words of a song. Then he grunted and left the bedroom.

David stared at the box. He didn't know much about models, but he knew that the Flying Fortress was The Big One. Even Simon had been working up to it in stages. The Everest of models in every sense. Size. Cost. Difficulty. The guns swivelled. The bomb bay doors opened. The vast and complex undercarriage went up and down. From the heights of such an achievement one could gaze serenely down at the whole landscape of childhood. David slid the box back into its large paper bag along with the paints and the glue and the knife. He put it down on the carpet and tried to concentrate on the agricultural revolution. The crumpled paper at the top of the bag made creepy crackling noises. He got up, put it in the bottom of his wardrobe and closed the door.

"How are you getting on with the model?" Dad asked him at tea two days later.

David nearly choked on a fish finger. He forced it down, the dry breadcrumbs sandpapering his throat. "I, I er—" He hadn't given the model any thought at all (just dreams and a chill of unease. A dark mountain to climb) since he'd put it away in the wardrobe. "I'm taking it slowly," he said. "I want to make sure I get it right."

Mum and Dad and Victoria returned to munching their food, satisfied for the time being.

After tea, David clicked his bedroom door shut and took the model out from the wardrobe. The paper bag crackled excitedly in his hands. He turned on Simon's light and sat down at the desk. Then he emptied the bag and bunched it into a tight ball, stuffing it firmly down into the wastepaper bin beside the chair. He lined the paints up next to the window. Duck egg green. Matt black. Silver. Silver. Silver . . . a neat row of squat little soldiers.

David took the craft knife and slit open the shining shrinkwrap covering. It rippled and squealed as he skinned it from the box. Then he worked the cardboard lid off. A clean, sweet smell wafted into his face. Like a new car (a hospital waiting room. The sudden taste of metal in your mouth as Mum's heirloom Spode tumbles towards the fireplace tiles) or the inside of a camera case. A clear plastic bag filled the box beneath a heavy wad of instructions. To open it he had to ease out the whole grey chittering weight of the model and cut open the seal, then carefully tease the innards out, terrified that he might lose a piece in doing so. When he'd finished, the unassembled Flying Fortress jutted out from the box like a huge pile of jack-straws. It took him another thirty minutes to get them to lie flat enough to close the lid. Somehow, it was very important that he closed the lid.

So far, so good. David unfolded the instructions. They got bigger and bigger, opening out into a vast sheet covered with dense type and arrows and numbers and line drawings. But he was determined not to be put off. Absolutely determined. He could see himself in just a few weeks' time, walking slowly down the stairs with the great silver bird cradled carefully in his arms. Every detail correct. The paintwork perfect. Mum and Dad and Victoria will look up as he enters the bright warm lounge. And soon there is joy on their faces. The Flying Fortress is marvellous, a miracle (even Simon couldn't have done better), a work of art. There is laughter and wonder like Christmas firelight as David demonstrates how the guns swivel, how the undercarriage goes up and down. And although there is no need to say it, everyone understands that this is the turning point. The sun will shine again, the rain will be warm and sweet, clear white snow will powder the winter and Simon will be just a sad memory, a glint of tears in their happy, smiling eyes.

The preface to the instructions helpfully suggested that it was best to paint the small parts before they were assembled. Never one to ignore sensible advice, David reopened the box and lifted out the grey clusters of plastic. Like coathangers, they had an implacable tendency to hook themselves onto each other. Every part was attached to one of the trees of thin plastic around which the model was moulded. The big pieces such as the sides of the aircraft and the wings were easy to recognise, but there were also a vast number of odd shapes that had no obvious purpose. Then, as his eyes searched along rows of thin bits, fat bits, star shaped bits and bits that might be parts of bombs, he saw a row of little grey men hanging from the plastic tree by their heads.

The first of the men was crouching in an oddly foetal position. When David pulled him off the plastic tree, his neck snapped instead of the join at the top of his head.

David spent the evenings and most of the weekends of the next month at work on the Flying Fortress.

"Junior," Dad said one day as he met him coming up the stairs, "you're getting so absorbed in that model of yours. I saw your light on last night when I went to bed. Just you be careful it doesn't get in the way of your homework."

"I won't let that happen," David answered, putting on his good-boy smile. "I won't get too absorbed."

But David was absorbed in the model, and the model was absorbed into him. It absorbed him to the exclusion of everything else. He could feel it working its way into his system. Lumps of glue and plastic, sticky sweet-smelling silver enamel worming into his flesh. Crusts of it were under his nails, sticking in his hair and to his teeth, his thoughts. Homework—which had been a worry to him—no longer mattered. He simply didn't do it. At the end-of-lesson bells he packed the exercise books into his satchel, and a week later he would take them out again for the next session, pristine and unchanged. Nobody actually took much notice. There was, he discovered, a group of boys and girls in his class who never did their homework—they just didn't do it. More amazing still, they weren't bothered about it and neither were the teachers. He began to sit at the back of the class with the cluster of paper-pellet flickers, boys who said Fuck, and lunchtime smokers. They made reluctant room for him, wrinkling their noses in suspicion at their new, paint-smelling, hollow-eyed colleague. As far as David was concerned, the arrangement was purely temporary. Once the model was finished he'd work his way back up the class, no problem.

The model absorbed David. David absorbed the model. He made mistakes. He learned from his mistakes and made other mistakes instead. In his hurry to learn from those mistakes he repeated the original ones. It took him aching hours of frustration and eye strain to paint the detailed small parts of the model. The Humbrol enamel would never quite go where he wanted it to, but unfailingly ended up all over his hands. His fingerprints began to mark the model, the desk and the surrounding area like the evidence of a crime. And everything was so tiny. As he squinted down into the yellow pool of light cast by Simon's neat lamp, the paintbrush trembling in one hand and a tiny piece of motor sticking to the fingers of the other, he could feel the minute, tickly itchiness of it drilling through the breathless silence into his brain. But he persevered. The pieces came and went; turning from grey to blotched and runny combinations of enamel. He arranged them on sheets of the *Daily Mirror* on the right-hand corner of his desk, peeling them off his fingers like half-sucked Murraymints. A week later the paint was still tacky: he hadn't stirred the pots properly.

The nights grew colder and longer. The monkey puzzle tree whispered in the wind. David found it difficult to keep warm in Simon's bed. After shivering wakefully into the grey small hours, he would often have to scramble out from the clinging cold sheets to go for a pee. Once, weary and fumbling with the cord of his pyjamas, he glanced down from the landing and saw Victoria sitting on the stairs. He tiptoed down to her, careful not to make the stairs creak and wake Mum and Dad.

"What's the matter?" he whispered.

Little Victoria turned to him, her face as expressionless as a doll's. "You're not Simon," she hissed. Then she pushed past him as she scampered back up to bed.

On Bonfire Night, David stood beneath a dripping umbrella as Dad struggled to light a Roman candle in a makeshift shelter of paving stones. Tomorrow, he decided, I will start to glue some bits together. Painting the rest of the details can wait. The firework flared briefly through the wet darkness, spraying silver fire and soot across the paving slab. Victoria squealed with fear and chewed her mitten. The after-image stayed in David's eyes. Silver, almost aeroplane-shaped.

The first thing David discovered about polystyrene cement was that it came out very quickly when the nozzle was pricked with a pin. The second was that it had a remarkable ability to melt plastic. He was almost in tears by the end of his first evening of attempted construction. There was a mushy crater in the middle of the left tailplane and grey smears of plastic all along the side of the motor housing he'd been trying to join. It was disgusting. Grey runners of plastic were dripping from his hands and he could feel the reek of the glue bringing a crushing headache down on him.

"Getting on alright?" Dad asked, poking his head around the door.

David nearly jumped out of his skin. He desperately clawed unmade bits of the model over to cover up the mess as Dad crossed the room to peer over his shoulder and mutter approvingly for a few seconds. When he'd gone, David discovered that the new pieces were now also sticky with glue and melting plastic.

David struggled on. He didn't like the Flying Fortress and would have happily thrown it away, but the thought of Mum and Dad's disappointment—even little Victoria screwing her face up in contempt — was now as vivid as his imagined triumph had been before. Simon never gave up on things. Simon always (David would show them) did everything right. But by now the very touch of the model, the tiny bumps of the rivets, the rough little edges where the moulding had seeped out, made his flesh crawl. And for no particular reason (a dream too bad to remember) the thought came to him that maybe even real Flying Fortresses (crammed into the rear gunner's turret like a corpse in a coffin. Kamikaze Zero Zens streaming out of the sky. Flames everywhere and the thick stink of burning. Boiling grey plastic pouring like treacle over his hands, his arms, his shoulders, his face. His mouth. Choking, screaming. Choking) weren't such wonderful things after all.

Compared with constructing the model, the painting— although a disaster—had been easy. Night after night, he struggled with meaningless bits of tiny plastic. And a grey voice whispered in his ear that Simon would have finished it now. Yes siree. And it would have been perfect. David was under no illusions now as to how difficult the model was to construct (those glib instructions to fit this part to that part that actually entailed hours of messy struggle. The suspicious fact that Airfix had chosen to use a painting of a real Flying Fortress on the box rather than a photograph of the finished model) but he knew that if anyone could finish it, Simon could. Simon could always do anything. Even dead, he amounted to more than David.

In mid November, David had a particularly difficult Thursday at Games. Mr Lewis wasn't like the other teachers. He didn't ignore little boys who kept quiet and didn't do much. As he was always telling them, he *Cared*. Because David hadn't paid much attention the week before, he'd brought along his rugger kit instead of his gym kit. He was the only boy dressed in green amid all the whites. Mr Lewis spotted him easily. While the rest of the class watched, laughing and hooting, David had to climb the ropes. Mr Lewis gave him a bruising push to get started. His muscles burning, his chest heaving with tears and exertion, David managed to climb a foot. Then he slid back. With an affable, aching clout, Mr Lewis shoved him up again. More quickly this time, David slid back, scouring his hands, arms and the inside of his legs red raw. Mr Lewis spun the rope; the climbing bars, the mat covered parquet floor, the horse and the tall windows looking out on the wet playground all swirled dizzily. He spun the rope the other way. Just as David was starting to wonder whether he could keep his dinner of liver, soggy chips and apple snow down for much longer, Mr Lewis stopped the rope again, embracing David in a sweaty hug. His face was close enough for David to count the big black pores on his nose—if he'd had a few hours to spare.

"A real softy, you are," Mr Lewis whispered. "Not like your brother at all. Now he was a proper lad." And then he let go.

David dropped to the floor, badly bruising his knees.

As he limped up the stairs that evening, the smell of glue, paint and plastic—which had been a permanent fixture in the bedroom for some time—poured down from the landing to greet him. It curled around his face like a caressing hand, fingering down his throat and into his nose. And there was nothing remotely like a Flying Fortress on Simon's old desk. But David had had enough. Tonight, he was determined to sort things out. Okay, he'd made a few mistakes, but they could be covered up, repaired, filled in. No one else would notice and the Flying Fortress would look (David, we knew you'd do a good job but we'd never imagined anything this splendid. We must ring Granny, tell the local press) just as a 1/72nd scale top-of-the-range Airfix model should.

David sat down at the desk. The branches of the monkey puzzle tree outside slithered and shivered in the rain. He stared at his yellow-lit reflection in the glass. The image of the rest of the room was dim, like something from the past. Simon's room. David had put up one or two things of his own now: a silver seagull mobile, a big Airlines of the World poster that he'd got by sending off ten Ski yoghurt foils; but, like cats in a new home, they'd never settled in.

David drew the curtains shut. He clicked the PLAY button on Simon's Sony portable and Dire Straits came out. He didn't think much of the music one way or another but it was nice to have a safe, predictable noise going on in the background. Simon's Sony was a special one that played one side of a cassette and then the other as often as you liked without having to turn it over. David remembered the trouble Simon had gone to to get the right machine at the right price, the pride with which he'd demonstrated the features to Mum and Dad, as though he'd invented them all himself. David had never felt that way about anything.

David clenched his eyes shut, praying that Simon's clever fingers and calm confidence would briefly touch him, that Simon would peek over his shoulder and offer some help. But the thought went astray. He sensed Simon standing at his shoulder alright, but it was Simon as he would be now after a year under the soil, his body still twisted like the frame of his bike, mossy black flesh sliding from his bones. David shuddered and opened his eyes to the grey plastic mess that was supposed to be a Flying Fortress. He forced himself to look over his shoulder. The room was smugly quiet.

Although there was still much to do, David had finished with planning and detail. He grabbed the obvious big parts of the plane that the interminable instructions (slot parts A, B, and C of the rear side bulkhead together, ensuring that the *upper* inside brace of the support joint fits into dovetail iv as illustrated) never got around to mentioning and began to push them together, squeezing out gouts of glue. Dire Straits droned on, "Love Over Gold," "It Never Rains," then back to the start of the tape. The faint hum of the TV came up through the floorboards. Key bits of plastic snapped and melted in his hands. David ignored them. At his back, the shadows of Simon's room fluttered in disapproval.

At last, David had something that bore some similarity to a plane. He turned its sticky weight in his hands and a great bird shadow flew across the ceiling behind him. One of the wings drooped down, there was a wide split down the middle of the body, smears of glue and paint were everywhere. It was, he knew, a sorry mess. He covered it over with an old sheet in case Mum and Dad should see it in the morning, then went to bed.

Darkness. Dad snoring faintly next door. The outline of Simon's body still there on the mattress beneath his back. David's heart pounded loudly enough to make the springs creak. The room and the Airfix-laden air pulsed in sympathy. It muttered and whispered (no sleep for you my boy. Nice and restless for you all night when everyone's tucked up warm and you're the only wide-awake person in the whole grey universe) but grew silent whenever he lay especially still and dared it to make a noise. The street light filtered though the monkey puzzle tree and the curtains on to Simon's desk. The sheet covering the model looked like a face. Simon's face. As it would be now.

David slept. He dreamed. The dreams were worse than waking.

When he opened his eyes to Friday morning, clawing up out of a nightmare into the plastic-scented room, Simon's decayed face still yawned lopsidedly at him, clear and unashamed in the grey wash of the winter dawn. He couldn't face touching the sheet, let alone taking it off and looking at the mess underneath. Shivering in his pyjamas, he found a biro in a drawer and used it to poke the yellowed cotton folds until they formed an innocuous shape.

It didn't feel like a Friday at school. The usual sense of sunny relief, the thought of two whole days of freedom, had drained away. His eyes sore from lack of sleep and the skin on his hands flaky with glue, David drifted through Maths and Art followed by French in the afternoon. At the start of Social Studies, the final lesson of the week, he sat down on a drawing pin that had been placed on his chair: now that Mr Lewis had singled him out, the naughty boys he shared the back of the class with were beginning to think of him as fair game. Amid the sniggers and guffaws, David pulled the pin out of his bottom uncomplainingly. He had other things on his mind. He was, in fact, a little less miserable about the Flying Fortress than he had been that morning. It probably wasn't as bad as he remembered (could anything really be that bad?) and if he continued tonight, working slowly, using silver paint freely to cover up the bad bits, there might still be a possibility that it would look reasonable. Maybe he could even hang it from the ceiling before anyone got a chance to take a close look. As he walked home through the wet mist, he kept telling himself that it would (please, please, O please God) be alright.

He peeled back the sheet, tugging it off the sticky bits. It was like taking a bandage from a scabby wound. The model looked dreadful. He whimpered and stepped back. He was sure it hadn't been that bad the night before. The wings and the body had sagged and the plastic had a bubbly, pimply look in places as though something was trying to erupt from underneath. Hurriedly, he snatched the sheet up again and threw it over, then ran downstairs into the lounge.

Mum glanced up from *The Price Is Right*. "You're a stranger down here," she said absently. "I thought you were still busy with that thing of yours."

"It's almost finished," David said to his own amazement as he flopped down, breathless, on the sofa.

Mum nodded slowly and turned back to the TV. She watched TV a lot these days. David had occasionally wandered in and found her staring at pages from Ceefax.

David sat in a daze, letting programme after programme go (as Simon used to say) in one eye and out of the other. He had no desire to go back upstairs to his (Simon's) bedroom, but when the credits rolled on *News at Ten* and Dad smiled at the screen and suggested it was time that Juniors were up in bed, he got up without argument. There was something less than affable about Dad's affable suggestions recently. As though if you didn't hop to it he might (slam your head against the wall until your bones stuck out through your face) grow angry.

After he'd found the courage to turn off the bedside light, David lay with his arms stiffly at his sides, his eyes wide open. Even in the darkness, he could see the pin marks on the ceiling where Simon had hung his planes. They were like tiny black stars. He heard Mum go up to bed, her nervous breathing as she climbed the stairs. He heard the whine of the TV as the channel closed, Dad clearing his throat before he turned it off, the sound of the toilet, the bedroom door closing. Then silence.

Silence. Like the taut skin of a drum. Dark pinprick stars on the grainy white ceiling like a negative of the real sky, as though the whole world had twisted itself inside out around David and he was now in a place where up was down, black was white and people slithered in the cracks beneath the pavement. Silence. He really missed last night's whispering voices. Expectant silence. Silence that screamed Something Is Going To Happen.

Something did. Quite matter-of-factly, as though it was as ordinary as the kettle in the kitchen switching itself off when it came to the boil or the traffic lights changing to red on the High Street, the sheet began to slide off the Flying Fortress. Simon's face briefly stretched into the folds, then vanished as the whole sheet flopped to the floor. The Fortress sat still for a moment, outlined in the light of the street lamp through the curtains. Then it began to crawl across the desk, dragging itself on its wings like a wounded beetle.

David didn't really believe that this could be happening. But as it moved it even made the sort of scratchy squeaky noises that a living model of a Flying Fortress might be expected to make. It paused at the edge of the desk, facing the window; it seemed to be wondering what to do next. As though, David thought with giggly hilarity, it hasn't done quite enough already. But the Fortress was far from finished. With a jerky, insectile movement, it launched itself towards the window. The curtain sagged and the glass went bump. Fluttering its wings like a huge moth, it clung on and started to climb up towards the curtain rail. Half way up, it paused again. It made a chittering sound and a ripple of movement passed along its back, a little shiver of pleasure: alive at last. And David knew it sensed something else alive in the room. Him. The Fortress launched itself from the curtains, setting the street light shivering across the empty desk and, more like a huge moth than ever, began to flutter around the room, bumping blindly into the ceiling and walls. Involuntarily, he covered his face with his hands. Through the cracks between his fingers he saw the grey flitter of its movement. He heard the shriek of soft, fleshy plastic. He felt the panicky breath of its wings. Just as he was starting to think it couldn't get any worse, the Fortress settled on his face. He felt the wings embracing him, the tail curling into his neck, thin grey claws scrabbling between his fingers, hungry to get at the liquid of his eyes and the soft flesh inside his cheeks.

David began to scream. The fingers grew more persistent, pulling at his hands with a strength he couldn't resist.

"David! What's the matter with you!"

The big light was on. Dad's face hovered above him. Mum stood at the bottom of the bed, her thin white hands tying and untying in knots.

". . ." He was lost for words, shaking with embarrassment and relief.

Mum and Dad stayed with him for a few minutes, their faces drawn and puzzled. Simon never pulled this sort of trick. Mum's hands knotted. Dad's made fists. Victoria's white face peered around the door when they weren't looking, then vanished again, quick as a ghost. All David could say was that he'd had a bad dream. He glanced across the desk through the bland yellow light. The Fortress was covered by its sheet again. Simon's rotting face grinned at him from the folds. You can't catch me out that easily, the grin said.

Mum and Dad switched off the big light when they left the room. They shuffled back down the landing. As soon as he heard their bedroom door clunk shut, David shot out of bed and clicked his light on again. He left it blazing all night as he sat on the side of the bed, staring at the cloth-covered model. It didn't move. The thin scratches on the backs of his hands were the only sign that anything had happened at all.

As David stared into his bowl of Rice Krispies at breakfast, their snap and crackle and pop fast fading into the sugary milk, Mum announced that she and Dad and Victoria were going to see Gran that afternoon for tea; did he want to come along? David said No. An idea had been growing in his mind, nurtured through the long hours of the night: with the afternoon free to himself, the idea became a fully fledged plan.

Saying he was off to the library, David went down to the Post Office on the High Street before it closed at lunchtime. The clouds were dark and low and the streets were damp. After waiting an age behind a shopkeeper with bags of ten-pence bits to change, he presented the fat lady behind the glass screen with his savings book and asked to withdraw everything but the one pound needed to keep the account open.

"That's a whole eleven pounds fifty-two pence," she said to him. "Have we been saving up for something special?"

"Oh, yes," David said, dragging his good-boy smile out from the wardrobe and giving it a dust-down for the occasion.

"A nice new toy? I know what you lads are like, all guns and armour."

"It's, um, a surprise."

The lady humphed, disappointed that he wouldn't tell her what it was. She took out a handful of dry roasted nuts from a drawer beneath the counter and popped them into her mouth, licking the salt off her fingers before counting out his money.

Back at home, David returned the savings book to the desk (his hands shaking in his hurry to get back out of the room, his eyes desperately focussed away from the cloth-covered model on the top) but kept the two five-pound notes and the change crinkling against his leg in the front pocket of his jeans. He just hoped that Dad wouldn't have one of his occasional surges of interest in his finances and ask to see the savings book. He'd thought that he might say something about helping out a poor schoolfriend who needed a loan for a new pair of shoes, but the idea sounded unconvincing even as he rehearsed it in his mind.

Fish fingers again for lunch. David wasn't hungry and slipped a few across the plastic tablecloth to Victoria when Mum and Dad weren't looking. Victoria could eat fish fingers until they came out of her ears. When she was really full up she sometimes even tried to poke a few in there to demonstrate that no more would fit.

Afterwards, David sat in the lounge and pretended to watch *Grandstand* while Mum and Dad and Victoria banged around upstairs and changed into their best clothes. He was tired and tense, feeling rather like the anguished ladies at the start of the headache-tablet adverts, but underneath there was a kind of exhilaration. After all that had happened, he was still determined to put up a fight. Finally, just as the runners and riders for the two o'clock Holsten Pils Handicap at rainswept Wetherby were getting ready for the off, Mum and Dad called Bye Bye and slammed the front door.

The doorbell rang a second later.

"Don't forget," Mum said, standing on the doorstep and fiddling with the strap of the black handbag she'd bought for Simon's funeral, "there's some fish fingers left in the freezer for your tea."

"No I won't," David said.

He stood and watched as the Cortina reversed out of the concrete drive and turned off down the estate road through a grey fog of exhaust.

It was a dark, moist afternoon, but the rain that was making the going heavy at Wetherby was still holding off. For once, the fates seemed to be conspiring in his favour. He took the old galvanized bucket from the garage and, grabbing the stiff-bristled outside broom for good measure, set off up the stairs towards Simon's bedroom. The reek of plastic was incredibly strong now—he wondered why no one else in the house hadn't noticed or complained.

The door to Simon's room was shut. Slippery with sweat, David's hand slid uselessly around the knob. Slowly, deliberately, forcing his muscles to work, he wiped his palms on his jeans and tried again. The knob turned. The door opened. The cloth face grinned at him through the stinking air. It was almost a skull now, as though the last of the flesh had been worried away, and the off-white of the sheet gave added realism. David tried not to think of such things. He walked briskly towards the desk, holding the broom out in front of him like a lance. He gave the cloth a push with it, trying to get rid of the face. The model beneath stirred lazily, like a sleeper awakening in a warm bed. More haste, less speed, he told himself. That was what Dad always said. The words became a meaningless jumble as he held the bucket beneath the lip of the desk and prodded the cloth-covered model towards it. More haste, less speed. Plastic screeched on the surface of the desk, leaving a wet grey trail. More waste, less greed. Little aircraft-shaped bumps came and went beneath the cloth. Hasting waste, wasting haste. The model plopped into the bucket; mercifully, the cloth still covered it. It squirmed and gave a plaintive squeak. David dropped the broom, took the bucket in both hands and shot down the stairs.

Out through the back door. Across the damp lawn to the black patch where Dad burnt the garden refuse. David tipped the bucket over quickly, trapping the model like a spider under a glass. He hared back into the house, snatching up a book of matches, a bottle of meths, firelighters and newspapers, then sprinted up the garden again before the model had time to think about getting out.

He lifted up the bucket and tossed it to one side. The cloth slid out over the blackened earth like a watery jelly. The model squirmed from the folds, stretching out its wings. David broke the cap from the meths bottle and tipped out a good pint over cloth and plastic and earth. The model hissed in surprise at the cool touch of the alcohol. He tried to light a match from the book. The thin strips of card crumpled.

The fourth match caught, but puffed out before he could touch it to the cloth. The model's struggles were becoming increasingly agitated. He struck another match. The head flew off. Another. The model started to crawl away from the cloth. Towards him, stretching and contracting like a slug. Shuddering and sick with disgust, David shoved it back with the toe of his trainer. He tried another match, almost dropping the crumpled book to the ground in his hurry. It flared. He forced himself to crouch down—moving slowly to preserve the precious flame—and touch it to the cloth. It went up with a satisfying *whooph*.

David stepped back from the cheery brightness. The cloth soon charred and vanished. The model mewed and twisted. Thick black smoke curled up from the fire. The grey plastic blistered and ran. Bubbles popped on the aircraft's writhing skin. It arched its tail in the heat like a scorpion. The black smoke grew thicker. The nextdoor neighbour, Mrs Bowen, slammed her bedroom window shut with an angry bang. David's eyes streamed as he threw on firelighters and balled-up newspapers for good measure.

The aircraft struggled in the flames, its blackened body rippling in heat and agony. But somehow, its shape remained. Against all the rules of the way things should be, the plastic didn't run into a sticky pool. And, even as the flames began to dwindle around it, the model was clearly still alive. Wounded, shivering with pain. But still alive.

David watched in bitter amazement. As the model had no right to exist in the first place, he supposed he'd been naive to imagine that an ordinary thing like a fire in the garden would be enough to kill it. The last of the flames puttered on the blackened earth. David breathed the raw, sick smell of burnt plastic. The model—which had lost what little resemblance it had ever had to a Flying Fortress and now reminded David more than anything of the dead seagull he once seen rotting on the beach at Blackpool—whimpered faintly and, slowly lifting its blistered and trembling wings, tried to crawl towards him.

He watched for a moment in horror, then jerked into action. The galvanized bucket lay just behind him. He picked it up and plonked it down hard on the model. It squealed: David saw that he'd trapped one of the blackened wings under the rim of the bucket. He lifted it up an inch, kicked the thing under with his trainer, then ran to find something to weigh down the bucket.

With two bricks on top, the model grew silent inside, as though accepting its fate. Maybe it really is dying (why haven't you got the courage to run and get the big spade from the shed like big brave Simon would do in a situation like this? Chop the thing up into tiny bits) he told himself. The very least he hoped for was that it wouldn't dig its way out.

David looked at his watch. Three-thirty. So far, things hadn't gone as well as he'd planned, but there was no time to stand around worrying. He still had a lot to do. He threw the book of matches into the bin, put the meths and the firelighters back where he had found them, hung the broom up in the garage, pulled on his duffle coat, locked up the house, and set off towards the High Street.

The greyness of a dull day was already sliding into the dark of evening. Pacing swiftly along the wet-leafed pavement, David glanced over privet hedges into warmly lit living rooms. Mums and Dads sitting on the sofa together, Big Sis doing her nails in preparation for a night down the pub with her boyfriend, little Jimmy playing with his He-Man doll in front of the fire. Be careful, David thought, seeing those blandly absorbed faces, things can fall apart so easily. Please, be careful.

He took the shortcut across the park where a few weary players chased a muddy white ball through the gloom and came out onto the High Street by the public toilets. Just across the road, the back tyres of the Pickfords lorry had rolled Simon into the next world.

David turned left. Woolworths seemed the best place to start. The High Street was busy. Cars and lorries grumbled between the numerous traffic lights, and streams of people dallied and bumped and pushed in and out of the fluorescent heat of the shops. David was surprised to see that the plate glass windows were already brimming with cardboard Santas and tinsel, but didn't feel the usual thrill of anticipation. Like the Friday-feeling and the Weekend-feeling, the Christmas-feeling seemed to have deserted him. Still, he told himself, there's plenty of time yet. Yes, plenty.

Everything had been switched around in Woolworths. The shelves where the models used to sit between the stick-on soles and the bicycle repair kits were now filled with displays of wine coolers and silk flowers. He eventually found them on a small shelf beside the compact disks, but he could tell almost at a glance that they didn't have any Flying Fortresses. He lifted out the few dusty boxes—a Dukes of Hazzard car, a skeleton, a Tyrannosaurus rex; kid's stuff, not the sort of thing that Simon would ever have bothered himself with—then set out back along the High Street towards W. H. Smiths. They had a better selection, but still no Flying Fortresses. A sign in black and orange suggested IF YOU CAN'T FIND WHAT YOU WANT ON DISPLAY PLEASE ASK AN ASSISTANT, but David was old and wise enough not to take it seriously. He tried the big newsagents across the road, and then Debenhams opposite Safeways where Santa Claus already had a pokey grotto of fairy lights and hardboard and the speakers gave a muffled rendition of Merry Christmas (War is Over). Still no luck. It was quarter to five now. The car lights, traffic lights, street lights and shop windows glimmered along the wet pavement, haloed by the beginnings of a winter fog. People were buttoning up their anoraks, tying their scarves and pulling up their detachable hoods, but David felt sweaty and tired, dodging between prams and slow old ladies and arm-in-arm girls with green punk hair. He was running out of shops. He was running out of time. Everyone was supposed to know about Airfix Flying Fortresses. He didn't imagine that the concerns of childhood penetrated very deeply into the adult world, but there were some things that were universal. You could go into a fish-and-chip shop and the man in the fat stained apron would say yes, he knew exactly what you meant, they just might have one out the back with the blocks of fat and the potatoes. Or so David had thought. A whole High Street without one seemed impossible. Once he'd got the model he would, of course, have to repeat the long and unpleasant task of assembling the thing, but he was sure that he'd make a better go of it a second time. In its latter stages the first model had shown tendencies which even Simon with his far greater experience of model making had probably never experienced. For a moment, he felt panic rising in his throat like sour vomit. The model, trapped under its bucket, squirmed in his mind. He forced the thought down. After all, he'd done his best. Of course, he could always write to Airfix and complain, but he somehow doubted whether they were to blame.

He had two more shops on his mental list and about twenty minutes to reach them. The first, an old-fashioned craft shop had, he discovered, become the new offices of a building society. The second, right up at the far end of the High Street beyond the near-legendary marital aids shop and outside his normal territory, lay in a small and less than successful precinct built as a speculation five years before and still half empty. David ran past the faded *To Let* signs into the square. There was no Christmas rush here. Most of the lights in the fibreglass pseudo-Victorian lamps were broken. In the near darkness a cluster of youths sat drinking Shandy Bass on the concrete wall around the dying poplar at the centre of the square. The few shops that were open looked empty and about to close. The one David was after had a window filled unpromisingly with giant nylon teddies in various shades of green, pink, and orange.

An old woman in a grubby housecoat was mopping the marleytiled floor and the air inside the shop was heavy with the scent of the same cheap disinfectant they used in the school toilets. David glanced around, pulling the air into his lungs in thirsty gulps. The shop was bigger than he'd imagined, but all he could see on display were a few dusty Sindy outfits, a swivel stand of practical jokes and a newish rack of Slime Balls "You Squeeze 'Em And They Ooze"; the fad of the previous summer.

The man standing with his beer belly resting on the counter glanced up from picking the dirt from under his nails. "Looking for something?"

"Um, models, er, please." David gasped. His throat itched, his lungs ached. He wished he could just close his eyes and curl up in a corner somewhere to sleep.

"Upstairs."

David blinked and looked around again. There was indeed a stairway leading up to another floor. He took it, three steps at a time.

A younger man in a leather-tasselled coat sat with his cowboy boots resting up on a glass counter, smoking and reading *Interview With A Vampire*. He looked even less like an assistant than the man downstairs, but David couldn't imagine what else he could be, unless he was one of the non-speaking baddies who hung around at the back of the gang in spaghetti westerns. A faulty fluorescent tube flickered on and off like lightning in the smoky air, shooting out bursts of unpredictable shadow. David walked quickly along the few aisles. Past a row of Transformer robots, their bubble plastic wrapping stuck back into the card with strips of yellowing Sellotape, he came to the model section. At first it didn't look promising, but as he crouched down to check along the rows, he saw a long box poking out from beneath a Revelle Catalina on the bottom shelf. There was an all-too-familiar picture on the side: a Flying Fortress. He pulled it out slowly, half expecting it to disappear in a puff of smoke. But no, it stayed firm and real. An Airfix Flying Fortress, a little more dusty and faded than the one Dad had given him, but the same grey weight of plastic, the same painting on the box, £7.75, glue and paints not included, but then he still had plenty of both. David could feel his relief fading even as he slowly drew the long box from the shelf. After all, he still had to make the thing.

The cowboy behind the counter coughed and lit up a fresh Rothmans from the stub of his old one. David glanced along the aisle. What he saw sent a warm jolt through him that destroyed all sense of tiredness and fatigue. There was a display inside the glass cabinet beneath the crossed cowboy boots. Little plastic men struck poses on a greenish sheet of artexed hardboard that was supposed to look like grass. There were neat little huts, a fuel tender and a few white dashes and red markers to indicate the start of a runway. In the middle of it all, undercarriage down and bomb bay doors open, was a silver Flying Fortress. His mouth dry, David slid the box back onto the shelf and strolled up to take a closer look, hands casually thrust into the itchy woolen pockets of his duffle coat, placing his feet down carefully to control the sudden trembling in his legs. It was finished, complete; it looked nothing like the deformed monstrosity he had tried to destroy. Even at a distance through the none-too-clean glass of the display case, he could make out the intricate details, the bright transfers (something he'd never been able to think about applying to his Fortress) and he could tell just from the look of the gun turrets that they would swivel up, down, sideways, any way you liked.

The cowboy re-crossed his boots and looked up. He raised his eyebrows questioningly.

"I er . . . just looking."

"We close now," he said, and returned to his book.

David backed away down the stairs, his eyes fixed on the completed Fortress until it vanished from sight behind a stack of Fisher-Price baby toys. He took the rest of the stairs slowly, his head spinning. He could buy as many models as he liked, but he was absolutely sure he would never be able to reach the level of perfection on display in that glass case. Maybe Simon could have done it better, but no one else.

David took another step down. His spine jarred; without noticing, he'd reached the ground floor. The man cleaning his nails at the desk had gone. The woman with the mop was working her way behind a pillar. He saw a door marked *PRIVATE* behind a jagged pile of unused shelving. He had an idea; the best he'd had all day.

Moving quickly but carefully so that his trainers didn't squeak, he crossed the shining wet floor, praying that his footsteps wouldn't show. The door had no handle. He pushed it gently with the tips of his fingers. It opened.

There was no light inside. As the door slid closed behind him, he glimpsed a stainless steel sink with a few mugs perched on the draining board, a couple of old chairs and a girlie calendar on the wall. It was a small room; there didn't seem to be space for anything else. Certainly no room to hide if anyone should open the door. David backed his way carefully into one of the chairs. He sat down. A spring boinged gently. He waited.

As he sat in the almost absolute darkness, his tiredness fought with his fear. The woman with the mop shuffled close by outside. She paused for a heart-stopping moment, but then she went on and David heard the clang of the bucket and the whine of the water pipes through the thin walls from a neighbouring room. She came out again, humming a snatch of a familiar but unplaceable tune. Da-de-da de-de-de dum-dum. Stevie Wonder? The Beatles? Wham? David felt his eyelids drooping. His head began to nod.

Footsteps down the stairs. Someone coughing. He wondered if he was back at home. And he wondered why he felt so happy to be there.

He imagined that he was Simon. He could feel the mannish strength inside him, the confident hands that could turn chaotic plastic into perfect machines, the warm, admiring approval of the whole wide world surrounding him like the glowing skin of the boy in the Ready Brek advert.

A man's voice calling goodnight and the clink of keys drew David back from sleep. He opened his eyes and listened. After what might have been ten minutes but seemed like an hour there was still silence. He stood up and felt for the door. He opened it a crack. The lights were still on at the windows but the shop was locked and empty. Quick and easy as a shadow, he made his way up the stairs. The Fortress was waiting for him, clean lines of silvered plastic, intricate and marvellous as a dream. He slid back the glass door of the case (no lock or bolt—he could hardly believe how careless people could be with such treasure) and took it in his hands. It was beautiful. It was perfect, and it lacked any life of its own. He sniffed back tears. That was the best thing of all. It was dead.

It wasn't easy getting the model home. Fumbling his way through the darkness at the back of the shop, he managed to find the fire escape door, but when he leaned on the lever and shoved it open an alarm bell started to clang close above his head. He stood rigid for a moment, drenched in cold shock, then shot out across the loading yard and along the road behind. People stared at him as he pounded the streets on the long, aching run home. The silver Fortress was far too big to hide. That—and the fact that the man in the shop would be bound to remember that he'd been hanging around before closing time—made David sure that he had committed a less than perfect crime. Like Bonnie and Clyde or Butch Cassidy, David guessed it was only a matter of time before the Law caught up with him. But first he would have his moment of glory; perhaps a moment glorious enough to turn around everything that had happened so far.

Arriving home with a bad cramp in his ribs and Mum and Dad and Victoria still out at Gran's, he found that the bucket in the garden still sat undisturbed with two bricks on top. Although he didn't have the courage to lift it up to look, there was nothing to suggest that the old Fortress wasn't sitting quietly (perhaps even dead) underneath. Lying on his bed and blowing at the model's propellers to make them spin, he could already feel the power growing within him. Tomorrow, in the daylight, he knew he'd feel strong enough to get the spade and sort things out properly.

All in all, he decided, the day had gone quite well. Things never happen as you expect, he told himself; they're either far better or far worse. This morning he'd never have believed that he'd have a finished Flying Fortress in his hands by the evening, yet here he was, gazing into the cockpit at the incredible detail of the crew and their tiny controls as a lover would gaze into the eyes of their beloved.

And the best was yet to come. Even as he smiled to himself, the lights of Dad's Cortina swept across the bedroom curtains. The front door opened. David heard Mum's voice saying shush, then Dad's. He smiled again. This was, after all, what he'd been striving for. He had in his hands the proof that he was as good as Simon. The Fortress was the healing miracle that would soothe away the scars of his death. The family would become one. The grey curse would be lifted from the house.

Dad's heavy tread came up the stairs. He went into Victoria's bedroom. After a moment, he stuck his head around David's door.

"Everything alright, Junior?"

"Yes, Dad."

"Try to be quiet. Victoria fell asleep in the car and I've put her straight to bed."

Dad's head vanished. He pulled the door shut. Opening and closing the bomb bay doors, David gazed up at the model. Dad hadn't noticed the Fortress. Odd, that. Still, it probably showed just how special it was.

The TV boomed downstairs. The start of *3–2–1*; David recognised the tune. He got up slowly from his bed. He paused at the door to glance back into the room. No longer Simon's room, he told himself—*His Room*. He crossed the landing and walked down the stairs. Faintly, he heard the sound of Victoria moaning in her sleep. But that was alright. Everything would be alright. The finished model was cradled in his hands. It was like a dream.

He opened the lounge door. The quiz show colours on the TV filled his eyes. Red and silver and gold, bright and warm as Christmas. Mum was sitting in her usual chair wearing her usual TV expression. Dad was stretched out on the sofa.

He looked up at David. "Alright, Junior?"

David held the silver Fortress out towards his father. The fuselage glittered in the TV light. "Look, I've finished the model."

"Let's see." Dad stretched out his hand. David gave it to him. "Sure . . . that's pretty good, Junior. You'll have to save up and buy something more difficult with that money you've got in the Post Office. . . . Here." He handed it back to David.

David took the Fortress. One of the bomb bay doors flipped open. He clicked it back into place.

On the TV Steve and Yvette from Rochdale were telling Ted Rogers a story about their honeymoon. Ted finished it off with a punchline that David didn't understand. The audience roared.

Dad scratched his belly, worming his fingers into the gaps between the buttons of his shirt. "I think your mother wanted a word with you," he said, watching as Steve and Yvette agonised over a question. He raised his voice a little. "Isn't that right, pet? Didn't you want a word with him?"

Mum's face turned slowly from the TV screen.

"Look," David said, taking a step towards her, "I've—"

Mum's head continued turning. Away from David, towards Dad. "I thought you were going to speak to him," she said.

Dad shrugged. "You found them, pet, you tell him . . . and move, Junior. I can't see the programme through you."

David moved.

Mum fumbled in the pocket of her dress. She produced a book of matches. "I found these in the bin," she said, looking straight at him. Through him. David had to suppress a shudder. "What have you been up to?"

"Nothing." David grinned weakly. His good-boy smile wouldn't come.

"You haven't been smoking?"

"No, Mum. I promise."

"Well, as long as you don't." Mum turned back to the TV. Steve and Yvette had failed. Instead of a Mini Metro they had won Dusty Bin. The audience was in raptures. Back after the break, said Ted Rogers.

David stood watching the bright screen. A grey tombstone loomed towards him. This is what happens, a voice said, if you get AIDS.

Dad gave a theatrical groan that turned into a cough. "Those queers make me sick," he said when he'd hawked his throat clear.

Without realising what he was doing, David left the room and went back upstairs to Simon's bedroom.

He left the lights on and re-opened the curtains. The monkey puzzle tree waved at him through the wet darkness; the rain from Wetherby had finally arrived. Each droplet sliding down the glass held a tiny spark of streetlight.

He sat down and plonked the Fortress on the desk in front of him. A propeller blade snapped; he hadn't bothered to put the undercarriage down. He didn't care. He breathed deeply, the air shuddering in his throat like the sound of running past railings. Through the bitter phlegm he could still smell the reek of plastic. Not the faint, tidy smell of the finished Fortress. No, this was the smell that had been with him for weeks. But now it didn't bring sick expectation in his stomach; he no longer felt afraid. Now, in his own way, he had reached the summit of a finished Flying Fortress, a high place from where he could look back at the remains of his childhood. Everything had been out of scale before, but now he saw, he really saw. 1/72nd scale; David knew what it meant now. The Fortress was big, as heavy and grey as the rest of the world. It was him that was tiny, 1/72nd scale.

He looked at the Fortress: big, ugly and silver. The sight of it sickened him more than the old model had ever done. At least that had been his. For all its considerable faults, he had made it.

David stood up. Quietly, he left the room and went down the stairs, past the lounge and the booming TV, into the kitchen. He found the waterproof torch and walked out into the rain.

The bucket still hadn't moved. Holding the torch in the crook of his arm, David removed the two bricks and lifted it up. For a moment, he thought that there was nothing underneath, but then, pointing the torch's rainstreamed light straight down, he saw that the model was still there. As he'd half expected, it had tried to burrow its way out from under the bucket. But it was too weak. All it had succeeded in doing was to cover itself in wet earth.

The model mewed gently and tried to raise itself up towards David.

This time he didn't step back. "Come on," he said. "We're going back inside."

David led the way, levelling the beam of the torch through the rain like a scaled-down searchlight, its yellow oval glistening on the muddy wet grass just ahead. The rain was getting worse; heavy drops rattling on David's skull and plastering his hair down like a wet swimming cap. The model moved slowly, seeming to weaken with every arch of its rotting fuselage. David clenched his jaw and tried to urge it on, pouring his own strength into the wounded creature. Once, he looked up over the roofs of the houses. Above the chimneys and TV aerials cloud-heavy sky seemed to boil. Briefly, he thought he saw shapes form, ghosts swirling on the moaning wind. And the ghosts were not people, but simple inanimate things. Clocks and cars, china and jewelry, toys and trophies all tumbling uselessly through the night. But then he blinked and there was nothing to be seen but the rain, washing his face and filling his eyes like tears.

He was wet through by the time they reached the back door. The concrete step proved too much for the model and David had to stoop and quickly lift it onto the lino inside, trying not to think of the way it felt in his hands.

In the kitchen's fluorescent light, he saw for the first time just how badly injured the creature was. Clumps of earth clung to its sticky, blistered wings and grey plastic oozed from gaping wounds along its fuselage. And the reek of it immediately filled the kitchen, easily overpowering the usual smell of fish fingers. It stank of glue and paint and plastic; but there was more. It also smelt like something dying.

It moved on, dragging its wings, whimpering in agony, growing weaker with every inch. Plainly, the creature was close to the end of its short existence.

"Come on," David whispered, crouching down close beside it. "There's not far to go now. Please try. Please . . . don't die yet."

Seeming to understand, the model made a final effort. David held the kitchen door open as it crawled into the hall, onwards toward the light and sound of the TV through the frosted lounge door.

"You made *that?*" An awed whisper came from half way up the stairs.

David looked up and saw little Victoria peering down at the limping model, her hands gripping the bannister like a prisoner behind bars. He nodded, feeling an odd sense of pride. It was, after all, his. But he knew you could take pride too far. The model belonged to the whole family as well. To Victoria sitting alone at night on the stairs, to Simon turning to mush and bones in his damp coffin—and to Mum and Dad. And that was why it was important to show them. David was old for a child; he knew that grownups were funny like that. If you didn't show them things, they simply didn't believe in them.

"Come on," he said, holding out his hand.

Victoria scampered quickly down the stairs and along the hall, stepping carefully over the model and putting her cold little hand inside his slightly larger one.

The model struggled on, leaving a trail of slimy plastic behind on the carpet. When it reached the lounge door, David turned the handle and the three of them went in together.

KARL EDWARD WAGNER

Cedar Lane

KARL EDWARD WAGNER has won both the British and World Fantasy Awards, and trained as a psychiatrist before becomming a full-time writer and editor.

His first book, *Darkness Weaves With Many Shades*, introduced readers to his offbeat heroic fantasy protagonist Kane, whose exploits he continued through three further novels and two collections.

More recently he has edited twelve volumes of *The Year's Best Horror Stories* (currently being reprinted in multi-edition hardcovers as *Horrorstory*), *Intensive Scare* and three volumes of *Echoes of Valor*.

With artist Kent Williams he has collaborated on a major graphic novel, *Tell Me, Dark*, published by DC Comics, and his new novel *The Fourth Seal* is due from Bantam.

"Cedar Lane" could be called "psychological science fiction", but however you want to describe it, it will leave you with a chill long after you've finished reading it.

Dream is a shadow of something real.
                    —from the Peter Weir film *The Last Wave*

H E WAS BACK AT CEDAR LANE again, in the big house where he had spent his childhood, growing up there until time to go away to college. He was the youngest, and his parents had sold the house then, moving into something smaller and more convenient in a newer and nicer suburban development.

A rite of passage, but for Garrett Larkin it truly reinforced the reality that he could never go home again. Except in dream. And dreams are what the world is made of.

At times it puzzled him that while he nightly dreamed of his boy-hood home on Cedar Lane, he never dreamed about any of the houses he had lived in since.

Sometimes the dreams were scary.

Sometimes more so than others.

It was a big two-story house plus basement, built just before the war, the war in which he was born. It was very solid, faced with thick stones of pink-hued Tennessee marble from the local quarries. There were three dormer windows thrusting out from the roof in front, and Garrett liked to call it the House of the Three Gables because he always thought the Hawthorne book had a neat spooky title. He and his two brothers each had his private hideout in the little dormer rooms—just big enough for shelves, boxes of toys, a tiny desk for making models or working jigsaw puzzles. Homework was not to intrude here, relegated instead to the big desk in Dad's never-used study in the den downstairs.

Cedar Lane was an old country lane laid out probably at the beginning of the previous century along dirt farm roads. Now two narrow lanes of much-repaved blacktop twisted through a narrow gap curtained between rows of massive cedar trees. Garrett's house stood well back upon four acres of lawn, orchards, and vegetable garden—portioned off from farmland as the neighborhood shifted from rural to suburban just before the war.

It had been a wonderful house to grow up in—three boys upstairs and a sissy older sister with her own bedroom downstairs across the hall from Mom and Dad. There were two flights of stairs to run down—the other leading to the cavernous basement where Dad parked the new car and had all his shop tools and gardening equipment, and where dwelt the Molochian coal furnace named Fear and its nether realm, the monster-haunted coal cellar. The yard was bigger than any of his friends had, and until he grew old enough to have to mow the grass and cuss, it was a limitless playground to run and romp with the dogs, for ball games and playing cowboy or soldier, for climbing trees and building secret clubhouses out of boxes and scrap lumber.

Garrett loved the house on Cedar Lane. But he wished that he wouldn't dream about it *every* night. Sometimes he wondered if he might be haunted by the house. His shrink told him it was purely a fantasy-longing for his vanished childhood.

Only it wasn't. Some of the dreams disturbed him. Like the elusive fragrance of autumn leaves burning, and the fragmentary remembrance of carbonizing flesh.

Garrett Larkin was a very successful landscape architect with his own offices and partnership in Chicago. He had kept the same marvelous wife for going on thirty years, was just now putting the youngest of their three wonderful children through Antioch, was looking forward to a comfortable and placid fifth decade of life, and had not slept in his bed at Cedar Lane since he was seventeen.

Garrett Larkin awoke in his bed in the house on Cedar Lane, feeling vaguely troubled. He groped over his head for the black metal cowboy-silhouette wall lamp mounted above his bed. He found the switch, but the lamp refused to come on. He slipped out from beneath the covers, moved through familiar darkness into the bathroom, thumbed the light switch there.

He was filling the drinking glass with water when he noticed that his hands were those of an old man.

An old man's. Not his hands. Nor his the face in the bathroom mirror. Lined with too many years, too many cares. Hair gray and thinning. Nose bulbous and flecked with red blotches. Left eyebrow missing the thin scar from when he'd totaled the Volvo. Hands heavy with calluses from manual labor. No wedding ring. None-too-clean flannel pajamas, loose over a too-thin frame.

He swallowed the water slowly, studying the reflection. It *could* have been him. Just another disturbing dream. He waited for the awakening.

He walked down the hall to his brothers' room. There were two young boys asleep there. Neither one was his brother. They were probably between nine and thirteen years in age, and somehow they minded him of his brothers—long ago, when they were all young together on Cedar Lane.

One of them stirred suddenly and opened his eyes. He looked up at the old man silhouetted by the distant bathroom light. He said sleepily, "What's wrong, Uncle Gary?"

"Nothing. I thought I heard one of you cry out. Go back to sleep now, Josh."

The voice was his, and the response came automatically. Garrett Larkin returned to his room and sat there on the edge of his bed, awaiting daylight.

Daylight came, and with the smell of coffee and frying bacon, and still the dream remained. Larkin found his clothes in the dimness, dragged on the familiar overalls, and made his way downstairs.

The carpet was new and much of the furniture was strange, but it was still the house on Cedar Lane. Only older.

His niece was bustling about the kitchen. She was pushing the limits of thirty and the seams of her housedress, and he had never seen her before in his life.

"Morning, Uncle Gary." She poured coffee into his cup. "Boys up yet?"

Garrett sat down in his chair at the kitchen table, blew cautiously over the coffee. "Dead to the world."

Lucille left the bacon for a moment and went around to the stairway. He could hear her voice echoing up the stairwell. "Dwayne! Josh! Rise and shine! Don't forget to bring down your dirty clothes when you come! Shake a leg now!"

Martin, his niece's husband, joined them in the kitchen, gave his wife a hug, and poured himself a cup of coffee. He stole a slice of bacon. "Morning, Gary. Sleep well?"

"I must have." Garrett stared at his cup.

Martin munched overcrisp bacon. "Need to get those boys working on the leaves after school."

Garrett thought of the smell of burning leaves and remembered the pain of vaporizing skin, and the coffee seared his throat like a rush of boiling blood, and he awoke.

Garrett Larkin gasped at the darkness and sat up in bed. He fumbled behind him for the cowboy-silhouette wall lamp, couldn't find it. Then there was light. A lamp on the night-stand from the opposite side of the king-size bed. His wife was staring at him in concern.

"Gar, are you okay?"

Garrett tried to compose his memory. "It's all right . . . Rachel. Just another bad dream is all."

"Another bad dream? *Yet* another bad dream, you mean. You sure you're telling your shrink about these?"

"He says it's just a nostalgic longing for childhood as I cope with advancing maturity."

"Must have been some happy childhood. Okay if I turn out the light now?"

And he was dreaming again, dreaming of Cedar Lane.

He was safe and snug in his own bed in his own room, burrowed beneath Mom's heirloom quilts against the October chill that penetrated the unheated upper storey. Something pressed hard into his ribs, and he awoke to discover his Boy Scout flashlight was trapped beneath the covers—along with the forbidden E.C. horror comic books he'd been secretly reading after bedtime.

Gary thumbed on the light, turning it about his room. Its beam was sickly yellow because he needed fresh batteries, but it zigzagged reassuringly across the bedroom walls—made familiar by their airplane posters, blotchy paint-by-numbers oil paintings, and (a seasonal addition) cutout Halloween decorations of jack-o'-lanterns and black cats, broom-riding witches, and dancing skeletons. The beam probed into the dormer, picking out the shelved books and treasures, the half-completed B-36 "Flying Cigar" nuclear bomber rising above a desk strewn with plastic parts and tubes of glue.

The flashlight's fading beam shifted to the other side of his room and paused upon the face that looked down upon him from beside his bed. It was a grown-up's face, someone he'd never seen before, ghastly in the yellow light. At first Gary thought it must be one of his brothers in a Halloween mask, and then he knew it was really a demented killer with a butcher knife like he'd read about in the comics, and then the flesh began to peel away in blackened strips from the spotlit face, and bare bone and teeth charred and cracked apart into evaporating dust, and Gary's bladder exploded with a rush of steam.

Larkin muttered and stirred from drunken stupor, groping beneath the layers of tattered plastic for his crotch, thinking he had pissed himself in his sleep. He hadn't, but it really wouldn't have mattered to him if he had. Something was poking him in the ribs, and he retrieved the half-empty bottle of Thunderbird. He took a pull. The wine was warm with the heat of his body, and its fumes trickled up his nose.

Larkin scooted farther into his cardboard box, to where its back propped against the alley wall. It was cold this autumn night—another bad winter, for sure—and he wondered if he maybe ought to crawl out and join the others around the trash fire. He had another gulp of wine, letting it warm his throat and his guts.

When he could afford it, Larkin liked to drink Thunderbird. It was a link to his boyhood. "I learned to drive in my old man's brand-new 1961 Thunderbird," he often told whoever was crouched beside him. "White 1961 Thunderbird with turquoise-blue upholstery. Power everything and fast as shit. Girls back in high school would line up to date me for a ride in that brand-new Thunderbird. I was ass-deep in pussy!"

All of that was a lie, because his father had never trusted him to drive the Thunderbird, and Larkin instead had spent his teenage years burning out three clutches on the family hand-me-down Volkswagen Beetle. But none of that really mattered in the long run, because Larkin had been drafted right after college, and the best part of him never came back from Nam.

V.A. hospitals, treatment centers, halfway houses, too many jails to count. Why bother counting? Nobody else gave a damn. Larkin remembered that he had been dreaming about Cedar Lane again. Not even rotgut wine could kill those memories. Larkin shivered and wondered if he had anything left to eat. There'd been some spoiled produce from a dumpster, but that was gone now.

He decided to try his luck over at the trash fire. Crawling out of his cardboard box, he pocketed his wine bottle and tried to remember if he'd left anything worth stealing. Probably not. He remembered instead how he once had camped out in the huge box from their new refrigerator on Cedar Lane, before the rains melted the cardboard into mush.

There were half a dozen or so of them still up, silhouetted by the blaze flaring from the oil drum on the demolition site. They weren't supposed to be here, but then the site was supposed to have been cleared off two years ago. Larkin shuffled over toward them—an identical blob of tattered refuse at one with the urban wasteland.

"Wuz happnin', bro?" Pointman asked him.

"Too cold to sleep. Had dreams. Had bad dreams."

The black nodded understandingly and used his good arm to poke a stick into the fire. Sparks flew upward and vanished into the night. "About Nam?"

"Worse." Larkin dug out his bottle. "Dreamed I was a kid again. Back home. Cedar Lane."

Pointman took a long swallow and backed the bottle back. "Thought you told me you had a happy childhood."

"I did. As best I can remember." Larkin killed the bottle.

"That's it," Pointman advised. "Sometimes it's best to forget."

"Sometimes I can't remember who I am," Larkin told him.

"Sometimes that's the best thing, too."

Pointman hooked his fingers into an old shipping crate and heaved it into the oil drum. A rat had made a nest inside the packing material and it all went up in a mushroom of bright sparks and thick black smoke.

Larkin listened to their frightened squeals and agonized thrashing. It only lasted for a minute or two. Then he could smell the burning flesh, could hear the soft popping of exploding bodies. And he thought of autumn leaves burning at the curbside, and he remembered the soft popping of his eyeballs exploding.

Gary Blaze sucked in a lungful of crack fumes and fought to hold back a cough. He handed the pipe to Dr Syn and exhaled. "It's like I keep having these dreams about back when I was a kid," he told his drummer. "And a lot of other shit. It gets really heavy some of the time, man."

Dr Syn was the fourth drummer during the two-decades up-and-down career of Gary Blaze and the Craze. He had been with the band just over a year, and he hadn't heard Gary repeat his same old stories quite so many times as had the older survivors. Just now they were on a very hot worldwide tour, and Dr Syn didn't want to go back to playing gigs in bars in Minnesota. He finished what was left of the pipe and said with sympathy, "Heavy shit."

"It's like some of the time I can't remember who I am," Gary Blaze confided, watching a groupie recharge the glass pipe. They had the air conditioner on full blast, and the hotel room felt cold.

"It's just all the years of being on the road," Dr Syn reassured him. He was a tall kid half Gary's age, with the obligatory long blond hair and heavy-metal gear, and getting a big start with a fading rock superstar couldn't hurt his own rising career.

"You know"—Gary swallowed a lude with a vodka chaser— "you know, sometimes I get up onstage, and I can't really remember whether I can play this thing." He patted his vintage Strat. "And I've been playing ever since I bought my first Elvis forty-five."

"*Hound Dog* and *Don't Be Cruel*, back in 1956," Dr Syn reminded him. "You were just a kid growing up in East Tennessee."

"And I keep dreaming about that. About the old family house on Cedar Lane."

Dr Syn helped himself to another hit of Gary's crack. "It's all the years on the road," he coughed. "You keep thinking back to your roots."

"Maybe I ought to go back. Just once. You know—see the old place again. Wonder if it's still there?"

"Make it sort of a bad-rocker-comes-home gig?"

"Shit!" Gary shook his head. "I don't ever want to see the place again."

He inhaled forcefully, dragging the crack fumes deep into his lungs, and he remembered how his chest exploded in a great blast of superheated steam.

Garrett Larkin was dreaming again, dreaming of Cedar Lane.

His mother's voice awoke him, and that wasn't fair, because he knew before he fell asleep that today was Saturday.

"Gary! Rise and shine! Remember, you promised your father you'd have the leaves all raked before you watched that football game! Shake a leg now!"

"All right," he murmured down the stairs, and he whispered a couple swear words to himself. He threw his long legs over the side of his bed, yawned and stretched, struggled into blue jeans and high school sweatshirt, made it into the bathroom to wash up. A teenager's face looked back at him from the mirror. Gary explored a few incipient zits before brushing his teeth and applying fresh Butch Wax to his flattop.

He could smell the sausage frying and the pancakes turning golden-brown as he thumped down the stairs. Mom was in the kitchen, all business in her apron and housedress, already serving up his plate. Gary sat down at the table and chugged his orange juice.

"Your father gets back from Washington tomorrow after church." Mom reminded him. "He'll expect to see that lawn all raked clean."

"I'll get the front finished." Gary poured Karo syrup over each pancake in the stack.

"You said you'd do it all."

"But, Mom! The leaves are still falling down. It's only under those maples where they really need raking." Gary bolted a link of sausage.

"Chew your food," Mom nagged.

But it was a beautiful October morning, with the air cool and crisp, and the sky cloudless blue. His stomach comfortably full, Gary attacked the golden leaves, sweeping them up in swirling bunches with the rattling leafrake. Blackie, his aged white mutt, swayed over to a warm spot in the sun to oversee his work. She soon grew bored and fell asleep.

He started at the base of the pink marble front of the house, pulling leaves from under the shrubs and rolling them in windrows beneath the tall sugar maples and then onto the curb. Traffic was light this morning on Cedar Lane, and cars' occasional whizzing passages sent spirals of leaves briefly skyward from the pile. It was going faster than Gary had expected it to, and he might have time to start on the rest of the yard before lunch.

"There's really no point in this, Blackie," he told his dog. "There's just a lot more to come down."

Blackie thumped her tail in sympathy, and he paused to pat her head. He wondered how many years she had left in her, hoped it wouldn't happen until after he left for college.

Gary applied matches to the long row of leaves at the curbside. In a few minutes the pile was well ablaze, and the sweet smell of burning leaves filled the October day. Gary crossed to the front of the house and hooked up the garden hose to the faucet at the base of the wall, just in case. Already he'd worked up a good sweat, and he paused to drink from the rush of water.

Standing there before the pink marble wall, hose to his mouth, Gary suddenly looked up into the blue sky.

Of course, he never really saw the flash.

There are no cedars now on Cedar Lane, only rows of shattered and blackened stumps. No leaves to rake, only a sodden mush of dead ash. No blue October skies, only the dead gray of a long nuclear winter.

Although the house is only a memory preserved in charcoal, a section of the marble front wall still stands, and fused into the pink stone is the black silhouette of a teenaged boy, looking confidently upward.

The gray wind blows fitfully across the dead wasteland, and the burned-out skeleton of the house on Cedar Lane still mourns the loss of those who loved it and those whom it loved.

Sleep well, Gary Larkin, and dream your dreams. Dream of all the men you might have become, dream of the world that might have been, dream of all the people who might have lived—had there never been that October day in 1962.

In life I could not spare you. In death I will shelter your soul and your dreams for as long as my wall shall stand.

> *What we see.*
> *And what we seem.*
> *Are but a dream.*
> *A dream within a dream.*
> —From the Peter Weir film of Joan Lindsay's novel
> *Picnic at Hanging Rock*

KIM ANTIEAU

At a Window Facing West

KIM ANTIEAU lives in the Pacific Northwest of America and is married to Canadian author Mario Milosevic, whom she met at the 1980 Clarion Writer's Workshop.

Her first story was published in 1983 in *Isaac Asimov's Science Fiction Magazine*. Since then she has appeared in various mainstream, horror, mystery, science fiction and fantasy publications, including *The Clinton Street Quarterly*, *Twilight Zone Magazine*, *The Magazine of Fantasy & Science Fiction*, *Fantasy Book*, *Cemetery Dance*, *Pulphouse*, *Shadows*, *The Year's Best Fantasy Stories*, *The Year's Best Horror Stories*, *Doom City*, *Borderlands II* and *The Ultimate Werewolf*. *Blossoms* was a short story paperback from Pulphouse Publishing.

She has recently written a science fiction novel, *Ruins*, and is at work on another, entitled *Fool's Child*. Meanwhile, *Deere Crossing* is the first volume in a new mystery series.

"At a Window Facing West" is another of those nightmare holiday stories that seem to crop up regularly in *Best New Horror* . . .

"I STILL CAN'T FIND THIS PLACE on the map," Rich said, smoothing out the coffee-stained map across the metal tabletop. "Don't worry about it," Maggie said. She squinted as she looked out across the Gulf of California. A pelican followed the line of waves for a moment before diving into the turquoise water.

"I don't like it here," Rich said. He leaned toward Maggie and Peter and whispered, "They all seem so poor."

Maggie took a sip of beer to keep herself from saying something cruel to Rich. They should never have suggested he come along on this trip. Because Rich could not bear to stray off the beaten path, they had spent over two weeks in tacky tourist towns. He did not trust waiters who could not speak English, and he turned pale at the sight of dirty children.

Peter glanced at Maggie. She put down her glass and squeezed lemon along the rim. She wished they had been able to find limes. Of course, she supposed, they had been lucky to find a restaurant at all. And hotel rooms. She doubted that many tourists came to this place—wherever it was.

"I wish I could do something for all those poor dirty little children," Rich said. He glanced about uncomfortably.

Maggie sighed. Peter shook his head at her.

"Give them money if you think they're so poor," Maggie said. "Or throw a bucket of water over them. That should clean up a few of them."

"Don't be nasty," Peter said.

Rich pushed away from the table. "It must be nice to be so fearless, Maggie." He strode from the table and the restaurant. He stopped at the edge of the dirt road leading back to the village center and looked in either direction. A truck rumbled by and covered him with a cloud of dust.

"I hope he finds his way back to the hotel," Peter said. "He can't help the way he is, Maggie. The divorce has really shaken him."

Two boys ran up to the table. One carried a bucket of dirty water; the other held a squeegee. "Windows! Windows!" they cried together. Good thing Rich was gone, Maggie thought; these kids would scare him to death. Maggie nodded to the boys, and they ran to Peter's blue van and began washing the windows.

"Your brother has always been like this," Maggie said. "My god, he is afraid of everything."

"He's led a sheltered life," Peter said. "Ann Arbor is a long way from Mexico."

Maggie shrugged and leaned back and closed her eyes. The sun felt nice on her face. The sound of water rolling across the sand was soothing. Now this was a vacation. She was going to stay here for a few days no matter what Rich thought.

The boys finished the windows and ran back to the table. Maggie glanced at the van as she pulled coins from the pocket of her jeans. Now the sides of the dusty van were streaked where water had run down from the windows. She gave the money to the boys, and they ran away.

"Rich is trying to be adventurous," Peter said. "He read *People's Guide to Mexico*." Peter grinned, and Maggie laughed.

"All right, all right," Maggie said. "I'll be nice to him."

For dinner, they sat outside the same restaurant at the same table. Inside, the restaurant was crowded and noisy. Music from the jukebox came from the open windows.

"See, Rich, Bruce Springsteen. We're not that far from civilization," Maggie said. Insects buzzed around the lantern on the table. Peter stared at the flame and smiled happily as he consumed several beers. The beach became dark, except for the restaurant lights and several bonfires in the distance. Figures danced in front of the fires, black shadows against gold light.

Rich lifted his bottle of beer in salute. "You were right and I was wrong, Maggie. I am a jerk. I can't help it. A character flaw." He laughed drunkenly. "While you were out protesting the war in college, I was doing my homework. While you were marching against chemical dumps, I was doing taxes for the dumpers. I am a spineless worthless piece of crap." He laughed again.

"I wouldn't go that far," Maggie said. She sipped her beer slowly. It appeared she would be driving them back to the hotel.

"You always fight the good fight," Rich said. "You are always politically correct; I am politically incorrect. You say terrorists, I say freedom fighters. You say freedom fighters, I say guerrillas."

"Don't get her started," Peter said, lifting his head to look away from the lantern. "I don't want to hear any political speeches tonight. I want peace and quiet, beer and pretzels."

"Oh, shut up, both of you," Maggie said. "I'm sitting here trying to enjoy my beer and I'm being attacked on both sides. I stand up for what I believe in, so what?"

Peter waved a hand. "It's too late, Rich. You've started her. She'll talk about which charities she donates to and why, and which ones you shouldn't donate to and why. She can tell you about repressed people everywhere. She's got it all right here." He tapped his head and grinned.

"The helper of the downtrodden! Patron of Mother Earth," Rich said, "we bow down to you." Rich and Peter dropped from their chairs onto the concrete porch and bowed in front of Maggie.

She laughed. "Go away. I'm trying to have a vacation."

196

Giggling, they pulled themselves into their chairs again. They sat quietly for several minutes. Rich drained his beer and then finished Peter's.

"We still don't know where we are," Rich said. The light from the lantern made his eyes red.

"I know where we are," Peter said.

"Mexico is not all that stable, you know," Rich continued, as if not hearing Peter. "People disappear here, too. Americans. United Statesians. Whatever we are. We disappear, too. They want our credit cards."

Maggie laughed. Rich stared angrily at her. "It's all so funny to you."

"They can have my plastic," Maggie said. "It's not really vogue for a political correspondent to carry around such things anyway."

"I think I'm going to be sick," Rich said, covering his mouth.

"Time to go home," Peter said. He stood up and put an arm across Rich's shoulder.

"You take him," Maggie said. "I'm not finished with my beer."

"Come on, Maggie," Peter said. "I've had too much to drink. You can come back after you've dropped us off if you want."

Maggie hesitated, and then she went inside the smoky restaurant to pay the bill. The conversation died for a moment as everyone stared at her. The cash register rang, and the conversations began again. Outside, Rich vomited on the left rear tire of the van.

Maggie sat at the window of their second story hotel room while Peter helped Rich into bed in his room. Their hotel was at the center of the village. Directly across the street, blocking the view of the ocean, was some sort of government building. Between the government building and the hotel was a statue of a man on a rearing horse at the center of a traffic circle. Some Mexican general. Maggie had read the inscription and then promptly forgotten it. Purple and yellow flowers grew at the back feet of the horse. No cars traveled around the circle now. A single light from the government building illuminated the man and the horse. The two boys who had washed the windows of the van sat on a nearby bench counting their money. Maggie wished she could still hear the ocean.

"He's almost asleep," Peter said as he came through the door. "He didn't want to stay alone. He's crying."

"What a baby."

Peter grabbed the doorknob and stared at her. "Sometimes you have absolutely no compassion."

Maggie turned from the window and sat on the bed.

"I wasn't expecting to babysit during our vacation," she said. "I wanted to relax and have fun."

"It hasn't been so terrible," he said. "He just gets afraid. He's never been alone. He was married to Jean right out of high school. He feels as though his entire life is crumbling."

"He shouldn't drink so much," Maggie said. "Though at least when he's drunk he's slightly amusing."

"Don't make fun of him," Peter said.

"I've made you angry," she said. "I'm sorry."

"And don't patronize me! He's known true fear; have you? I don't see you running down to Nicaragua and El Salvador, or Guatemala or any of those places you write about so eloquently. Perhaps you're just as frightened as all of us and you won't admit it. You don't really care about anything, do you? You just stay on the sidelines and write about it and pretend you're fighting the good fight." Peter pulled open the door again. "I'm staying with Rich until he feels better."

"That could be for the rest of his life," Maggie said. She sighed. "I want to explore the beach first thing tomorrow morning."

"Rich wants to leave this place," Peter said.

Maggie chewed her cheek. "Why am I being made out to be the bad guy here? I want a few days of relaxation before I go back to work. I think I've really been very accommodating to your brother."

"Good night, Maggie." Peter left, shutting the door behind him.

Maggie took off her clothes, put on a nightgown, and turned off the light. She slid under the covers. They were staying; she didn't care how Rich felt.

Maggie opened her eyes. For a moment she did not know where she was. The dark room had an unfamiliar smell—kerosene? Peter was not asleep next to her. Someone screamed.

Maggie threw off her covers and ran to the window. Below, at the center of the traffic circle, a woman struggled to get away from two men dressed in uniforms with batons and pistols strapped to their legs. Each held an arm of the woman. They spoke loudly but too rapidly for Maggie to understand. Black hair covered the woman's face as she screamed. She pulled at her hair, and her cries became desperate whimpers.

"Help me," she cried.

Maggie stepped back from the window. Had she heard those words in English or Spanish? She leaned forward slightly. The woman kicked one of the men. He pulled out his baton. He was going to hit her. Maggie covered her mouth; she felt ill. The man dropped the baton. The woman screamed again.

Maggie's heart raced. They would kill the woman if someone did not stop them. The woman had screamed for help and no one had answered. Everyone hid behind closed doors. Everyone.

Maggie had to do something, but she felt frozen in place. The woman went limp, becoming a dead weight in the men's arms. They dragged her past the roaring horse. The woman screamed again, long and loud, a pathetic wail. "Help me," she sobbed. They pulled her toward the government building and out of view of the hotel window. The sound of her cries died, and the night was quiet again. A dog barked in the distance. A seagull mewed.

Maggie stared out the window. She had watched two armed men drag someone away, and she had done nothing to stop them. The helper of the downtrodden. Patron of Mother Earth.

She had watched passively.

She backed away until the edge of the bed touched her thighs. She sat on the bed. Her legs and hands trembled.

What if they came after her next? Or Peter? She listened closely. No unusual sounds. Perhaps Rich had been right all along. Perhaps they were not safe here.

Noiselessly, Maggie packed their clothes. Then she sat on the bed and waited for sunrise.

Peter kissed her cheek, and she opened her eyes. Bright sunshine came through the open window. A warm breeze brought in the smells of the ocean.

"Sorry about last night," Peter said.

Maggie sat up. She was still nauseated.

"Did you hear anything last night?" Maggie asked.

Peter shook his head. "Not a thing. Rich's ready to explore the beach with us this morning. He's even hungry after all that drinking." Peter smiled. "Come to think of it, Rich said he thought he heard something in the night. A scream, maybe. You could ask him. Why?"

Maggie walked slowly to the window until she could just see the place where the woman and men had struggled. The scene flashed before her. She closed her eyes. What if someone had seen her watching, doing nothing? They could report her, arrest her. She breathed deeply. This was all stupid. She was in a foreign country, what could she have done?

"I thought I saw something last night, that's all," Maggie said.

"You've packed." Peter put his hands on Maggie's shoulders. "What's wrong? You look scared to death."

"I had a bad night," she snapped. She shook off his hands. "What did you expect with you in the other room while I was alone in this macho country?"

"You've never been afraid to be alone before."

"I wasn't afraid! Can we drop this?" Was the woman across the street now in that building being tortured? Maggie should go to the police and

report what she saw. She should do something before it was too late.

She shivered. "I want to leave," Maggie said. "I want to go home."

Maggie lay across the back seat while Peter drove. Rich sat next to him looking out the window.

"I hope you're not leaving because of me," Rich said quietly.

"It's time to go home, that's all," Peter answered.

Maggie closed her eyes. She did not want to hear them. Peter the peacemaker. Rich the whiner. She wanted to curl up into a little ball and cry. She could have helped that woman last night, but she hadn't. She knew the woman had been destroyed. Killed, tortured, driven insane, something. All because Maggie had stood there and watched and done absolutely nothing.

She awakened in a sweat, the woman's screams echoing inside her head. She sat up. There was still something she could do to help. She could go back and tell someone what she had seen.

The idea terrified her. "Are we almost to the border?" Maggie asked.

"Soon, Maggie, soon," Peter answered.

Maggie was relieved to be in their familiar apartment again. The pictures on the walls, the carpeting, the television set, the view of the city. She ran her fingers across the kitchen table. She did not even mind that Rich had to stay a few days because his plane was not scheduled to leave until the end of the week.

"I'll make dinner," Rich said, sounding more certain of himself again. "What would you like, Maggie?"

"Sleep," she said. She smiled wearily. "I'm tired. You two stay up and have fun."

Peter turned on the television. Time for the news. Maggie quickly went into the bedroom and closed the door. She rubbed her stomach and went to the bathroom and splashed her face with cold water.

"It's not important," Maggie said as she looked at her reflection. "Whatever happened, happened; end of story." She had never seen fear in her own eyes before. It looked unnatural.

She stripped off her clothes and crawled, naked, under the covers. It would all be better after she slept.

She was in her own bed, but the window looked down upon the statue of the horse and its general. Beneath the statue, the woman lay. The horse shook itself alive and pummeled the prone woman with its hooves. Maggie backed away from the window.

"Maggie, Maggie." Peter's voice was close to her ear. "You were crying out in your sleep. Are you all right?"

Maggie opened her eyes. The room came into focus. She put her arms around Peter and held him tightly.

"Are you ever afraid?" she asked.

He laughed.

"I'm serious," she said, pulling away from him.

"Of course I'm afraid," he said. "Everyone's afraid. It's normal. That's what life is all about. What's wrong with you? You've been acting strange ever since we left Mexico. You hardly said anything in the car."

"I've never been afraid before," Maggie said. "Rich was right. I was fearless."

"Ignorant," Peter said. "You just never really looked at the world." He smoothed a strand of hair off her face. "Dinner's ready." He got up from the bed and left the room.

After a few minutes, Maggie got dressed and followed him out.

She was certain Rich knew what she had done by the way he watched her. He had heard the screams, too, even though he denied it when she asked him. He had done nothing, too. That was part of his character. It was not supposed to be part of hers. She was the fighter. The believer.

Easy to march in protests with all of those people around you, someone had told her once. Easy to believe in peace when no one holds a gun to your head. Who said that? Maggie stared at Rich across the dinner table. He had said it, hadn't he? During one of his drunken lectures in Mexico. Easy to believe when you are not afraid.

Maggie listened to the sounds of Rich and Peter eating, to the refrigerator sighing, to the traffic in the distance. Was the woman still screaming?

She did not want to sleep. She knew she would hear the screams again. She sat in her study at the typewriter. Maybe she could write about what happened to the woman. Make it part of her column. That would vindicate her. The world would know what had happened.

Maggie shook her head and turned off the typewriter. No, she knew nothing about the woman. All she could write about was her own fear and fall from grace.

She went into the darkened living room and curled up on the couch. She switched on the light and sat with her back to the curtained window. She did not want to hear or see anything as she flipped through the pages of *Vegetarian Times*.

Rich and Peter went to Disneyland the following day. Maggie kept the curtains closed and watched soap operas. She scanned the Los Angeles *Times* for any information about a missing woman in Mexico. She found nothing.

She dozed once in the afternoon and woke herself up quickly before the woman could find her. That night, she drank coffee and read magazines at the kitchen table while Peter and Rich slept.

"Maggie, it's four in the morning," Peter said. "Why are you still up? You haven't slept in days." He rubbed his eyes and pulled out a chair and sat next to her.

"I can't," Maggie said.

"Why?"

Maggie bit her lip. Tears streamed down her face.

"I'm afraid," she said.

"Of what?" Peter asked.

"I can't tell you," she said. "You'd hate me. You'd think I was a coward."

He shook his head. "No, I wouldn't. I don't know what's wrong with you, but you've got to stop this. You don't look or sound good. So you're afraid. Don't you know that everyone is afraid? That's what life is, Maggie. Living is going on despite the fear. Rich does that every day. He's terrified, but most of the time he just faces his fears and carries on."

"But I think I may have . . ." She stopped. She could not tell him. She could not explain what she had done because she did not understand it. She had let them take away the woman and she had done nothing to stop them. "Shhh," she said to Peter. "Do you hear that?"

Peter listened silently. "No, I don't hear anything," he finally said.

Maggie started to cry again. "I still hear her screaming."

Maggie waited until Peter and Rich left the apartment for the airport. Then she packed a bag and got into the car and began the drive to Mexico. Peter was right. People had to face their fears. She had to find out what had happened to the woman. Then maybe the screaming would stop.

She drove into the night. She stopped once for coffee. She heard the sounds of the woman's screams, and she quickly returned to the car and started driving again. She cried as she traveled through Mexico; Rich said it was not safe at night. She took a wrong turn and had to double back. Then she was at the village. She stopped the car in front of the police station.

She climbed out of the car. The night was quiet. The air was damp and fishy smelling. She heard the waves stroking the sand. No one screamed.

She walked into the police station. It was a small room. Two officers sat behind desks, their feet up, talking and laughing together. They both stood when she came into the room. Her legs trembled. Her vision blurred. I have to sleep, she thought; I have to eat.

"How may we help you?" one of the men asked, speaking English. She stared at them. They were the men who had taken away the woman. She put out a hand to steady herself. It was the middle of the night and she was alone with the two men who had killed the woman.

Someone screamed. Maggie looked out toward the traffic circle. It was empty.

"May we help you?" the man repeated. A baton and gun were strapped to his leg.

"I—I saw a woman here, three or four days ago," Maggie said. She slowly backed out of the office. "In the middle of the night. You took her away."

The men looked at each other, puzzled. "I am sorry but you must be mistaken," the man said. "We have no woman. Was she a friend of yours?"

The woman screamed again. Maggie put her hands over her ears. This had to stop. She stumbled out of the office.

"You look tired. Are you well?" The officer followed her into the street.

Maggie looked over at the statue. Were the horse's hooves moving? Was there blood staining the metal? I should have helped her, Maggie thought. I could have saved her. Evil flourishes where good people do nothing. Who said that? Maggie ran toward the statue. Edmund Burke? William Shakespeare? The woman screaming in her ear?

The screams were shrill, heartbreaking. Maggie shook her head as she raced toward the statue. She had to get the cries out of her brain. She had to find the woman and save her.

She stood near the horse. The world spun. The horse moved. She opened her mouth and screamed. The police officers were beside her, trying to calm her. "It's all right," they both said in Spanish. "You will be fine." Each of them took an arm. "We will take you to the hospital. You will be fine."

Maggie screamed. Fear overwhelmed her. How could she have lived her entire life without seeing—without realizing how terrifying everything was? "Help me!" she cried. She kicked the police officer. He pulled out his baton and then dropped it. The horse's bloody hooves beat the air. The woman still screamed. Maggie pulled at her hair.

"Help me!" she screamed one more time before the officers dragged her away, out of sight of the hotel window where a woman sat watching.

203

GARRY KILWORTH

Inside the Walled City

ALTHOUGH ONE OR TWO of his earlier stories have been called horror, Garry Kilworth admits he wrote them as fantasy or science fiction, and he has only recently ventured into the horror short fiction field.

Born in York, England, his formative years were spent in South Arabia and he currently lives in Hong Kong. The author's short stories have been published in such magazines and anthologies as *Omni*, *Fantasy & Science Fiction*, *Fantasy Tales*, *Twilight Zone*, *Interzone*, *Isaac Asimov's Science Fiction Magazine*, *Other Edens*, *Beyond the Lands of Never* and the *15th Fontana Book of Great Horror Stories*.

Collections of his own fiction include *The Songbirds of Pain*, *In the Hollow of the Deep-Sea Wave* and *Dark Hills, Hollow Clocks*, while *Hunter's Moon* and *Midnight's Sun* are recent novels.

The following story obviously draws upon the writer's travels, but beneath the rich texture of character and setting lurks a powerful fear and a nasty twist . . .

THEY HAD BEEN LOUD-HAILING the place for days, and it certainly looked empty, but John said you can't knock down a building that size without being absolutely sure that some terrified Chinese child wasn't trapped in one of the myriad of rooms, or that an abandoned old lady wasn't caught in some blocked passageway, unable to find her way out. There must have been elderly people who had set up home in the center of this huge rotten cheese, and around whom the rest of the slum was raised over the years. Such people would have forgotten there *was* an outside world, let alone be able to find their way to it.

"You ready?" he asked me, and I nodded.

It was John Speakman's job, as a Hong Kong Police inspector, to go into the empty shell of the giant slum to make sure everyone was out, so that the demolition could begin. He had a guide of course, and an armed escort of two locally born policemen, and was accompanied by a newspaper reporter—me. I'm a free-lance whose articles appear mainly in the *South China Morning Post*.

You could say the Walled City was many dwellings, as many as seven thousand, but you would be equally right to call it a single structure. It consisted of one solid block of crudely built homes, all fused together. No thought or planning had gone into each tacked-on dwelling, beyond that of providing shelter for a family. The whole building covered the approximate area of a football stadium. There was no quadrangle at its center, nor inner courtyard, no space within the ground it occupied. Every single piece of the ramshackle mass, apart from the occasional fetid airshaft, had been used to build, up to twelve stories high. Beneath the ground, and through every part of this monstrous shanty, ran a warren of tunnels and passageways. Above and within it, there were walkways, ladders, catwalks, streets, and alleys, all welded together as if some junk artist like the man who built the Watts Towers had decided to try his hand at architecture.

Once you got more than ten feet inside, there was no natural light. Those within used to have to send messages to those on the edges to find out if it was day or night, fine or wet. The homemade brick and plaster was apt to rot and crumble in the airless confines inside and had to be constantly patched and shored up. In a land of high temperatures and humidity, fungus grew thick on the walls and in the cracks the rats and cockroaches built their own colonies. The stink was unbelievable. When it was occupied, more than fifty thousand people existed within its walls.

John called his two local cops to his side, and we all slipped into the dark slit in the side of the Walled City, Sang Lau the guide going first. Two *gwailos*—whites—and three Chinese, entering the forbidden place, perhaps for the last time. Even Sang Lau, who knew the building as well as any, seemed anxious to get the job over and done with. The son of an illegal immigrant, he had been raised in this block of hovels, in the muck and darkness of its intestines. His stunted little body was evidence of that fact, and he had only volunteered to show us the way in exchange for a right to Hong Kong citizenship for members of his family still without Hong Kong citizenship. He and his immediate family had taken advantage of the amnesty that had served to empty the city of its inhabitants. They had come out, some of them half-blind through lack of light, some of them sick and crippled from the disease and bad air, and now Sang Lau had been asked to return for one last time. I guessed how he would be feeling: slightly nostalgic (for it was his birthplace), yet wanting to get it over with, so that the many other unsavory remembrances might be razed along with the structure.

The passage inside was narrow, constantly twisting, turning, dipping, and climbing, apparently at random. Its walls ran with slick water and it smelled musty, with pockets of stale-food stink, and worse. I constantly gagged. Then there were writhing coils of hose and cable that tangled our feet if we were not careful: plastic water pipes ran alongside wires that had once carried stolen electricity. When the rotten cables were live and water ran through the leaking hoses, these passageways must have been death traps. Now and again the beam from the lamp in my helmet transfixed a pointed face, with whiskers and small eyes, then the rat would scuttle away, into its own maze of tunnels.

Every so often, we paused at one of the many junctions or shafts, and one of the Chinese policemen, the stocky, square-faced one, would yell through a megaphone. The sound smacked dully into the walls, or echoed along corridors of plasterboard. The atmosphere was leaden, though strangely aware. The massive structure with all its holes, its pits and shafts, was like a beast at the end of its life, waiting for the final breath. It was a shell, but one that had been soaked in the feverish activity of fifty thousand souls. It was once a holy city, but it had been bled, sweated, urinated, and spat on not only by the poor and the destitute, but also by mobsters, hoodlums, renegades, felons, runaways, refugees, and fugitives, until no part of it remained consecrated. It pressed in on us on all sides, as if it wanted to crush us, but lacked the final strength needed to collapse itself. It was a brooding, moody place and terribly alien to a *gwailo* like myself. I could sense spirits clustering in the corners: spirits from a culture that no Westerner has ever fully understood. More than once, as I stumbled along behind the others, I said to myself, *What am I doing here? This is no place for me, in this hole.*

The stocky policeman seemed startled by his own voice, blaring from the megaphone: he visibly twitched every time he had to make his announcement. From his build I guessed his family originally came from the north, from somewhere around the Great Wall. His features and heavy torso were Mongol rather than Cantonese, the southerners having a tendency toward small, delicate statures and moon-shaped faces. He probably made a tough policeman out on the streets, where his build would be of use in knocking heads together, but in here his northern superstitions and obsessive fear of spirits made him a liability. Not for the first time I wondered at John Speakman's judgment in assessing human character.

After about an hour of walking, and sometimes crawling, along tunnels the size of a sewer pipe, John suggested we rest for a while.

I said, "You're not going to eat sandwiches in here, are you?"

It was supposed to be a joke, but I was so tense, it came out quite flat, and John growled, "No, of course not."

We sat cross-legged in a circle, in what used to be an apartment: It was a hardboard box about ten-by-ten feet.

"Where are we?" I asked the torchlit faces. "I mean in relation to the outside." The reply could have been "the bowels of the earth" and I would have believed it. It was gloomy, damp, fetid, and reeked of prawn paste, which has a odor reminiscent of dredged sludge.

Sang Lau replied, "Somewhere near east corner. We move soon, toward middle."

His reply made me uneasy.

"*Somewhere* near? Don't you know exactly?"

John snapped, "Don't be silly, Peter. How can he know *exactly*? The important thing is he knows the way out. This isn't an exercise in specific location."

"Right," I said, giving him a mock salute, and he tipped his peaked cap back on his head, a sure sign he was annoyed. If he'd been standing, I don't doubt his hands would have been on his hips in the classic "*gwailo* giving orders" stance.

John hadn't been altogether happy about taking a "civilian" along, despite the fact that I was a close friend. He had a very poor opinion of those who did not wear a uniform of some kind. According to his philosophy, the human race was split into two: There were the protectors (police, army, medical profession, firemen, et al.) and those who needed protection (the rest of the population). Since I apparently came under the second category, I needed looking after. John was one of those crusty bachelors you find in the last outposts of faded empires: a living reminder of the beginning of the century. Sheena, my wife, called him "the fossil," even to his face. I think they both regarded it as a term of endearment.

However, he said he wanted to do me a favor, since he knew that my job was getting tough. Things were getting tight in the free-lance business, especially since Australia had just woken up to the fact that Hong Kong, a thriving place of business where money was to be made hand over fist, was right on its doorstep. The British and American expatriates equaled each other for the top slot, numerically speaking, but Aussie professionals were beginning to enter—if not in droves, in small herds. With them they brought their own parasites, the free-lancers, and for the first time I had a lot of competition. It meant I had to consolidate friendships and use contacts that had previously been mostly social. Sheena and I were going through a bit of a rough time too, and one thing she would not put up with was a tame writer who earned less than a poorly paid local clerk. I could sense the words "proper job" in the air, waiting to condense.

Even the darkness in there seemed to have substance. I could see the other young policeman, the thin, sharp Cantonese youth, was uncomfortable too. He kept looking up, into the blackness, smiling nervously. He and his companion cop whispered to each other, and I heard "Bruce Lee" mentioned just before they fell into silence again, their grins fixed. Perhaps they were trying to use the memory of the fabled martial-arts actor to bolster their courage? Possibly the only one of us who was completely oblivious, or perhaps indifferent, to the spiritual ambience of the place was John himself. He was too thick-skinned, too much the old-warrior expat, to be affected by spooky atmospheres. I thought he might reassure his men though, since we both knew that when Chinese smiled under circumstances such as these, it meant they were hiding either acute embarrassment or abject terror. They had nothing to be embarrassed about, so I was left with only one assumption.

John, however, chose to ignore their fear.

"Right, let's go," he said, climbing to his feet.

We continued along the passageways, stumbling after Sang Lau, whose power over us was absolute in this place, since without him we would certainly be lost. It was possible that a search party might find us, but then again, we could wander the interior of this vast wormery for weeks without finding or being found.

A subtle change seemed to come over the place. Its resistance seemed to have evaporated, and it was almost as if it were gently drawing us on. The tunnels were getting wider, more accessible, and there were fewer obstacles to negotiate. I have an active imagination, especially in places of darkness, notorious places that are steeped in recent histories of blood and founded on terror. Far from making me feel better, this alteration in the atmosphere made my stomach knot, but what could I say to John? I wanted to go back? I had no choice but to follow where his guide led us, and hope for an early opportunity to duck out if we saw daylight at any time.

Although I am sensitive to such places, I'm not usually a coward. Old churches and ancient houses bother me, but I normally shrug and put up with any feeling of spiritual discomfort. Here, however, the oppressive atmosphere was so threatening and the feeling of dread so strong, I wanted to run from the building and to hell with the article and the money I needed so much. The closer we got to the center, the more acute became my emotional stress, until I wondered whether I was going to hyperventilate. Finally, I shouted, "John!"

He swung round with an irritated "What is it?"

"I've—I've got to go back. . . ."

One of the policemen grabbed my arm in the dark, and squeezed it. I believed it to be a sign of encouragement. He too wanted to turn round, but he was more terrified of his boss than of any ghost. From the strength of the grip I guessed the owner of the fingers was the Mongol.

"Impossible," John snapped. "What's the matter with you?"

"A pain," I said. "I have a pain in my chest."

He pushed past the other men and pulled me roughly to one side.

"I knew I shouldn't have brought you. I only did it for Sheena—she seemed to think there was still something left in you. Now pull yourself together. I know what's the matter with you, you're getting the jitters. It's claustrophobia, nothing else. Fight it, man. You're scaring my boys with your stupid funk."

"I have a pain," I repeated, but he wasn't buying it.

"Crap. Sheena would be disgusted with you. God knows what she ever saw in you in the first place."

For a moment all fear was driven out of me by an intense fury that flooded my veins. How *dare* this thickskinned, arrogant cop assume knowledge of my wife's regard for me! It was true that her feelings were not now what they had been in the beginning, but she had once fully loved me, and only a rottenness bred by superficial life in the colony had eaten away that love. The mannequins, the people with plaster faces, had served to corrode us. Sheena had once been a happy woman, full of energy, enthusiasms, color. Now she was pinched and bitter, as I was myself: made so by the shallow *gwailos* we consorted with and had become ourselves. Money, affairs and bugger-thy-neighbor were the priorities in life.

"You leave Sheena's name out of this," I said, my voice catching with the anger that stuck in my throat. "What the *hell* do you know about our beginnings?"

Speakman merely gave me a look of contempt and took up his position in the front once more, with the hunchbacked Lau indicating which way he should go when we came to one of the many junctions and crossroads. Occasionally, the thin one, who now had the megaphone, would call out in Cantonese, the sound quickly swallowed by the denseness of the structure around us. Added to my anxiety problem was now a feeling of misery. I had shown my inner nature to a man who was increasingly becoming detestable to me. Something was nagging at the edge of my brain too, which gradually ate its way inward, toward an area of comprehension.

God knows what she ever saw in you in the first place.

When it came, the full implication of these words stunned me. At first I was too taken aback to do anything more than keep turning the idea over in my mind, in an obsessive way, until it drove out any other thought. I kept going over his words, trying to find another way of interpreting them, but came up with the same answer every time.

Finally, I could keep quiet no longer. I had to get it out. It was beginning to fester. I stopped in my tracks, and despite the presence of the other men, shouted, "You bastard, Speakman, you're having an affair with her, aren't you?"

He turned and regarded me, silently.

"You bastard," I said again. I could hardly get it out, it was choking me. "You're supposed to be a friend."

There was utter contempt in his voice.

"I was never your friend."

"You *wanted* me to know, didn't you? You wanted to tell me in here."

He knew that in this place I would be less than confident of myself. The advantages were all with him. I was out of my environment and less able to handle things than he was. In the past few months he had been in here several times, was more familiar with the darkness and the tight, airless zones of the Walled City's interior. We were in an underworld that terrified me and left him unperturbed.

"You men go on," he ordered the others, not taking his eyes off me. "We'll follow in a moment."

They did as they were told. John Speakman was not a man to be brooked by his Asiatic subordinates. When they were out of earshot, he said, "Yes, Sheena and I had—had some time together."

In the light of my helmet lamp I saw his lips twitch, and I wanted to smash him in the mouth.

"*Had?* You mean it's over?"

"Not completely. But there's still you. You're in the way. Sheena, being the woman she is, still retains some sort of loyalty toward you. Can't see it myself, but there it is."

"We'll sort this out later," I said, "between the three of us."

I made a move to get past him, but he blocked the way.

Then a second, more shocking realization hit me, and again I was not ready for it. He must have seen it in my face, because his lips tightened this time.

I said calmly now, "You're going to lose me in here, aren't you? Sheena said she wouldn't leave me, and you're going to make sure I stay behind."

"Your imagination is running away with you again," he snapped back. "Try to be a little more level-headed, old chap."

"I am being level-headed."

His hands were on his hips now, in that *gwailo* stance I knew so well. One of them rested on the butt of his revolver. Being a policeman, he of course carried a gun, which I did not. There was little point in my trying force anyway. He was a good four inches taller than I and weighed two stone more, most of it muscle. We stood there, confronting one another, until we heard the scream that turned my guts to milk.

The ear-piercing cry was followed by a scrabbling sound, and eventually one of the two policemen appeared in the light of our lamps.

"Sir, come quick," he gasped. "The guide."

Our quarrel put aside for the moment, we hurried along the tunnel to where the other policeman stood. In front of him, perhaps five yards away, was the guide. His helmet light was out, and he seemed to be standing on tiptoe for some reason, arms hanging loosely by his sides. John stepped forward, and I found myself going with him. He might have wanted *me* out of the way, but I was going to stick closely to him.

What I saw in the light of our lamps made me retch and step backward quickly.

It would seem that a beam had swung down from the ceiling, as the guide had passed beneath it. This had smashed his helmet lamp. Had that been all, the guide might have got away with a broken nose, or black eye, but it was not. In the end of the beam, now holding him on his feet, was a curved nail-spike. It had gone through his right eye, and was no doubt deeply imbedded in the poor man's brain. He dangled from this support loosely, blood running down the side of his nose and dripping onto his white tennis shoes.

"Jesus Christ!" I said at last. It wasn't a profanity, a blasphemy. It was a prayer. I called for us, who were now lost in a dark, hostile world, and I called for Sang Lau. Poor little Sang Lau. Just when he had begun to make it in life, just when he had escaped the Walled City, the bricks and mortar and timber had reached out petulantly for its former child and brained it. Sang Lau had been one of the quiet millions who struggle out of the mire, who evolve from terrible beginnings to a place in the world of light. All in vain, apparently.

John Speakman lifted the man away from the instrument that had impaled him, and laid the body on the floor. He went through the formality of feeling for a pulse, and then shook his head. To give him his due, his voice remained remarkably firm, as if he were still in control of things.

"We'll have to carry him out," he said to his two men. "Take one end each."

There was a reluctant shuffling of feet, as the men moved forward to do as they were told. The smaller of the two was trembling so badly he dropped the legs straight away, and had to retrieve them quickly under Speakman's glare.

I said, "And who the hell is going to lead us out, now he's gone?"

"I am," came the reply.

"And I suppose you know which way to go?"

"We're near the heart of the place, old chap. It doesn't really matter in which direction we go, as long as we keep going straight."

That, I knew, was easier said than done. When passageways curve and turn, run into each other, go up and down, meet forks and crossroads and junctions with choices, how the hell do you keep in a straight line? I said nothing for once. I didn't want the two policemen to panic. If we were to get out, we had to stay calm. And those on the outside wouldn't leave us here. They would send in a search party, once nightfall came.

Nightfall. I suppressed a chill as we moved into the heart of the beast.

Seven months ago Britain agreed with China that Hong Kong would return to its landlord country in 1997. It was then at last decided to clean up and clean out the Walled City, to pull it down and rehouse the inhabitants. There were plans to build a park on the ground then covered by this ancient city within a city, for the use of the occupants of the surrounding tenement buildings.

It stood in the middle of Kowloon on the mainland. Once upon a time there *was* a wall around it, when it was the home of the Manchus, but Japanese invaders robbed it of its ancient stones to build elsewhere. The area on which it stood is still known as the Walled City. When the Manchus were there, they used it as a fort against the British. Then the British were leased the peninsula, and it became an enclave for China's officials, whose duty it was to report on *gwailo* activities in the area to Peking. Finally, it became an architectural nightmare, a giant slum. An area not recognized by the British, who refused to police it, and abandoned by Peking, it was a lawless labyrinth, sometimes called the Forbidden Place. It was here that unlicensed doctors and dentists practiced and every kind of vice flourished. It was ruled by gangs of youths, the Triads, who covered its inner walls with blood. It is a place of death, the home of ten thousand ghosts.

For the next two hours we struggled through the rank-smelling tunnels, crawling over filth and across piles of trash, until we were all exhausted. I had cuts on my knees, and my hair felt teeming with insects. I knew there were spiders, possibly even snakes, in these passageways. There were certainly lice, horseflies, mosquitoes and a dozen other nasty biters. Not only that, but there seemed to be projections everywhere: sharp bits of metal, cables hanging like vines from the ceiling and rusty nails. The little Cantonese policeman had trodden on a nail, which had completely pierced his foot. He was now limping and whining in a small voice. He knew that if he did not get treatment soon, blood poisoning would be the least of his troubles. I felt sorry for the young man, who in the normal run of things probably dealt with the tide of human affairs very competently within his range of duties. He was an official of the law in the most densely populated area of the world, and I had seen his type deal cleanly and (more often than not) peacefully with potentially ugly situations daily. In here, however, he was over his head. This situation could not be handled by efficient traffic signals or negotiation, or even prudent use of a weapon. There was something about this man that was familiar. There were scars on his face: shiny patches that might have been the result of plastic surgery. I tried to recall where I had seen the Cantonese policeman before, but my mind was soggy with recent events.

We took turns to carry the body of the guide. Once I had touched him and got over my squeamishness, that part of it didn't bother me too much. What did was the weight of the corpse. I never believed a man could be so heavy. After ten minutes my arms were nearly coming out of their sockets. I began by carrying the legs, and quickly decided that the man at the head, carrying the torso, had the best part of the deal. I suggested a change round, which was effected, only to find that the other end of the man was twice as heavy. I began to hate him.

After four hours I had had enough.

"I'm not humping him around anymore," I stated bluntly to the cop who was trying to take my wife from me. "You want him outside, you carry him by yourselves. You're the bloody boss man. It's your damn show."

"I see," John said. "Laying down some ground rules, are we?"

"Shove it up your arse," I replied. "I've had you up to here. I can't prove you planned to dump me in here, but *I* know, pal, and when we get out of this place, you and I are going to have a little talk."

"*If* we get out," he muttered.

He was sitting away from me, in the darkness, where my lamplight couldn't reach him. I could not see his expression.

"If?"

"Exactly," he sighed. "We don't seem to be getting very far, do we? It's almost as if this place were trying to keep us. I swear it's turning us in on ourselves. We should have reached the outside long ago."

"But they'll send someone in after us," I said.

And one of the policemen, added. "Yes. Someone come."

"'Fraid not. No one knows we're here." It came out almost as if he were pleased with himself. I saw now that I *had* been right. It had been his intention to drop me off in the middle of this godforsaken building, knowing I would never find my own way out. I wondered only briefly what he planned to do with the two men and the guide. I don't doubt they could be bribed. The Hong Kong Police Force has at times been notorious for its corruption. Maybe they were chosen because they could be bought.

"How long have we got?" I asked, trying to stick to practical issues.

"About five more hours. Then the demolition starts. They begin knocking it down at six A.M."

Just then, the smaller of the Chinese made a horrific gargling sound, and we all shone our lights on him instinctively. At first I couldn't understand what was wrong with him, though I could see he was convulsing. He was in a sitting position, and his body kept jerking and flopping. John Speakman bent over him, then straightened, saying, "Christ, not another one . . ."

"What?" I cried. "What is it?"

"Six-inch nail. It's gone in behind his ear. How the hell? I don't understand how he managed to lean all the way back on it."

"Unless the nail came out of the wood?" I said.

"What are you saying?"

"I don't know. All I know is two men have been injured in accidents that seem too freakish to believe. What do you think? Why can't we get out of this place? Shit, it's only the area of a football stadium. We've been in here *hours*."

The other policeman was looking at his colleague with wide, disbelieving eyes. He grabbed John Speakman by the collar, blurting. "We go now. We go outside now," and then a babble of that tonal language, some of which John might have understood. I certainly didn't.

Speakman peeled the man's stubby fingers from his collar and turned away from him, toward the dead cop, as if the incident had not taken place. "He was a good policeman," he said. "Jimmy Wong. You know he saved a boy from a fire last year? Dragged the child out with his teeth, hauling the body along the floor and down the stairs because his hands were burned too badly to clutch the kid. You remember. You covered the story."

I remembered him now. Jimmy Wong. The governor had presented him with a medal. He had saluted proudly, with heavily bandaged hands. Today he was not a hero. Today he was a number. The second victim.

John Speakman said, "Good-bye, Jimmy."

Then he ignored him, saying to me, "We can't carry both bodies out. We'll have to leave them. I . . ." but I heard no more. There was a quick tearing sound, and I was suddenly falling. My heart dropped out of me. I landed heavily on my back. Something entered between my shoulder blades, something sharp and painful, and I had to struggle hard to get free. When I managed to get to my feet and reached down and felt along the floor, I touched a slim projection, probably a large nail. It was sticky with my blood. A voice from above said, "Are you all right?"

"I—I think so. A nail . . ."

"What?"

My light had gone out, and I was feeling disoriented. I must have fallen about fourteen feet, judging from the distance of the lamps above me. I reached down my back with my hand. It felt wet and warm, but apart from the pain I wasn't gasping for air or anything. Obviously, it had missed my lungs and other vital organs, or I would be squirming in the dust, coughing my guts up.

I heard John say, "We'll try to reach you," and then the voice and the lights drifted away.

"*No!*" I shouted. "Don't leave me! Give me your arm." I reached upward. "Help me up!"

But my hand remained empty. They had gone, leaving the blackness behind them. I lay still for a long time, afraid to move. There were nails everywhere. My heart was racing. I was sure that I was going to die. The Walled City had us in its grip, and we were not going to get out. Once, it had been teeming with life, but we had robbed it of its soul, the people that had crowded within its walls. Now even the shell was threatened with destruction. And we were the men responsible. We represented the authority who had ordered its death, and it was determined to take us with it. Nothing likes to die alone. Nothing wants to leave this world without, at the very least, obtaining satisfaction in the way of revenge. The ancient black heart of the Walled City of the Manchus, surrounded by the body it had been given by later outcasts from society, had enough life left in it to slaughter these five puny mortals from the other side, the lawful side. It had tasted *gwailo* blood, and it would have more.

My wound was beginning to ache, and I climbed stiffly and carefully to my feet. I felt slowly along the walls, taking each step cautiously. Things scuttled over my feet, whispered over my face, but I ignored them. A sudden move and I would find myself impaled on some projection. The stink of death was in the stale air, filling my nostrils. It was trying to drive fear into me. The only way I was going to survive was by remaining calm. Once I panicked, it would all be over. I had the feeling that the building could kill me at any time, but it was savoring the moment, allowing it to be my mistake. It wanted me to dive headlong into insanity, it wanted to experience my terror, then it would deliver the *coup de grace*.

I moved this way along the tunnels for about an hour: Neither of us, it seemed, was short of patience. The Walled City had seen centuries, so what was an hour or two? The legacy of death left by the Manchus and the Triads existed without reference to time. Ancient evils and modern iniquity had joined forces against the foreigner, the *gwailo*, and the malodorous darkness smiled at any attempt to thwart its intention to suck the life from my body.

At one point my forward foot did not touch ground. There was a space, a hole, in front of me.

"Nice try," I whispered, "but not yet."

As I prepared to edge around it, hoping for a small ledge or something, I felt ahead of me, and touched the thing. It was dangling over the hole, like a plumb-line weight. I pushed it, and it swung slowly.

By leaning over and feeling carefully, I ascertained it to be the remaining local policeman, the muscled northerner. I knew that by his Sam Browne shoulder strap: Speakman had not been wearing one. I felt up by the corpse's throat and found the skin bulging over some tight electrical cords. The building had hanged him.

Used to death now, I gripped the corpse around the waist and used it as a swing to get myself across the gap. The cords held, and I touched ground. A second later, the body must have dropped, because I heard a crash below.

I continued my journey through the endless tunnels, my throat very parched now. I was thirsty as hell. Eventually, I could stand it no longer and licked some of the moisture that ran down the walls. It tasted like wine. At one point I tongued up a cockroach, cracked it between my teeth, and spit it out in disgust. Really, I no longer cared. All I wanted to do was get out alive. I didn't even care whether John and Sheena told me to go away. I would be happy to do so. There wasn't much left, in any case. Anything I had felt had shriveled away during this ordeal. I just wanted to live. Nothing more, nothing less.

At one point a stake or something plunged downward from the roof and passed through several floors, missing me by an inch. I think I actually laughed. A little while later, I found an airshaft with a rope hanging in it. Trusting that the building would not let me fall, I climbed down this narrow chimney to get to the bottom. I had some idea that if I could reach ground-level, I might find a way to get through the walls. Some of them were no thicker than cardboard.

After reaching the ground safely, I began to feel my way along the corridors and alleys, until I saw a light. I gasped with relief, thinking at first it was daylight, but had to swallow a certain amount of disappointment in finding it was only a helmet with its lamp still on. The owner was nowhere to be seen. I guessed it was John's: He was the only one left, apart from me.

Not long after this, I heard John Speakman's voice for the last time. It seemed to come from very far below me, in the depths of the underground passages that wormholed beneath the Walled City. It was a faint pathetic cry for help. Immediately following this distant shout was the sound of falling masonry. And then, silence. I shuddered, involuntarily, guessing what had happened. The building had lured him into its underworld, its maze below the earth, and had then blocked the exits. John Speakman had been buried alive, immured by the city that held him in contempt.

Now there was only me.

I moved through an inner darkness, the beam of the remaining helmet lamp having faded to a dim glow. I was Theseus in the Labyrinth, except that I had no Ariadne to help me find the way through it. I stumbled through long tunnels where the air was so thick and damp I might have been in a steam bath. I crawled along passages no taller or wider than a cupboard under a kitchen sink, shared it with spiders and rats and came out the other end choking on dust, spitting out cobwebs. I knocked my way through walls so thin and rotten a single blow with my fist was enough to hole them. I climbed over fallen girders, rubble, and piles of filthy rags, collecting unwanted passengers and abrasions on the way.

And all the while I knew the building was laughing at me.

It was leading me round in circles, playing with me like a rat in a maze. I could hear it moving, creaking and shifting as it readjusted itself, changed its inner structure to keep me from finding an outside wall. Once, I trod on something soft. It could have been a hand—John's hand—quickly withdrawn. Or it might have been a creature of the Walled City, a rat or a snake. Whatever it was, it had been alive.

There were times when I became so despondent I wanted to lie down and just fade into death, the way a primitive tribesman will give up all hope and turn his face to the wall. There were times when I became angry, and screeched at the structure that had me trapped in its belly, remonstrating with it until my voice was hoarse. Sometimes I was driven to useless violence and picked up the nearest object to smash at my tormentor, even if my actions brought the place down around my ears.

Once, I even whispered to the darkness:

"I'll be your slave. Tell me what to do—any evil thing—and I'll do it. If you let me go, I promise to follow your wishes. Tell me what to do. . . ."

And still it laughed at me, until I knew I was going insane.

Finally, I began singing to myself, not to keep up my spirits like brave men are supposed to, but because I was beginning to slip into that crazy world that rejects reality in favor of fantasy. I thought I was home, in my own house, making coffee. I found myself going through the actions of putting on the kettle, and preparing the coffee, milk and sugar, humming a pleasant tune to myself all the while. One part of me recognized that domestic scene was make-believe, but the other was convinced that I could not possibly be trapped by a malevolent entity and about to die in the dark corridors of its multisectioned shell.

Then something happened, to jerk me into sanity.

The sequence of events covering the next few minutes or so are lost to me. Only by concentrating very hard and surmising can I recall what *might* have happened. Certainly, I believe I remember those first few moments, when a sound deafened me, and the whole building rocked and trembled as if in an earthquake. Then I think I fell to the floor and had the presence of mind to jam the helmet on my head. There followed a second (what I now know to be) explosion. Pieces of building rained around me: bricks were striking my shoulders and bouncing off my hard hat. I think the only reason none of them injured me badly was because the builders, being poor, had used the cheapest materials they could find. These were bricks fashioned out of crushed coke, which are luckily light and airy.

A hole appeared, through which I could see blinding daylight. I was on my feet in an instant, and racing toward it. Nails appeared out of the woodwork, up from the floor, and ripped and tore at my flesh like sharp fangs. Metal posts crashed across my path, struck me on my limbs. I was attacked from all sides by chunks of masonry and debris, until I was bruised and raw, bleeding from dozens of cuts and penetrations.

When I reached the hole in the wall, I threw myself at it, and landed outside in the dust. There, the demolition people saw me, and one risked his life to dash forward and pull me clear of the collapsing building. I was then rushed to hospital. I was found to have a broken arm and multiple lacerations, some of them quite deep.

Mostly, I don't remember what happened at the end. I'm going by what I've been told, and what flashes on and off in my nightmares, and using these have pieced together the above account of my escape from the Walled City. It seems as though it might be reasonably accurate.

I have not, of course, told the true story of what happened inside those walls, except in this account, which will go into a safe place until after my death. Such a tale would only have people clucking their tongues and saying, "It's the shock, you know—the trauma of such an experience," and sending for the psychiatrist. I tried to tell Sheena once, but I could see that it was disturbing her, so I mumbled something about, "Of course, I can see that one's imagination can work overtime in a place like that," and never mentioned it to her again.

I did manage to tell the demolition crew about John. I told them he might still be alive, under all that rubble. They stopped their operations immediately and sent in search parties, but though they found the bodies of the guide and policemen, John was never seen again. The search parties all managed to get out safely, which has me wondering whether perhaps there is something wrong with my head—except I have the wounds, and there are the corpses of my traveling companions. I don't know. I can only say now what I think happened. I told the police (and stuck rigidly to my story) that I was separated from the others before any deaths occurred. How was I to explain two deaths by sharp instruments, and a subsequent hanging? I let them try to figure it out. All I told them was that I heard John's final cry, and that was the truth. I don't even care whether or not they believe me. I'm outside that damn hellhole, and that's all that concerns me.

And Sheena? It is seven months since the incident. And it was only yesterday that I confronted and accused her of having an affair with John, and she looked so shocked and distressed and denied it so vehemently that I have to admit I believe that nothing of the kind happened between them. I was about to tell her that John had admitted to it, but had second thoughts. I mean, had he? He certainly inferred that there had been something between them, but perhaps he was just trying to goad me? Maybe I had filled in the gaps with my own jealous fears? To tell you the truth, I can't honestly remember, and the guilt is going to be hard to live with. You see, when they asked me for the location of John's cry for help, I indicated a spot . . . well, I *think* I told them to dig—I said . . . anyway, they didn't find him, which wasn't surprising, since I . . . well, perhaps this is not the place for full confessions.

John is still under there somewhere, God help him. I have the awful feeling that the underground ruins of the Walled City might keep him alive in some way, with redirected water, and food in the form of rats and cockroaches. A starving man will eat dirt, if it fills his stomach. Perhaps he is still below, in some pocket created by that underworld? Such a slow, terrible torture, keeping a man barely alive in his own grave, would be consistent with that devious, nefarious entity I know as the Walled City of the Manchus.

Some nights when I am feeling especially brave, I go to the park and listen—listen for small cries from a subterranean prison—listen for the faint pleas for help from an *oubliette* far below the ground.

Sometimes I think I hear them.

JEAN-DANIEL BREQUE

On the Wing

JEAN-DANIEL BREQUE was born in Bordeaux, France. After studying to become a Math teacher and spending five years working in a Dunkirk tax-office, he decided to become a full-time translator in 1987, moving to Paris where he still lives and works.

Most of his translation work has been in the horror field, and he has worked on books and stories by such well-known names as Clive Barker, Brian Lumley, Ramsey Campbell, Graham Masterton, Dean R. Koontz, Raymond E. Feist, David Morrell, Charles L. Grant and Garfield Reeves-Stevens, amongst others. He has recently translated stories by Stephen King, Fritz Leiber, Richard Matheson, Richard Christian Matheson, Nicholas Royle, Ramsey Campbell, Edward Bryant and others for the new anthology series *Territoires de l'Inquietude*, edited by Alain Doremieux.

"On the Wing" was the first story he wrote, although it waited five years to be published. For its initial appearance in English it was translated by Nicholas Royle, who appears elsewhere in this volume with his own, equally powerful story of disquietude.

THE BEGINNING OF SUMMER in Merignac: dry pine needles cracking underfoot, petals lying shrivelled on the ground, the numbing din of crickets in the trees. Robin cleared a path through the thicket, scratching himself on the broom and getting his fingers sticky with resin, searching for the track which led to the little quarry, and to the pool. Just like every summer, the anarchic advent of plants and foliage of all kinds had almost completely hidden the track shaped by their feet the previous year. Etched day after day by their wanderings, it never kept exactly the same outline from one summer to the next, and its landmarks became muddled in their minds: was it last year or the year before that this twisted pine tree had materialised a turn?

Robin stopped short before a square of sandy earth, in which shallow circular depressions had been dug. He smiled; for a long time, he had thought these holes were footprints left by some mysterious creature roaming the thicket, silently following him. Then, one day, he had seen a sparrow bathing itself in the soil, and he had been almost ashamed by the vagaries of his mind.

He recognised a pile of dead branches encroached upon by clumps of moss; the scents of resin and broom swept over him with sudden violence. Close by, a pine tree had been blown over by the wind, and he had to stoop under it to get to the quarry. A bush next to him crackled dryly and a black bird made an abrupt swoop toward the sky. In front of him, the surface of the pool sparkled in the sunlight.

He was alone.

Taken aback, Robin stepped onto the little beach of blackish sand. He stopped a moment to take off his tennis shoes, then proceeded to test the water. Slowly, he directed his gaze around the pool, stopping at each tree in the surrounding woods. No one. So where were the others? Where were Gérard and Michel? This was not the first time they had decided to do something together without bothering to tell him, leaving him alone, feeling stupid and understanding nothing. Asshole, he said in a low voice, embarrassed by his crudeness. There's no one to hear you, he continued. No one. He walked a little way and saw marks left by bare feet on the sand: they had already been here, in the morning or more likely the day before, without saying anything to him, without letting him know; and today, the first real day of the holidays, they were not here. Robin had never dared play truant from school.

He got undressed quickly, placed his shirt and shorts on a rock next to his trainers, stepped into the water and swam towards the centre of the pool. He came to a halt, gently moving his arms to keep himself in position. He half-expected to see Michel or Gérard dart out from behind a bush and run towards his clothes, to seize them and throw them into the water; Michel and Gérard, who had perfected the crawl

223

and would catch up with him in less than five seconds, while he was scarcely able to remain afloat.

Once, he had tried to dive, forced into it by their incessant, almost spiteful teasing. On the other side of the quarry stood a thirty-foot rock, from the top of which he had taken flight with his eyes closed. Breaking the surface, he had seen a fine laceration running right down his leg, and as the water cleared, it had revealed a metal girder rusting away at the bottom of the pool.

The sun snatched flashes of light from the waves, and he shut his eyes against the glare, but beneath his closed eyelids, white patches danced on a dark velvet backcloth. The soft warmth of the air and the water's biting chill battled to dominate the skin over his ribs and thighs; he let himself drift slowly across the shimmering surface of the pool, floating in search of some undefined shoreline. He could have believed himself captured in a cocoon, isolated from the outside world, were it not for the light breeze which caressed his chest from time to time and the rattling of the pines which gradually faded into silence. Opaque light glimmered across his inner eye, mingled with darting shadows in an unceasing ballet. He felt an immediate presence and opened his eyes. A black shape blocked his view. He screamed, covered his face with his arms, and dropped straight down. When he rose to the surface again, the crow had disappeared.

After putting his bicycle away, Robin carefully closed the garage door and walked to the house. His hair was still a bit damp and he stopped a moment to rub his head. Nestling in the pines, the house revealed only a part of its squat outline and would be easily missed by someone who did not know it was here. His parents were not back and he did not have a key. He sat on the ground, picked up a handful of pine needles and began to weave them into a wreath; either too supple or too brittle, they evaded his grasp and he hurled them away.

He got up and walked around the outside of the house. His bedroom window had been left open. His hand rested against the pine tree nearest the house. Could he possibly . . .? He made a sudden decision, left his towel on a branch and began to climb. A few minutes later, he was perched on the branch which brushed against his window, the branch which his father had to trim each spring. Crouched on the ledge, he gazed at the carefully made bed, the bookcase full of books worn-out from so many readings, and the cupboard stuffed full of toys he no longer touched.

He imagined himself surprising his parents: they would enter the house somewhat taken aback, wondering if they had left him locked in all afternoon. Then he recalled his father making vague remarks about cutting the tree down. He took a book from his bookcase, then climbed back down again.

He spread out the towel on the carpet of needles, in the sun, and lay down to read.

The cry of a bird flying just above woke him. No, it was his parents' car horn. In a tone of forced joviality, they asked him questions which he grumpily evaded.

He went to the kitchen and got himself a glass of ice-cold Coke, while his parents sat down in front of the television. A sumptuously dressed woman was slitting the throat of a tuxedo-clad prince while the detective jotted down notes. *Una paloma blanca.* He went up to his room.

Next to the window, the branch seemed to provoke him. Had he really climbed up here? He leaned out and was seized by giddiness. At a loose end, he turned to the cupboard, which he jerked open. Something pale and hairy fell on his face, making him jump. His heart in his mouth, he looked at the wig lying on the floor. Three or four years ago, he was not really sure when, his schoolteacher had organised an end-of-the-year show. Disguised as cherubs, he and a dozen other kids had bustled about pathetically on stage, to the great delight of their assembled parents. That summer, Gérard and Michel, who were moving up to high school in the autumn, never stopped their mocking cries of "little angel".

He threw the wig back on the shelf and closed the cupboard. He no longer wanted to play. The book he took from the bookcase was already open when he noticed his mother had come into the room.

"What is it, Robin? Is there something wrong?"

"No, no. I'm fine."

"Where did you go this afternoon? To the pool?"

He grunted.

"Answer me. Were you off with those friends of yours again?" She pronounced "friends" in her most cutting voice. Robin was silent. "Answer me, will you."

"No. I was alone."

"Good. I prefer that. You know, it would be better if you saw them a little less. After all, they are older than you. Can't you find friends of your own age? What about Antoine, for instance?" Who still plays with little plastic cowboys, Robin thought to himself. He lay on the bed and opened his book. "And don't sprawl on your bed like that, if you don't mind. How many times do I have to tell you?" Grumbling, he got up and sat in the chair, his head buried in his book.

He squirmed, ill at ease, when his mother leaned over to give him a kiss. The long black curtain of her hair imprisoned his head, plunging him into suffocating darkness. She murmured something unintelligible, then left the room.

He was floating motionless in the pool, but the light had disappeared. The surface of the water reflected only the blind shadows of a starless night. His eyes were wide open, but he could not distinguish anything; nothing detached itself from the darkness. Silence. Somewhere deep within him, his heart beat a hurried rhythm, but the pulse did not reach his brain. A flash. A glimmer, a pinprick piercing the shadows, accompanied by an even darker indistinct shape. The crow landed on his chest.

Robin did not move. Had he wanted to move, to brush the bird away with his arm, he would not have been able to. An icy flash of light revealed the eye of the crow, its beak poised over Robin's throat and striking now repeatedly with little dry pecks, like a child's kisses, gradually becoming more urgent, more violent, more painful. Hot liquid flowed over his chest. The crow lifted its blood-darkened beak, uttered a shrill cry, and dug once more into the proffered throat.

He woke up, soaking in sweat, and stifled a scream. Had he noticed movement on the tree outside? That cry, was it the cry of a bird? Trembling, he got up and went to the window. Nothing. He lowered his gaze. The branch was grooved with dark scratches.

He went back to bed and noticed he had torn the cover of the bolster, gripping it with his nails; several white feathers lay on the sheets. He shook his head. Was he dreaming? As he looked at them, the feathers grew steadily darker, seeming to quiver, almost flying away. He closed his eyes and opened them again. They had gone. The tear was still there in the bolster, but the feathers had disappeared.

Should he tell his parents? He half-opened his bedroom door, but did not step outside. Downstairs, the light was still on in the living room. He heard his mother's voice.

"—not that he should be shut in here all day, no, but I'd rather he stopped hanging around with those little louts. After all, you know very well what happened at the school last spring."

He could not hear his father's reply.

"Oh right! You're not going to tell me you were like them at their age?" Again, an indistinct murmur. "No, he was at the pool on his own, at least that's what he told me, and he didn't sound like he was lying, he just sounded annoyed. Fortunately, I think they want to stop seeing him. Anyway, according to what I've been told, it's in the evening they meet at that wretched quarry, to . . . to . . ."

Robin was not listening anymore to his mother's recriminations. So, Michel and Gerard hadn't been at the pool in the daytime, but during the night. And they no longer wanted him to take part in their games.

He lay down again. It was too late to do anything now, but tomorrow . . . Tomorrow . . .

His parents both worked all day, and he was alone when he got up. His mother had come to kiss him before leaving, but he had pretended to be asleep; he had kept his face still when her long black hair had lightly brushed his throat. He quickly gulped down his breakfast and went to the garage. No, he wouldn't take his bicycle today. He'd go on foot.

He had a canvas bag, which he began to fill with pebbles. When he decided it was heavy enough, he set off to the pool. No problem, until he got to the secondary road; afterwards, he started to leave markers at regular intervals. He reached the thicket about midday and paused there: the path was not yet cleared and the others would probably need to look at the ground in order to find their way; was there not a risk that they would find his markers? He had a sudden idea. He put his bag on the ground and climbed up a tree. When he had taken his bearings, he cut a notch in a branch with his knife. He proceeded in the same manner, marking about a dozen trees, before reaching his destination.

Robin walked on the beach for a moment and looked at the surface of the pool. Beneath the calm water, something seemed to be spying on him. In the middle of the pool, a black shape was floating. Floating? No, it was just the reflection of a crow gliding over his head. Alarmed, he took cover behind a bush. The bird tirelessly described a perfect circle, cawing shrilly from time to time.

Unnerved, without quite knowing why, Robin retraced his steps and returned home.

"You're going up already?"

"Yeah."

"Don't you want to stay with us and watch the TV?"

"No. I've already seen this movie."

Robin hurried upstairs, catching only snatches of conversation coming from the living room. "—deliberately to annoy me—" "—always hope he'll do what you want. He is twelve now, after all."

He closed his bedroom door and leant against it for a moment. Nothing. Without wasting any time, he went to his bed, arranged the bolster on the mattress, covered it with his pyjama jacket, and to complete the illusion, carefully placed the angel's wig on the head of the makeshift dummy. He folded over the blanket and stepped back to judge the effect. It would do. Quietly, he opened the window, jumped onto the branch, climbed down the tree, and made off. It was still day, but dusk was approaching. Gradually, the shadows took possession of the bushes and trees.

Once past the secondary road, he quickly found his first track-markers, but he soon had to use his torch to locate the later ones.

Approaching the thicket, he stood still when he heard something cry out. What was happening? He moved forwards cautiously, now and again climbing a tree to find the notches he had carved that afternoon. Soon, there was only a bush separating him from the bank. Shapes moved about vaguely in the half-darkness. A stifled cry; the crack of broken glass; a high-pitched laugh. He squinted in vain; nothing was distinguishable. He could not catch any intelligible words; nothing but rumblings and eructations.

He moved lightly to the left and cried out abruptly. The crow had darted into his face, flaying his skin with claws and beak. All was quiet on the beach, then came several shouts of surprise. Robin broke into a run, the fetid breath of the bird still lingering in his throat. He charged onwards, blindly.

He found himself back on the secondary road without knowing how he had got there. Behind him, the exclamations were becoming fainter; he must have lost them.

Slowing down, he walked toward the house. His parents were still watching television and he took every precaution as he climbed up the tree, advanced along the branch, opened the window, and slipped into his bedroom.

The bed was empty.

He had the sensation of plunging into a bottomless abyss. His mother must have come up to see if he was sleeping well, and discovered his trickery. It would be pointless to act as if nothing had happened. He opened the door and went downstairs; the tears which mingled with the blood on his cheeks had a sour taste.

The glimmer of the television danced on the furniture and on the walls, carving up deep shadows swirling in the hidden recesses of the room. Facing the set, his mother and father, their back to him, and a third person. Who was it? The stranger, conscious of being watched, turned his gaze toward him, exchanged a look with his mother, who nodded her head, and got up.

Robin stood paralysed on the threshold of the living room. The other, who had his build and wore his pyjamas, advanced toward him in silence. He refused to look at his face. The other stopped in front of him and lifted a hand toward his throat. He felt his

228

flesh being crumpled and torn. The hand withdrew, covered with bloody feathers. Shaking, as if on the edge of a chasm of dark shadows, he saw them rise slowly in the air, thrown up by the stranger in a contemptuous gesture. They fluttered a moment, stars faintly flickering in a fading velvet sky, and then there was only the dark.

J. L. COMEAU

Firebird

JUDITH LYNN COMEAU was born in Washington D.C. and is a full-time writer. Her interests include ancient music, 18th and 19th century English novels, anthropology and, of course, "all things dark and horrible."

Since 1987 her fiction has been published in such magazine and anthologies as *Grue*, *Haunts*, *Twisted Night Slivers*, *Dreams & Nightmares*, *The Women Who Walk Through Fire*, *Women of the West*, *Borderlands II* and *The Year's Best Horror Stories*. She has recently completed her first novel, entitled *Haunted Landscapes*.

"Firebird" is a fast-paced blend of police procedural and witchcraft that is guaranteed to make your palms sweat . . .

C ONCENTRATION IS THE THING.
   You have to block out everything but the task at hand if you want to succeed. In my mind, I am the Firebird, soaring above the ashes of my own extinction.

Ignoring the sweat pouring down my face, I stand before the mirrored wall, one hand lightly touching the barre. I bring my knee up steadily and lay it alongside my nose, then ever so slowly extend the calf, arching my toes toward the ceiling.

Technique, line, proportion, balance: these are the classical elements of the dance. Ballet is a celebration of the physical instrument, a ruthless, brutal discipline from which mastery of movement emerges. I try to think only of the dance as I push away from the barre and glissade to the center of the cold, silent studio.

I want to pretend that it is not nearly four a.m., that I am not exhausted, that I am not courting injury by pushing myself too hard. Going up on pointe, I turn a dozen mad fourettes, one-legged spins that confuse the mind and challenge the spirit. I want to forget what happened last night. I want to fill my empty soul with the dance.

I keep my balance by means of light and gravity. I focus on the staccato *tock-tock-tock* of my toeshoes against the hardwood floor. I will myself to forget, but even as my body transcends exhaustion and pushes into the realm of pure bliss, I remember . . . I remember . . .

The dream is always the same: I'm charging through a long, dim hallway surrounded by shadowy blue figures running ahead and beside me. Blood crashing in my temples all but obliterates the thunder of our heavy boots as we approach a scarred metal door at the end of the hall. Amid angry shouts and confusing clamor, the door suddenly bursts open. (At this point in the dream, I start struggling to awaken myself because I can't bear to see what I know waits in that apartment.) My screams reach out of my dream and into my consciousness. I awaken on my feet, engulfed in a blind panic.

The dream is a remnant of the other side of my life. Of necessity, most dancers live two-sided lives. Foremost always is the grand passion—the dance—but unless one is a principal dancer in a large company, there is also a full-time outside job that pays the rent and buys the toeshoes.

When I'm not dancing, I work for the city. I'm one of a five-member tactical assault team the Detroit Police Department secretly calls "The Nut Squad". We're specifically trained to respond to barricade situations, which are often precipitated by emotionally disturbed persons, hence the nickname.

My given name is Julianna Christine Larkin. At the dance studio, I'm addressed as Julianna, but inside the police department, I'm often referred to as "Twinkletoes" or "The Sugarplum Fairy" behind my back. At one time, the guys on my squad gave me a hard time, making ballerina jokes and crude references to my gender. Now they simply call me Larkin, and that suits me just fine.

When I pack up my toeshoes and go out with my squad, the mandatory gear is decidedly different. Instead of a skimpy leotard, I wear heavy pads of flexible armor covering my chest, back and groin. A spidery two-way radio headset with multiple channels allows us to communicate quietly. We each carry a different weapon: a shotgun for support fire, an M16 A-2 automatic rifle for close-range management, a .223-caliber assault rifle for long-range control. I carry the A-2, which is relatively light but effective. We also have hydraulic jacks to crack open locked doors, systems to deliver tear gas canisters, and a contraption that shoots explosive diversion devices called "Thunder Flashers".

Like ballet, tactical police work requires agility, strength, endurance and a rigorous training schedule, so the two are not quite so disparate as they might at first seem. These are the areas where I excel. It's a grasp of social competence that has so far eluded me.

For me, adolescence was a nightmare. Girls who reach a height of six feet by junior high school might as well have leprosy. But after a full day of peer indifference or outright scorn at school, I would become a swan in dance class, envied for my length of limb.

"Stand tall, Julianna! Reach for the clouds!" Madame Jedinov would bark from the back of the studio as she pounded her baton in time to the music. "Arch the neck! Extend the arm!"

In the grace and beauty of the dance I found pleasure in being me.

There is a certain grace and beauty to be found in the savage Detroit inner city streets as well. Instead of a joyous dance of life, it is a desperate dance of death, beautiful in its own wretched way.

My first police assignment was a barricade situation located in a shabby, drug-riddled housing project downtown. When I arrived, the building had been pinned to the night sky by spotlights and ringed by armed personnel.

Lieutenant Steven Brophy, my squad leader and veteran of two tours of combat in Vietnam, told me, "I want you to stay in back of the team, young lady. Don't want any trouble on this one. We've got our hands full and we don't need to be babysitting you."

His doubts about my competence did not annoy me—I was having my own misgivings. Everyone in the department was aware that I had received my placement in the unit to squelch a rash of sexual discrimination suits filed against the city. I thought I would be able prove myself when the time came, but right then, I was just plain rabbit scared.

As I adjusted my radio headset, a sharp cry pulled my attention to the third floor apartment window where something dangled beneath the windowsill. Pushing my hair up under my cap I saw that it was a child—a baby!—being held by one ankle, bobbing precariously above the bleak tundra of the courtyard thirty feet below.

The baby screamed in terror, windmilling its little arms, arching its back. My heart froze. Seconds later, the child was jerked roughly back through the window and disappeared from view. Only its wails echoed in the cold night air.

"That's right," Brophy said as he motioned for me to follow him toward the equipment truck. "We got us a maniac, little girl."

After handing me a heavy hydraulic jack, which I would carry during the assault, we joined the rest of the squad for a fast briefing. It was terrifying. Unconfirmed reports indicated that there was a psycho in apartment 302 named Ralph Esposito who had taken his former wife and children hostage. Sporadic gunfire heard earlier in the evening was shortly followed by the ejection of an object from the window which was later identified as his ex-wife's head. Of the six children presumed to be inside the apartment with him, it was unsure how many survived. The situation had been deteriorating rapidly for several hours and the life of the single known surviving hostage, the baby, had reached an unacceptable level of risk.

Our task: Full-Assault Scenario/Termination of Suspect Authorized.

We crept into the building past a dozen uniformed officers and waited for one breathless minute at the end of the third floor hallway until Lieutenant Brophy gave the signal to move. At that point, I was so frightened and everything started moving so fast that the whole sequence of events always comes back to me in blurs and flashes:

Midnight blue figures hustling down the hallway—the sound of our boots against the linoleum floor—halting outside the door to 302—handing the jack to Fred Zaluta, second in command— dragging my A-2 off my back, throwing the safety—the door buckling and bursting open—gunfire—Zaluta on the floor, writhing—I know he's moaning, but all I can hear is my own blood crashing in my ears—a naked man, clotted with gore, pointing a rifle at me—*no!*—the end of the barrel explodes with light and something punches me hard in the shoulder—I start to go down, sure that I'm already dead—automatically, I train the red dot of my laser aiming device on the center of the madman's forehead and squeeze off a fast burst.

As I go down, I see the top of the suspect's head lift off and explode in hundreds of shards and droplets that fan out in every direction—swiveling my head, I see another spray of dark blood pumping out of the torn meat of my shoulder—I think very clearly, "Where's the baby?" as I hit the floor—there is shouting and commotion—I lay injured and dazed, but not actually registering pain yet—the medical people swarm over me, lift me onto a stretcher that puts me at eye level with a strange object that looks like a raw roast beef pinned to the wall with a big cooking fork.

Time twists and stretches now, slowing to a crawl.

How odd, I think, running my eyes over the blue veins marbling the strangely shaped piece of meat. Rivulets of blood trace down the dingy wall beneath. How very, very odd.

People talk to me as I'm carried toward the door, but all I can hear is the hushed voice of one uniformed policeman addressing another officer.

"That's the way it goes with these screwballs," he was saying, shaking his head sadly. "The bastard killed every one of them. Skinned the baby alive and staked it to the wall with a fork right before the rescue unit got in. Five more minutes might have saved it. Ain't that a shame?"

When I start screaming, the ambulance attendant jabs me with a needle. Fadeout.

The first thing I thought of when I woke up in the hospital was that poor mutilated baby fastened to the wall, and I've thought about it every day for the past two years. I learned afterwards from the reports that the man I'd . . . killed . . . had a history of mental problems and had been released from a state hospital that same morning because of budgetary cutbacks. Ralph Esposito. The sound of his name makes my neck prickle. The baby he murdered along with his ex-wife and five other children was named Carmelita. Carmelita. Such a musical name. So full of laughter and promise. I can't stop hearing it in my mind.

Well, months of sweaty work in the dance studio and the department gym healed my shoulder. I've always been able to handle the physical demands of life. It's my head that keeps giving me trouble. If I could only banish the image of that poor child . . . poor Carmelita, from my dreams.

The guys on my squad welcomed me whole-heartedly into the unit when I came back to work. I was no longer considered an irksome political placement to bolster the department's image.

Lieutenant Fred Zaluta, who was also wounded during the raid on 302, became my champion. He still insists that I saved his life, but I don't know—I was just doing my job. He knows I live alone in a coldwater flat downtown, so he and his wife invite me over for a home-cooked meal with them and their three kids at least once a month. I love watching the Zalutas together. They're a volatile group, always fighting and bickering, but you can feel the love radiating from every cluttered corner of their home. I was raised an only child. My parents' house was cool and hushed, the corners immaculately bare.

My squad leader, Lieutenant Brophy, and the other two men on the team, Parks and Channing, treat me equitably, but we don't socialize. While we've become an extremely tight working unit, the prevailing wisdom is that it's dangerous to become emotionally involved. I guess Zaluta and I are just asking for trouble, but I can't imagine losing those wonderful evenings with his family. I'm willing to risk it.

When I first started having the dream about the raid on 302, I asked Zaluta if he thought I was going crazy.

"Naw," he said. I could tell by the way he wouldn't look me in the eye that discussing it troubled him. "We all get dreams. I heard once that the only way to get rid of one entirely is to replace it with something even worse."

"You have one, too?"

"Aw, sure. There was a raid back in seventy-two. A psycho twisted some pitiful old lady's head around two full turns while I stood there with my mouth hanging open. I always thought maybe I could have saved her if I hadn't been so green and scared. I don't dream about it as much as I used to, though. It gets better little by little, Larkin. You'll see."

I nodded, disturbed by the way his shoulders sagged and his broad face had grown pinched. I decided not to mention the subject again.

These past two years since the raid on 302 have rocketed past. I divide my time between police work and ballet and, usually, that's enough . . . until I key the lock to the dreary little closet I rent downtown. At some point, even cops and ballerinas have to go home. Maybe someday I'll buy some curtains, or a cat . . .

Detroit is often referred to as "Murder City" by the press, and from my own vantage point, the inner city resembles a monstrous, diseased organism that seems to grow exponentially by feeding on its own overabundance of poverty and rage. I don't know if a cure exists—I just help fight the symptoms: teenage gangs warring over drug turf, crazies strung out on crack and PCP, plus the usual family violence. Automatic weapons like Uzis and Baretta handguns equipped with 100-round banana clips are common in the rougher projects downtown. Drug turf battles are dangerous, but I would much rather respond to a gang war barricade then a nut barricade. Gang members usually surrender quickly—they're willing to trade their machismo for survival. But the whackos, they just don't give a damn, which makes them infinitely more treacherous.

Whatever the particular scenario happens to be, each assault is virtually the same, a tightly choreographed dance that never becomes routine. It's the part of my job I dread the most and love the best. The sweats and the jitters I experience seconds before an assault are indistinguishable from the butterflies I get backstage just before dancing in front of an audience. It's thrilling and terrifying at once.

When poised for an assault on a barricaded house or apartment, my heart is always in my mouth right before the door goes down. We never know what we'll find inside. When the door gives and we rush in, I go dead cool. Instinct and training kick in and, one way or the other, it's all over in a matter of minutes. Afterward, just like after a ballet performance, I experience an intensely gratifying rush of physical and emotional satisfaction we call the "afterburn" back in the squad room. It's what drives me, makes me push myself to the very limit of my capabilities, what clouds my judgement at times, but always, always satisfies . . . for the moment.

Zaluta says everyone is chasing the afterburn in one form or another, and I think he's right.

Sometimes I worry that I have some kind of weird attraction to brutality. Violence is integral to police work, of course, but not many people recognize the inherent self-inflicted violence of the ballet. Ballerinas look like fragile, fairy-like creatures who rest on satin pillows when not dancing—that's the illusion. Pink satin toeshoes and opaque tights usually conceal feet that look like raw hamburger and ugly surgical scars criss-crossing sprung knees and ankles.

Personally, I'm terrified of injuries and pain, but I keep running head-on at the possibility, nonetheless. I don't know, maybe there's something wrong with me. I've never been a particularly introspective woman, but after what happened last night . . . everything has changed. I've changed.

I had just showered up and was busy stowing gear in my squad locker yesterday evening when the call came in. It's unusual for an off team to get called back on duty since there are three other teams working on rotating shifts. When we arrived at the scene, it was already dark and cruelly cold as only a Detroit winter night can be. A large crowd of spectators had gathered across the street from a five story tenement building, brilliantly hideous against the black winter sky lit by rows of huge, smoking kleig lights. The crowd was clearly agitated, surging behind the phalanx of uniformed police officers who were having some difficulty keeping them in order.

"They've got my Momma!" A young black man wearing a flimsy grey sweatshirt shouted, trying to break past the sawhorse barrier.

An elderly woman shrieked, "Help me, God!" and collapsed in a faint, disappearing into the rippling sea of bodies.

It struck me as odd that none of the people who had assembled across the street were behaving like the usual gawkers who always turn out for a barricade. Instead of the typical good-natured spectators looking for a little excitement, each appeared to have something personal at stake.

Most of the women and a good number of the men were sobbing and moaning; none took their eyes from the floodlit building.

I knew then that it was going to be bad. Very bad.

When I heard Lieutenant Brophy summoning our squad for a briefing, I almost didn't want to hear what was going on. Christ, I thought, just let me do my job and get out of here. Then, as I was turning to join my team, the crowd stopped their frantic milling and shoving all at once. It made my flesh creep the way they stood like zombies, faces pale and distorted as they stared up at the building.

When I turned, I entered a waking nightmare.

Wailing in terror, little Carmelita Esposito, my nightmare child, was being dangled three stories above the sidewalk by a wild-eyed man. There was no doubt in my mind that the man was her father, Ralph Esposito, the man I'd killed two years before.

I went hot all over despite the frigid night wind. I felt like I weighed a thousand pounds, petrified.

I might still be standing there if Zaluta hadn't gripped my arm and started shouting, "Holy Jesus, Larkin! It's the old woman I told you about! Mother of God, her head's on backward and she's still alive! Oh, Jesus!"

I swung around and looked at Zaluta. His face was twisted in anguish as he watched the building. I shook his arm hard and he looked at me. I don't know how long we stood holding onto each other, but when we turned our eyes back to the building, whatever it was we'd seen had vanished.

All hell broke loose. The crowd behind us became a hysterical mob, screaming and pushing against the barriers, demanding that something be done. A two-way radio in a nearby squad car squawked something about assembly of a riot control unit. Curling clouds of frosty vapor rose before our faces as we breathed into the numbingly cold air, my own lungs pumping fast and heavy. A couple of teenage boys broke through the police barrier and made a run at the building, but were stopped and strong-armed back behind the line by one gigantic uniformed officer.

"I don't see any of the other assault teams around," I remarked to Zaluta as we headed for the equipment truck to pick up our gear. "I thought we were all supposed to be out here."

"I overheard the Chief telling Brophy that the other units were getting in place and ready to go. They're just waiting for a signal from the point team."

"Who's on point?" I asked.

"I don't know, but I'm glad it's not us."

I nodded as we pulled on our armor. "I'd like to know what the hell's going on. We're hallucinating or something worse. I feel like I'm dreaming."

"I *wish* you were dreaming," Zaluta said, hoisting his Heckler and Koch 9mm submachine gun, a real brute of a weapon that was just too heavy for me to handle. "If you were dreaming, we'd all be at home."

While we were adjusting our radio headsets, the rest of our team, Brophy, Parks and Channing, climbed into the back of the truck and joined us, their faces grim and pasty behind frosty crimson lips and noses.

"This is the deal," Lieutenant Brophy said, rubbing his hands together. "Something fucking weird is going on in that building."

Everyone snickered but Brophy, who cracked a sideways grin. Having successfully loosened us up, his mouth fell into a frown and his eyes narrowed. "Nobody knows what we've got in there. I guess I don't have to tell you that whatever is happening, we're all witnessing some pretty strange stuff."

Everyone nodded.

"Okay. Here's the plan. Earl Cook's unit is the point team. They're going to make an assault in a few minutes. We're last up, so we're just here for backup. We won't be called out unless the other teams fail to resolve this situation."

We all fell silent for a long moment.

"Here's what I know," Brophy continued. "Around six this evening, the department started receiving frantic calls from a number of hysterical people, all claiming to have seen a different event occurring at this address. Four uniformed officers entered the building shortly after six-thirty. Evidently, they never came out."

Carefully adjusting the armor protecting his groin, Brophy said, "Let's not bust our nuts worrying until we get a reconnaissance report from the point team, okay?" He looked up at me. "And you, Larkin, don't bust whatever it is you got to bust."

We laughed and shook our heads, then slowly filed out of the truck. Parks went to get everyone some hot coffee, and the rest of us took positions behind the rows of squad cars parked in a semicircle in front of the building. Then we waited. And waited. The tension was bone-crushing. There was a lot of fidgeting, shifting, and dry-throated coughs.

Behind us, the crowd rumbled like thunder, their collective growl a continual roar that rose and fell, punctuated by shrill cries and hoarse shouts. At the time, I considered that unruly throng as much of a threat to life and limb as the situation inside the building.

As it turned out, I was very much mistaken.

Then things started popping. The first team went in like gangbusters, detonating a number of small, grenade-shaped devices called Thunder

Flashers that explode harmlessly, but mimic miniature atomic bombs. You can't help but be disoriented momentarily, even when you know it's coming. Under cover of this diversionary blitzkrieg, they entered the building.

When the sound of the flash-bombs finally stopped reverberating in my ears, I could hear what was going on inside through the command radio hooked into the teams' two-way sets. There was gunfire mixed with the most gut-wrenching shrieks and screams I have ever heard, and which I suspect I'll be hearing in my head for a long, long time. I clenched my fists so tightly my fingernails punctured my palms. Wedged in between the screams were a few frantic words that I could just barely make out:

". . . outta here!" one of them yelled in a high-pitched squeal.

". . . fuckin dogs! . . . *No!* . . . *Jesus!* . . ."

The gunfire finally ceased, but the screams continued for at least another minute. Then there was a crackling silence.

After that terrible pause, everyone starting talking at once, and Brophy had to shout us down to make himself heard. Once we quieted, he said simply, "Unit Two is preparing to enter," and turned away.

Whispering close to my ear, Zaluta said, "That was Kellerman screaming about dogs on the radio. He's been scared shitless of dogs since a crack dealer holed up in a motel released a doberman on him a few years back."

We stared at each other. Everyone in the vicinity was experiencing his or her own private nightmare.

"Are we being purposely manipulated? Is this even *real*?" I asked, hearing my voice becoming shrill.

Zaluta shrugged his shoulders wearily and patted me on the arm. He was only in his late thirties, but he already looked like an old man. "I don't know, Larkin. I don't know."

The crowd was working itself into another frenzy when the second assault team silenced them by plunging into the building amid another round of booms and flashes.

Again, the radio crackled with shouts and gunfire. But this time, when the chaos died down, one distinct voice rose out of the background hiss, a trembly but jubilant voice declaring victory.

"I got the murdering bastard!" he cried. "I'm bringing him back alive, folks, so don't blow my ass off when we come out. And send in the medics stat, people. We've got a slaughterhouse in here. Okay, hold your fire now, we're exiting the building."

Hot relief swept over me. I spun around to face the building and began to cheer and clap with the others when two figures emerged.

"It's Delroy Stanton," Parks said.

The wild applause dwindled and died away slowly when it became apparent that something was amiss. Instead of driving a suspect at gunpoint, Stanton was dragging an inert, profusely bleeding man by the tattered collar of a midnight-blue shirt—an assault team shirt.

The prisoner appeared to be a member of his own unit.

"See?" Stanton shouted deliriously as a pair of medics rushed him and pulled away his prisoner. A group of officers, including Lieutenant Brophy, swarmed around him. His eyes were wild, rolling back to show white. "It's the *boogeyman*!" He fell to his knees and started to sob. "Oh, God! It's not even *human*!"

Too quickly for anyone to stop him, Stanton raised his handgun and placed it in his mouth.

"No!" Brophy shouted, charging at Stanton, hands stretching for the pistol.

I squeezed my eyes shut a split-second before the crack of the gun discharging racketed into the night, echoing through the cold streets.

Beside me, Zaluta moaned.

Complete pandemonium ensued. The crowd behind the lines went berserk, shrieking and throwing empty bottles and other debris as the policemen fought to hold them back. In our own camp, professional decorum evaporated. Angry demands for full disclosure raced through our ranks. Two of us were known dead, twelve more lives were probably lost inside the building.

A tenured officer named Detrick clambered atop a squad car with a bull horn and blared, "*Assault teams three and four report to command post at once!*"

"That's us," Zaluta said.

Following behind Zaluta, I was struck by the surreal quality of my perceptions. Even the shiny black heels of Zaluta's boots flashing and ebbing as he walked ahead of me looked strange somehow. Brighter . . . more textured. Sounds lost their sharp edges and became rounded, hollow.

When we arrived at the Command Post, a jerry-rigged open-air office on the far side of the police lines, Lieutenant Brophy and his Team Three counterpart were busy talking with the Chief and his people. Amidst the chattering department personnel was an odd little man dressed in a long black tunic covering tightly fitted black trousers. He stood solemnly, clutching a battered leather portfolio case to his narrow chest. As I stared at him, he swiveled his head and looked directly at me, pegging me to the spot with his luminous dark eyes.

We surveyed each other for a long moment, until the spell was broken by the strident voice of Mel Anderson, a flashy, balding department spokesman whose job it was to deal with the media.

"All right, people," Anderson called out, waving his arms and making his storm jacket bunch up around his neck. "Let's have some *quiet*! I have some information to pass along to you assault personnel, so listen up."

Lieutenant Brophy, standing behind Anderson, rolled his eyes and shook his head slightly, affirming his widely known dislike of the man we privately called "Captain Video".

"Now what we've got is this," Anderson continued, referring to a yellow legal pad in his left hand. "Two officers confirmed casualties, twelve officers missing in action and an unknown number of tenants inside the building, condition unknown. Identity of suspect or suspects unconfirmed. Causative factors, unconfirmed." He paused, delivering his patented Concerned Countenance, which I'd often seen him wear on the evening news. "We don't know exactly what's going on, so what we've done is bring in an expert on paranormal occurrences."

Putting his hands up to quell the rising buzz of indignant murmurs, he added, "Now, you all know that Homicide Division occasionally employs the services of psychics when they've hit a wall with their inquiries—"

"Oh, come on, man!" someone shouted.

"We ain't no Ghostbusters!" someone else yelled.

"Look!" Anderson said angrily, pointing a finger at us. "If any of you hotshots have the answer to what's going on in that goddamned building, step right up!"

Silence.

"Fine," he said, adjusting his tie. "Now shut up and listen." He extended an arm toward the little man in the black tunic, who walked over and stood next to Anderson. "Mr Chase has graciously consented to lend his expertise to the department and to work with us on this case. And it is therefore expected that all personnel will treat Mr Chase with the utmost dignity and respect." Turning a baleful eye toward us, he growled, "Is that *understood*?"

This is getting too weird, I thought, thanking Channing as he handed me a styrofoam cup of bitter-smelling coffee.

"I would like to speak to the young lady," Chase said in a thin voice tinged with an rolling accent.

Like everyone else, I started looking around for the alleged "young lady", but when my eyes returned to the strange little man the department had brought in, I was surprised to find that he was pointing at *me*.

I touched my chest and Mr Chase nodded. "Oh, Christ," I said under my breath, gulping my coffee down in three swallows.

Amid much hooting and laughter from the guys, I followed Mr Chase, Lieutenant Brophy and Mel Anderson to one of the squad cars and climbed into the back seat with Mr Chase.

"This is Corporal Larkin," Brophy said, twisting around in the front seat to face me. I noted the silent apology in his eyes. "What do you want with her?"

"She is the only person I saw with the aptitude to remedy this unfortunate occurrence," Mr Chase responded measuredly.

"What do you mean, 'aptitude'?" Anderson asked. "We've got plenty of men out there."

"My point exactly," Chase said. "Corporal Larkin's obvious aptitude, in this case, is her gender."

"Now, wait just a minute—" Brophy started, but was interrupted by Anderson.

"Mr Chase," Anderson said, "We need some answers here. We're laying the department's credibility on the line by inviting you into this matter, so if you can tell us something, please be clear."

The little man nodded his head politely and cleared his throat. "It is my firm belief that this disturbance is being caused by a drude," he announced. "'Drude' is an Old English expression for a nightmare fiend. According to most authorities, a young witch becomes a drude when she reaches the age of forty and then assumes the power to haunt any victim she chooses with terrible visions. Sometimes, this new power drives them mad, which is precisely what I believe has occurred here. And in order to put an end to her malicious activity, she must be destroyed. That is your answer, gentlemen."

He inclined his lips slightly, apparently amused by our dumbstruck expressions. He patted my forearm and added, "Males are powerless against drudes. You are therefore chosen, Corporal."

"Oh, this is *nuts*!" Brophy shouted. "Do you think I'm going to allow Larkin to go in there after two heavily armed squads have failed?"

Anderson had just opened his mouth to respond when every single window in the barricaded building exploded outward with a terrible shattering sound and sprayed a hundred foot perimeter with glittering shards of broken glass.

"Maybe we ought to hear Mr Chase out," Anderson said.

After we'd listened to Chase's incredible plan, Brophy looked at me with tired eyes and said, "It's up to you Larkin. It's your ass—you call it. I'm telling you right now that I think it stinks, but like Anderson says, the Chief will overrule me on this one for sure." He sneered at Anderson. "You guys will try anything to protect your public image, won't you?"

Anderson ignored him. "Our next best alternative is to send the two remaining squads anyway, Larkin. What if Mr Chase is right? All those lives . . . ?"

"Hey!" Brophy said, his face red with rage. He grabbed Anderson roughly by the collar.

"You better cool off, Brophy," Anderson said. "It's out of your hands."

"We'll see about that!" Brophy shouted, releasing Anderson's collar before slamming out of the squad car.

I appreciated Brophy's gesture, but I knew even then that it wouldn't make any difference. I was going into the building alone. It was simply a fact. I knew it in my heart. I saw it in Chase's ebony eyes. Some things are inevitable. So I said, "All right."

After a few more careful instructions from Mr Chase, I went over to the equipment truck to check out my radio and pick up some extra gear. If I refused the assignment and more people died as a result, it wouldn't be worth the effort to live. I had to do it.

But I was scared. Good Christ, I was scared.

Once I had made up my mind, Brophy and the rest of the guys quit trying to talk me out of it, but I thought I saw tears in Zaluta's eyes as I came down the ramp leading out of the truck. That's when I nearly backed out; I came so close to backing out . . .

But then Mr Chase was affixing something to the collar of my shirt. "This is the only thing that will work," he whispered.

I lifted my collar and saw an old fashioned hat pin inserted through the fabric. It was silver, about seven inches long and was topped with what looked like an enormous black pearl.

I looked down at Mr Chase. "The heart," he said. "Remember the heart."

I nodded, wondering who was crazier, him or me.

"Keep your focus," Chase continued. "None of it is real. Only the drude. But she cannot alter her own appearance before another formidable woman. Ignore everything else. Remember the signs I told you to look for and you'll find her."

Fastening a string of small explosive charges to my vest and snapping a clip into a 9mm Baretta semiautomatic handgun equipped with a flashlight attachment, I figured that I would be carrying nearly seventy pounds. My antiballistic armor weighed forty eight pounds alone. The additional weight of the handgun, clips and my A-2 was finally the limit I could bear and still move.

I had never really considered the utter strangeness of what I do for a living until I walked across that cold lot toward the building, the arsenal I carried swaying in time to my steps. I'm sure I must have looked like a erstwhile Valkyrie, except there was no Valhalla waiting for me—I was going in after a deranged *witch* who had taken up residence in a Detroit project building.

The radio buzzed and cracked in my ears. I adjusted the earpieces one last time before I stepped across the lines and crossed the lot toward the building. Hustling as fast as I was able, I crossed the open area of the courtyard until I hugged the icy bricks forming the base of the building. I got a quick glimpse of Zaluta crouched beside a nearby trash dumpster, his face was turned up, his mouth open wide.

Across the street, the crowd convulsed.

I tilted my head back just in time to see a plastic trash can teetering on the ledge of a third floor window being turned over. Before I could move, I was struck full in the face with a splattering gush of hot, clotting blood. When I could get my eyes open, I saw my nemesis, Ralph Esposito, leaning over the windowsill, leering at me past the edge of the dripping can.

I turned away, revolted and terrified. I tensed my body, trying not to retch, ignoring the shouting voice on the radio. *Concentrate*! I told myself. *It's not real*!

My breathing slowed and I looked down at myself. Clean and dry. Not a speck of blood. Chase had been right. It was going to be a battle of wills, not weapons. I looked up at the window. Nothing.

"It's all right," I whispered into the radio mouthpiece. "I'm going in."

Having thus committed myself, I trotted up to the fire-blasted front entryway and slipped into the building. It was similar to other project apartment houses I'd been in, except for one thing: a naked overhead bulb glared across the writhing floor of the entry hall. I found myself standing up to my ankles in snakes.

Something darted near my eyes and I instinctively batted it away with one hand. Panting, I watched my radio headset tumble into a thrashing reptilian mass at my feet. *Stupid*! I thought. I'd let myself be fooled into losing my communications. There were no snakes. Clamping down on my terror, I tried to concentrate, *concentrate* . . .

I blinked my eyes and the snakes vanished.

Not wanting to waste the time it would take to rehook my headset, I left it lying on the filthy grey linoleum. The building was still as a tomb. There wasn't a sign of a single living soul. Remembering Chase's instructions, I strained to hear a high-pitched keening sound, and I thought I could hear something fading in and out like a remote radio signal, a fluttering wail hovering on the far edge of my audial range. It was coming from above. I headed for the stairs.

When I reached the second floor, I edged around the corner and stood against the wall at the end of the corridor. Nothing moved. A coppery tang hung in the air, a salty odor I recognized instantly. Above it rode the sharp smell of cordite. Most of the lightbulbs lining the ceiling had been long since smashed or stolen, so the corridor lay in an eerie half-light. Hugging the wall, I inched down the corridor to find that all of the apartment doors had been left standing ajar.

Toeing open the first door, I discovered the bodies of several people strewn like smashed mannequins across the dimly lit living room. One of the dead, a large man with a rough beard, lay sprawled on his back, his hand still clutching a plastic handled steak knife with which he'd apparently slashed his own throat.

Feeling sick and lightheaded, I turned away from the carnage, taking deep draughts of air into my lungs. Back in the corridor, I leaned against the wall for a moment trying to regain my bearings and wondered what my odds of escape might be if I made a dash for the stairs.

I was thinking, *shit on this—I'm bailing out*, when I heard something behind me move.

I couldn't help screaming when I turned and faced the dark, bloodied figures that shambled toward me from the interior of the apartment. They jerked and hobbled as if drawn along by some mad puppeteer, eyes glazed and fixed on nothing.

Flashes of fire began strobing in front of me and there was thunder in my ears. A bitter cloud of blue smoke rose near my face, through which I could see the advancing corpses exploding and flying apart. It wasn't until after I'd expended my entire 30-round clip that I realized I had been firing my A-2 through the apartment doorway.

And they were still coming.

I turned and made a panicky run for it, breaking for the stairs. Honor and duty be damned. I couldn't think of anything but getting the hell out. I didn't care what happened as long as I got away.

I only made it as far as the top of the stairs when I heard a familiar voice call my name.

"Julianna," it barked in a familiar tone.

And I knew goddamned well that if I turned around, it would be a stupid, perhaps fatal, mistake. But I couldn't help it. I just had to look.

There in the filthy tenement corridor, not ten feet behind me, stood Madame Jedinov, starkly majestic in her wispy dancing skirts, baton in hand, a fierce look on her stern Baltic face.

I stared, astonished, as a huge black tongue snaked out of her mouth like lightning, wrapping itself around my neck and yanking me off my feet. I hit the linoleum floor like a sack of cement and my A-2 skittered out of my hands and bounced down the stairs. As the constriction around my neck tightened, I could hear braying laughter booming over my head.

No, I thought as little lights danced in my head. *I won't go down like this.* Clamping down on every fiber of my imagination, I forced myself to concentrate. *It's not real. It can't hurt me.*

When the corridor swam back into focus, I found myself on my knees with my own hands clenched around my throat. Releasing them,

I stood, coughing, and looked down the hallway. It was silent and empty. The buzzing in my head cleared until all that was left was that strange, electrical keening sound I'd first detected downstairs, stronger now.

I touched the collar of my uniform and found I'd almost dislodged the hatpin that Chase had inserted there. So that was the game: Get Rid of the Pin. The bitch was *scared*.

Jamming the pin tightly into my collar, I glanced down at my A-2 lying at the bottom of the stairs. I wouldn't be needing it. In my mind, I conjured up an image of a bent, hideous crone wearing a peaked black hat and focused on it. Placing my boot squarely on the first step leading to the third floor, I silently called out, *I'm coming for you*.

Soft laughter echoed above. A shimmering image appeared on the stairway, an abortive, half-formed horror that I was able to sweep away with a wave of my hand. *I'm wise to you now*.

Confident of my own power to dispel the drude's best efforts to fake me out, I jogged up the stairs, heart racing, hot for the game. *Go ahead*, I thought wildly. *Hit me with your best shot, honey*.

When I reached the third floor, I stopped dead in my tracks. Suspended from the overhead light fixtures that lined the ceiling were eight large, meticulously skinned human bodies. It was obscene. They swung like smokehouse hams in small, lazy circles spotlighted by naked bulbs above their dreadfully glazed, fleshy heads.

My hands flew to my mouth and I gagged. Looking away, I called back the imagery of the witch-crone and concentrated upon it, hating her, crowding out the revulsion and terror with rage. With a strangled cry, I turned and charged down the hallway directly at the swaying atrocities the drude had conjured to stop me. I would reduce them to vapor like the one on the stairs.

It's impossible to describe how horrible, how shocking, how loathsome it was when I collided with that cold, wet slab of human meat. I struck it hard, bouncing backward off of it and hitting the floor hard. I lay there looking up, seeing that terrible dripping thing dangling over me, trying to get my breath back.

There was a soft popping noise and the corpse, evidently released from its mooring, toppled from the ceiling and collapsed on top of me.

A woman's shrieking laughter filled the corridor, drowning out my screams as I struggled to get out from under the inert body pinning me on my back, holding me in a repugnant embrace.

Her laughter racketed in my ears, making it impossible to think. My heart pounded painfully hard, forcing great pulsing torrents though my body. My will and concentration had been pushed to the wall. I was unsure if I possessed the emotional strength to handle my predicament. Surely my spirit could not survive one more shock.

And then the lights went out.

Silence. Not a sound except my own breathing. I managed to push away the thing on top of me and it hit the floor with a wet, slapping noise that reverberated oddly, like in a cavern.

Grabbing the handgun out of my belt holster, I flicked on the flashlight attachment and swung the beam out across a domed roof that undulated with the squirming bodies of huge brown bats. One of them disentangled itself from the seething mass and flew at me, striking my chest, snapping at my throat.

As I grappled with it, trying to tear it away, I dragged my left hand across the point of the pin in my collar, painfully ripping open the skin of my palm. *Remember the pin! The drude is trying to get the hatpin*, I thought wildly. *There's no cave, no bats. Concentrate.*

The cavern rippled and shimmered, then faded into the walls of the tenement corridor. Arcing my flashlight to the end of the hallway, I saw that the shadows pooling there seemed to be alive, thrashing like storm clouds. This was a sign, according to Mr Chase. She couldn't bear the light, he'd said, and threw out darkness like a squid expels ink. Being careful to avoid contact with the remaining bodies suspended from the ceiling, I followed the beam to the end of the hall. I flashed the light on the door. The numbers on the scarred metal fire door read, "302".

I should have known.

This is it, I told myself as I pressed a small clay charge beneath the doorknob. Standing well to one side of the door, I triggered the charge. The door blew open and stood ajar, smoking.

Edging past the door, I played the beam of my flashlight around the room, but the darkness was so thick that the light scarcely cut three feet into the gloom. A bright pain blossomed in my heart with each breath I took. My soul was exhausted and damaged. I truly did not think I would be alive much longer, and the unadorned reality of that absolute belief somehow washed away my dread of death, filling me with one burning conviction: to make my last act on earth a meaningful one.

I was going to take that crazy bitch down with me.

"Where are you, you fucking *hag*?" I shouted, ignoring the tears blurring my vision. I whipped the flashlight beam back and forth, until it fell upon a pale figure standing in the whirling darkness.

His naked body was very white where it was not splashed with blood. My own personal nightmare, Ralph Esposito, stood with a viciously gleeful smile on his mad face. In front of him, he clutched a beautiful little girl by her dark hair, holding a dimestore pocket knife to her throat.

Little Carmelita begged me to save her with desolate brown eyes.

"I'll peel her like a grape if you take one more step," her father growled.

I didn't have the strength to banish the delusion, so I let it play itself out. Sobbing like a child, I moved forward.

Ralph Esposito drew the blade evenly across her smooth neck. She went rigid and shrieked as a crimson trickle necklaced her tender throat.

"*Stop it!*" I screamed. I couldn't stand it. I couldn't bear the child's agony, real or imagined. Dropping to my knees, I begged, "*please . . .*"

I felt the light touch of a hand on my back. I turned to face whatever new demon had been summoned to torment me and looked into the jet black eyes of a divinely beautiful goldenhaired woman.

"You're tired," she murmured. "So tired."

Her sympathy drained me. I slumped at her feet, my face against the silken fabric of her long skirt. If I could close my eyes and rest a while . . .

I felt her hand slide to my collar and gently tug at the pin, but her soothing voice lulled me into a dreamy fantasy. I was wearing a crystalline costume, dancing on a mirror in a child's jewel box, spinning round and round—

A sudden thunder pounded overhead, shaking the floor beneath me, jarring me awake. I reached up and grasped the hand fumbling with my collar.

The drude screeched in my ear and tore at my face with her free hand. Feeling her nails tear deep furrows across my cheek, I jerked my handgun up until the barrel jammed under her chin and emptied the clip into her head.

The drude screamed with laughter and knocked the gun out of my hand, the flashlight beam pinwheeling through the roiling dark and coming to rest beyond my reach. If anything, she had grown even stronger, fighting like a wildcat. Though barely half my size, she possessed at least twice my strength. And she was choking the life out of me. I couldn't allow her get hold of the pin.

The bass thrumming overhead increased, filling the room with its heavy pulsations.

The sound distracted her for a scant moment and I took advantage of it, knocking her off balance as she sat on my chest. Whipping my leg around, I caught her across her neck and levered her onto her back.

Above us, the booming throb increased to a deafening intensity.

I yanked the hatpin out of my collar and held it out before me. The drude disappeared into the shadows.

I spun around, my heart banging painfully in my chest. She could be anywhere, ready to pounce on me from behind. I edged over to where my gun lay and picked it up, flashing the beam around me.

The building pulsed and shook. *Whop-whop-whop.*

I found her. She was cowering in a dark corner, shielding her eyes from the light, making pitiful mewling sounds.

She looked up, her lovely face stricken with pain and fear. "Please," she whimpered. "Please. Don't kill me."

Her anguish caught me by surprise and that one moment of hesitation on my part was all she wanted.

She sprang at me with blinding speed, but I was ready for her. When she grabbed my wrist, I felt bones splinter but held fast to the hatpin. It was her own hand that helped drive the pin up beneath her ribcage and into her heart.

She stiffened, her black eyes wide with surprise. Exhaling a gust of foul breath into my face, she went limp and her knees buckled. I went down with her, driving the pin hard, setting it deep.

Pulling myself to my feet, I looked down at her small, crumpled form. There was no victory here. The swirling darkness receded, leaving the room in its former dingy, trash-strewn verity. Above the thunderous pandemonium roaring over my head, I heard the wail of a baby.

Emerging from a cluttered corner, Carmelita Esposito, the most beautiful child ever born on this planet, wobbled unsteadily toward me on pudgy toddler's legs, arms outstretched.

A indescribably intense rush of joy surged through me when I picked that precious baby up and held her in my arms. She was safe. She was mine. I would never let her go. *Never.*

Hugging her close, I sidled up to a bare window where jagged shards of windowpane rattled in the casement from the bedlam outside. Gales of cold wind blew into our faces, bright lights shone down from overhead. I recognized the insectile outlines of the black shape hovering over us.

A Chinook helicopter hung above the building, its rotors roaring and throbbing.

What are they doing up there? I wondered, certain that any rescue operation would certainly be ground-based.

Something was being lowered from the side of the chopper, something that looked like a large coffee can on a wire.

A bomb. They were going to bomb the building! Images of the Philadelphia MOVE house bombing, the explosion and subsequent conflagration leaped into my mind.

The chopper eased up to a higher altitude, readying for the drop. There would be no time to escape from the building's entrance door. I screamed up at them, but my voice was lost in the chopper's backwash. There was only one alternative left for Carmelita and me, and not a very good one.

My mind set, I kicked the remaining glass out of the window and looked down. At least a thirty foot drop to frozen turf. If I wrapped myself around the child and let my legs take the impact, she might not be injured. My legs would be shattered. The dance . . .

"Fuck it!" I shouted, ripping off my teflon vestpiece and wrapping Carmelita in it. Her big brown eyes flickered with light.

Holding her tightly to my chest, I climbed over the casement and pushed out, leaping into the cold, cold night.

As if suspended, we seemed to drift like a feather. I saw the ground coming up slowly, slowly.

As we fell, the top floor of the building exploded behind us in a gigantic fireball of mortar and steel.

The ground surged to meet us. I felt a tremendous impact as my legs slammed into the ground. I could sense that the big bones had shattered on contact, but there was no pain.

Then silence.

Lying on my back, I couldn't raise my head, I couldn't move. Then I felt the light pressure of a small hand on my face and Carmelita's sweet face rose over mine.

I remember smiling, then spinning down, down into blackness.

I came around slowly, my blurred vision focusing itself on Zaluta's worried face.

"Is the baby all right?" I asked.

"Baby?" Zaluta said, then motioned to someone beyond my visual range.

A white-coated medic kneeled down beside me and flicked a penlight beam across my eyes. I pushed it away, angry now.

"The baby! Is she *all right*?"

Zaluta looked at the medic and shrugged. "Looks like she took a pretty hard lick from that bottle."

"What?" I demanded, becoming extremely upset with him.

"One of those jerks in the crowd lobbed a bottle at us and it caught you in the back of the head, Larkin. Knocked you silly for a couple seconds, but you're going to be okay," Zaluta explained.

"Wait a minute," I said, sitting up and rubbing the painful knot near the base of my skull. I looked at my legs: straight and healthy. I stood up. I was behind the barrier with the rest of the police personnel. "What's happened?"

Not understanding my question, Zaluta said, "False alarm, kiddo. They dragged us out here for nothing. The situation's been resolved."

"You mean it's all over?"

He nodded. "Team One went in and found the suspect dead. Suicide. They're bringing her out now."

"Her?"

"Yeah, some woman on the third floor caused a ruckus then offed herself. Stabbed herself to death with some kind of long pin, can you imagine? A neighbor said it was the woman's fortieth birthday. Happy birthday, huh?"

We watched them wheel out the gurney with the body bag strapped across it; I didn't need to see the dead woman. I knew her face. I just wanted to go to the studio and try to dance away the empty feeling in the pit of my stomach.

I dumped my gear and walked through the dark Detroit nightstreets toward the studio. A light sprinkling of snow drifted down from the swirling black sky and glittered like diamonds in the harsh glow of street lamps.

I stood out in front of the old warehouse housing the dance studio watching the snow obliterate the grey ugliness of the city, trying to remember how little Carmelita's hand had felt against my face. But I couldn't get it back. The dream was gone.

Sighing, I turned and unlocked the warehouse door and flicked on the lights. The stairs to the dance studio seemed unusually steep as I trudged up to the dressing room. Released from the confinement of my uniform, I pulled three pairs of legwarmers over my tights to protect my ankles and calves against the unheated chill of the building. There was a dull ache in my chest as I laced the pink ribbons of my toeshoes and tested the firmness of the pointes.

When I went to close my locker, I noticed a black velvet case resting on the top shelf. Picking it up, I found a plain white note card concealed beneath it. The note read:

> Remember the heart.
> Your fond admirer,
> D. Chase

Inside the case lay a silver hatpin topped with a huge black pearl.

Technique, line, proportion, balance: it is clear to me now that these things apply in all areas of life. I dance feverishly, spinning and leaping, thinking of my bleak rented room, my bleak heart.

Enough. Dripping perspiration, I cool myself down with a series of slow barre exercises. Mopping my neck with a towel as I leave the studio, I stop in the wardrobe room and inspect my costume for tonight's performance of Stravinsky's *Firebird*. It is exquisite; leotard and headpiece ablaze with flashing orange and red sequins and streaming yellow feathers.

Dancing the principal role this evening, I will feel like Pavlova. It makes no difference that this performance will take place in a elementary school auditorium. It's the dance that matters, not the stage. Zaluta and his family will be in the first row and, instead of dancing for myself, tonight I am going to dance for them.

And when the dance is finished, I will sleep. I will not wake up afraid in the night. There is nothing left to fear. Tomorrow I will remind myself that life is more than a series of choreographed movements. I must learn to open my heart. It will be difficult, I know, but I have always enjoyed a challenge.

Concentration is the thing.

DAVID J. SCHOW

Incident on a Rainy Night in Beverly Hills

DAVID J. SCHOW is probably getting bored with being described as the man who coined the term "splatterpunk"—his own fiction far outstrips the "guts and gore" mentality foistered on readers by some members of that would-be movement.

Schow won the *Twilight Zone Magazine's* readers poll for his short story, "Coming Soon to a Theatre Near You", and recent anthology appearances include *The Year's Best Horror Stories, Book of the Dead, Pulphouse 7, Fantasy Tales, Dark Voices 3* and *The Mammoth Book of Terror*.

Besides a string of TV novelizations written under a pseudonym, his books include the novels *The Kill Riff* and *The Shaft* and the collections *Seeing Red* and *Lost Angels*. He has edited the anthology *Silver Scream* and co-authored the non-fiction study, *The Outer Limits: The Official Companion*.

David Schow also scripted the movies *Leatherface The Texas Chainsaw Massacre III* and *Critters 3* and *4*. With his insider's knowledge of Hollywood, the story that follows just could be more than fiction . . .

J ONATHAN BRILL WAS THINKING: *The last time I saw Haskell Hammer, he was dead set on becoming a famous writer of screenplays in Hollywood.*

The siren song of Southern California has always been the Big Break—a litany everyone babbles and no one truly believes. The Big Break. According to myth, you stumble across it by accident . . . or it mows you down on purpose. The thing in which people believe is the tease, the promise of the litany.

Rain droplets crawled down the windowpanes and blurred the view from the den. Jonathan permitted his gaze to defocus. Across his west lawn was his cul-de-sac; in it was parked his Mercedes. Sensible businessman's gray had been his choice of car color. The driveway beyond meandered down Carla Ridge and insulated him from the old Trousdale Estates branch of Beverly Hills.

Among his home's fourteen rooms, Jonathan Brill's favorite was his den. He inventoried it in terms of matériel: wood, glass, paper, fiber, canvas, metal.

Teak was for the paneling, mahogany for the sprawling three-quarter administrator's desk, thick oak planks for the pegged library shelving that dominated half the wall space. The narrow tinted windows through which he watched the rain were Nadia Charas commission work featuring her characteristic lozenge-shaped leaded panes. Floor to ceiling, in ordered ranks, stood the books. Behind the desk was a long, low buffet groaning with reference and overpriced showoff volumes; near the windows was a sideboard with sliding glass doors entombing a matched complement of leatherbound first editions. The carpet was a lush pile in a sober dark brown, directionally combed. Jonathan had been dramatic about arranging the few paintings he liked beneath pinlight spots. The originals included a Picasso ink wash and a Franz von Stuck from the turn of the century—one of the German Symbolist's terrifically popular *Sin* series, mostly forgotten now. It depicted a voluptuary encoiled by a giant, malevolent snake, the sort of thing Freud would have a field day with. As with the Bruckner aluminum sculpture brooding down from its special nook, to Jonathan the acquisition held meaning beyond art. When admirers mentioned *worth*, he thought *price*, and had long ago chosen to make the best of this unfortunate incapacity. The edition of *Moby Dick* he held cradled to his chest as he stood by the windows had cost one thousand dollars in 1979. It was a miracle of thoughtful book-bindery. It was a *thousand-dollar book*, an investment, more stable than the messier forms of human transaction that had left Jonathan with his fourteen-room home all to himself this year. Any journeyman shrink could point his or her pipe at Jonathan's overdone den and quack "compensatory surrogate," and they'd be right, but Jonathan found he relished the feeling of control he got from rattling around his house all by himself after the hired help had come and gone. He already knew most of the punchlines that his colleagues would apply to his life—his *new* life—and dismissed them. They were just envious. His divorce from Janice was history, and now he was free of her forever.

And the last time Haskell Hammer saw me, I was going to grow up to be a successful analyst. He held his thousand-dollar book in one hand and a slug of Grand Marnier in the other, holding his contemplative pose by the rainspattered windows. *Shrink to the brats of the stars, he had kidded me. Elbow to the ribs. Ha-ha, sho' nuff.*

The pleasant music of his door chimes soured when cycled over and over. The help had clocked out for the day; Jonathan had finally answered the door himself, prepared to dispense with some lunatic Jehovah's Witness or door-to-door Scientologist. Instead he found his old buddy Haskell Hammer crutched against the glowing button, looking as though a bus had mistakenly dropped him off in hell and he had hoofed it through miles of brimstone just to get back to Hollywood.

Haskell's opening dialogue had seemed depressingly melodramatic. *This was the only place I could come . . . you're the only person who'll understand . . . they've choked off my escape avenues . . . they're after me. . . .*

After a beat of honest shock, Jonathan's professional face slid into position. The personal, the emotional, the reactionary aspects of his anima retreated behind the shield of persona. Ego beats id. Diploma wraps stone.

Haskell had nearly swooned into his arms. Then followed, like a bad movie cliché, the restorative pop of cognac and the sudden clearing of Haskell's eyes that denoted a return to the universe of the rational. He would, of course, have a story to tell. This narrative was to be revealed as soon as he emerged from the shower in Jonathan's guest bathroom, where he had been holed up for nearly half an hour.

Far to the south, lightning belabored Century City. A shudder of thunder freed speckles of water to roll earthward along the panes. Jonathan considered his own reflection, the professional at ease, a still life of sober erudition with his leatherbound tome and balloon glass full of overpriced joy juice. All day the sky had retained the ominous hue of old newsprint; now it was as black and dense as the leaded ornamentation sectioning the glass panes.

He added half an inch to his snifter and slipped the special Arion edition of *Moby Dick* into its precise vacancy on the oak bookshelf. Melville was just the sort of intimidating bulwark of literature—pronounced *lich-ri-cha*—that no person of style or means would ever browse idly. The public schools had propagandized against

Melville, poor bastard. Even Jonathan would only pick up the book to hold his grand in his hand. It would remain undisturbed on the shelf.

Lightning tines, closer this time, colored the sky again. In the window Jonathan saw the reflection of a silhouette filling the den doorway, behind him. Haskell's hair was slicked blackly back in a wet pompadour and the smell of a fresh cleansing radiated from him. Jonathan dashed a few fingers of cognac into a new glass.

"Can we close the curtains?"

The talk barrier had been broken. Good. Jonathan already knew the window was not visible from the road, but kept it to himself. He drew a thin cord and the burgundy drapes swished grandly together, compressing the den, making it a bit more claustrophobic. This was to be a backstage interview.

"Not paranoia, Jon, I swear," he said. Yet his movements seemed nervous and furtive. He accepted the brandy snifter, then jumped away like a suspicious dog; when he moved to the cluster of sofa and chairs near the window, he immediately selected a corner seat that kept his back to the bookshelves and left him in a position to keep a jumpy watch on both the windows and the entrance to the den. "Not paranoia. I'm not crazy, either. Just cautious."

Jonathan stopped down a wince of disappointment. *Oh, christ,* INVASION OF THE BODY SNATCHERS, *gimme a break!*

Sensing this, Haskell perked up. "God, don't I know what *that* sounds like. When people babble under stress, their dialog would offend the worst B-movie hack. Ever wonder if you were a mouthpiece for some keyboard-basher's rotten cosmic screenplay? You work in Hollywood long enough, you realize that what life needs is pacing, better camera angles, less exposition, and a crack editor to re-order the whole mess into something interesting. And dénouements."

"Stay in my neighborhood long enough," said Jonathan, "And you begin analyzing reflex conversation, plumbing the sordid, crazed, anal-retentive depths of *have a nice day*." He felt a flush of guilt. Haskell had been his friend. After a rush of years he had come to him for help out of the night, obviously as a barrel-bottom last resort. If Jonathan could not fix things, what in hell was his purpose on the planet? "Don't start at the beginning," he said. "Start with whatever is of the most importance."

"Simplicity," said Haskell, uttering a harsh little laugh. "The Conclave."

"Which is?"

"A phalanx of men and women you've never read about in *Variety*. Consummate business folk. A tiny, elite federation. Compressed, efficient. Mother, are they ever efficient. . . ."

"Movers and shakers. What are they into?"

"Movies, what else?" said Haskell as though it was obvious to a child. "They 'make' movies, by helping movies make money. They make reputations. They deal in success, not excess. It's the only game in this town."

"You mean they're a production group?"

"No." Haskell struggled against a vast and insubstantial void, realizing the futility of wrestling with a ghost. He used up dead time by looking from the curtains to the door to Jonathan. He sipped his cognac. With a sigh of frustration—the sound of a drowning man who sees that rescuers do not notice him—he fought to find a way to encapsulate the ideas in his head and push them out into the light for examination. Jonathan could see the ideas were massy and unwieldy, involving an obvious danger that was easily overlooked, like a hostile gray bull elephant lurking against a gray building. When Jonathan considered that simile, he noticed that Haskell himself had grayed quite a lot in the years since they'd last talked. The black hair was interrupted by frequent striations of dead marble whiteness, where composure had seemingly been bleached away. Where Haskell's hip self-confidence had been bartered away in some devil's pact that left ashes in the soul and a red rime of fear crusting the eyes.

"Jon," he said finally. "Did you ever notice those white vans all over Los Angeles, the ones with the microwave dishes on the roof, and the highbeam transmitters that look like someone made a science fiction prop out of two oversized shotgun microphones? Sometimes you see them on residential streets, just sitting there, or parked next to the newspaper machines outside a restaurant. Ever wonder what they're for?"

Jonathan hoped his smile was encouraging. "I've always shrugged them off as TV news, or CIA, or cable-service trucks. Always unmarked. No panel windows, and what glass there is is heavily reflectorized." Two words nattered in his brain, and they were *conspiracy paranoia*.

"And sometimes with no external gear at all. Just another faceless white van. But in your gut you know they're all kin."

"Right." Jonathan remained casual. It would not do for Haskell to think he was being humored.

"Ever see the film *Gimme Shelter*?" Haskell was deadpan.

Non sequitur? Jonathan raced to make identification while he kept his face relaxed and friendly. "Yes. A long while ago. The Rolling Stones documentary of the Altamont Speedway concert. Lots of narrative by Melvin Belli, the attorney. Raw, spontaneous footage of a man getting knifed right in front of the stage."

"You remember the story they used to tell about *Ben-Hur*, the industry story for stuntmen?"

"That's one I'm not familiar with."

"Rumor had it that during the film's climactic chariot race a stuntman was run over by his own chariot after a muffed fall. Killed. For years, people insisted that if you looked closely enough at the finished footage, you'd actually see the poor son of a bitch getting crushed in living color."

"Just like the stabbing at Altamont."

"Or the riot footage from the Chicago Democratic Convention in Wexler's *Medium Cool*. Real head bashings; blood you *knew* wasn't Karo Syrup and food dye. When a truncheon bounces off a head in that film, you *feel* it pulverizing bone and tissue." He was rolling now, albeit with queasy uncertainty, the kind that treads softly in the psyche. He did not want Jonathan to dismiss him before he reached the crux. His job had always been to make such stories palatable, whether they were true or not, to live creatively through a typewriter. It would be an absurd shame if he botched it with the truth. "Let's escalate now, shall we? *Snuff*. You've heard of it, I'm sure. Purports to be an actual filmed record of torture and murder. The people you see being killed actually *were* killed—or so the myth goes. Tell me, Jon, just offhand, what's the current moneymaker playing all over Hollywood and Westwood?"

"Having not made it out to the movies in about three weeks, I'd say that movie *The Nam*, because it's been on the news so much."

"Uh-huh. Why?"

"Well, because—" Jonathan stopped and sought Haskell's eyes, his glass hesitating midway to his mouth. "Because of that TV actor who was killed during filming. Supposedly you can see him getting blown to smithereens. It got a lot of media. Three-ring coverage."

"Supposedly you can also see the guy's blood on the camera lens. But the only reality you can be sure of is that because of that scene, the film is now minting money fist over asshole, as my little brother used to say." He finished his drink.

"But did that actor—did he . . .?"

"His name was Pepperdine," said Haskell.

"Did he really die, or not?"

"There you go, Jon, off down the slide. In your eyes, right now, I can see the thing that's making *The Nam* such a hit. The lust to know, coupled with the proximity of death, the most undeniable thing there is. Yes, Pepperdine died. What you see in the movies is real. But no accident."

"You're suggesting that this man's death was arranged, premeditated in order that a motion picture could pull in more bucks at the box office?" He was flustered and incredulous. "For god's sake . . ."

"Not only was it arranged," said Haskell, motioning for more cognac. "But it's a perfect example of how I've been making my living for going on five years now."

The Grand Marnier bottle sat on the table between them like an obscenely large salad cruet. The cognac's pleasant orange taste went flat and tacky in Jonathan's mouth.

He rediscovered his voice. "You can't be serious," he said to the curtains as lightning flared outside. Dramatic sting.

"Now *you* sound like one of those bad B-movie characters." For the first time, a phantom smile wisped past Haskell's lips.

"Backtrack, Haskell. You're going to confess to me that spectacular fluke deaths connected to the movie industry are being engineered for the sole purpose of profit?" He tried to juggle the concept in his head and chanced across a good example. "That, say, the disaster at Three Mile Island was *set up* so that *The China Syndrome* would be a hit film?!"

"Wait, Jon, just a second. I never asked you to believe me, or anything I'm about to tell you. I've got one reason for coming here."

"Shoot." Ha-ha, another cinematic pun.

Haskell seemed anything but crazy now. Ragged, and harried, and on the brink of some inner breakdown of spirit, yes, but not bereft of sanity. "You predate my involvement with the Conclave by years," he said, fingers laced, contemplating the floor. "We were friends back in our idealistic youth. This whole Conclave thing weighs on my brain; I want to get it out of my head and push it away from me. Because I might not have a whole lot of time left, and like a character in a shabby B-movie—one with simple, easily encapsulated motives—I want to clear my conscience in whatever cheap, shabby way I can. I lucked across your name. I'll get to that later. But I lucked across it, and remembered you'd made a go of your aspiration to psychiatry—shrink to the stars' kids, remember?—so I decided to despoil your doorstep in the dead of night."

"No problem for a friend. And I *am* a professional ear. It would look like you chose correctly. So let's have it."

"Thank god. I'd hoped you'd cut around the bullshit and deal with the core." He rose, refilled his snifter, and drank down another thunderbolt of liquor. "Cigarettes anywhere?"

Jonathan lit Haskell's and decided against one for himself. Haskell inhaled strength and urgency; expelled psychic cinders and decay. Another guarded glance at the window, and he spoke.

"They propositioned me right after Maureen died. I was ripe with ideas for films, stories, articles, projects . . . all with no takers. Maureen had a stroke. I blamed it on the hours her own career hustling imposed on her—the tryouts, the auditions, the commercial shoots. When she died, I was reactionary and bitter—cannon fodder for any good scheme. The Conclave recognized a good vengeance motive and exploited mine. I wanted to make 'the Industry' pay for my loss of Maureen. After nine months I began to wonder if the Conclave had somehow set up her death in the first place, just because they had a slot on the table of Scripters that needed filling. But by then it didn't matter—that was how my thinking had changed."

"Scripters?"

"That was what they called us. Seven of us. It turned out they had read every unfilmed script I'd ever written, and every page of every story I'd ever submitted anywhere. They said my kind of story logic was what they needed. I wound up helping them to blueprint formulae whereby events are programmed to yield maximum profit. Simply stated, that was our sole aim. Scripters, as opposed to writers. You won't find the vocation on an IRS form anywhere."

"Nor any mention of the Conclave, I gather."

Haskell coughed, and with the attitude of a true nicotine addict, puffed his cigarette for relief. "We were tax immune anyway. The money we got paid never existed. Do you recall the legal flap several years ago concerning the profit breakdown on that space monster film—the one that cost ten million to make, grossed fifteen times that much, and didn't show a profit?"

"I remember. Lawsuits flew like chaff in a typhoon." The *Variety* rule of thumb stated that a film had to gross two and a half times its cost to break even. The estimate had recently been revised upward to 2.7, but either way it meant that in this particular case there was a boatload of cash that needed to be answered for.

"Conclave smoke," said Haskell. "Haven't you ever stopped to wonder why Hollywood continues to bash its head against the impenetrable brick wall of movie musicals? They *never* make money—*Grease* was a fluke—and yet every year we get two or three bombs like *Song of Norway* or *Lost Horizon* or *Annie*. Why? Same reason the alien monster movie didn't make any cash until it got too big to hide."

"Sounds like a whopper of a petty-cash till."

"*Studio Advisory Overhead* covers a lot of yardage in contractese." He shrugged. "Scripters have to be well paid."

Jonathan tilted his head solemnly. Any elite profession that had only seven experts would *have* to pay by the shovelful.

"It was a minor vogue among the Scripters themselves to be paid in gold bullion, direct to Swiss accounts. None of us would touch American dollars with a cattleprod. And payment of that sort suited the Conclave just peachy. It gave them both secrecy and control."

"It was enough money to compensate for all the Hollywood ego tripping the job itself denied you?" Jonathan paused a beat, and then said, "Dumb question, I'll wager."

"Their leverage exceeds monetary power," said Haskell. "That's why I'm sitting here spilling this to you, instead of to the law enforcement agencies of our fair state. The Conclave *likes* fascist governors, and I suppose you've noticed that our own current chief executive is just another creation of the media." He cut loose a harsh, jagged laugh. "Metro cops that go for thirty large per year don't even provide nuisance value."

"Money and power," mused Jonathan. "It's almost impossible for me to conceive of that much . . ."

"Incentive? It's easy." Bitterness flushed Haskell's face as he overrode his friend. "Is there anyone you know whose life is worth ten million to you? Or the six, nine, twelve million spent on prints and publicity? Nope. It gets easy to say it: he, she, or it dies . . . if that's what you need to make money, to keep everyone employed and grinning."

The operational clarity of the Conclave was classically pragmatic. Chilling. It demanded utter ruthlessness up front, a petcock shutoff of human emotions.

Said the siren song: *Do us a trick and we'll make you a star. But then you have to do us a bigger trick.*

"All sorts of ideas fell from the creative hats of the Scripters. When I left, things were turning evil. Let me run some ideas past you, to give you a bigger picture." His tone was now maddeningly reasonable. He might have been discussing market futures. In a way, he was. "Posited: a romanticized gang movie. We set up shootings and knifings at selected theatres with high news visibility. Grownup news commentators frowned, and word of mouth made the film a blockbuster. Remember the first manufactured controversy over gory horror films, that whole riff that they were misogynistic, sexist? A Scripter I worked with, a woman, thought that one up over lunch one afternoon. The more simplistic pop critics ate it whole and regurgitated it to their audiences. It's been more than a decade now, and those goddamn movies are still minting cash!

"Occasionally, the Conclave votes that a chosen actor should *expire*—never say die. They graph boxoffice draw over a span of years and pull a final jolt of income by killing off the actor. Funny how John Wayne died of cancer right after making a film about a cowboy who dies of cancer . . . See Blah-Blah's *final film*! They—we—called it the Rockstar Formula."

"Death equals increased album sales," Jonathan said. "Like with Jim Morrison, or—"

"Yeah, well, I don't know about John Lennon or Henry Fonda. Some recent occurrences—look at the Natalie Wood thing—have the earmarks of Conclave jobs but I sure as hell couldn't tell you if they were bona fide or not. You gain an eye for the techniques after a while, but the Conclave is always refining and modifying their approach, in case some outsider starts adding up facts. And sometimes fate intercedes—I think that was the case with Lennon. Random acts still happen, even in the 1980s. But Lennon's death was a profit setup from square one whether it was programmed that way or not."

Jonathan said nothing.

"You have that expression on your face again, Jon. What you're thinking is what I've mulled over a billion times. It is cold. You have to turn yourself off, function only on the medulla level. You consider a problem dispassionately, the way a mathematician faces down an equation."

"You did all this for money?" Suddenly Jonathan was rudely aware of his stained-glass windows, and expensive desk, and sybaritic carpeting, and the things he had done to get them. His eyes picked out his thousand-dollar copy of *Moby Dick* on the costly oak and peg shelf.

"Not just for money. I'm not sure I can explain why the opportunity appealed to me—explain in any sane way, I mean." He let his open hands fall into his lap.

"I'm not as dumb as you may think," Jonathan said colorlessly. "I've got a pretty fair idea of why you or any other creative mind would go for it: Hollywood doesn't break ground anymore. It's a creative dry well. Screenplays are infinitely rewritable so that studio middle management can stay employed. Directors find their final cuts being edited by the PR department and their endings being dictated by know-nothing preview audiences. The studios have all co-opted each other, and the whole circus has been inside the tight fists of the accountants for at least the past thirty years. People don't watch films today, they watch corporate deal-making in action. Once, filmmakers made their films and then sold them. Now it's the other way around—money isn't to make movies, movies are to make money. The screenplay, as manipulable as hamburger, is just a formality amid formulaic, simpleminded formats, 'name' stars, 'name' directors, and 'hot properties.' The accountants add these raw materials together exactly like mathematicians—and label the result their 'product.' It's borne a system in which any film that doesn't gross a hundred million dollars is deemed a failure. In such a system, the last bastion of true creativity is the guy who can figure out how to present such tired garbage in such a way that it is a success, thanks to millions of moviegoers being conned into believing it is something fresh and original and moving."

Jonathan had an absurd picture of the archetypal Hollywood Meeting. Haskell was pitching the idea for a dark little film indeed, and Jonathan was examining the concept from all angles, trying to decide whether to buy it. "The most creative intellect, therefore," he decided, "would be the person who could compose social events or sculpt media attention unobtrusively. Real death can lure a jaded and reactionary public, and the scenarios must be increasingly complex in order to remain convincingly 'real.' The challenge to any creative mind is obvious: while your legitimate screenplays and ideas were considered disposable, your dictates as a Scripter would have to be elaborate, meticulous, loophole free . . . and absolute. You see? At last the *creator* gains control over one facet of the moviemaking business." The ictus of Jonathan's heartbeat was making his throat throb. "Tell me if I'm warm," he said without humor.

Haskell's gaze abstracted toward the curtains again. "That was the original idea. But like everything in Hollywood, it didn't take too long before the original idea got adulterated."

"That's why you had to leave?"

"That's why I went *mad*." He drew the last word out into a long hiss. The cognac, it seemed, had displaced some of his itchy caution. "Wouldn't a job like that drive you . . . mad?"

Jonathan shook his head. "You're not moonblind. As far as I can see. And I'm an expert at picking out the walnuts, my diplomas all say so. Besides, Haskell, I flat-out don't believe that you've actually snuffed anybody. And that leaves me in a quandary. If the Conclave is real, then you must be lying about your participation—you're no murderer."

"That returns us to the weird white vans. Scripters are creative talent only. The boogeymen in the white vans execute the janitorial work per se."

"You're afraid a van-load of hitmen is going to tool up my drive? Nobody knows you're here."

"Ascribe it to the caution of the insane. That was how I evaded their clutches, you see. It does no good to run, so I went mad. I went mad to get out and buy time to make sure the Conclave couldn't erase me."

"After you became disenchanted with the . . . adulterations." Jonathan's own voice sounded ominous and melodramatic, and he tried to downshift his attitude into the brand of uncondescending sympathy peculiar to the analyst's calling.

"Actually, the change in the Conclave was fundamental and perfectly predictable," said Haskell. "Their aims became corrupted. People in such a position of power should *never* acknowledge a higher authority. And yes, I realize it sounds horrible to describe their original aims as pure, but I can't come up with a better description."

"Well, viewed objectively—pragmatically—the Conclave's object-ives were pure, I daresay. Uncompromisingly pure." Jonathan was fascinated by the idea.

"Like every bloodydamn thing in the industry, it wasn't satisfied with enough. Greed caused them to start monkeying around with chemicals. Additives to the junk movie audiences buy at theatre snackbars. Tiny jolts of light hypnotics, to render the viewer more receptive to planted visual subliminals. The first tryouts were merchandise-oriented—T-shirts, toys, novelizations, dolls, that whole farrago. Screenplays included a lot of subsurface pressure-point stroking for the median consumer. The suggestions, combined with the test drugs, ensured that audiences would buy tie-in merchandise like lab mice sucking up Violet Number Two—all it took was a squirt of mind-booze into the popcorn, and the funny thing was that the whole program was very cheap. Remember when popcorn butter was replaced by that orange, vegetable-oil glop at the snackbar?"

"That greasy stuff that comes in gallon cans and solidifies at room temperature, like candle wax?"

"We phased it under the guise of economization. Every household in America is sympathetic to the idea of frugality, and it was accepted as a necessary evil. Easy as a bread sandwich." Pride still tinged Haskell's voice, perversely. They were, after all, discussing his creativity.

"But so far the orientation was still profit. Money."

"Things changed." Haskell lifted his empty glass and slid it around on the tabletop in a ritualistic pattern. "About the time the government reinstituted draft registration, things began to change. The Conclave was contracted—I *think*—to apply our usual tactics, plus what we learned from the Popcorn Scenario, to find out if there was a cost-effective way to remilitarize the youth of the country, in order that they might accept the planned reinstatement of the draft itself more readily. The government set the stage economically by informing everyone that we were in a depression period, with very pointed allusions to the 1930s. The period just prior to our last 'good' war."

"And the Conclave . . .?"

"Boiled down, our objective was to make killing and military life seem like adventurous fun, so for our inspiration we went back to the thirties as well. It was pure serendipity. Inside one of the Scripter offices there was an old copy of Doc Smith's first *Lensman* space opera. It turned out that audiences in the 1970s were more receptive to the sort of thing they scoffed at as juvenilia in the 1930s. Our drugs conditioned them to repeat viewings, simultaneously serving the ends of profit and positive reinforcement. The movie we came up with stroked all the correct psychological triggers. The fact that it grossed more money than any film in history at the time proves how on-target our approach was."

"Oh my god . . ." said Jonathan, his mouth stalling in the open position.

"Six months afterward we ripped ourselves off and got secondary reinforcement onto television. We pulled a 40 share. The year after that we phased in the video games, experimenting with non-narcotic hypnosis, using electrical pulses, body capacitance, and keying the pleasure centers of the brain with low-voltage shocks. Jesus, Jonathan, can you *see* what we accomplished? In something under half a decade, we've programmed an entire generation of warm bodies to go to war for us and love it. They buy what we tell them to. Music, movies, whole lifestyles. And they hate who we tell them to. Khomeini, Quaddaffi. Ever notice how the leader of a country we oppose automatically becomes a lunatic? It's simple to make our audiences slaver for blood; that past hasn't changed since the days of the Colosseum. We've conditioned a whole population to live on the rim of Apocalypse and love it. They want to kill the enemy, tear his heart out, go to war so their gas bills will go down! They're all primed for just that sort of dénouement, to satisfy their need for linear storytelling in the fictions that have become their lives! The system perpetuates itself. Our own guinea pigs pay us money to keep the mechanisms grinding away. If you don't believe that, just check out last year's big hit movies . . . then try to tell me the target demographic audience isn't waiting for marching orders."

Haskell rubbed his eyes, making them bloodshot and teary. "Not long after *that* masterstroke, I decided to take my leave of the whole cesspool. I didn't feel so goddamned superior anymore. To see the manipulation of the masses as something cleaner than outright murder, one-to-one, takes the keenest kind of egomania. I couldn't lie anymore—especially to myself. So, as I've said, I went mad."

To Jonathan, Haskell looked deflated now, slightly shrunken, as if decanting his angst had left him physically diminished. He had become his job. He had been engulfed by his own obsession to leave footprints in the world of cinema, and now was kicking the underpinnings from the obsession itself and cannibalizing his existence. Consuming himself via confession. Jonathan half expected his old friend to dissolve away like a cinematic special effect, leaving a Cheshire cat rictus that would hold for a single, meaningful beat before fading to permanent black. He appraised Haskell through steepled fingers. After a precarious moment of silence he figured it out. "You didn't really lose your mind."

Haskell nodded, perking up. "I got angry, not crazy. It was to my advantage to convince the Conclave that one was the other." He used the tabletop to resume the liquor and cigarettes ritual, then leaned conspiratorially closer to Jonathan. "After the dazzle of the pay scale diminishes, you begin wondering what happens when Scripters say that's *enough*—like I was about to. We all just assumed that a letter of resignation could be tendered, everybody would shake hands, and the retiree would traipse off to Monaco to spend his Swiss balance. Four Scripters announced their intentions to quit and did so, amid quite a lot of good cheer, during my tenure. Their replacements were introduced in a matter of days, as if the Conclave had a card file *full* of emotionally vulnerable hardcases . . . like me, like I had been. Even Scripting gets mundane after a few years, right?"

Jonathan nodded, although he could not see how it could possibly get dull. He wanted more cognac for himself but the bottle was drained clean.

"Then I stopped thinking like a schmuck and started thinking like a Scripter again," said Haskell, pointing. "Wouldn't it be much simpler for the Conclave to dispatch a white van to take care of the old blood? And juggle Swiss numbers so the ex-Scripter's balance slides right back into the Conclave coffers? And thereby gain a fail-safe procedure against ex-Scripters multiplying, becoming a goddamned minority practically, and having one of them inevitably spilling the beans the way I'm doing right now?" His smile was sickly but expressive, the smile of a terminal cancer patient laughing at a tumor joke. "So yes, I did go mad. The mad are unpredictable, and if there is one quality the Conclave hates, it's mad unpredictability—because it falls outside the realm of demographics and flowcharts."

"No by-the-book solutions," said Jonathan, understanding Haskell's drift immediately. "No cut-and-dried solutions. Each case is different—almost random, like the real-life, accidental deaths versus the Conclave's planned ones. Yes." He said *yes* again to himself as he rose and rummaged through the low cherrywood cabinet for another bottle of something suitable. Tension was chewing at his knotted muscles. A pulsing in his head made him aware that his jaws had been squeezing together, grinding his teeth for at least half an hour. Giving up on the cabinet, he said, "Wait a second. Got to go to the kitchen."

Wandering back from his empty kitchen, he stopped in his empty bathroom and forced himself to urinate five drops, and while staring at the brandy bottle he'd scared up, balanced on the tank lid of the toilet, he told himself that he had encountered no real problems. Haskell did not seem violent although he did seem delusional. There was no foreseeable trouble.

Haskell was peering through a slit in the den curtains when he returned. Jonathan dashed a fresh taste into a clean crystal highball glass for himself and made a point of setting the brandy bottle down on the low table near Haskell's empty snifter.

"The rain's letting up."

"You're not finished yet, Haskell," Jonathan urged calmly.

He turned. "Yeah. Permit me to tell you how and why I went bonkers, Jon."

"That's not what I meant. You told me how you got into the mess with the Conclave, now I presume you're going to tell me how you got out of it. I take it you evaded the guys in the white vans pretty expertly. You're here, after all."

"Yes." Haskell fingered the flap pocket of his shirt.

"You must have outfoxed them, or found blackmail leverage against them, or both. If they were killing everyone else—"

"I had no desire to spend the rest of my life looking over my shoulder. I plotted my escape as a Scripter, not a fugitive. I took a lot of evidence against them—documents—and I ran to earth, and then I let them find me, apparently insensate . . . without the documents. They didn't dare kill or lobotomize me in case I'd socked away something that would tip over their monolith in the event of my demise. So they tucked me away in a very cozy asylum, to keep an eye on me for a while. Rather, I *let* them do it."

"It was all a bluff?"

"No. I went north with two knapsacks full of cash and documents. Both still exist as I speak."

"What, then?" Jonathan was inwardly exasperated. "Your brilliant plan was to finish out your days in a nuthouse?" He nearly startled himself with the word *nuthouse*.

"Jon, I'm not there now, am I? Haven't you read the papers lately?"

Jonathan stopped to review.

Haskell's eyes glinted with something like sick glee. "I'll give you a hint. They're still shoveling corpses out of the wreckage and ashes."

"Briar Lane," Jonathan murmured. "Good god, they filed you away in Briar Lane?"

"Can you think of a more exclusive nuthouse? They keep the patient's entire medical history right at hand there—even the dental records." He resumed his seat, now fiddling with an unidentifiable metal knickknack he'd taken out of his pocket to play with.

"*You* started the fire at Briar Lane?" Jonathan wanted more alcohol, but cut short his body's urge to reach for the bottle.

"It was a classic old mansion, Jon. Ultra-wealthy incurables only. Pyromaniacs need not apply. The Conclave paid my freight—nothing but the best for those who might turn on you—and access to the files proves pretty goddamn easy if you're not really crazy. Or if you're crazy in the right direction."

"Do you really expect the Conclave to be fooled by the old Hitler ploy? A body charred to unrecognizability and a set of labeled dental proofs, charred or not, are not going to reassure them much . . . from what you've said."

"On the other hand, it's been over a year now since I went 'nuts' and they've seen no provocative action from my presumed blackmail securities. I want them to understand that the Briar Lane incident is their escape valve regarding me—that they should relax, pursue their new projects, maybe even write me off. They don't hurt me and I don't hurt them. Just let me fade, with the money I've stockpiled."

"Can't they connect you to the money?"

"Assumed name," Haskell said, with the air of repeating prepared answers.

"The period during which you vanished? 'Ran to earth'?" Jonathan was aware of his own sharpened, inquisitive gaze, of his more aggressive posture in the chair. He was automatically grilling Haskell. To atone he added, "Said the devil's advocate," and Haskell's eyebrows arched.

"Jon, the Conclave doesn't believe in what insurance companies call acts of God. They always try to anticipate what sort of scam will be run on them. I'm not the first to try, though I may be the first to succeed. The trick is knowing when to *stop* thinking like a Scripter. I planned not to plan, and wound up doing the sort of entirely random thing that would never be accepted in fiction. I took my knapsacks full of *incriminata* and hitchhiked. While I was riding my thumb, they went berserk scouring California, checking banks, monitoring LAX and municipal skyports and bus depots and Union Station and car rental agencies and I wasn't even in California! But California is where they caught me. After I'd come back." His eyes were aglint with some private joke, some fundamental trivium he was purposefully omitting from his story.

"Without the knapsacks." Jonathan tried to sum the bits and orts of information in order to extrapolate.

Haskell stood up again and paced like Sherlock Holmes about to finger a murderer from suspects congregated before a Victorian hearth. "I know what you're thinking, Jon—with a setup like I've described, it would seem reckless of me to just drop in on you after all these years, entirely by chance, right?"

"I was going to ask why me."

"When I infiltrated the files at Briar Lane, I found a doctors' directory—you know, that binder thing they constantly update with inserts. I looked up your name and hot damn, there you were. It was just like we'd speculated. I'd become a screenwriter—a Scripter—and you'd become a shrink. It even had your home address."

"Conveniently enough," said Jon. "A paranoid mind might see a plot brewing in a simple fact like that."

"Oh yeah. My first thought. I guess that confirms me as a sicko. But consider, Jon: if you'd been seduced by the Conclave, you would've put me under with a drug in the cognac and remanded me to the boys in the white vans for pumping . . . except for one thing. The one thing they weren't able to get out of me when they had me, through drugs or threats or promises, and the one thing they might be desperate enough to try subterfuge to win. The one thing I haven't mentioned yet—the location of the blackmail material. Where I went when I took my little excursion."

"My office could have been bugged without my knowledge, Haskell."

"*Now* you're thinking like a Scripter. Tempting job, isn't it? At least, the way it looks from the outside. Mass manipulation of entire populations would especially intrigue a psychiatrist or a sociologist. I saw your sheepskins on both, Jon. They're right behind the desk." He watched Jonathan's eyes track to the frames on the wall and back. "But I don't think they'd try something as superhuman as bugging each of my past acquaintances in all of Los Angeles. The Conclave prefers buying people to equipment."

Jonathan gestured impatiently, urging Haskell to get on with it. "So what's the punchline, Haskell? You going to string me along, or tell me whether you trust me or not?"

Haskell smiled. "Ah, *now* you're in character—do you see? The concerned analyst banking on his patient's faith; just the right amount of deep sobriety and interest." He held his thumb and forefinger an inch apart. "Just enough irritation to prompt the patient to reassure him with the truth." He moved to the closed curtains, arms spread as though entreating an unseen audience. "Is he playing a role?" He brought his hands together in one swift clap. "Or is he for real?"

"All right, Haskell, goddamnit!" His fingers were clawed across the chair arms like marble spiders; his face was indignantly flushed. "I'll play this stupid game just to help you!" He pointed his finger like a weapon. "Here it comes, look out for it! What did you do with the blackmail material?" His eyes were bulging, and when his lips stopped speaking they curled back, loading a full clip of invective.

"*The question*!" Haskell shouted. "At last! And you know what, Jon? I'll answer your question honestly if you'll answer one of mine honestly." He buried his hands in his pockets and leaned against one of the bookcases. "If you're really my pal, then I've gotten this story out of my guts and into the ear of a real human being unlike those bloodless slugs in the Conclave. Plus I've gained a reliable fail-safe for my blackmail material; something very desirable and worth a risk like coming here and exposing myself. Right?"

"Ask." His gaze had turned metallic.

"Have you ever heard of the Conclave before tonight?" Now Haskell had folded his arms. All humor had fled from his face.

"No!"

"Why haven't you had any of the brandy you brought from the kitchen, Jon?"

Jonathan grew flustered. "I thought you—" He stopped, wiped his face. "I was waiting to get rid of the Grand Marnier a bit before I had some." The brandy bottle Jonathan had brought into the room sat untouched, as did Jonathan's highball glass.

"Why don't you have some right now?" Haskell's voice was level, reasoned. Strangely, he looked much healthier now than when he'd stumbled across Jonathan's threshold earlier this evening.

"In good time, Haskell." He sighed, stabbing his finger in the air again. "I refuse to get angry with you. You're—"

"Come off it, Jonathan!" Haskell spun, ran his finger along the spines of the books against which he had been leaning, and drew out Jonathan's thousand-dollar Arion edition of Moby Dick. He let the front cover drop open, revealing a hollow that had been sliced out of the thickness of pages. Secured within the hollow was a small Sanyo tape recorder. Haskell slammed the book shut, dropped it to the carpet with a thump, and pulled from his pocket a cassette tape, waving it in the air. "I took this out while you were in the *john*, Jonathan! Over half an hour ago!"

Jonathan's mouth was open but his teeth were not clenched anymore. His face went pale and he lost whatever words he had prepared.

"Your eyes went right from the book to the telephone, Jon. You know the number as well as I do: 727–3933. The numbers make a word, Jonathan, that's how we remember it. Punch in that number and a white van will roll up your drive in a neat five minutes." He shook his head slowly. "I was hoping you might not sell me down the river, Jon." He made a furious, frustrated motion with his fist. "Shit! It couldn't have been the money. It had to have been the control they offered you. Had to be."

Jonathan pushed himself slowly up from the recliner. "The tape is part of my hardware, Haskell; it's SOP for anybody who talks to me in as disturbed a state as you brought through the door with you. No plot, no boobytrap . . ." His voice had turned authoritarian and succoring. He was back in character.

"Have a jolt of brandy, Jonathan," Haskell said, indicating the untouched bottle, perceiving in his heart the kind of arrogance it took to carve a hole in a thousand-dollar book for the purpose of subterfuge.

"I will not." Teacher to unruly delinquent. Jonathan turned his back on Haskell and moved toward the desk. He heard Haskell catch up with him, felt his hand grasp his own fore-arm, expected to be turned back certainly, to be struck possibly. His fancied control of the situation admitted nothing further.

"I'm afraid I'll have to insist," said Haskell, grasping, and spinning, and striking him, but not in the way he expected.

Jonathan saw Haskell's flat, openhanded blow coming, with little real velocity to cause pain. He could weather the impact and remain standing. Then he saw the metal knickknack from Haskell's pocket between his index and middle fingers, flying to meet him. He felt a sharp needle pain in the muscles of his neck. Haskell jumped away. Jonathan's openhanded grab came up empty.

"*Damn!*" The tiny puncture stung, enraging him. He lifted the receiver of the desk phone and punched two digits before his hand swelled up and got too fat to function. He dropped the receiver. It clunked on the desktop and fell to the floor, uncoiling the cable. He pawed for the desk edge with an incredulous expression on his face, missed, and followed the phone to the floor, where he lolled like some armless, legless thing attempting locomotion. Haskell stood by the sofa, near the curtains.

"The CIA calls this thing a sting-bee, Jonathan. Like king bee, I guess. Most of your motor coordination will be out for about an hour. As you're discovering, your eyes will still focus and you can hear me perfectly . . . but that's it." He parted the curtains for another check.

"I've done a little deduction, too, Jonathan, with the result of leaving you in another quandary, as you said. Sorry. But here it is: I guessed the Conclave would appeal to you. They must have propositioned you right after your divorce from Janice—same as me. As an acid test, an invitation, they want you to snare me for them, and they give you my story. You arrange for your name to be planted at Briar Lane as a memory key—it's easily predictable, like giving someone a university yellow pages. You'd automatically look up your old compatriots, well, so did I, and this was a specific listing of psychiatrists, which made it a pretty sure thing. In return, you promise to uncover for the Conclave the location of the blackmail leverage, having gained in confidence from me. After all, I'm years in your past; easy enough to screw over for the right kind of carrot.

"But you'd better start worrying about this, Jon: what if I'm a loyalty test for you? My whole story could have been fabricated as a Conclave gambit to test your resiliency—how far do old friendships reach? Did I escape tonight, or did you let me get away? Think about it, when you're explaining to the Conclave why I'm not here and why you don't have what they want. That's part one of your dilemma. Part two is this—if I'm not a test, then you're going to have to cover for me. I anticipated this because I'm a veteran and you're a tyro at this game. You're going to have to dance pretty fast to convince them I'm either dead for real, or impotent as a threat to them, because if you don't, they'll kill *you* for botching things.

"If you succeed in snowing them, then you'll be in. You'll get to be a Scripter. And after a year, three years, five, you'll get just as sick of it as I have. You see, Jon, you're exactly as I was when I went in. I know how you'll react. And perhaps a few years from now we'll run into each other out there in the wilderness somewhere. As for now, I've just relieved myself out of the onus of paranoia that's dogged me ever since I opted out. I've given it to you. And with that shadow hanging over your shoulder, you'll learn how horrible the Conclave really is—you'll learn it in the only meaningful way to be had, and maybe it'll turn you into an ally eventually. As for right now—"

He pulled out Jonathan's billfold, extracted the cash, and replaced it. Jonathan's body was a wet, composureless mail sack. His eyes glared, beaten, amazed, and helpless. Drool rolled out of one corner of his slack mouth and was absorbed into the expensive carpeting.

Haskell ducked out of the den and reappeared with a can of Dr Pepper from Jonathan's refrigerator, emptying it quickly. "Talk like this always makes me thirsty. Don't worry, Jon, I'm gone, untraceably, just as soon as I make a phone call."

He collected the phone from the floor and tapped the cradle impatiently until he got a dial tone. "You remember the word, of course, Jon? The word they gave us so we'd never forget the phone number? SCREWED."

When he heard the connection go through, Haskell placed the open receiver on the desktop, tossed the prone form of Jonathan a little mocking salute, and left. Jonathan heard the back door slam, could even feel its vibrations against his cheek through the floor. That was all he could do. Haskell had thoughtfully extinguished the house lights on his way out, and he could see nothing.

Five minutes later, van headlights flashed against the backside of the den's curtains. Then the house fell dark again.

POPPY Z. BRITE

His Mouth Will Taste of Wormwood

POPPY Z. BRITE spent her earliest years in New Orleans, the setting for the atmospheric story that follows, and describes the city as able "to make death seem romantic even to the most hard-hearted." She has lived all over the American South and has worked as a candy maker, an artist's model, a gourmet cook, a mouse caretaker, and an exotic dancer.

Her first fiction was published in *The Horror Show* magazine between 1985 and 1990 and, in the Fall 1987 issue, she was featured as a "Rising Star" of modern horror. More recently her stories have appeared in the anthologies *Borderlands*, *Women of Darkness II*, *Dead End: City Limits* and *Still Dead* (*Book of the Dead II*). She has completed her first novel, and she longs to travel to India.

"To THE TREASURES AND THE PLEASURES OF THE GRAVE," said my friend Louis, and raised his goblet of absinthe to me in drunken benediction.

"To the funeral lilies," I replied, "and to the calm pale bones." I drank deeply from my own glass. The absinthe cauterized my throat with its flavor, part pepper, part licorice, part rot. It had been one of our greatest finds: more than fifty bottles of the now-outlawed liqueur, sealed up in a New Orleans family tomb. Transporting them was a nuisance, but once we had learned to enjoy the taste of wormwood, our continued drunkenness was ensured for a long, long time. We had taken the skull of the crypt's patriarch, too, and it now resided in a velvet-lined enclave in our museum.

Louis and I, you see, were dreamers of a dark and restless sort. We met in our second year of college and quickly found that we shared one vital trait: both of us were dissatisfied with everything. We drank straight whiskey and declared it too weak. We took strange drugs, but the visions they brought us were of emptiness, mindlessness, slow decay. The books we read were dull; the artists who sold their colorful drawings on the street were mere hacks in our eyes; the music we heard was never loud enough, never harsh enough to stir us. We were truly jaded, we told one another. For all the impression the world made upon us, our eyes might have been dead black holes in our heads.

For a time we thought our salvation lay in the sorcery wrought by music. We studied recordings of weird nameless dissonances, attended performances of obscure bands at ill-lit filthy clubs. But music did not save us. For a time we distracted ourselves with carnality. We explored the damp alien territory between the legs of any girl who would have us, sometimes separately, sometimes both of us in bed together with one girl or more. We bound their wrists and ankles with black lace, we lubricated and penetrated their every orifice, we shamed them with their own pleasures. I recall a mauve-haired beauty, Felicia, who was brought to wild sobbing orgasm by the rough tongue of a stray dog we trapped. We watched her from across the room, drug dazed and unstirred.

When we had exhausted the possibilities of women we sought those of our own sex, craving the androgynous curve of a boy's cheekbone, the molten flood of ejaculation invading our mouths. Eventually we turned to one another, seeking the thresholds of pain and ecstasy no one else had been able to help us attain. Louis asked me to grow my nails long and file them into needle-sharp points. When I raked them down his back, tiny beads of blood welled up in the angry tracks they left. He loved to lie still, pretending to submit to me, as I licked the salty blood away. Afterward he would push me and attack me with his mouth, his tongue seeming to sear a trail of liquid fire into my skin.

But sex did not save us either. We shut ourselves in our room and saw no one for days on end. At last we withdrew to the seclusion of Louis's ancestral home near Baton Rouge. Both his parents were dead—a suicide pact, Louis hinted, or perhaps a murder and a suicide. Louis, the only child, retained the family home and fortune. Built on the edge of a vast swamp, the plantation house loomed sepulchrally out of the gloom that surrounded it always, even in the middle of a summer afternoon. Oaks of primordial hugeness grew in a canopy over the house, their branches like black arms fraught with Spanish moss. The moss was everywhere, reminding me of brittle gray hair, stirring wraithlike in the dank breeze from the swamp. I had the impression that, left too long unchecked, the moss might begin to grow from the ornate window frames and fluted columns of the house itself.

The place was deserted save for us. The air was heady with the luminous scent of magnolias and the fetor of swamp gas. At night we sat on the veranda and sipped bottles of wine from the family cellar, gazing through an increasingly alcoholic mist at the will-o'-the-wisps that beckoned far off in the swamp. Obsessively we talked of new thrills and how we might get them. Louis's wit sparkled liveliest when he was bored, and on the night he first mentioned grave robbing, I laughed. I could not imagine that he was serious.

"What would we do with a bunch of dried-up old remains? Grind them to make a voodoo potion? I preferred your idea of increasing our tolerance to various poisons."

Louis's sharp face snapped toward me. His eyes were painfully sensitive to light, so that even in this gloaming he wore tinted glasses and it was impossible to see his expression. He kept his fair hair clipped very short, so that it stood up in crazy tufts when he raked a nervous hand through it. "No, Howard. Think of it: our own collection of death. A catalog of pain, of human frailty—all for us. Set against a backdrop of tranquil loveliness. Think what it would be to walk through such a place, meditating, reflecting upon your own ephemeral essence. Think of making love in a charnel house! We have only to assemble the parts—they will create a whole into which we may fall."

(Louis enjoyed speaking in cryptic puns; anagrams and palindromes, too, and any sort of puzzle appealed to him. I wonder whether that was not the root of his determination to look into the fathomless eye of death and master it. Perhaps he saw the mortality of the flesh as a gigantic jigsaw or cross-word which, if he fitted all the parts into place, he might solve and thus defeat. Louis would have loved to live forever, though he would never have known what to do with all his time.)

He soon produced his hashish pipe to sweeten the taste of the wine, and we spoke no more of grave robbing that night. But the thought preyed upon me in the languorous weeks to come. The smell of a freshly opened grave, I thought, must in its way be as intoxicating as the perfume of the swamp or a girl's most intimate sweat. Could we truly assemble a collection of the grave's treasures that would be lovely to look upon, that would soothe our fevered souls?

The caresses of Louis's tongue grew languid. Sometimes, instead of nestling with me between the black satin sheets of our bed, he would sleep on a torn blanket in one of the underground rooms. These had originally been built for indeterminate but always intriguing purposes—abolitionist meetings had taken place there, Louis told me, and a weekend of free love, and an earnest but wildly incompetent Black Mass replete with a vestal virgin and phallic candles.

These rooms were where our museum would be set up. At last I came to agree with Louis that only the plundering of graves might cure us of the most stifling ennui we had yet suffered. I could not bear to watch his tormented sleep, the pallor of his hollow cheeks, the delicate bruiselike darkening of the skin beneath his flickering eyes. Besides, the notion of grave robbing had begun to entice me. In ultimate corruption, might we not find the path to ultimate salvation?

Our first grisly prize was the head of Louis's mother, rotten as a pumpkin forgotten on the vine, half shattered by two bullets from an antique Civil War revolver. We took it from the family crypt by the light of a full moon. The will-o'-the-wisps glowed weakly, like dying beacons on some unattainable shore, as we crept back to the manse. I dragged pick and shovel behind me; Louis carried the putrescent trophy tucked beneath his arm. After we had descended into the museum, I lit three candles scented with the russet spices of autumn (the season when Louis's parents had died), while Louis placed the head in the alcove we had prepared for it. I thought I detected a certain tenderness in his manner. "May she give us the family blessing," he murmured, absently wiping on the lapel of his jacket a few shreds of pulpy flesh that had adhered to his fingers.

We spent a happy time refurbishing the museum, polishing the inlaid precious metals of the wall fixtures, brushing away the dust that frosted the velvet designs of the wallpaper, alternately burning incense and charring bits of cloth we had saturated with our blood, in order to give the rooms the odor we desired—a charnel perfume strong enough to drive us to frenzy. We traveled far for our collections, but always we returned home with crates full of things no man had ever been meant to possess. We heard of a girl with violet eyes who had died in some distant town; not seven days later we had those eyes in an ornate cut-glass jar, pickled in formaldehyde. We scraped bone dust and nitre from the bottoms of ancient coffins; we stole the barely withered heads and hands of children fresh in their graves, with their soft little fingers and their lips like flower petals. We had baubles and precious heirlooms, vermiculated prayer books and shrouds encrusted with mold. I had not taken seriously Louis's talk of making love in a charnel house—but neither had I reckoned on the pleasure he could inflict with a femur dipped in rose-scented oil.

Upon the night I speak of—the night we drank our toast to the grave and its riches—we had just acquired our finest prize yet. Later in the evening we planned a celebratory debauch at a nightclub in the city. We had returned from our most recent travels not with the usual assortment of sacks and crates, but with only one small box carefully wrapped and tucked into Louis's breast pocket. The box contained an object whose existence we had only speculated upon previously. From certain half-articulate mutterings of an old blind man plied with cheap liquor in a French Quarter bar, we traced rumors of a certain fetish or charm to a Negro graveyard in the southern bayou country. The fetish was said to be a thing of eerie beauty, capable of luring any lover to one's bed, hexing any enemy to a sick and painful death, and (this, I think, was what intrigued Louis the most) turning back tenfold on anyone who used it with less than the touch of a master.

A heavy mist hung low over the graveyard when we arrived there, lapping at our ankles, pooling around the markers of wood and stone, abruptly melting away in patches to reveal a gnarled root or a patch of blackened grass, then closing back in. By the light of a waning moon we made our way along a path overgrown with rioting weeds. The graves were decorated with elaborate mosaics of broken glass, coins, bottle caps, oyster shells lacquered silver and gold. Some mounds were outlined by empty bottles shoved neck downward into the earth. I saw a lone plaster saint whose features had been worn away by years of wind and rain. I kicked half-buried rusty cans that had once held flowers; now they held only bare brittle stems and pestilent rainwater or nothing at all. Only the scent of wild spider lilies pervaded the night.

The earth in one corner of the graveyard seemed blacker than the rest. The grave we sought was marked only by a crude cross of charred and twisted wood. We were skilled at the art of violating the dead; soon we had the coffin uncovered. The boards were warped by years of burial in wet, foul earth. Louis pried up the lid with his spade and, by the moon's meager and watery light, we gazed upon what lay within.

Of the inhabitant we knew almost nothing. Some said a hideously disfigured old conjure woman lay buried here. Some said she was a young girl with a face as lovely and cold as moonlight on water, and a soul crueler than Fate itself. Some claimed the body was not a woman's at all, but that of a white voodoo priest who had ruled the bayou. He had features of a cool, unearthly beauty, they said, and a stock of fetishes and potions that he would hand out with the kindest blessing . . . or the direst curse. This was the story Louis and I liked best; the sorcerer's capriciousness appealed to us, and the fact that he was beautiful.

No trace of beauty remained on the thing in the coffin—at least not the sort of beauty that a healthy eye might cherish. Louis and I loved the translucent parchment skin stretched tight over long bones that seemed to have been carved from ivory. The delicate brittle hands folded across the sunken chest, the soft black caverns of the eyes, the colorless strands of hair that still clung to the fine white dome of the skull—to us these things were the poetry of death.

Louis played his flashlight over the withered cords of the neck. There, on a silver chain gone black with age, was the object we had come seeking. No crude wax doll or bit of dried root was this. Louis and I gazed at each other, moved by the beauty of the thing; then, as if in a dream, he reached to grasp it. This was our rightful night's prize, our plunder from a sorcerer's grave.

"How does it look?" Louis asked as we were dressing.

I never had to think about my clothes. On an evening such as this, when we were dressing to go out, I would choose the same garments I might wear for a night's digging in the graveyard—black, unornamented black, with only the whiteness of my face and hands showing against the backdrop of night. On a particularly festive occasion, such as this, I might smudge a bit of kohl round my eyes. The absence of color made me nearly invisible: if I walked with my shoulders hunched and my chin tucked down, no one except Louis would see me.

"Don't slouch so, Howard," said Louis irritably as I ducked past the mirror. "Turn around and look at me. Aren't I fine in my sorcerer's jewelry?"

Even when Louis wore black, he did it to be noticed. Tonight he was resplendent in narrow-legged trousers of purple paisley silk and a silvery jacket that seemed to turn all light iridescent. He had taken our prize out of its box and fastened it around his throat. As I came closer to look at it, I caught Louis's scent: rich and rather meaty, like blood kept too long in a stoppered bottle.

Against the sculpted hollow of Louis's throat, the thing on its chain seemed more strangely beautiful than ever. Have I neglected to describe the magical object, the voodoo fetish from the churned earth of the grave? I will never forget it. A polished sliver of bone (or a tooth, but what fang could have been so long, so sleekly honed, and still have somehow retained the look of a *human tooth*?) bound by a strip of copper. Set into the metal, a single ruby sparkled like a drop of gore against the verdigris. Etched in exquisite miniature upon the sliver of bone, and darkened by the rubbing in of some black-red substance, was an elaborate vévé—one of the symbols used by voodooists to invoke their pantheon of terrible gods. Whoever was buried in that lonely bayou grave, he had been no mere dabbler in swamp magic. Every cross and swirl of the vévé was reproduced to perfection. I thought the thing still retained a trace of the grave's scent—a dark odor like potatoes long spoiled. Each grave has its own peculiar scent, just as each living body does.

"Are you certain you should wear it?" I asked.

"It will go into the museum tomorrow," he said, "with a scarlet candle burning eternally before it. Tonight its powers are mine."

The nightclub was in a part of the city that looked as if it had been gutted from the inside out by a righteous tongue of fire. The street was lit only by occasional scribbles of neon high overhead, advertisements for cheap hotels and all-night bars. Dark eyes stared at us from the crevices and pathways between buildings, disappearing only when Louis's hand crept toward the inner pocket of his jacket. He carried a small stiletto there, and knew how to use it for more than pleasure.

We slipped through a door at the end of an alley and descended the narrow staircase into the club. The lurid glow of a blue bulb flooded the stairs, making Louis's face look sunken and dead behind his tinted glasses. Feedback blasted us as we came in, and above it, a screaming battle of guitars. The inside of the club was a patchwork of flickering light and darkness. Graffiti covered the walls and the ceiling like a tangle of barbed wire come alive. I saw bands' insignia and jeering death's-heads, crucifixes bejeweled with broken glass, and black obscenities writhing in the stroboscopic light.

Louis brought me a drink from the bar. I sipped it slowly, still drunk on absinthe. Since the music was too loud for conversation, I studied the clubgoers around us. A quiet bunch, they were, staring fixedly at the stage as if they had been drugged (and no doubt many of them had—I remembered visiting a club one night on a dose of hallucinogenic mushrooms, watching in fascination as the guitar strings seemed to drip soft viscera onto the stage). Younger than Louis and myself, most of them were, and queerly beautiful in their thrift shop rags, their leather and fishnet and cheap costume jewelry, their pale faces and painted hair. Perhaps we would take one of them home with us tonight. We had done so before. "The delicious guttersnipes," Louis called them. A particularly beautiful face, starkly boned and androgynous, flickered at the edge of my vision. When I looked, it was gone.

I went into the rest room. A pair of boys stood at a single urinal, talking animatedly. I stood at the sink rinsing my hands, watching the boys in the mirror and trying to overhear their conversation. A hairline fracture in the glass seemed to pull the taller boy's eyes askew. "Caspar and Alyssa found her tonight," he said. "In some old warehouse by the river. I heard her skin was *gray*, man. And sort of withered, like something had sucked out most of the meat."

"Far out," said the other boy. His black-rimmed lips barely moved.

"She was only fifteen, you know?" said the tall boy as he zipped his ragged trousers.

"She was a cunt anyway."

They turned away from the urinal and started talking about the band—Ritual Sacrifice, I gathered, whose name was scrawled on the walls of the club. As they went out, the boys glanced at the mirror and the tall one's eyes met mine for an instant. Nose like a haughty Indian chief's, eyelids smudged with black and silver. Louis would approve, I thought—but the night was young, and there were many drinks yet to be had.

When the band took a break we visited the bar again. Louis edged in beside a thin dark-haired boy who was bare chested except for a piece of torn lace tied about his throat. When he turned, I knew his was the androgynous and striking face I had glimpsed before. His beauty was almost feral, but overlaid with a cool elegance like a veneer of sanity hiding madness. His ivory skin stretched over cheekbones like razors; his eyes were hectic pools of darkness.

"I like your amulet," he said to Louis. "It's very unusual."

"I have another one like it at home," Louis told him.

"Really? I'd like to see them both together." The boy paused to let Louis order our vodka gimlets, then said, "I thought there was only one."

Louis's back straightened like a string of beads being pulled taut. Behind his glasses, I knew, his pupils would have shrunk to pinpoints: the light pained him more when he was nervous. But no tremor in his voice betrayed him when he said, "What do you know about it?"

The boy shrugged. On his bony shoulders, the movement was insouciant and drop-dead graceful. "It's voodoo," he said. "I know what voodoo is. Do you?"

The implication stung, but Louis only bared his teeth the slightest bit; it might have been a smile. "I am *conversant* in all types of magic," he said, "at least."

The boy moved closer to Louis, so that their hips were almost touching, and lifted the amulet between thumb and forefinger. I thought I saw one long nail brush Louis's throat, but I could not be sure. "I could tell you the meaning of this vévé," he said, "if you were certain you wished to know."

"It symbolizes power," Louis said. "All the power of my soul." His voice was cold, but I saw his tongue dart out to moisten his lips. He was beginning to dislike this boy, and also to desire him.

"No," said the boy so softly that I barely caught his words. He sounded almost sad. "This cross in the center is inverted, you see, and the line encircling it represents a serpent. A thing like this can trap your soul. Instead of being rewarded with eternal life . . . you might be doomed to it."

"Doomed to eternal life?" Louis permitted himself a small cold smile. "Whatever do you mean?"

"The band is starting again. Find me after the show and I'll tell you. We can have a drink . . . and you can tell me all you know about voodoo." The boy threw back his head and laughed. Only then did I notice that one of his upper canine teeth was missing.

The next part of the evening remains a blur of moonlight and neon, ice cubes and blue swirling smoke and sweet drunkenness. The boy drank glass after glass of absinthe with us, seeming to relish the bitter taste. None of our other guests had liked the liqueur. "Where did you get it?" he asked. Louis was silent for a long moment before he said, "It was sent over from France." Except for its single black gap, the boy's smile would have been as perfect as the sharp-edged crescent moon.

"Another drink?" said Louis, refilling both our glasses.

When I next came to clarity, I was in the boy's arms. I could not make out the words he was whispering; they might have been an incantation, if magic may be sung to pleasure's music. A pair of hands cupped my face, guiding my lips over the boy's pale parchment skin. They might have been Louis's hands. I knew nothing except this boy, the fragile movement of the bones beneath the skin, the taste of his spit bitter with wormwood.

I do not remember when he finally turned away from me and began lavishing his love upon Louis. I wish I could have watched, could have seen the lust bleeding into Louis's eyes, the pleasure wracking his body. For, as it turned out, the boy loved Louis so much more thoroughly than ever he loved me.

When I awoke, the bass thump of my pulse echoing through my skull blotted out all other sensations. Gradually, though, I became aware of tangled silk sheets, of hot sunlight on my face. Not until I came fully awake did I see the thing I had cradled like a lover all through the night.

For an instant two realities shifted in uneasy juxtaposition and almost merged. I was in Louis's bed; I recognized the feel of the sheets, their odor of silk and sweat. But this thing I held—this was surely one of the fragile mummies we had dragged out of their graves, the things we dissected for our museum. It took me only a moment, though, to recognize the familiar ruined features—the sharp chin, the high elegant brow. Something had desiccated Louis, had drained him of every drop of his moisture, his vitality. His skin crackled and flaked away beneath my fingers. His hair stuck to my lips, dry and colorless. The amulet, which had still been around his throat in bed last night, was gone.

The boy had left no trace—or so I thought until I saw a nearly transparent thing at the foot of the bed. It was like a quantity of spiderweb, or a damp and insubstantial veil. I picked it up and shook it out, but could not see its features until I held it up to the window. The thing was vaguely human shaped, with empty limbs trailing off into nearly invisible tatters. As the thing wafted and billowed, I saw part of a face in it—the sharp curve left by a cheekbone, the hole where an eye had been—as if a face were imprinted upon gauze.

I carried Louis's brittle shell of a corpse down into the museum. Laying him before his mother's niche, I left a stick of incense burning in his folded hands and a pillow of black silk cradling the papery dry bulb of his skull. He would have wished it thus.

The boy has not come to me again, though I leave the window open every night. I have been back to the club, where I stand sipping vodka and watching the crowd. I have seen many beauties, many strange wasted faces, but not the one I seek. I think I know where I will find him. Perhaps he still desires me—I must know.

I will go again to the lonely graveyard in the bayou. Once more—alone, this time—I will find the unmarked grave and plant my spade in its black earth. When I open the coffin—I know it, I am sure of it!—I will find not the mouldering thing we beheld before, but the calm beauty of replenished youth. The youth he drank from Louis. His face will be a scrimshaw mask of tranquility. The amulet—I know it; I am sure of it—will be around his neck.

Dying: the final shock of pain or nothingness that is the price we pay for everything. Could it not be the sweetest thrill, the only salvation we can attain . . . the only true moment of self-knowledge? The dark pools of his eyes will open, still and deep enough to drown in. He will hold out his arms to me, inviting me to lie down with him in his rich wormy bed.

With the first kiss his mouth will taste of wormwood. After that it will taste only of me—of my blood, my life, siphoning out of my body and into his. I will feel the sensations Louis felt: the shriveling of my tissues, the drying up of all my vital juices. I care not. The treasures and the pleasures of the grave? They are his hands, his lips, his tongue.

KIM NEWMAN

The Original Dr Shade

KIM NEWMAN is fast building a reputation as a writer, with his acclaimed short stories published in *Interzone*, *Fantasy Tales* and *New Worlds*, amongst other titles, and regular appearances in various "Year's Best" anthologies.

His first novel, *The Night Mayor*, was recently optioned by Hollywood, and two subsequent books, *Bad Dreams* and *Jago* look set to be equally successful. As "Jack Yeovil" he has published a number of gaming novelisations set in offbeat fantasy and futuristic milieus.

In 1990, he won the Horror Writers of America Award for *Horror: 100 Best Books*, which he co-edited with Stephen Jones, and other non-fiction books under his byline include *Ghastly Beyond Belief* (with Neil Gaiman), *Nightmare Movies* and *Wild West Movies*. He is currently working on an original anthology with Paul J. McAuley.

"The Original Dr Shade" is a darkly downbeat novella that mixes Thatcherite Britain, comics fans, and an unusual type of haunting into a highly original horror tale. However, that didn't stop it winning the 1991 British Science Fiction Award for Best Short Story.

Like a shark breaking inky waters, the big black car surfaced out of the night, its searchlight headlamps freezing the Bolsheviks en tableau as they huddled over their dynamite. Cohen, their vile leader, tried to control his raging emotions, realizing that yet again his schemings to bring about the ruination of the British Empire were undone. Borzoff, his hands shaking uncontrollably, fell to his ragged-trousered knees and tried one last prayer to the God whose icons he had spat upon that day in the mother country when he had taken his riflebutt to the princess' eggshell-delicate skull. Petrofsky drooled into his stringy beard, his one diseased eye shrinking in the light like a slug exposed to salt, and uselessly thumb-cocked his revolver.

The canvas top of the Rolls Royce "Shadowshark" raised like a hawk's eyelid, and a dark shape seemed to grow out of the driver's seat, cloak billowing in the strong wind, twin moons reflected in the insectlike dark goggles, wide-brimmed hat at a jaunty angle.

Petrofsky raised his shaking pistol, and slammed back against the iron globe of the chemical tank, cut down by another silent dart from the doctor's famous airgun. In the distance, the conspirators could hear police sirens, but they knew they would not be taken into custody. The shadowman would not allow them to live out the night to further sully the green and fruitful soil of sacred England with their foul presence.

As the doctor advanced, the headlamps threw his expanding shadow on the Bolsheviks.

Israel Cohen, the Mad Genius of the Revolution, trembled, his flabby chins slapping against his chest, sweat pouring from his ape-like forehead down his protuberant nose to his fleshy, sensual lips. He raised a ham-sized fist against the doctor, sneering insane defiance to the last:

"Curse you, Shade!"

—Rex Cash, *Dr Shade Vs the Dynamite Boys* (1936)

T HEY ATE AN EXPENSIVELY minimalist meal at Alastair Little's in Frith Street, and Basil Crosbie, Leech's Art Editor, picked up the bill with his company card. Throughout, Tamara, his agent, kept reminding Crosbie of the Eagle awards Greg had gained for *Fat Chance*, not mentioning that that was two years ago. As with most restaurants, there was nowhere that could safely accommodate Greg's yardsquare artwork folder, and he was worried the sample strips would get scrunched or warped. He would have brought copies, but wanted to put himself over as sharply as possible. Besides, the ink wasn't dry on the pieces he had finished this morning. As usual, there hadn't been time to cover himself.

Whenever there was dead air in the conversation, Tamara filled it with more selected highlights from Greg's career. Greg guessed she had invited herself to this lunch to keep him under control. She remembered, but was carefully avoiding mention of, his scratchy beginnings in the '70s—spiky strips and singletons for punk fanzines like *Sheep Worrying*, *Brainrape* and *Kill Your Pet Puppy*—and knew exactly how he felt about the Derek Leech organization. She probably thought he was going to turn up in a ripped rubbish bag, with lots of black eyeliner and safety-pins through his earlobes, then go for Crosbie with a screwdriver. Actually, while the *Sex Pistols* were swearing on live television and gobbing at gigs, he had been a neatly-dressed, normal-haired art student. It was only at the easel, where he used to assemble police-brutality collages with ransom note captions, that he had embodied the spirit of '77.

If Tamara would shut up, he thought he could get on with Crosbie. Greg knew the man had started out on the *Eagle*, and filled in on *Garth* once in a while. He had been a genuine minor talent in his day. Still, he worked for Leech, and if there was one artefact that summed up everything Greg loathed about Britain under late Thatcherism, it was Leech's *Daily Comet*. The paper was known for its Boobs 'n' Pubes, its multi-million Giveaway Grids, its unflinching support of the diamond-hard right, its lawsuit-fuelled muckraking, and prose that read like a football hooligan's attempt to imitate the *Janet and John* books. It was Britain's fastest-growing newspaper, and the hub of a communications empire that was putting Leech in the Murdoch-Maxwell bracket. In Madame Tussaud's last annual poll, the statue of Derek Leech had ranked eighth on the Most Admired list, between Gorbachev and Prince Charles, and second on the Most Hated and Feared chart, after Margaret Thatcher but before Adolf Hitler, Colonel Quadaffi, Count Dracula and the Yorkshire Ripper.

Crosbie didn't start talking business until eyedropper-sized cups of coffee arrived. With the plates taken away, the Art Editor opened his folder on the table, and brought out a neatly paperclipped set of notes. Tamara was still picking at her fruit salad, five pieces of pale apple and/or pear floating in a steel bowl of water with a solitary grape. She and Crosbie had been drinking dry white wine with the meal, but Greg stuck to mineral water. The gritty coffee gave him quite a punch, and he felt his heart tighten like an angry fist. Since *Fat Chance*, he hadn't done anything notable. This was an important meeting for him. Tamara might not dump him if it didn't come out right, but she might shift him from her A-list to her B-list.

"As you probably know," Crosbie began, "Leech United Kingdom is expanding at the moment. I don't know if you keep up with the trades, but Derek has recently bought up the rights to a lot of defunct titles with a view to relaunch. It's a lot easier to sell something familiar than something new. Just now, Derek's special baby is the *Evening Argus*."

"The Brighton paper?" Greg asked.

"No, a national. It folded in 1953, but it was very big from the '20s through to the War. Lord Badgerfield ran it."

"I have heard of it," Greg said. "It's always an *Argus* headline in those old films about Dunkirk."

"That's right. The paper had what they used to call 'a good War'. Churchill called it 'the voice of true democracy'. Like Churchill, it was never quite the same after the War . . . but now, what with the interest in the 50th anniversary of the Battle of Britain and all that, we think the time is right to bring it back. It'll be nostalgia, but it'll be new too . . ."

"Gasmasks and rationing and the spirit of the Blitz, eh?"

"That sort of thing. It'll come out in the Autumn, and we'll build up to it with a massive campaign. 'The voice is back.' We'll cut from this ovaltine-type '40s look to an aggressive '90s feel, yuppies on carphones, designer style, full-colour pages. It'll be a harder news paper than the *Comet*, but it'll still be a Leech UK product, populist and commercial. We aim to be the turn-of-the-century newspaper."

"And you want a cartoonist?"

Crosbie smiled. "I liked your *Fat Chance* work a lot, Greg. The script was a bit manky for my taste, but you draw with clean lines, good solid blocks of black. Your private eye was a thug, but he looked like a real strip hero. There was a bit of Jeff Hawke there. It was just what we want for the *Argus*, the feel of the past but the content of the present."

"So you'll be wanting Greg to do a *Fat Chance* strip for the new paper?"

Greg had made the connection, and was cracking a smile.

"No, Tamara, that's not what he wants. I've remembered the other thing I know about the *Argus*. I should have recognized the name straight off. It's a by-word . . ."

Crosbie cut in, "that's right. The *Mirror* had Jane and Garth, but the *Argus* had . . ."

Greg was actually excited. He thought he had grown up, but there was still a pulp heart in him. As a child, he had pored through second- and third-hand books and magazines. Before *Brainrape* and *Fat Chance* and *PC Rozzerblade*, he had tried to draw his other heroes: Bulldog Drummond, the Saint, Sexton Blake, Biggles, and . . .

"Dr Shade."

"You may haff caught me, *Herr Doktor Schatten*, but ze glory off ze Sird Reich vill roll over zis passetic country like a tchuggernaucht. I die for ze greater glory off Tchermany, off ze Nazi party and off Adolf Hitler . . ."

"That's where you're wrong, Von Spielsdorf. I wouldn't dirty my hands by killing you, even if it is what you so richly deserve."

"Ain't we gonna ice the lousy stinkin' rat, Doc?" asked Hank the Yank. The American loomed over the German mastermind, a snub-nosed automatic in his meaty fist.

"Yours is a young country, Henry," said Dr Shade gently, laying a black-gloved hand of restraint upon his comrade's arm. "That's not how we do things in England. Von Spielsdorf here may be shot as a spy, but that decision is not ours to make. We have courts and laws and justice. That's what this whole war's about, my friend. The right of the people to have courts and laws and justice. Even you, Von Spielsdorf. We're fighting for your rights too."

"Pah, decadent *Englische Scheweinhund!*"

Hank tapped the German on the forehead with his pistol-grip, and the saboteur sat down suddenly, his eyes rolling upwards.

"That showed him, eh, Doc?"

Dr Shade's thin, normally inexpressive lips, curled in a slight smile.

"Indubitably, Henry. Indubitably."

> —Rex Cash, "The Fiend of the Fifth Column",
> *Dr Shade Monthly* No 111 [May, 1943]

The heart of Leech UK was a chrome-and-glass pyramid in London docklands, squatting by the Thames like a recently-arrived flying saucer. Greg felt a little queasy as the minicab they had sent for him slipped through the pickets. It was a chilly Spring day, and there weren't many of them about. Crosbie had warned him of "the Union Luddites" and their stance against the new technology that enabled Leech to put out the *Comet* and its other papers with a bare minimum of production staff. Greg hoped none of the placard-carriers would recognize him. Last year, there had been quite a bit of violence as the pickets, augmented by busloads of radicals as annoyed by Leech's editorials as his industrial relations policies, came up against the police and a contingent of the *Comet*-reading skinheads who were the backbone of Leech's support. Now, the dispute dragged on but was almost forgotten. Leech's papers had never mentioned it much, and the rest of the press had fresher strikes, revolutions and outrages to cover.

The minicab drove right into the pyramid, into an enclosed reception area where the vehicle was checked by security guards. Greg was allowed out and issued with a blue day pass that a smiling girl in a smart uniform pinned on his lapel.

Behind her desk were framed colour shots of smiling girls without uniforms, smart or otherwise, their nipples like squashed cherries, their faces cleanly unexpressive. The *Comet Knock-Outs* were supposed to be a national institution. But so, according to the *Comet*, were corporal punishment in schools, capital punishment for supporters of Sinn Fein, and the right to tell lies about the sexual preferences of soap opera performers. Greg wondered what Penny Stamp—Girl Reporter, Dr Shade's sidekick in the old strip, would have made of a *Comet Knock-Out*. Penny had always been rowing with the editor who wanted her to cover fashion shows and garden parties when she would rather be chasing crime scoops for the front page; perhaps her modern equivalent should be a pin-up girl who wants to keep her clothes on and become Roger Cook or Woodward and Bernstein?

He rode up to the 23rd floor, which was where Crosbie had arranged to meet him. The girl downstairs had telephoned up, and her clone was waiting for him in the thickly-carpeted lobby outside the lift. She smiled, and escorted him through an open-plan office where telephones and computers were being installed by a cadre of workmen. At the far end were a series of glassed-off cubicles. She eased him into one of these, and asked if he wanted tea or coffee. She brought him instant coffee, the granules floating near the bottom of a paper cupful of hot brown water. There was a dummy edition of the *Evening Argus* on the desk. The headline was "IT'S WAR!" Greg didn't have time to look at it.

Crosbie came in with a tall, slightly stooped man, and ordered more coffee. The newcomer was in his 70s, but looked fit for his age. He wore comfortable old trousers and a cardigan under a new sports jacket. Greg knew who he was.

"Rex Cash?" he asked, his hand out.

The man's grip was firm. "One of him," he said. "Not the original."

"This is Harry Lipman, Greg."

"Harry," Harry said.

"Greg. Greg Daniels."

"*Fat Chance*?"

Greg nodded. He was surprised Harry had kept up with the business. He had been retired for a long time, he knew.

"Mr Crosbie told me. I've been looking your stuff out. I don't know much about the drawing side. Words are my line. But you're a talented young man."

"Thanks."

"Can we work together?" Harry was being direct. Greg didn't have an answer.

"I hope so."

"So do I. It's been a long time. I'll need someone to snip the extra words out of the panels."

Harry Lipman had been Rex Cash from 1939 to 1952, taking over the name from Donald Moncrieff, the creator of Dr Shade. He had filled 58 Dr Shade books with words, 42 novels and 135 short stories, and he had scripted the newspaper strip all the while, juggling storylines. Several of the best-known artists in British adventure comics had worked on the Dr Shade strip—Mack Bullivant, who would create *Andy of the Arsenal* for *British Pluck*, Tommy Wrathall, highly regarded for his commando and paratroop stories in *Boys' War*, and, greatest of all, Frank FitzGerald, who had, for six years, made Dr Shade dark, funny and almost magical. They were all dead now. Harry was the last survivor of those days. And so the *Argus* was calling in Greg to fill the footprints.

"Harry has been working up some storylines," said Crosbie. "I'll leave you to talk them through. If you need more coffee, give Nicola a buzz. I'll be back in a few hours to see how you're doing."

Crosbie left. Harry and Greg looked at each other and, for no reason, started laughing like members of a family sharing a joke they could never explain to an outsider.

"Considering Dr Shade must be about 150 now," Harry began, "I thought we'd start the strip with him trying to get the DHSS to up his heating allowance for the winter . . ."

SHADE, DOCTOR Scientific vigilante of mysterious origins, usually hidden behind a cloak and goggle-like dark glasses, although also a master of disguise with many other identities. Operating out of an outwardly dilapidated but inwardly luxurious retreat in London's East End, he employs a group of semi-criminal bully boys in his neverending war against foreign elements importing evil into the heart of the British Empire. Originally introduced (under the name "Dr Jonathan Shadow") as a minor character in *The Cur of Limehouse* (1929), a novel by Rex Cash (Donald Moncrieff), in which he turns up in the final chapters to help the aristocratic pugilist hero Reggie Brandon defeat the East End opium warlord Baron Quon. The character was so popular with the readers of *Wendover's Magazine*, the monthly publication in which the novel was serialized, that Moncrieff wrote several series of short adventures, later collected in the volumes *Dr Shadow and the Poison Goddess* (1931) and *Dr Shadow's Nigger Trouble* (1932). In 1934, alleging plagiarism of their character, The SHADOW, Street and Smith threatened to sue Badgerfield, publishers of *Wendover's* and of the collections, and, to appease the American firm, the character was renamed Dr Shade.

A semi-supernatural, ultra-patriotic avenger whose politics would seem to be somewhat to the right of those of Sapper's Bulldog DRUMMOND or the real-life Oswald Mosley (of whom Moncrieff was reputed to be a great admirer), Dr Shade is much given to executing minor villains with his airgun or gruesomely torturing them for information. He appeared in nearly 100 short novels, all credited to Rex Cash, written for *Dr Shade Monthly*, a pulp periodical issued by Badgerfield from 1934 until 1947. The house pseudonym was also used by a few other writers, mostly for back-up stories in the 1930s, when the prolific Moncrieff's inspiration flagged. The character became even more popular when featured in a daily strip in the *Evening Argus*, most famously drawn by Frank FitzGerald, from 1935 to 1952. Moncrieff, after a bitter dispute with Lord Badgerfield, stopped writing Dr Shade in 1939, and the strip was taken over by Harry Lipman, a writer who had done a few Dr Shade stories for the magazine. By the outbreak of war, Lipman had effectively become Rex Cash, and was producing stories and novels for the magazine as well as scripting the comic.

Lipman's Dr Shade is a less frightening figure than Moncrieff's. Although his uniform and gadgets are unchanged, Lipman's hero was an official agent of the British government who refrained from sadistically mistreating his enemies the way Moncrieff's had. It was revealed that Dr Shade is really Dr Jonathan Chambers, an honest and dedicated general practitioner, and the supernatural elements of the strip were toned down. During WW II, Dr Shade's politics changed; as written by Moncrieff, he is an implacable foe of the non-white races and international communism, but Lipman's hero is a straightforward defender of democracy in the face of the Nazi menace. Moncrieff's Moriarty figure, introduced in *Dr Shade and the Whooping Horror* (1934), is Israel Cohen, a stereotypically Jewish master criminal in league with Russian anarchists and Indian Thuggees in a plot to destroy Britain's naval superiority. During the War, Cohen was retired—although he returned in the late 1940s as a comic East End nightclub owner and *friend* of Dr Shade—and the penumbral adventurer, joined by two-fisted American OSS agent Harry Hemingway and peppy girl reporter Penny Stamp, concentrated exclusively on licking Hitler.

Moncrieff's Dr Shade novels include *Dr Shade Vs the Dynamite Boys* (1936), *A Yellow Man's Treachery* (1936), *Dr Shade's Balkan Affair* (1937), *To the Last Drop of Our British Blood* (1937), *The Bulldog Bites Back* (1937), *The International Conspirators* (1938) and *Dr Shade in Suez* (1939), while Lipman's are *Dr Shade's Home Front* (1940), *Underground in France* (1941), *Dr Shade Takes Over* (1943), *Dr Shade in Tokyo* (1945), *Dr Shade Buries the Hatchet* (1948) and *The Piccadilly Gestapo* (1951). The character also featured in films, beginning with *Dr Shade's Phantom Taxi Mystery* (1936; dir. Michael Powell), in which he was played by Raymond Massey, while Francis L. Sullivan was a decidedly non-Semitic Israel Cohen, renamed "Idris Kobon." Valentine Dyall took the role in a BBC Radio serial from 1943 to 1946, and Ronald Howard wore the cloak in a 1963 Rediffusion TV serial, *Introducing Dr Shade . . .*, with Elizabeth Shepherd as Penny Stamp and Alfie Bass as Israel Cohen.

See also: Dr Shade's associates: Reggie BRANDON, Lord Highbury and Islington; Henry HEMINGWAY (Hank the Yank); Penny STAMP, Girl Reporter; and his enemies: Israel COHEN, the Mad Genius of the Revolution; ACHMET the Almost Human; Melchior Umberto GASPARD, Prince of Forgers; Professor IZAN, the Führer's Favourite.

—David Pringle, *Imaginary People:*
A Who's Who of Modern Fictional Characters (1987)

Greg and Harry Lipman met several times over the next few weeks,
mainly away from the Leech building. In Soho pubs and cheap
restaurants, they discussed the direction of the new Dr Shade
strip. Greg had liked Harry immediately, and came to admire
his still-quick storyteller's mind. He knew he could work with
this man. Having taken Dr Shade over from Donald Moncrieff, he
didn't have a creator's obsessive attachment to the property, and
was open to suggestions that would change the frame of the strip.
Harry agreed that there was no point in producing a '40s pastiche.
Their Dr Shade had to be different from all the character's previous
incarnations, but still maintain some of the continuity. Gradually, their
ideas came together.

In keeping with the *Argus'* stated old-but-new approach, they
decided to set the strip in the near future. Everybody was talking
about the turn of the century. They would have Dr Shade come
out of retirement, disenchanted with the post-war world he fought
for back in the old days, and assembling a new team of adventurers
to tackle up-to-the-moment villains against a backdrop of urban
decay and injustice. Greg suggested pitting the avenging shadowman
against rapacious property speculators laying waste to his old East
End stamping grounds, a Crack cartel posing as a fundamentalist
religious sect, corporate despoilers of the environment, or unethical
stock-brokers with Mafia connections.

"You know," Harry said one afternoon in The Posts, sipping his
pint, "if Donald were writing these stories, Dr Shade would be on
the side of those fellers. He died thinking he'd lost everything, and
here we are, half a century later, with a country the original Dr Shade
would have been proud of."

Nearby, a bored mid-afternoon drinker, swallows tattooed on his
neck, zapped spaceships, his beeping deathrays cutting into the piped
jazz. Greg pulled open his bag of salt-and-vinegar crisps. "I don't know
much about Moncrieff. Even the reference books are pretty sketchy.
What was he like?"

"I didn't really know the man, Greg. To him, Lipmans were like
Cohens . . . not people you talked to."

"Was he really a fascist?"

"Oh yes," Harry's eyes got a little larger. "Nobody had a shirt
blacker than Donald Moncrieff. The whole kit and kaboodle, he
had: glassy eyes, toothbrush moustache, thin blonde hair. Marched
through Brixton with Mosley a couple of times. Smashed up my
brother's newsagent's shop, they did. And he went on goodwill
jaunts to Spain and Germany. I believe he wrote pamphlets for the
British Union of Fascists, and he certainly conned poor old Frank

into designing a recruiting poster for the Cause."

"Frank FitzGerald?"

"Yes, your predecessor with the pencils. Frank never forgave Donald for that. During the war, the intelligence people kept interrogating Frank whenever there was a bit of suspected sabotage. You know the line in *Casablanca*? 'Round up the usual suspects.' Well, Donald put Frank on the list of 'usual suspects'."

The space cadet burned out. He swore and thumped the machine as it flashed its "Game Over" sneer at him.

"Were you brought in specifically to change Dr Shade?"

"Oh yes. Badgerfield was an appeasement man right up until Munich, but he was a smart newspaper boy and saw the change in the wind. He dumped a lot of people—not just fascists, lots of pacifists got tarred with the same brush—and about-faced his editorial policy. You'd think he'd overlook the comic strip, but he didn't. He knew it was as much a part of the *Argus* as the editorial pages and his own 'Honest Opinion' column. My orders when I took over were quite blunt. He told me to 'de-Nazify' Dr Shade."

"What happened to Moncrieff?"

"Oh, he sued and sued and sued, but Badgerfield owned the character and could do what he wanted. When the War started, he became very unpopular, of course. He spent some time in one of those holiday camps they set up for Germans and Italians and sympathizers. They didn't have much concrete on him, and he came back to London. He wrote some books, I think, but couldn't get them published. I heard he had a stack of Dr Shade stories he was never able to use because only His Lordship had the right to exploit the character. Then, he died . . ."

"He was young, wasn't he?"

"Younger than me. It was the Blitz. They tried to say he was waving a torch in the blackout for the *Lüftwaffe*, but I reckon he was just under the wrong bomb at the wrong time. I saw him near the end, and he was pretty cracked. Not at all the privileged smoothie he'd been in the '30s. I didn't like the feller, of course, but you had to feel sorry for him. He thought Hitler was Jesus Christ, and the War just drove him off his head. Lots of Englishmen like that, there were. You don't hear much about them these days."

"I don't know. They all seem to be in Parliament now."

Harry chuckled. "Too right, but Dr Shade'll see to 'em, you bet, eh?"

They raised their drinks and toasted the avenging shadow, the implacable enemy of injustice, intolerance and ill-will.

IN PRAISE OF BRITISH HERO'S

Those of us PROUD TO BE BRITISH know that in this nations HOUR OF DIREST NEED, the True Blue BRITISH HERO'S will appear and STAND TALL TOGETHER to WIPE FROM THE FACE OF THIS FAIR FLOWER OF A LAND those who BESMERCH IT'S PURITY. With the WHITE BRITON'S in danger of drowning under the tidal wave of COLOUREDS, and the dedicated and law-upholding BRITISH POLICE going unarmed against the SEMITEX BOMBS, OOZY MACHINE GUNS and ROCKET LAUNCHERS of the KINK-HAIRED NIGGER'S, MONEY-GRUBBING YIDS, ARSE-BANDIT AID'S-SPREADERS, SLANT-EYED KUNGFU CHINKIE'S, LONG-HAIRED HIPPY RABBLE, LOONY LEFT LESBIONS, and RAGHEADED MUSSULMEN, the time has come for KING ARTHUR to return from under the hill, for the CROSS OF ST GEORGE to fly from the banners of the CRUSADERS OF CHRISTENDOM, for ROBIN HOOD to come back from the greenwood of Avalon, for the archers of CRECY to notch up their arrows on the orders of GOOD KING HENRY THE FIFTH, for ADMIRAL HORATIO NELSON to take command of the STOUTHEARTED FLEET, for RAJAH BROOKE OF SARA-WAK to show the coons and gooks and spooks and poofs whats what, for the MURDER of GENERAL GORDON to be avenged with the blood of AY-RAB troublemakers, for DICK TURPIN to rob the JEW-INFESTED coffers of the INVADING IMMIGRANT VERMIN AND FILTH, for DR SHADE to use his airgun on the enemies of WHITE LIBERTY . . .

The time will come soon when all GOOD BRITISH MEN will have to dip their FISTS in PAKKYNIGGERYIDCHINK-AY-RAB BLOOD to make clean for the healthy WHITE babies of our women this sacred island. The STINKING SCUM with their DOG-EATING, their DIS-GUSTING UNCHRISTIAN RITUAL PRACTICES, their PIG-SCREWING, CHILD-RAPING, MARRIAGE-ARRANGING, DISEASE-SPREADING habits will be thrown off the WHITE cliffs of Dover and swept out to sea as we, THE TRUE INHABITANTS OF GREAT BRITAIN, reclame the homes, the jobs, the lands and the women that are ours by DIVINE RIGHT.

KING ARTHUR! ST GEORGE! DR SHADE!

Today, go out and glassbottle a chinkie waiter, rapefuck a stinking coon bitch, piss burning petrol in a pakky news-agent, stick the boot to a raghead, hang a queer, shit in a sinnagog, puke on a lesbion. ITS YOUR LEGAL RIGHT! ITS YOUR DUTY! ITS YOUR DESTINY!

ARTHUR is COMING BACK! DR SHADE WILL RETURN!

Our's is the RIGHT, our's is the GLORY, our's is the ONLY TRUE JUSTICE! We shall PREVALE!

We are the SONS OF DR SHADE!

—"Johnny British Man," *Britannia Rules* fanzine,
Issue 37, June 1991.
(Confiscated by police at a South London football fixture.)

Harry had given him a map of the estate, but Greg still got lost. The place was one of those '60s wastelands, concrete slabs now disfigured by layers of spray-painted hatred, odd little depressions clogged with rubbish, more than a few burned-out or derelict houses. There was loud Heavy Metal coming from somewhere, and teenagers hung about in menacing gaggles, looking at him with empty, hostile eyes as they compared tattoos or passed bottles. One group was inhaling something—glue?—from a brown paper bag. He looked at them a moment or two longer than he should have, and they stared defiance. A girl whose skin haircut showed the odd bumps of her skull flashed him the V sign.

He kept his eyes on the ground and got more lost. The numbering system of the houses was irregular and contradictory, and Greg had to go round in circles for a while. He asked for directions from a pair of henna-redheaded teenage girls sitting on a wall, and they just shrugged their shoulders and went back to chewing gum. One of the girls was pregnant, her swollen belly pushing through her torn T-shirt, bursting the buttons of her jeans fly.

Greg was conscious that even his old overcoat was several degrees smarter than the norm in this area, and that that might mark him as a mugging target. He also knew that he had less than ten pounds on him, and that frustrated muggers usually make up the difference between their expectations and their acquisitions with bare-knuckle beatings and loose teeth.

It was a summer evening, and quite warm, but the estate had a chill all of its own. The block-shaped tiers of council flats cast odd shadows that slipped across alleyways in a manner that struck Greg as being subtly wrong, like an illustration where the perspective is off or the light sources contradictory. The graffiti wasn't the '80s hip-hop style he knew from his own area, elaborate signatures to absent works of art, but was bluntly, boldly blatant, embroidered only by the occasional swastika (invariably drawn the wrong way round), football club symbol or Union Jack scratch.

CHELSEA FC FOREVER. KILL THE COONS! NF NOW. GAS THE YIDS! UP THE GUNNERS. FUCK THE IRISH MURDERERS! HELP STAMP OUT AIDS—SHOOT A POOF TODAY. And the names of bands he had read about in *Searchlight*, the anti-fascist paper: SCREWDRIVER, BRITISH BOYS, WHITE-WASH, CRUSADERS. There was a song lyric, magic markered on a bus stop in neat primary school writing: "Jump down, turn around, kick a fucking nigger. Jump down, turn around, kick him in the head. Jump down, turn around, kick a fucking nigger. Jump down, turn around, kick him till he's dead . . ."

You would have thought that the Nazis had won the War, and installed a puppet Tory government. The estate could easily be a '30s science-fiction writer's idea of the ghetto of the future, clean-lined and featureless buildings trashed by the bubble-helmeted brownshirts of some interplanetary axis, Jews, blacks and Martians despatched to some concentration camp asteroid. This wasn't the Jubilee Year. Nobody was even angry any more, just numbed with the endless, grinding misery of it all.

Eventually, more or less by wandering at random, he found Harry Lipman's flat. The bell button had been wrenched off, leaving a tuft of multi-coloured wires, and there was a reversed swastika carved into the door. Greg knocked, and a light went on in the hall. Harry admitted him into the neat, small flat, and Greg realized the place was fortified like a command bunker, a row of locks on the door, multiple catches on the reinforced glass windows, a burglar alarm fixed up on the wall between the gas and electricity meters. Otherwise, it was what he had expected: bookshelves everywhere, including the toilet, and a pleasantly musty clutter.

"I've not had many people here since Becky died"—Greg had known that Harry was a widower—"you must excuse the fearful mess."

Harry showed Greg through to the kitchen. There was an Amstrad PCW 8256 set up on the small vinyl-topped table, a stack of continuous paper in a tray on the floor feeding the printer. The room smelled slightly of fried food.

"I'm afraid this is where I write. It's the only room with enough natural light for me. Besides, I like to be near the kettle and the Earl Gray."

"Don't worry about it, Harry. You should see what my studio looks like. I think it used to be a coal cellar."

He put down his art folder, and Harry made a pot of tea.

"So, how's Dr Shade coming along? I've made some drawings."

"Swimmingly. I've done a month's worth of scripts, giving us our introductory serial. In the end, I went with the East End story as the strongest to bring the Doctor back . . ."

The East End story was an idea Harry and Greg had developed in which Dr Jonathan Chambers, miraculously not a day older than he was in 1952 (or in 1929, come to that) when he was last seen, returns from a spell in a Tibetan Monastery (or somewhere) studying the mystic healing arts (or something) to discover that the area where he used to make his home is being taken over by Dominick Dalmas, a sinister tycoon whose sharp-suited thugs are using violence and intimidation to evict the long-time residents, among whom are several of the doctor's old friends. Penelope Stamp, formerly a girl reporter but now a feisty old woman, is head of the Residents' Protection Committee, and she appeals to Chambers to resume his old crime-fighting alias and to investigate Dalmas. At first reluctant, Chambers is convinced by a botched assassination attempt to put on the cloak and goggles, and it emerges that Dalmas is the head of a mysterious secret society whose nefarious schemes would provide limitless future plotlines. Dalmas would be hoping to build up a substantial powerbase in London with the long-term intention of taking over the country, if not the world. Of course, Dr Shade would thwart his plots time and again, although not without a supreme effort.

"Maybe I'm just old, Greg," Harry said after he had shown him the scripts, "but this Dr Shade feels different. People said that when I took over from Donald, the strip became more appealing, with more comedy and thrills than horror and violence, but I can't see much to laugh about in this story. It's almost as if someone were trying to force Dr Shade to be Donald's character, by creating a world where his monster vigilante makes more sense than my straight-arrow hero. Everything's turned around."

"Don't worry about it. Our Dr Shade is still fighting for justice. He's on the side of Penny Stamp, not Dominick Dalmas."

"What I want to know is whether he'll be on the side of Derek Leech?"

Greg really hadn't thought of that. The proprietor of the Argus would, of course, have the power of veto over the adventures of his cartoon character. He might not care for the direction Greg and Harry wanted to take Dr Shade in.

"Leech is on the side of money. We just have to make the strip so good it sells well, then it won't matter to him what it says."

"I hope you're right, Greg, I really do. More tea?"

Outside, it got dark, and they worked through the scripts, making minor changes. Beyond the kitchen windows, shadows crept across the tiny garden towards the flat, their fingers reaching slowly for the concrete and tile. There were many small noises in the night, and it would have been easy to mistake the soft hiss of an aerosol paintspray for the popping of a high-powered airgun.

AUSSIE SOAP STAR GOT ME ON CRACK: Doomed schoolgirl's story—EXCLUSIVE—begins in the *Comet* today.

THE *COMET* LAW AND ORDER PULL-OUT. We ask top coppers, MPs, criminals and ordinary people what's to be done about rising crime?

BRIXTON YOBS SLASH WAR HERO PENSIONER: Is the birch the only language they understand? "Have-a-Go" Tommy Barraclough, 76, thinks so. A special *Comet* poll shows that so do 69% of you readers.

DEREK LEECH TALKS STRAIGHT: Today: IMMIGRATION, CRIME, UNEMPLOYMENT.

"No matter what the whingers and moaners say, the simple fact is that Britain is an island. We are a small country, and we only have room for the British. Everybody knows about the chronic housing shortage and the lack of jobs. The pro-open door partisans can't argue with the facts and figures.

"British citizenship is a privilege not a universal right. This simple man thinks we should start thinking twice before we give it away to any old Tom, Dick or Pandit who comes, turban in hand, to our country, hoping to make a fortune off the dole . . ."

WIN! WIN! WIN! LURVERLY DOSH! THE *COMET* GIVE AWAY GRID DISHES OUT THREE MILLION KNICKER! THEY SAID WE'D NEVER DO IT, BUT WE DID! MILLIONS MORE IN LURVERLY PRIZES MUST GO!

This is BRANDI ALEXANDER, 17, and she'll be seen without the football scarf in our ADULTS ONLY Sunday edition. BRANDI has just left school. Already, she has landed a part in a film, *Fiona Does the Falklands*. The part may be small, but hers aren't . . .

CATS TORTURED BY CURRYHOUSE KING?: What's really in that vindaloo, Mr Patel?

DID ELVIS DIE OF AIDS?: Our psychic reveals the truth!

GUARDIAN ANGEL KILLINGS CONTINUE: Scotland Yard Insiders Condemn Vigilante Justice.

The bodies of Malcolm Williams, 19, and Barry Tozer, 22, were identified yesterday by the Reverend Kenneth Hood, a spokesman for the West Indian community. The dead men were dumped in an underpass on the South London Attlee Estate. Both were shot at close range with a smallbore gun, execution-style. Inspector Mark Davey of the Metropolitan Police believes that the weapon used might be an airgun. The incident follows the identical killings of five black and Asian youths in recent months.

Williams and Tozer, like the other victims, had extensive police records. Williams served three months in prison last year for breaking and entering, and Tozer had a history of mugging, statutory rape, petty thieving and violence. It is possible that they were killed shortly after committing an assault. A women's handbag was found nearby, its contents scattered. Witnesses report that Williams and Tozer left The Flask, their local, when they couldn't pay for more drinks, and yet they had money on them when they were found.

The police are appealing for any witnesses to come forward. In particular, they would like to question the owner of the bag, who might well be able to identify the "Guardian Angel" executioner. Previous appeals have not produced any useful leads.

A local resident who wishes to remain anonymous told our reporter, "I hope they never catch the Guardian Angel. There are a lot more n*gg*r b*st*rds with knives out there. I hope the Angel gets them all. Then maybe I can cash my pension at the post-office without fearing for my life."

Coming Soon: BRITAIN'S NEW-OLD NEWSPAPER. CHURCHILL's FAVOURITE READING IS BACK. DR SHADE WILL RETURN. At last, the EVENING has a HERO.
—From the *Daily Comet*, Monday July the 1st, 1991

Saturday mornings were always quiet at comics conventions. Every time Greg went into the main hall there was a panel. All of them featured three quiet people nodding and chuckling while Neil Gaiman told all the jokes from his works-in-progress. He had heard them all in the bar the night before, and kept leaving for yet another turn around the dealers' room. They had him on a panel in the evening about reviving old characters: they were bringing back Tarzan, Grimly Feendish and Dan Dare, so Dr Shade would be in good company. At the charity auction, his first attempts at designing a new-look Dr Shade had fetched over £50, which must mean something.

He drifted away from the cardboard boxes full of overpriced American comic books in plastic bags to the more eccentric stalls which offered old movie stills, general interest magazines from the '40s and '50s (and, he realized with a chill, the '60s and '70s), odd items like *Stingray* jigsaws (only three pieces missing, £12.00) and *Rawhide* boardgames (£5.00), and digest-sized pulp magazines.

A dealer recognized him, probably from an earlier con, and said he might have something that would interest him. He had the smugly discreet tone of a pimp. Bending down below his trestle table, which made him breathe hard, he reached for a tied bundle of pulps and brought them up.

"You don't see these very often . . ."

Greg looked at the cover of the topmost magazine. *Dr Shade Monthly*. The illustration, a faded FitzGerald, showed the goggled and cloaked doctor struggling with an eight-foot neanderthal in the uniform of an SS officer, while the blonde Penny Stamp, dressed only in flimsy '40s foundation garments and chains, lay helpless on an operating table. INSIDE: "Master of the Mutants" a complete novel by REX CASH. Also "Flaming Torture," "The Laughter of Dr Shade" and "Hank the Yank and the Hangman of Heidelberg." April, 1945. A

Badgerfield Publication.

Greg had asked Harry Lipman to come along to the con, but the writer had had a few bad experiences at events like this and said he didn't want to "mix with the looneys." He knew Harry didn't have many of the old mags with his stuff in, and that he had to buy these for him. Who knows, there might be a few ideas in them that could be re-used.

"Ten quid the lot?"

He handed over two fives, and took the bundle, checking the spines to see that the dealer hadn't slipped in some *Reader's Digests* to bulk out the package.

No, they were all *Dr Shades*, all from the '40s. He had an urge to sit down and read the lot.

Back in the hall, someone was lecturing an intently interested but pimple-plagued audience about adolescent angst in *The Teen Titans* and *X-Men*, and Greg wondered where he could get a cup of tea or coffee and a biscuit. Neil Gaiman, surrounded by acolytes, grinned at him and waved from across the room, signalling. Greg gestured his thanks. Neil had alerted him to the presence of Hunt Sealey, a British comics entrepreneur he had once taken to court over some financial irregularities. Greg did not want to go through that old argument again. Avoiding the spherical Sealey, he stepped into a darkened room where a handful of white-faced young men with thick glasses were watching a Mexican horror-wrestling movie on a projection video. The tape was a third- or fourth-generation dupe, and the picture looked as if it were being screened at a tropical drive-in during the monsoon.

"Come, Julio," said a deep American voice dubbed over the lip movements of a swarthy mad doctor, "help me carry the cadaver of the gorilla to the incinerator."

Nobody laughed. The video room smelled of stale cigarette smoke and spilled beer. The kids who couldn't afford a room in the hotel crashed out in here, undisturbed by the non-stop Z-movie festival. The only film Greg wanted to see—a French print of Georges Franju's *Les Yeux sans Visage*—was scheduled at the same time as his panel. Typical.

On the assumption that Sealey, who was known for the length of time he could hold a grudge, would be loitering in the hall harassing Neil, Greg sat on a chair and watched the movie. The mad doctor was transplanting gorilla hearts, and a monster was terrorizing the city, ripping the dresses off hefty *senoritas*. The heroine was a sensitive lady wrestler who wanted to quit the ring because she had put her latest opponent in a coma.

Greg got bored with the autopsy footage and the jumpy images, and looked around to see if anyone he knew was there. The audience were gazing at the screen like communicants at mass, the video mirrored in their spectacles, providing starlike pinpoints in the darkness.

He had been drawing a lot of darkness recently, filling in the shadows around Dr Shade, only the white of his lower face and the highlights of his goggles showing in the night as he stalked Dominick Dalmas through the mean streets of East London. His hand got tired after inking in the solid blacks of the strip. Occasionally, you saw Dr Chambers in the daytime, but 95% of the panels were night scenes.

There was a glitch on the videotape, and the film vanished for a few seconds, replaced by Nanette Newman waving a bottle of washing-up liquid. Nobody hooted or complained, and the mad doctor's gorilla-man came back in an instant. A tomato-like eyeball was fished out, gravyish blood coursing down the contorted face of a bad actor with a worse toupee. Stock music as old as talking pictures thundered on the soundtrack. If it weren't for the violence, this could easily have been made in the '30s, when Donald Moncrieff's Dr Shade was in the hero business, tossing mad scientists out of tenth-storey windows and putting explosive airgun darts into Bolshies and rebellious natives.

Although his eyes were used to the dark, Greg thought he wasn't seeing properly. A corner of the room, behind the video, was as thickly black as any of his panels. To one side of the screen, he could dimly see the walls with their movie posters and fan announcements, a fire extinguisher hung next to a notice. But the other side of the room was just an impenetrable night.

He had a headache, and there were dots in front of his eyes. He looked away from the dark corner, and back again. It didn't disappear. But it did seem to move, easing itself away from the wall and expanding towards him. A row of seats disappeared. The screen shone brighter, dingy colours becoming as vivid as a comic-book cover.

Greg clutched his *Dr Shades*, telling himself this was what came of too much beer, not enough food and too many late nights in the convention bar. Suddenly, it was very hot in the video room, as if the darkness were burning up, suffocating him . . .

A pair of spectacles glinted in the dark. There was someone inside the shadow, someone wearing thick sunglasses. No, not glasses. Goggles.

He stood up, knocking his chair over. Somebody grumbled at the noise. On the screen, the Mexico City cops had shot the gorilla man dead, and the mad doctor—his father—was being emotional about his loss.

The darkness took manshape, but not mansize. Its shadow head, topped by the shape of a widebrimmed hat, scraped the ceiling, its arms reached from wall to wall.

Only Greg took any notice. Everyone else was upset about the gorilla man and the mad doctor. Somewhere under the goggles, up near the light fixtures, a phantom white nose and chin were forming around the black gash of a humourless mouth.

Greg opened the door, and stepped out of the video room, his heart spasming in its cage. Slamming the door on the darkness, he pushed himself into the corridor, and collided with a tall, cloaked figure.

Suddenly angry, he was about to lash out verbally when he realized he knew who the man was. The recognition was like an ECT jolt.

He was standing in front of Dr Shade.

The Jew fled through the burning city, feeling a clench of dread each time a shadow fell over his heart. There was nowhere he could hide. Not in the underground railway stations that doubled as bomb shelters, not in the sewers with the other rats, not in the cells of the traitor police. The doctor was coming for him, coming to avenge the lies he had told, and there was nothing that could be done.

The all-clear had sounded, the drone of the planes was gone from the sky, and the streets were busy with firemen and panicking Londoners. Their homes were destroyed, their lilywhite lives ground into the mud. The Jew found it in his heart to laugh bitterly as he saw a mother in a nightdress, calling for her children outside the pile of smoking bricks that had been her house. His insidious kind had done their job too well, setting the Aryan races at each other's throats while they plotted with the Soviet Russians and the heathen Chinee to dominate the grim world that would come out of this struggle. Germans dropped bombs on Englishmen, and the Jew smiled.

But, in this moment, he knew that success of the Conspiracy would mean nothing to him. Not while the night still had shadows. Not while there was a Dr Shade . . .

He leaned, exhausted, against a soot-grimed wall. The mark of Dr Shade was on him, a black handprint on his camelhair coat. The doctor's East End associates were dogging him, relaying messages back to their master, driving him away from the light, keeping him running through the night. There was no one to call him "friend."

A cloth-capped young man looked into the alley, ice-blue eyes penetrating the dark. He put his thumb and forefinger to his mouth and gave a shrill whistle.

"'Ere, mateys, we gots us a Yid! Call fer the doc!"

There was a stampede of heavy boots. Almost reluctant to keep on the move, wishing for it all to be over, the murdering filth shoved himself away from the wall and made a run for the end of the alley. The wall was low, and he hauled himself up it onto a sloping roof. The East End boys were after him, broken bottles and shivs in their hands, but he made it ahead of them. He strode up the tiles, feeling them shift under his feet. Some came loose and fell behind him, into the faces of Shade's men.

Using chimneys to steady himself, the stinking guttershite ran across the rooftops. He had his revolver out, and fired blindly into the darkness behind him, panic tearing him apart from the inside. Then, he came to the end of his run.

He stood calmly, arms folded, his cloak flapping in the breeze, silhouetted sharply against the fiery skyline. The thin lips formed a smile, and the child-raping libellous Israelite scum knew he was justly dead.

"Hello, Harry," said Dr Shade.

—Donald Moncrieff, "Dr Shade, Jew Killer"
(unpublished, 1942)

"Hello, Harry," said Greg, jiggling the phone in the regulation hopeless attempt to improve a bad connection, "I thought we'd been cut off . . ."

Harry sounded as if he were in Jakarta, not three stops away on the District Line. "So there I was, face to goggles with Dr Shade."

He could make it sound funny now, hours later.

"The guy was on his way to the masquerade. There are always people in weird outfits at these things. He had all the details right, airgun and all."

Greg had called Harry from his hotel room to tell him about all the excitement the Return of Dr Shade was generating with the fans. Kids whose parents hadn't been born when the Argus went out of business were eagerly awaiting the comeback of the cloaked crimefighter.

"Obviously, the Doc has percolated into our folk memory, Harry. Or maybe Leech is right. It's just time to have him back."

His panel had gone well. The questions from the audience had almost all been directed at him, and he had had to field some to the other panelists so as not to hog the whole platform. The fans had been soliciting for information. Yes, Penny Stamp would be back, but she wouldn't be a girl reporter any more. Yes, the Doctor's Rolls Royce "Shadowshark" would be coming out of the garage, with more hidden tricks than ever. Yes, the Doctor would be dealing with the contemporary problems of East London. When someone asked if the proprietor of the paper would be exerting any influence over the content of the strip, Greg replied "well, he hasn't so far," and got cheers by claiming, "I don't think Dr Shade is a *Comet* reader, somehow." Somebody even knew enough to ask him to compare the Donald Moncrieff Rex Cash with the Harry Lipman Rex Cash. He had conveyed best wishes to the con from Harry, and praised the writer's still-active imagination.

At the other end of the line, Harry sounded tired. Sometimes, Greg had to remind himself how old the man was. He wondered whether the call had woken him up.

"We've even had some American interest, maybe in republishing the whole thing as a monthly book, staggered behind the newspaper series. I'm having Tamara investigate. She thinks we can do it without tithing off too much of the money to Derek Leech, but rights deals are tricky. Also, Condé Nast, the corporate heirs of Street and Smith, have a long memory and still think Moncrieff ripped off The Shadow in the '30s. Still, it's worth going into."

Harry tried to sound enthusiastic.

"Are you okay, Harry?"

He said so, but somehow Greg didn't believe him. Greg checked his watch. He had agreed to meet Neil and a few other friends in the bar in ten minutes. He said goodnight to Harry, and hung up.

Wanting to change his panelist's jacket for a drinker's pullover, Greg delved through the suitcase perched on the regulation anonymous armchair. He found the jumper he needed, and transferred his convention badge from lapel to epaulette. Under the suitcase, he found the bundle of *Dr Shade Monthlies* he had bought for Harry. He hadn't mentioned them on the phone.

Harry couldn't have got back to bed yet. He'd barely be in the hall. Greg stabbed the REDIAL button, and listened to the clicking of the exchange. Harry's phone rang again.

The shadows in the room seemed longer. When Harry didn't pick up immediately, Greg's first thought was that something was wrong. He imagined coronaries, nasty falls, fainting spells, the infirmities of the aged. The telephone rang. Ten, twenty, thirty times.

Harry couldn't have got back to bed and fallen into a deep sleep in twenty seconds.

You also couldn't get a wrong number on a phone with a REDIAL facility.

The phone was picked up at the other end.

"Hello," said a female voice, young and hard, "who's this then?"

"Harry," Greg said. "Where's Harry?"

"'E's got a bit of a problem, mate," the girl said. "But we'll see to 'im."

Greg was feeling very bad about this. The girl on the phone didn't sound like a concerned neighbour. "Is Harry ill?"

A pause. Greg imagined silent laughter. There was music in the background. Not Harry Lipman music, but tinny Heavy Metal, distorted by a cheap boombox and the telephone. Suddenly, Greg was down from his high, the good feeling and the alcohol washed out of his system.

"Hello?"

"Still here," the girl said.

"Is Harry ill?"

"Well, I'll put it this way," she said, "we've sent for the doctor."

Evidence has come to light linking Derek Leech, the man at the top of the pyramid, with a linked chain of dubious right-wing organizations here and abroad. A source inside the Leech organization, currently gearing up to launch a new national evening paper, revealed to our reporter, DUNCAN EYLES, that while other press barons diversify into the electronic media and publishing, Derek Leech has his eye on a more direct manner of influencing the shape of the nation.

"Derek has been underwriting the election campaigns of parliamentary candidates in the last few by-elections," the source told us. "They mostly lost their deposits. Patrick Massinghame, the Britain First chairman who later rejoined the Tories, was one. The idea was not to take a seat, but to use the campaigns to disseminate propaganda. The *Comet* has always been anti-immigration, pro-law-and-order, anti-anything-socialist, pro-hanging-and-flogging, pro-military spending, pro-political-censorship. But the campaigns were able to be rabidly so."

Leech, who has regularly dismissed similar allegations as "lunatic conspiracy theories," refused to comment on documents leaked to us which give facts and figures. In addition to funding Patrick Massinghame and others of his political stripe, Leech has contributed heavily to such bizarre causes as the White Freedom Crusade, which channels funds from British and American big business into South Africa, the English Liberation Front, who claim that immigrants from the Indian Sub-Continent and the Caribbean constitute "an army of occupation" and should be driven out through armed struggle, the Revive Capital Punishment lobby, and even Caucasian supremacist thrashmetal band Whitewash, whose single "Blood, Iron and St George" was banned by the BBC and commercial radio stations but still managed to reach Number 5 in the independent charts.

Even more disturbing in the light of these allegations, is the paramilitary nature of the security force Leech is employing to guard the pyramid that is at the heart of his empire. Recruiting directly from right-wing youth gangs, often through advertisements placed in illiterate but suspiciously well produced and printed fanzines distributed at football matches, the Leech organization has been assembling what can only be described as an army of yobs to break the still-continuing print-union pickets in docklands. Our source informs us that the pyramid contains a well-stocked armoury, as if the proprietor of the *Comet* and the forthcoming *Argus* were expecting a siege. Rumour has it that Leech has even invested in a custom-made Rolls Royce featuring such unusual extras as bullet-proof bodywork, James Bond-style concealed rocket launchers, a teargas cannon and bonnet-mounted stilettos.

Derek Leech can afford all the toys he wants. But perhaps it's about time we started to get worried about the games he wants to play . . .

—*Searchlight*, August 1991.

*

The minicab driver wouldn't take him onto the estate no matter what he offered to pay, and left him stranded at the kerb. At night, the place was even less inviting than by day. There were wire-mesh protected lights embedded in concrete walls every so often, but skilled vandals had got through to them. Greg knew that dashing into the dark maze would do no good, and forced himself to study the battered, graffiti-covered map of the estate that stood by the road. He found Harry's house on the map easily. By it, someone had drawn a stickman hanging from a gallows. It was impossible to read a real resemblance into the infant's scrawl of a face, but Greg knew it was supposed to represent Harry.

He walked towards the house, so concerned for Harry Lipman that he forgot to be scared for himself. That was a mistake.

They came from an underpass, and surrounded him. He got an impression of Union Jack T-shirts and shaven heads. Studded leather straps wrapped around knuckles. They only seemed to hit him four or five times, but it was enough.

He turned his head with the first blow, and felt his nose flatten into his cheek. Blood was seeping out of his instantly swollen nostrils, and he was cut inside his mouth. He shook his head, trying to dislodge the pain. They stood back, and watched him yelp blood onto his chest. He was still wearing his convention tag.

Then one of them came in close, breathed foully in his face, and put a knee into his groin. He sagged, crying out, and felt his knees going. They kicked his legs, and he was on the ground. His ribs hurt.

"Come on, P," one of them said, "'e's 'ad 'is. Let's scarper."

"Nahh," said a girl—the one he had talked to on the telephone?—as she stepped forwards. "'e's not properly done yet."

Greg pressed his nostrils together to stanch the blood, and realized his nose wasn't broken. There was a lump rising on his cheek, though. He looked into the girl's face.

She was young, maybe fifteen or sixteen, and there was blonde fur on her skull. Her head was lumpy, and the skinhead cut made her child's face seem small, as if painted on an Easter egg. He had seen her the last time he was here. She wore Britannia earrings, and had a rare right-way-round swastika tattooed in blue on her temple.

"Come on . . ."

P smiled at him, and licked her lips like a cat. "Do you need telling any more, Mr Artist?"

The others were bunched behind her. She was small and wiry, but they were like hulks in the shadows.

"Do you get the picture?"

Greg nodded. Anything, just so long as they let him alone. He had to get to Harry.

"Good. Draw well, 'cause we'll be watching over you."

Lights came on in a house opposite, and he got a clearer look at their faces. Apart from P, they weren't kids. They were in the full skinhead gear, but on them it looked like a disguise. There were muffled voices from the house, and the lights went off again.

"Kick 'im, Penelope," said someone.

P smiled again. "Nahh, Bazzo. 'e knows what's what, now. We don't want to hurt 'im. 'e's important. Ain't ya, Mr Artist?"

Greg was standing up again. There was nothing broken inside his head, but he was still jarred. His teeth hurt, and he spat out a mouthful of blood.

"Dirty beast."

His vision was wobbling. P was double-exposed, a bubble fringe shimmering around her outline.

"Goodnight," said P. "Be good."

Then they were gone, leaving only shadows behind them. Greg ran across the walkway, vinegar-stained pages of the *Comet* swirling about his ankles. Harry's front door was hanging open, the chain broken, and the hallway was lit up.

Greg found him in his kitchen, lying on the floor, his word processor slowly pouring a long manuscript onto him. The machine rasped as it printed out.

He helped Harry sit up, and got him a teacup of water from the tap. They hadn't hurt him too badly, although there was a bruise on his forehead. Harry was badly shaken. Greg had never seen him without his teeth in, and he was drooling like a baby, unconsciously wiping his mouth on his cardigan sleeve. He was trying to talk, but couldn't get the words out.

The phone was ripped out of the wall. The printer was scratching Greg's nerves. He sat at the desk, and tried to work out how to shut it off without losing anything. He wasn't familiar with this model.

Then, he looked at the continuous paper. It was printing out a draft of the first month of new Dr Shade scripts. Greg couldn't help but read what was coming out of the machine.

It wasn't what he had been working on. It wasn't even in script form. But Harry had written it, and he would be expected to draw it.

Unable to control his shaking, Greg read on.

"I'm sorry," said Harry. "It was Him. They brought Him here. He was here before Donald started writing Him. He'll always be here."

Greg turned to look at the old man. Harry was standing over him, laying a hand on his shoulder. Greg shook his head, and Harry sadly nodded.

"It's true. We've always known, really."

Beyond Harry was his hallway. Beyond that, the open door allowed Greg to see into the night. The shadowman was out there, laughing . . .

. . . the laughter faded into the noise of the printer.

Greg read on.

He thought for a moment before selecting the face he would wear tonight. The Chambers identity was wearing thin, limiting him too much. These were troubled times, and stricter methods were required. He considered all the people he had been, listed the names, paged through their faces.

Sitting behind the desk at the tip of the glass and steel pyramid, he felt the thrill of power. Out there in the night cowered the Crack dealers and the anarchists, the blacks and the yellows, the traitors and the slackers. Tonight they would know he was back.

The press baron was a useful face. It had helped him gain a purchase on these new times, given him a perspective on the sorry state of the nation.

He thought of the true patriots who had been rejected. Oswald Mosley, Unity Mitford, William Joyce, Donald Moncrieff. And the false creatures who had succeeded them. This time, things would be different. There would be no bowing to foreign interests.

He fastened his cloak at his throat, and peeled off the latest mask. Smiling at the thin-lipped reflection in the dark mirror of the glass, he pulled on the goggles.

The private lift was ready to take him to the Shadowshark. He holstered his trusty airgun.

Plunging towards his destiny, he exulted in the thrill of the chase. He was back.

Accept no pale imitations. Avoid the lesser men, the men of wavering resolves, of dangerous weaknesses.

He was the original.

—Rex Cash, "The Return of Dr Shade" (1991)

Greg was at his easel, drawing. There was nothing else he could do. No matter how much he hated the commission, he had to splash the black ink, had to fill out the sketches. It was all he had left of himself. In the panel, Dr Shade was breaking up a meeting of the conspirators. African communists were infiltrating London, foully plotting to sabotage British business by blowing up the Stock Exchange. But the Doctor would stop them. Greg filled in the thick lips of Papa Dominick, the voodoo commissar, and tried to get the fear in the villain's eyes as the shadowman raised his airgun.

"Did you hear," P said, "they're giving me a chance to write for the *Argus*. The Stamp of Truth, they'll call my column. I can write about music or politics or fashion or anything. I'll be a proper little girl reporter."

Crosbie told him Derek Leech was delighted at the way the strip was going. Dr Shade was really taking off. There was Dr Shade graffiti all over town, and he had started seeing youths with Dr Shade goggles tattooed around their eyes. A comics reviewer who had acclaimed *Fat Chance* as a masterpiece described the strip as "racist drivel." He hadn't been invited to any conventions recently, and a lot of his old friends would cross the street to avoid him. Greg's telephone rang rarely, now. It was always Crosbie. To his surprise, Tamara had cut herself out of the 10% after the first week of the *Argus* and told him to find other representation. He never heard from Harry, just received the scripts by special messenger. Greg could imagine the writer disconsolately tapping out stories in Donald Moncrieff's style at his Amstrad. He knew exactly how the other man felt.

He had the radio on. The riots were still flaring up. The police were concerned by a rash of airgun killings, but didn't seem to be doing much about them. It appeared that the victims were mainly rabble-rousing ringleaders, although not a few West Indian and Asian community figures had been killed or wounded. Kenneth Hood, a popular vicar, had tried to calm down the rioters and been shot in the head. He wasn't expected to live, and two policemen plus seven "rioters" had died in the violent outburst that followed the attempt on his life. Greg imagined the shadowman on the rooftops, taking aim, hat pulled low, cloak streaming like demon wings.

Greg drew the Shadowshark, sliding through the city night, hurling aside the petrol-bomb-throwing minions of Papa Dominick. "The sun has shone for too long on the open schemes of the traitors," Harry had written, "but night must fall . . . and with the night comes Shade."

Early on, Greg had tried to leave the city, but they were waiting for him at the station. The girl called P, and some of the others. They had escorted him home. They called themselves Shadeheads now, and wore hats and cloaks like the doctor, tattered black over torn T-shirts, drainpipe jeans and steel-toed Doc Martens.

P was with him most of the time now. At first, she had just been in the corner of his vision, watching over him. Finally, he'd given in and called her over. Now, she was in the flat, making her calls to the Doctor, preparing his meals, warming his single bed. They'd pushed him enough, and now he had to be reassured, cajoled. He worked better that way.

Derek Leech was on the radio now, defending the record of his security staff during the riots. He had pitched in to help the police, using his news helicopters to direct the action, and sending his people into the fighting like troops. The police were obviously not happy, but public opinion was forcing them to accept the tycoon's assistance. Leech made a remark about "the spirit of Dr Shade," and Greg's hand jumped, squirting ink across the paper.

"Careful, careful," said P, dipping in with a tissue and delicately wiping away the blot, saving the artwork. Her hair was growing out. She'd never be a *Comet* Knock-Out, but she was turning into a surprisingly housewifely, almost maternal, girl. In the end, Shadeheads believed a woman's place was with her legs spread and her hands in dishwater.

In the final panel, Dr Shade was standing over his vanquished enemies, holding up his fist in a defiant salute. White fire was reflected in his goggles.

The news was over, and the new Crusaders single came on. "There'll Always Be an England." It was climbing the charts.

Greg looked out of the window. He imagined fires on the horizon.

He took a finer pen, and bent to do some detail work on the strip. He wished he had held out longer. He wished he'd taken more than one beating. Sometimes, he told himself he was doing it for Harry, to protect the old man. But that was bullshit. They hadn't been Reggie Barton and Hank Hemingway. Imaginative torture hadn't been necessary, and they hadn't sworn never to give in, never to break down, never to knuckle under. A few plain old thumps and the promise of a few more had been enough. Plus more money a month than either of them had earned in any given three years of their career.

Next week, the Doctor would execute Papa Dominick. Then, he would do something about the strikers, the scroungers, the slackers, the scum . . .

A shadow fell over the easel, cloak spreading around it. Greg turned to look up at the goggled face of his true master.

Dr Shade was pleased with him.

D. F. LEWIS

Madge

D.F. LEWIS is perhaps the most prolific published author working in the horror field today. While that's no idle boast, it's easier to understand when you realize that most of his stories only cover a few pages at most.

"Madge" is no exception, yet despite its brief length, Des Lewis manages to pack as much of a punch into his sparse prose as many horror writers take a whole book to achieve.

Recent outlets for his fiction have included such small press publications as *Winter Chills, BBR, Cobweb, Dementia 13, Flickers 'n' Frames, Peeping Tom, Dreams & Nightmares, Dark Star, Deathrealm, Arrows of Desire, Dream, Overspace* and *After Hours*, along with appearances in *The Year's Best Horror Stories* and, of course, *Best New Horror*.

T HE WOMAN SAT THERE CROONING of one she loved.
 The sea's roar was backdrop to the song, those listening
swaying with its rhythms, their hair forking in the tumbling winds;
they'd heard the song several times before, supposedly understanding
the deep sorrow it betokened, but never so plangent, never so heart-
felt as now.

The woman caught her breath momentarily, wrapped her shawl
tighter against the seaspray that was borne as far inland tonight as it
ever had; and she took up some new verses heretofore unsung, except
when on her own late at night, to lull herself into fitful sleep.

Those listening ceased swaying, tankards poised upon their lips, not
drinking, but ready to drink when the song ended . . . but the end now
was so unpredictable. Many held their breath; but amid such winds
as blew along those coasts, it was possible for the lungs to respire
without the consent of mind or body.

The song entered areas to which none would dare listen, given the
choice. Many hoped that the growing thunder of the encroaching seas
would deafen . . .

Later, in her cot, as the storm neared its peak, she attempted lullaby
after lullaby, not only to take sleep upon herself from the pitch
darkness, but also gently to entice her partner for the night into a
rest which, he told her, would help him to work the trawler through
the next week or so. They had loved long and hard since day-repair,
so surely sleep would be easy.

He whispered:

"Your song was hard to bear, this night, Madge."

"I could hardly bear it myself, but I was determined to get through
all the verses . . ."

"The others did not know where to put their faces . . . But I hoped,
I really hoped, you would choose me tonight, and you must have read
as much in my eyes, for here I be."

"I needed someone strong this night of all nights, not only because
the storm is fiercer than I at least can remember, but my mother once
told me that if I sang the song straight through, without break, he of
which it speaks will know he can finally rest—but will need to see me
for the last time. And, if he comes tonight, I want him to know I'm
happy, strongly serviced by the likes of you."

"Madge, don't you think he'll be bitter seeing me share your
cot?"

"Ghosts can never be bitter, man, they can only hope for the
happiness of those they leave behind. That's where all the tales and
songs be wrong."

"If you say so . . ."

The storm hurtled louder than the quaking of the Earth at the end of time.

She wrapped herself tighter into his arms, feeling that his breath was staunched, like hers, for the duration of the moment's sanctity.

Day-break, with the storm quickly passing over, the rest of the village woke to hear her renewed crooning. This time it was with a morning's melody and lightsome words.

Madge's mother found her still locked in the twine of the man's white unmoving limbs, as she carolled of a new ghost . . .

The tides were too far out to hear. But, when her song was done, she listened to the squelch of boots as men mumbled into their beards and dragged their boats through new-made troughs to the distant sea.

CHERRY WILDER

Alive in Venice

CHERRY WILDER is a New Zealander who lives in Germany. Her first story was published in 1974 and, although she is better known as a science fiction writer, a number of her recent tales have been in the horror genre.

Her work has appeared in such anthologies and magazines as *New Terrors*, *Dark Voices*, *Skin of the Soul*, *Interzone*, *Omni* and *Isaac Asimov's Science Fiction Magazine*, while her books include *Second Nature*, the *Torin* and *Rulers of Hylor* trilogies, and *Cruel Designs*, the latter a horror novel set in her adopted country.

Like "The House on Cemetery Street" by the same author, which was one of the most popular stories in our first volume, "Alive in Venice" is a deceptively quiet story in which the horror builds slowly and surely to a powerful resolution.

THE PENSIONE GUARDI WAS A SOMBRE BUILDING fifteen minutes' brisk walk from the Accademia. It stood at the end of a brick tunnel, a *sottoportego*, on the banks of a canal that had long been filled in. The Pensione was crushed up against the rambling rear walls of a palace . . . perhaps it had once been an annex of the more splendid edifice. When Susan Field looked out of her bedroom window, craning her neck to the right, she could see the wings and rump of a stone lion, outlined against blue sky.

The bedroom was very small and mercifully it was around one corner of the corridor from the larger bedroom inhabited through the langorous summer nights by Jamie and Olive. Susan was not ignorant of the "facts of life". Fate, she saw, had played her brother and sister-in-law a cruel trick. Bad enough to have a family misfortune which banished their wedding to a country church in Oxfordshire but worse, far worse to go on honeymoon accompanied by—ugh—the groom's fourteen-year-old sister.

Honeymooners, as everyone knew, needed to be alone. Susan was not sure what this "alone" really meant. Alone in bed together? Far away from their families and friends? Venice was crowded and the young couple would not have dreamed of travelling without Kidson, a dour woman of fifty, Olive's personal maid.

Susan set out to be good and self-effacing. She succeeded so well that she became a sort of ghost; Jamie and Olive jumped when she spoke or tugged them by the sleeve. She was surprised when confronted by her own reflection in one of a thousand mirrors, framed in gold. She hung back in the teeming streets, became lost and found herself again. At the Pensione she explored all the rooms in which she could reasonably spend time by herself. Her favourite was the writing room.

It had faded gilt furniture, a desk topped in dove-grey leather, and a soft watery light from the eastern windows. No one ever seemed to write although the inkwells were full and there was a sand shaker as well as blotting paper. She would not have been surprised to find a quill pen and a roll of parchment. She bought postcards but because of her peculiar situation she had no one to send them to except herself. She addressed them to the London house which was quite empty now and thought of them falling through the letter-box on to the mat with a ghostly Susan running down the stairs to pick them up.

One wall of the room was unpapered and had no windows; it was of grey stone relieved by four large woven panels. Three of these panels were covered with a repeating pattern of arabesques and flowers, but the larger central panel was a tapestry picture of two ladies stepping down into a gondola. Masked revellers watched them idly from a bridge; the moon was rising; servants carried a ribboned mandolin, a lap-dog, a basket of flowers. It was an interesting picture and she sat watching it by the hour. She decided that the ladies—one of them was really a young girl—were going home after a visit. Perhaps they had been at a party or a masquerade; the older woman wore a half-mask and powdered hair.

Sometimes people came to fetch her from the writing room.

"Oh there you are, Tuppence!" said Jamie, still her teasing big brother.

"They're waiting, Miss!" said Kidson, stiff with disapproval.

"Ah, *poverina* . . ." sighed the Signora, who had red hair and a comfortable figure. Worst of all was Mrs Porter, wife of Canon Porter, who had struck up an acquaintance at breakfast in the courtyard. This good woman had a most particular interest in Susan herself and had offered to "mind" her while the young couple went off by themselves. Mrs Porter had read the London papers, even the more gruesome ones, and when the girl was in her clutches she asked questions. Susan, crimson in the face, refused to answer.

Luckily Mrs Porter had a heavy tread and a habit of calling before she reached the door. Susan found a place to hide behind one of the patterned panels; there was a recess in the wall, an old doorway. When Mrs Porter had seen the room empty and gone away Susan could slip out into the corridor, run down a little back stair to the courtyard and take her place beside Jamie and Olive. She sat in the shadows, they smiled and yawned in the sunshine. Mrs Porter, bustling in to say that the child was nowhere to be found, stared as if she had seen a ghost.

There was no one else who mattered at the Pensione Guardi: two families of Germans, a group of art students from the Slade School, jolly Bohemian girls who were suspected of smoking cigarettes. Then there was the American with whom Jamie had a nodding acquaintance from Cambridge. Hadley, he said, was a bit of a dry stick who studied old buildings, wrote books about them in fact. No need to worry about old Hadley knowing anything; he lived in a dream. Susan looked enviously at Hadley, who was neither Bohemian nor jolly, lounging in the shade of the oleanders. She had written, on a postcard to herself, *Sometimes I think I am living in a nightmare.*

During the endless summer they went many times to the Piazza San Marco. They glimpsed Hadley in the distance gazing at the empty space left by the Campanile, which had fallen down something over a year ago. A golden age had ended for Susan at about this time: the London house was decorated for the coronation but Father—what else could she call him—went to stay at his club. Her mother wept in a darkened room. Mrs Field was not at home to anyone ever again except the doctor and nurse who bore her away, by night, in a closed carriage.

Now, inside the glittering cavern of the cathedral, they all hid from their neighbours, the Farquhars, and some acquaintances of Olive's family, the Misses Black. The pillars behind which they loitered until the coast was clear were of porphry, writhing upwards like the serpents that crushed Laocoön.

Once, in a smaller church, they simply hid Susan, the living proof that things were not as they should be. The honeymooners presented themselves (Olive all softness and blushes, Jamie with his shoulders back) to disarm the Misses Black, while Susan slipped into a side chapel. It was here that she recognized the presence for the first time.

She crouched down low in one of the little black chairs for worshippers. There were a few candles, a picture of the saint with the Virgin and angels. Candlelight penetrated the small glass box on the altar which contained a relic. A splinter of black bone lay on folds of apricot satin embroidered in turquoise and gold. The colour brought back associations which were so warm and vivid that Susan caught her breath with longing. Why, it was her dream again and it was the tapestry in the writing room.

The dream was not quite a dream of home. Better than that. She was driven in a closed carriage up to a pillared portico. Golden light streamed out and a low, sweet voice cried: "*Cara mia . . .*" She ran up the steps into the lady's arms, was half-smothered in soft folds of cloth of exactly this colour. Then there were crowds of people, the hallway was full and someone else said: "We are so awfully pleased to see you!" She knew that she was being rewarded for some heroic deed; she had been a great help to some absolutely splendid person who was under a cloud.

In the writing room again—she had been impatient to get back to the Pensione—she saw that the lady with the mask wore a cloak of the same shade. It came to her that the scene showed the beginning of some adventure, not the end. The lady with the mask was drawing her companion out of the gondola towards the door of the palazzo. The young girl hung back a little; the maskers on the bridge, Harlequin, Columbine and one with a death's head, seemed to say: "Oh go along, silly goose! Why are you so shy?"

On summer afternoons, during the long siesta, Susan left her bedroom and stole through the empty corridors to the writing room. She lay down on a striped sofa near the windows. Currents of warm air curled through the room lifting the upper edges of the tapestry panels and tinkling the lusters upon the chandelier. Once there was a soft sound as if one of these glass prisms had fallen down. She went to look and found a silver chain with a broken clasp lying in a heap against the stone wall. Next time it was a tiny bottle of Murano glass, white and gold, with a stopper in the shape of a fish. Days passed and she found, in more or less the same area of the room, a miniature fan with black lacquer sticks. Unfolded it was no bigger than the palm of her hand.

Susan could see that the tapestry panels hung upon the stone wall like banners, each with a rod and cord suspended from a hook. Higher than this, in the shadows, there were two outcrops in the stone in the shape of lions' heads. During the siesta when no one was likely to come in she lay full length upon the carpet and saw that the lions' heads, as she suspected, covered small dark openings in the wall. They were or had been ventilators. She blinked, as motes of dust fell from the tapestries. Right before her eyes a flying fish, a strip of paper with its ends ingeniously slotted together, came twirling down from the second lion's head, over the picture.

She jumped up and ran to the last panel. The door in the recess was locked but she did not think it was bolted; it moved slightly when she turned the handle and pushed against it. Something rattled in the half darkness above her head. She bent the tapestry aside and the sleepy afternoon light showed her the large key, hanging on a hook against the wall.

About this time there was a harsh intrusion from the real world. A packet of letters from London was sent to James Field, Poste Restante, at the post office where he picked up his copies of *The Times*. Tremendously embarrassed he took Susan aside and sat with her on a stone bench. At a distance Olive stared out over the lagoon and unfurled her sunshade. One letter was for Susan herself, on stiff cream paper, written out in copperplate by a stranger, a lawyer's clerk.

The letter must have been difficult to begin ... what could be written at the top? The compromise was sensible: "To Susan—", with a suggestively long dash. "In view of the findings of the court" it was preferable for all concerned that she should be known henceforth as Susan Anne Markham. She would be entered in August at Madame Kerr's School in Berne, Switzerland, under this name and it would be as well if she learned to get along with the new arrangement.

The letter had the air of an act of God. She believed for a few seconds that it had been written by a lawyer or even a judge. The full horror of the thing was contained in the last lines of copperplate and in the familiar signature. "Your mother is still under the care of Dr Rassmussen at Malvern Spa. Yours truly, H.B.L. Field."

It was the way that he signed his letters to tradespeople; the pain of his disavowal broke over her like a black wave; she trembled and clutched Jamie's arm. Markham was their mother's maiden name and they had distant Markham cousins.

"The Guvnor is going too far," said Jamie wretchedly. "He can't really make you do this, legally and all that."

"He means," said Susan, "to cast me off."

James Field made an effort to explain the disaster that had struck their house but it was very nearly too late.

"You see, Tuppence," he brought out, "the whole thing may not be true. Mother is very sick, the doctors say she has . . . she has lost her reason. Ladies sometimes accuse themselves of . . . of things that are not true."

Susan felt herself blushing again. Mrs Porter had asked her if she knew the meaning of the word adultery.

"If Mummy is mad," she said, "why is Father so dreadfully unkind to her . . . and to me?"

Jamie shook his head, it was becoming too difficult; Olive looked back impatiently. His father's "unkindness", his habitual and quite natural unfaithfulness, was at the root of the whole thing.

"He wanted to be free," said Jamie. "Divorced."

He was keeping an eye on a seller of knick-knacks with a ribboned tray who now approached Olive. Jamie bounced up and went to shoo the little bounder away. The happy pair stood close together under the sunshade; Susan saw them veiled in a sparkling mist that rose off the water. All around her floated the domes and colonnades of the unreal city. An elderly couple sat on the stone bench and fed the pigeons. She felt sure that they could not see her at all.

She drifted away to buy a postcard. As she put the letter into her purse she touched the little bottle of Murano glass, cold as the green depths of the sea. Out of the corner of her eye, there by the pillar topped with a crocodile, she caught a flash of apricot satin. She could not make out if they were both there, the young woman and the older one who wore a mask. When she turned her head they were gone. A gentleman bowed to her:

"Good morning, Miss Field!"

It was Hadley, the American. He saw her plain and she gave him a grateful smile.

Soon afterwards James and Olive went off for five days to do Padua. Kidson went with them, of course, and Susan was left in the capable hands of Mrs Porter. She gave no trouble and indeed the good woman seemed to have lost interest in her case. Susan appeared promptly at breakfast with her hair well brushed and it was accepted that she was going to "moon about the pension with a book". Canon Porter went so far as to lend her his own copy of *Travels with a Donkey*.

Susan mooned about heavy with secret knowledge. She could not tell when it had come to her . . . it had not been a sudden revelation. She knew that she must take the risk of telling one of the adults. Her choice had narrowed: the jolly student girls had moved on to Florence. It was easy enough to dawdle over breakfast and then, when they were alone in the courtyard, to move to Hadley's table.

Ashton Hadley did have some memory of a scandal in the London papers. It struck him as vaguely indecent that a schoolgirl should accompany Field and his new bride. They were a handsome couple and the sensual aura that surrounded them impressed even Hadley, who liked to think of himself as world-weary. Now here was the young girl, irreproachably English, an adolescent Alice, and in her innocent way she was "making up" to him. Only seven years or so separated this half-formed creature from Olive, who glowed like Venus rising from the waves. He was overwhelmed by painful memories of a family of young American girls, his cousins, who had romped and flirted with arrogant assurance and then married other fellows.

He had no wish to be unkind; he agreed that he did have a moment to spare and that he knew about old buildings. His lips twitched a little as she swore him to secrecy; he began to be intrigued.

"There is a lady imprisoned," said Susan, "in the old palazzo, behind the wall of the writing room."

Hadley shut his Ruskin and stared. The girl was perfectly serious. "Imprisoned?"

"She can't get out. She is being kept there," said Susan. "She sends . . . messages, through the wall."

He began to see that the poor thing was mad. She was very pale and there were shadows under her blue eyes. Hadley was out of his depth, he wanted to hand her over as quickly as possible to a parent or guardian. He thought of the ghastly Mrs Porter and hesitated. It struck him for the first that Susan Field was unusually alone.

"I know it sounds pretty unbelievable," she said, "but it is true."

"My dear Miss Field . . ."

"Susan," she said. "I can show you the evidence."

Hadley made a despairing effort.

"Why would this person be . . . shut up?"

"I could think of reasons," said Susan, "but that would be my imagination. I will show you . . ."

She reached into her white kid purse and carefully laid a number of small objects on the marble table top. Ashton Hadley was drawn to the glass bottle which was old and finely worked. He laughed uneasily and polished his eyeglasses.

"What's that?"

She unfolded it gravely. Across the faded paper of the miniature fan a word was written in bronzed ink: *Soccorso*.

"Where did you get these things?"

"They came through the lions' heads," said Susan. "The ventilators high up on the wall of the writing room. They reach right back into some room on the other side of the wall. In the palazzo."

She delved into her purse again and drew out three strips of paper with crossed ends slotted together. She held one of these constructions high above her head and it floated, twirling gently, down to the stones of the courtyard.

"I call them flying fish," she whispered.

Hadley retrieved the strip of paper; with a fold at the front and the crossed ends forming a tail it did have a fish shape. It was of blue-green writing paper, not new, and inscribed on the outer surface was another word in the same bronzed ink: *Hilfe*. The two remaining fish were just as laconic: *Help me*, said one, *Au secours* the other. He felt sure that the girl had written these words.

"Came through the lions' heads?" he said quizzically.

"I swear it!"

She knotted her hands together.

"No," said Hadley, as gently as he could. "Susan, it is all a nonsense. Even if someone were there . . ."

"Someone *is* there, Mr Hadley!"

"They may be confined for a good reason," he said, "by relatives. Someone old perhaps, or unbalanced. What do you want me to do?"

He could see that what she wanted from him was some piece of knight-errantry.

"I would like to know who sent these things," she said. "Perhaps we could help the lady."

"Why must it be a lady?" demanded Hadley. "Why not children playing games?"

Why not, he thought, a certain young person trying to attract attention.

"Look here," he said slyly, "I think you read rather a lot."

"No," she said, "not as much as people think."

"You've read *Jane Eyre* I expect?"

"The mad wife in that book is frightening and horrid," she said, blushing.

"And you think this . . . lady is not?" he said, smiling.

"You don't believe me!"

Susan lifted her chin proudly; she swept all the evidence back into her purse. The Signora looked into the courtyard from the kitchen and turned back to give a stream of instruction to one of the maids. As Susan hurried off Hadley called:

"Wait, Miss Field!"

She lowered her head and went away without a backward glance. Hadley was already late for his appointment with Monsignore Venier, head of an architectural committee, but he spent a moment outside the Pensione Guardi staring up at its junction with the Palazzo Castell-Giordano. The larger building, stemming mainly from the seventeenth century, was not of much interest to him and it was not open to the public. He felt sure that certain relicts of one or other of the families still lived in its draughty chambers. On his way to the Accademia bridge he glanced at the palazzo's modest façade, in a side canal, almost a backwater. It would be easy enough, with his architectural connections, to make some enquiries and satisfy the poor girl's curiosity.

Susan had known all along that Hadley would fail her. Her appeal to him had been simply a nod in the direction of rational behaviour. In her bedroom for several days now she had kept a small lamp with a glass shade burning before a picture of the Madonna. Her white purse did not seem right for such an expedition but she put all her evidence into the right hand pocket of her sailor blouse and a stump of candle into the other. When the Pensione Guardi sank into its long siesta she took the lamp and set out.

The writing room was full of moving shadows. She was very much afraid and cast a last long glance at the tapestry picture for reassurance. "Go along, silly goose!" whispered the masqueraders. She went up close and laid her hand upon the satiny expanse of the lady's cloak. Then she slipped into the recess and wrestled with the heavy key until it turned in the lock.

The door grated open an inch at a time and behind it there was a misty thread of daylight. She was in some kind of no man's land between high walls; there was a strong odour of sea-damp and rotting wood. The place reeked of Venice. There were two ways to go: the stairs, which were pitch black, and a kind of landing, greenish and slippery, where light struggled down from above. She went this way for a few steps and fell down, desperately trying to save the lamp.

The little guttering flame did not go out; she looked into evil-smelling depths, full of the roar of water. Slowly she drew back and moved to the stairway. The surface of each step was hazardous, covered with lumps of fallen masonry. She went up slowly, pressing against an inner wall. There was no banister; the staircase seemed to hover over an abyss.

Her fear, which had been a little in abeyance, returned in a sickening black wave. She trembled at every step. There was nothing anywhere that she could bear to touch. Beyond the feeble light from her lamp the world was sharp and hard with a cutting edge or else damp and foul. An icy wind played on her face and neck. She was terrified that she might have to stop, sink down on the filthy stairway and cry for help. She pictured Mrs Porter, gloating like a harpy at the daughter of a mad mother, and it gave her strength. One step, two and a whiff of perfume came to her on the cold wind. There was a door at the top of the stairs and a thread of golden light under the door. Susan dragged herself upwards and laid a timid hand on the door; it swung inwards at her touch.

Light and warmth flooded over her. It would have been wrong or at least disappointing if she had been accompanied by Mr Hadley; she knew all this was for her alone. There was soft carpet under her muddy shoes; she bumped against a chair; her cold hand touched velvet. The Lady shone more brightly than the candles; she was all softness, her satins and pearls glowed with an inner light.

"*Cara mia* . . ."

Susan ran to her embrace and it was dreamlike, incorporeal. At the same time she was aware of her own body, naked under her clothes; she drew back a little and the Lady did the same. They were parted yet they spoke together in shared thoughts and broken phrases. Susan had been very brave; the Lady knew how much she had suffered. Rescue? Yes, rescue for both of them. It was a new beginning; a world waited for her, full of warmth, adventure, love.

"But is it *life*?" asked Susan.

A long life, came the answer. She found herself gazing into one of the mirrors in the secret chamber. There was no sign of her own reflection or of the Lady but she saw a huge bed, a four-poster, with filmy curtains drawn back. Propped up on her pillows there was a very old woman, a stranger, her features peacefully composed.

"She was the sister of my soul," said the Lady. "You will be guarded just as tenderly."

Susan put out a hand towards the mirror and said in a loud shaking voice:

"Am I allowed to say no?"

There was a gentle sigh and the presence was withdrawn. She stood alone in the midst of a small hot room under the leads of the palazzo. It had been a lady's dressing room; the candles were long burnt out, the only light came from her own oil lamp, still burning on a commode, and from the curtained door to a roof-garden. In the dusty mirror she saw a faint reflection, a girl who might become invisible at any minute. Who was there left in all the world to care for such a girl? A faint glow of light arose in a corner, near the inner door that led into the palazzo. Susan spread her arms and cried out softly:

"Oh come back! Come back! Don't leave me!"

The light grew around her and the Lady smiled. For a moment she was displaced, afraid, shrinking down inside herself, then some mysterious balance was achieved; they were one. In the glass there was Susan, bright-eyed, smiling now, smoothing her tangled hair. She could hear people outside on the landing. "Are there others?" "Our true servants . . ." She saw her own hand reach out firmly and open the door into the palace.

The search for the young English girl, Susan Field, went on for several months. The Venetian authorities were, in their own way, more thorough and more discreet than the Anglo-Saxon visitor might have expected. Even so it was a harrowing experience for young Field and his new wife. As the days went by, poor Olive Field, her bloom quite gone, became increasingly nervous and distressed. She went home alone, accompanied only by her maid, another bad omen for the marriage.

Ashton Hadley watched poor James Field trying to do his duty. He felt an obscure satisfaction when Jamie raised his fists to a senior police official who again questioned Susan's innocence. A young girl's disappearance suggested to the Venetians, at least, elopement or abduction as alternatives to violation and murder. These suspicions tainted the victim herself and dishonoured her family. There was only one fate for a lost girl and that worse than death. Female suicides were generally supposed to have been seduced and abandoned. Hadley stood by James Field on three occasions when they were called to examine the bodies of drowned women.

Hadley took the opportunity of insulting the egregious Mrs Porter. When she offered information about the family tragedy which had resulted in Susan's trip to Venice he called her a scandal-monger and a pharisee. She went thumping out of the writing room where this encounter had taken place and Hadley gave way to despair. In fact he blamed himself for the girl's disappearance. He knew that he would be haunted for a lifetime by his failure to respond to her last appeal.

The writing room had changed since the day Susan was lost. There seemed to be more light; the door in the wall stood open and its tapestry panel had been removed. Signora Ruffino had come first to Hadley with her anxiety as he sat reading in his bedroom. It was nearly midnight and the girl had gone; she was nowhere in the Pensione. Soon the Porters would return from the opera and the alarm would have to be raised.

He spoke at once of the door in the wall. Yes, the English Miss had mentioned this entry into the old palazzo. Was it possible that she had gone exploring? The Signora crossed herself and talked of the cloaca. They went at once, secretly, taking lamps. The Signora called him to witness that the key was in the lock; it usually hung upon the wall.

So they came into a tiny courtyard, crowded by the extension of the building that was now the Pensione. There was a gaping hole that led to the cloaca, a deep, swift underground waterway that carried waste into the canals and eventually into the sea. If Susan Field *had* come exploring it was possible that she had slipped into this oubliette and drowned, her body being swept away. There were marks on the slippery green paving stones but it was difficult to say when they had been made.

Hadley had turned his attention to the staircase at the junction of the two buildings. He called Susan and her name reverberated between the high walls. Who lived in the Palazzo Castell-Giordano? Signora Ruffino knew of the aged Contessa and a few servants. The room at the top of the staircase had been the antechamber to an old altana or roof terrace where the ladies went, in former times, to bleach their hair in the sun.

At last Hadley made the ascent as quickly as he could and held his lamp for the Signora, gamely following. The door at the top of the stairs had a broken catch and yielded to his touch. He held up his light on the threshold: the room was empty. He stepped in gingerly hoping for footprints in the dust but the room was not especially dusty. It was not a bedroom but it had the quality of a boudoir, a particularly feminine room, old and long disused.

Hadley set down his lamp on a commode; the Signora brought hers to a higher shelf and opened the door to the roof terrace revealing stone urns for plants and old wooden cages from which the birds had flown. In silence they looked about for clues and stared apprehensively at the inner door. Hadley noticed the lions' heads: there they were, repeated on this side of the wall, quite low down in the low-ceilinged room. They could be reached by standing on a chair. Absently he drew open the drawers of the commode and found in one a few sheets of writing paper . . . the wrong shade.

"Signor Hadley . . ." said the Signora quietly.

She had picked from the velvet surface of a chair two or three long golden hairs tangled with a scrap of black thread. It was all they ever found and there was nothing to say that the hair had not come from the head of some long-dead lady of the Castell-Giordano household.

Then light appeared under the inner door and Hadley dared to knock. The door was opened by an old man in antique servant's dress of solemn black. He was Baldassare, the Major Domo; the female servants had heard noises and sent him to investigate. He heard their urgent appeal but shook his head. No, a young English girl had not been seen. The palazzo was in mourning; the Contessa Giordano had at last given up the ghost.

They apologized again and Baldassare watched them negotiate the difficult staircase. The alarm was raised. In the course of the search the police went through the palazzo and questioned the servants, all without result. Yet Hadley was secretly convinced beyond all reason and beyond all doubt that Susan Field *had* been up there in that musky forgotten chamber.

She had been there . . . so ran his obsession . . . and she had passed through the door into the palazzo. Her fate was bound up in his mind, from the first, with the rejection and neglect she appeared to have suffered. In those first night hours he and the Signora rushed into the girl's bedroom . . . neat, virginal; later a lamp appeared to be missing. On the dressing table lay the purse of white leather that Hadley remembered but the "evidence" she had shown him was all gone. There was nothing but a letter which he read at once and found quite remarkably cruel. After that he measured the good-natured Jamie against that old brute, Field the Elder, who withdrew his paternity after fourteen years and consigned Susan to social oblivion.

He stayed on after James, his poor friend, had left, but Venice, which he had loved, became threatening. Terrible enough if Susan Field was dead, but if she were still alive? He began to see visions, in fact to look out for them. A young woman in deep mourning, heavily veiled, riding in a gondola towards the cemetery islands. An old man—was it Baldassare?—buying postcards on the Piazza? In a dream he saw a young girl dressed unequivocally as a courtesan; her mask was a death's head. She said, "Oh, much curiouser than that, Mr Hadley!" and under the mask it was Susan, unscathed, bright-eyed.

He kept her secret; it had become his own. The girl, abandoned, *had* been seduced . . . lured away and by a Lady. In his despair, in the writing room, he stared again at an expensive but hideous tapestry panel, woven after some detail of a larger painting. Guardi of course or "school of Guardi". What could the scene be called? *The House of Assignation* or even *The Procuress*. A wordly older woman in a mask urged a young girl towards a palace while other dubious masquers leered from a bridge.

Hadley went so far as to question Monsignore Venier concerning the Palazzo Castell-Giordano and its inhabitants. Yes, in one respect the family was almost unique. As a reward for doing the state some service the title and the depleted estate might devolve upon the female line. No hint of scandal in recent times but in the fifteenth century a notorious accusation of witchcraft, a Contessa who remained young and beautiful for so long that it became embarrassing. But in the end she too grew old and it was whispered that her demon would leave her. Possession? Yes, certainly, there was still some belief in such things. One scholar—a Venetian, of course—had suggested that the condition of being possessed need not be unpleasant or destructive. The Monsignore quoted, smiling:

"Who has not wished for a twin soul?"

Sixteen years later, Hadley, grey-haired and wearing his medals, took his young wife to a performance of *The Tales of Hoffmann* at the Paris Opera. He became impatient with the second act and left the box to stretch his legs. The lovely melody of the Venetian baccarole pursued him into the marble halls. A tall woman in an enveloping evening cloak brushed past him then stood still until he caught up with her. She was serene, beautiful, her hair, cut short, stood out in a stiff golden aureole around her head. She smiled, looking deep into his eyes.

"Ah, Signor Hadley, we have known the real Venice . . ."

He could not afterwards recall if she had spoken English or Italian. While he smiled uncertainly she pressed some small object into his hand and swept on down the grand staircase to where a party of ladies and gentlemen waited, their faces eagerly upturned. Hadley stood wondering what he had seen. He found himself clutching a miniature fan with black lacquer sticks. It was new and unmarked but he remembered seeing its twin; opened it was not so big as the palm of his hand.

GREGORY FROST

Divertimento

GREGORY FROST has been favourably compared by *The Washington Post Book World* to J.R.R. Tolkien, Evangeline Walton and T.H. White. Born in Des Moines, Iowa, he now lives in Philadelphia with a huge cat named 'Poot'.

The author of such fantasy novels as *Lyrec*, *Tain* and *Remscela*, his short fiction has been published in *The Magazine of Fantasy & Science Fiction*, *Asimov's*, *Whispers*, *The Twilight Zone Magazine*, *Night Cry*, *Liavek*, *Tropical Chills* and *Ripper!*, amongst others.

"Divertimento", like his story in our previous volume, was first published in a science fiction magazine. However, we believe it has now found its rightful place—between the covers of a horror anthology.

for Sycamore Hill, 1987

I N THE CENTER OF A RING OF THIRTY or more tourists, a polished
clavichord stood, solitary. Although heavy drapes were drawn
across the windows all around the room, dazzlingly bright highlights
reflected off the clavichord's surfaces. The tourists cleared their throats,
muttered expectantly to one another, and shifted from foot to foot
while they waited. They had been told not to sit just yet. Most had
little idea of what exactly they were about to see.

Their host—a stocky man with a heavy black beard just starting to
gray, and wearing 18th century dress—entered the room. His name
was Peter Tellier. He nodded to them, and took his place in one of
two large chairs of walnut and upholstery set up directly behind the
performer's bench. At his signal, the tourists sat, too. The Beidermeier
armchair beside him remained empty.

A few moments later, directly in front of Peter Tellier, a boy
appeared out of thin air and walked toward the keyboard. He
seated himself imperiously upon the bench. Like Peter, he wore
period clothing. His red coattails dangled lazily over the small bench.
He crossed his ankles. Then, with eyes glistening, the boy, Mozart,
glanced over his shoulder, directly at Peter.

After the first few times he had seen these actions repeated, Peter
Tellier had dragged a chair to the spot, so that their eyes—his and
Mozart's—would meet when the young composer looked around.
He had hoped they would see each other, and maybe make friends.
He would so have liked a playmate but had long since stopped
pretending that such a thing could happen. That secret glance did
communicate something wonderful, but not to him. Who was this
look of pride meant for? Sister? Father? The doddering Archbishop?
Peter had come to believe, having looked things up in a decrepit music
encyclopedia, that it was Michael Haydn being promised something
wonderful. Haydn would have had good cause to hope.

Such heavy eyelids, thought Peter. The eyes seemed too large for
Mozart's small face. His little powdered wig curled into a ridge
running around the back of his head from ear to ear. Peter thought
of him as a little sheep. "Safely grazing," he mumbled, then glanced
around self-consciously, but no one had noticed. His sister wasn't
going to make this performance; probably she didn't even know what
time it was. The other mismatched chairs, gathered from abandoned
buildings nearby, were arranged in a half-circle that kept everyone at
a distance from Peter and Susanne. "Lamb of God," he said, almost in
prayer, "sacrificed upon the altar of Salzburg." It was a line from the
crumbling encyclopedia that had stuck in his mind; it might as easily
have described him as Mozart.

Mozart began playing. The sound of the clavichord was incredibly piercing. Tellier beamed at the beauty of it. He wished he knew how to play. His parents had lacked the money for lessons, and he had never really thought about it back then. Now, for all his wishing, the matter had been irreversibly resolved.

The piece Mozart played was a practice, a test, though not for the him—he had written it and knew it so well that he needed no scrap of music before him. It was a trial run for a female singer. The opening was meant to be sung by a choir, but none existed in this performance. Instead, playing off each other's voices, the singer and Mozart would carry the opening together in a duet. Peter had hired a choral group once to see if he could draw a bigger crowd, but the cluster of singers took up too much space and blocked much of the view of the phenomenon, and he lost money. The crowds had thinned even further. He had come to believe since that the eeriness of the unaccompanied performance was what made it so riveting.

The long introduction, one day to be carried out by a small orchestra, neared its end. Tellier knew it by heart now: *Regina Coeli*, Kochel 127. He sat more stiffly. His hands were sweating. Mozart turned his eager young face to the side, addressing the woman no one else could see.

She began. She sounded as if she were standing just to the right of the clavichord. Her pure voice echoed like the ringing of a distant bell. Peter was pretty sure the voice belonged to Maria Lipp, wife to Michael Haydn. Haydn, so he believed, was sitting or standing right about where the two chairs were. Peter wished Maria Lipp would manifest there with Mozart, but he doubted that would ever happen. All the resurrections he'd heard of had arrived in single lumps, as finished or unfinished as they could ever be. He wished they would stop arriving altogether: Crowds this size were becoming the exception.

She sang out with Mozart: "Regina coeli laetare." They repeated it—all of it, parts of it—weaving around each other until the line ended, as did all the lines of the piece, in an "alleluja" meant for the complete chorus.

"Queen of heaven, rejoice," said Peter, sharing what he could. The crowd had fliers, in seven languages, translating the text; they didn't need his help but he couldn't keep it to himself. After so many performances, he had to show off just a little. He lowered his head, pretending to lose himself in the music.

The performance went on for a little over ten minutes, after which, unaware of the audience's applause, an excited Mozart got up and dashed right at Peter. An instant before he reached the big chair, he vanished. The crowd gasped as one—Mozart had become real to them. Peter thought sometimes that he could feel Mozart passing through him on his journey back in time, but he knew he was making that all up.

The applause thinned out quickly: With the performer nonexistent, who was there to clap for? Peter, after all, had done nothing more than tell them when to sit.

The crowd rose to leave, mumbling, grabbing their coats, thanking Peter as he held open the door for them, some enthusiastically, but most with an air of doubt, as if suspecting the whole thing to have been a hoax. Did any of them, he wondered, even know the story of this house?

When the last of them was gone, Peter stood briefly at the door, looking down the narrow slush-covered street toward the snowy heights of Kapuzinerberg for a sign of Susanne; but she was nowhere to be seen. She'd be out there somewhere, not very far away. Her playtime wanderings always worried him. If something should happen while she was out there, he might never know about it. He searched for her footprints but the tourists had stamped out all traces. His breath steamed. The cold stung his face. He closed the door and headed back inside. On the way down the hall, he dimmed the lights, then drifted back to his chair. Such weariness overcame him that he thought, with a spark of fear, he might be wearing out.

In the empty circle another performance would soon begin, but no more audiences were scheduled for today. He'd had them all week, five times a day, and that was enough. Too much. But the take had been exceptional. Enough to buy more medical help for Susanne. He looked at the dark space where the clavichord would shortly reappear.

He sat awhile in the dark, his thoughts going nowhere in particular. The smell coming from the kitchen was of warm chocolate. Behind him, the door banged open and his sister shuffled in. Filthy snow slid from her black boots; snow speckled her thermal-weave pantlegs. Peter tried not to show his great relief, because it would have revealed his concern at her absence. He thought she might have grown tired of the music. But of course that was absurd—Susanne had no idea how long she had been gone. One performance was any performance to her.

She had been making chocolate lace by pouring hot caramel into snowbanks. Undoubtedly she had wandered off with her pan of caramel to find just the right pile of snow. She had forgotten the pan outside somewhere in order to carry the product in—a pile of fragile amber sheets, crisscrossed patterns lying like pages of an open hymnal on her mittened palms. The whole world for Susanne at present consisted of getting the hardened caramel to the kitchen, where melted chocolate waited to receive each layer, thereby creating the time-honored confectionery wonder.

Susanne was younger than Peter by a year and a half, but she could easily have been his mother, even his grandmother. The device that had torn Mozart out of antiquity had detonated much nearer Susanne than her brother. The particles that had passed through her had slowed and lost energy by the time they reached Peter. As a result, her genetic material had received much higher exposure. She would have been dead, a memory, except that their parents—the first ones struck—had inadvertently shielded her somewhat with their bodies. Both parents turned from tissue to dust almost instantly. Cheeks caved in, eyes crackled back into the wrinkling lids, bodies doubled over, folding like accordions to the ground, where they puffed up a cloud of brown smoke. All of this in a second or two while their children writhed in a torment of stretching bones, growing teeth, sprouting hair—human ecosystems wildly out of control. Peter could still hear his parents' cries go creaking into oblivion and remember how in agony he thought his fingertips would pop open to let his skeleton expand.

He understood little about the "time bombs", as the press had dubbed them. The bombs had exploded in a few places around the world, but mostly here in Salzburg. No one knew why, just as no one knew for certain their source. Experts from Boston to Beijing speculated that the creators of the bombs, themselves from the future, had no idea of the destructive capacity of these devices. They might, in fact, be early experiments in time travel, the first unmanned capsules, inadvertently creating catastrophe by hauling a bit of future matter into the present. There was talk of prototachyonic pulses, of bombardment and loops, of matter and antimatter, of fission. None of it meant much to Peter. What no one talked about was the horrible pain of being eleven-years-old and watching your parents molder in front of your eyes. No one had ever consoled him over that. They were afraid of him and Susanne—absurdly afraid that what had happened might be contagious.

Though his hair and beard showed patches of gray and his eyes were dry and pouchy, Peter Tellier had only recently turned fifteen. Susanne, with her trembling arthritic hands, was thirteen but as a result of the time bomb had jumped all of adulthood to an immediate, doddering second childhood of perhaps eighty, perhaps more. Her deterioration seemed daily more evident to her helpless brother. Her body was racing to its end. Mozart—the sole means of support for the two children—was both the eldest and the youngest in the room at sixteen.

While her brother looked on, Susanne hobbled out of the kitchen. Chocolate stained her mouth and fingers. Tucked up under her like a football, she carried a feather duster.

The clavichord sat glowing in the center of the room, having reappeared for another performance, and Susanne intended to clean it. Peter sighed, inwardly aching on her behalf. She had been to so many specialists but no one had helped her. They probed her, studied her, probably wore her out faster with their poking and prodding than if he'd just let her deteriorate in peace, but he still sought for some cure. He recalled the way they had looked at him the last time, unable to cope with the idea of a little boy who was in appearance their senior. They often spoke to him about his sister as they might have spoken to his father, and for brief periods he became his father, acted the way his father might have done.

A scary kind of fame surrounded the time bombs; less respectable journals wrote outrageous things regarding them. The attention brought the crowds, certainly. They had to pay a lot to get in here, and they paid it without a whimper, because nowhere else would they ever see the real live Mozart ... unless, of course, another bomb released another segment of the composer's life. Peter refused anyone the chance to record the event, although a few had offered him substantial money to do so. What he couldn't understand was why some world network hadn't come forward with millions for exclusive rights. It was what he'd dreamt of, but no one had fulfilled that dream. There were other places he might have taken Susanne, with that kind of money.

As she neared the keyboard, Susanne disrupted the image. Static sparks danced on the feather duster, traveled up her arm. The clavichord rippled. Heedless, Susanne went right on dusting. Peter could read pain in every tiny movement that she made. She was, he conceded, getting much worse.

Peter suddenly found that he couldn't stand it any longer. "It's time," he called to her to let her know that Mozart would be coming out in a moment.

She turned around, shifting her weight from one hip to the other, wincing but denying it, too. She smiled at him. Half her teeth had dissolved. "What will he play for us today?"

"I don't know. Why don't you come and sit, and find out."

"He likes my cleaning up. He always gives me such a look before he starts, just to tell me that he's pleased."

"Yes, he does, doesn't he?" They'd had almost this same conversation a hundred times. Each repetition weighed him down more; he'd end up stoop-shouldered the way his father had always said he would if he didn't stand up straight.

He got up and helped his sister to her chair. He took an afghan from the back of the chair, unfolded it and laid it across her lap. She leaned around him to watch Mozart emerge on his way to the clavichord.

"Look, he's going to nod to me, Petey," she said. Peter looked down at her eyes full of delight and his face grew hot. He dodged around his own chair and walked off quickly, hoping to escape before the playing started.

At the door he snatched his coat from a peg, hastily wrestled his way into it on the way out the door.

The cold sliced under his skin. Outside, the orange haze of the sky framed baroque shadows and bombed-out buildings. In the further depths behind him, the keys of the clavichord "spanged" under Mozart's fingers, the introduction moving into the first verse of the *Regina Coeli*. How lonely the tiny voice sounded. It seemed to echo through the austere environment. Where had all the tourists gone? To the hotels, no doubt, on the other side of Kapuzinerburg, the living side. No bombs had gone off there as of the last Peter had heard. Smoke and lights sparkled in the early twilight over across the river. Hardly any showed down the street here. Or maybe the tourists had gone to the Cathedral Square. He had read about a time bomb there, that killed twenty and brought to life a piece of the "Everyman" play that long ago had been performed there every year. No doubt he'd lost paying customers to that event. To him that was the real cruelty of the bombs—that they wrought their damage without purpose or plan, robbing a life and then robbing the chance to rebuild that life.

The spirit woman sang, "Quia quem meruisti portare . . ."

Peter walked away from the sound. The snow crunched beneath his feet. He pretended to be his father, engaged in conversation with him. "You are fifteen now," the father said, "too old to play make-believe games anymore. You and your sister can hardly get along now. Where will you go when the money is gone? When the tourists stop coming altogether? You haven't saved enough, Peter. You're living like sick people. You have your food delivered, and you never leave the house except to take your sister out sometimes. You've grown up afraid. Afraid of the world."

"I have Mozart," Peter replied, a little scared by what he was revealing from within. "Maybe we could go with him."

"Does your Mozart know that he's here? Does he know that you're here? Or Susie? No. You're playing games, Peter. Mozart's dead, and you and your sister are catching up with him."

"Stop it," Peter said. He stopped walking. The "voice" went away. It hadn't been his father at all. He turned and saw how far from the house he had gone in just a few minutes. He had nearly reached the other end of the street and the arrow sign he had put up. From there, the house looked no different than any of the other uninhabited dwellings surrounding it. Hurriedly, he walked back toward it. Look at the place. Without the sign how could the tourists know in which house Mozart played? No wonder the crowds had thinned out. He'd been so busy with Susanne's care that he had let the house rot around him.

As he neared, he could hear Maria Lipp singing repeatedly, "Resurrexit," then both she and Mozart launched into a series of joyous "Allelujahs".

Peter closed the door, then stood leaning against it, as if to keep something evil out. His breathing wheezed and little sparkles danced in the air. He couldn't believe such a short run had drained him so much.

The beautiful voice floated through "Ora pro nobis Deum." Peter thought, *please, yes, pray for us to God*.

He hung on there until the last "allelujah" was sung. Susanne began clapping gaily. Peter peered through the doorway at her, as Mozart came running only to vanish just before reaching her. He wondered, did Mozart know she was there? Could he, from his side of time, see a bit of the present?

Seeming to sense his presence, Susanne glanced back at him. "Hello, Petey," she said. "Would you like some of my chocolate lace? It ought to be hard now."

He nodded. His face had gone dull with dissembling to hide from all the fears that churned inside him. He watched her climb up to shuffle across to the kitchen, obviously in great pain. The feather duster fell from her lap but she made no attempt to pick it up. She looked more withered than when she had sat down, only minutes before. When she was out of sight, he took off his coat and hung it back in the hallway.

"We can share it with Mozart, okay?" she called out to him.

"Fine." The word squeaked out of his knotted throat.

Susanne came shambling out of the kitchen, nearly doubled over with the effort of supporting her treat. It lay, a dark doily across her hands. Delight glistened in her cataracted eyes, senility blocking pain. "Lookit, isn't it nice?"

Peter stared at her and saw no one that he recognized. The sister he knew had gone into the kitchen; this creature had emerged, cut loose finally from his memories of her. What had happened to his sister? "Susie," he lamented. He walked swiftly forward, reaching out to take the chocolate.

Susanne's brows knitted. She glanced down at her breastbone. "Bee bite," she said. Uncomprehending, Peter drew up for a moment. Then Susanne swayed and her head went back with a look like that of ecstasy on her face.

Peter cried out and rushed forward. The chocolate lace slid off her hand and dropped. The fragile, woven strands shattered as they hit the floor, scattering fragments in every direction. Peter clutched her to him, his feet crunching on the glassy bits of caramel. "No, Susanne."

"Petey, I'm funny," she said. Tellier dragged her to her chair and set her down in it. "Where's momma, she here?" Her voice had gone thick. One side of her mouth twisted up as if trying to grin.

"She's coming," he answered quickly, searching her softening face for a hint of the little sister he could barely remember. "Be here in a minute."

For all the death he'd experienced, for all that he knew this would come, Peter Tellier retained a childlike incomprehension of how someone so close could slip away while he watched, while he held her.

She was only dozing between performances, he told himself. She often did that. She would be all right. He straightened her up, tucked the afghan across her lap. He found a few large pieces of the chocolate lace and placed them on her lap, too.

Behind him, the clavichord fluttered into being. He turned and stared at it as at some horrible and totally alien object. He could not stand to hear that music again. Not ever again.

He forgot his jacket but climbed down into the snow like a figure out of history himself, in lace and velvet and trousers that buttoned just below the knee. The lights of civilization lay across the water, down the hill. He wondered if he would survive the walk.

Within, the house stood silent for a time.

Dust motes dancing in the sunbeams settled on the clavichord. The girl with the feather duster skipped over to it and began whisking at the surfaces, the keys, the bench, until young Mozart in red waistcoat came marching out and angrily ordered her away. Mozart shooed her along as if herding a cow. She pranced ahead of him, smiling blissfully as if he were proclaiming undying love. Mozart vanished as she settled into the Beidermeier chair with coquettish grace. In the other chair, the ghost of Michael Haydn glanced reprovingly her way.

Mozart returned from behind the chair and headed for the clavichord. To the right of it, with both hands clasped beneath her bosom, Maria Lipp watched him for her cue to begin.

Susanne heard a little noise behind her and looked around to find her older brother closing the doors with great care. He was dressed in a wonderful costume just like Mozart's, but he put one finger to his lips to silence any outburst she might have had, then tiptoed into the shadows. She glanced surreptitiously at Haydn but he hadn't noticed Peter's arrival.

Susanne leaned down and placed her feather duster on the floor. Her feet dangled above it. She gripped the arms of her chair tightly, as if the chair were about to soar into the sky and carry her away to fabulous lands. "Regina coeli," she named herself, then closed her eyes as Mozart's slender hands descended upon the keys.

F. PAUL WILSON

Pelts

F. PAUL WILSON had his first short fiction first published in 1971, while he was still studying to become a doctor. Since then he has gone on to appear in most of the major science fiction and fantasy magazines, and over two million copies of his books are in print in America.

His novels include *The Keep* (unsuccessfully filmed in 1983), *The Tomb*, *The Touch*, *Black Wind*, *The Tery*, *Sibs*, *Reborn* and its sequel, *Reprisals*, while his short fiction has been collected in *Soft & Others*.

"Pelts" was originally published as an individual booklet, and all royalties from the novella are being donated by the author to the charity Friends of Animals. An assured chiller that doesn't let its message get in the way of the horror, it was nominated for a Bram Stoker Award by the Horror Writers of America.

" I 'M SCARED, PA."

"Shush!" Pa said, tossing the word over his shoulder as he walked ahead.

Gary shivered in the frozen predawn dimness and scanned the surrounding pines and brush for the thousandth time. He was heading for his twentieth year and knew he shouldn't be getting the willies like this but he couldn't help it. He didn't like this place.

"What if we get caught?"

"Only way we'll get caught is if you keep yappin', boy," Pa said. "We're almost there. Wouldna brought you along 'cept I can't do all the carryin' myself! Now hesh up!"

Their feet crunched though the half-inch shroud of frozen snow that layered the sandy ground. Gary pressed his lips tightly together, kept an extra tight grip on the Louisville Slugger, and followed Pa through the brush. But he didn't like this one bit. Not that he didn't favor hunting and trapping. He liked them fine. Loved them, in fact. But he and Pa were on Zeb Foster's land today. And everybody knew that was bad news.

Old Foster owned thousands of acres in the Jersey Pine Barrens and didn't allow nobody to hunt them. Had "Posted" signs all around the perimeter. Always been that way with the Fosters. Pa said old Foster's granpa had started the no-trespassing foolishness and that the family was likely to hold to the damn stupid tradition till Judgment Day. Pa didn't think he should be fenced out of any part of the Barrens. Gary could go along with that most anywheres except old Foster's property.

There were stories . . . tales of the Jersey Devil roaming the woods here, of people poaching Foster's land and never being seen again. Those who disappeared weren't fools from Newark or Trenton who regularly got lost in the Pines and wandered in circles till they died. These were experienced trackers and hunters, Pineys just like Pa . . . and Gary.

Never seen again.

"Pa, what if we don't come out of here?" He hated the whiny sound in his voice and tried to change it. "What if somethin' gets us?"

"Ain't nothin gonna get us! Didn't I come in here yesterday and set the traps? And didn't I come out okay?"

"Yeah, but—"

"Yeah, but *nothin'!* The Fosters done a good job of spreadin' stories for generations to scare folk off. But they don't scare me. I know bullshit when I hear it."

"Is it much farther?"

"No. Right yonder over the next rise. A whole area crawlin' with coon tracks."

Gary noticed they were passing through a thick line of calf-high vegetation, dead now; looked as if it'd been dark and ferny before winterkill had turned it brittle. It ran off straight as a hunting arrow into the scrub pines on either side of them.

"Looky this, Pa. Look how straight this stuff runs. Almost like it was planted."

Pa snorted. "That wasn't planted. That's spleenwort—ebony spleenwort. Only place it grows around here is where somebody's used lime to set footings for a foundation. Soil's too acid for it otherwise. Find it growin' over all the vanished towns."

Gary knew there were lots of vanished towns in the Barrens, but this must have been one hell of a foundation. It was close to six feet wide and ran as far as he could see in either direction.

"What you think used to stand here, Pa?"

"Who knows, who cares? People was buildin' in the Barrens afore the Revolutionary War. And I hear tell there was crumblin' ruins already here when the Indians arrived. There's some real old stuff around these parts but we ain't about to dig it up. We're here for coon. Now hesh up till we get to the traps!"

Gary couldn't believe their luck. Every damn leg-hold trap had a coon in it! Big fat ones with thick, silky coats the likes of which he'd never seen. A few were already dead, but most of them were still alive, lying on their sides, their black eyes wide with fear and pain; panting, bloody, exhausted from trying to pull loose from the teeth of the traps, still tugging weakly at the chains that linked the trap to its stake.

He and Pa took care of the tuckered-out ones first by crushing their throats. Gary flipped them onto their backs and watched their striped tails come up protectively over their bellies. I *ain't after your belly, Mr Coon*. He put his heel right over the windpipe, and kicked down hard. If he was in the right spot he heard a satisfying *crunch* as the cartilage collapsed. The coons wheezed and thrashed and flopped around awhile in the traps trying to draw some air past the crushed spot but soon enough they choked to death. Gary had had some trouble doing the throat crush when he started at it years ago, but he was used to it by now. It was just the way it was done. All the trappers did it.

But you couldn't try that on the ones that still had some pepper in them. They wouldn't hold still enough for you to place your heel. That was where the Gary and his Slugger came in. He swung at one as it snapped at him.

"The head! The *head*, dammit!" Pa yelled.

"Awright, awright!"

"Don't mess the pelts!"

Some of those coons were tough suckers. Took at least half a dozen whacks each with the Slugger to kill them dead. They'd twist and squeal and squirm around and it wasn't easy to pound a direct hit on the head every single time. But they weren't going nowhere, not with one of their legs caught in a steel trap.

By the time he and Pa reached the last trap, Gary's bat was drippy red up to the taped grip, and his bag was so heavy he could barely lift it. Pa's was just about full too.

"Damn!" Pa said, standing over the last trap. "Empty!" Then he knelt for a closer look. "No, wait! Lookit that! It's been sprung! The paw's still in it! Musta chewed it off!"

Gary heard a rustle in the brush to his right and caught a glimpse of a gray-and-black striped tail slithering away.

"There it is!"

"Get it!"

Gary dropped the sack and went after the last coon. No sweat. It was missing one of its rear paws and left a trail of blood behind on the snow wherever it went. He came upon it within twenty feet. A fat one, waddling and gimping along as fast as its three legs would carry it. He swung but the coon partially dodged the blow and squalled as the bat glanced off its skull. The next shot got it solid but it rolled away. Gary kept after it through the brush, hitting it again and again, until his arms got tired. He counted nearly thirty strikes before he got in a good one. The big coon rolled over and looked at him with glazed eyes, blood running from its ears. He saw the nipples on its belly—a female. As he lifted the Slugger again, it raised its two front paws over its face—an almost human gesture that made him hesitate for a second. Then he clocked her with a winner. He bashed her head ten more times for good measure to make sure she wouldn't be going anywhere. The snow around her was splattered with red by the time he was done.

As he lifted her by her tail to take her back, he got a look at the mangled stump of her hind leg. Chewed off. God, you really had to want to get free to do something like that.

He carried her back to Pa, passing all the other splotches of crimson along the way. Looked like some bloody-footed giant had stomped through here.

"Whooeee!" Pa said when he saw the last one. "That's a beauty! They're *all* beauties! Gary, m'boy, we're gonna have money to burn when we sell these!"

Gary glanced at the sun as he tossed the last one into the sack. It was rising brightly into a clear sky.

"Maybe we shouldn't spend it until we get off Foster's land."

"You're right," Pa said, looking uneasy for the first time. "I'll come back tomorrow and rebait the traps." He slapped Gary on the back. "We found ourselfs a goldmine, son!"

Gary groaned under the weight of the sack, but he leaned forward and struck off toward the sun. He wanted to be gone from here. Quick like.

"I'll lead the way, Pa."

"Look at these!" Pa said, holding up two pelts by their tails. "Thick as can be and not a scar or a bald spot anywhere to be seen! Primes, every single one of them!"

He swayed as he stood by the skinning table. He'd been nipping at the applejack bottle steadily during the day-long job of cutting, stripping, and washing the pelts, and now he was pretty near blitzed. Gary had taken the knife from Pa early on, doing all the cutting himself and leaving the stripping for the old man. You didn't have to be sober for stripping. Once the cuts were made—that was the hard part—a strong man could rip the pelt off like husking an ear of corn.

"Yeah," Gary said. "They're beauts all right. Full winter coats."

The dead of winter was, naturally, the best time to trap any fur animal. That was when the coats were the thickest. And these were *thick*. Gary couldn't remember seeing anything like these pelts. The light gray fur seemed to glow a pale metallic blue when the light hit it right. Touching it gave him a funny warm feeling inside. Made him want to find a woman and ride her straight on till morning.

The amazing thing was that they were all identical. No one was going to have to dye these babies to make a coat. They all matched perfectly, like these coons had been one big family.

These were going to make one *hell* of a beautiful full-length coat.

"Jake's gonna *love* these!" Pa said. "And he's gonna pay pretty for 'em, too!"

"Did you get hold of him?" Gary asked, thinking of the shotgun he wanted to buy.

"Yep. Be round first thing in the morning."

"Great, Pa. Whyn't you hit the sack and I'll clean up round here."

"You sure?"

"Sure."

"You're all right, son," Pa said. He clapped him on the shoulder and staggered for the door.

Gary shivered in the cold blast of wind that dashed past Pa on his way out of the barn. He got up and threw another log into the pot-bellied stove squatting in the corner, then surveyed the scene.

There really wasn't all that much left to be done. The furs had all been washed and all but a few were tacked up on the drying boards. The guts had been tossed out, and the meat had been put in the cold shed to feed to the dogs during the next few weeks. So all he had to—

Gary's eyes darted to the bench. Had something moved there? He watched a second but all was still. Yet he could have sworn one of the unstretched pelts piled there had moved. He rubbed his eyes and grinned.

Long day.

He went to the bench and spread out the remaining half dozen before stretching them. Most times they'd nail their catches to the barn door, but these were too valuable for that. He ran his hands over them. God, these were special. Never had he seen coon fur this thick and soft. That warm, peaceful, horny feeling slipped over him again. On a lark, he draped it over his arm. What a coat this was gonna—

The pelt moved, rippled. In a single swift smooth motion its edges curled and wrapped snugly around his forearm. A gush of horror dribbled away before he could react, drowned in a flood of peace and tranquility.

Nothing unusual here. Everything was all right . . . all right.

He watched placidly as the three remaining unstretched furs rippled and began to move toward him. Nothing wrong with that. Nothing wrong with the way they crawled over his hands and wrists and wrapped themselves around his arms. Perfectly natural. He smiled. Looked like he had caveman arms.

It was time to go back to the house. He got up and started walking. On the way out the door, he picked up the Louisville Slugger.

Pa was snoring.

Gary poked him with the bat and called to him. His own voice seemed to come from far away.

"Pa! Wake up, Pa!"

Finally Pa stirred and opened his bloodshot eyes. "What is it, boy? What the hell you want?"

Gary lifted the bat over his head. Pa screamed and raised his hands to protect himself, much like that last coon this morning. Gary swung the bat with everything he had and got Pa on the wrist and over the right ear as he tried to roll away. Pa grunted and stiffened, but Gary didn't wait to see what happened. He swung again. And again. And again, counting. His arms weren't tired at all. The pelts snuggling around them seemed to give him strength. Long before the fortieth swing, Pa's head and brains were little more than a huge smear of currant jelly across the pillows.

Then he turned and headed for the back door.

Back in the barn, he stood by the stretching boards and looked down at the gore-smeared bat, clutched tightly now in both of his fists. A small part of him screamed a warning but the rest of him knew that everything was all right. Everything was fine. Everything was—

He suddenly rotated his wrists and forearms and smashed the bat against his face. He staggered back and would have screamed if his throat had only let him. His nose and forehead were in agony! But everything was all right—

No! Everything was *not* all right! This was—

He hit himself again with the bat and felt his right cheek cave in. And again, and again. The next few blows smeared his nose and took out his eyes. He was blind now, but the damn bat wouldn't stop!

He fell backwards onto the floor but still he kept battering his own head. He heard his skull splinter. But still he couldn't stop that damn bat!

And the pain! He should have been knocked cold by the first whack but he was still conscious. He felt *everything*!

He prayed he died before the bat hit him forty times.

II

No one answered his knocking at the house—house, shmouse, it was a hovel—so Jake Feldman headed for the barn. The cold early morning air chilled the inexorably widening bald spot that commanded the top of his scalp; he wrapped his unbuttoned overcoat around his ample girth and quickened his pace as much as he dared over the icy, rutted driveway.

Old man Jameson had said he'd come by some outstanding pelts. Pelts of such quality that Jake would be willing to pay ten times the going price to have them. Out of the goodness of Jameson's heart and because of their long-standing business relationship, he was going to give Jake first crack at them.

Right.

But the old Piney gonif's genuine enthusiasm had intrigued Jake. Jameson was no bullshitter. Maybe he really had something unique. And maybe not.

This better be worth it, he thought as he pulled open the barn door. He didn't have time to traipse down to the Jersey Pine Barrens on a wild goose chase.

The familiar odor of dried blood hit him as he opened the barn door. Not unexpected. Buy fresh pelts at the source for a while and you soon got used to the smell. What was unexpected was how cold it was in the barn. The lights were on but the wood stove was cold. Pelts would freeze if they stayed in this temperature too long.

Then he saw them—all lined up, all neatly nailed out on the stretching boards. The fur shimmered, reflecting glints of opalescence from the incandescent bulbs above the cold fire from the morning light pouring through the open door behind him. They were exquisite. *Magnificent!*

Jake Feldman knew fur. He'd spent almost forty of his fifty-five years in the business, starting as a cutter and working his way up till he found the *chutzpah* to start his own factory. In all those years he had never seen anything like these pelts.

My God, Jameson, where did you get them and are there any more where these came from?

Jake approached the stretching boards and touched the pelts. He had to. Something about them urged his fingers forward. So soft, so shimmery, so incredibly beautiful. Jake had seen, touched, and on occasion even cut the very finest Siberian sable pelts from Russia. But they were nothing compared to these. These were beyond quality. These were beautiful in a way that was almost scary, almost . . . supernatural.

Then he saw the boots. Big, gore-encrusted rubber boots sticking out from under one of the stretching boards. Nothing unusual about that except for their position. They lay on the dirt floor with their toes pointing toward the ceiling at different angles, like the hands of a clock reading five after ten. Boots simply didn't lie like that . . . unless there were feet in them.

Jake bent and saw denim-sheathed legs running up from the boots. He smiled. One of the Jamesons—either old Jeb or young Gary. Jake bet on the elder. A fairly safe bet seeing as how old Jeb loved his Jersey lightning.

"Hey, old man," he said as he squeezed between two of the stretching boards to get behind. "What're you doing back there? You'll catch your death of—"

The rest of the sentence clogged in Jake's throat as he looked down at the corpse. All he could see at first was the red. The entire torso was drenched in clotted blood—the chest, the arms, the shoulders, the—dear Lord, the head! There was almost nothing left of the head! The face and the whole upper half of the skull had been smashed to a red, oozing pulp from which the remnant of an eye and some crazily angled teeth protruded. Only a patch of smooth, clean-shaven cheek identified the corpse as Gary, not Jeb.

But who could have done this? And why? More frightening than the sight of the corpse was Jake's sudden grasp of the ungovernable fury behind all the repeated blows it must have taken to cave in Gary's head like that. With what—that baseball bat? And after pounding him so mercilessly, had the killer wrapped Gary's dead fingers around the murder weapon? What sick—?

Jeb! Where was old Jeb? Surely he'd had nothing to do with this!

Calling the old man's name, Jake ran back up to the house. His cries went unanswered. The back door was open. He stood on the stoop, calling out again. Only silence greeted him. The shack had an *empty* feel to it. That was the only reason Jake stepped inside.

It didn't take him long to find the bedroom. And what was left of Jeb.

A moment later Jake stood panting and retching in the stretch between the house and the barn.

Dead! Both dead!

More than dead—battered, crushed, *smeared*!

. . . but those pelts. Even with the horrors of what he'd just seen raging through his mind, he couldn't stop thinking about those pelts.

Exquisite!

Jake ran to his car, backed it up to the barn door, popped the trunk. It took him a while but eventually he got all the pelts off the stretching boards and into his trunk. He found a couple of loose ones on the floor near Gary's body and he grabbed those too.

And then he roared away down the twin ruts that passed for a road in these parts. He felt bad about leaving the two corpses like that, but there was nothing he could do to help the Jamesons. He'd call the State Police from the Parkway. Anonymously.

But he had the pelts. That was the important thing.

And he knew exactly what he was going to do with them.

After getting the pelts safely back to his factory in New York's garment district, Jake immediately went about turning them into a coat. He ran into only one minor snag and that was at the beginning: The Orientals among his cutters refused to work with them. A couple of them took one look at the pelts and made a wide-eyed, screaming dash from the factory.

That shook him up for a little while, but he recovered quickly enough. Once he got things organized, he personally supervised every step: the cleaning and softening, the removal of the guard hairs, the letting-out process in which he actually took a knife in hand and crosscut a few pelts himself, just as he'd done when he started in the business; he oversaw the sewing of the let-out strips and the placement of the thousands of nails used in tacking out the fur according to the pattern.

With the final stitching of the silk lining nearing completion, Jake allowed himself to relax. Even unfinished, the coat—*That Coat*, as he'd come to call it—was stunning, unutterably beautiful. In less than an hour he was going to be the owner of the world's most extraordinary raccoon coat. Extraordinary not simply because of its unique sheen and texture, but because you couldn't tell it was raccoon. Even the cutters and tackers in his factory had been fooled; they'd agreed that the length of the hair and size of the pelts were similar to raccoon, but none of them had ever seen raccoon like this, or *any* fur like this.

Jake wished to hell he knew where Jameson had trapped them. He'd be willing to pay almost anything for a regular supply of those pelts. What he could sell those coats for!

But he had only one coat now, and he wasn't going to sell it. No way. This baby was going to be an exhibition piece. It was going to put Fell Furs on the map. He's bring it to the next international show and blow the crowd away. The whole industry would be buzzing about That Coat. And Fell Furs would be known at the company with That Coat.

And God knew the company needed a boost. Business was down all over the industry. Jake couldn't remember furs ever being discounted as deeply as they were now. The animal lovers were having a definite impact. Well, hell, he was an animal lover too. Didn't he have a black lab at home?

But animal love stopped at the bottom line, bubby.

If he played it right, That Coat would turn things around for Fell Furs. But he needed the right model to strut it.

And he knew just who to call.

He sat in his office and dialed Shanna's home number. Even though she'd just moved, he didn't have to look it up. He knew it by heart already. He should have. He'd dialed it enough times.

Shanna . . . a middle-level model he'd seen at a fur show two years ago. The shoulder length black hair with the long bangs, the white skin and knockout cheekbones, onyx eyes that promised everything. And her body—Shanna had a figure that set her far apart from the other bean-poles in the field. Jake hadn't been able to get her out of his mind since. He wanted her but it seemed like a lost cause. He always felt like some sort of warty frog next to her, and that was just how she treated him. He'd approached her countless times and each of those times he'd been rebuffed. He didn't want to own her, he just wanted to be near her, to touch her once in a while. And who knew? Maybe he'd grow on her.

At least now he had a chance. That Coat would open the door. This time would be different. He could feel it.

Her voice, soft and inviting, came on the line after the third ring.

"Yes?"

"Shanna, it's me. Jake Feldman."

"Oh." The drop in temperature within that single syllable spoke volumes. "What do you want, Jake?"

"I have a business proposition for you, Shanna."

Her voice grew even cooler. "I've heard your propositions before. I'm not the least—"

"This is straight down the line business," he said quickly. "I've got a coat for you. I want you to wear it at the international show next week."

"I don't know." She seemed the tiniest bit hesitant now. "It's been a while since I've done a fur show."

"You'll want to do them again when you see this coat. Believe me."

Maybe some of his enthusiasm for the coat was coming over the phone. Jake sensed a barely detectable thaw in her voice.

"Well . . . call the agency."

"I will. But I want you to see this coat first. You've got to see it."

"Really Jake—"

"You've got to see it. I'll bring it right down."

He hung up before she could tell him no and hurried out to the work room. As soon as the last knot was tied in the last stitch he boxed That Coat and headed for the door.

"What kind of coat you buy, Mister?" someone said as soon as he stepped out onto the sidewalk.

Oh, shit. Animal lovers. A bunch of them holding signs, milling around outside his showroom.

Somebody shoved a placard in his face:

> *The only one who can wear a fur*
> *coat gracefully and beautifully*
> *is the animal to whom it belongs.*

"How many harmless animals were trapped and beaten to death to make it?" said a guy with a beard.

"Fuck off!" Jake said. "You're wearing leather shoes, aren't you?"

The guy smiled, "Actually, I'm wearing sneakers, but even if they were leather it wouldn't be for pure vanity. Cows are in the human food chain. Beavers, minks, and baby seals are not."

"So what?"

"It's one thing for animals to die to provide food—that's the law of nature. It's something entirely different to kill animals so you can steal their beauty by draping yourself with their skins. Animals shouldn't suffer and die to feed human vanity."

A chant began.

"Vanity! Vanity! Vanity . . ."

Jake flipped them all the bird and grabbed a cab downtown.

Such a beautiful girl living in a place like this, Jake thought as he entered the lobby of the converted TriBeCa warehouse where Shanna had just bought a condo. Probably paid a small fortune for it too. Just because it was considered a chic area of town.

At the "Elevator" sign he found himself facing a steel panel studded with rivets. Not sure of what to do, he tried a pull on the lever under the sign. With a clank the steel panel split horizontally, dividing into a pair of huge metal doors that opened vertically, the top one sliding upward, the bottom sinking. An old freight elevator. Inside he figured out how to get the contraption to work and rode the noisy open car up to the third level.

Stepping out on the third floor he found a door marked 3B straight ahead of him. That was Shanna's. He knocked, heard footsteps approaching.

"Who's there?" said a muffled voice from the other side. Shanna's voice.

"It's me. Jake. I brought the coat."

"I told you to call the agency."

Even through the door he could sense her annoyance. This wasn't going well. He spotted the glass lens in the door and that gave him an idea.

"Look through your peephole, Shanna."

He pulled That Coat from the box. The fur seemed to ripple against his hands as he lifted it. A few unused letting-out strips fell from the sleeve, landing in the box. The looked like furry caterpillars; a couple of them even seemed to move on their own. Strange. They shouldn't have been in the coat. He shrugged it off. It didn't matter. That Coat was all that mattered. And getting past Shanna's door.

"Just take a gander at this coat. Try one peek at this beauty and then tell me you don't want to take a closer look."

He heard the peephole cover move on the other side. Ten seconds later, the door opened. Shanna stood there staring. He caught his breath at the sight of her. Even without make-up, wearing an old terry cloth robe, she was beautiful. But her wide eyes were oblivious to him. They were fixed on That Coat. She seemed to be in a trance.

"Jake, it's . . . it's beautiful. Can I . . .?"

As she reached for it, Jake dropped the fur back into its box and slid by her into the apartment.

"Try it on in here. The light's better."

She followed him into the huge, open, loft-like space that made up the great room of her condo. Too open for Jake's tastes. Ceilings too high, not enough walls. And still not finished yet. The paper hangers were halfway through a bizarre mural on one wall; their ladders and tools were stacked by the door.

He turned and held That Coat open for her.

"Here, Shanna. I had it made in your size."

She turned and slipped her arms into the sleeves. As Jake settled it over her shoulders he noticed a few of those leftover fur strips clinging to the coat. He plucked them off and bunched them into his palm to discard later. Then he stepped back to look at her. The fur had been breathtaking before, but Shanna enhanced its beauty. And vice versa. The two of them seemed made for each other. The effect brought tears to Jake's eyes.

She glided over to a mirrored wall and did slow turns, again and again. Rapture glowed in her face. Finally she turned to him, eyes bright.

"You don't have to call the agency," she said. "I'll call. I want to show this coat."

Jake suddenly realized that he was in a much better bargaining position than he had ever imagined. Shanna no longer had the upper hand. He did. He decided to raise the stakes.

"Of course you do," he said offhandedly. "And there's a good chance you'll be the model we finally settle on."

Her face showed concern for the first time since she'd laid eyes on the coat.

" 'A good chance'? What's that supposed to mean?"

"Well, there are other models who're very interested. We have to give them a chance to audition."

She wrapped the fur more tightly around her.

"I don't want anyone else wearing this coat!"

"Well . . ."

Slowly Shanna pulled open the coat, untied the terry cloth robe beneath it, and pulled that open too. She wore nothing under the robe. Jake barely noticed her smile.

"Believe me," she said in that honey voice, "this is the only audition you'll need."

Jake's mouth was suddenly too dry to speak. He could not take his eyes off her breasts. He reached for the buttons on his own coat and found the fur strips in his right hand. As he went to throw them away, he felt them move, wiggling like furry worms. When he looked, they had wrapped themselves around his fingers.

Tranquility seeped through him like fine red wine. It didn't seem odd that the strips should move. Perfectly natural. Funny even.

Look. I've got fur rings.

He pulled at his coat and shirt until he was bare from the waist up. Then he realized he needed to be alone for a minute.

"Where's your bathroom?"

"That door behind you."

He needed something sharp. Why?

"Do you have a knife? A sharp one?" The words seemed to form on their own.

Her expression was quizzical. "I think so. The paperhangers were using razor blades—"

"That'll be fine." He went to the work bench and found the utility knife, then headed for the bathroom. "I'll only be a minute. Wait for me in the bedroom."

What am I doing?

In the bathroom he stood before the mirror with the utility knife gripped in the fur-wrapped fingers of his right hand. A sudden wave of cold shuddered through him. He felt half-frozen, trapped, afraid. Then he saw old Jameson's whiskered face, huge in the mirror, saw his monstrous foot ram toward him. Jake gagged with the crushing pain in his throat, he was suffocating, God, he couldn't breathe—!

And then just as suddenly he was fine again. Everything was all right. He pushed the upper corner of the utility blade through the skin at the top of his breast bone, just deep enough to pierce its full thickness through to the fatty layer beneath. Then he drew the blade straight down the length of his sternum. When he reached the top of his abdomen he angled the cut to the right, following the line of the bottom rib across his flank. He heard the tendons and ligaments in his shoulder joint creak and pop in protest as his hand extended the cut all the way around his waist to his back, but he felt no pain, not from the shoulder, not even from the gash that had begun to bleed so freely. Something within him was screaming in horror but it was far away. Everything was all right here. Everything was fine.

When he had extended the first cut all the way back to his spine he switched the blade to his left hand and made a similar cut from the front toward the left, meeting the first cut at the rear near the base of his spine. Then he made a circular cut around each shoulder—over the top and through the armpit. Then another all the way around his neck. When that was done, he gripped the edges on each side of the incision he had made over the breast bone and yanked. Amid sprays of red, the skin began to pull free of the underlying tissues.

Everything was all right . . . all right . . .

Jake kept tugging.

III

Where the hell is he?

Wrapped in the coat, Shanna stood before her bedroom mirror and waited for Jake.

She wasn't looking forward to this. No way. The thought of that flabby white body flopping around on top of her made her a little ill, but she was going through with it: Nothing was going to keep her from wearing this fur.

She snuggled the coat closer about her but it kept falling away, almost as if it didn't want to touch her. Silly thought.

She did a slow turn before the mirror.

Looking good, Shanna!

This was it. This was one of those moments you hear about when your whole future hinges on a single decision. Shanna knew what that decision had to be. Her career was stalled short of the top. She was making good money but she wanted more—she wanted her face recognized everywhere. And this coat was going to get her that recognition. A couple of international shows and she'd be known the world over as the girl in the fabulous fur. From then on she could write her own ticket.

In spite of her queasy stomach, Shanna allowed herself a sour smile. This wouldn't be the first time she'd spread to get something she wanted. Jake Feldman had been leching after her for years; if letting him get his jollies on her a couple of times assured her of exclusive rights to model his coat, tonight might be the *last* time she ever had to spread for anyone like Jake Feldman.

What was he doing in the bathroom—papering it? She wished he'd get out of there and get this over with. Then she could—

She heard the bathroom door open, heard his footsteps in the great room. He was shuffling.

"In here, Jake!" she called.

Quickly she pulled free of the coat long enough to shed the robe, then slipped back into it and stretched out on the bed. She rolled onto her side and propped herself up on one elbow but the fur kept falling away from her. Well, that was okay too. She left it open, arranging the coat so that her best stuff was displayed to the max. She knew all the provocative poses. She'd done her share of nudie sessions to pay her bills between those early fashion assignments.

Outside the door the shuffling steps were drawing closer. What was he doing—walking around with his pants around his ankles?

"Hurry up, honey! I'm waiting for you!"

Let's get this show on the road, you fat slob!

Suddenly she was cold, her leg hurt, she saw a boyish-faced giant looming over her with a raised club, saw it come crashing down on her head. As she began to scream she suddenly found herself back in her condo, sprawled on her bed with the fur.

Jake was shuffling through the door.

Shanna's mind dimly registered that he was holding something, but her attention was immediately captured by the red. Jake was all red—*dripping* red—his pants, the skin of his arms, his bare—

Oh God it was blood! He was covered with blood! And his chest and upper abdomen—they were the bloodiest. Christ! The skin was gone! Gone! Like someone had ripped the hide off his upper torso.

"I . . ." His voice was hoarse. A croak. His eyes were wide and glazed as he shuffled toward her. "I made this vest for you."

And then Shanna looked at what he held out to her, what drooped from his bloody fingers—fingers that seemed to be covered with fur.

It was indeed a vest. A white, blood-streaked, sleeveless vest. Between the streaks of blood she could see the wiry chest hairs straggling across the front . . . whorling around the nipples . . .

Shanna screamed and rolled off the bed, hugging the coat around her. She wished she could have pulled it over her head to hide the sight of him.

"It's for you," he said, continuing his shuffle toward her. "You can wear it under the coat . . ."

Whimpering in fear and revulsion, Shanna ran around the bed and dashed for the door. She ran across the great room and out into the hall. The elevator! She had to get away from that man, that *thing* who'd cut his skin into a—

The shuffling. He was coming!

She pressed the down button, pounded on it. Behind the steel door she heard the winches whir to life. The elevator was on its way. She turned and gagged as she saw Jake come through her apartment door and approach her, leaving a trail of red behind him, holding the bloody skin out as if expecting her to slip her arms through the openings.

A clank behind her. She turned, pulled the lever that opened the heavy steel doors, and leaped inside. An upward push on the inner lever brought the outer doors down with a deafening clang, shutting out the sight of Jake and his hideous offering.

Clutching the coat around her bare body Shanna sank to her knees and began to sob.

God, what was happening here? Why had Jake cut his skin off like that? *How* had he done it?

"Shanna, please," said that croaking voice from the other side of the doors. "I made it for you."

And then the doors started to open! Before her eyes a horizontal slit was opening between the outer doors, and two bloody arms with fur-wrapped fingers were thrusting the loathsome vest toward her through the gap.

Shanna's scream echoed up and down the open elevator shaft as she hit the *Down* button. The car lurched and started to sink.

Thank you, God!

But the third floor doors continued to open. As she passed the second floor and continued her descent, Shanna's eyes were irresistibly

350

drawn upward. Through the open ceiling of the car she watched the ever-widening gap, watched as the two protruding arms and the vest were joined by Jake's head and upper torso.

"Shanna! It's for you!"

The car stopped with a jolt. First floor. Shanna yanked up the safety grate and pulled the lever. Five seconds . . . five seconds and she'd be running for the street, for the cops. As the outer doors slowly parted, that voice echoed again through the elevator shaft.

"Shanna!"

She chanced one last look upward.

The third floor doors had retracted to the floor and ceiling lines. Most of Jake's torso seemed to be hanging over the edge.

"It's for—"

He leaned too far.

Oh, shit, he's falling!

"—yoooooouuuuu!"

Shanna's high-pitched scream of "Noooo!" blended with Jake's voice in a fearful harmony that ended with his head striking the upper edge of the elevator car's rear wall. As the rest of his body whipped around in a wild, blood-splattering, pinwheeling sprawl, his shoed foot slammed against Shanna's head, knocking her back against the door lever. Half-dazed, she watched the steel doors reverse their opening motion.

"No!"

And Jake . . . Jake was still moving, crawling toward her an inch at a time on twisted arms, broken legs, his shattered head raised, trying to speak, still clutching the vest in one hand, still offering it to her.

The coat seemed to ripple around her, moving on its own. She had to get *out* of here!

The doors! Shanna lunged for the opening, reaching toward the light from the deserted front foyer. She could make it through if—

She slipped on the blood, went down on one knee, still reaching as the steel doors slammed down on her wrist. Shanna heard her bones crunch as pain beyond anything she had ever known ran up her arm. She would have screamed but the agony had stolen her voice. She tried to pull free but she was caught, tried to reach the lever but it was a good foot beyond her grasp.

Something touched her foot. Jake—it was what was left of Jake holding his vest out to her with one hand, caressing her bare foot with one of the fur strips wrapped around the fingers of his other hand. She kicked at him, slid herself away from him. She couldn't let him get near her. He'd want to put that vest on her, want to try to do other things to her. And she was bare-ass naked under this coat. She had to get free, get free of these doors, anything to get free!

She began chewing at the flesh of her trapped wrist, tearing at it, unmindful of the greater pain, of the running blood. It seemed the natural thing to do, the *only* thing to do.

Free! She had to get *free*!

IV

Juanita wasn't having much luck tonight. She'd just pushed her shopping cart with all her worldly belongings the length of a narrow alley looking for a safe place to huddle for the night, an alcove or deep doorway, someplace out of sight and out of the wind. A good alley, real potential, but it was already occupied by someone very drunk and very nasty. She'd moved on.

Cold. Really felt the cold these days. Didn't know how old she was but knew that her bones creaked and her back hurt and she couldn't stand the cold like she used to. If she could find a place to hide her cart, maybe she could sneak into the subway for the night. Always warmer down there. But when she came up top again all her things might be gone.

Didn't want to be carted off to no shelter, neither. Even a safe one. Didn't like being closed in, and once they got you into those places they never let you go till morning. Liked to come and go as she pleased. Besides, she got confused indoors and her mind wouldn't work straight. She was an outdoors person. That was where she did her clearest thinking, where she intended to stay.

As she turned a corner she spotted all the flashing red and blue lights outside a building she remembered as a warehouse but was now a bunch of apartments. Like a child, she was drawn to the bright, pretty lights to see what was going on.

Took her a while to find out. Juanita allowed herself few illusions. She knew not many people want to explain things to someone who looks like a walking rag pile, but she persisted and eventually managed to pick up half a dozen variations on what had happened inside. All agreed on one thing: a gruesome double murder in the building's elevator involving a naked woman and a half-naked man. After that the stories got crazy. Some said the man had been flayed alive and the woman was wearing his skin, others said the man had cut off the woman's hand, still others said she'd *chewed* her own hand off.

Enough. Shuddering, Juanita turned and pushed her cart away. She'd gone only a few yards when she spotted movement as she was passing a shadowed doorway. Not human movement; too low to the ground. Looked like an animal but it was too big for a rat, even a New York City rat. Light from a passing EMS wagon glinted off the thing and Juanita was struck by the thickness of its fur, by the way the light danced and flickered over its surface.

Then she realized it was a coat—a fur coat. Even in the dark she could see that it wasn't some junky fun fur. This was the real thing, a true, blue, top-of-the-line, utterly fabulous fur coat. She grabbed it and held it up. *Mira!* Even in the dark she could see how lovely it was, how the fur glistened.

She slipped into it. The coat seemed to ripple away from her for a second, then it snuggled against her. Instantly she was warm. So warm. Almost as if the fur was generating its own heat, like an electric blanket. Seemed to draw the cold right out of her bones. Must've been ages since she last felt so toasty. But she forced herself to pull free of it and hold it up again.

Sadly, Juanita shook her head. No good. Too nice. Wear this thing around and someone'd think she was rich and roll her but good. Maybe she could pawn it. But it was probably hot and that would get her busted. Couldn't take being locked up ever again. A shame, though. Such a nice warm coat and she couldn't wear it.

And then she had an idea. She found an alley like the one she'd left before and dropped the coat onto the pavement, fur side down. Then she knelt beside it and began to rub it into the filth. From top to bottom she covered the fur with any grime she could find. Practically cleaned the end of the alley with that coat. Then she held it up again.

Better. Much better. No one would recognize it and hardly anybody would bother trying to take it from her the way it looked now. But what did she care how she looked in it? As long as it served its purpose, that was all she asked. She slipped into it again and once more the warmth enveloped her.

She smiled and felt the wind whistle through the gaps between her teeth.

This is living! she thought. Nothing like a fur to keep you warm. And after all, for those of us who do our living in the outdoors, ain't that what fur is for?

DAVID SUTTON

Those of Rhenea

DAVID SUTTON'S horror and dark fantasy fiction has been published in such anthologies and magazines as *Final Shadows*, *Cold Fear*, *Taste of Fear*, *Skeleton Crew*, *Ghosts & Scholars*, *Grue*, *2AM*, *Kadath* and others.

He has written *Earthchild*, a novel of elemental forces, Aboriginal myths and drugs, and is currently at work on a second, tentatively titled *Feng Shui*, set in Hong Kong.

He was one of the originators of The British Fantasy Society, has worked extensively to promote fantasy and horror in the UK since the late '60s, and was instrumental in beginning the British Fantasy Conventions.

He is a winner of the World Fantasy Award and eight-time recipient of the British Fantasy Award for his co-editorship of *Fantasy Tales* with Stephen Jones. The same team is also responsible for *The Best Horror from Fantasy Tales* and two volumes of *Dark Voices: The Pan Book of Horror*. His other anthologies include *New Writings in Horror and the Supernatural 1* and *2* and *The Satyr's Head and Other Tales of Terror*.

Another example of holiday horrors, the following story may put you off package trips to Greece for quite some time . . .

E XCEPT WHEN SHE THOUGHT ABOUT IT, the frenzy of Athens was a million miles away. When she did, flashes of its rampant lifestyle tore through Elizabeth's brain like an express locomotive.

The recent elections had daubed the city with myriadfold banners, hung between every available lamp-post and tree, or across buildings, advocating this party or the other. The equally strident calls to the faithful from the various political headquarters in Ormonia Square—their loudspeakers issuing the usual pre-election promises interspersed with Greek muzak at an ear-stinging rate of decibels—were guaranteed to inflame the heart of any Hawkwind fan. If it wasn't the noise of the political canvassing, from which you were even at risk on the trolley buses, from leafleteers, it was the incessant roar of traffic.

Elizabeth's hotel, the Alexandros, was just off Vas Sofias, up by the American Embassy, and the noise from the omnipresent automobiles and their obligatory horns had, in the end, become almost restful. Twenty-four hours a day Athens is penetrated, she thought, like some symbolic whore, by motor cars driving across the city at dizzying speeds. By night and the street lamps, the polluting fog of carbon monoxide fumes lay like a thick pale yellow duvet over the lower parts of the city.

Now though, Athens was a half-remembered dream. She had met Steve at a bar in Syntagma Square—no emotional entanglement so far, thank God—and they had both found they were going to Naxos in two days' time. Although the largest of the islands in the Cyclades, Naxos had no airport, which Steve had found surprising. Elizabeth was initally pleased, she didn't look forward to flying. The ten-hour ferry trip had, however, been crowded and unpleasant, with an unhelpful Greek crew. Only the barman made any attempt at friendliness and Elizabeth had been glad of Steve's company.

From the Venetian charm of Naxos town—it seemed that every Greek island had at one time bent to the maritime will of the great Italian empire—Steve persuaded Elizabeth on a boat trip to fabled Delos.

Steve had won her over with his surprised-looking, but attractive crew-cut, his cheap black plastic sunglasses, his camera and his anecdotes from Greek Mythology. He was on a sabbatical from Boston University and had plenty of time for travel, and he seemed to like to keep moving, even when he was staying in one place. She'd have been just as happy to stay on the beaches soaking up the sun, and Naxos was relaxing, but a boat trip appealed to her, so long as it wasn't akin to the crossing from Piraeus.

The only thing which dampened her enthusiasm, albeit briefly, was the curious incident in the National Museum of Antiquities, which had taken place the day before their departure from Athens. The day after she'd met Steve, he took her to lunch and then to the museum. It was a vast, staggering array of treasures and she'd felt dwarfed by the sculpture, the gold, the decorative eloquence of Greek history.

For his part, Steve was less interested in the magnificence of Agamemnon's gold death-mask, or the bronze statue of Poseidon, and more inclined to the less dramatic pieces. Especially two steatite pyxis, flat trinket boxes. He lingered long over the cabinet in which they resided along with other, similar artefacts, looking at the items, labelled as having been discovered in a grave on Delos.

"See the carving on those lids?" he said to Elizabeth, who was itching to move on.

"Mmm." She was sure her growing boredom was beginning to show. It was, after all, merely grooves cut or chiselled into the lids.

"A spiral pattern. Very simple." He paused. What was he trying to say, Elizabeth wondered.

"Very like . . . *very* like spiral carvings in Britain and Ireland from four-thousand years ago."

"Is there a connection, then?" Elizabeth asked.

"A mystery at least," he replied mysteriously. "Prehistoric, pagan symbology . . ."

Elizabeth was about to say something, but noticed that Steve was lost, hypnotised, transfixed by the objects. She stared down at them too, trying to see what it was that he was finding *so* fascinating. Then she was subjected to an optical illusion, or so she thought at first. As when sometimes a particular type of pattern in carpet or wallpaper defies the eye's usual ability to see two-dimensionality, and parts of the design assume a three-dimensional region of space between the observer and the flatness of the motif itself. Shake your head, but it still insists in occupying space where the logical mind tells you it isn't. These coils were doing that to her. She wondered if that was why Steve was particularly taken with them.

She was about to phrase that question when she was overcome by a dizzy spell. The spirals, two maze-like hummocks, swum round making her feel as if she was turning in the opposite direction. A sensation of nausea tensed her stomach. Her legs were beginning to swing clear of the floor. Her arms flailed out to stop the unwanted motion.

"The breasts of the queen of ghosts," a voice spoke, though it did not sound like Steve's; it was harsher, rasping, ugly. The words stole over her emotions, taking on a weight far heavier than the mere syllables themselves. The voice continued:

"Are they not compelling?" It was spoken rhetorically. "The unwary traveller may succumb to her ways."

The malignant voice was gone as suddenly as it had appeared and so too had the illusion. Elizabeth found she was leaning into Steve's supporting arms.

"You all right?" he asked, his eyes expressing concern.

"Mmm. Dizzy, just a dizzy spell. It must be too warm in here."

"Well, let's sit you down for a while, eh?" Steve was leading her by the elbow to a nearby bench.

"No, really, Steve. I feel so silly. I'm okay. Really." Several people were staring and she felt slightly embarrassed. They sat nevertheless and Elizabeth was grateful to be able to feel cool marble walls at her back.

"You look like you're about to ask me a question?" Steve was rummaging in a bag for the guidebook.

Elizabeth was about to ask him whether the wormy carvings had had a similar effect on him. Instead, she said, "Who, or what is the 'queen of ghosts'?"

"Quite a question for someone with a professed lack of mythological knowledge," he replied.

She looked at him, smiled sweetly at his expression of mock disdain and said nothing. He finally relented. "She, the queen of ghosts, is Hecate, a minor deity in Greek myth, but she's assumed a wider influence world-wide—darkly linked to the ghastly underworld," he added with an amused, sinister flourish.

"Any connection with those trinket boxes?" Elizabeth found herself asking despite the thought of having to explain to him her auditory hallucination.

"Well, not that I'm aware of . . . Might be worth a little research though. But—"

Elizabeth knew what was coming and interrupted. "Well, I'm feeling much better now. Fancy a trip down Mycenae way? It's the next room . . ."

"I'm not too good in the sun," he had said, talking about sunbathing. Naturally, Elizabeth had thought, his freckled body that had made him so attractive to her in the first place. And that wiry red hair. She also liked the soft New England accent in his voice and his lack of brashness. It was interesting to discover a man less outgoing and more reserved than her, especially in an American. Her own job, in catering, meant she led a busy lifestyle, travelling and talking to clients about menus and venues; preparing the food and presentation with her small staff, and so on. Elizabeth's idea of a holiday, therefore, was to keep off her feet as much as possible.

The boat swayed rhythmically on a calm Aegean sea. The sensation was hypnotic. Elizabeth relaxed on a spare bit of deck in her bikini, her brown body deliciously warm, and she could almost feel her auburn hair becoming bleached in the hot sun. The mix of voices from the other passengers provided a background drone along with the sputtering of the boat's engines. It was dreamy and pleasurable.

She felt herself drifting off, hypnagogic, aware of a dream she was about to have, a strange encounter on Delos, deep into the phantasmal past when Zeus chained the wandering island to the bottom of the Aegean with adamantine chains.

"Here, hold this," Zeus said, his voice a soft lilt for such a god. Elizabeth stirred, unwilling to allow the waking dream to finish, but Zeus—no, it was Steve—shook her shoulder. "Don't fall asleep in this sun!" She opened her soft brown eyes and frowned at him.

"I was just about to have a good time with Zeus," she said, smiling. "And don't worry about me—it's you who needs to keep out of the sun, Steve."

"Don't bother about that now, here, take hold of this." He handed her his rucksack loaded with camera equipment. "It might slip off the boat." He then turned to the rail and pointed his lens seaward. In the distance were islands. You couldn't escape them in this part of the world, but the tour guide was telling everyone that they could now observe Delos.

"There she blows," Steve puffed as he pushed his sunglasses back on his head, squinting his pale blue eyes briefly before hiding them behind the camera. Tourists were stirring, their lethargy over as the distant island closed towards them.

The dusky female Greek voice boomed from the loudspeaker once more. "Well ladees and chentlemen, we are nearly at the ancien' islan' of Delos. I c'hope you will enjoy your afternoon here. Remember, please," she continued while Elizabeth pulled on a pale pink blouse and shorts, "you belonck here only four 'ours and you mus' return back to the boat by four-thirty. Thankyou."

Within half an hour they had all disembarked from a small jetty and began to wander slowly inland under the dry, burning sun. Steve was risking his arms, exposed from the sleeves of a tee-shirt, but he wore jeans and hot-looking hiking boots. Elizabeth began to wonder briefly if her flat shoes were the right choice after all, looking at the terrain. Some people, she observed, had gone straight to the small museum to be in the shade or to find refreshments. Delos might well be an unmissable stop for Greek history, Elizabeth thought, but four hours in this heat, with virtually no shade, was almost frightening. The island spread out in front of them as Steve headed for the Agora, the large, worn grey blocks of the old market place reminding her that time had stood still here. In the distance the gentle slope of Mount Cynthus rose up out of the small island. Steve's camera began to click, providing a counterpoint to the never-ending rasp of the cicadas hidden in the sparse, sun-bleached grasses that grew between the tumbled blocks of the ruins.

It had been hot in Athens, but this! Elizabeth began to perspire. How did Steve manage in those clothes, and the rucksack, she asked herself. Cynthus' domed peak was hazed by the rising heat and it made her think back to that evening, the lovely cool evening on Lykabettos where Steve had taken her after the museum. At night the distant lights of Athens had spread below them, a twinkling, moving wash of jewels. They had drunk some wine at the restaurant and felt the cool breeze while moths flitted around the lamps. And, she thought, they'd gone up Lykabettos hill in the cable car. Mount Cynthus had no such luxury to reach its ancient theatre and sprawling ruins. No cool wind either, but instead an open blue sky through which the sun flared, white-hot.

The heat-haze was apparently making arabesques in front of Elizabeth before she realised she was walking on the ancient floor of a house, its remarkably preserved mosaic surface a disturbingly familiar labyrinthine pattern. Steve had sat by the remains of a wall and was changing film. "Did you know," he said, "that this place was once *the* cultural and trading empire of the Greeks?" He clicked the back of the camera shut. "Got it." Elizabeth had heard the tour guide on the boat, but knew that Steve probably had even greater knowledge about the island. She sighed. It wasn't that she lacked interest, but the heat . . .

A lizard, the palest green colour, scuttled across marble walls. Cicadas hummed. Suddenly, she realised that there was no one else, other than Steve, nearby. The harbour was invisible, hidden by the contours of the land. The only sound was the island's ancient insect inhabitants. They stood between what remained of the walls of what was probably a merchant's house, on hot mosaics, with a well in the corner. Elizabeth looked down to see black water deep below, as unmoving as the fugitive shadow she glimpsed within it. Other crumbling buildings surrounded them, with a profusion of tall, yellow grass finding hospitality everywhere.

Steve stood up and began looking at his guidebook. "The French first started excavating here in eighteen-seventy-three," he offered. "And it's continued right up to the present day."

"Yes I know. This place is 'second only to Pompeii for archeological completeness,' " Elizabeth quoted. "I heard the guide tell us." The parched grass was so still, like a photograph. Nothing stirred.

"But isn't it magnificent," Steve added, apparently unaware of an atmosphere Elizabeth was too easily detecting. "The shrines and temples and houses of a cosmopolitan city . . ."

"It's beginning to give me the creeps."

"What?" Click went the shutter. "It's all ruins. There's nobody here except us tourists."

"Where are they then?" She shuddered, despite the burning she felt on her legs. Elizabeth struggled with her thoughts, to find coherence, but the nagging worry didn't surface. "There might be snakes." It was the first thing she could think of saying.

"Well there are supposed to be poisonous snakes here . . ." Steve suddenly thought better of continuing. He put his arm round Elizabeth's shoulders and kissed her lightly on the lips. They embraced. No emotional entanglements, she reminded herself. She'd never see him again after her holiday. Nevertheless, she found the press of his body against hers comforting amidst those dry, ancient, watchful ruins.

Mount Cynthus' human artefacts climbed in front of them. Both Steve and Elizabeth were sweltering, sweating profusely now. The island was spreading out behind and below them, the sea a rich blue, invitingly cool. Steve was running through his films, this time using a zoom lens, back down to the distant architecture of the Terrace of the Lions and the four remaining columns of the Poseidoniasts building. Elizabeth could at last see people, in the distance, like gaily coloured ants crawling about, and behind them the reassuring harbour and the tourist boats, lazily bobbing.

"Those lions used to border a sacred lake which was fed from a spring somewhere on this mountain, if you can call it a mountain." Elizabeth mumbled that she *had* heard as they stumbled on upwards, past the half-moon of the amphitheatre. She could hardly believe there had ever been surface water on such a desiccated island.

"Who was it again," she asked, "that this island was sacred to?"

Steve turned back to face her, his sunglasses a burnished black, hiding his weak eyes. "Delos was the birthplace of Apollo and Artemis, you know, the offspring of Zeus and the mortal, Leto." Wasn't Artemis related in some way to Hecate? Steve asked himself inconsequentially.

"God of the Sun and Goddess of the Moon?"

"Yeah!" He was pleased that at last she seemed to be taking an interest in their expedition.

On a different tack Elizabeth sat and said, "D'you mind if we have a rest, Steve?"

He didn't say anything, but stood wiping the sheen of wet from his reddened brow. They had been on the island for an hour and a half and to her it had seemed forever. It was a fascinating place, of that there was no doubt, but the sun was merciless and the quiet stillness unnerved Elizabeth. It was so unlike the ruins in Athens, those ponderous columns and temples, full of people, surrounded by the heartening life of the modern city. Here a dreamlike atmosphere washed over her and curious, unsurfaced fears slowly paced the depths of her mind. She had heard of the unseen presences supposed to stalk the island, Steve had told her that. She could believe it.

"Why did they take away all the graves?" Elizabeth asked. It was merely one mystery, if not another, but those thoughts disturbed her, especially now they had almost become part of Delos. The rest of the four hours might be an eternity.

"In five-forty BC Delos was purified and all corpses removed from ground visible from the Sanctuary," Steve recapitulated his Greek history, nodding to the peak of the hill. "Then later all ancient tombs were excavated and removed. Since then," he added, "no births or deaths have been allowed on the island, nobody is allowed to stay permanently."

"And nobody lives here now . . ."

"They were all taken to Rhenea."

"Who, the inhabitants?" She removed a wet-wipe from her bag and breathed a languid sigh as she wiped her face with the cold tissue. Dust scrambled as her foot slid quickly away from an unusually inquisitive lizard. A few forlorn poppies stood out against the stones from whose cracks they grew.

"No," he answered, "the cadavers. They were re-buried over there, behind Hecate's Isle." There was that name again! He pointed to the nearby island which was clearly visible from the hill. It looked much like any small Greek island from where they sat, but Elizabeth thought it would be better not to visit such a place. She hoped that there was not some additional boat trip available to Rhenea. It was unlikely. After all, they'd only two hours left on Delos before their little Greek craft would drift, seemingly unaided, back to Naxos by way of Myconos. That deep Aegean sea beckoned to her, a safe haven from the morbid marble statuary of Delos.

It was with a feeling of immense relief to Elizabeth when finally they reached the sanctuary area, despite its history of despoiled graves and disinterred corpses. That last few minutes and she thought she might pass out. Mount Cynthus had been beaten on one of the hottest days of the season. She could see that Steve was also visibly wilting. His camera had for some time hung unused from its neck strap, swinging slightly as he negotiated the tumbled terrain. The panorama below them was magnificent, but Elizabeth was in no mood to appreciate it. She headed numbly for the sanctuary.

She had expected something more imposing, but it was merely more tumbled masonry. There was a cave, however, albeit one man-made. It consisted of a natural fissure with a pitched roof of large, dressed granite slabs forming a peak about six feet high. At the entrance there were also a number of smaller stones forming a wall and leaving a narrow passage into its short twelve foot length. The most immediate thing Elizabeth noticed was that it offered the one thing that the whole of the rest of Delos did not—shade. She gratefully scrambled inside.

"I wonder if we'll have time to look round the museum?" Steve slid in beside her.

Elizabeth looked at her watch, frowning at the thought of a hasty scramble back down the hillside. "I don't think there's time . . ." She began to feel terribly tired and wanted most of all to sleep, just forty winks before venturing out. "I must have a breather, Steve." Her worried frown caught his wandering attention.

"Sorry, Liz, I wasn't thinking. We've still got an hour. You relax here for twenty minutes." He stood up. "I'll do a bit more exploring—around the old boneyard! Here—" He opened his ruck-sack and took out a couple of cans of beer, still reasonably cool despite the temperature to which they had been subjected.

"Oh, manna!"

"Forgot I'd brought them until now. Delos is a pretty striking place!" Steve gave her one of his idiotic waves from his brow with his head leaning to one side and a half-sick smile on his face. Elizabeth smiled at him encouragingly. He departed the cave, for a moment his body engulfing the light and making the interior suddenly very dark.

Elizabeth relaxed, savouring the relative coolness of the cave. She took the rucksack and bundled it behind her head, stretching out. Gritty dust clung to the film of perspiration on the back of her legs, but she forgot any discomfort as sleep insisted her eyes close and her mind begin to drift right-brain-wards, slowly spiralling into slumber, down like a journey back through time's indefinable continuum. She snapped back alert briefly, her left brain rightly reminding her that she had not quenched her undoubted thirst with one, or possibly both the cans of beer. The moment passed unfulfilled and sleep gratefully came.

"Oh no!"

"Mmnn . . .?" Elizabeth was, curiously she thought for her, quickly pulling off her shorts. Bits of sharp stone cut into her buttocks. A figure leaned over her in darkness, its face totally obscured. She could feel heat coming from its body and she knew it was a golden, beautiful body, like a classical Greek statue. She gasped as the masculine shape moved forwards.

"Wake up!" She felt her shoulder being shaken vigorously, but not the expected penetration.

"Oh . . . Oh! Steve . . .?" She was at last awake and didn't much like the timing. "What's the matter with you?" It was only then that she noticed that in reality it was nearly as dark as in the dream. "What time—"

"We've missed it, damn!" he cursed. Elizabeth stood and ran to the cave's entrance. Dusk was beginning to carpet the distant sea a rich, wine-dark red from the setting sun. So, they'd missed their boat back to civilisation.

"Where've you been, Steve?" Elizabeth felt slightly angry, but it was tempered with a desire to laugh at the absurdity of their situation.

He looked her her sheepishly. "I fell asleep as well." No more explanation was necessary. Delos had secured their undivided attention for at least the next eighteen hours.

"Perhaps they're still waiting," Elizabeth said as the realisation sunk in, but no, she could still see the harbour and it was deserted. Nearby the museum building was in darkness. They were the only people left on Delos.

"I'm sorry, Liz." He looked like he genuinely was too. "We can sleep in this cave and be down at the harbour by midday tomorrow. We'll be back on Naxos in time for dinner."

Elizabeth examined her surroundings, but the dream she'd half remembered had decided her. "I'd rather not," she answered him. "Can't we find a place nearer the shore?" But of course to trek down the hill in near darkness was foolish, it was bad enough trying to avoid the ankle-twisting, overgrown chunks of Delos' former glory in daylight. Before he could answer, she said, jokingly, "No. I know this is the safest place to stay now. At least we have shelter should it rain!"

They both sat quietly for a hour, saying very little. The sun finally gave up the day and the night was blacker than they could ever have imagined, except that there were stars in the sky, and over on Rhenea a few lights twinkled. A far cry, Elizabeth recalled, from Athens' bejewelled night, where every precious gem's colour was represented by streetlamps, houses, automobiles, displays, and sudden diamond-sparks from trolleybus cables.

Dinner consisted of a can of beer each—how glad Elizabeth was that sleep had saved them!—and a few biscuits and pistachios Steve found in his rucksack. They both ate and drank slowly; there was a long night ahead and it was still quite early. There'd be no browsing down by the quayside to find a suitable taverna. No embarrassed look around the owner's kitchen to choose their meal. No lingering, warm wash of wine and calm sea to lull the senses.

Later, the quietness began to make Elizabeth's flesh crawl. The atmosphere didn't appear to affect Steve, who was leaning, like herself, at the entrance to the grotto, breathing deeply and gazing enigmatically at the starry heavens. For some reason the expected rasp of the cicadas was absent and the sea was so calm and distant that any sounds it issued did not reach them. She felt far from sleep now, yet yearned for a dream as powerful as that she had had earlier, as eloquent as all her dreams had been whilst on vacation. She hoped that the cool night would not drive her inside the cave. There might be snakes in there now. She was reminded of the serpentine forms that writhed beautifully, yet balefully she thought, in mosaics on the floor of one of the roofless temples they'd visited; of scorpions and the whole spectrum of beasts which, to modern Western minds, held evil intent but which soared to god-like heights in the ancients' collective mind.

When she looked up again out of her reverie, Steve was no longer there. Now where had he gone?

"Steve," she called gently towards the cave. There was no answer. The answer, she smiled, was simple: a call of nature. A small breeze cracked the dry grass at her feet and whispered around the sanctuary like a primeval, probing oread, wandering up the hill from its pleasures among the ruins and wondering at the strange being sitting in front of the antrum where once Apollo had been worshipped. Maybe that mountain nymph had never seen human-kind for hundreds of years on those desolate Delos nights?

A mist was drifting up the hill and before he knew it, Steve was engulfed in its clammy caress. If anyone had asked why he had wandered off just then, he doubted he could consciously say. It felt the right thing to do, but the grey swathes curling around him were nightmarishly unreal on this warm night. He ought to return to Liz and try to settle down and get some sleep. Nothing could be done until morning. If he turned carefully he could easily grope his way back without getting lost.

He took cautious steps, fretfully searching the ground for pitfalls and in his concentration the lone, quiet yowl of a dog went unheard. Had he heard the sound, his myth-imbued mind would immediately have realised its portent. It was made only once, though, before the hag came to him. Hecate, the Goddess that Appears on the Way, was monstrously garbed in the raimant of a cadaver, her dark hair like strings of snakes, her face dry and mummified, her eyes luminous shards. Under a shroud of fine-spun silk her withered breasts were clearly visible. His eyes met hers through the fog and he knew that time and reality had finally become spent forces for him. If the ritual purifications of Delos had been started by the Priests, these things were now continued under the guidance of Gods. Delos was still a place where no living being lingered after dark and if the dead returned, it was to ensure that sanctity was forever preserved.

Steve was surprised at his mind's ability to think rationally as the corpse approached. Large hands, talons of aged flesh, reached to grasp his skull and he managed to scream only briefly as the cold, hard white thumbs forced their way between his lips and pressed his vibrating tongue down the back of his throat.

As the breeze died away a noise below startled Elizabeth, somewhere on the darkened slope of Cynthus. It sounded like tumbling stones or loose footfalls among the debris. Why would Steve go that far for a pee?

The night held a beauty that transcended her mundane thoughts. Its beauty was dark and alien, thousands of years old and still breathing a life as real as the lambent lights which now played over the remains of the cemetery. Elizabeth peered through the gloom, puzzling at the sudden flickering, flame-like flashes of light. Fireflies, maybe.

A glow seemed to lift above Hecate's Isle, or it may have been over Rhenea beyond. Immediately Elizabeth thought about the purification pit where Delos' long dead were re-lain. Loose chippings of stone began again to tumble down the slope, with the loud clarity only former silence can imbue such sounds with.

"Steve . . .?" Elizabeth stood and glanced around, finding only fear in her inability to penetrate the darkness. It was almost as if he'd never been here, a form as hallucinatory to her now as the city of Athens was. She began to feel anger at her descent into irrationality, but that descent was inexorable, driven by a growing terror at the dreamlike predicament she was in. She wanted to shout, to scream out Steve's name, he must be nearby. He must . . . Had he caught the boat back to Naxos and left her stranded with a mischievious hallucination of himself for a companion? It dawned on Elizabeth that Steve may never have been real—

Now she was being absurd!

She finally overcame her fear of the benighted hill and took to the friendless maw of the cave. She felt her way in, choking on the dust her shoes raised. Something—only for a second did her mind feel relief that Steve had returned—with strong, cold hands grabbed her arms and she could smell an obnoxious, a poisonous fetor from the darkness a little above her face. "Ste—!" But it wasn't, couldn't have been him.

The invisible figure was merciless in its actions, which Elizabeth quickly realised were those of something not living. Above all, the stench of death was forced into her nostrils and dry, crumbling flesh pressed down upon her. She was saved by the darkness from seeing the face that belonged to the hard, cold, half-slimy tongue which opened her lips and forced its attentions upon her own. Elizabeth felt silken fabric between her and the pressure of iron-hard breasts; and the posturing proboscis opening her jaws to cracking point while long-dead saliva dribbled down her throat. The sensation sent her reeling into the safe haven of unconsciousness, but not before her mind induced her to believe that this visitant to Delos was one of Rhenea's long dead guardians.

Dawn was like a red curse over the slopes of Delos. Steve and Elizabeth mused over it as they gazed hypnotically across the bay. They didn't really appreciate their changed viewpoint or their new flesh, such as it was. The vista from Rhenea was very familiar and had been for millenia. They sighed together, and gathering up age-tattered robes, made their way back down a long underground tunnel to join their purified dead as the sun's strong light began to bask the empty slopes of distant Cynthus. They knew that Apollo's birthplace could never harbour the dead, or the living, for long . . .

GENE WOLFE

Lord of the Land

GENE WOLFE was born in New York and grew up in Houston, where he attended Edgar Allan Poe Elementary School, an accident which he admits seems to have shaped much of his life.

In 1984 he resigned from his position as senior editor of *Plant Engineering Magazine* to write full time. Besides the four volumes that make up the award-winning "The Book of the New Sun" (*The Shadow of the Torturer, The Claw of the Conciliator, The Sword of the Lictor* and *The Citadel of the Autarch*), his books include *The Fifth Head of Cerberus, The Devil in a Forest, Peace, Free Live Free, Soldier of the Mist, The Urth of the New Sun, There Are Doors, Soldier of Arete* and *Castleview.*

Some of his short fiction has been collected in *The Island of Doctor Death and Other Stories and Other Stories* ("that's the title," he points out, "not a typo"), *Gene Wolfe's Book of Days, Storeys* ("ditto") *From the Old Hotel* and *Endangered Species.* His most recent book is *Pandora By Holly Hollander*, a mystery novel, and a new science fiction volume, titled *Nightside the Long Sun*, is forthcoming.

"Lord of the Land" is the author's tribute to both Edgar Allan Poe and particularly H.P. Lovecraft, who he describes as "the only writer of stature to extend the tradition in horror Poe created."

THE NEBRASKAN SMILED WARMLY, leaned forward, and made a sweeping gesture with his right hand, saying, "Yes indeed, that's exactly the sort of thing I'm most interested in. Tell me about it, Mr Thacker, please."

All this was intended to keep old Hop Thacker's attention away from the Nebraskan's left hand, which had slipped into his left jacket pocket to turn on the miniature recorder there. Its microphone was pinned to the back of the Nebraskan's lapel, the fine brown wire almost invisible.

Perhaps old Hop would not have cared in any case; old Hop was hardly the shy type. "Waul," he began, "this was years an' years back, the way I hear'd it. Guess it'd have been in my great granpaw's time, Mr Cooper, or mebbe before."

The Nebraskan nodded encouragingly.

"There's these three boys, an' they had an old mule, wasn't good fer nothin' 'cept crowbait. One was Colonel Lightfoot— course didn't nobody call him colonel then. One was Creech an' t'other 'un . . ." The old man paused, fingering his scant beard. "Guess I don't rightly know. I *did* know. It'll come to me when don't nobody want to hear it. He's the one had the mule."

The Nebraskan nodded again. "Three young men, you say, Mr Thacker?"

"That's right, an' Colonel Lightfoot, he had him a new gun. An' this other 'un—he was a friend of my grandpaw's or somebody—he had him one everybody said was jest about the best shooter in the county. So this here Laban Creech, he said *he* wasn't no bad shot hisself, an' he went an' fetched his'un. He was the 'un had that mule. I recollect now.

"So they led the ol' mule out into the medder, mebbe fifty straddles from the brake. You know how you do. Creech, he shot it smack in the ear, an' it jest laid down an' died, it was old, an' sick, too, didn't kick or nothin'. So Colonel Lightfoot, he fetched out his knife an' cut it up the belly, an' they went on back to the brake fer to wait out the crows."

"I see," the Nebraskan said.

"One'd shoot, an' then another, an' they'd keep score. An' it got to be near to dark, you know, an' Colonel Lightfoot with his new gun an' this other man that had the good 'un, they was even up, an' this Laban Creech was only one behind 'em. Reckon there was near to a hundred crows back behind in the gully. You can't jest shoot a crow an' leave him, you know, an' 'spect the rest to come. They look an' see that dead 'un, an' they say, Waul, jest look what become of *him*. I don't calc'late to come anywheres near *there*."

The Nebraskan smiled. "Wise birds."

"Oh, there's all kinds of stories 'bout 'em," the old man said. "Thankee, Sarah."

His granddaughter had brought two tall glasses of lemonade; she paused in the doorway to dry her hands on her red-and-white checkered apron, glancing at the Nebraskan with shy alarm before retreating into the house.

"Didn't have a lick, back then." The old man poked an ice cube with one bony, somewhat soiled finger. "Didn't have none when I was a little 'un, neither, till the TVA come. Nowadays you talk 'bout the TVA an' they think you mean them programs, you know." He waved his glass. "I watch 'em sometimes."

"Television," the Nebraskan supplied.

"That's it. Like, you take when Bud Bloodhat went to his reward, Mr Cooper. Hot? You never seen the like. The birds all had their mouths open, wouldn't fly fer anything. Lost two hogs, I recollect, that same day. My paw, he wanted to save the meat, but 'twasn't a bit of good. He says he thought them hogs was rotten 'fore ever they dropped, an' he was 'fraid to give it to the dogs, it was that hot. They was all asleepin' under the porch anyhow. Wouldn't come out fer nothin'."

The Nebraskan was tempted to reintroduce the subject of the crow shoot, but an instinct born of thousands of hours of such listening prompted him to nod and smile instead.

"Waul, they knowed they had to git him under quick, didn't they? So they got him fixed, cleaned up an' his best clothes on an' all like that, an' they was all in there listenin', but it was terrible hot in there an' you could smell him pretty strong, so by an' by I jest snuck out. Wasn't nobody payin' attention to *me*, do you see? The women's all bawlin' an' carryin' on, an' the men thinkin' it was time to put him under an' have another."

The old man's cane fell with a sudden, dry rattle. For a moment as he picked it up, the Nebraskan glimpsed Sarah's pale face on the other side of the doorway.

"So I snuck out on the stoop. I bet it was a hundred easy, but it felt good to me after bein' inside there. That was when I seen it comin' down the hill t'other side of the road. Stayed in the shadow much as it could, an' looked like a shadow itself, only you could see it move, an' it was always blacker than what they was. I knowed it was the soul-sucker an' was afeered it'd git my ma. I took to cryin', an' she come outside an' fetched me down the spring fer a drink, an' that's the last time anybody ever did see it, far's I know."

"Why do you call it the soul-sucker?" the Nebraskan asked.

"'Cause that's what it does, Mr Cooper. Guess you know it ain't only folks that has ghosts. A man can see the ghost of another man, all right, but he can see the ghost of a dog or a mule or anythin' like that, too. Waul, you take a man's, 'cause that don't make so much argyment. It's his soul, ain't it? Why ain't it in Heaven or down in the bad place like it's s'possed to be? What's it doin' in the haint house, or walkin' down the road, or wherever 'twas you seen it? I had a dog that seen a ghost one time, an' that'n was another dog's, do you see? *I* never did see it, but he did, an' I knowed he did by how he acted. What was it doin' there?"

The Nebraskan shook his head. "I've no idea, Mr Thacker."

"Waul, I'll tell you. When a man passes on, or a horse or a dog or whatever, it's s'pposed to git out an' git over to the Judgment. The Lord Jesus Christ's our judge, Mr Cooper. Only sometimes it won't do it. Mebbe it's afeared to be judged, or mebbe it has this or that to tend to down here yet, or anyhow reckons it does, like showin' somebody some money what it knowed about. Some does that pretty often, an' I might tell you 'bout some of them times. But if it don't have business an' is jest feared to go, it'll stay where 'tis—that's the kind that haints their graves. They b'long to the soul-sucker, do you see, if it can git 'em. Only if it's hungered it'll suck on a live person, an' he's bound to fight or die." The old man paused to wet his lips with lemonade, staring across his family's little burial plot and fields of dry cornstalks to purple hills where he would never hunt again. "Don't win, not particular often. Guess the first 'un was a Indian, mebbe. Somethin' like that. I tell you how Creech shot it?"

"No you didn't, Mr Thacker." The Nebraskan took a swallow of his own lemonade, which was refreshingly tart. "I'd like very much to hear it."

The old man rocked in silence for what seemed a long while. "Waul," he said at last, "they'd been shootin' all day. Reckon I said that. Fer a good long time anyhow. An' they was tied, Colonel Lightfoot an' this here Cooper was, an' Creech jest one behind 'em. 'Twas Creech's time next, an' he kept on sayin' to stay fer jest one more, then he'd go an' they'd all go, hit or miss. So they stayed, but wasn't no more crows 'cause they'd 'bout kilt every crow in many a mile. Started gittin' dark fer sure, an' this Cooper, he says, Come on, Lab, couldn't nobody hit nothin' now. You lost an' you got to face up.

"Creech, he says, waul, 'twas my mule. An' jest 'bout then here comes somethin' bigger'n any crow, an' black, hoppin' 'long the ground like a crow will sometimes, do you see? Over towards that dead mule. So Creech ups with his gun. Colonel Lightfoot, he allowed afterwards he couldn't have seed his sights in that dark. Reckon he jest sighted 'longside the barrel. 'Tis the ol' mountain way, do you see, an' there's lots what swore by it.

"Waul, he let go an' it fell over. You won, says Colonel Lightfoot, an' he claps Creech on his back, an' let's go. Only this Cooper, he knowed it wasn't no crow, bein' too big, an' he goes over to see what 'twas. Waul, sir, 'twas like to a man, only crooked-legged an' wry neck. 'Twasn't no man, but like to it, do you see? Who shot me? it says, an' the mouth was full of worms. Grave worms, do you see?

"Who shot me? An' Cooper, he said Creech, then he hollered fer Creech an' Colonel Lightfoot. Colonel Lightfoot says, boys, we got to bury this. An' Creech goes back to his home place an' fetches a spade an' a ol' shovel, them bein' all he's got. He's shakin' so bad they jest rattled together, do you see? Colonel Lightfoot an' this Cooper, they seed he couldn't dig, so they goes hard at it. Pretty soon they looked around, an' Creech was gone, an' the soul-sucker, too."

The old man paused dramatically. "Next time anybody seed the soul-sucker, 'twas Creech. So he's the one I seed, or one of his kin anyhow. Don't never shoot anythin' without you're dead sure what 'tis, young feller."

Cued by his closing words, Sarah appeared in the doorway. "Supper's ready. I set a place for you, Mr Cooper. Pa said. You sure you want to stay? Won't be fancy."

The Nebraskan stood up. "Why, that was very kind of you, Miss Thacker."

His granddaughter helped the old man rise. Propped by the cane in his right hand and guided and supported by her on his left, he shuffled slowly into the house. The Nebraskan followed and held his chair.

"Pa's washin' up," Sarah said. "He was changin' the oil in the tractor. He'll say grace. You don't have to get my chair for me, Mr Cooper, I'll put on till he comes. Just sit down."

"Thank you." The Nebraskan sat across from the old man.

"We got ham and sweet corn, biscuits, and potatoes. It's not no company dinner."

With perfect honesty the Nebraskan said, "Everything smells wonderful, Miss Thacker."

Her father entered, scrubbed to the elbows but bringing a tang of crankcase oil to the mingled aromas from the stove. "You hear all you wanted to, Mr Cooper?"

"I heard some marvelous stories, Mr Thacker," the Nebraskan said.

Sarah gave the ham the place of honor before her father. "I think it's truly fine, what you're doin', writin' up all these old stories 'fore they're lost."

Her father nodded reluctantly. "Wouldn't have thought you could make a livin' at it, though."

"He don't, pa. He teaches. He's a teacher." The ham was followed by a mountainous platter of biscuits. Sarah dropped into a chair. "I'll fetch our sweet corn and potatoes in just a shake. Corn's not quite done yet."

"O Lord, bless this food and them that eats it. Make us thankful for farm, family, and friends. Welcome the stranger 'neath our roof as we do, O Lord. Now let's eat." The younger Mr Thacker rose and applied an enormous butcher knife to the ham, and the Nebraskan remembered at last to switch off his tape recorder.

Two hours later, more than filled, the Nebraskan had agreed to stay the night. "It's not real fancy," Sarah said as she showed him to their vacant bedroom, "but it's clean. I just put those sheets and the comforter on while you were talkin' to Grandpa." The door creaked. She flipped the switch.

The Nebraskan nodded. "You anticipated that I'd accept your father's invitation."

"Well, he hoped you would." Careful not to meet his eye, Sarah added, "I never seen Grandpa so happy in years. You're goin' to talk to him some more in the mornin'? You can put the stuff from your suitcase right here in this dresser. I cleared out these top drawers, and I already turned your bed down for you. Bathroom's on past Pa's room. You know. I guess we seem awful country to you, out here."

"I grew up on a farm near Fremont, Nebraska," the Nebraskan told her. There was no reply. When he looked around, Sarah was blowing a kiss from the doorway; instantly she was gone.

With a philosophical shrug, he laid his suitcase on the bed and opened it. In addition to his notebooks, he had brought his well-thumbed copy of *The Types of the Folktale* and Schmit's *Gods Before the Greeks*, which he had been planning to read. Soon the Thackers would assemble in their front room to watch television. Surely he might be excused for an hour or two? His unexpected arrival later in the evening might actually give them pleasure. He had a sudden premonition that Sarah, fair and willow-slender, would be sitting alone on the sagging sofa, and that there would be no unoccupied chair.

There was an unoccupied chair in the room, however; an old but sturdy-looking wooden one with a cane bottom. He carried it to the window and opened Schmit, determined to read as long as the light lasted. Dis, he knew, had come in his chariot for the souls of departed Greeks, and so had been called the Gatherer of Many by those too fearful to name him; but Hop Thacker's twisted and almost pitiable soul-sucker appeared to have nothing else in common with the dark and kingly Dis. Had there been some still earlier deity who clearly prefigured the soul-sucker? Like most folklorists, the Nebraskan firmly believed that folklore's themes were, if not actually eternal, for the most part very ancient indeed. *Gods Before the Greeks* seemed well indexed.

Dead, their mummies visited by An-uat, 2.

The Nebraskan nodded to himself and turned to the front of the book.

An-uat, Anuat, "Lord of the Land (the Necropolis)," "Opener to the North." Though frequently confused with Anubis, to whom he lent his form, it is clear that An-uat the jackal-god maintained a separate identity into the New Kingdom period. Souls that had refused to board Ra's boat (and thus to appear before the throne of the resurrected Osiris) were dragged by An-uat, who visited their mummies for this purpose, to Tuat, the lightless, demon-haunted valley stretching between the death of the old sun and the rising of the new. An-uat and the less threatening Anubis can seldom be distinguished in art, but where such distinction is possible, An-uat is the more powerfully muscled figure. Van Allen reports that An-uat is still invoked by the modern (Moslem or Coptic) magicians of Egypt, under the name Ju'gu.

The Nebraskan rose, laid the book on his chair, and strode to the dresser and back. Here was a five-thousand-year-old myth that paralleled the soul-sucker in function. Nor was it certain by any means that the similarity was merely coincidental. That the folklore of the Appalachians could have been influenced by the occult beliefs of modern Egypt was wildly improbable, but by no means impossible. After the Civil War the United States Army had imported not only camels but camel drivers from Egypt, the Nebraskan reminded himself; and the escape artist Harry Houdini had once described in lurid detail his imprisonment in the Great Pyramid. His account was undoubtedly highly colored—but had he, perhaps, actually visited Egypt as an extension of some European tour? Thousands of American servicemen must have passed through Egypt during the Second World War, but the soul-sucker tale was clearly older than that, and probably older than Houdini.

There seemed to be a difference in appearance as well; but just how different were the soul-sucker and this Ju'gu, really? An-uat had been depicted as a muscular man with a jackal's head. The soul-sucker had been . . .

The Nebraskan extracted the tape recorder from his pocket, rewound the tape, and inserted the earpiece.

Had been "like to a man, only crooked-legged an' wry neck." Yet it had not *been* a man, though the feature that separated it from humanity had not been specified. A dog-like head seemed a possibility, surely, and An-uat might have changed a good deal in five thousand years.

The Nebraskan returned to his chair and reopened his book, but the sun was already nearly at the horizon. After flipping pages aimlessly for a minute or two, he joined the Thackers in their living room.

Never had the inanities of television seemed less real or less significant. Though his eyes followed the movements of the actors on the screen, he was in fact considerably more attentive to Sarah's warmth and rather too generously applied perfume, and still more to a scene that had never, perhaps, taken place: to the dead mule lying in the field long ago, and to the marksmen concealed where the woods began. Colonel Lightfoot had no doubt been a historical person, locally famous, who would be familiar to the majority of Mr Thacker's hearers. Laban Creech might or might not have been an actual person as well. Mr Thacker had—mysteriously, now that the Nebraskan came to consider it—given the Nebraskan's own last name, Cooper, to the third and somewhat inessential marksman.

Three marksmen had been introduced because numbers greater than unity were practically always three in folklore, of course; but the use of his own name seemed odd. No doubt it had been no more than a quirk of the old man's failing memory. Remembering *Cooper*, he had attributed the name incorrectly.

By imperceptible degrees, the Nebraskan grew conscious that the Thackers were giving no more attention to the screen than he himself was; they chuckled at no jokes, showed no irritation at even the most insistent commercials, and spoke about the dismal sitcom neither to him nor to one another.

Pretty Sarah sat primly beside him, her knees together, her long legs crossed at their slender ankles, and her dishwater-reddened hands folded on her apron. To his right, the old man rocked, the faint protests of his chair as regular, and as slow, as the ticking of the tall clock in the corner, his hands upon the crook of his cane, his expression a sightless frown.

To Sarah's left, the younger Mr Thacker was almost hidden from the Nebraskan's view. He rose and went into the kitchen, cracking his knuckles as he walked, returned with neither food nor drink, and sat once more for less than half a minute before rising again.

Sarah ventured, "Maybe you'd like some cookies, or some more lemonade?"

The Nebraskan shook his head. "Thank you, Miss Thacker; but if I were to eat anything else, I wouldn't sleep."

Oddly, her hands clenched. "I could fetch you a piece of pie."

"No, thank you."

Mercifully, the sitcom was over, replaced by a many-colored sunrise on the plains of Africa. There sailed the boat of Ra, the Nebraskan reflected, issuing in splendor from the dark gorge called Tuat to give light to mankind. For a moment he pictured a far smaller and less radiant vessel, black-hulled and crowded with the recalcitrant dead, a vessel steered by a jackal-headed man: a minute fleck against the blazing disk of the African sun. What was that book of Von Daniken's? *Ships*—no, *Chariots of the Gods*. Spaceships none the less—and that was folklore, too, or at any rate was quickly passing into folklore; the Nebraskan had encountered it twice already.

An animal, a zebra, lay still upon the plain. The camera panned in on it; when it was very near, the head of a huge hyena appeared, its jaws dripping carrion. The old man turned away, his abrupt movement drawing the Nebraskan's attention.

Fear. That was it, of course. He cursed himself for not having identified the emotion pervading the living room sooner. Sarah was frightened, and so was the old man—horribly afraid. Even Sarah's father appeared fearful and restless, leaning back in his chair, then forward, shifting his feet, wiping his palms on the thighs of his faded khaki trousers.

The Nebraskan rose and stretched. "You'll have to excuse me. It's been a long day."

When neither of the men spoke, Sarah said, "I'm 'bout to turn in myself, Mr Cooper. You want to take a bath?"

He hesitated, trying to divine the desired reply. "If it's not going to be too much trouble. That would be very nice."

Sarah rose with alacrity. "I'll fetch you some towels and stuff."

He returned to his room, stripped, and put on pajamas and a robe. Sarah was waiting for him at the bathroom door with a bar of Zest and half a dozen towels at least. As he took the towels the Nebraskan murmured, "Can you tell me what's wrong? Perhaps I can help."

"We could go to town, Mr Cooper." Hesitantly she touched his arm. "I'm kind of pretty, don't you think so? You wouldn't have to marry me or nothin', just go off in the mornin'."

"You are," the Nebraskan told her. "In fact, you're very pretty; but I couldn't do that to your family."

"You get dressed again." Her voice was scarcely audible, her eyes on the top of the stairs. "You say your old trouble's startin' up, you got to see the doctor. I'll slide out the back and 'round. Stop for me at the big elm."

"I really couldn't, Miss Thacker," the Nebraskan said.

In the tub he told himself that he had been a fool. What was it that girl in his last class had called him? A hopeless romantic. He could have enjoyed an attractive young woman that night (and it had been months since he had slept with a woman) and saved her from . . . what? A beating by her father? There had been no bruises on her bare arms, and he had noticed no missing teeth. That delicate nose had never been broken, surely.

He could have enjoyed the night with a very pretty young woman—for whom he would have felt responsible afterward, for the remainder of his life. He pictured the reference in *The Journal of American Folklore:* "Collected by Dr Samuel Cooper, U. Neb., from Hopkin Thacker, 73, whose granddaughter Dr Cooper seduced and abandoned."

With a snort of disgust, he stood, jerked the chain of the white rubber plug that had retained his bath water, and snatched up one of Sarah's towels, at which a scrap of paper fluttered to the yellow bathroom rug. He picked it up, his fingers dampening lined notebook filler.

Do not tell him anything grandpa told you. A woman's hand, almost painfully legible.

Sarah had anticipated his refusal, clearly; anticipated it, and coppered her bets. *Him* meant her father, presumably, unless there was another male in the house or another was expected—her father almost certainly.

The Nebraskan tore the note into small pieces and flushed them down the toilet, dried himself with two towels, brushed his teeth and resumed his pajamas and robe, then stepped quietly out into the hall and stood listening.

The television was still on, not very loudly, in the front room. There were no other voices, no sound of footsteps or of blows. What had the Thackers been afraid of? The soul-sucker? Egypt's mouldering divinities?

The Nebraskan returned to his room and shut the door firmly behind him. Whatever it was, it was most certainly none of his business. In the morning he would eat breakfast, listen to a tale or two from the old man, and put the whole family out of his mind.

Something moved when he switched off the light. And for an instant he had glimpsed his own shadow on the window blind, with that of someone or something behind him, a man even taller than he, a broad-shouldered figure with horns or pointed ears.

Which was ridiculous on the face of it. The old-fashioned brass chandelier was suspended over the center of the room; the switch was by the door, as far as possible from the windows. In no conceivable fashion could his shadow—or any other—have been cast on that shade. He and whatever he thought he had glimpsed would have to have been standing on the other side of the room, between the light and the window.

It seemed that someone had moved the bed. He waited for his eyes to become accustomed to the darkness. What furniture? The bed, the chair in which he had read—that should be beside the window where he had left it—a dresser with a spotted mirror, and (he racked his brain) a nightstand, perhaps. That should be by the head of the bed, if it were there at all.

Whispers filled the room. That was the wind outside; the windows were open wide, the old house flanked by stately maples. Those windows were visible now, pale rectangles in the darkness. As carefully as he could he crossed to one and raised the blind. Moonlight filled the bedroom; there was his bed, here his chair, in front of the window to his left. No puff of air stirred the leaf-burdened limbs.

He took off his robe and hung it on the towering bedpost, pulled top sheet and comforter to the foot of the bed, and lay down. He had heard something—or nothing. Seen something—or nothing. He thought longingly of his apartment in Lincoln, of his sabbatical—almost a year ago now—in Greece. Of sunshine on the Saronic Gulf. . .

Circular and yellow-white, the moon floated upon stagnant water. Beyond the moon lay the city of the dead, street after narrow street of silent tombs, a daedal labyrinth of death and stone. Far away, a jackal yipped. For whole ages of the world, nothing moved; painted likenesses with limpid eyes appeared to mock the empty, tumbled skulls beyond their crumbling doors.

Far down one of the winding avenues of the dead, a second jackal appeared. Head high and ears erect, it contemplated the emptiness and listened to the silence before turning to sink its teeth once more in the tattered thing it had already dragged so far. Eyeless and desiccated, smeared with bitumen and trailing rotting wrappings, the Nebraskan recognized his own corpse.

And at once he was there, lying helpless in the night-shrouded street. For a moment the jackal's glowing eyes loomed over him; its jaws closed, and his collarbone snapped. . .

The jackal and the moonlit city vanished. Bolt upright, shaking and shaken, he did not know where. Sweat streamed into his eyes.

There had been a sound.

To dispel the jackal and the accursed, sunless city, he rose and groped for the light switch. The bedroom was—or at least appeared to be—as he recalled it, save for the damp outline of his lanky body on the sheet. His suitcase stood beside the dresser; his shaving kit lay upon it; *Gods Before the Greeks* waited his return on the cane seat of the old chair.

"*You must come to me.*"

He whirled. There was no one but himself in the room, no one (as far as he could see) in the branches of the maple or on the ground below. Yet the words had been distinct, the speaker—so it had seemed—almost at his ear. Feeling an utter fool, he looked under the bed. There was nobody there, and no one in the closet.

The doorknob would not turn in his hand. He was locked in. That, perhaps, had been the noise that woke him: the sharp click of the bolt. He squatted to squint through the old-fashioned keyhole. The dim hallway outside was empty, as far as he could see. He stood; a hard object gouged the sole of his right foot, and he bent to look.

It was the key. He picked it up. Somebody had locked his door, pushed the key under it, and (possibly) spoken through the keyhole.

Or perhaps it was only that some fragment of his dream had remained with him; that had been the jackal's voice, surely.

The key turned smoothly in the lock. Outside in the hall, he seemed to detect the fragrance of Sarah's perfume, though he could not be sure. If it had been Sarah, she had locked him in, providing the key so that he could free himself in the morning. Whom had she been locking out?

He returned to the bedroom, shut the door, and stood for a moment staring at it, the key in his hand. It seemed unlikely that the crude, outmoded lock would delay any intruder long, and of course it would obstruct him when he answered—

Answered whose summons?

And why should he?

Frightened again, frightened still, he searched for another light. There was none: no reading light on the bed, no lamp on the nightstand, no floorlamp, no fixture upon any of the walls. He turned the key in the lock, and after a few seconds' thought dropped it into the topmost drawer of the dresser and picked up his book.

Abaddon. The angel of destruction dispatched by God to turn the Nile and all its waters to blood, and to kill the first-born male child in every Egyptian family. Abaddon's hand was averted from the Children of Israel, who for this purpose smeared their doorposts with the blood of the paschal lamb. This substitution has frequently been considered a foreshadowing of the sacrifice of Christ.

Am-mit, Ammit, "Devourer of the Dead." This Egyptian goddess guarded the throne of Osiris in the underworld and feasted upon the souls of those whom Osiris condemned. She had the head of a crocodile and the forelegs of a lion. The remainder of her form was that of a hippopotamus, Figure 1. Am-mit's great temple at Henen-su (Herakleopolis) was destroyed by Octavian, who had its priests impaled.

An-uat, Anuat, "Lord of the Land (the Necropolis)," "Opener to the North." Though frequently confused with Anubis—

The Nebraskan laid his book aside; the overhead light was not well adapted to reading in any case. He switched it off and lay down.

Staring up into the darkness, he pondered An-uat's strange title, Opener to the North. Devourer of the Dead and Lord of the Land seemed clear enough. Or rather Lord of the Land seemed clear once Schmit explained that it referred to the necropolis. (That explanation was the source of his dream, obviously.) Why then had Schmit not explained Opener to the North? Presumably because he didn't understand it either. Well, an opener was one who went before, the first to pass in a certain direction. He (or she) made it easier for others to follow, marking trails and so on. The Nile flowed north, so An-uat might have been thought of as the god who went before the Egyptians when they left their river to sail the Mediterranean. He himself had pictured An-uat in a boat earlier, for that matter, because there was supposed to be a celestial Nile. (Was it the Milky Way?) Because he had known that the Egyptians had believed there was a divine analog to the Nile along which Ra's sun-boat journeyed. And of course the Milky Way actually was—really is in the most literal sense—the branching star-pool where the sun floats. . .

The jackal released the corpse it had dragged, coughed, and vomited, spewing carrion alive with worms. The Nebraskan picked up a stone fallen from one of the crumbling tombs, and flung it, striking the jackal just below the ear.

It rose upon its hind legs, and though its face remained that of a beast, its eyes were those of a man. "This is for you," it said, and pointed toward the writhing mass. "Take it, and come to me."

The Nebraskan knelt and plucked one of the worms from the reeking spew. It was pale, streaked and splotched with scarlet, and woke in him a longing never felt before. In his mouth, it brought peace, health, love, and hunger for something he could not name.

Old Hop Thacker's voice floated across infinite distance: "Don't never shoot anythin' without you're dead sure what 'tis, young feller."

Another worm and another, and each as good as the last.

"We will teach you," the worms said, speaking from his own mouth. "Have we not come from the stars? Your own desire for them has wakened, Man of Earth."

Hop Thacker's voice: "Grave worms, do you see?"

"*Come to me.*"

The Nebraskan took the key from the drawer. It was only necessary to open the nearest tomb. The jackal pointed to the lock.

"If it's hungered, it'll suck on a live person, an' he's bound to fight it or die."

The end of the key scraped across the door, seeking the keyhole.

"*Come to me, Man of Earth. Come quickly.*"

Sarah's voice had joined the old man's, their words mingled and confused. She screamed, and the painted figures faded from the door of the tomb.

The key turned. Thacker stepped from the tomb. Behind him his father shouted, "Joe, boy! Joe!" And struck him with his cane. Blood streamed from Thacker's torn scalp, but he did not look around.

"Fight him, young feller! You got to fight him!"

Someone switched on the light. The Nebraskan backed toward the bed.

"Pa, *don't*!" Sarah had the huge butcher knife. She lifted it higher than her father's head and brought it down. He caught her wrist, revealing a long raking cut down his back as he spun about. The knife, and Sarah, fell to the floor.

The Nebraskan grabbed Thacker's arm. "What is this!"

"It is love," Thacker told him. "That is your word, Man of Earth. It is love." No tongue showed between his parted lips; worms writhed there instead, and among the worms gleamed stars.

With all his strength, the Nebraskan drove his right fist into those lips. Thacker's head was slammed back by the blow; pain shot along the Nebraskan's arm. He swung again, with his left this time, and his wrist was caught as Sarah's had been. He tried to back away; struggled to pull free. The high, old-fashioned bed blocked his legs at the knees.

Thacker bent above him, his torn lips parted and bleeding, his eyes filled with such pain as the Nebraskan had never seen. The jackal spoke: "*Open to me.*"

"Yes," the Nebraskan told it. "Yes, I will." He had never known before that he possessed a soul, but he felt it rush into his throat.

Thacker's eyes rolled upward. His mouth gaped, disclosing for an instant the slime-sheathed, tentacled thing within. Half falling, half rolling, he slumped upon the bed.

For a second that felt much longer, Thacker's father stood over him with trembling hands. A step backward, and the older Mr Thacker fell as well—fell horribly and awkwardly, his head striking the floor with a distinct crack.

"Grandpa!" Sarah knelt beside him.

The Nebraskan rose. The worn brown handle of the butcher knife protruded from Thacker's back. A little blood, less than the Nebraskan would have expected, trickled down the smooth old wood to form a crimson pool on the sheet.

"Help me with him, Mr Cooper. He's got to go to bed."

The Nebraskan nodded and lifted the only living Mr Thacker onto his feet. "How do you feel?"

"Shaky," the old man admitted. "Real shaky."

The Nebraskan put the old man's right arm about his own neck and picked him up. "I can carry him," he said. "You'll have to show me his bedroom."

"Most times Joe was just like always." The old man's voice was a whisper, as faint and far as it had been in the dream-city of the dead. "That's what you got to understand. Near all the time, an' when—when he did, they was dead, do you see? Dead or near to it. Didn't do a lot of harm."

The Nebraskan nodded.

Sarah, in a threadbare white nightgown that might have been her mother's once, was already in the hall, stumbling and racked with sobs.

"Then you come. An' Joe, he made us. Said I had to keep on talkin' an' she had to ask you fer supper."

"You told me that story to warn me," the Nebraskan said.

The old man nodded feebly as they entered his bedroom. "I thought I was bein' slick. It was true, though, 'cept 'twasn't Cooper, nor Creech neither."

"I understand," the Nebraskan said. He laid the old man on his bed and pulled up a blanket.

"I kilt him didn't I? I kilt my boy Joe."

"It wasn't you, Grandpa." Sarah had found a man's bandana, no doubt in one of her grandfather's drawers; she blew her nose into it.

"That's what they'll say."

The Nebraskan turned on his heel. "We've got to find that thing and kill it. I should have done that first." Before he had completed the thought, he was hurrying back toward the room that had been his.

He rolled Thacker over as far as the knife handle permitted and lifted his legs onto the bed. Thacker's jaw hung slack; his tongue and palate were thinly coated with a clear, glutinous gel that carried a faint smell of ammonia; otherwise his mouth was perfectly normal.

"It's a spirit," Sarah told the Nebraskan from the doorway. "It'll go into Grandpa now, 'cause he killed it. That's what he always said."

The Nebraskan straightened up, turning to face her. "It's a living creature, something like a cuttlefish, and it came here from—" He waved the thought aside. "It doesn't really matter. It landed in North Africa, or at least I think it must have, and if I'm right, it was eaten by a jackal. They'll eat just about anything, from what I've read. It survived inside the jackal as a sort of intestinal parasite. Long ago, it transmitted itself to a man, somehow."

Sarah was looking down at her father, no longer listening. "He's restin' now, Mr Cooper. He shot the old soulsucker in the woods one day. That's what Grandpa tells, and he hasn't had no rest since, but he's peaceful now. I was only eight or 'bout that, and for a long time Grandpa was 'fraid he'd get me, only he never did." With both her thumbs, she drew down the lids of the dead man's eyes.

"Either it's crawled away—" the Nebraskan began.

Abruptly, Sarah dropped to her knees beside her dead parent and kissed him.

When at last the Nebraskan backed out of the room, the dead man and the living woman remained locked in that kiss, her face ecstatic, her fingers tangled in the dead man's hair. Two full days later, after the Nebraskan had crossed the Mississippi, he still saw that kiss in shadows beside the road.

STEVE RASNIC TEM

Aquarium

STEVE RASNIC TEM lives with his wife, the writer Melanie Tem, in a supposedly haunted Victorian house in Denver, Colorado.

A prolific author of short stories and poems for the small press field and numerous anthology markets, recent or upcoming appearances include *Fantasy Tales 4*, *Pulphouse 7*, *Psycho Paths 2*, *New Crimes 3*, *Stalkers 3*, and books without numbers on them such as *The Fantastic Robin Hood*, *Tales of the Wandering Jew*, *Dark At Heart* and *The Year's Best Fantasy and Horror*. A collection of stories, *Ombres sur la route*, was published in France by Denoel, and collaborations with Melanie appear in *The Ultimate Frankenstein* and *The Ultimate Dracula*.

Roadkill Press has published his chapbook *Fairytales*, and another is due from Haunted Library entitled *Absences: Charlie Goode's Ghosts*.

We are pleased to welcome him back to *Best New Horror* with another fine example of his mastery of the short form . . .

IN THE ORPHANAGE THEY'D HAD AN AQUARIUM. A wooden model of the ancient, sprawling orphanage itself, open at the top, had served as a frame for the ordinary glass aquarium inside.

The orphanage was always receiving unusual gifts like that— giant gingerbread men, dolls with some president's face, doll houses modeled after some famous building. There'd be an article in the paper each time with a picture of the donor and his gift, surrounded by dozens of children with practiced smiles.

Other benefactors hosted special events. The SeaHarp used to throw parties for the children of the orphanage every year, parties that sometimes lasted for days, with the children sleeping in the hotel. Michael knew he had attended several of them, but he had been so young at the time—not more than four or five—he really couldn't remember them.

The aquarium had had a little brass plaque: "Gift of Martin O'Brien." Michael had heard that the fellow had been some sort of fisherman, and himself an orphan. Many of the gifts were supposedly from former residents of the orphanage. But Michael never actually believed that there was such a thing a former resident; the place marked you forever. Sometimes he would wonder what he would give to the orphanage when he got old and successful.

Sometimes the fish would swim up to the tiny model windows and look out. One of the older boys said that fish could barely see past their mouths, but they sure looked like they were peering out at you. As if you were a prospective parent and today was visitor's day. That's the way the children always looked on visitor's day, Michael thought: staring wide-eyed out the windows and moving their gills in and out nervously. Trying to look like whoever these prospective parents expected you to look like. Trying to look like you'd fit right into their family. Sometimes when the light was right in the aquarium room you could see your own reflection in these windows, superimposed over the fish. Looking in, and looking out. Waiting.

In the orphanage Michael used to dream that he had no face. He was waiting for someone to choose a face for him. Until then, he had the open-mouthed, wide- and wet-eyed face of a fish.

Now, in Greystone Bay, Michael got into a green cab that said "Two Crazy Brothers Cab Co." on the door. He wondered if that meant there were two identical cabs, a brother driving each one, or perhaps only one cab with which they alternated shifts—Greystone Bay was, after all, a relatively small place. Or perhaps there were dozens of such cabs, and the brothers didn't drive anymore, being president and vice-president of the company, or perhaps co-vice-presidents, their mother or father taking the largely honorary presidential post. It was difficult to know exactly who his driver was, and what he expected from him.

"Not many go to the SeaHarp this time o' year," the driver said.

Michael glanced at the rear-view mirror and fixed on the driver's eyes. Seeing just the slice of face holding the eyes bothered him. He'd never been able to tell much from eyes— people's eyes had always seemed somewhat interchangeable. Seeing just that cut-out of someone's eyes led him to imagine that they were his own eyes, transplanted somehow into someone else's shadowy face. A social worker at the orphanage had once given him a toy that rearranged slices of faces like that, a chin, a mouth, a nose, eyes, hair, all from different characters mixed and matched. After a while the particular arrangement hadn't seemed to matter. It was the very act of changing which had been important.

"You must like a quiet holiday," the cab driver said.

Michael looked at the mirror eyes which might have been his own. He wondered what the driver's mouth was like, whether it conveyed a message different from that of the eyes. "Why do you say that?"

"Like I said. Before. Nobody much comes to the SeaHarp this time of year. Thanksgiving through Christmas, right up 'til the party on New Year's Eve. Then the whole town turns out. But up 'til then, that's their dead season. People are home with their families, not in some hotel."

"Well, I don't have a family, I'm afraid."

The driver was silent a moment. Then, "Didn't think you did."

Michael held himself stiff, eyes motionless. They always seem to know. How do they always know? Then he forced himself to relax, wondering what it was the cab driver might like to see. What kind of passenger he might like and admire. Just like a good orphan. He could feel the themes of independence and "good business" entering his relaxed facial muscles, his posture.

"Too busy building a career, I guess." He let slip a self-amused chuckle. "A fellow my age, his career takes up most of his time."

"Your age?"

"Twenty-five." He'd lied by twelve years, but he could see in the mirror eyes that the driver believed him, apparently not seeing all the age signs that made that unlikely. People believed a good orphan. "I'm an architect."

A sudden, new respect in those mirror eyes. "Really? They planning to expand up there at the SeaHarp? Maybe they know some things about money coming into the Bay us regular working folk don't?"

"I really couldn't say . . ."

"Or maybe they're going to remodel. You gonna give that old lady a facelift?"

"Really. I couldn't."

"Hey, I get ya. I understand." One of the mirror eyes half-winked.

The driver offered to carry his bags up the steps to the hotel, but Michael told him that wasn't necessary. "Travel light in my business." The driver nodded as if he knew exactly what Michael was talking about. Michael gave him a generous tip anyway; he had to. Walking up the steps he wondered if he had enough expense money left.

In the dark, the SeaHarp was magnificent. Its classical lines flowed sweetly into the shadows left and right; its silhouette climbed smoothly out of the porchlight with very few of the architectural afterthoughts that spoiled the proportions of so many of its type. Outside lighting had been kept to a minimum, forcing the night-time visitor to focus on the windows—so many windows—exaggerating the width of that first floor.

But then most old buildings looked impressive in the dark. He hoped it lived up to its promise in the less forgiving daylight. That's when you could tell just how much of the SeaHarp's budget had been alloted to maintenance and repair over the years. By mid-morning he'd be able to spot any dryrot or sagging wood. He could already tell the SeaHarp had been fitted with Dutch gutters in spots—the downspouts went right up into the enclosed eaves—a real problem with water damage if they hadn't been refurbished recently.

Something bothered him about the windows. It was silly, and these little naggings he was prey to now and then made him angry; he didn't like to think of himself as irrational. Rationality had always meant safety. All the kids he'd grown up with in the orphanage and all their dreams—it had given them nothing but a crib of pain as far as he could see.

And yet he took the few steps up onto the porch and stopped, compelled to examine these windows before entering.

The glass was extraordinarily clean. A good omen. In fact the glass was so clean you'd hardly know it was there. It was an invisible barrier separating what was in—the contents, the atmosphere of the hotel—from what was out. Michael imagined the heavy pressure of that atmosphere—the accumulated breath and spirit of all those visitors over all those years—pushing mightily against that glass which had to be so strong, so finely crafted. Like an aquarium.

He stepped closer to the glass. Inside, the furniture and the carpets were of sea colors, blue and blue-green, the wall-paper a faded blue. The guests moved slowly from setting to setting. As if asleep. Or as if underwater. Their faces, blue and green, pumping the heavy, ancient hotel air. Michael wondered if they could see him outside the glass, peering into their underwater world, seeing his own face in the faces of all these fish.

He walked gingerly to the main door and opened it, took a deep breath. The moist air quickly escaped, pushing over the porch and wetting his face and hair. Stepping inside, he pulled the door tightly, sealing himself in.

He forced himself to remember who he was and the nature of the task he had been hired for.

He was pleased to see that much of the furniture in the lobby and other public areas dated back to the original construction of the hotel; whether it was original to the SeaHarp itself, of course, remained to be seen. And there was so *much* of it. On impulse he crouched as low as possible for a child's eye view, and peered along the floor at a sea of Victorian furniture legs: rosewood and black walnut with the characteristic cabriole carving and rudimentary feet supporting a Gallic ornateness of leaved, flowered, and fruited moldings and upholsteries. Here and there among the Victorian legs there were the occasional modern, straight-legged anachronisms, or, stranger still, legs of curly maple and cherry, spirally reeded or acanthus-leaf carved American Empire pieces, or, going back even further, Sheraton mahogany with satinwood. Michael wondered if the original builder—Bolgran he believed was the name—had brought some older, family pieces into the hotel when he moved in.

No one appeared to be watching, so Michael went down to his knees, lowering his head to scan the floor even better. And then he remembered: four years old, and all the legs and furniture had been trees and caves to him, as he raced across the lobby on hands and knees, so fast that Mr Dobbins, the supervisor that day, had been unable to catch him. Every time Dobbins had gotten close Michael had hidden under a particularly well-stuffed item, sitting there trying not to giggle while Dobbins called and pleaded with increasing volume. Dobbins' tightly-panted gabardine legs—old, stiff, a bit crooked—seemed like all those other legs of the forest while he was still, and once he moved it was as if the whole forest of legs moved, and when other adult legs joined the search, it felt like a forest in a hurricane, legs sliding across the floor, crashing to the floor, old voices cracking with alarm. At the time he'd thought about staying in that forest forever, maybe grabbing a few of his friends and living there, but then Dobbins had lifted the chair from over him, there was daylight and thunder overhead, and Michael was lifted skyward.

He stood up, dusted off his pants, and headed toward the desk. Still looking around. No one had noticed. Good. He made himself look professional.

Numerous secretaries and writing desks lined the far wall of the lobby, including two excellent drop-fronts of the French *secrétaire à abattant* type, built all in one piece, which must have been brought up from New Orleans at no small expense. He couldn't wait to open them up and examine the insides.

He continued to the registration desk, his eyes alert for the odd detail, the surprise.

Victor Montgomery sat motionless on the other side of his desk. He seemed strangely out of place, and yet Michael could not imagine this man being anywhere else. Perhaps it was the clothes: all of them a size too large, including the collar. But the knot of the tie was firm and tight, and the suit wasn't particularly wrinkled from enclosing a body too small for it. It was as if Montgomery had shrunk after putting the suit on. The desk appeared too large for him, as well. As did the black phone, the blotter, the desk lamp with the green glass shade. They seemed huge to Michael. And Victor Montgomery seemed an infant, forcing his small wrinkled head out of the huge collar, his baby face glowing red from the exertion, his small eyes having difficulty focusing.

"There is quite a lot to catalogue," Montgomery said, his baby eyes straying. "The furniture in all the rooms, the public areas, the storage cellars. As well as all the art and accessory items, of course. You will not be inventorying the family's private quarters or the attics, however, nor will you be permitted access to a few odd rooms. But those are locked, in any case. If there is any question, I expect you to ask."

"I can assure you there will be no problem completing the inventory in the allotted time. Perhaps even sooner." Michael permitted just a hint of laughter into his voice, thinking it might show enthusiasm.

Montgomery looked like a baby startled by a sudden noise. "I did not expect there would be."

"No, of course not. I just thought that if you were leaving the family quarters, the attics, or any other areas off my assignment for fear of the time they would take, I should reassure you that they would be no problem as well. I have done a number of these hotel inventories and have become quite efficient, I assure you."

"Any furniture in those off-limit areas I wanted inventoried has already been moved into rooms 312 and 313. You will evaluate each piece, make recommendations as to which should remain part of the SeaHarp collection—whether because of historical interest, rarity, or to illustrate a particular theme, I do not care—and which might be sold at auction. Any marginal items of dubious functionality should be disposed of as quickly and inexpensively as possible. Most importantly, I want a complete record and evaluation of all items in the hotel. I am quite sure we have been pilfered in the past and am determined to put a stop to it."

Michael nodded, doodling in his pad as if he had recorded every word. The infant's head was frighteningly red. "May I start tonight?"

"If you wish. In fact I would suggest that you do much of your work at night. That will avoid distracting the help from their work, not to mention attracting their curiosity."

"And that would be a problem?"

"I do not want them to think I distrust them. Although, of course, I do. You will be eating Thanksgiving dinner here."

Michael didn't know if that was a question or an order. "I had planned on it, if possible."

"What of your family?"

"I have none. And no other place to go this holiday."

The infant looked vaguely distressed, as if it had filled its diapers. "I am sorry to hear that. A family is a great source of strength. It is important to belong." Michael waited for him to say something specific about his own family, but he did not.

"I feel I am a member of the family of man," Michael lied.

The infant looked confused. "An orphan?"

"Yes, in fact the children of the orphanage came here over a number of years for a kind of holiday. Even I . . ."

"I was away at school most of those years," Montgomery said.

"Yes, yes, of course."

"There are no more orphanages, are there? In the United States, I mean?" Montgomery said.

"No, I don't believe there are."

"Foster homes and such, I believe. The poor orphans get real families now," Montgomery said. Michael simply nodded. The infant Montgomery was suddenly struggling to his feet, lost in his clothes, his baby's head lost in the voluminous collar. The interview was over. "I will make sure the staff prepares a suitable Thanksgiving repast for you tomorrow. After that you will have the hotel essentially to yourself. The staff will be home with their families. We Montgomerys will remain in our quarters for the following two days, at the end of which time I expect to be able to review your full report."

"Certainly." Montgomery was moving slowly around his huge desk. He seemed to be extending one sleeve. For a panicked second Michael thought he was extending his hand to him, but the infant's arms were so short Michael would never be able to find the hand, lost in the huge folds of the coat sleeve.

"One more thing." The infant yawned and its eyes rolled. Up past his bedtime, Michael mused. "Any remaining furniture should *fit* the hotel. It is very important that things fit, find their proper place. I hired you because you supposedly know about such things."

"I do, sir."

The infant lolled its head in the huge collar, then waddled off to bed.

Michael took a long, rambling, post-midnight tour of the SeaHarp's floors to get a preliminary feel for the place. He didn't at all mind working at night. Most nights he was unable to get to sleep until three or four in the morning anyway. There never seemed to be any particular reason for his insomnia—his mind simply was not yet ready for sleep. And he had no wife or children to be bothered by his sleeplessness.

The walls of the SeaHarp's public areas were well-supplied with art. There was a number of pieces by British painters in the German Romantic style. Michael had a working familiarity with art but knew he'd have to call in someone else for a proper appraisal: Reynolds from Boston or perhaps J.P. Jacobs in Providence, although Jacobs was often a bit too optimistic in his appraisals for Michael's taste. And Montgomery would want a conservative appraisal, the more conservative the better. So maybe it would have to be Reynolds. Reynolds would have a field day: there were several excellent examples of the outline style, after Retzsch. Also some nice small sculptures he was sure Reynolds could identify—if the sculptors were worth identifying—the pieces looked nice enough but Michael was out of his area here. The themes seemed to be typically classical: Venus and Cupid, Venus and Mercury. The Death of Leander. And several small pieces of children. Cupid, no doubt. But the faces were so worn. Expressionless, as if left too long underwater.

Along one stretch of wall there were so many of these small, near-featureless sculptures, raised on pedestals or recessed in alcoves, that Michael was compelled to stop and ponder. But there seemed to be no reason for it. He could not understand the emphasis of these damaged, ill-colored pieces. Literally ill-colored, he thought, for the stone was a yellowish-white, like diseased flesh, like flesh kept half-wet and half-dry for a long time. Even when he left this area he could feel the sculptures clamoring for his attention, floating into his peripheral vision like distorted embryos.

The door to room 312 creaked open. He pawed through a fur of dust for the lightswitch, and when he finally got the light on he discovered more dust hanging in strings from the ceiling, and from antique furniture stacked almost to the ceiling, obscuring the glass fixture which itself appeared to have been dipped into brown oil. Obviously, Montgomery had had the furniture moved here some time ago. He wondered why it had taken the man so long to finally decide on getting an appraiser. Or maybe it was a matter of finding the *right* appraiser. That thought made him get out of the chill of the hall and completely into the room, however dim and dusty. The sound of the door shutting was muted by the thick skin of dust over the jamb. Michael slipped the small tape recorder out of his coat pocket.

A good deal of the furniture in the room predated the hotel, late eighteenth century to early nineteenth. Bought as collectors' pieces, no doubt, by some past manager. Most of them were chairs: Chippendale mahogany wing chairs and armchairs of the Martha Washington type, late Sheraton side chairs and a few Queen Anne wing and slippers. But they varied widely in quality. Most of the Sheratons were too heavy, with rather awkward carving on the center splat, but there was one boasting a beautifully carved spread eagle and fine leg lines, worth a good ten times more than the others. The Chippendales were all too boxy and vertical in the back. Most of the Martha Washingtons suffered from shapeless arms or legs that were too short, seats often too heavy in relation to the top part of the chair, but there were two genuine masterpieces among those: finely scooped arms, serpentine crests, beautifully proportioned all around.

Some of the chairs had been virtually ruined by amateurish restoration efforts: the arms crudely embellished, mismatched replacement of a crest rail or stretcher, the legs shortened to give the chair an awkward stance. And something odd about one of the altered pieces. Michael clicked on his recorder:

"A metal rod has been added to the top of the chair, with leather straps attached." He brushed off the leather and leaned in for a closer look. "It appears to be some sort of chin strap. Another, wider leather strap has been attached to the seat. Like a seat belt, I'd say, but poorly designed. It would be much too tight, even for a child."

He gradually worked his way around the room, not trying to catalog everything, but simply trying to get a feel for the range of the pieces, highlighting anything that looked interesting. "An English Tall Clock, with a black japanned case embellished with colored portraits of both George III and George Washington. An excellent matching highboy and lowboy with cabriole legs. An early eighteenth-century high chest of drawers. Ruined because one of the cup turned legs has been lost and replaced at some point with a leg trumpet turned. A very nice India side chair with Flemish scrolls and feet . . ."

He stopped once he discovered he was standing by the window. A heavy fog had come in from the bay, had crept like steaming gray mud over the trees, and was now filling the yard to surround and isolate the SeaHarp. It seemed only fitting for such obsessive, lonely work. On the evening before his solitary Thanksgiving meal. It had been only recently that Michael realized he had no practical use for the antiques he valued so much. These were heirlooms, family icons and embodiments. Made for a family to use, for fathers and mothers to pass down to children and grandchildren. And he was someone who had no place to go for Thanksgiving. A wet fish trapped inside the aquarium. He was haunted by mothers and fathers, grandparents, generations of ancestors who—as far as he could tell—had never existed.

He had no fixed place. He was, forever, the rootless boy who cannot get along.

He got down on his hands and knees and rooted like a pig through the dust of ages. He pretended to be a professional. He examined the pieces of patina, wear, and tool marks. His fingers delicately traced the grain for the track of the jack plane. He crawled around and under the pieces, seeking out construction details. He made constant measurements, gauging proportion and dimension. "A sofa in the Louis XV style with a scroll-arched rail and a center crest of carved fruits and flowers with foliage," he chanted into the recorder held to his lips, like a singer making love to his microphone.

But in fact he was a dirty little boy, four or five, hiding in a forest of legs and upholstery. Now and then he would try out a chair or sofa, sitting the way he was supposed to sit, sitting like a grownup in uncomfortable furniture that broke the back and warped the legs and changed the body until it fit the furniture, and nothing was more important than fitting in however painful the process. "A Philadelphia walnut armchair, mid-eighteenth century, with a pierced back and early cresting." Yellow-pale, distorted children with featureless heads were strapping themselves into the chairs around him, trying to sit pretty with agreeable smiles so that visiting adults would choose them. "Three Victorian side chairs after the French style of Louis XV, both flower and fruit motifs, black walnut." Wet children with eyes bigger than their mouths pressed tighter and tighter against the glass. "Belter chair with a scroll-outlined concave back and central upholstered panel crowned by a crest of carved foliage, flowers and fruit."

He examined the wall nearer the floor. Letters were scratched into the baseboard, by something sharp. Perhaps a pocket knife. Perhaps a fingernail grown too long. V.I. He imagined a child on his knees, scratching away at the baseboard with his torn and bleeding fingernail. V.I.C.T.O.R, the baseboard cried.

The next morning he woke up from a series of strange dreams he could not remember, in the rough chair with the straps, the cracked leather chinstrap caressing his cheek like a lover's dry hand.

The morning's disorientation continued throughout the day.

Thanksgiving dinner in the Dining Room was a solitary affair; he quickly discovered that the last of the hotel's guests had left that morning and, other than two or three staff members and the Montgomerys hidden away in their quarters at the top of the hotel, he had been left to himself. An elderly waiter poured the wine.

"Compliments of Mr Montgomery, Suh," the old man creaked out.

"Well, please tell Mr Montgomery how much I appreciate it."

"Mr Montgomery feels badly that you should dine alone. And on *Thanksgiving*."

"Well, I *do* appreciate his concern." Michael tried not to look at the old man.

"Mr Montgomery says a family is a very important thing to a man. 'Families make us human,' he says."

"How interesting." Michael bolted his wine and held up his glass for more. The elderly waiter obliged. "He is close to his family, is he? And was he close to his father as well, when he was alive?"

"Mr Simon Montgomery had a strong *interest* in child-rearing. He was always looking for ways to improve his children, and read extensively on the subject. You can find some of his reading material still in the library, in fact."

"Is that why he brought the children from the orphanage here over the years?" Again, Michael bolted his wine, and again the old waiter replenished his glass.

"I suppose. Did you enjoy yourselves?"

Michael stared up at the waiter. The old man's tired red eyes were watching him carefully. Michael wanted to reach up and break through the glass wall that had suddenly surrounded him, and throttle this ancient Peeping Tom. But he couldn't move. "I don't remember," he finally said.

After dinner Michael spent several hours in the library trying to sober up so that he could continue his cataloguing. He was particularly interested in the older books, of course, and in the course of his examinations discovered the German title *Kallipädie*, 1858, by a Dr Daniel Schreber. Michael's German was rather rusty, but the book's illustrations were clear enough. A figure-eight shoulder band that tied the child's shoulders back so they wouldn't slump forward. A "Geradhalter"—a metal cross attached to the edge of a table—that prevented the child from leaning forward during meals or study. Chairs and beds with straps and halters to prevent "squirming" or "tossing and turning," guaranteed to keep the young body "straight."

Off in the distance, in some other room, Michael could hear the pounding of tiny knees on the carpet, the thunder of the old men trying to catch them.

Michael made his way down to the cellars via a door in the wall on the north side of the back porch. That door led him to a descending staircase, and the cellars. The main part of these cellars consisted of the kitchen, laundry, furnace and supply rooms, and various rooms used by the gardeners and janitors. But hidden on one end, seldom-used, were the storage cellars.

In the cellars had been stored a treasure of miscellaneous household appurtenances: some of the most ornate andirons Michael had ever seen, with dogs and lions and elephants worked into their designs; shuttlecocks and beakers; finely painted bellows and ancient bottles and all manner of brass ware (ladles, skimmers, colanders, kettles, candlesticks and the like); twenty-two elaborately stenciled tin canisters and a chafing dish in the shape of a deer (necessary to keep the colonials' freshly slain venison suitably warm); dozens of rolls of carpet which had been ill-preserved and fell into rotted clumps when he tried to examine them; a half-dozen crocks, several filled with such odd hardware as teardrop handles, bat's-wing and willow mounts, rosette knobs and wrought-iron hinges, and the largest with an assortment of wall and furniture stencils; another half-dozen pieces of Delft ware from Holland (also called "counterfeit china"); a dripping pan and a dredging box; a variety of flesh hooks and graters and latten ware and patty pans, all artifacts from earlier versions of the SeaHarp's grand kitchen; a jack for removing some long-dead gentleman's boots; a finely-made milk keeler and several old jack mangles for smoothing the hotel's linen; a rotting bag full of crumbling pillow cases (sorting through these Michael liked to imagine all the young maids' hands which had smoothed them and fluffed their pillows—they would have been calling them "pillow bears" back then); skewers and skillets; trays and trenchers; and a great wealth of wooden ware, no doubt used by some past manager in an attempt to hold down costs.

He could spend a full week cataloguing it all, which wasn't really what he wanted to do during his time at the hotel. After seeing just these more common, day-to-day, bits and pieces, he was more anxious than ever to go through the other rooms. But he could tell from his finds in the cellars that there was quite a bit of antique wealth here. If the sales were handled properly they could bring the Montgomerys a fair amount of money. And the beauty of it, of course, was that these relics were now of little use in the actual running of the hotel.

That evening Michael began his inventories of the guest rooms themselves. Most could be handled very quickly as there was little of value or interest. The only thing that slowed him was a continuation of the vague sense of disorientation he'd felt since awakening that morning. Things—most recognizably the faceless cupid statues he'd encountered his first night—hovered at the periphery of his vision, and then disappeared, much like the after-effects of some drug-induced alertness. He began to wonder if there had been something wrong with his Thanksgiving dinner—perhaps it had been the wine the old waiter had delivered so freely—and he became very careful of the things he ate, examining each glass of beverage or piece of bread or meat minutely—for consistency, pattern, tool-marks, style—before consumption.

"A tea-table with cabriole legs and slipper feet tapering finely to the toe. Like some stylish grandmother dancing. Perhaps my own, undiscovered, grandmother dancing. Second quarter of the eighteenth century, probably from Philadelphia."

The orphans squealed with delight, their tiny knees raw and bleeding from carpet burns.

"This kettledrum base desk is obviously pregnant. A portrait of my mother bearing me? Its sides swell out greatly at the bottom. A block front."

In two rooms he found painted Pennsylvania Dutch rocking chairs. The pale yellow children rocked them so vigorously he thought they might take off, fueled by their infant dreams.

When it finally came time to retire, Michael of course had his choice of many beds. But many of the beds were of the modern type and therefore of little interest to him. Where there were antique beds they were usually Jenny Linds with simple spool-turned posts or the occasional Belter bed with its huge headboard carved with leaves and tendrils.

Michael finally settled for a bed with straps, so many straps it was like sleeping in a cage. But he felt secure, accepted. He began a dream about a forest full of children, tying one another to the trees. The crackling noises in the walls of his bedroom jarred his nerves, but eventually he was able to fall asleep. That night, as always, he had a boy's dreams. No business or marital worries informed them.

It was only upon waking that Michael discovered this room had a stenciled wall. This was of course a surprise in a structure from the 1850s, with the number of manufactured wallpapers available, but he supposed it might have been done—no doubt using old stencils—for uniqueness, to preserve some individual effect. Michael was surprised to find that it had survived the many small repaintings and remodellings that had occurred over the years. Usually a later owner would find the slight imperfections normal to a stencilled wall irritating, and the patterns crude, as certainly they often were.

But Michael liked them; there was a lot to be said for the note of individuality they added to a room. He suspected the only reason this particular wall had been saved, however, was because the guests hadn't the opportunity to see it. Looking around the walls—at their shabbiness, and the crude nature of the furniture—he felt sure this room was not normally rented. So an owner would not be embarrassed.

The pattern was an unusual one. The border was standard enough: leaves and vines and pineapples, quite similar to the work of Moses Eaton, Jr. Some of the wall stencils Michael had found in the cellar matched these shapes. Within these borders, however, was a grove of trees. Most of them were large stencils of weeping willows, but still fairly standard, again derived from Eaton's work. But here and there among the willows was another sort of tree: an oak, perhaps, but he wasn't sure, tied or bound by a large rope, or maybe it was a snake wrapping around the trunk and through the branches. Bound was the proper description, because the branches seemed pulled down or otherwise diverted from their natural direction by the rope or snake, and the trunk *twisted* from the upright—a dramatic violation of the classical symmetry one usually found in wall designs.

The design of this particular tree was obviously too intricate to have been done with a single stencil. There had to have been several, overlapping. But the color was too faded and worn to make out much of the detail, as if some past cleaning woman had tried to remove the bound trees, though not the willows, with an abrasive.

He got down on his hands and knees. The baseboard was covered with scratches, the signatures of dozens of different children. He could hear a distant thundering in the hall outside, hundreds of orphan limbs, pounding out a protest that grew slowly in its articulateness. *Choose me. Me me me.* He began to doubt that Victor Montgomery had ever been away to school, that he had ever left this hotel, and his father's watchful eye, at all. The voices in the hall seemed strangely distorted. *Distorted embryos.* As if under water. The scratches in the baseboard tore at his fingertips.

Michael crawled out the door and down several flights of stairs. The faceless children all crowded him, jostled him, and yet he still kept his knees moving. He maneuvered through a mass of legs, odd items of furniture stacked and jammed wall-to-wall, all eager to grab him with their straps and wooden arms and bend him to their shape. He cried when their sharp legs kicked him, and covered his face when hurricanes swept through the woods and shouted like old men.

He stopped at the front windows and floated up to the glass. A crowd of people watched him, pointed, tapped the glass. Sweat drenched him and fogged the glass wall. His eyes grew bigger than his mouth. And yet no matter how hard he peered at the ones outside, he could find no face that resembled his own.

GAHAN WILSON

Mister Ice Cold

GAHAN WILSON is best known as one of America's most popular cartoonists, his macabre work appearing regularly in *The New Yorker*, *Playboy*, *The Magazine of Fantasy & Science Fiction*, *National Lampoon*, *Punch* and *Paris Match*, amongst others. He illustrated Edgar Allan Poe's *The Raven and Other Poems* for the first issue of the new Classics Illustrated comics, and contributed all the artwork to *Weird Tales* No. 300, a special Robert Bloch issue.

His short fiction has recently appeared in such diverse outlets as *Omni* and the *Lovecraft's Legacy* anthology, among his own books are *Gahan Wilson's Graveside Manner*, *Is Nothing Sacred?*, *Nuts*, *Eddy Deco's Last Caper*, *Everybody's Favourite Duck* and several children's volumes, including a series on *Harry, The Fat Bear Spy*.

Wilson reveals that he was officially declared born dead by the attending physician in Evanston, Illinois. Rescued by another medico who dipped him alternately in bowls of hot and cold water, he survived to become the first student at the School of the Art Institute in Chicago to admit he was going there to learn how to become a cartoonist.

He is well known for his wicked and perverse sense of humour, both of which you will find aplenty in the poignant little tale that follows . . .

L ISTEN, CHILDREN! Hear the music? Hear its bright and cheerful chiming coming down the street? Hear it playing its pretty little tune—dingy di-ding, dingy di-ding—as it sings softly through the green trees, through the blue sky overhead, as it sings through the thick, still, sultry summer heat? It's Mister Ice Cold coming in his truck! Mister Ice Cold and his nice ice cream! Fat, round, cool balls of it plopped into cones! Thick, juicy slabs of it covered in frozen chocolate frosting and stuck on sticks! Soft, pink, chilly twirls of it oozed into cups!

The music's coming closer through the heat—dingy di-ding, dingy di-ding—and excitement starts stirring where all was lazy and drowsy just a sweaty blink before! Bobby Martin's no longer lying flat on the grass, staring up at a slow-moving summer cloud without seeing it at all; he's scrambled to his feet and is running over the thick summer grass to ask his mother—nodding on the porch over a limp magazine almost slipped from her fingers—if he can have enough money to buy a frozen lime frog. And Suzy Brenner's left off dreamily trying to tie her doll's bonnet over her cat's head (much to the cat's relief) and is desperately digging into her plastic, polka-dot purse to see if there's enough change in there to buy her a cup of banana ice cream with chocolate sprinkles. Oh, she can taste the sweetness of it! Oh, her throat can feel its coolness going down! And you, you've forgotten all about blowing through a leaf to see if you can make it squeak the way you saw Arnold Carter's older brother do it; now you're clawing feverishly with your small hands in both pockets, feeling your way past that sandy shell you found yesterday on the beach, and that little ball chewed bounceless by your dog, and that funny rock you came across in the vacant lot which may, with luck, be full of uranium and highly radioactive, and so far you have come up with two pennies and a quarter and you think you've just touched a nickel. Meantime Mister Ice Cold's truck is rolling closer—dingy di-ding, dingy di-ding—and Martin Walpole, always a show-off, wipes his brow, points, and calls out proudly, "I see it! There it is!"

And sure enough, *there it is*, rolling smoothly around the corner of Main and Lincoln, and you can see the shiny, fat fullness of its white roof gleaming in the bright sun through the thick, juicy-green foliage of the trees, which have, in the peak of their summer swelling, achieved a tropical density and richness more appropriate to some Amazonian jungle than to midwestern Lakeside, and you push aside one last, forgotten tangle of knotted string in your pocket and your heart swells for joy because you've come across another quarter and that means you've got enough for an orange icicle on a stick which will freeze your fillings and chill your gut and stain your tongue that gorgeous, glowing copper color which never fails to terrify your sister!

Now Mister Ice Cold's truck has swept into full view, and its dingy di-ding sounds out loud and clear and sprightly enough, even in this steaming, muggy air, to startle a sparrow and make it swerve in its flight.

Rusty Taylor's dog barks for a signal, and all of you come running quick as you can from every direction, coins clutched in your sweaty fingers and squeezed tightly as possible in your damp, small palms, and every one of you is licking your lips and staring at the bright blue lettering painted in frozen ice cubes that spells out MISTER ICE COLD over the truck's sides and front and back, and Mister Ice Cold himself gives a sweeping wave of his big, pale hand to everyone from behind his wheel and brings his vehicle and all the wonders it contains to a slow, majestic halt with the skill and style of a commodore docking an ocean liner.

"A strawberry rocket!" cries fat Harold Smith, who has got there way ahead of everyone else as usual, and Mister Ice Cold flips open one of the six small doors set into the left side of the truck with a click and plucks out Harold's rocket and gives it to him and takes the change, and before you know it he has glided to the right top door of the four doors at the truck's back and opened it, click, and Mandy Carter's holding her frozen maple tree and licking it and handing her money over all at the same time, and now Mister Ice Cold is opening one of the six small doors on the right side of the truck, click, and Eddy Morse has bitten the point off the top of his bright red cinnamon crunchy munch and is completely happy.

Then your heart's desire is plucked with a neat click from the top middle drawer on the truck's right side, which has always been its place for as long as you can remember, and you've put your money into Mister Ice Cold's large, pale, always-cool palm, and as you step back to lick your orange icicle and to feel its coolness trickle down your throat, once again you find yourself admiring the sheer smoothness of Mister Ice Cold's movements as he glides and dips, spins and turns, bows and rises, going from one small door, click, to another, click, with never a stumble, click, never a pause, click, his huge body leaving a coolness in the wake of his passing, and you wish you moved that smoothly when you run over the gravel of the playground with your hands stretched up, hoping for a catch, but you know you don't.

Everything's so familiar and comforting: the slow quieting of the other children getting what they want, your tongue growing more and more chill as you reduce yet another orange icicle, lick by lick, down to its flat stick, and the heavy, hot summer air pressing down on top of it all.

But this time it's just a little different than it ever was before because, without meaning to, without having the slightest intention of doing it, you've noticed something you never noticed before. Mister Ice Cold never opens the bottom right door in the back of the truck.

He opens all the rest of them, absolutely every one, and you see him doing it now as new children arrive and call out what they want. Click, click, click, he opens them one after the other, producing frozen banana bars and cherry twirls and all the other special favorites, each one always from its particular, predictable door.

But his big, cool hand always glides past that *one door* set into the truck's back, the one on the bottom row, the one to the far right. And you realize now, with a funny little thrill, that you have never—not in all the years since your big brother Fred first took you by the hand and gave Mister Ice Cold the money for your orange icicle because you were so small you couldn't even count—you have never *ever* seen that door open.

And now you've licked the whole orange icicle away, and your tongue's moving over and over the rough wood of the stick without feeling it at all, and you can't stop staring at that door, and you know, deep in the pit of your stomach, that you have to open it.

You watch Mister Ice Cold carefully now, counting out to yourself how long it takes him to move from the doors farthest forward back to the rear of the truck, and because your mind is racing very, very quickly, you soon see that two orders in a row will keep him up front just long enough for you to open the door which is never opened, the door which you are now standing close enough to touch, just enough time to take a quick peek and close it shut before he knows.

Then Betty Deane calls out for a snow maiden right on top of Mike Howard's asking for a pecan pot, and you know those are both far up front on the right-hand side.

Mister Ice Cold glides by you close enough for the cool breeze coming from his passing to raise little goose bumps on your arms. Without pausing, without giving yourself a chance for any more thought, you reach out.

Click! Your heart freezes hard as anything inside the truck. There, inside the square opening, cold and bleached and glistening, are two tidy stacks of small hands, small as yours, their fingertips reaching out toward you and the sunlight; their thin, dead young arms reaching out behind them, back into the darkness. Poking over the top two hands, growing out of something round and shiny and far back and horribly still, are two stiff golden braids of hair with pretty frozen bows tied onto their ends. But you have stared too long in horror and the door is closed, click, and almost entirely covered by Mister Ice Cold's hand, which seems enormous, and he's bent down over you with his huge, smiling face so near to yours you can feel the coolness of it in the summer heat.

"Not that door," he says, very softly, and his small, neat, even teeth shine like chips from an iceberg, and because of his closeness now you know that even his breath is icy cold. "Those in there are not for you. Those in there are for me."

Then he's standing up again and moving smoothly from door to door, click, click, click, but none of the other children see inside, and none of them will really believe you when you tell them, though their eyes will go wide and they'll love the story, and not a one of them saw the promise for you in Mister Ice Cold's eyes. But you did, didn't you? And some night, after the end of summer, when it's cool and you don't want it any cooler, you'll be lying in your bed all alone and you'll hear Mister Ice Cold's pretty little song coming closer through the night, through the dead, withered autumn leaves.

Dingy di-ding, dingy di-ding . . .

Then, later on, you just may hear the first click. But you'll never hear the second click. None of them ever do.

ELIZABETH HAND

On the Town Route

ELIZABETH HAND lives on the Maine coast with novelist Richard Grant and their daughter Callie Anne. She is the author of the novels *Winterlong* (a nominee for the Philip K. Dick Award) and *Aestival Tide*, and is currently at work on *Waking the Moon*. Her short stories have appeared in numerous magazines and anthologies such as *The Year's Best Horror Stories*, *Full Spectrum II* and *Twilight Zone*. She is a Contributing Editor to *Science Fiction Eye* and her book reviews and criticism are published in *The Washington Post*, *Penthouse*, *The Detroit Metro Times* and the feminist quarterly, *Belles Lettres*.

The powerful slice of dark fantasy which follows is based on the author's real-life experiences on the town route in Green County, Virginia, several years ago. "Like Julie Dean," she notes, "I ate too many Bomb Pops, smoked too many cigarettes, and met the people you'll find in this story, including the bearded lady and Sam and Little Eva. And as anyone who's spent much time in those mountains can tell you, some truly weird stuff happens there."

I MET THE BEARDED LADY the first day I rode with Cass on the town route. That sweltering afternoon I sprawled across my mattress on the floor. A few inches from my nose lay the crumpled notice of the revocation of my scholarship. Beside it a less formally worded letter indicated that in light of my recent lack of interest in the doings of The Fertile Mind Bookstore, my services there would no longer be needed, and would I please return the *Defries Incunabula* I had "borrowed" for my thesis immediately? From downstairs thumped the persistent bass line of the house band's demo tape. Then another, more insistent thudding began outside my room. I moaned and pulled my pillow onto my head. I ignored the pounding on the door, finally pretended to be asleep as Cass let himself in.

"Time to wake up," he announced, kneeling beside the mattress and sliding a popsicle down my back. "Time to go on the ice cream truck."

I moaned and burrowed deeper into the bed. "Ow—that hurts—"

"It's ice cream, Julie. It's supposed to hurt." Cass dug the popsicle into the nape of my neck, dripping pink ice and licking it from my skin between whispers. "Snap out of it, Jules. You been in here two whole weeks. Natalie at the bookstore's worried."

"Natalie at the bookstore fired me." I reached for a cigarette and twisted to face the window. "You better go, Cass. I have work to do."

"Huh." He bent to flick at the scholarship notice, glanced at yet another sordid billet: UNDERGRADUATE ACADEMIC SUS-PENSION in bold red characters. Beneath them a humorlessly detailed list of transgressions. "You're not working on your thesis. You're not doing *anything*. You got to get out of here, Julie. You promised. You said you'd come with me on the truck and you haven't gone once since I started." He stalked to the door, kicking at a drift of unpaid bills, uncashed checks, unopened letters from my parents, unreturned phone messages from Cass Tyrone. "You don't come today, Julie, that's it. No more ice cream."

"No more Bomb Pops?" I asked plaintively.

"Nope." He sidled across the hall, idly nudging a beer bottle down the steps.

"No more Chump Bars?"

"Forget it. And no Sno-Cones, either. I'll save 'em for Little Eva." Reaching into his knapsack, he tossed me another popsicle and waited. I unpeeled it and licked it thoughtfully, applying it to my aching forehead. Then I stood up.

"Okay. I'm coming."

Outside, on the house's crumbling brick, someone had spraypainted *Dog Is Glove* and *You Are What You Smell*, along with some enthusiastic criticism of the house band written by Cass himself. A few steps farther and the truck stood in a vacant parking lot glittering with squashed beer cans and shattered bottles. Before I could climb in, Cass made me walk with him around the rusted machine. He patted the flaking metal signs and kicked the tires appraisingly. The truck settled ominously into the gravel at this attention and Cass sighed. "Damn. Hope we don't get another flat your first time out."

Once it had been a Good Humor truck. Ghostly letters still glowed balefully above a phantom ice cream bar, since painted over with the slogan *Jolly Times*. One side of the cab was plastered with ancient decals displaying mottled eclairs twisted into weird shapes and faded, poisonous colors. I grimaced, then clambered in after Cass.

As the engine wheezed, the ancient cab rattled like a box of marbles, empty pop bottles and freezer cartons rolling underfoot as I tried to clear a place to lean against the freezer. Cass lit a cigarette, dropping the match into a grape puddle.

"You ready?" he shouted, and the truck lurched forward. I braced myself against the freezer lid, my hands sticking to the cool metal. Cass glanced back and apologized. "Sorry about that. Left a Chump Bar there last night. First stop's Tandy Court."

The truck hurtled through the university town of Zion, past the college lawn and the student ghettos, past tiny churches where clots of the faithful stirred listlessly on brown lawns, fanning themselves with Sunday bulletins. Cass and I sucked popsicles to cool off, the sticks piling on the floor between us like chicken bones at a barbecue. Above the dashboard dangled a string of rusty bells. Occasionally Cass tugged at an old gray shoelace to ring them, frowning at the wan metallic gargle. He hunched over the steering column, like a rodeo clown clinging to that great ugly hulk. Then he whooped, jangled the bells, and gunned the motor.

The road narrowed to a silvery track stretching before us, churches and homes falling away as we left the town limits. About us began the slow steady erosion of village into farmland, farmland into open country, the furrows of ploughed fields plunging into the ravines and ancient hollows of the Blue Ridge. We turned off the highway, bouncing across train tracks. I breathed the cloudy sweet scents of anthracite and honeysuckle and laughed, suddenly elated.

Below us perched a dozen trailer homes, strewn among stands of poplar and red oak like a doll village sprung from a sandbox. Old pickups and junked Chevys rusted side by side like Tonka Toys. The truck crept gingerly between ruts and boulders until we reached a little midden where an inflated Yogi Bear hung from a broom handle, revolving lazily in the breeze.

Cass shook his head, bemused. "Lot of toys on this route." He pointed to a shiny new trailer shell, its brown pocket of lawn vivid with red plastic tulips and spinning whirligigs. In the trailer's windows huddled small figures, brown and green and pink, staring out with shiny black eyes. More toys peered from other trailers as we crept by, rag dolls and inchworms abandoned in back lots. Only the pickups and motorcycles parked between Big Wheel bikes hinted that there might be adults somewhere.

"So where are all the kids?" I demanded, unwrapping a Neapolitan sandwich.

Cass halted the truck in a cul-de-sac. "Watch this."

The bells jingled, echoing against the mountainside until the hollow chimed. Silence, except for distant birdsong.

Then another sound began, a clamorous tide of screen doors slamming open and shut, door after door creaking, booming, hissing closed. Drawers banged, coins jingled. And the children came, big ones dragging smaller ones, toddlers dragging dolls, galloping dogs and kittens scampering beneath the stalled truck. Cass fell into his seat, grinning. "Ready to sell some ice cream?" He threw open the freezer drawers, nodding to the group outside.

"Here's the three Kims," he commented, hefting an unopened carton. Three girls in cut-offs and T-shirts squirmed to the side of the truck, eyeing me warily.

"Hi," whispered the prettiest girl, staring at Cass boldly enough to belie her soft voice. "Give me a ee-clair."

Cass winked as he reached into the freezer. "Eclair? That's a new one. Anything for your momma?"

She shook her head, clinked down two quarters and slipped away.

"What about you, Kim?" asked Cass. "Same thing?"

"Kim*ber*ly," lisped the second girl. She had protruding front teeth and a true harelip, her split upper lip glowing pink and wet as bubblegum when she smiled. "Fudgesicle."

He handed her a fudgesicle, and then the remaining children piled forward, yelling requests as I dredged ice cream from the freezer, frost billowing around me like steam. After the last child darted off, Cass wheeled the truck around and we plunged back up the road.

From one side of the mountain to the other I watched the same scene, an endless procession of children unwinding beneath the blinding sun. I felt sick from too many cigarettes and ice cream bars. My eyes ached; the landscape looked flat and bright, overexposed, the streams of children a timelapsed film: first the tiniest boys and girls, grinning and dirty as if freshly pulled from a garden. Then their older brothers and sisters, feral creatures with slanted eyes yellowed in the sunlight, bare arms and legs sleek and golden as perch. Girls just past puberty, one with her mother's bra flapping loosely around her thin chest. An occasional boy, rude and bashful, a wad of chewing tobacco plumping his cheek. And finally another baby stumbling to the truck behind a mother ungraced by a gold ring, the two of them leaving naked footprints in the road.

"Wild girls," Cass said softly as we watched them run from the truck, to swing over fences or perch there for an instant, staring back at us with glittering eyes. "Like dragonflies," he murmured. I saw them as he did, shining creatures darting between the pines. A flicker in the trees and they were gone, their pretty husks crumbled in the sun.

Farther up and farther in we drove. The houses grew older, more scattered. There were no more telephone poles. The truck scaled tortuous roads so narrow I wondered how we'd get back down after dark. I stood beside the driver's seat, balancing myself so that I could watch the sun dance in and out of the distant mountaintops. In front of me Cass fidgeted in his seat, chainsmoking.

"Count and see if we got enough for a case of beer when we get back," he yelled over the droning motor.

My hands were stained in minutes, counting streaked pennies and quarters sticky with tar and gum and more lint than I cared to think about. I felt rather than saw the difference in one coin, so heavy I thought at first it was a silver dollar.

"What's this?"

I tossed it gingerly into my other hand, extending it to Cass. The face was worn to a dull moon, but letters still caught the afternoon light and flashed as Cass took it from me. "Look: it's not even in English."

He shut one eye and regarded it appraisingly. "Another one? She gives me those sometimes. It's real silver."

I took it back, weighed it in my fist. "They worth anything?"

"Worth their weight in silver," Cass replied brusquely, and he reddened. "I told Sam. But he wouldn't take 'em back," he added defensively. He bent to trace the characters on the coin with one finger. "They're Greek. And they're real, real old. I bring them to the stamp shop in Zion and the guy there gives me twenty bucks apiece. You can keep that one. I haven't seen any for awhile."

"I bet they're worth more than twenty bucks," I said, but Cass only shrugged.

"Not in Zion. And up here they're only worth fifty cents." And laughing he lit a cigarette.

"We're almost at the bearded lady's," he announced. "You'll meet Sam there. That's always my last stop. I found her place by mistake," he went on, pounding the dashboard for emphasis. "We're not even supposed to go *down* this road."

He pointed his cigarette at the dusty track winding before us, so narrow that branches poked through the windows, raking my arms as the truck crept down the hill.

"No one lives here. Just the kids, they're always around. Come to play with Little Eva. But I never see anyone in these houses," he mused, slowing the truck as it drifted past two dilapidated cottages, caved in upon themselves like an old man's gums. Cass yanked on the shoelace and the bells rang faintly.

From the shadowy verdure appeared a tiny white house, stark and precise as a child's drawing chalked against the woodlands. Here the dirt road straightened and the hill ended, as if too exhausted to go on. The truck, too, grated to a stop.

Behind the house stretched woods and fallow farmland, ochre clay, yellow flax fading into the silvery horizon where a distant silo wavered in the heat like a melting candle. From an unseen bog droned the resolute thud of a croaking bullfrog, the splash of a heron highstepping through the marsh. Shrill tuneless singing wafted from inside the house.

A kitten lay panting beneath the worn floorboards of a little porch, ignoring a white cabbage butterfly feebly beating its wings in the scant shade. The singing stopped abruptly and I heard a radio's blare.

"Watch," Cass whispered. He lit another cigarette and rang the bells. The kitten sprang from beneath the porch, craning to watch the front door.

One moment the doorway was black. The next a girl stood there, her hair a spiky orange nimbus flared about a white face. Barefoot, a dirty white nightgown flapping around legs golden with dust and feet stained brick red from the clay. She smiled and jigged up and down on her heels, glancing back at the house. The kitten ran to her, cuffing her ankle—I could have circled one of those ankles with my thumb and forefinger and slid a pencil between. Her thin arm lashed out and grabbed the kitten by its nape, dangling it absently like a pocketbook.

"Hi," called Cass, blowing a smoke ring out the window. "Little Eva."

The girl beamed, stepping towards the road, then stopped to squint back at the doorway. "She's real shy," Cass muttered. "Hey, Eva—"

He flourished a green and yellow popsicle shaped like a daisy. "I saved this for you. The three Kims wanted it but I told 'em, no way, this one's for Little Eva."

Giggling, she shuffled down the dirt walk, her feet slipping between paving stones and broken glass. I smiled, nodding reassuringly as she took the popsicle and squatted beside Cass on the truck's metal side-steps. He opened a can of grape pop and drained it in one pull, then tossed the empty into the back of the truck. "Where's your mom, Eva?"

"Right there." She pointed with her ice pop, dropping and retrieving it from the dirt in one motion. The kitten scrambled from her arms and disappeared in the jewelweed.

From the shadows of the doorway stepped a woman, small and fat as a bobwhite, wearing a baggy blue shift like a hospital gown. Long greasy hair was bunched in a clumsy ball at the back of her neck; long black hairs plastered her forehead. From her chin curled thick tufts of black hair, coarse as a billy goat's beard. A pair of glasses pinched her snub nose, thick-lensed glasses with cheap black plastic frames—standard county issue. Behind the grimy lenses her eyes glinted pale cloudy yellow. When she spoke, her voice creaked like burlap sacking and her head bobbed back and forth like a snake's. It was a whole minute before I realized she was blind.

"Little Eva," she yelled, her twang thick and muddy as a creek bottom. "Who's it?"

"Ice cream man," drawled Eva, and she poked her popsicle into the woman's hand. "He give me this. Get money from Sam."

Cass nodded slowly. "It's Cass Tyrone, Maidie." He thumped a heavy carton on the side of the truck. "I got you a box of eclairs here. That what you want?"

Her hands groped along the side of the truck, pouncing on the frost-rimed box. "Sam," she shrilled. "Ice cream man."

Someone else shuffled onto the porch then, wiping his hands on the front of a filthy union suit. Much older than Maidie, he wore only those greasy coveralls and a crudely drawn tattoo. He took very small steps to the edge of the porch—such small steps that I glanced down at his feet. Bare feet, grub white and hardly bigger than Little Eva's.

How he walked on those feet was a mystery. He was very fat, although there was something deflated about his girth, as though the weight had somewhere slipped from him, leaving soft folds and ripples of slack papery skin. His head and neck looked as though they'd been piped from pastry cream, ornate folds and dimples of white flesh nearly hiding his features. Even his tattoo was blurred and softened by time, as though it had shrunk with him, like the image on a deflated balloon. I turned my head to keep from laughing nervously. But the old man turned his head as well, so that I stared into a pair of vivid garter-blue eyes fringed with lashes black as beetles. I coughed, embarrassed. He smiled at me and I drew back, my skin prickling.

Such a beautiful smile! Perfect white teeth and lips a little too red, as though he'd been eating some overripe fruit. I thought of Ingrid Bergman—that serene glow, those liquid eyes with their black lashes fluttering beneath a shock of grimy white hair. He was irresistible.

Shyly I smiled back, and in a very soft voice he said, "Hello, Ice Cream."

He was the ugliest man I had ever seen.

Cass nudged me, explaining, "That's what he calls me. 'Ice Cream.' Like you call a blacksmith Smith, or a gardener Gardner." I nodded doubtfully, but Sam smiled, tilting his head to Little Eva as he bent to tug her gently by the ear.

"You want a cigarette, Sam?" drawled Cass, handing him an Old Gold. Sam took it without a word.

"That's my girl, Sam." Cass sighed mournfully. "Julie Dean: she's awful mean. Maidie, that's my girl."

The bearded lady wagged her head, then thumped her hand on the side of the truck, palm up, until I stuck my own hand out the window. She grabbed it and nearly yanked me out into the road.

"Maidie," I said loudly, wincing as I heard my fingers crackle in her grip. "I'm Julie."

She shook her head, staring eagerly at the roof of the truck. "I knowed all about you. He told me. He got this girl . . ." Her voice ebbed and she turned to Sam, wildly brandishing her box of eclairs as she shouted, "Take 'em, Sam! That Ice Cream's girl?"

Sam smiled apologetically as he enfolded the box in one great soft paw. "I don't know, Maidie," he told her, then whispered to me, "She don't see much people." He spoke so slowly, so gently, that I wondered if he was dim-witted; if he'd ever been off the mountain. Ice Cream," he murmured, and reached to stroke my hand. "Ice Cream, this your girl?"

Cass grabbed me, shaking me until my hair flew loose from my bandana and my jaw rattled. "This is her. The one and only. What you think, Sam?"

Sam stared at me. I saw a light flare and fade in his iris: the pupils pulsed like a pair of flexing black wings, then shrank to tiny points once more. I shrugged, then nodded uneasily.

"Julie," he whispered. "You his girl?"

I shook my head, stammering, and shrank from the window.

"Julie Dean. I'll remember," whispered Sam. He slid his hand over mine, his skin smooth and dry and cool as glass. "You know, Ice Cream is awful good to us."

"I thought everybody hated the ice cream man," I remarked, grinning.

Sam shook his head, shocked. "*We love* ice cream."

Cass grinned. "Hear that? They love me. Right, Maidie? Right, Eva?"

Maidie giggled sharply, tilting her head so that I saw the moles clustered beneath her chin, buried like dark thumbprints in that fleshy dewlap where the hairs grew thickest. I shuddered, thinking of cancers, those dark little fingers tickling her throat in the middle of the night. Little Eva laughed with her mother, clutching the truck's fender.

"Ice Cream!" she shrieked. "Give me ice cream!"

Cass beamed and scooped another popsicle from the freezer, tossing it to her like a bear slapping a trout to shore. The kitten flashed from the grass, tumbling the pop in mid-air so it fell at Maidie's feet.

"I'll be by tomorrow," Cass called to Sam, and he started back into the truck. "You catch me then."

"I got money," Sam muttered. He wriggled his hand into a pocket, then opened his palm to display a handful of tarnished coins, age-blackened and feathered with verdigris. Cass scrutinized the coins, finally picked out three. Eva giggled, baring a mouthful of green-iced teeth.

"Okay," he said. "But I got to go now. Kiss, Little Eva?"

She fled tittering to the porch, pausing to spin and wave like one of those plastic whirligigs, bobbing goodbye before she skipped indoors. Cass started the truck and waved.

"So long, Maidie, Sam. Anything special tomorrow?"

Maidie yelled, "Eclairs," then waddled back to the porch. For another minute Sam lingered, stroking the rusted metal of the truck's headlights. "You'll be back?" he finally asked.

"Sure, Sam," Cass shouted above the motor. "Tomorrow."

Sam nodded, lifting his hand and opening it a single time in measured farewell. "Tomorrow," he repeated, and stepped back from the cloud of dirt and grass that erupted behind us. A minute later and they were gone from sight, hidden behind the oaks and serpentine road. Cass grinned like a dog, twisting in his seat to face me. "What'd you think?"

I lit a cigarette, staring at the fields streaming red and gold in the twilight, the tumbledown walls and rotting fenceposts. I waited a long time before answering him, and then I only said, "I thought it was sad," and tossed my cigarette across the road.

"Sad?" said Cass, puzzled. "You thought Little Eva was sad?"

"Christ, they're so poor. Like they haven't had a real meal in months."

"Sad?" he repeated. "Sad?" And he stomped the gas pedal. "I thought they'd make you happy."

"Cass!" I shook my head, kicking at an empty beer bottle. "You're *feeding* them."

"I don't give them anything," he protested. "They buy that ice cream."

"Cass, I saw you give him a box of eclairs."

He shook his head violently, jerking the wheel from side to side. "He bought that, Julie. He paid for it."

"Fifty cents for ten bucks worth of eclairs."

"What are you saying? Just what are you saying?" Cass demanded. "I sold him that ice cream." His face glowed bright pink, the stubble on his face a crimson fuzz. I hunched back against the freezer and looked away stubbornly.

"Look, Cass, I don't care what you do with your money—"

"Shut up. Just shut up. What the hell do you know? They don't need that ice cream. They *love* it. That's why I go there. Not like—" He stopped, furious, switching the radio on and then off again.

We rode in silence. It grew darker as we traced our way back down again. Night leaked like black water to fill the rims and ridges of the mountains. The first stars gleamed as the trees began to bow before a cool rising wind. I reached over to roll up the window, as much to shut out the night itself as the chill air; but the handle was broken. I rubbed my arms and wished I'd brought a sweater. Silently Cass groped beneath his seat with one hand, then tossed me a dirty sweatshirt. I pulled it on gratefully and leaned forward to kiss him.

"Am I your girl? Is that what you tell them?"

He shrugged and shifted gears. He drove with his face pressed right up to the gritty windshield, shoving his glasses against the bridge of his nose as if that might make his eyes strong enough to pierce the dark tunnel of pine and shivering aspen. "Damn," he muttered. "This place gets dark."

I nodded, huddling into his sweatshirt as I peered into the night. It was like day was something that could be peeled away, and now the black core of the mountain, the pith and marrow of it, throbbed here. I saw averted eyes, heard wings and the rustle of pokeweed where something loped alongside us for a few yards before veering off into the bracken. I stuck my head out the window and saw reflected in the scarlet taillights a fox, one black foreleg raised as he watched us pass.

Then came a long stretch where the road flattened out and stretched before us like a solid shaft of darkness flying into the heart of the country. Overhead, branches linked and flowers dangled against the windshield, laving us in their dreamy scent. Cass cut back the engine and the truck glided down this gentle slope, headlights guttering on rabbits that did not run, but stopped to regard us with gooseberry eyes from the roadside. I yawned and let my arms droop out the window.

"Poison ivy," warned Cass; but he did the same thing, sparks from his cigarette singeing sphinx moths and lacewings. Great white blossoms belled from the trees and I reached to grab a handful of flowers, yanking them through the window until the branch snapped and showered us with pollen and dew.

"Look," I gasped, breathless from the cold spray. "What are they?"

Cass poked sagely at his glasses, leaning over to inhale.

411

"Moonflowers," he announced.

"Really?" I lifted my face and shook the branch, spattering more dew on my sunburned cheeks. "They smell like heaven."

"Nah. I don't know what they are, really. White things—asphodel, moonflowers," he finished, yawning. "They do smell like—"

He choked on the word, twisting the wheel sharply. "Sweet Jesus . . ."

In the road before us crouched a child, her eyes incandescent in the highbeams. I shouted and lunged for the wheel, tearing it from Cass's hands. With a shearing sound the wheel spun free and the truck plowed forward.

There was no way we could avoid hitting her. The soft thump was almost a relief, the gentle slap of a great wave against a dinghy. The truck shuddered to a stop and Cass groaned, knocking me aside as he staggered through the door to land on his knees in the dirt. I followed and collapsed beside him.

She was dead, of course. A vivid russet bruise smeared her face from neck to shoulder, staining her torn T-shirt. At first I didn't recognize the face beneath the speckled dirt and blood. Then I noticed the tiny pink cleft above her teeth, the blood pooling there to trickle into her mouth. Cass dabbed at her chin with his shirt sleeve, halted and began to cry. His keening rose higher and higher until I covered my ears against his screams, too stunned to calm him. I didn't think to go for help. We knelt there a long time, and I dully brushed away the insects that landed on the child's face.

Behind us something moved. A silhouette cut off the headlights' beam. I stared at my hand splayed against the girl's clenched fist, afraid to turn and face the figure standing in the light. Instead I waited for the cry that would drown out Cass's voice: mother, father, searching sister.

But the voice was laconic, dull as dust. "What you crying for?"

I lifted my head and saw Maidie feeling her way along the front of the truck, balancing clumsily by grabbing the grill above one headlight. Cass stared at her and choked, clutching wildly at my knee. "She can't see," he gasped, and suddenly pushed at the girl's body. "Julie—"

Maidie stood in front of the truck, her blue shift glowing in the backlight. I stammered loudly, "Maidie—we got trouble—Kimberly—we hit her."

She stumbled towards us, smacking the grill and kicking violently at stones in her path. A rock bounded against the child's forehead and Cass gagged, drawing closer to me. I rose to my knees and reached to halt the blind woman.

"Maidie. You better go back . . ."

Then she was on her knees beside us, groping in the dirt until she grasped the crushed shoulder, the head lolling like an overripe peach. "Hurt that pore old head," she laughed, and her yellow eyes rolled behind glinting lenses. "Bang."

I drew back in disgust, then squeezed Cass's hand as I stood. "Don't leave," I warned him. "I'm getting help."

Maidie leaned over the child, brushing the girl's hair from her forehead. "Poor old head," she chortled. Then she spat on her fingers and rubbed the dirt from the girl's mouth, all the while staring blankly into the glaring headlights.

For a moment I hesitated, watching the gleam of light on her beard, the flash of her glasses like two bright coins. Then I turned to leave. Where the circle of light ended I paused, blinking as I tried to see where the road twisted. Behind me Cass hissed and Maidie giggled, the two sounds like a bird's call. I glanced back once again.

Between Cass and the bearded woman the child stirred, thrashing at the ground until she heaved herself upright to stare at them sleepy-eyed. She shook her head so that her hair shone in a blur of dust, the face beneath that mane a sticky mess of blood and dirt. Then she stuck her finger in her mouth, blinking in the painful light, and asked doubtfully, "You the ice cream man?"

Cass nodded, dazed, pulled his glasses from his nose, put them back, stared from Maidie to the child once more. Then he laughed, hooting until the mountain rang, and I heard an owl's mournful reply. "Jesus, you scared me! Kim, you all right?"

"Kim*ber*ly," she murmured, rubbing her shoulder. She glanced at her bloody hand and wiped it on her shorts. "I sure fell," she said. "Can I have a Sno-Cone?"

Cass staggered to his feet and sprinted to the truck. From inside he tossed Sno-Cones, eclairs, a frozen Moon-Pie. A can of pop exploded on the ground in a cherry mist and he stopped, seeing me for the first time. He ran his hands through his hair. "Sno-Cone," he repeated.

"I just want an e-clair," Maidie called petulantly, and she pounded the road with her palm. "We got to get back, Kimberly." She lumbered to her feet and hobbled to the truck, the girl beside her scratching. Cass stepped down and put a Sno-Cone in each small hand, turned and handed Maidie an eclair. The bearded lady grabbed Kimberly by the neck and pushed her impatiently. "Take me home," she rasped, and Kimberly started to walk up the road, limping slightly. Maidie kicked the stones from her path as they plodded past me, trailing melting ice cream. At the edge of light they disappeared from view, the soft uneven pad of their feet fading into the pines.

From the doorway Cass squinted after them, and I stared at him, both of us silent. Cass trembled so that the cigarette he lit flew off into the darkness like a firefly. In the road melted a dozen Sno-Cones and eclairs, pooling white and red and brown in the clay. I stepped towards the truck and knelt to inspect a slender rillet of blood. Already tiny spiders skated across the black surface and moths lit there to rest their wings, uncoiling dark tongues to feed. With one finger I touched the sticky surface and raised my hand to the light.

There was too much blood. She had not been breathing. The right side of her face had paled to the color of lilacs, and I had glimpsed the rim of bone beneath her cheek, the broken lip spilling blood into the earth. Now behind me two sets of footprints marked the mountain road, and I could hear a woman's distant voice, a child's faint reply. I wiped the blood from my finger, and slowly returned to the truck to help Cass up the steps. Gently I eased him onto the freezer, pushing his shoulders until he sat there quietly. Then I settled myself beside the wheel. I started the engine, tentatively pressing pedals until the truck heaved forward, and drove crouched at the edge of the seat, squinting into the halo of light that preceded us. Behind me Cass toyed with his glasses, dropping them once and retrieving them from the floor. I saw him reflected in the truck's mirror like a trick of the light, his eyes fixed upon the passing hollows, the dark and tossing trees that hid from us a wonder.

After that I rode with Cass every morning on the town route. And as each afternoon struggled to its melancholy peak we'd start for the bearded lady's house. Sometimes we'd take one or two of the children with us, Kimberly and June Bug flanking me atop the freezer or playing with the radio dials. But usually we'd just find them all waiting for us when we arrived, racing through the tall grass behind Eva: Little Eva always running, running to hug Cass's knees and slip slyly past me when I stooped to greet her. Cass would bring a six-pack of True Blue Beer, and we'd squat beside Sam on the flimsy back porch, drinking and watching the children play.

The months marched past slowly. Our afternoons lingered into evenings when we took our cue from the hoarse voices of mothers hailing their children home. One night we stayed until moonrise, waving good-bye to the children as they took their hidden paths through the pinegroves. Their chatter was of school starting in the valley: new clothes and classrooms, a new teacher. The three Kims were the last to leave, and Cass handed each a popsicle as they passed the truck.

"Too cold," Kimberly squealed, and tossed hers into the weeds. Cass nodded sadly as we walked back to the porch, tugging at his collar against the evening chill. Eva sat yawning in Sam's lap, and the old man stroked her hair, humming to himself. I could scarcely see

Maidie where she stood at the edge of the field, her face upturned to the lowering sky. Cass and I settled beside Sam, Cass reaching to take Eva into his arms.

"Will you miss me when it's too cold for ice cream, Eva?" he asked mournfully. "When the three Kims are all drinking hot chocolate?"

She stared at him solemn-eyed for a moment as he gazed wistfully across the field. Then she slid from his lap, pursing her lips to kiss his chin, and pulled at Sam's shoulder. "Show him what you can do, Sam," she said imperiously. "That thing. Show Cass."

Sam smiled and looked away.

"Show him!" She bounced against his side, pulling his union suit until he nodded and rose sighing, like a bear torn from his long sleep. Cass looked at me with mock alarm as Sam lumbered down the steps to the willow tree.

"Watch!" Eva shrilled, and Maidie turned to face us, her white face cold and impassive.

About the willow tree honeysuckle twined, wreathing it in gold and ivory trumpets. Sam reached and gently stripped the tiny blooms from a vine, disturbing the cicadas that sang there. In his hands the flowers glowed slightly in the dusk. I glanced up and marked where bats stitched the sky above him, and pointed for Eva to look.

"I see," she said impatiently, pulling away from me. "*Watch*, Cass."

Sam wheeled to face us, inclined his head to Eva and smiled. Then he flung his arms upwards, sending a stream of flowers into the air.

"See them?" cried Eva, clinging to Cass's hand.

I saw nothing. Beside me Cass squinted, adjusting his glasses. Sam tore more honeysuckle from the willow and flung another handful into the air.

A black shape broke from the sky, whipped towards Sam's face and fell away so quickly it looked like it was moving backwards. Another flicker of darkness inches from Sam's face, and another; and they were everywhere, chasing the blossoms he hurled into the night, flitting about his face like great black moths. A faint rush of air upon my cheek: I saw the bluish sheen of wings, the starpoint reflection of one tiny eye as a bat skimmed past. I shuddered and drew closer to Cass. Eva laughed and darted away from the porch, joining Sam and gathering the broken flowers from the grass. She stood with face tilted to where the tiny shadows whirled, striking at flowers and craneflies.

"Can you hear them, Cass?" she called. He stood, eyes and mouth wide as he looked from the two of them to me, and nodded.

"I do," he murmured.

Beside him I gripped the porch rail and shrank from them, the soft rush of wings and their plaintive song: a high thin sound like wires snapping. "Cass," I whispered. "Cass—let's go."

But he didn't hear me; only stood and watched until Maidie called to Eva and her sharp voice sent the bats flurrying into the night. Her voice stirred Cass as well; he turned to me blinking, shaking his head.

"Let's go," I urged him, and he took my hand, nodding dazedly: Sam walked to the porch steps and looked up at us.

"You be by tomorrow," he said, and for a moment he held my other hand. His fingers were cold and damp, and when he withdrew them I found a green tendril in my palm, its single frail blossom crushed against my skin. "To say good-bye."

"We'll be here," Cass called back as I led him towards the truck.

When we drove up the following afternoon it was late, the sun already burning off the tops of the mountains. Cass had bought a case of True Blue back in Zion. We'd been drinking most of the day, mourning the end of summer, the first golden leaves on the tulip poplars. From the top of the rise Maidie's house looked still, and as we coasted down the hill I saw no one on the porch. The chairs and empty beer bottles were gone. So was the broom that Cass had made into a hobby-horse for Eva, and the broken pots and dishes that had been her toys. Cass parked the truck on the grass and looked at me.

"What the hell is this?" he wondered, and opened another beer. For several minutes we sat, waiting for Sam or Eva to greet us. Finally he finished his beer and said lamely, "Guess we better go find out."

On the porch Eva's half-grown kitten mewled, scampering off when Cass bent to pick it up. "Jeez," he muttered, pushing tentatively at the screen door. It gave gently, and we hesitated before entering. Inside there was nothing: not a chair, not a rag, not a glass. Cass stared in disbelief, but put on a nonchalant expression when Sam trudged in.

"Looks like you been doing your spring cleaning," Cass said uneasily.

Sam nodded. "I got to go. This time of year . . . take the girl with me." He smiled vacantly and crossed to the back door. Cass and I looked at each other, perplexed. Sam said nothing more and stepped outside. I followed him, peering into the single other room that had held a cot and mattress. Empty.

I found Cass outside, weaving slightly as he followed Sam to the porch's crumbling edge. "Where're you going?" he asked plaintively, but Sam only shook his head in silence, leaning on the splintered rail and gazing out at the field.

There was no sign of Maidie, but I could hear Eva chanting tunelessly to herself in the thicket of jewelweed at wood's edge. Cass heard, too, and called her name thickly. The golden fronds, heavy with blossoms and bees, twitched and crackled; and then Eva raced out, breathless, her face damp with excitement.

"Cass!" she cried, and scrambled up the porch steps to hug him. "We got to go."

"Where?" he asked again, resting his beer against her neck as he smoothed her tangled hair. "You going off to school?"

She shook her head. "No. Sam's place." Eva hugged his legs and looked up at him imploringly. "You come too. Okay, Cass? Okay?"

Cass finished his beer and threw the bottle recklessly towards the field, to crash and shatter on stone. "I wish someone'd tell me where you all are going," he insisted, turning to Sam.

The old man shrugged and eyed Little Eva. "You about ready?"

Eva shook her head fiercely. For the first time since I'd known her I saw her eyes blister with tears. "Sam—" she pleaded, yanking Cass's hand at each word. "I want Cass too."

"You know that ain't up to me," Sam replied bluntly, and he turned and went back inside.

Cass grinned then, and winked at me. "Just like a girl," he remarked, tousling her hair.

Faint high voices called from the woods. From the brush scrambled the three Kims, tearing twigs from their hair and yelling to us as they clambered over the fence. Beside me Little Eva stiffened, slipping her hand from Cass's as she watched her friends waving. Suddenly she let out a yell and sprang to meet them with arms flung wide, her hair a blazing flag in the sunset. Cass called after her, amused.

"That kid," he laughed, then stopped and cocked his head.

"What?" I glanced back at the sagging porch door, wondering where Maidie and Sam had gone.

"Hear that?" Cass murmured. He looked at me sharply. "You hear that?"

I shook my head, smoothing the hair from my ears. "No. The kids?" I pointed to the girls greeting Eva in the tall grass.

"Singing," Cass said softly. "Someone's singing." He stared intently after Eva.

Above the field the sun candled the clouds to an ardent sea. A chill breeze rose from the west, lifting a shimmering net of bees from the jewelweed and rattling the willow leaves. In the grass the girls shrieked and giggled, and as we watched the other children joined them for their evening games of Gray Wolf and Shadow-Tag, small white shapes slipping from the darkening trees with their mongrels romping underfoot. Eva pelted her friends with goldenrod while the boys tussled in furrows, their long blue shadows dancing across the grass until they were swallowed by the willow's roots. Cass watched

417

them, entranced, his head tilted to catch some faint sound on the wind.

"What is it?" I asked, but he only shook his head.

"Can't you hear?" He looked at me in wonder, then turned away and walked across the field towards the children.

"Cass!" I called after him; but he ignored me. For several minutes I waited, and finally stepped back to the door. And stopped.

Someone *was* singing. Perhaps I had already heard without realizing, or mistaken the refrain for the cry of the crickets or nightjars. I cocked my head as Cass had done and tried to trace the music; but it was gone again, drowned by the children's voices. I caught the bellow of Cass's laughter among their play, then faint music once more: a woman's voice, but wordless or else too far off for me to understand her song. At the doorway I paused and looked out at the field. The sun scarcely brushed the horizon now above the cirrus archipelago. Lightning bugs sparked the air and the children spilled through their trails, Cass lumbering among them with first Kim and then Little Eva hugging his narrow shoulders. For a long while I watched them, until only Eva's amber hair and Cass's white shirt flashed in the dusk. Finally Cass looked up and, seeing me for the first time, beckoned me to join them. I smiled and waved, then bounded down the steps and across the field.

From the grass hundreds of leafhoppers flew up as I passed, the click of their wings a soft and constant burr. Last light silvered the willow bark and faded. The wind was stronger now, and with the children's voices it carried that faint music once more, ringing clearly over the whir of insects. I halted, suddenly dizzy, and stared at my feet as I tried to steady myself.

When I glanced up the children had fallen still. They stood ranged across the field, their dogs beside them motionless, ears pricked. I turned to see what held them.

As though storm-riven the willow thrashed, branches raking the sky as if to hurl the first stars earthward. I swore and stepped back in disbelief. Beneath me the ground shuddered, buckling like rotten bark. Then with a steady grinding roar the earth heaved. A rich spume of dirt and clover sprayed me as the ground beneath the tree split like a windfall apple.

The roaring stopped. A second of utter silence; and then song poured from the rift like a flock of swans. I clapped my hands to my ears and fell to my knees.

The dogs heard first. I felt the heat of their flanks as they streamed past me, heard their panting and faint whimpers. I forced myself to look up, brushing dirt from my face.

Above a gaping mouth in the red earth the willow reared. In its shadow stood Maidie, arms outstretched. She was singing, and the dogs streamed past her, vaulting into the darkness at her feet. I stared amazed. Then from behind me I heard voices, the soft stir of footsteps. I glanced back.

The field lay in gray half-light. Abruptly the darkness itself shivered, broken where the children ran laughing across the field, in twos and threes, girls clutching hands to form a chain across the waving grass, the littlest clinging to the bigger boys shouting in excitement. I yelled to them, but my voice was drowned by their laughter. They did not see me as they raced past.

She drew them, head thrown back as she sang on and on and on, her voice embracing stone and tree and hound and stars, until her song was the children and she sang them all into the earth. Her glasses fell from her face, the gaze she turned upon the children no longer blind but blinding: eyes like golden flowers, like sunrise, like autumn wheat. My hands were raw from kneading the clay as I stared, boys and girls rushing to her and laughing as they disappeared one by one into the rift at her feet. Her hands moved over and over again in a ceaseless welcoming wave, as though she gathered armfuls of bright blossoms to her breast. But I could not move: it was as if I had become that tree, and rooted to the earth.

Final footsteps pattered on the grass. Cass and Eva passed me, running hand in hand to join the rest, now gone beneath the willow. I screamed his name and they halted. Cass stared back dimly, shaking his head as though trying to recognize me. The woman I had known as Maidie raised her arms and fell silent. Then she called out a word, a name. Little Eva smiled at Cass, standing on tiptoe to kiss him. He smiled and kissed her forehead, then gathered her into his arms to carry her the last few steps to the willow. I watched as the woman waiting there took his hands; and lost him forever.

Another figure stepped from the tree's shadow. He stooped to take the child from Cass's arms. I saw Cass turn from Sam to the woman beside him, the woman whose wheat-gold eyes held a terrible sorrow. And suddenly I understood: knew the mother's eternal anguish at losing the child again to him, that bleak consort, He Who Receives Many; knew why she gathered this bright harvest of playmates for a sunless garden, attendants for the girl no more a girl, the gentle maiden doomed to darkness the rest of the turning year.

One last moment they remained. The child raised her hand to me and opened it, once, in a tiny farewell. The ground trembled. A sound like rushing water rent the air. The willow tree crashed into darkness. A crack like granite shattering; a smell like ash and grinding stone. They were gone; all gone.

The night was silent. Before me stretched the empty field, an abandoned cottage. Then from the woods echoed a poorwill's wail and its mate's echoing lament. I stumbled to the fallen tree and, kneeling between its roots, wept among the anemones hiding children in the earth.

STEPHEN JONES & KIM NEWMAN

Necrology: 1990

ONCE AGAIN, IT IS TIME to remember those writers, artists, performers and film-makers who made many important contributions to the genre of the *fantastique* during their lifetimes, and who passed away in 1990 . . .

AUTHORS/ARTISTS

After battling lymphatic cancer for more than a year, **Robert Adams** died at his home in Florida on January 4th. He was 56. Author of 18 novels and editor of several anthologies in the best-selling 'Horseclans' series, which began with *The Coming of the Horseclans* in 1975, he also wrote six volumes in the 'Castaways in Time' series and completed two out of three outlined novels in another series, 'Stairway to Forever'.

Poet and writer of short supernatural fiction, **Joseph Payne Brennan** died from acute leukemia on January 28th, aged 71. His first published poem appeared in *The Christian Science Monitor* (1940) and his first supernatural story, 'The Green Parrot' was published in *Weird Tales* in 1952. Among his best-known books are the Arkham House collections *Nine Horrors and a Dream, Stories of Darkness and Dread* and *Nightmare Need* (verse), as well as *The Shapes of Midnight* and three volumes featuring his psychic detective Lucius Leffing.

Playwright and screenwriter **Arnaud D'Usseau** died from stomach cancer on January 29th, aged 73. A big Broadway name (*Tomorrow the World*) and minor Hollywood writer (*The Man Who Wouldn't Die*) in the '40s, he was driven abroad by the the blacklist and contributed under 'front' pseudonyms to numerous European movies, including *Horror Express*.

Julia Fitzgerald, the author of a number of historical romances with fantasy elements, such as *Beauty to the Devil*, *Taboo* and *Earth Queen, Sky King*, died from cancer on February 5th.

Commercial artist and fantasy author **Carl Sherrell** died on February 7th from aneurism in his esophagus, aged 60. He had been suffering from a heart condition complicated by leukemia. His first novel, *Raum*, appeared in 1977, and other books include *Skraelings, Arcane, The Space Prodigal* and *Dark Flowers*.

Popular SF cartoonist **Arthur "ATOM" Thomson** died from a blood clot on February 8th. He was 62. He discovered fandom in 1954 and contributed to a number of professional magazines during the '50s, although he preferred to work for fanzines.

The same day singer/songwriter **Del Shannon** died from a self-inflicted gunshot wound. His '60s hit *Runaway* was used in both *Children of the Corn* and TV's *Crime Story*.

Wendayne Ackerman, 76, German-born wife of collector/ editor/ historian Forrest J Ackerman, died on March 5th after a long illness. She translated 137 novels of the German space opera 'Perry Rhodan', as well as books by Stanislaw Lem, Pierre Barbet and the Strugatsky brothers, and wrote one of the most popular and often-reprinted features in *Famous Monsters of Filmland*: 'Rocket to the Rue Morgue'.

Pulp magzine publisher and founder of Popular Library, **Ned L. Pines** died in Paris on May 14th, aged 84. After creating the 'Thriller' pulps in the early '30s, he added the weird menace title *Thrilling Mystery* in 1935 and the following year bought the ailing *Wonder Stories* from Hugo Gernsback and retitled it *Thrilling Wonder Stories*. A companion magazine, *Startling Stories*, started in 1939 and by the end of the decade Pines Publications had 44 titles on the newsstands, including *Captain Future, Fantastic Story Magazine* and *Wonder Story Annual*.

Children's author **Lucy M. Boston** died on June 1st. She was 97, and is best known for the 'Green Knowe' series of fantasies, beginning with *The Children of Green Knowe* in 1954 and followed by five more volumes between 1958–76.

Film journalist and novelist **Geoff Simm** died on June 11th from AIDS. He was 40, and contributed to such specialist magazines as *Shock Xpress* and *Starburst*, as well as working as a technician on several recent UK movies.

Playwright and director **Paul Giovanni** died on June 17th of pneumonia with complications. He was 57. In 1978 Giovanni wrote and staged the Tony Award nominated Sherlock Holmes pastiche, *The Crucifer of Blood*, filmed in 1990 with Charlton Heston as Holmes.

Screenwriter **Sidney Boehm**, whose credits include *When Worlds Collide, The Atomic City* and *Shock Treatment*, died on June 25th, aged 82. He won an Edgar Award for his script for *The Big Heat*.

Argentinian magic realist author **Manuel Puig** died from a heart attack following complications after surgery on July 22nd. He was 57. His best-known novel was *Kiss of the Spider Woman*, which was filmed in 1985.

Ed Emshwiller, one of the top science fiction artists of the 1950s and '60s died of cancer on July 27th, aged 65. He began illustrating for *Galaxy* in 1951, signing his paintings 'Emsh'. For the past decade he was involved in multi-media productions on film and video, and was the visual consultant on the TV movie *The Lathe of Heaven*.

Cartoonist **B. (Bernard) Kliban**, whose bestselling books of weird artwork included *Cats, Never Eat Anything Bigger Than Your Head, Whack Your Porcupine* and *Two Guys Fooling Around With the Moon*, died on August 12th, two weeks after undergoing heart surgery. He was 55.

Screenwriter **Edmund H. North** died August 28th from pneumonia, aged 79. Among his two dozen screenplays was the classic 1951 SF movie, *The Day the Earth Stood Still*. He won an Oscar for *Patton*.

Comics writer **Jerry Iger** died on September 5th. He was 87. Amongst the characters he created were Sheena, Queen of the Jungle (which became a 1950s TV series and a 1984 movie), Blue Beetle, Wonder Boy and The Ray.

Fan, author, editor and publisher **Donald A. Wollheim** died in his sleep from an apparent heart attack on November 2nd, two years after suffering a stroke. He was 76. One of the most important figures in science fiction, he became an early member of fandom in the mid-1930s and by the early '40s was editing such pulp magazines as *Stirring Science Stories* and *Cosmic Stories*. In 1943 he edited the first mass-market SF anthology, *The Pocket Book of Science Fiction*, and between 1947 and 1952 edited 18 issues of *The Avon Fantasy Reader*, reprinting the cream of *Weird Tales*-type material. He went on to become the *entire* editorial staff at Avon Books and, in 1952, he started Ace Books with A.A. Wyn. In 1971, three years after Wynn's death, Wollheim resigned from Ace and formed DAW Books, the first mass-market publisher solely devoted to science fiction, fantasy and horror. He discovered and developed many new writers and continued to edit anthologies until his stroke.

Gothic and historical novelist **Anya Seton** died on November 8th from heart failure. She was 86. One of her best-known novels was *Dragonwyck*, filmed in 1946 starring Vincent Price.

Bestselling author **Roald Dahl** died on November 23rd, aged 74. Several of his children's books, such as *Willy Wonka and the Chocolate Factory*, *The Witches* and *The BFG* were made into films, he scripted *Chitty Chitty Bang Bang* and the James Bond adventure *You Only Live Twice*, and hosted the TV series *Way Out* and *Roald Dahl's Tales of the Unexpected*.

Playwright and novelist **Dorothy (Dodie) Smith** died on November 24th, aged 94. Her most famous book for children was *One Hundred & One Dalmatians*, filmed by Disney in 1961.

Pulp publisher **Henry Steeger III**, who co-founded Popular Publications in 1930 with Harold Goldsmith, died on December 25th, aged 87. At its height, Popular published over 300 individual titles, including *Horror Stories*, *Terror Tales*, *The Spider*, *Operator 5*, *G-8 and His Battle Aces*, *Fantastic Mysteries*, *Fantastic Novels*, and *A. Merritt's Fantasy*.

Screenwriter **Warren Skaaren** died of bone cancer, aged 44, on December 28th. He co-wrote the scripts for *Beetlejuice*, *Top Gun*, *Beverly Hills Cop II* and *Batman*, and completed the script for *Beetlejuice 2* just before his death.

ACTORS/ACTRESSES

Character actor **Alan Hale, Jr.** died on January 2nd from cancer of the thymus, aged 71. Best-known for his TV work in such series as *Gilligan's Isle*, *Casey Jones*, *Wild, Wild West* and *Land of the Giants*, he also starred in such low-budget gems as *The Crawling Hand* and *The Giant Spider Invasion*.

Actress **Lydia Bilbrooke** died on January 4th, aged 101. Her film credits include *The Picture of Dorian Gray*, *The Spider Woman*, *Mr Peabody and the Mermaid* and *The Brighton Strangler*.

Arthur Kennedy died on January 5th from a brain tumor. He was 75. Amongst his many movie credits are *Fantastic Voyage*, *The Living Dead at the Manchester Morgue*, *The Antichrist*, *The Sentinel* and *The Humanoid*.

Best known for his starring role in *Chariots of Fire*, British actor **Ian Charleson** died on January 6th from AIDS. He was 40, and also appeared in *Opera* and *Greystoke: The Legend of Tarzan, Lord of the Apes*.

Veteran comedy actor **Terry-Thomas** died on January 8th, aged 78. He had been suffering from Parkinson's disease for many years.

His long list of credits includes *tom thumb*, *The Wonderful World of the Brothers Grimm*, *Munster Go Home!*, *Danger: Diabolik*, *The Abominable Dr Phibes*, *Dr Phibes Rises Again*, *The Hound of the Baskervilles* (1977) and *Vault of Horror*.

Film and TV actor **Gordon Jackson** died on January 15th, aged 66. His many film appearances include *Meet Mr Lucifer*, *The Quatermass Experiment*, *Scrooge*, *Madam Sin*, *Spectre*, *The Medusa Touch* and *The Masks of Death*.

Veteran actress **Barbara Stanwyck** died on January 20th from congestive heart failure. She was 82. She appeared in *Flesh and Fantasy* and William Castle's *The Night Walker* as well as the early '70s TV movies *The House That Would Not Die* and *A Taste of Evil*.

Madge Bellamy, who co-starred with Bela Lugosi in *White Zombie* (1932) died on January 24th, aged 89.

Hollywood actress **Ava Gardner**, once voted the world's most beautiful woman, died of pneumonia at her London home on January 25th. She was 67. The star of more than 60 films, her credits include *Spooks Run Wild* and *Ghosts on the Loose* (both with Bela Lugosi), *One Touch of Venus*, *Pandora and the Flying Dutchman*, *On the Beach*, *Seven Days in May*, *Earthquake*, *The Bluebird* (1976) and *The Sentinel*.

The same day, British character actor **Ian Dudley Hardy** was killed near London when a tree uprooted by the storms struck his car. He was aged 79 and was featured in the 1936 *Things to Come*.

German-born actor **Henry Brandon** died of a heart attack in Los Angeles on February 13th, aged 77. He portrayed Captain Lasca in the 1939 serial *Buck Rogers* with Buster Crabbe and the following year played the oriental mastermind in *The Drums of Fu Manchu*. His numerous other film credits include Laurel & Hardy's *Babes in Toyland*, *Doomed to Die*, *Tarzan and the She-Devil*, *War of the Worlds*, *The Land Unknown*, *Scared Stiff*, *Captain Sinbad*, *Search for the Evil One* and *Assault on Precinct 13*.

Character actor **Gary Merrill** died on March 5th from cancer. He was 74. His numerous credits include *The Mysterious Island*, *The Woman Who Wouldn't Die*, *Destination Inner Space*, *Earth II* and *The Power*.

French model and actress **Capucine** (Germaine Lefebvre) killed herself on March 17th. She was 57. Among her many international films were *The Pink Panther* and *Arabian Adventure* (with Christopher Lee and Peter Cushing).

Hollywood goddess **Greta Garbo** died on April 15th from undisclosed causes. She was 84. Born Greta Gustafson in Sweden, she starred in a number of movies for MGM during the late 1920s and early '30s until her early retirement in 1941. She appeared with

Bela Lugosi in *Ninotchka* (1939) and turned up in the 1974 gay sex film *Adam and Yves*.

Paulette Goddard, actress and former wife of Charlie Chaplin and Burgess Meredith (amongst four husbands), died on April 23rd after a brief illness. She starred in more than forty movies, including Chaplin's *Modern Times* and alongside Bob Hope in the two classic horror comedies, *The Cat and the Canary* (1939) and *The Ghost Breakers* (1940). Her last film was the 1972 TV movie, *The Snoop Sisters*.

Actor **Albert Salmi** and his wife were found shot dead on April 23rd in an apparent murder-suicide. He was 62, and his credits include *The Ambushers*, *Escape from the Planet of the Apes*, *Empire of the Ants*, *Dragonslayer*, *Kung Fu II*, *The Coming* and *Superstition* (aka *The Witch*).

David Rappaport, the diminutive star of *Time Bandits*, TV's *The Wizard* and the nine-hour National Theatre version of *Illuminatus*, committed suicide on May 2nd in Los Angeles. The 38-year-old, 3 ft 11 ins actor was suffering from depression and was found dead from a gunshot wound. His other movies include *The Bride* and *Sword of the Valiant*.

Actress **Susan Oliver** died on May 10th of cancer, aged 53. Amongst her many TV credits was the *Star Trek* pilot *The Cage/Menagerie* as well as such films as *The Monitors*, *Change of Mind* and *Murder By Decree*.

Singer and entertainer **Sammy Davis, Jr.** died on May 16th from throat cancer. He appeared in *One More Time* and *Poor Devil* (both with Christopher Lee), *Alice in Wonderland* (1985) and episodes of TV's *Wild, Wild West*, *Batman*, *I Dream of Jeannie* and *Fantasy Island*.

Jill Ireland, British-born actress and wife of Charles Bronson, died of cancer on May 18th, aged 54. She began her career as a Rank starlet and married actor David McCallum in 1957. They divorced ten years later. Her films include *Someone Behind the Door*, *The Karate Killers* and TV's *The Girl, the Gold Watch and Everything*, along with episodes of *Voyage to the Bottom of the Sea*, *Star Trek* and *Night Gallery*.

Comedian and actor **Max Wall** died on May 22nd after falling outside a restaurant in London's Strand. He was aged 82. His movie credits include the Pythonesque fantasy *Jabberwocky*.

Debonair British actor **Sir Rex Harrison** died from pancreatic cancer on June 2nd, aged 82. Although his career alternated between stage and film productions on both sides of the Atlantic, he is best remembered for his Oscar-winning role as Professor Higgins in *My Fair Lady* (1964). His other movie credits include *Blithe Spirit*, *The Ghost and Mrs Muir*, *Midnight Lace* and *Doctor Dolittle*.

Veteran character actor **Jack Gilford** died the same day from cancer. He was 81. His many credits include *They Might Be Giants*, *Catch 22*, *Caveman*, *Cocoon* and *Cocoon the Return*.

British character actor **Raymond Huntley** died in June, aged 86. He played Dracula on the stage between 1928–30, and he appeared in such movies as *The Ghost of St Michaels*, *The Ghost Train*, *Passport to Pimlico*, *I'll Never Forget You*, *Meet Mr Lucifer*, *The Black Torment* and Hammer's remake of *The Mummy* (1959).

Actor **Leonard Sachs** died from kidney failure on June 15th, aged 82. His occasional film appearances included *Taste of Fear* (aka *Scream of Fear*), *The Gamma People*, *The Giant Behemoth*, *Konga* and *Thunderball*, as well as TV's *Dr Who* and *1984*.

British actress **Anna Palk** died on July 1st from cancer. She was 48. Her many credits include *The Earth Dies Screaming*, *The Skull*, *Fahrenheit 451*, *The Frozen Dead*, *Tower of Evil* (aka *Horror of Snape Island*) and *The Nightcomers*.

Actor **Howard Duff** died on July 8th of a heart attack, aged 76. He appeared in the 1953 film *Spaceways*, plus *Oh, God Book II*, *Monster in the Closet* and numerous TV series.

Irene Champlin, who played Dale Arden in the 1950s *Flash Gordon* TV series, died on July 10th, aged 59.

Leading lady **Margaret Lockwood** died on July 15th. She was 73. Despite attracting the attention of Hollywood with her starring role in Hitchcock's *The Lady Vanishes*, most of her films were made in Britain, including *Dr Syn* (1937), *A Place of One's Own* and *The Slipper and the Rose*.

American comic actor **Eddie Quillan**, aged 83, died on July 19th of cancer. Besides appearing in *Mutiny on the Bounty* (1935) and *The Grapes of Wrath*, he also turned up in *Brigadoon*, *The Ghost and Mrs Chicken*, *Angel in My Pocket*, *Jungle Queen*, *Jungle Raiders* and TV's *The Darker Side of Terror*.

Actress **Elizabeth Allan**, who co-starred with Bela Lugosi in *Mark of the Vampire* and also appeared in *The Phantom Fiend* (aka *The Lodger*, 1935), died on July 27th. She was 80.

Jill Esmond died on July 28th. The 82-year-old actress was the first wife of Laurence Olivier, and her credits include *FP1 Does Not Reply* and *13 Women*.

Actor **Maurice Braddell** died the same day, aged 89. He played Dr Harding in the 1936 version of *Things to Come*.

Nina Bara, who portrayed the regular villainess, Tonga, in the '50s TV show *Space Patrol*, died on August 15th of cancer. She was 66. She also starred in *Missile to the Moon*.

Black actor **Raymond St Jacques**, aged 60, died on August 27th from cancer of the lymph glands. He portrayed Martin Luther King in

The Private Files of J. Edgar Hoover, and other credits include *Change of Mind*, *The Eyes of Laura Mars*, *They Live* and *Search for the Gods*, as well as numerous TV appearances.

Hollywood star of the 1930s and '40s **Irene Dunne** died on September 4th from heart failure at the age of 88. She appeared in *13 Women*, *A Guy Named Joe*, *It Grows on Trees* and the James Whale version of *Showboat*.

British character actress **Athene Seyler** died on September 11th, aged 101. She appeared in the 1935 version of *Scrooge* and played Mrs Karswell in *Night of the Demon* (aka *Curse of the Demon*).

Former child actor **Jackie Moran** died on September 20th from cancer, aged 65. Best remembered as Buddy Wade in the original *Buck Rogers* serial (1939), he also featured in *Meet Mr Christian*, *Henry Aldrich Haunts a House* and *Hop Harrigan*.

British actress **Jill Bennett** committed suicide on October 4th, aged 59. She appeared in *The Skull*, *The Nanny*, *Britannia Hospital*, *For Your Eyes Only*, *The Anatomist* and *Full Circle* (aka *The Haunting of Julia*).

Radio entertainer and straight man **Richard Murdoch** died of a heart attack on October 9th. He was 83, and his film credits include *The Terror* (1938) and *The Ghost Train* (1941).

Tough-guy character actor **Robert Tessier** died on October 11th from cancer, aged 56. With his shaved head and muscular build, he often portrayed villains in such movies as *The Velvet Vampire*, *Doc Savage The Man of Bronze*, *Starcrash*, *Billion Dollar Threat*, *The Sword and the Sorcerer*, *The Lost Empire* and *Double Exposure*.

French leading actress **Delphine Seyrig** died from lung disease on October 15th, aged 58. She appeared in *Last Year in Marienbad*, *Mr Freedom*, *The Milky Way*, *Donkey Skin*, *Discreet Charm of the Bourgeoisie*, *Dorian Gray in the Mirror of the Popular Press* (as Frau Dr Mabuse) and the haunting *Daughters of Darkness* (as the vampirish Countess Bathory).

Hollywood star **Joel McCrea** died on October 20th of pulmonary complications. He was 84. In a career that spanned four decades, he appeared in such classics as *Sullivan's Travels* and *Ride the High Country*, as well as *The Most Dangerous Game*, *Bird of Paradise* (with Lon Chaney, Jr) and *The Unseen*.

Character actress **Freda Jackson** died the same day at the age of 82. During the 1960s she appeared in a number of horror and fantasy movies including *Shadow of the Cat*, Hammer's *The Brides of Dracula*, *Die, Monster, Die!* (aka *Monster of Terror*, with Boris Karloff), plus two Ray Harryhausen extravaganzas: *Valley of Gwangi* and *Clash of the Titans*.

Italian leading actor **Ugo Tognazzi** died from a cerebral haemorrhage on October 27th, aged 68. He appeared in *Toto in the Moon*, *My Friend Dr Jekyll*, *The Ape Woman*, *Barbarella* (as Mark Hand), *The Master and Margarita* and *La Grande Bouffe*, amongst others.

Spanish-American bandleader **Xavier Cugat** died on the same day from heart failure, aged 90. He appeared in many of the MGM musicals of the '40s, as well as *The Monitors* and *The Pyx*.

Veteran character actor **Harry Lauter** died on October 30th, aged 76, from heart failure. His numerous movie credits include *The Flying Disc Man from Mars*, *The Day the Earth Stood Still*, *Canadian Mounties vs. Atomic Invaders*, *It Came from Beneath the Sea*, *Earth vs. the Flying Saucers*, *The Creature with the Atom Brain*, *The Werewolf*, *Escape from the Planet of the Apes* and *Superbeast*.

British actress **Valerie French** died on November 3rd from leukaemia. She was 59. Amongst her credits were *The 27th Day*, *The Four Skulls of Jonathan Drake* and TV's *The Prisoner*.

Musical comedy star **Mary Martin** died the same day of cancer, aged 76. The mother of actor Larry Hagman, she first starred on Broadway in *One Touch of Venus* and went on to be identified in the American public's mind as the definitive Peter Pan.

Will Kuluva died from an embolism on November 6th. He was 73. In 1964 he appeared in the Leo G. Carroll role in *The Man from UNCLE* TV pilot, which later became the feature *To Trap a Spy*. His many other small screen credits include *Twilight Zone*, *Wild, Wild West* and *Beauty and the Beast*.

American comedienne and original Ziegfeld girl **Eve Arden** (Eunice Quedens) died on November 12th from heart disease, aged somewhere between 78 and 88. She appeared in *Whistling in the Dark*, *One Touch of Venus*, *Sergeant Deadhead*, *The Strongest Man in the World* and *Pandemonium* as well as the boxoffice hit *Grease* and TV's *Alice in Wonderland*.

Meghan Robinson, actress and founding member of Charles Busch's Theater-in-Limbo, died on November 18th of AIDS. She was 35 and co-starred with Busch in the off-Broadway comedies *Psycho Beach Party* and *Vampire Lesbians of Sodom*.

David White, who portrayed Larry Tate in the long-running TV series *Bewitched*, died on November 26th of a heart attack. He was 74.

31-inch tall actress **Tamara de Treaux**, who played the title role in *E.T. The Extra-Terrestrial*, died from heart and respiratory problems on November 28th. She was 31. She also appeared in *Ghoulies* and *Rockula*.

Leading film and TV actor **Robert Cummings**, aged 80, died of kidney failure and pneumonia on December 2nd. He began his film career in 1935 and starred in *Flesh and Fantasy, The Lost Moment, Heaven Only Knows, For Heaven's Sake, Free for All, Dial M for Murder* and *Five Golden Dragons* (with Christopher Lee).

Veteran character actor **Edward Binns** died on December 4th from a heart attack. He was 74. Amongst his numerous credits are *Curse of the Undead, Fail Safe, Hunter, The Power Within* and *Diary of the Dead*.

Hollywood leading lady **Joan Bennett** died of a heart attack on December 7th, aged 80. She made her movie debut in 1915 and appeared in *Alice in Wonderland* (1927 short), *The Man Who Reclaimed His Head, The Secret Beyond the Door, For Heaven's Sake, House of Dark Shadows* and *Suspiria*. Between 1966–71 she played Elizabeth Collins Stoddard in the TV series *Dark Shadows*, and also appeared in the TV movies *The Eyes of Charles Sand* and *This House Possessed*.

Tough-guy actor and pro-wrestler **Mike Mazurki** (Mikhail Mazurski) died on December 9th, aged 82, after a long illness. He made his screen debut in 1934 and went on to appear in *Dr Renault's Secret, Henry Aldrich Haunts a House, The Canterville Ghost* (1943), *Murder, My Sweet* (as Moose Malloy), *Dick Tracy* (1945, as Splitface), *The Horn Blows At Midnight, Sinbad the Sailor, Around the World in 80 Days, Zotz!, Alligator, Amazon Women On the Moon* and Warren Beatty's *Dick Tracy* (1990).

FILM/TV TECHNICIANS:

"The dean of Hollywood art directors", **Lyle Wheeler**, died of pneumonia on January 10th, aged 84. During a career that spanned 25 years and more than 400 films, he received 24 Academy Award nominations and won 5 times. His numerous credits include *Gone With the Wind, Rebecca, Journey to the Centre of the Earth, Cleopatra* and *Marooned*.

Low budget director **William J. Hole, Jr.** died from respiratory failure on February 11th. He was 71. Among his credits are *The Ghost of Dragstrip Hollow, The Devil's Hand, Face of Terror* and *Man in Outer Space*.

Acclaimed British screenwriter, director and producer **Michael Powell** died on February 19th of prostate cancer. He was 84. With the late Emeric Pressburger he made 14 movies, including the classic fantasies *A Matter of Life and Death* (aka *Stairway to Heaven*), *The Red Shoes, Tales of Hoffman* and *The Boy Who Turned Yellow*. His other credits included the Academy Award-winning 1940 fantasy *The Thief of Bagdad* and the 1960 chiller *Peeping Tom*.

Writer/producer **Aubrey Wisberg** died of cancer in New York on March 14th. He was 78. Besides being involved with such diverse projects as *The Horn Blows at Midnight* (1945) with Jack Benny and *Hercules in New York* (1969) with Arnold Schwarzenegger, he formed Mid-Century Productions with Jack Pollexfen in 1950. Over the next few years they turned out such "classics" as *The Man from Planet X*, *Captive Women*, *The Neanderthal Man* and *Port Sinister*.

Cinematographer **Karl Brown** died March 25th, aged 93. He created double printing, first used in D.W. Griffith's *Intolerance* (1916) and helped develop the minature projection system used for *King Kong* (1933). During the late '30s and early '40s Brown wrote several low budget films featuring Boris Karloff as a mad scientist, including *The Man They Could Not Hang*, *The Man With Nine Lives* and *Before I Hang*.

Milton S. Gelman, producer and chief writer on NBC-TV's *The Man from UNCLE* for nearly four years, died on May 2nd following heart surgery. He was 70.

British film designer **Tony Masters**, aged 70, died in May in the South of France. Married to actress Heather Sears, he entered the film industry in 1946 and was production designer on more than 60 movies including *2001: A Space Odyssey*, for which he won a BAFTA Award and was nominated for an Oscar.

Puppeteer and creator of the Muppets, **Jim Henson**, died of a bacterial infection on May 17th, aged 53. After working in television during the late 1950s and early '60s, his career took off with *Sesame Street* and *The Muppet Show*. Later television shows included *Fraggle Rock*, *The Ghosts of Faffner Hall* and *The Storyteller*, while his movie credits boasted *The Muppet Movie*, *The Great Muppet Caper*, *The Muppets Take Manhatten*, *The Dark Crystal*, *Labyrinth*, *Dreamchild*, *The Witches* and *Teenage Mutant Ninja Turtles*.

Early special effects expert **Theodore J. Lydecker** died from cancer on May 25th, aged 81. Best known for his work with his brother Howard (who died in 1969) on the Republic serials of the 1930s–'50s, his credits include *Dick Tracy* (1937), *The Adventures of Captain Marvel*, *Captain America*, *The Lady and the Monster*, *The Catman of Paris*, *Valley of the Zombies*, *King of the Rocket Men*, *The Invisible Monster*, *Zombies of the Stratosphere*, *Tobor the Great* and *Panther Girl of the Congo*, amongst numerous others.

Sir James Carreras, who headed Hammer Films from 1949–1980, died on June 9th. He was 81. Carreras built Hammer during the post-war years, but it was the release of *The Quatermass Experiment* (aka *The Creeping Unknown*) in 1955 that gave the company its direction and success, finally resulting in the Queens Award to Industry during the late '60s.

Veteran Disney art director **Al Roelofs** died on July 2nd from a stroke. He was 83, and his many credits include *The Island At the Top of the World*, *Charley and the Angel*, *Escape from Witch Mountain*, *The Black Hole*, *Tron* etc.

Still photographer/montage expert **Robert Coburn** died on July 3rd, aged 90. He worked on *King Kong* (1933).

TV director **Philip Leacock** died on July 14th from collapsed lungs, aged 73. His numerous credits include *Baffled*, *When Michael Calls*, *Dying Room Only*, *The Curse of King Tut's Tomb* and *Three Sovereigns for Sarah*.

Pioneer special effects cameraman **Bud Thackery** died on July 15th. He was 87, and directed the process photography on *King Kong* (1933) as well as working on *Noah's Ark* (1928), *The Jazz Singer*, *The Most Dangerous Game*, *Scarface*, *The Phantom Empire* and many other movies.

Alan Clarke, who directed *Billy the Kid and the Green Baize Vampire*, died on July 24th, aged 54.

Best known as a major western director and creator of TV's *Gunsmoke*, writer/producer **Charles Marquis Warren** died on August 11th of heart aneurysm. He was 77, and his film credits include *Back from the Dead* and *The Unknown Terror*.

Manly P. Hall, who hypnotized Bela Lugosi on the set of *Black Friday* (1941) for his dramatic death scene, died August 29th, aged 89. He also performed the wedding ceremony for Lugosi's fifth and final wedding.

Top 1930s dancer/choreographer **Hermes Pan** died from an apparent stroke on September 19th, aged 80. Amongst the films he worked on are *Top Hat*, *Swing Time*, *Shall We Dance*, *Kiss Me Kate*, *Finian's Rainbow* and *Lost Horizon* (1973).

Special effects director **Scott Bartlett** died on September 29th from complications following a kidney-liver transplant. He was 47, and his credits include *Starman*, *The Jupiter Menace*, *Altered States* and *Sheena*.

Veteran animator **Grim Natwick** died on October 7th from pneumonia-heart disease. He was 100 years old. Besides creating cartoon character Betty Boop, he worked on such movies as *Snow White and the Seven Dwarfs*, *Gulliver's Travels*, *Raggedy Ann and Andy*, *The Thief and the Cobbler*, and with Popeye, Crusader Rabbit, Mr Magoo and Woody Woodpecker.

3-D expert and cinematographer **Howard Schwartz** died on October 25th from a heart attack, aged 71. His films include *Bwana Devil* and *House of Wax*.

French film-maker **Jacques Demy** died from leukaemia on October 27th. He was 59 and directed *The Umbrellas of Cherbourg*, *Donkey Skin* and *The Pied Piper*, amongst others.

British director **Don Chaffey** died on November 13th from heart disease, aged 72. His movie credits include *The 3 Lives of Thomasina*, *Jason and the Argonauts*, *One Million Years B.C.*, *Creatures the World Forgot*, *Persecution* (aka *The Terror of Sheba*) and *Pete's Dragon*.

Italian screenwriter and director **Sergio Corbucci** died on December 2nd from a heart attack. He was 80. His many credits include *Duel of the Titans*, *The Son of Spartacus*, *Goliath and the Vampires*, *Django* and the 1965 remake of *The Man Who Laughs*.

Film and TV writer/director **Richard Benner** died the same day from AIDS, aged 47. He wrote and directed *Outrageous* and *Outrageous Too*, both of which starred female impersonator Craig Russell (who died of AIDS on October 30th) as well as several episodes of TV's *Tales From the Darkside*.

TV director **Richard Irving** died following heart surgery on December 30th, aged 73. Amongst his many credits were the pilot film for *The Six Million Dollar Man* and *Exoman*.